nickelodeon

GARFIELD

Full Course

BY JIM DAVIS

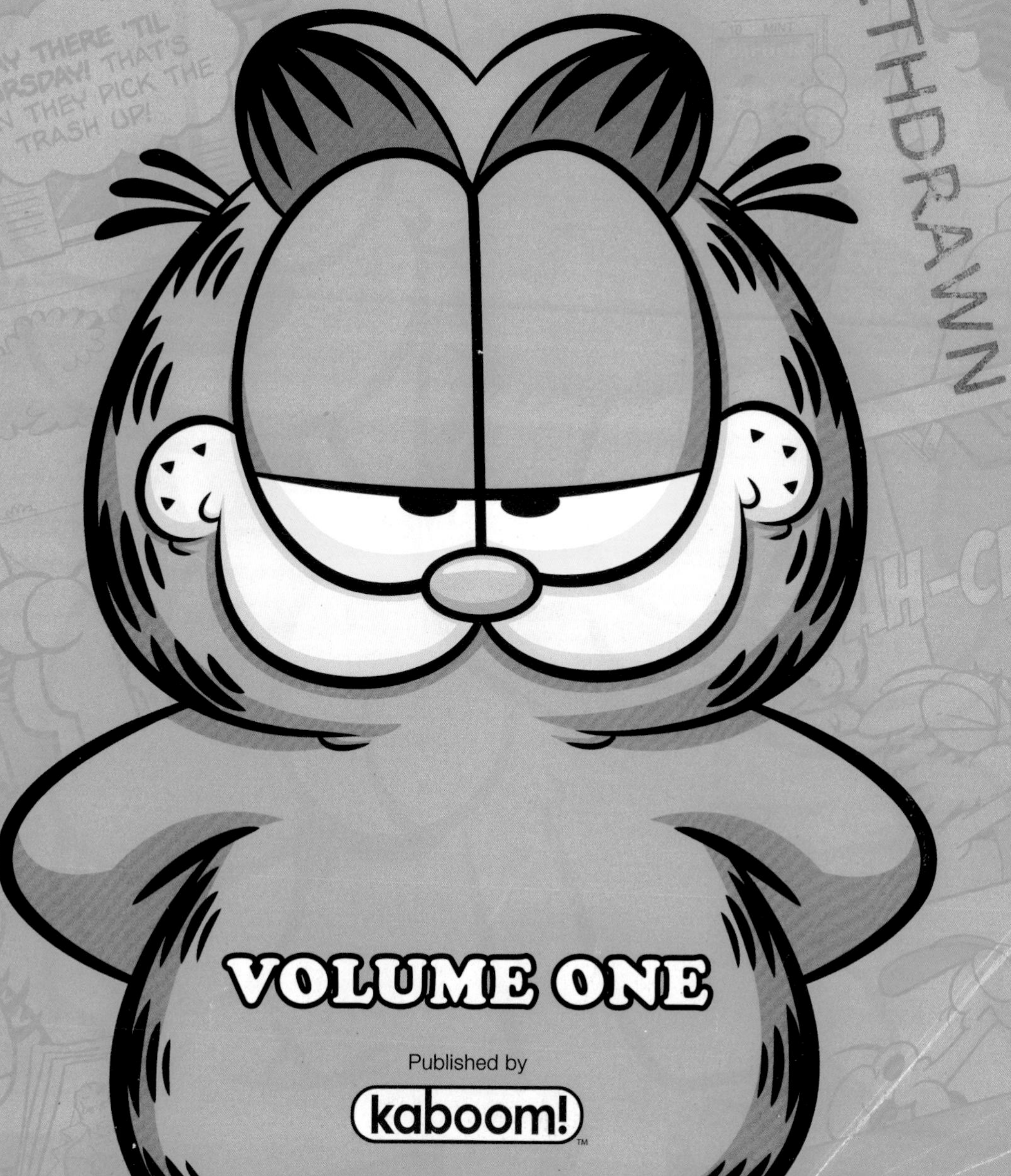

VOLUME ONE

Published by
kaboom!

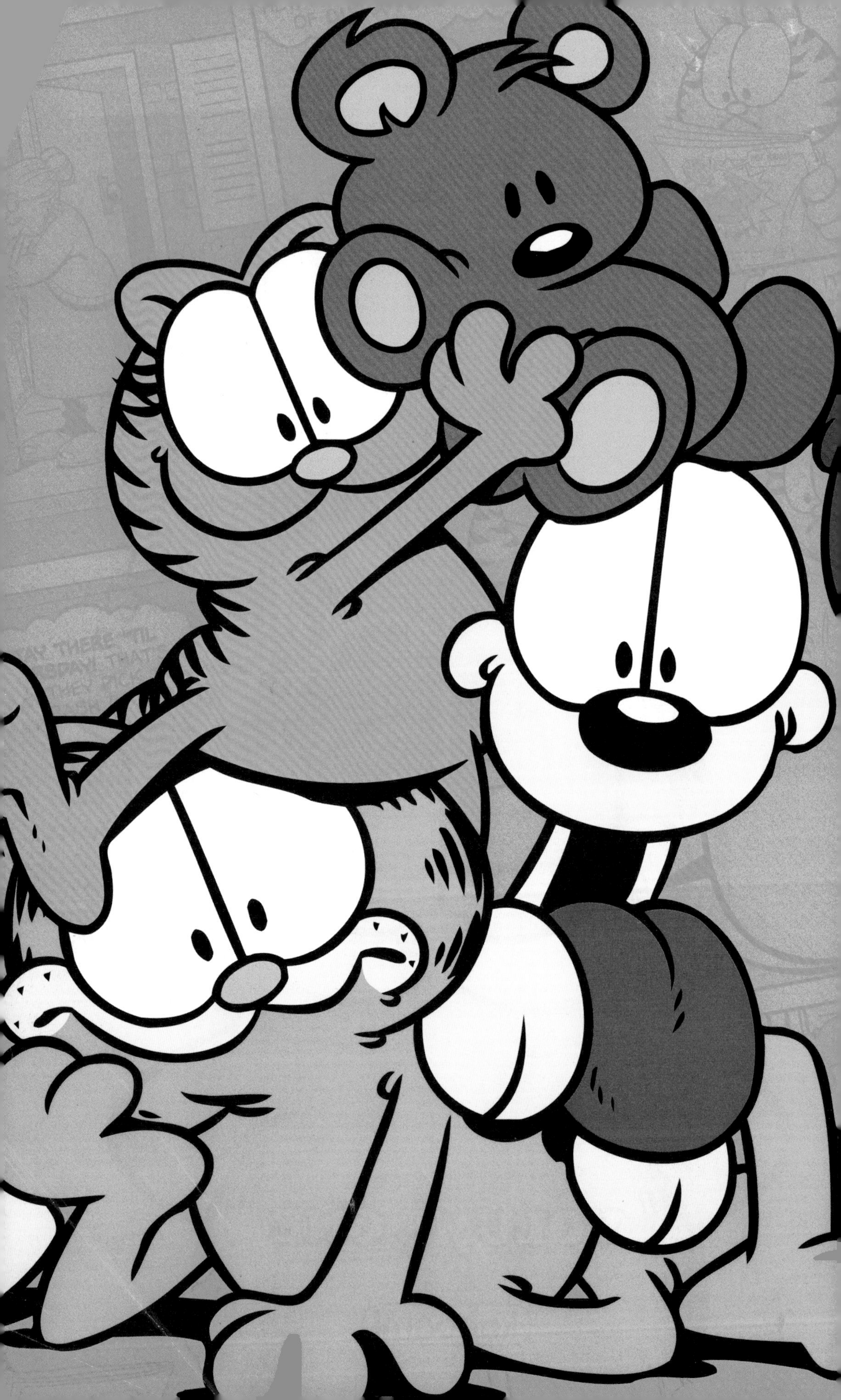

Created by
JIM DAVIS

Written by
MARK EVANIER
SCOTT NICKEL

Art by
GARY BARKER
DAN DAVIS
MIKE DeCARLO
ANDY HIRSCH
MARK & STEPHANIE HEIKE

Colors by
BRADEN LAMB
LISA MOORE

Letters by
STEVE WANDS

Cover Design by
MARIE KRUPINA

Original Series Assistant Editor

CHRIS ROSA

Original Series Editor

MATT GAGNON

Collection Editor

SHANTEL LaROCQUE

Collection Designer

ARMANDO ELIZONDO

Special Thanks to Scott Nickel, David Reddick, and the entire Paws, Inc. team, and Jeff Whitman, Micol Hiatt, and Claire Posner-Greco at Paramount.

kaboom! **nickelodeon**™

GARFIELD: FULL COURSE **Volume One**. November 2023. Published by KaBOOM!, a division of Boom Entertainment, Inc. ©2023 by Paws, Inc. All Rights Reserved. "GARFIELD" and the GARFIELD characters are trademarks of Paws, Inc. Nickelodeon is a trademark of Viacom International Inc. Based on the Garfield® characters created by Jim Davis. Originally published in single magazine form as GARFIELD No. 1-8. ™ & © 2012 Boom Entertainment, Inc. and PAWS, INCORPORATED. All rights reserved. KaBOOM!™ and the KaBOOM! logo are trademarks of Boom Entertainment, Inc., registered in various countries and categories. All characters, events, and institutions depicted herein are fictional. Any similarity between any of the names, characters, persons, events, and/or institutions in this publication to actual names, characters, and persons, whether living or dead, events, and/or institutions is unintended and purely coincidental. KaBOOM! does not read or accept unsolicited submissions of ideas, stories, or artwork.

BOOM! Studios, 6920 Melrose Avenue, Los Angeles, CA 90038-3306. Printed in Canada. First Printing.

ISBN: 978-1-60886-128-6, eISBN: 978-1-93986-750-6

45th Anniversary Edition ISBN 978-1-60886-129-3

FOREWORD

It's incredible to see that after all this time, Garfield continues to be a big, fat, and hairy deal! It's been 45 years since my first *Garfield* comic was published and fans are still in love with him—sassy cattitude and all. I suspect that the fact that there's a little Garfield in each of us has helped to capture hearts around the world. However this cat-next-door has impacted your life, it's been an honor to be part of this global phenomenon. As we celebrate this anniversary with the release of KaBOOM!'s earliest *Garfield* comic stories, may your Mondays be moody, your naps be long, and your lasagna large!

JIM DAVIS

CATTITUDE

noun
cat•ti•tude

1: Thoughts and feelings of general annoyance; sarcastic, laidback.

2: See also – Garfield

TABLE OF CONTENTS

CHAPTER ONE

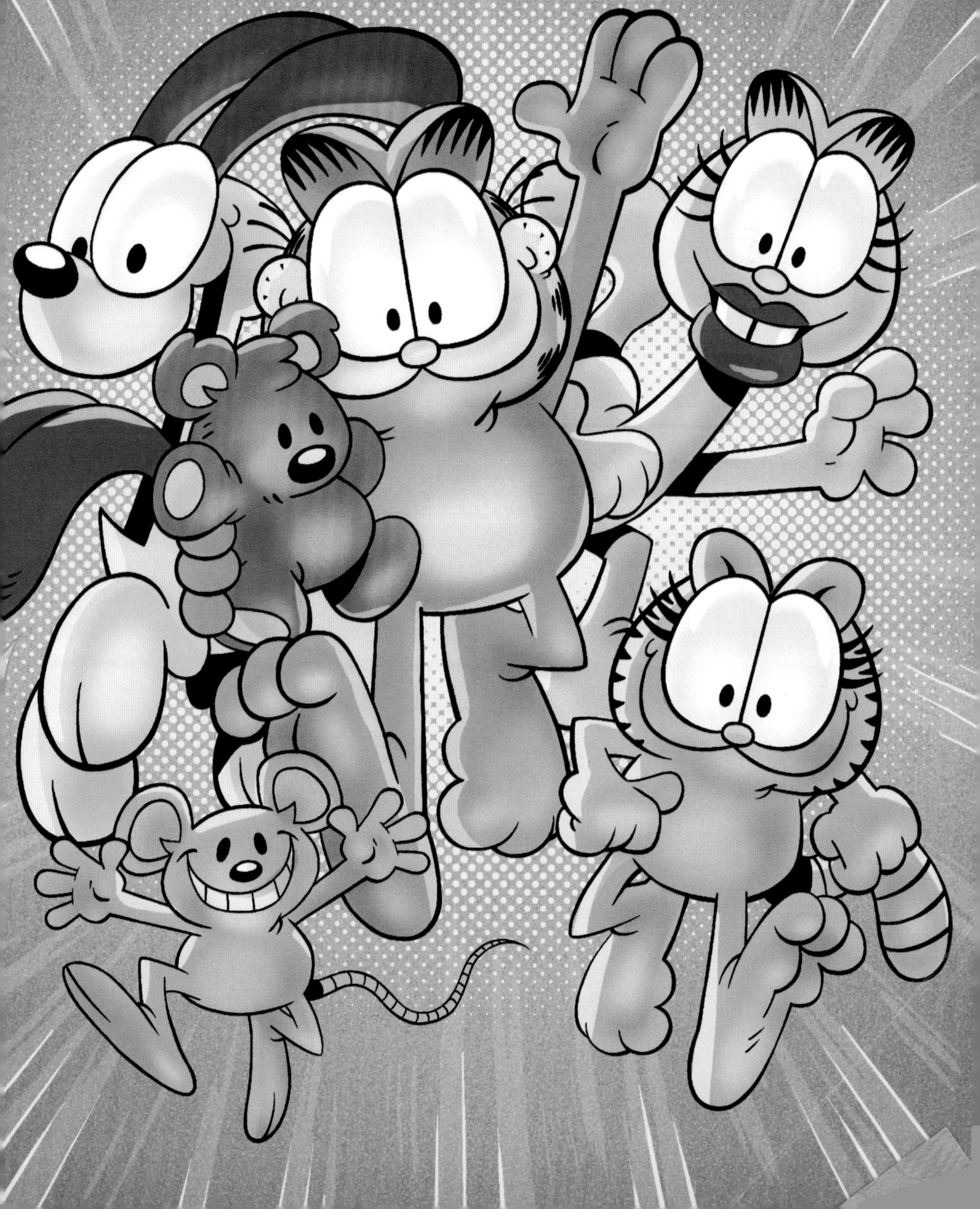

COLLECTORS
CLASSIC
BIG MOUSE MEAL

Written by
MARK EVANIER

Art by
GARY BARKER

Colors by
BRADEN LAMB

Chapter Break Art by
GARY BARKER
WITH BRADEN LAMB

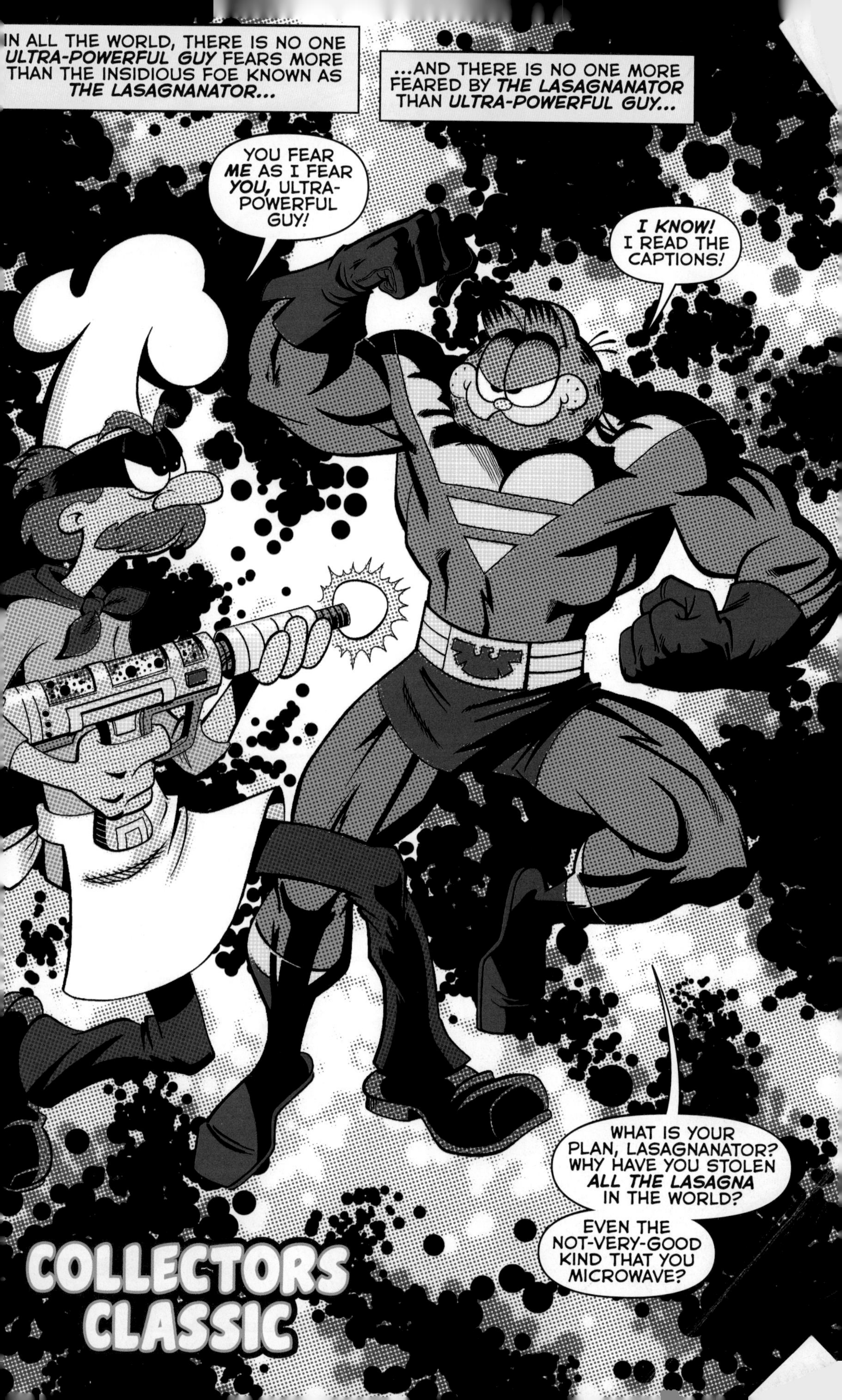
IN ALL THE WORLD, THERE IS NO ONE ULTRA-POWERFUL GUY FEARS MORE THAN THE INSIDIOUS FOE KNOWN AS THE LASAGNANATOR...
...AND THERE IS NO ONE MORE FEARED BY THE LASAGNANATOR THAN ULTRA-POWERFUL GUY...
YOU FEAR ME AS I FEAR YOU, ULTRA-POWERFUL GUY!
I KNOW! I READ THE CAPTIONS!
WHAT IS YOUR PLAN, LASAGNANATOR? WHY HAVE YOU STOLEN ALL THE LASAGNA IN THE WORLD?
EVEN THE NOT-VERY-GOOD KIND THAT YOU MICROWAVE?
COLLECTORS CLASSIC

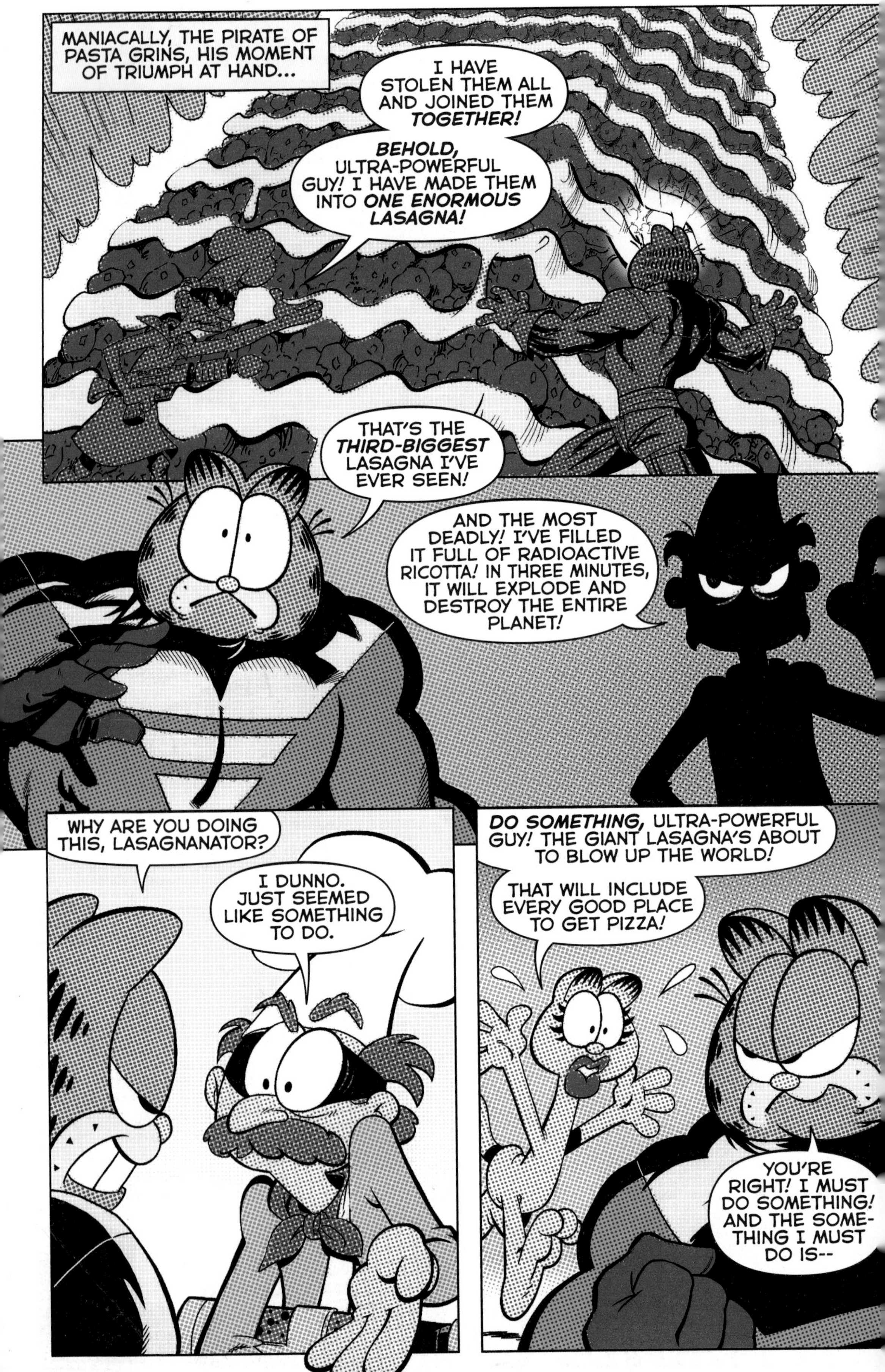
MANIACALLY, THE PIRATE OF PASTA GRINS, HIS MOMENT OF TRIUMPH AT HAND...
I HAVE STOLEN THEM ALL AND JOINED THEM TOGETHER!
BEHOLD, ULTRA-POWERFUL GUY! I HAVE MADE THEM INTO ONE ENORMOUS LASAGNA!
THAT'S THE THIRD-BIGGEST LASAGNA I'VE EVER SEEN!
AND THE MOST DEADLY! I'VE FILLED IT FULL OF RADIOACTIVE RICOTTA! IN THREE MINUTES, IT WILL EXPLODE AND DESTROY THE ENTIRE PLANET!
WHY ARE YOU DOING THIS, LASAGNANATOR?
I DUNNO. JUST SEEMED LIKE SOMETHING TO DO.
DO SOMETHING, ULTRA-POWERFUL GUY! THE GIANT LASAGNA'S ABOUT TO BLOW UP THE WORLD!
THAT WILL INCLUDE EVERY GOOD PLACE TO GET PIZZA!
YOU'RE RIGHT! I MUST DO SOMETHING! AND THE SOMETHING I MUST DO IS--

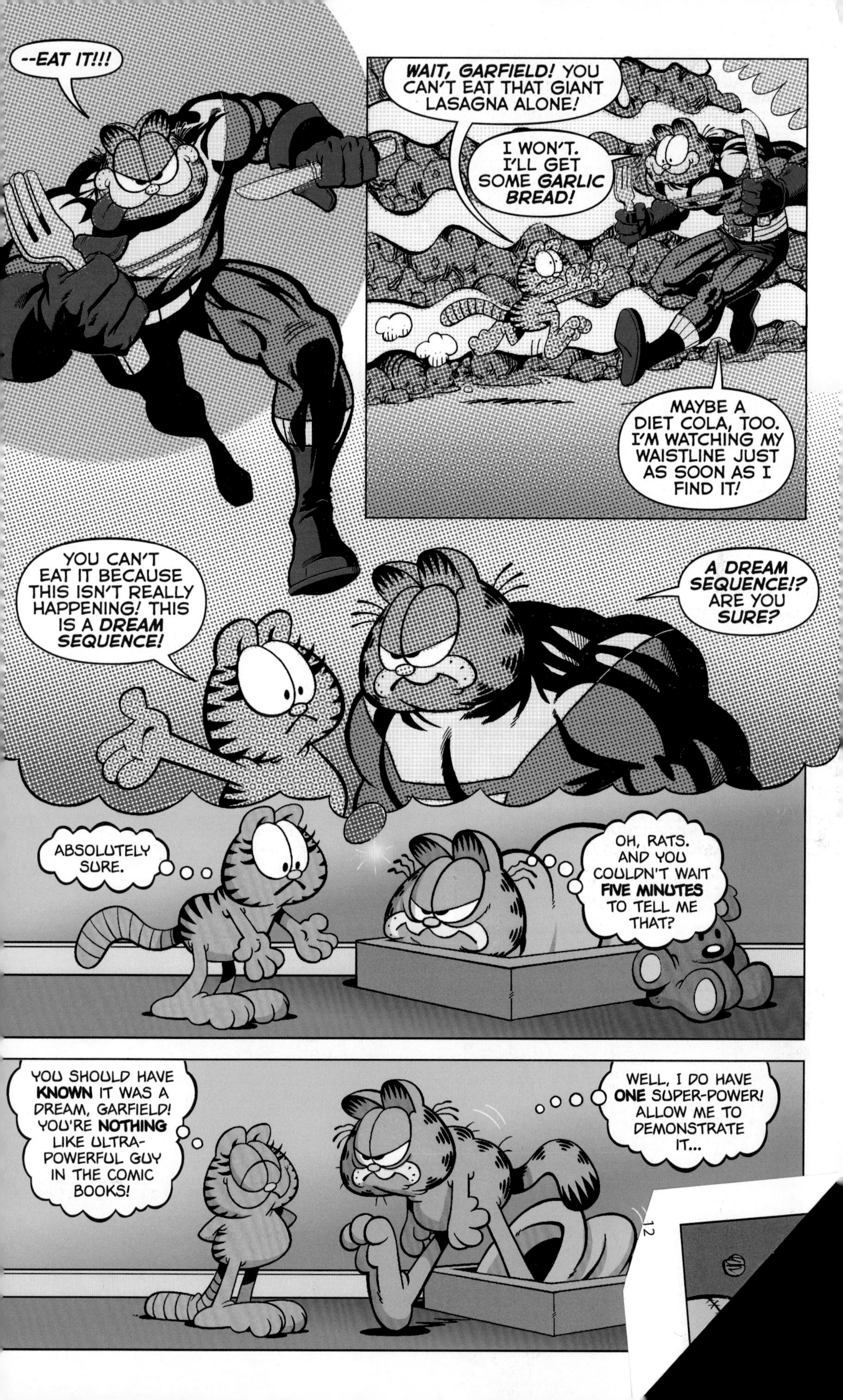
--EAT IT!!!
WAIT, GARFIELD! YOU CAN'T EAT THAT GIANT LASAGNA ALONE!
I WON'T. I'LL GET SOME GARLIC BREAD!
MAYBE A DIET COLA, TOO. I'M WATCHING MY WAISTLINE JUST AS SOON AS I FIND IT!
YOU CAN'T EAT IT BECAUSE THIS ISN'T REALLY HAPPENING! THIS IS A DREAM SEQUENCE!
A DREAM SEQUENCE!? ARE YOU SURE?
ABSOLUTELY SURE.
OH, RATS. AND YOU COULDN'T WAIT FIVE MINUTES TO TELL ME THAT?
YOU SHOULD HAVE KNOWN IT WAS A DREAM, GARFIELD! YOU'RE NOTHING LIKE ULTRA-POWERFUL GUY IN THE COMIC BOOKS!
WELL, I DO HAVE ONE SUPER-POWER! ALLOW ME TO DEMONSTRATE IT...
12

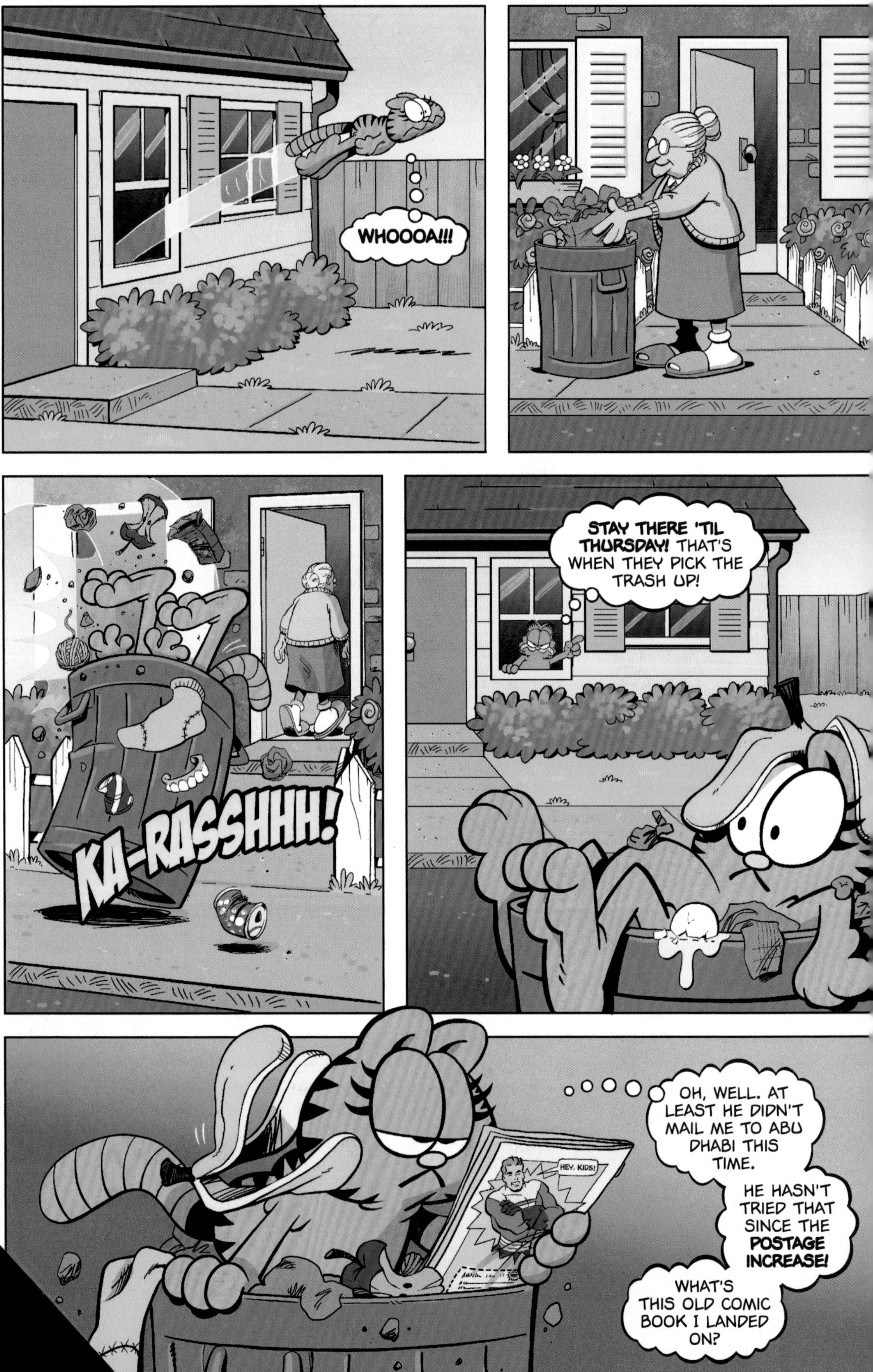
WHOOOA!!!
STAY THERE 'TIL THURSDAY! THAT'S WHEN THEY PICK THE TRASH UP!
KA-RASSHHH!
OH, WELL. AT LEAST HE DIDN'T MAIL ME TO ABU DHABI THIS TIME.
HE HASN'T TRIED THAT SINCE THE POSTAGE INCREASE!
WHAT'S THIS OLD COMIC BOOK I LANDED ON?
HEY, KIDS!

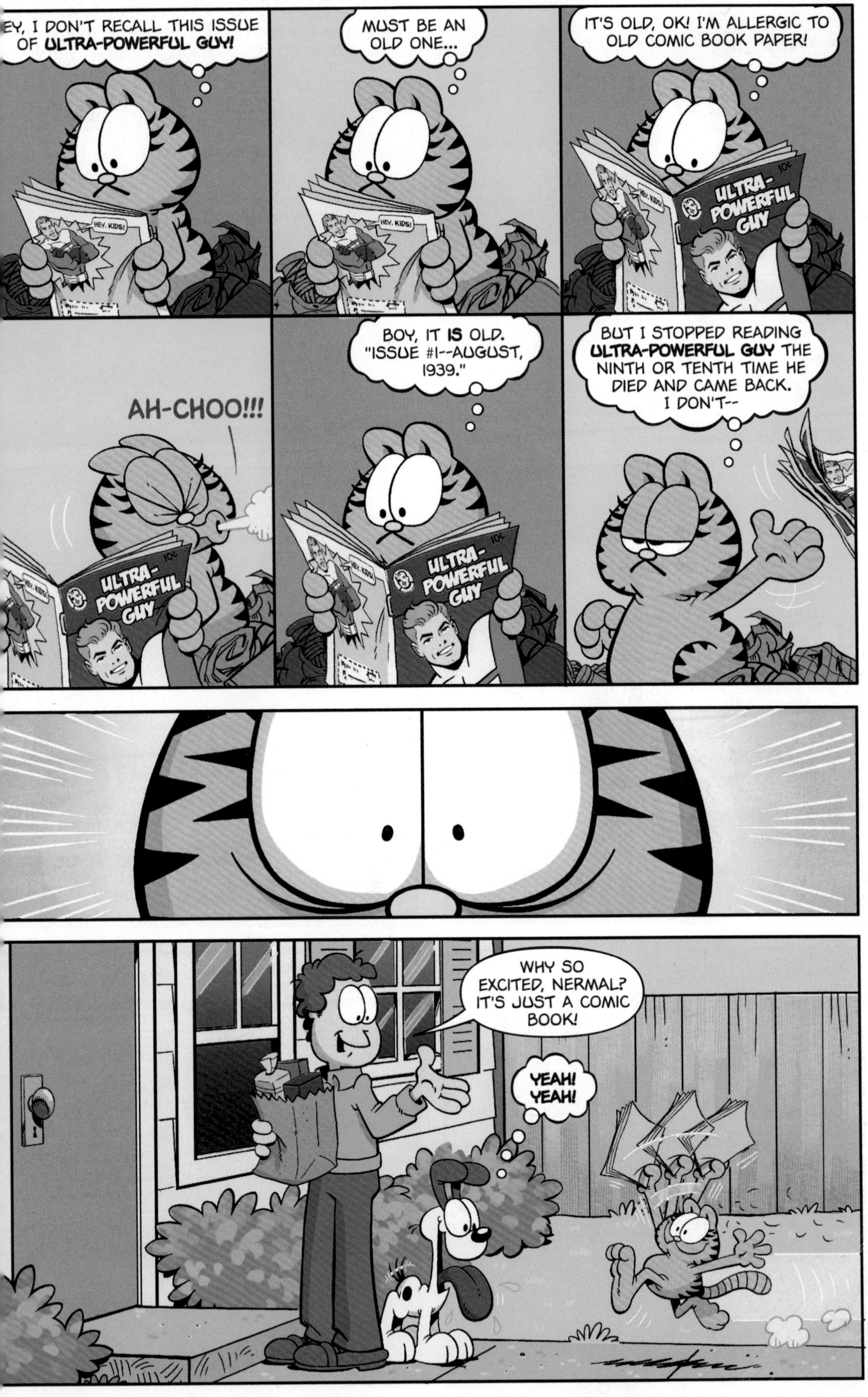
EY, I DON'T RECALL THIS ISSUE OF ULTRA-POWERFUL GUY!
HEY, KIDS!
MUST BE AN OLD ONE...
IT'S OLD, OK! I'M ALLERGIC TO OLD COMIC BOOK PAPER!
ULTRA-POWERFUL GUY
10¢
AH-CHOO!!!
BOY, IT IS OLD. "ISSUE #1--AUGUST, 1939."
BUT I STOPPED READING ULTRA-POWERFUL GUY THE NINTH OR TENTH TIME HE DIED AND CAME BACK. I DON'T--
WHY SO EXCITED, NERMAL? IT'S JUST A COMIC BOOK!
YEAH! YEAH!

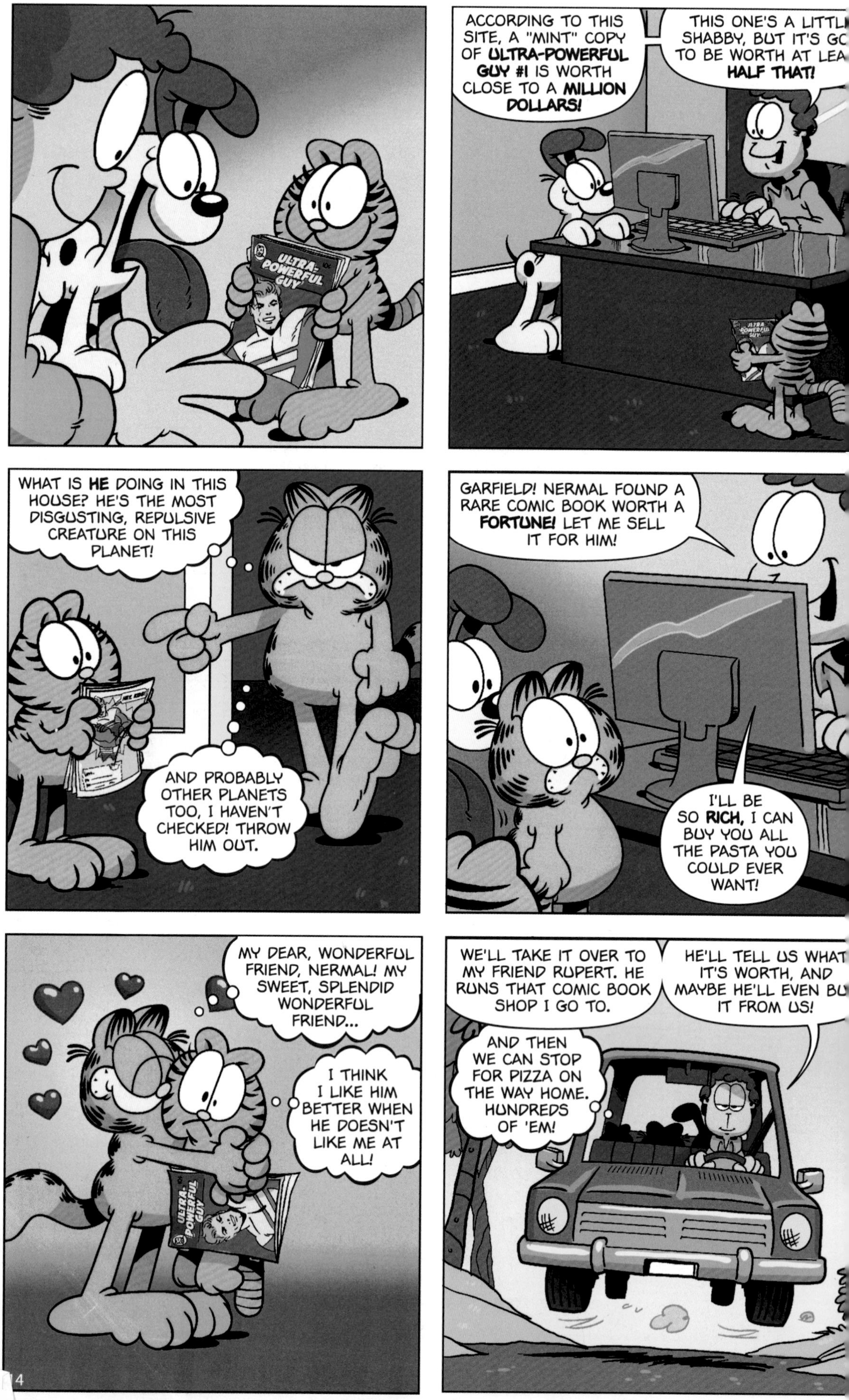

ACCORDING TO THIS SITE, A "MINT" COPY OF ULTRA-POWERFUL GUY #1 IS WORTH CLOSE TO A MILLION DOLLARS!
THIS ONE'S A LITTL SHABBY, BUT IT'S GO TO BE WORTH AT LEA HALF THAT!
ULTRA-POWERFUL GUY
WHAT IS HE DOING IN THIS HOUSE? HE'S THE MOST DISGUSTING, REPULSIVE CREATURE ON THIS PLANET!
AND PROBABLY OTHER PLANETS TOO, I HAVEN'T CHECKED! THROW HIM OUT.
GARFIELD! NERMAL FOUND A RARE COMIC BOOK WORTH A FORTUNE! LET ME SELL IT FOR HIM!
I'LL BE SO RICH, I CAN BUY YOU ALL THE PASTA YOU COULD EVER WANT!
MY DEAR, WONDERFUL FRIEND, NERMAL! MY SWEET, SPLENDID WONDERFUL FRIEND...
I THINK I LIKE HIM BETTER WHEN HE DOESN'T LIKE ME AT ALL!
ULTRA-POWERFUL GUY
WE'LL TAKE IT OVER TO MY FRIEND RUPERT. HE RUNS THAT COMIC BOOK SHOP I GO TO.
HE'LL TELL US WHAT IT'S WORTH, AND MAYBE HE'LL EVEN BU IT FROM US!
AND THEN WE CAN STOP FOR PIZZA ON THE WAY HOME. HUNDREDS OF 'EM!

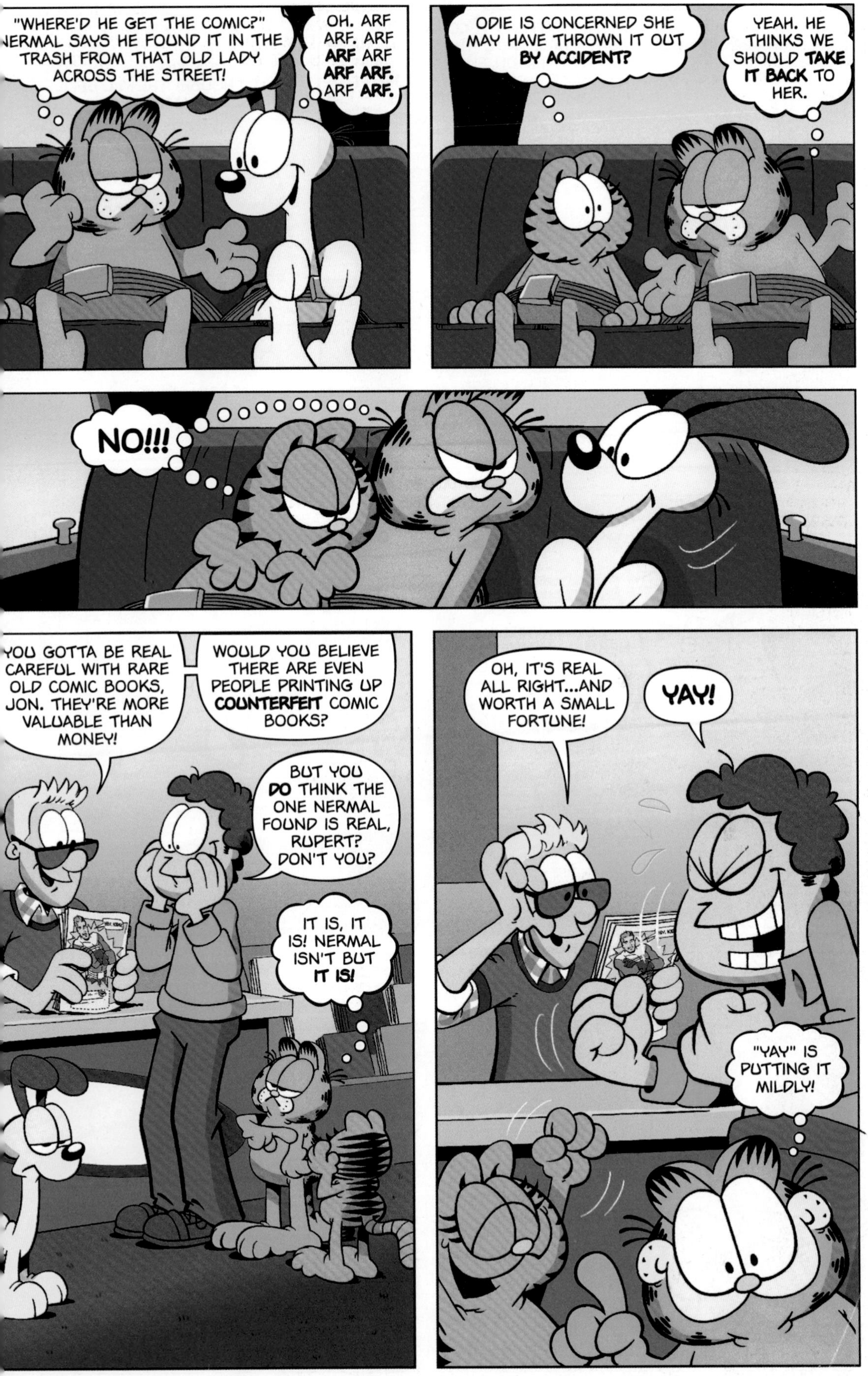
"WHERE'D HE GET THE COMIC?" NERMAL SAYS HE FOUND IT IN THE TRASH FROM THAT OLD LADY ACROSS THE STREET!
OH. ARF ARF. ARF ARF ARF ARF ARF. ARF ARF. ARF ARF.
ODIE IS CONCERNED SHE MAY HAVE THROWN IT OUT BY ACCIDENT?
YEAH. HE THINKS WE SHOULD TAKE IT BACK TO HER.
NO!!!
YOU GOTTA BE REAL CAREFUL WITH RARE OLD COMIC BOOKS, JON. THEY'RE MORE VALUABLE THAN MONEY!
WOULD YOU BELIEVE THERE ARE EVEN PEOPLE PRINTING UP COUNTERFEIT COMIC BOOKS?
BUT YOU DO THINK THE ONE NERMAL FOUND IS REAL, RUPERT? DON'T YOU?
IT IS, IT IS! NERMAL ISN'T BUT IT IS!
OH, IT'S REAL ALL RIGHT...AND WORTH A SMALL FORTUNE!
YAY!
"YAY" IS PUTTING IT MILDLY!

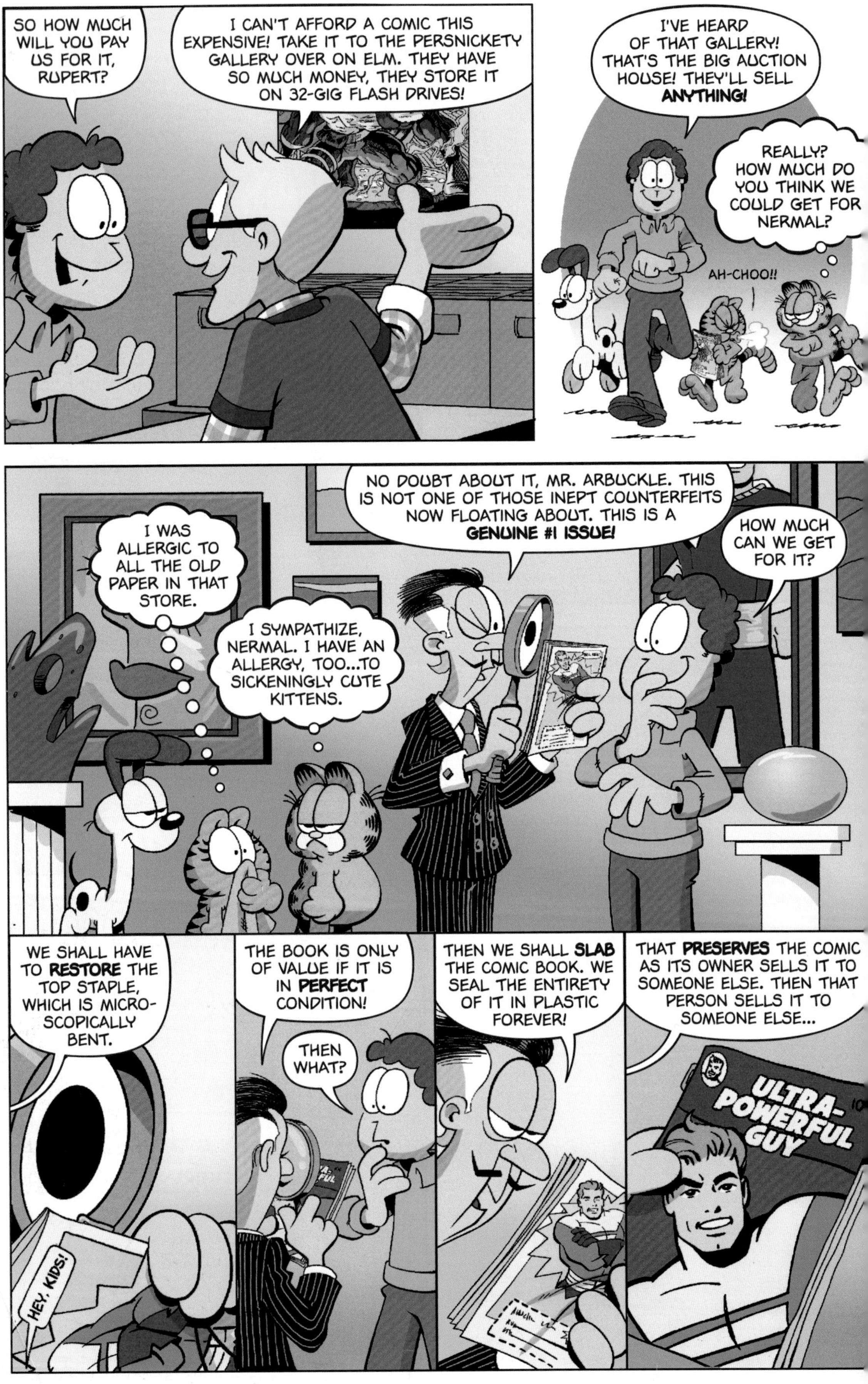
SO HOW MUCH WILL YOU PAY US FOR IT, RUPERT?
I CAN'T AFFORD A COMIC THIS EXPENSIVE! TAKE IT TO THE PERSNICKETY GALLERY OVER ON ELM. THEY HAVE SO MUCH MONEY, THEY STORE IT ON 32-GIG FLASH DRIVES!
I'VE HEARD OF THAT GALLERY! THAT'S THE BIG AUCTION HOUSE! THEY'LL SELL **ANYTHING!**
REALLY? HOW MUCH DO YOU THINK WE COULD GET FOR NERMAL?
AH-CHOO!!
NO DOUBT ABOUT IT, MR. ARBUCKLE. THIS IS NOT ONE OF THOSE INEPT COUNTERFEITS NOW FLOATING ABOUT. THIS IS A **GENUINE #1 ISSUE!**
I WAS ALLERGIC TO ALL THE OLD PAPER IN THAT STORE.
I SYMPATHIZE, NERMAL. I HAVE AN ALLERGY, TOO...TO SICKENINGLY CUTE KITTENS.
HOW MUCH CAN WE GET FOR IT?
WE SHALL HAVE TO **RESTORE** THE TOP STAPLE, WHICH IS MICRO-SCOPICALLY BENT.
HEY, KIDS!
THE BOOK IS ONLY OF VALUE IF IT IS IN **PERFECT** CONDITION!
THEN WHAT?
THEN WE SHALL **SLAB** THE COMIC BOOK. WE SEAL THE ENTIRETY OF IT IN PLASTIC FOREVER!
THAT **PRESERVES** THE COMIC AS ITS OWNER SELLS IT TO SOMEONE ELSE. THEN THAT PERSON SELLS IT TO SOMEONE ELSE...
ULTRA-POWERFUL GUY

YES, BUT WHEN DOES ANYONE GET TO **READ** IT?

WHY ON EARTH WOULD ANYONE WANT TO DO **THAT?**

HERE, YOU ADORABLE MINT-CONDITION KITTEN. HANDLE IT CARE-FULLY.

10 MINT

Garfield

WE JUST SLABBED EVERY SINGLE COPY OF A NEWLY RELEASED #1 ISSUE EXCEPT FOR **ONE** COPY!

IN FACT, OUR COMPUTERS TELL US THAT RIGHT THIS MOMENT, SOMEONE IS READING THAT ONE COPY!

REALLY?

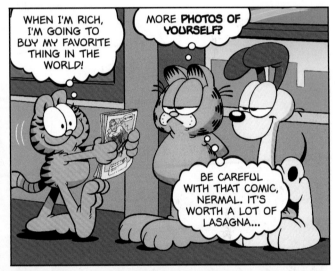

WHEN I'M RICH, I'M GOING TO BUY MY FAVORITE THING IN THE WORLD!

MORE **PHOTOS OF YOURSELF?**

BE CAREFUL WITH THAT COMIC, NERMAL. IT'S WORTH A LOT OF LASAGNA...

AH-CHOO!!

YOWP!

NERMAL! YOU JUST SNEEZED OUR FORTUNE **OUT** THE WINDOW!

IT WASN'T MY FAULT! I'M **ALLERGIC!**

IF WE DON'T FIND IT, YOU'D BETTER HOPE YOU'RE NOT ALLERGIC TO BEING MAILED TO ABU DHABI!

I CAN SMELL THE POSTAGE STAMPS ALREADY!

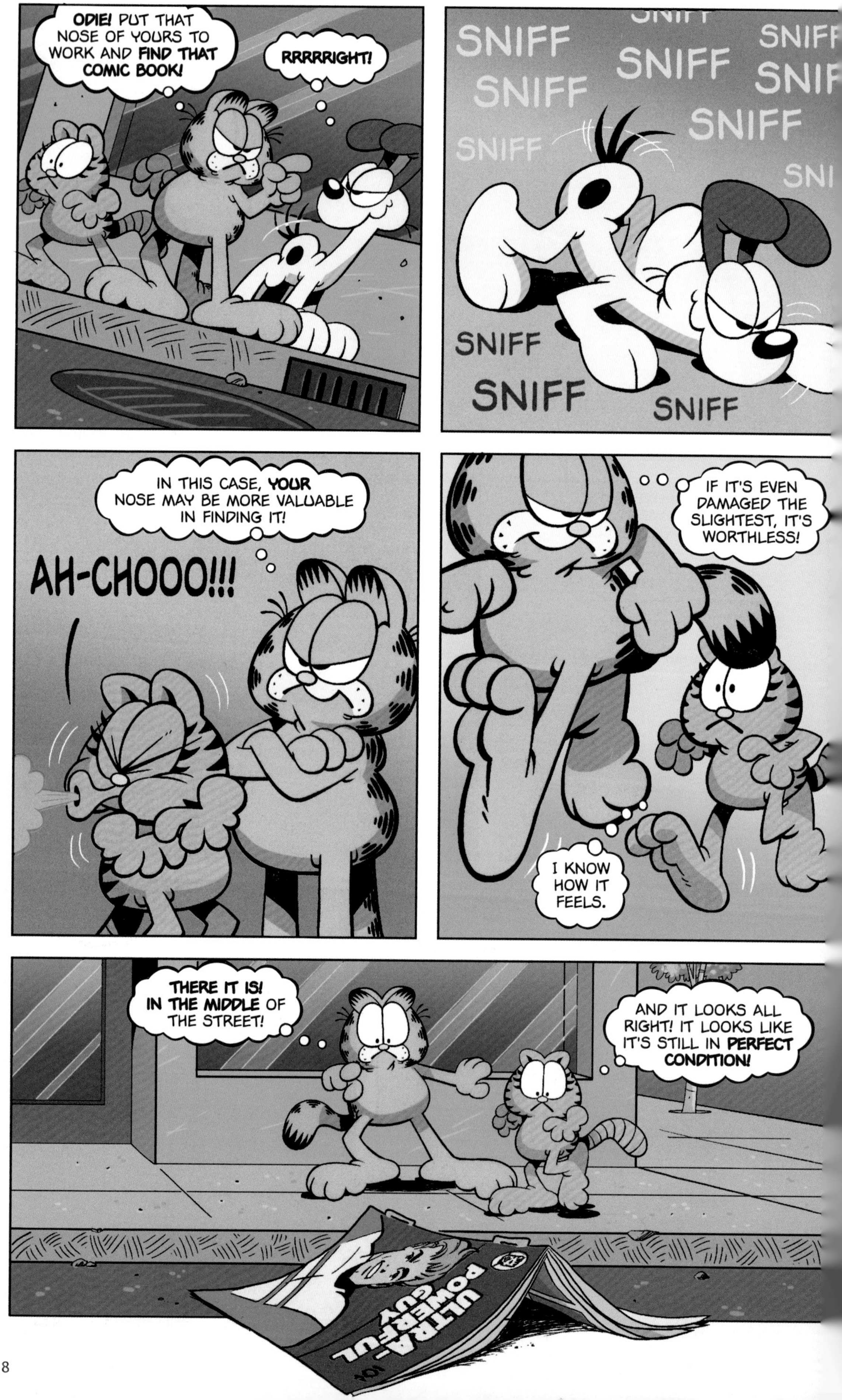
ODIE! PUT THAT NOSE OF YOURS TO WORK AND FIND THAT COMIC BOOK!
RRRRRIGHT!
SNIFF
SNIFF
SNIFF
SNIFF
SNIFF
SNIFF
SNIFF
SNIFF
SNIFF
SNIFF
IN THIS CASE, YOUR NOSE MAY BE MORE VALUABLE IN FINDING IT!
AH-CHOOO!!!
IF IT'S EVEN DAMAGED THE SLIGHTEST, IT'S WORTHLESS!
I KNOW HOW IT FEELS.
THERE IT IS! IN THE MIDDLE OF THE STREET!
AND IT LOOKS ALL RIGHT! IT LOOKS LIKE IT'S STILL IN PERFECT CONDITION!

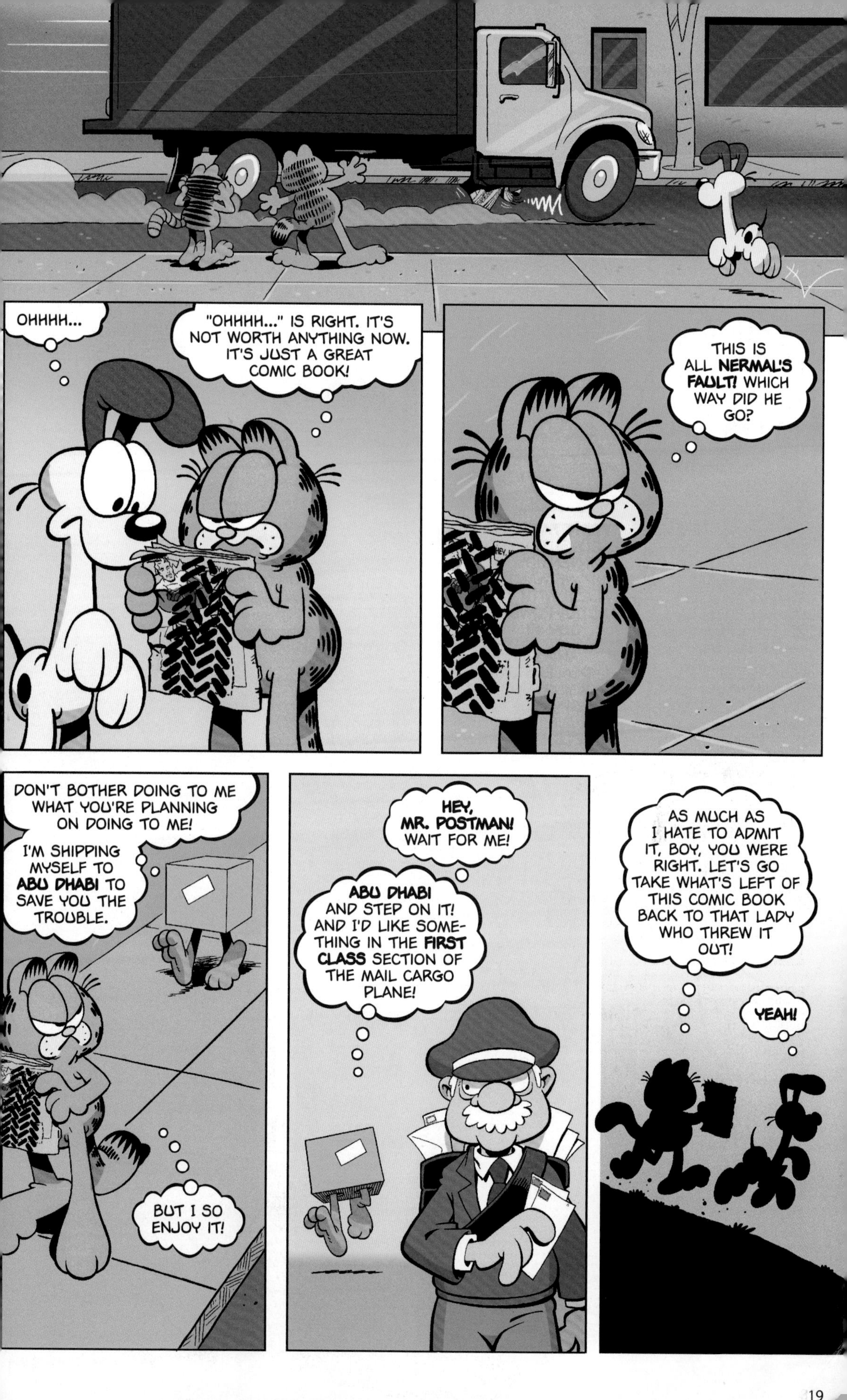

OHHHH...
"OHHHH..." IS RIGHT. IT'S NOT WORTH ANYTHING NOW. IT'S JUST A GREAT COMIC BOOK!
THIS IS ALL NERMAL'S FAULT! WHICH WAY DID HE GO?
DON'T BOTHER DOING TO ME WHAT YOU'RE PLANNING ON DOING TO ME!
I'M SHIPPING MYSELF TO ABU DHABI TO SAVE YOU THE TROUBLE.
BUT I SO ENJOY IT!
HEY, MR. POSTMAN! WAIT FOR ME!
ABU DHABI AND STEP ON IT! AND I'D LIKE SOMETHING IN THE FIRST CLASS SECTION OF THE MAIL CARGO PLANE!
AS MUCH AS I HATE TO ADMIT IT, BOY, YOU WERE RIGHT. LET'S GO TAKE WHAT'S LEFT OF THIS COMIC BOOK BACK TO THAT LADY WHO THREW IT OUT!
YEAH!

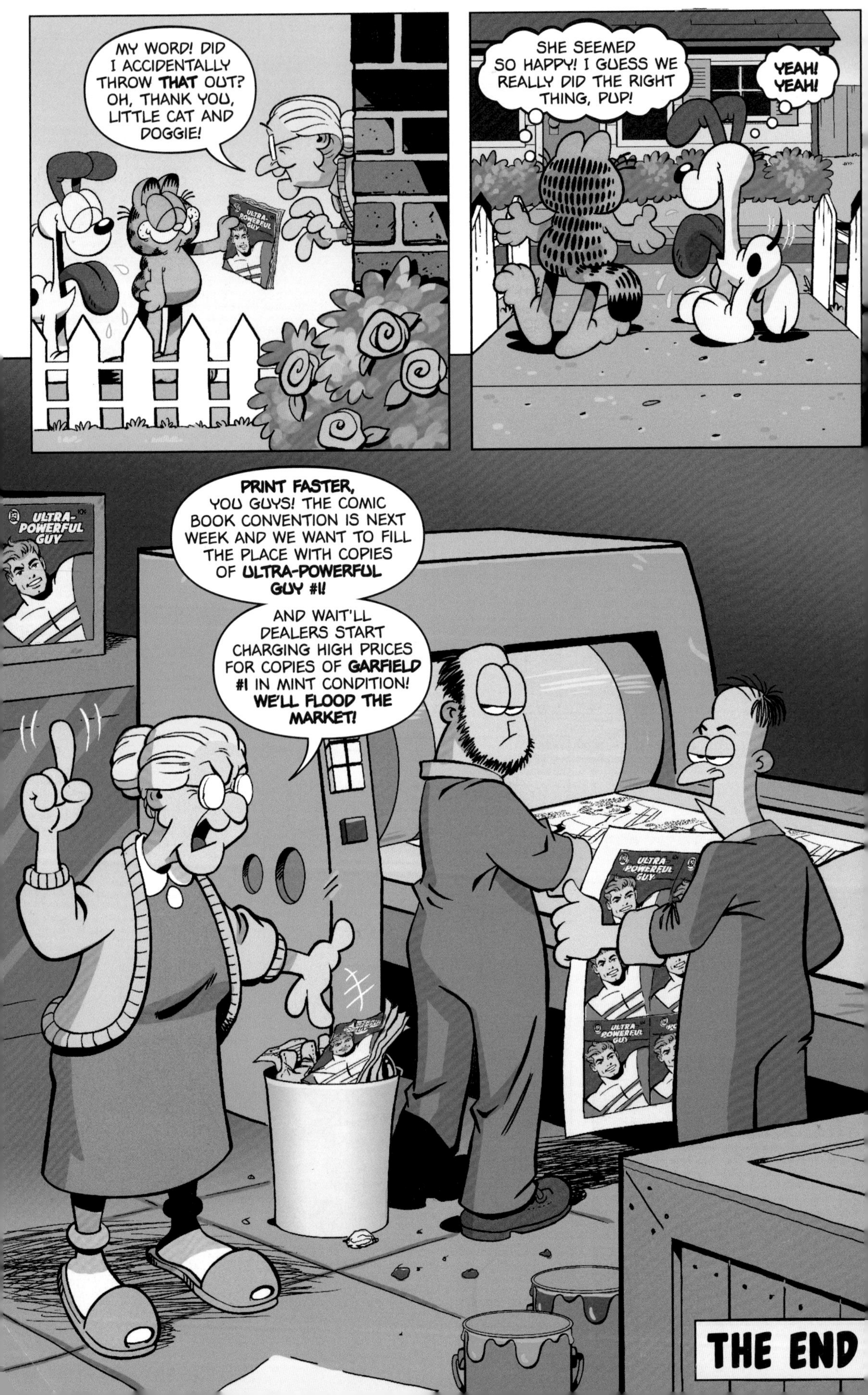
MY WORD! DID I ACCIDENTALLY THROW **THAT** OUT? OH, THANK YOU, LITTLE CAT AND DOGGIE!
ULTRA-POWERFUL GUY
SHE SEEMED SO HAPPY! I GUESS WE REALLY DID THE RIGHT THING, PUP!
YEAH! YEAH!
ULTRA-POWERFUL GUY
PRINT FASTER, YOU GUYS! THE COMIC BOOK CONVENTION IS NEXT WEEK AND WE WANT TO FILL THE PLACE WITH COPIES OF **ULTRA-POWERFUL GUY #1!**
AND WAIT'LL DEALERS START CHARGING HIGH PRICES FOR COPIES OF **GARFIELD #1** IN MINT CONDITION! **WE'LL FLOOD THE MARKET!**
ULTRA-POWERFUL GUY
THE END

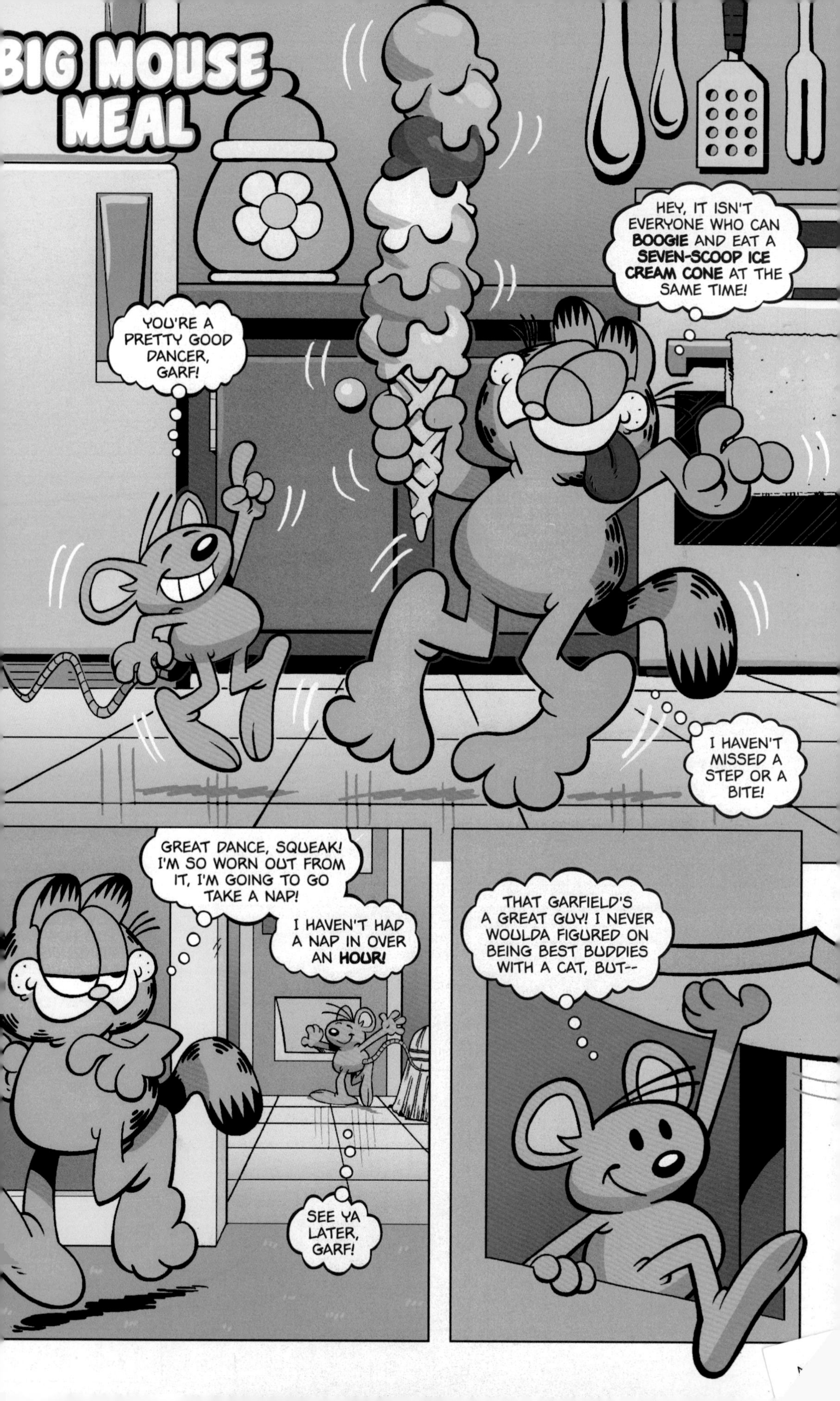

BIG MOUSE MEAL
YOU'RE A PRETTY GOOD DANCER, GARF!
HEY, IT ISN'T EVERYONE WHO CAN BOOGIE AND EAT A SEVEN-SCOOP ICE CREAM CONE AT THE SAME TIME!
I HAVEN'T MISSED A STEP OR A BITE!
GREAT DANCE, SQUEAK! I'M SO WORN OUT FROM IT, I'M GOING TO GO TAKE A NAP!
I HAVEN'T HAD A NAP IN OVER AN HOUR!
SEE YA LATER, GARF!
THAT GARFIELD'S A GREAT GUY! I NEVER WOULDA FIGURED ON BEING BEST BUDDIES WITH A CAT, BUT--

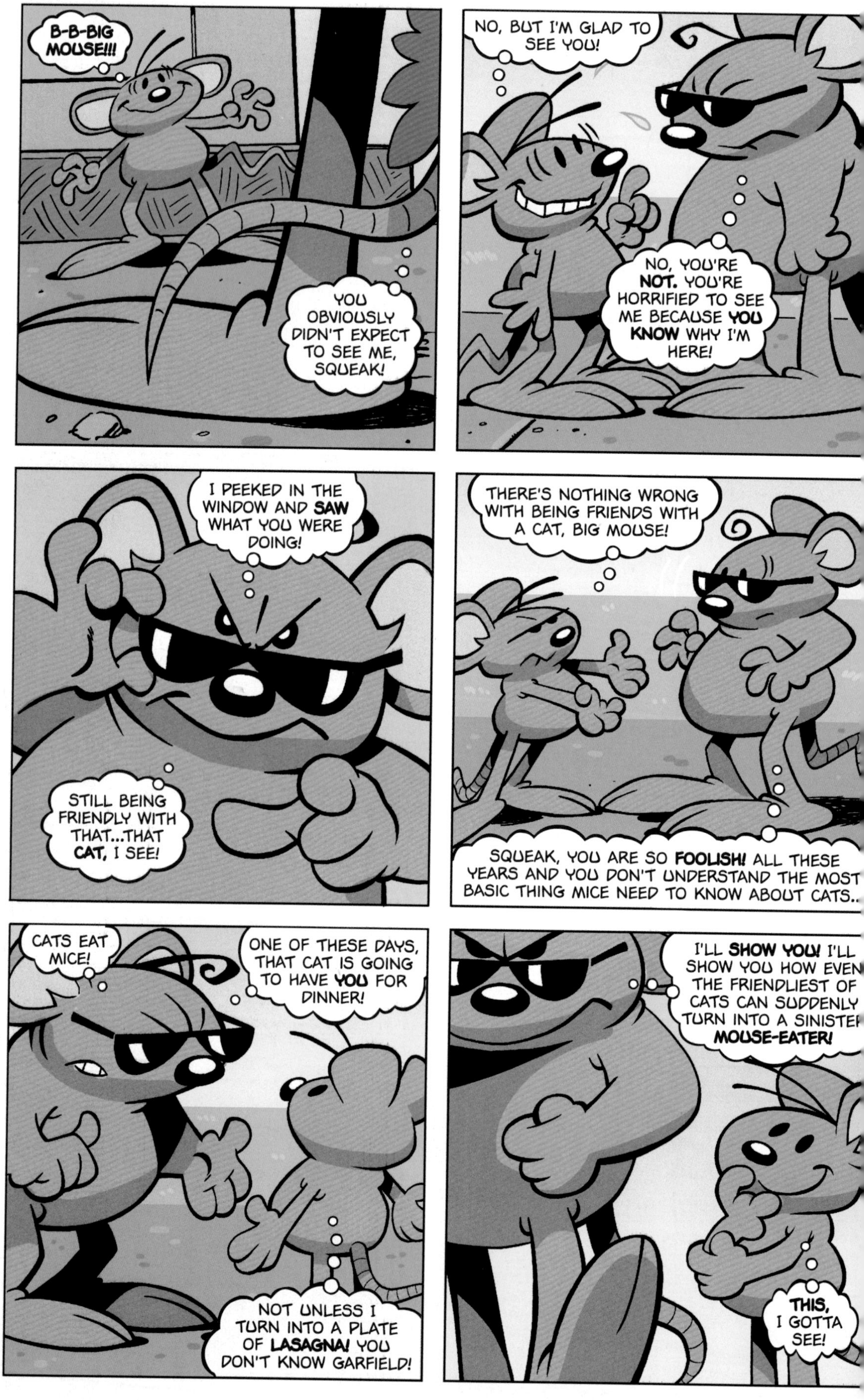
B-B-BIG MOUSE!!!
YOU OBVIOUSLY DIDN'T EXPECT TO SEE ME, SQUEAK!
NO, BUT I'M GLAD TO SEE YOU!
NO, YOU'RE NOT. YOU'RE HORRIFIED TO SEE ME BECAUSE YOU KNOW WHY I'M HERE!
I PEEKED IN THE WINDOW AND SAW WHAT YOU WERE DOING!
STILL BEING FRIENDLY WITH THAT...THAT CAT, I SEE!
THERE'S NOTHING WRONG WITH BEING FRIENDS WITH A CAT, BIG MOUSE!
SQUEAK, YOU ARE SO FOOLISH! ALL THESE YEARS AND YOU DON'T UNDERSTAND THE MOST BASIC THING MICE NEED TO KNOW ABOUT CATS...
CATS EAT MICE!
ONE OF THESE DAYS, THAT CAT IS GOING TO HAVE YOU FOR DINNER!
NOT UNLESS I TURN INTO A PLATE OF LASAGNA! YOU DON'T KNOW GARFIELD!
I'LL SHOW YOU! I'LL SHOW YOU HOW EVEN THE FRIENDLIEST OF CATS CAN SUDDENLY TURN INTO A SINISTER MOUSE-EATER!
THIS, I GOTTA SEE!

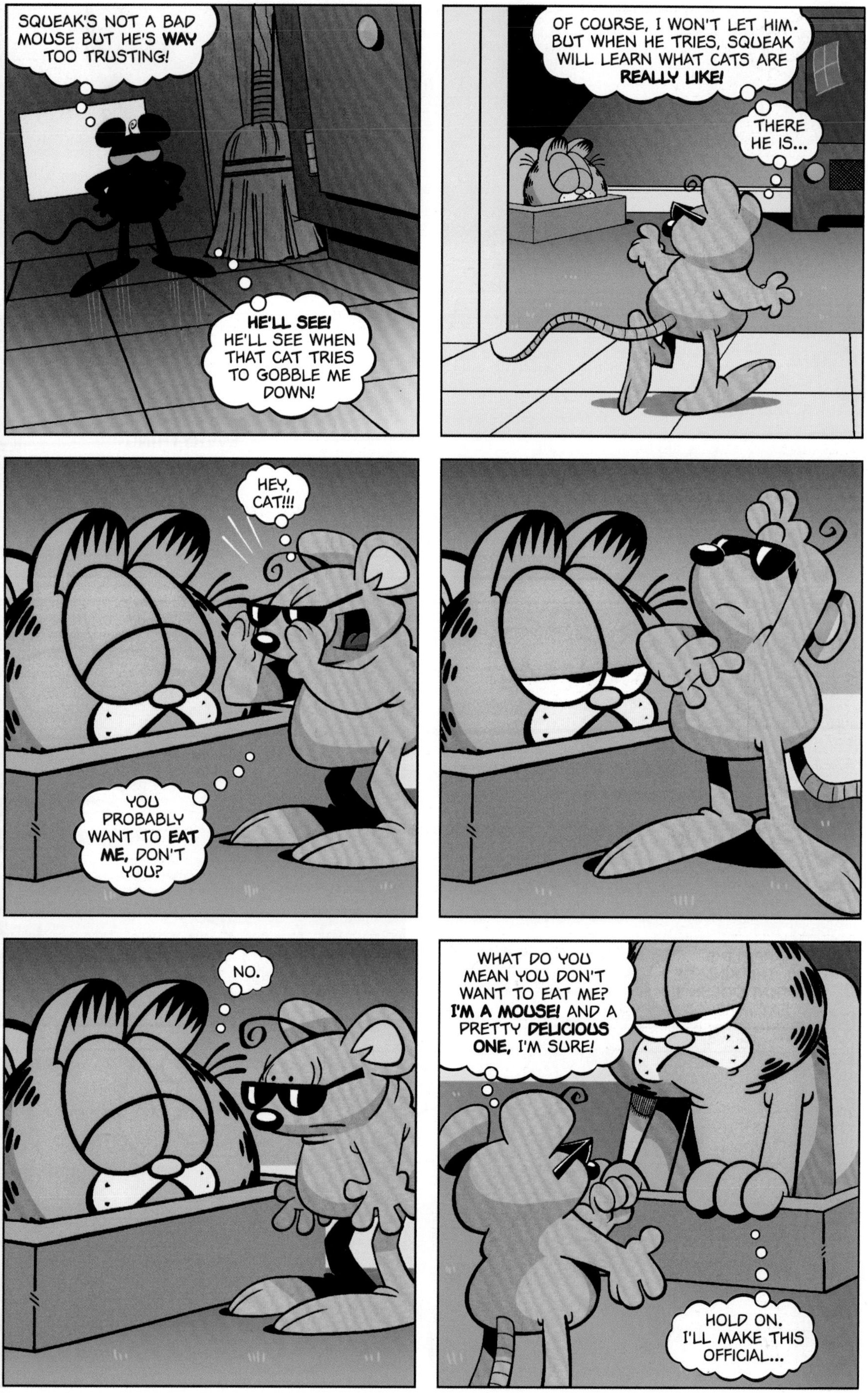

SQUEAK'S NOT A BAD MOUSE BUT HE'S **WAY** TOO TRUSTING!
HE'LL SEE! HE'LL SEE WHEN THAT CAT TRIES TO GOBBLE ME DOWN!
OF COURSE, I WON'T LET HIM. BUT WHEN HE TRIES, SQUEAK WILL LEARN WHAT CATS ARE **REALLY LIKE!**
THERE HE IS...
HEY, CAT!!!
YOU PROBABLY WANT TO **EAT ME,** DON'T YOU?
NO.
WHAT DO YOU MEAN YOU DON'T WANT TO EAT ME? **I'M A MOUSE!** AND A PRETTY **DELICIOUS ONE,** I'M SURE!
HOLD ON. I'LL MAKE THIS OFFICIAL...

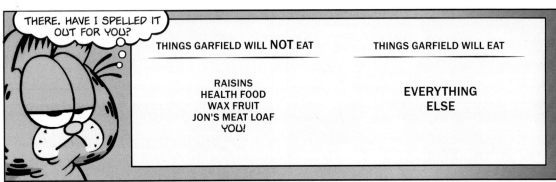

THERE. HAVE I SPELLED IT OUT FOR YOU?

THINGS GARFIELD WILL **NOT** EAT	THINGS GARFIELD WILL EAT
RAISINS HEALTH FOOD WAX FRUIT JON'S MEAT LOAF YOU!	EVERYTHING ELSE

TOLD YA!

THERE'S **NO SUCH** ANIMAL!

GARFIELD'S JUST THE KIND OF CAT THAT DOESN'T EAT MICE!

HE'S A CAT! **CATS** EAT MICE!

I'M GOING TO PROVE THAT TO SQUEAK IF IT'S THE LAST THING I DO!

I THINK I NEED A PRE-NAP SANDWICH, BUT I DON'T KNOW WHAT KIND...

MAYBE PEANUT BUTTER...MAYBE TURKEY...

MAYBE PEANUT BUTTER **AND** TURKEY...

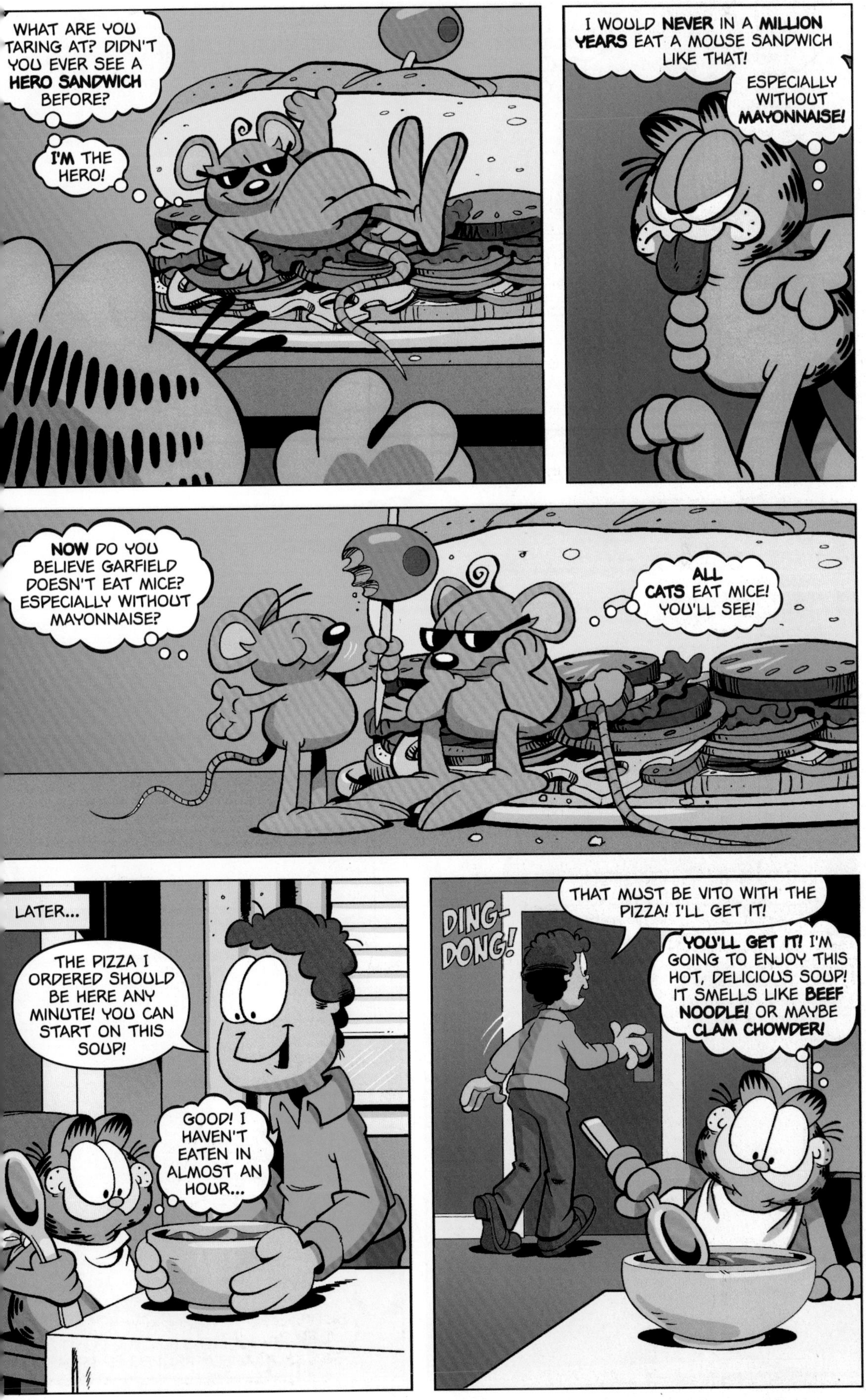

WHAT ARE YOU TARING AT? DIDN'T YOU EVER SEE A **HERO SANDWICH** BEFORE?
I'M THE HERO!
I WOULD **NEVER** IN A **MILLION YEARS** EAT A MOUSE SANDWICH LIKE THAT!
ESPECIALLY WITHOUT **MAYONNAISE!**
NOW DO YOU BELIEVE GARFIELD DOESN'T EAT MICE? ESPECIALLY WITHOUT MAYONNAISE?
ALL CATS EAT MICE! YOU'LL SEE!
LATER...
THE PIZZA I ORDERED SHOULD BE HERE ANY MINUTE! YOU CAN START ON THIS SOUP!
GOOD! I HAVEN'T EATEN IN ALMOST AN HOUR...
DING-DONG!
THAT MUST BE VITO WITH THE PIZZA! I'LL GET IT!
YOU'LL GET IT! I'M GOING TO ENJOY THIS HOT, DELICIOUS SOUP! IT SMELLS LIKE **BEEF NOODLE!** OR MAYBE **CLAM CHOWDER!**

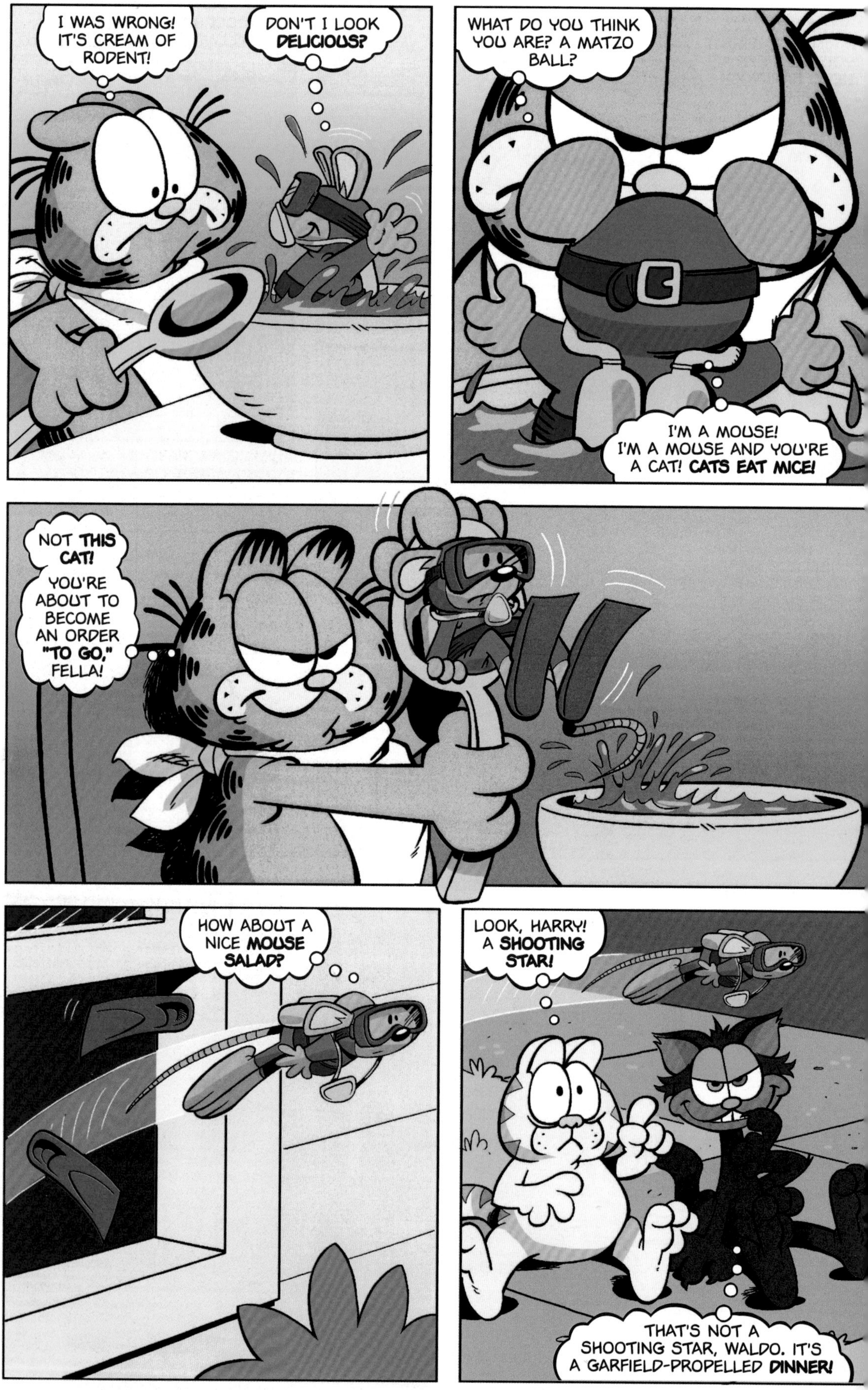
I WAS WRONG! IT'S CREAM OF RODENT!
DON'T I LOOK **DELICIOUS?**
WHAT DO YOU THINK YOU ARE? A MATZO BALL?
I'M A MOUSE! I'M A MOUSE AND YOU'RE A CAT! **CATS EAT MICE!**
NOT **THIS CAT!** YOU'RE ABOUT TO BECOME AN ORDER **"TO GO,"** FELLA!
HOW ABOUT A NICE **MOUSE SALAD?**
LOOK, HARRY! A **SHOOTING STAR!**
THAT'S NOT A SHOOTING STAR, WALDO. IT'S A GARFIELD-PROPELLED **DINNER!**

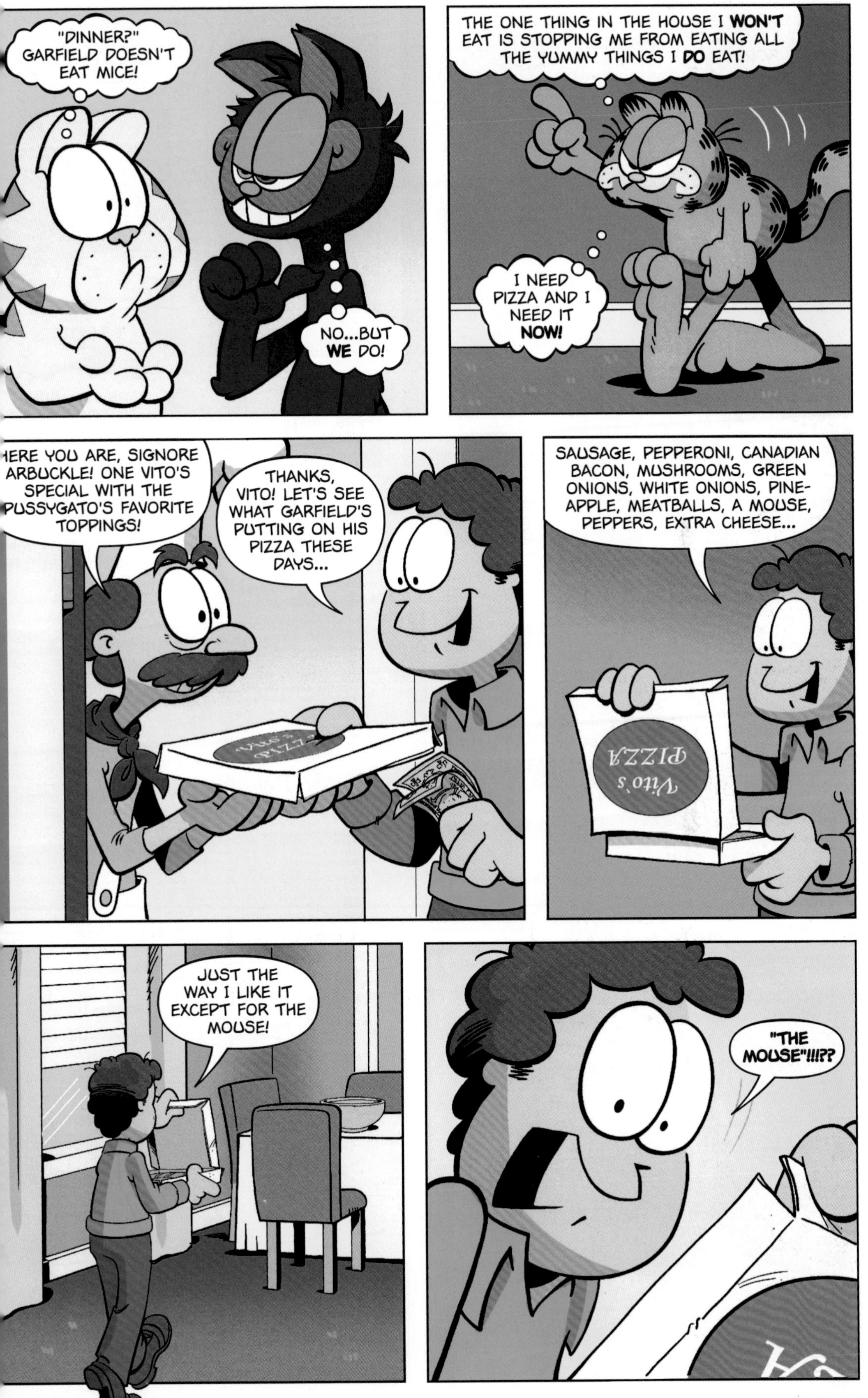
"DINNER?" GARFIELD DOESN'T EAT MICE!
NO...BUT **WE** DO!
THE ONE THING IN THE HOUSE I **WON'T** EAT IS STOPPING ME FROM EATING ALL THE YUMMY THINGS I **DO** EAT!
I NEED PIZZA AND I NEED IT **NOW!**
HERE YOU ARE, SIGNORE ARBUCKLE! ONE VITO'S SPECIAL WITH THE PUSSYGATO'S FAVORITE TOPPINGS!
THANKS, VITO! LET'S SEE WHAT GARFIELD'S PUTTING ON HIS PIZZA THESE DAYS...
SAUSAGE, PEPPERONI, CANADIAN BACON, MUSHROOMS, GREEN ONIONS, WHITE ONIONS, PINE-APPLE, MEATBALLS, A MOUSE, PEPPERS, EXTRA CHEESE...
JUST THE WAY I LIKE IT EXCEPT FOR THE MOUSE!
"THE MOUSE"!!!??

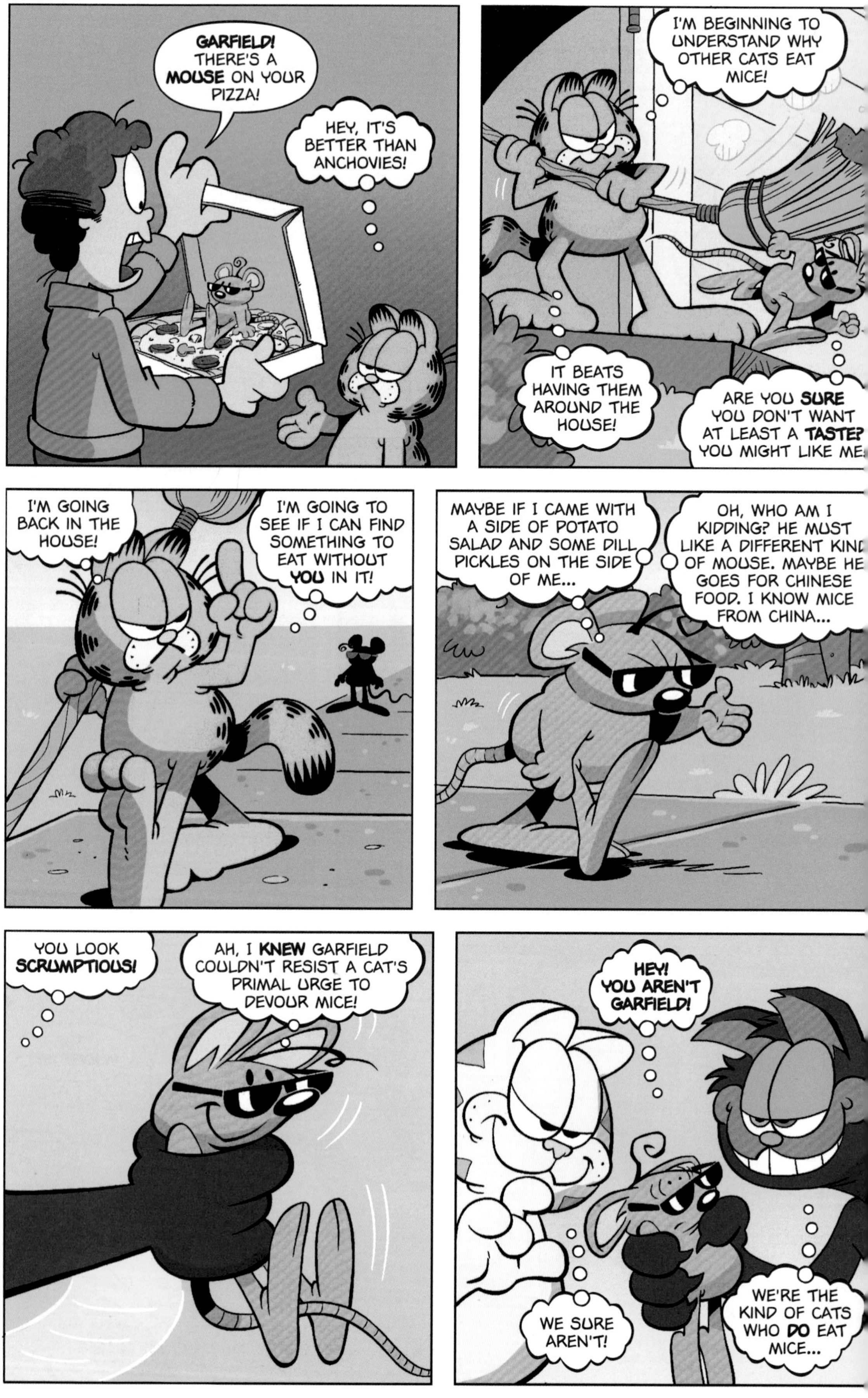
GARFIELD! THERE'S A MOUSE ON YOUR PIZZA!
HEY, IT'S BETTER THAN ANCHOVIES!
I'M BEGINNING TO UNDERSTAND WHY OTHER CATS EAT MICE!
IT BEATS HAVING THEM AROUND THE HOUSE!
ARE YOU SURE YOU DON'T WANT AT LEAST A TASTE? YOU MIGHT LIKE ME.
I'M GOING BACK IN THE HOUSE!
I'M GOING TO SEE IF I CAN FIND SOMETHING TO EAT WITHOUT YOU IN IT!
MAYBE IF I CAME WITH A SIDE OF POTATO SALAD AND SOME DILL PICKLES ON THE SIDE OF ME...
OH, WHO AM I KIDDING? HE MUST LIKE A DIFFERENT KIND OF MOUSE. MAYBE HE GOES FOR CHINESE FOOD. I KNOW MICE FROM CHINA...
YOU LOOK SCRUMPTIOUS!
AH, I KNEW GARFIELD COULDN'T RESIST A CAT'S PRIMAL URGE TO DEVOUR MICE!
HEY! YOU AREN'T GARFIELD!
WE SURE AREN'T!
WE'RE THE KIND OF CATS WHO DO EAT MICE...

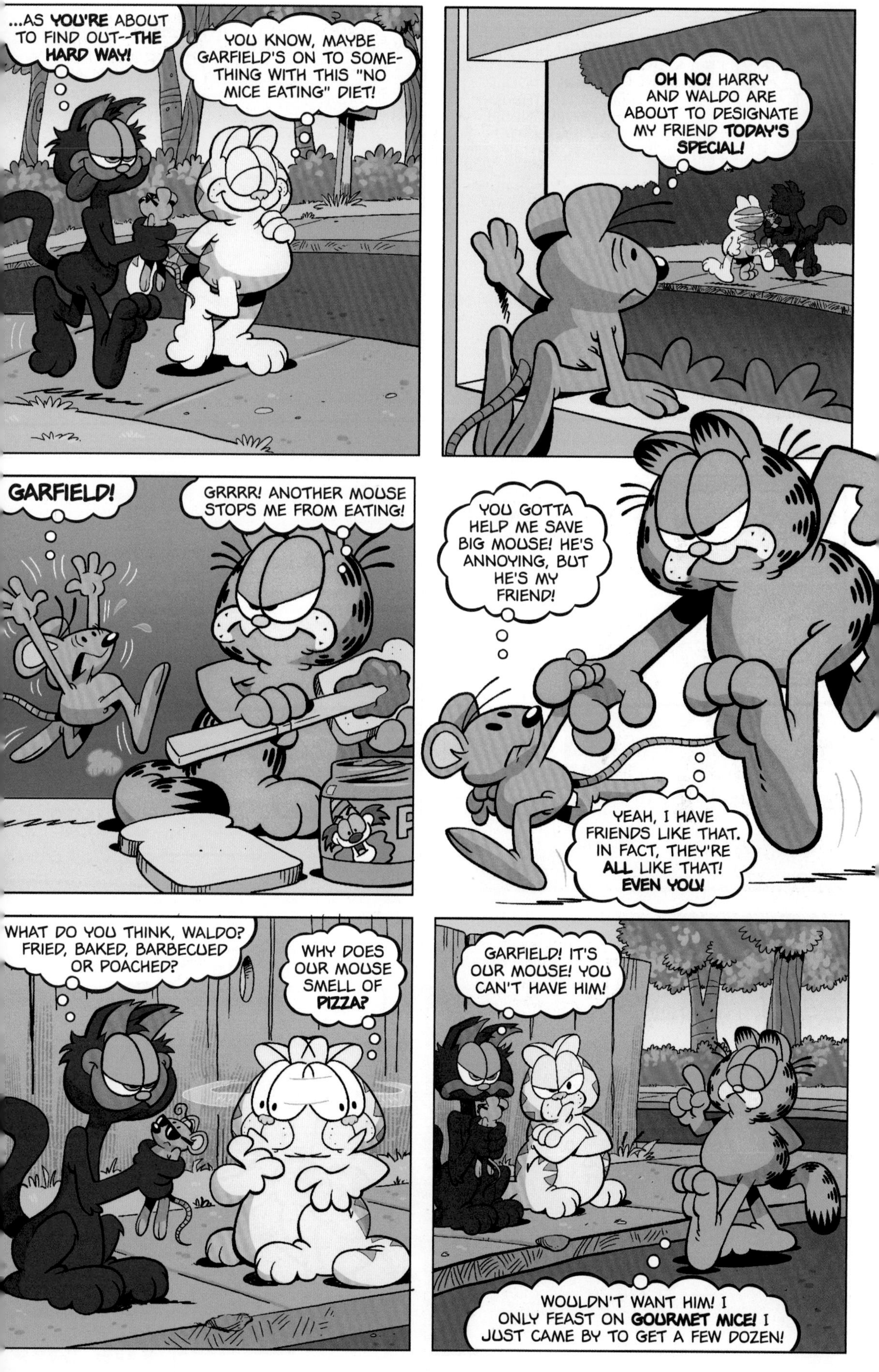
...AS YOU'RE ABOUT TO FIND OUT--THE HARD WAY!
YOU KNOW, MAYBE GARFIELD'S ON TO SOMETHING WITH THIS "NO MICE EATING" DIET!
OH NO! HARRY AND WALDO ARE ABOUT TO DESIGNATE MY FRIEND TODAY'S SPECIAL!
GARFIELD!
GRRRR! ANOTHER MOUSE STOPS ME FROM EATING!
YOU GOTTA HELP ME SAVE BIG MOUSE! HE'S ANNOYING, BUT HE'S MY FRIEND!
YEAH, I HAVE FRIENDS LIKE THAT. IN FACT, THEY'RE ALL LIKE THAT! EVEN YOU!
WHAT DO YOU THINK, WALDO? FRIED, BAKED, BARBECUED OR POACHED?
WHY DOES OUR MOUSE SMELL OF PIZZA?
GARFIELD! IT'S OUR MOUSE! YOU CAN'T HAVE HIM!
WOULDN'T WANT HIM! I ONLY FEAST ON GOURMET MICE! I JUST CAME BY TO GET A FEW DOZEN!

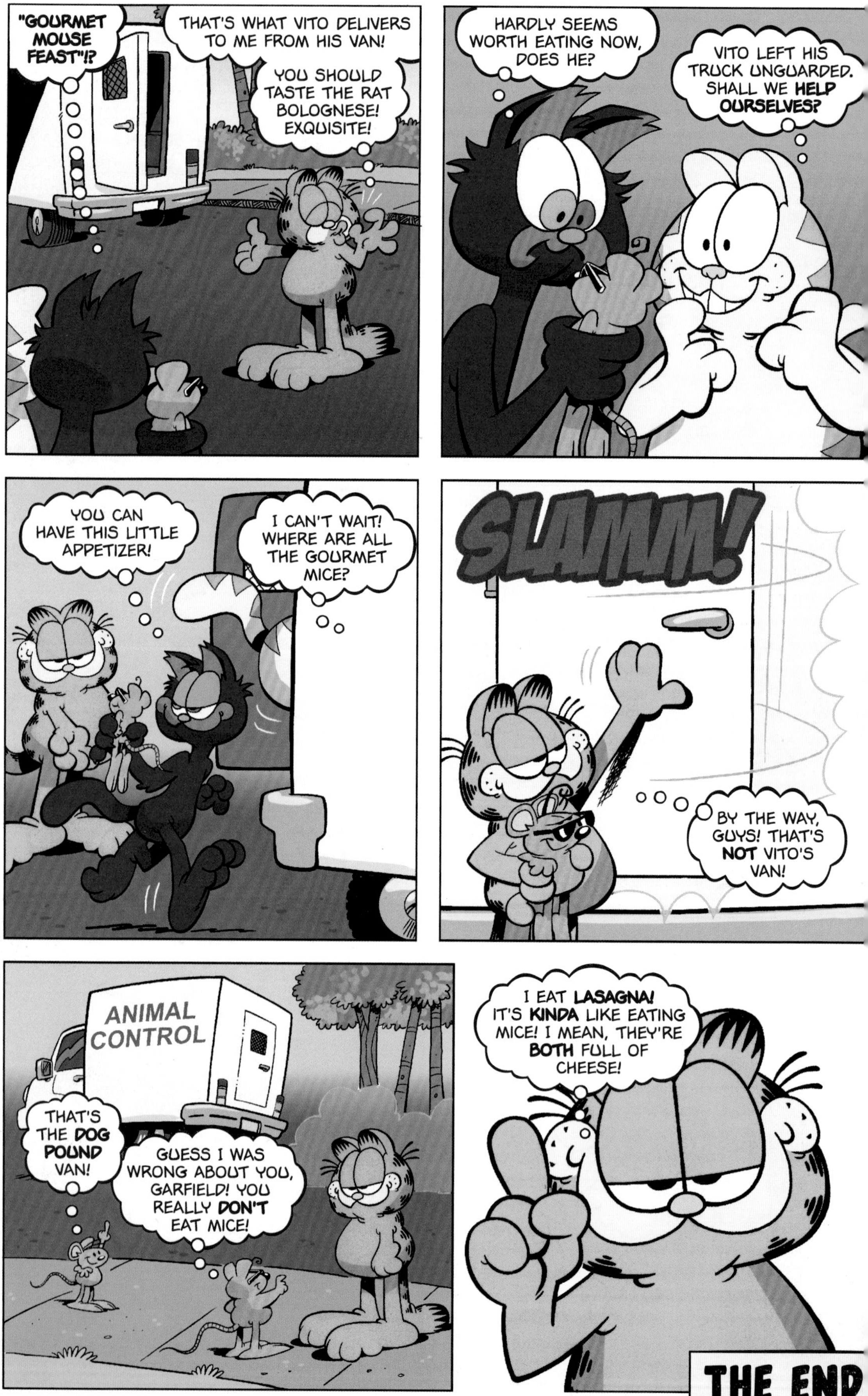
"GOURMET MOUSE FEAST"!?
THAT'S WHAT VITO DELIVERS TO ME FROM HIS VAN!
YOU SHOULD TASTE THE RAT BOLOGNESE! EXQUISITE!
HARDLY SEEMS WORTH EATING NOW, DOES HE?
VITO LEFT HIS TRUCK UNGUARDED. SHALL WE **HELP OURSELVES?**
YOU CAN HAVE THIS LITTLE APPETIZER!
I CAN'T WAIT! WHERE ARE ALL THE GOURMET MICE?
SLAMM!
BY THE WAY, GUYS! THAT'S **NOT** VITO'S VAN!
ANIMAL CONTROL
THAT'S THE **DOG POUND** VAN!
GUESS I WAS WRONG ABOUT YOU, GARFIELD! YOU REALLY **DON'T** EAT MICE!
I EAT **LASAGNA!** IT'S **KINDA** LIKE EATING MICE! I MEAN, THEY'RE **BOTH** FULL OF CHEESE!
THE END

CHAPTER TWO

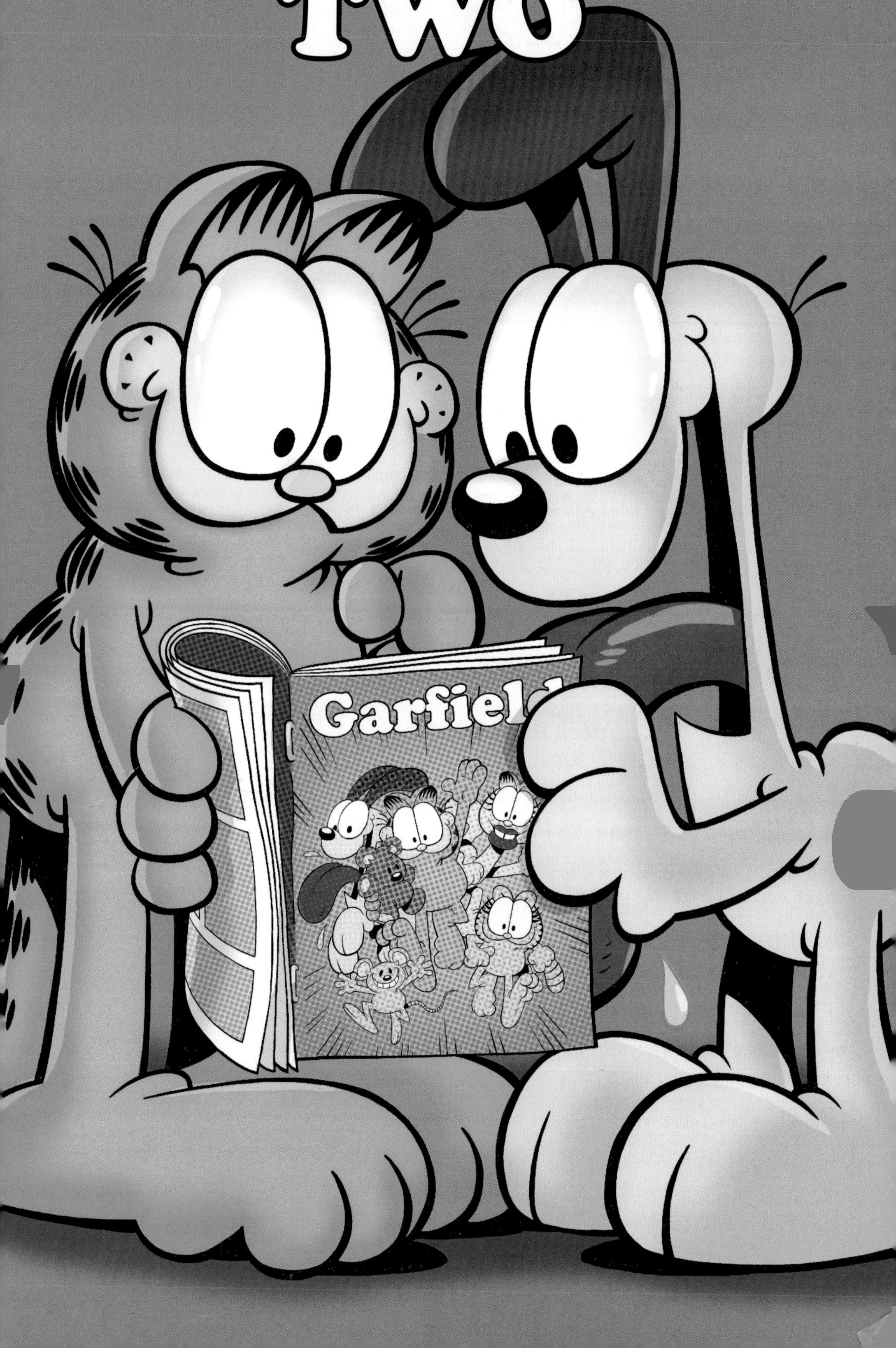
Garfield

STICKING POINT
DOWN FOR
THE COUNT

Written by
MARK EVANIER

Art by
GARY BARKER
AND DAN DAVIS

Colors by
LISA MOORE

Chapter Break Art by
GARY BARKER
WITH BRADEN LAMB

STICKING POINT

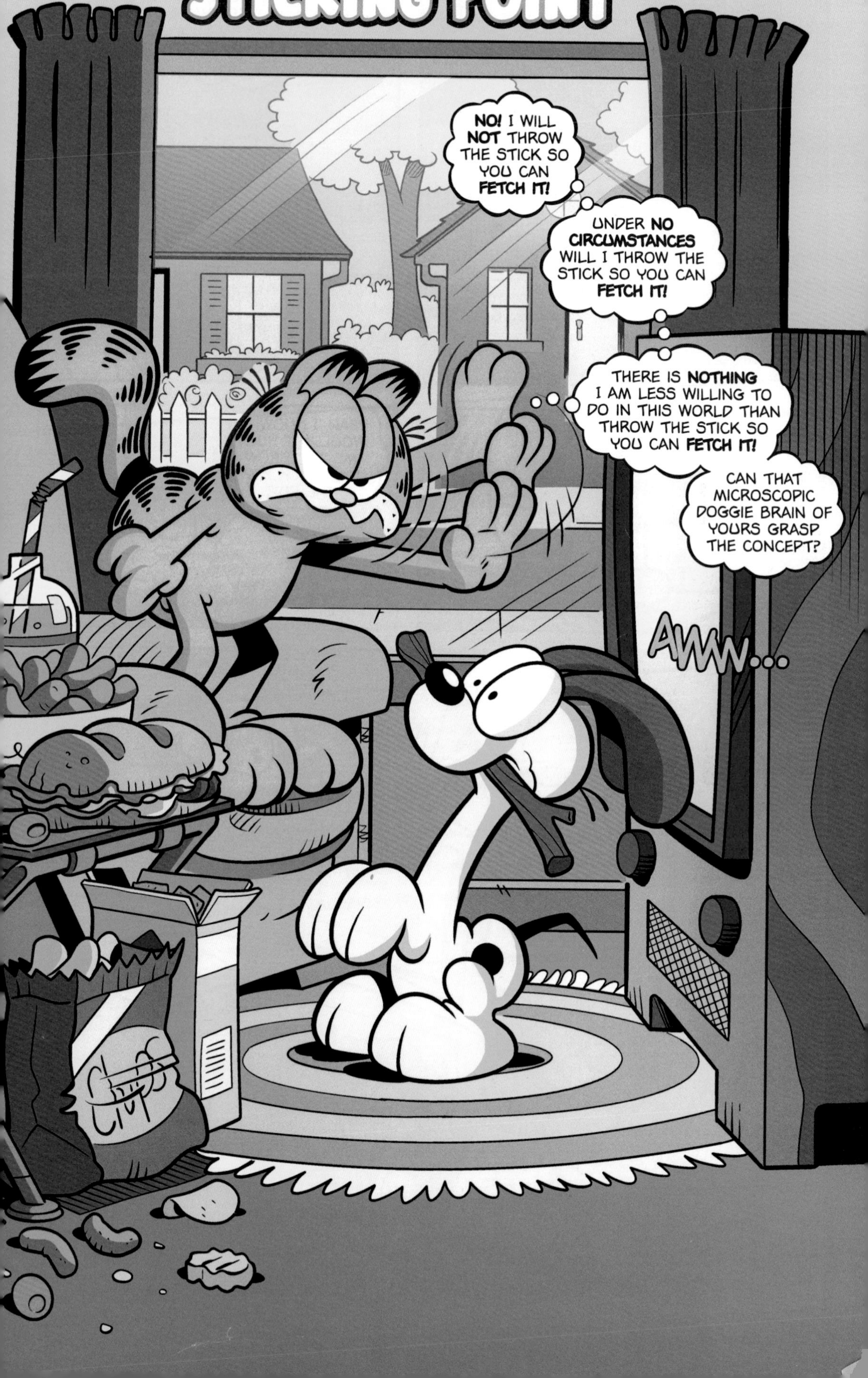
NO! I WILL NOT THROW THE STICK SO YOU CAN FETCH IT!
UNDER NO CIRCUMSTANCES WILL I THROW THE STICK SO YOU CAN FETCH IT!
THERE IS NOTHING I AM LESS WILLING TO DO IN THIS WORLD THAN THROW THE STICK SO YOU CAN FETCH IT!
CAN THAT MICROSCOPIC DOGGIE BRAIN OF YOURS GRASP THE CONCEPT?
AWW...
CHIPS

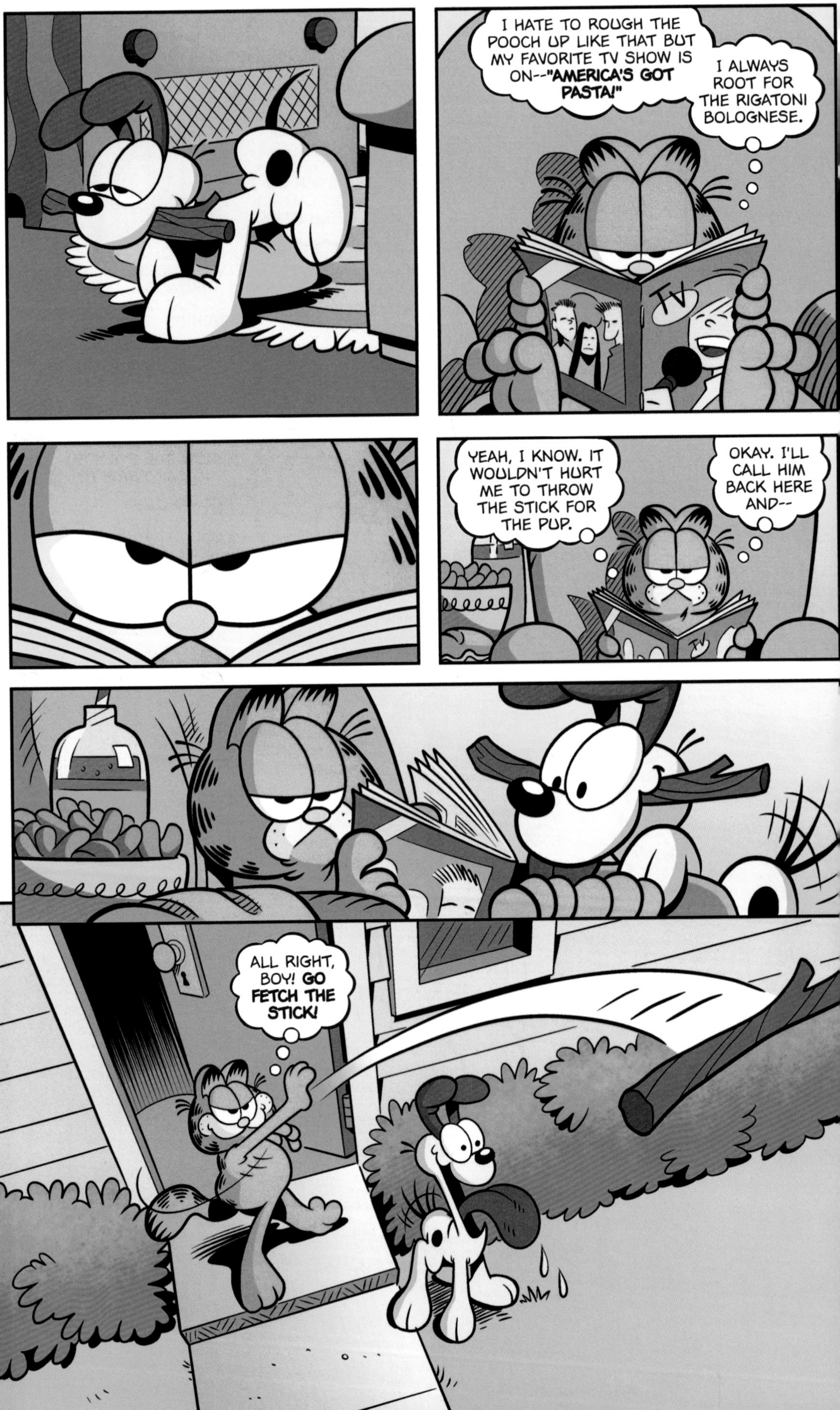
I HATE TO ROUGH THE POOCH UP LIKE THAT BUT MY FAVORITE TV SHOW IS ON--"AMERICA'S GOT PASTA!"
I ALWAYS ROOT FOR THE RIGATONI BOLOGNESE.
TV
YEAH, I KNOW. IT WOULDN'T HURT ME TO THROW THE STICK FOR THE PUP.
OKAY. I'LL CALL HIM BACK HERE AND--
ALL RIGHT, BOY! GO FETCH THE STICK!

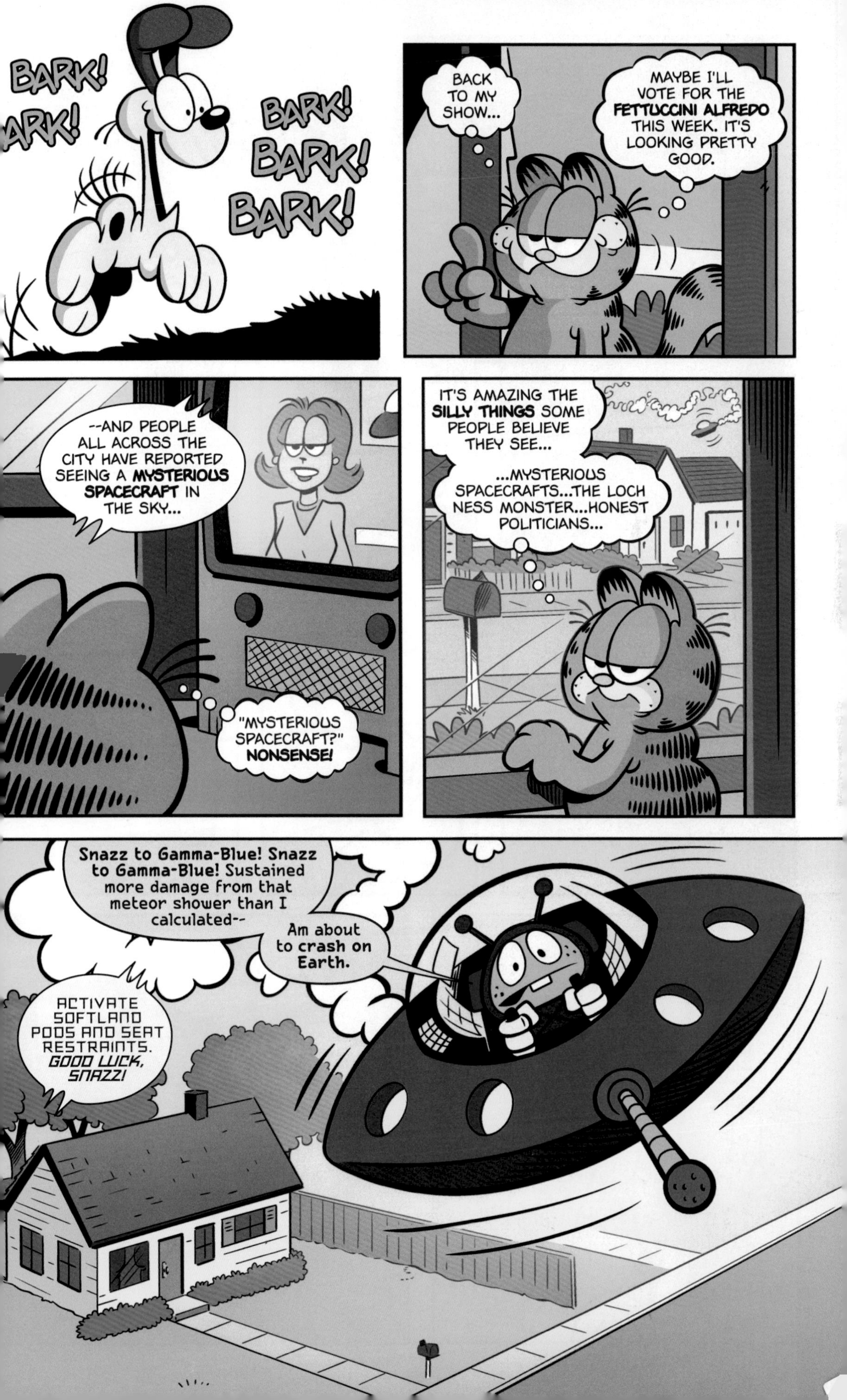
BARK!
BARK!
BARK!
BARK!
BARK!
BACK TO MY SHOW...
MAYBE I'LL VOTE FOR THE FETTUCCINI ALFREDO THIS WEEK. IT'S LOOKING PRETTY GOOD.
--AND PEOPLE ALL ACROSS THE CITY HAVE REPORTED SEEING A MYSTERIOUS SPACECRAFT IN THE SKY...
"MYSTERIOUS SPACECRAFT?" NONSENSE!
IT'S AMAZING THE SILLY THINGS SOME PEOPLE BELIEVE THEY SEE...
...MYSTERIOUS SPACECRAFTS...THE LOCH NESS MONSTER...HONEST POLITICIANS...
Snazz to Gamma-Blue! Snazz to Gamma-Blue! Sustained more damage from that meteor shower than I calculated--
Am about to crash on Earth.
ACTIVATE SOFTLAND PODS AND SEAT RESTRAINTS. GOOD LUCK, SNAZZ!

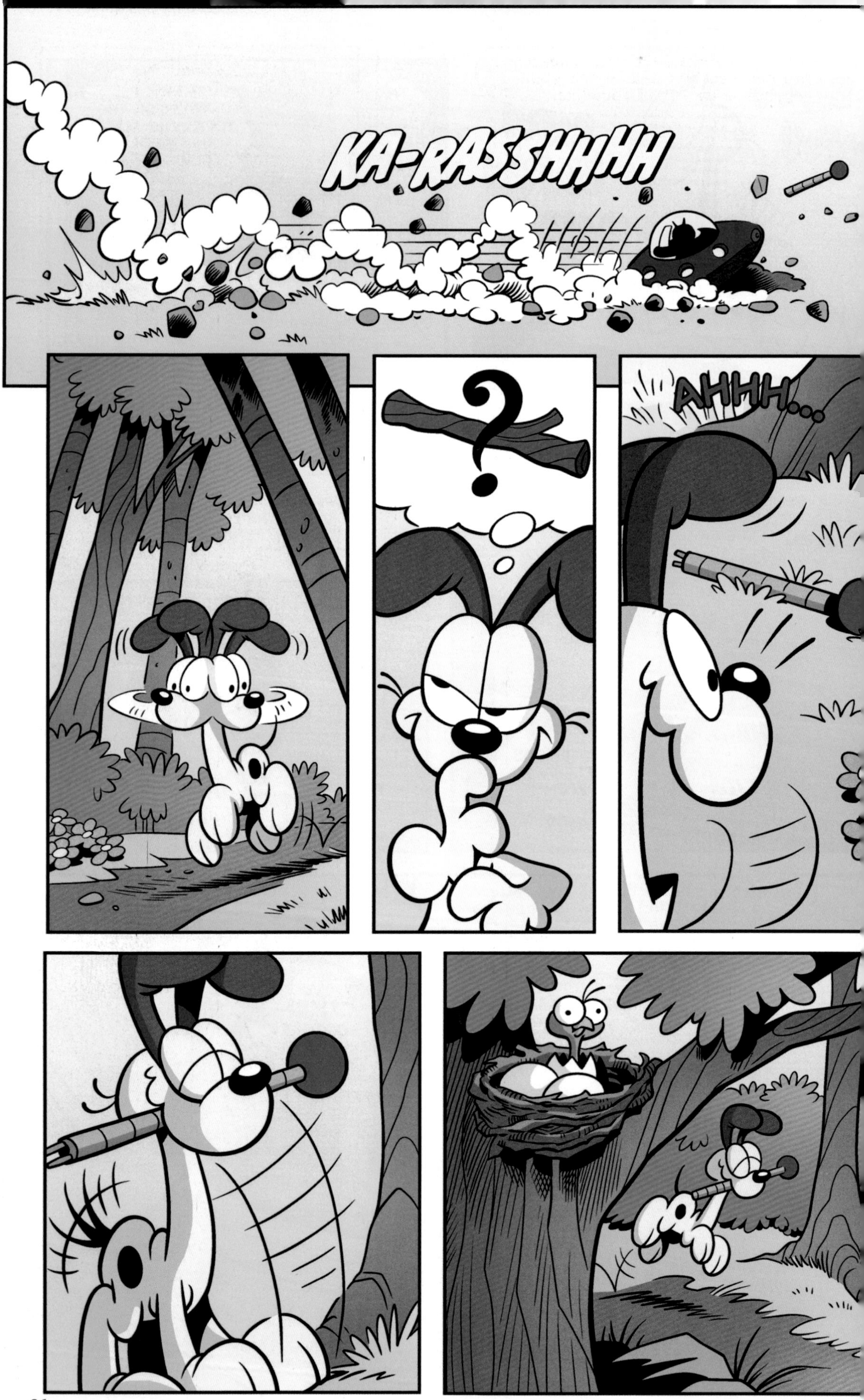
KA-RASSHHHH
AHHH...

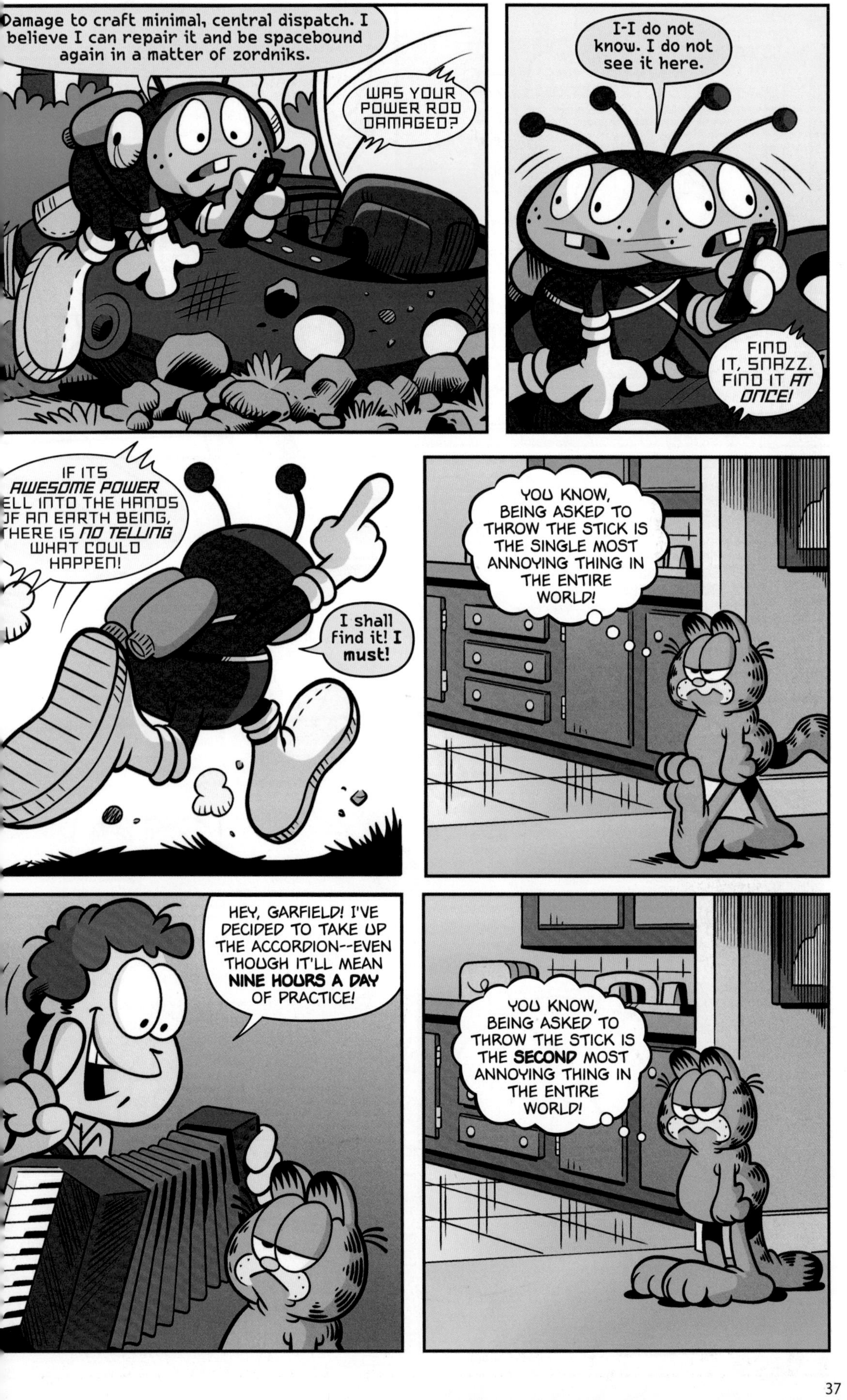

Damage to craft minimal, central dispatch. I believe I can repair it and be spacebound again in a matter of zordniks.
WAS YOUR POWER ROD DAMAGED?
I-I do not know. I do not see it here.
FIND IT, SNAZZ. FIND IT AT ONCE!
IF ITS AWESOME POWER ELL INTO THE HANDS F AN EARTH BEING, HERE IS NO TELLING WHAT COULD HAPPEN!
I shall find it! I must!
YOU KNOW, BEING ASKED TO THROW THE STICK IS THE SINGLE MOST ANNOYING THING IN THE ENTIRE WORLD!
HEY, GARFIELD! I'VE DECIDED TO TAKE UP THE ACCORDION--EVEN THOUGH IT'LL MEAN NINE HOURS A DAY OF PRACTICE!
YOU KNOW, BEING ASKED TO THROW THE STICK IS THE SECOND MOST ANNOYING THING IN THE ENTIRE WORLD!

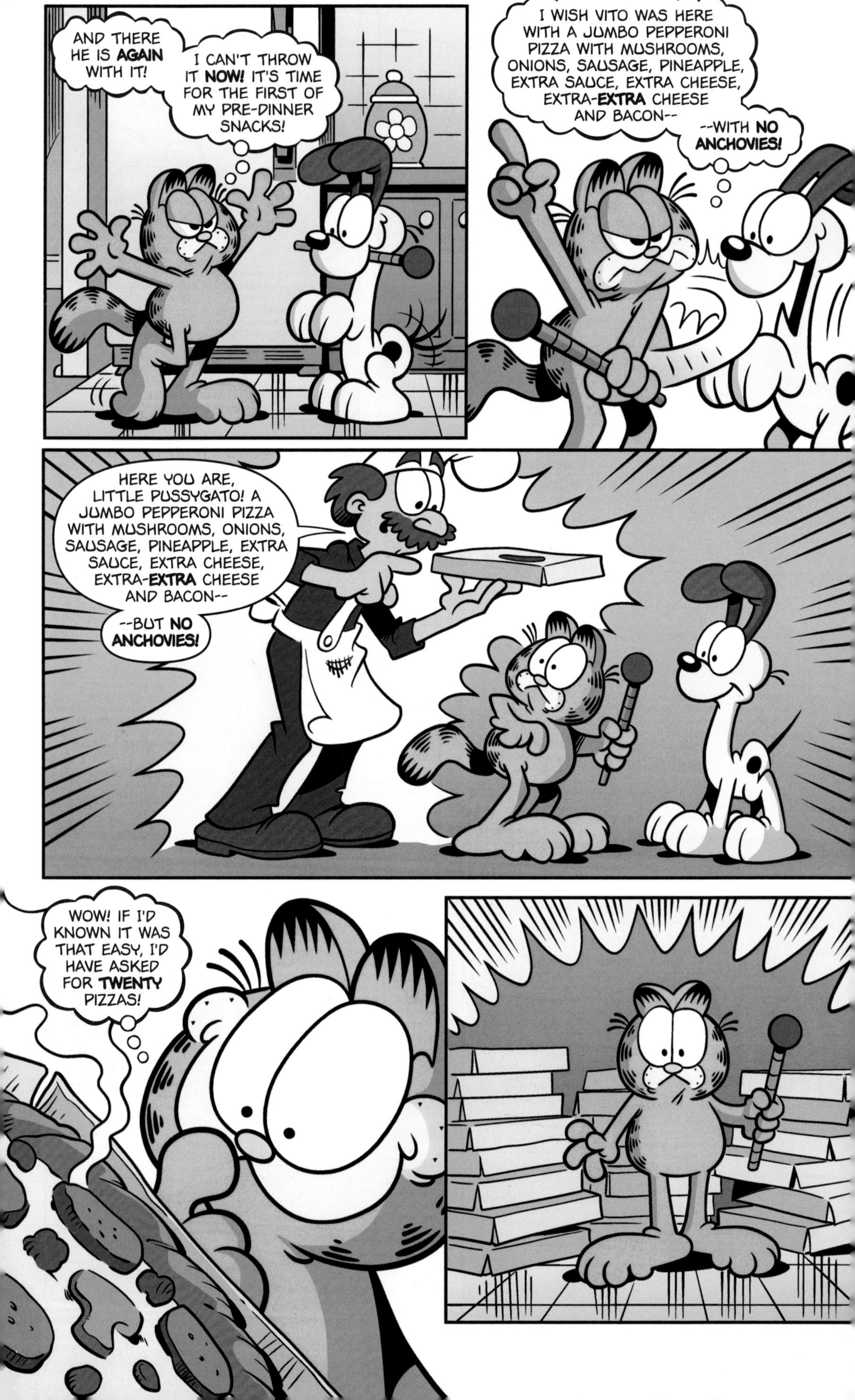

AND THERE HE IS **AGAIN** WITH IT!
I CAN'T THROW IT **NOW!** IT'S TIME FOR THE FIRST OF MY PRE-DINNER SNACKS!
I WISH VITO WAS HERE WITH A JUMBO PEPPERONI PIZZA WITH MUSHROOMS, ONIONS, SAUSAGE, PINEAPPLE, EXTRA SAUCE, EXTRA CHEESE, EXTRA-**EXTRA** CHEESE AND BACON--
--WITH **NO ANCHOVIES!**
HERE YOU ARE, LITTLE PUSSYGATO! A JUMBO PEPPERONI PIZZA WITH MUSHROOMS, ONIONS, SAUSAGE, PINEAPPLE, EXTRA SAUCE, EXTRA CHEESE, EXTRA-**EXTRA** CHEESE AND BACON--
--BUT **NO ANCHOVIES!**
WOW! IF I'D KNOWN IT WAS THAT EASY, I'D HAVE ASKED FOR **TWENTY** PIZZAS!

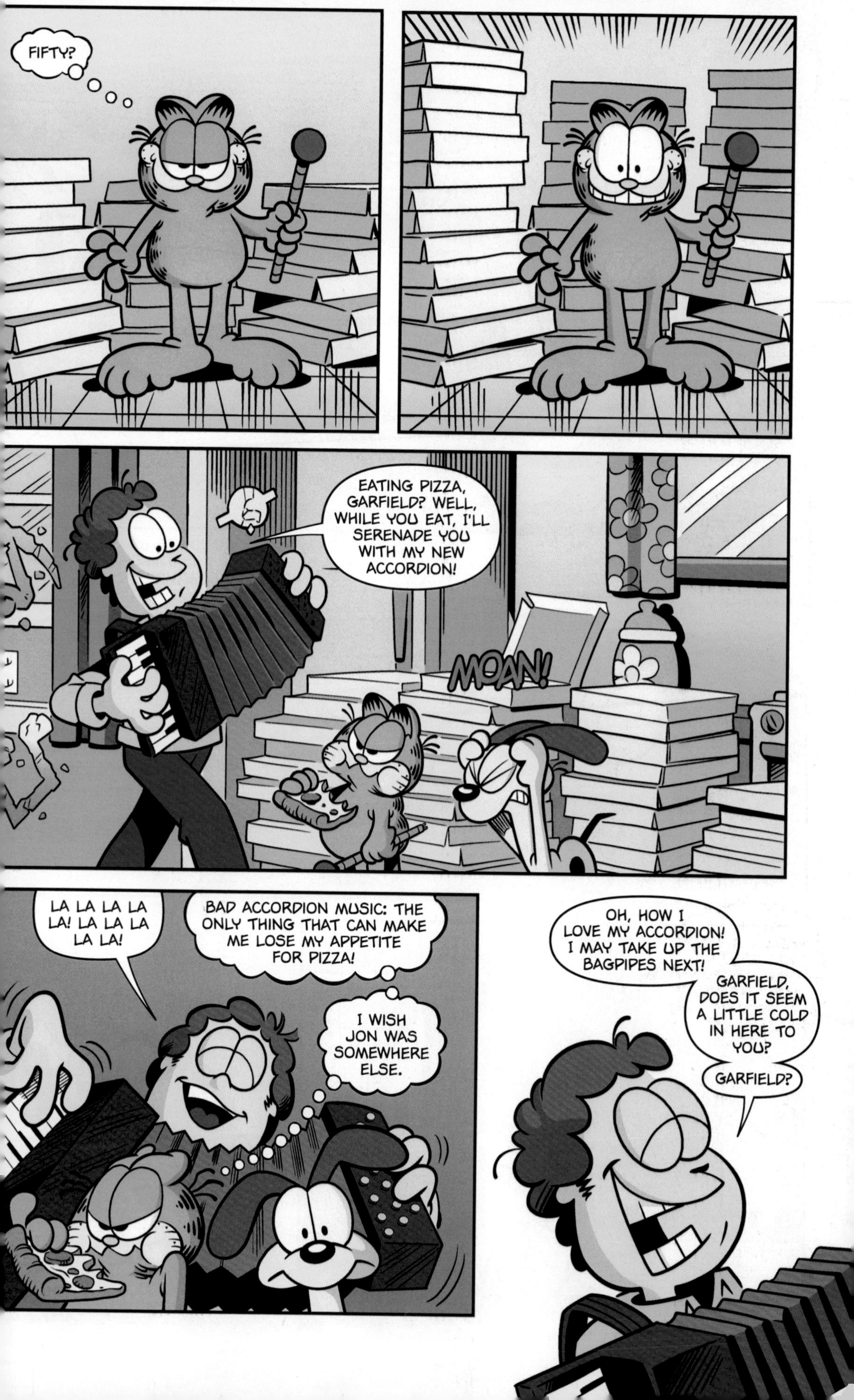
FIFTY?
EATING PIZZA, GARFIELD? WELL, WHILE YOU EAT, I'LL SERENADE YOU WITH MY NEW ACCORDION!
MOAN!
LA LA LA LA LA! LA LA LA LA LA!
BAD ACCORDION MUSIC: THE ONLY THING THAT CAN MAKE ME LOSE MY APPETITE FOR PIZZA!
I WISH JON WAS SOMEWHERE ELSE.
OH, HOW I LOVE MY ACCORDION! I MAY TAKE UP THE BAGPIPES NEXT!
GARFIELD, DOES IT SEEM A LITTLE COLD IN HERE TO YOU?
GARFIELD?

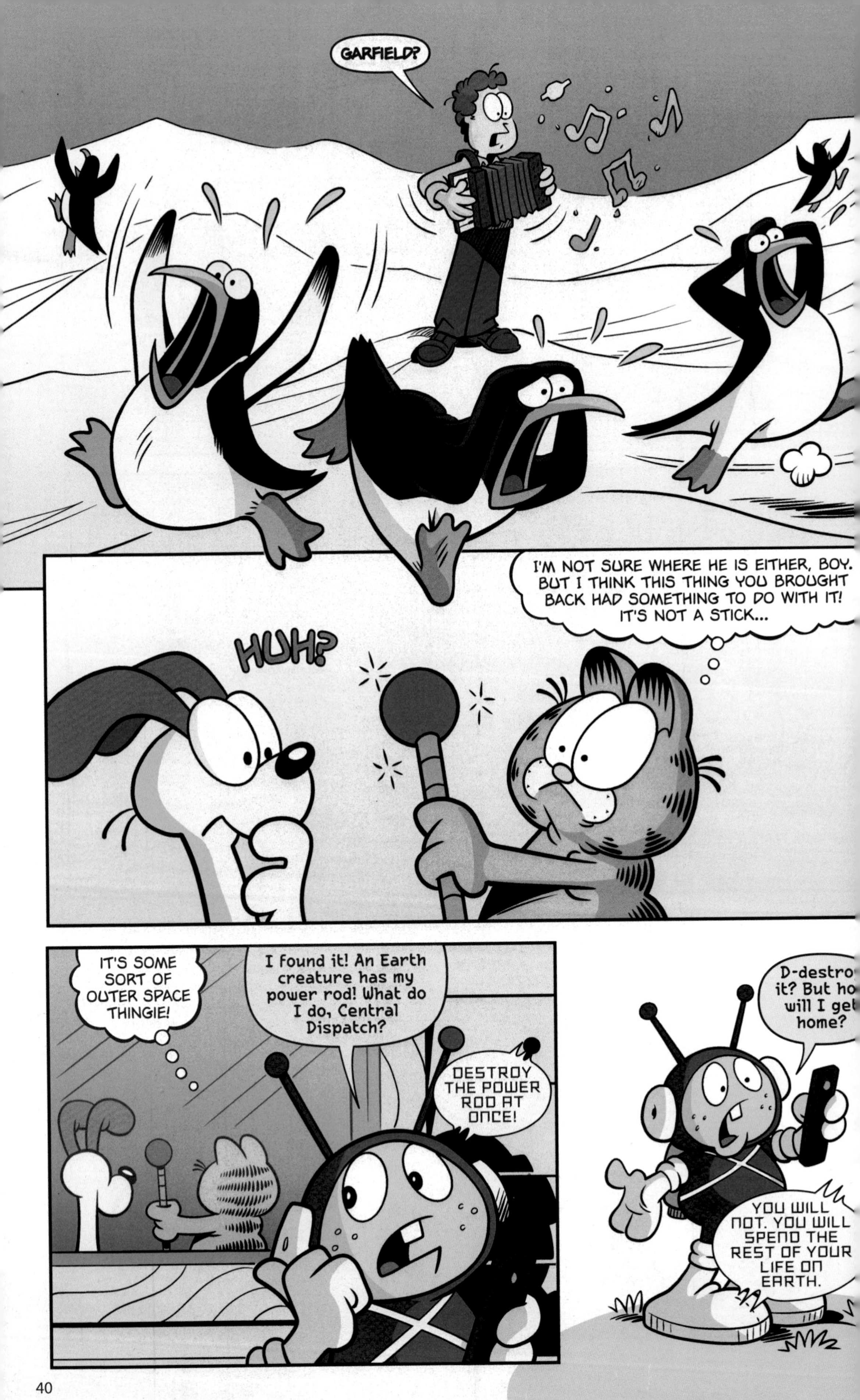
GARFIELD?
I'M NOT SURE WHERE HE IS EITHER, BOY. BUT I THINK THIS THING YOU BROUGHT BACK HAD SOMETHING TO DO WITH IT! IT'S NOT A STICK...
HUH?
IT'S SOME SORT OF OUTER SPACE THINGIE!
I found it! An Earth creature has my power rod! What do I do, Central Dispatch?
DESTROY THE POWER ROD AT ONCE!
D-destro it? But ho will I ge home?
YOU WILL NOT. YOU WILL SPEND THE REST OF YOUR LIFE ON EARTH.

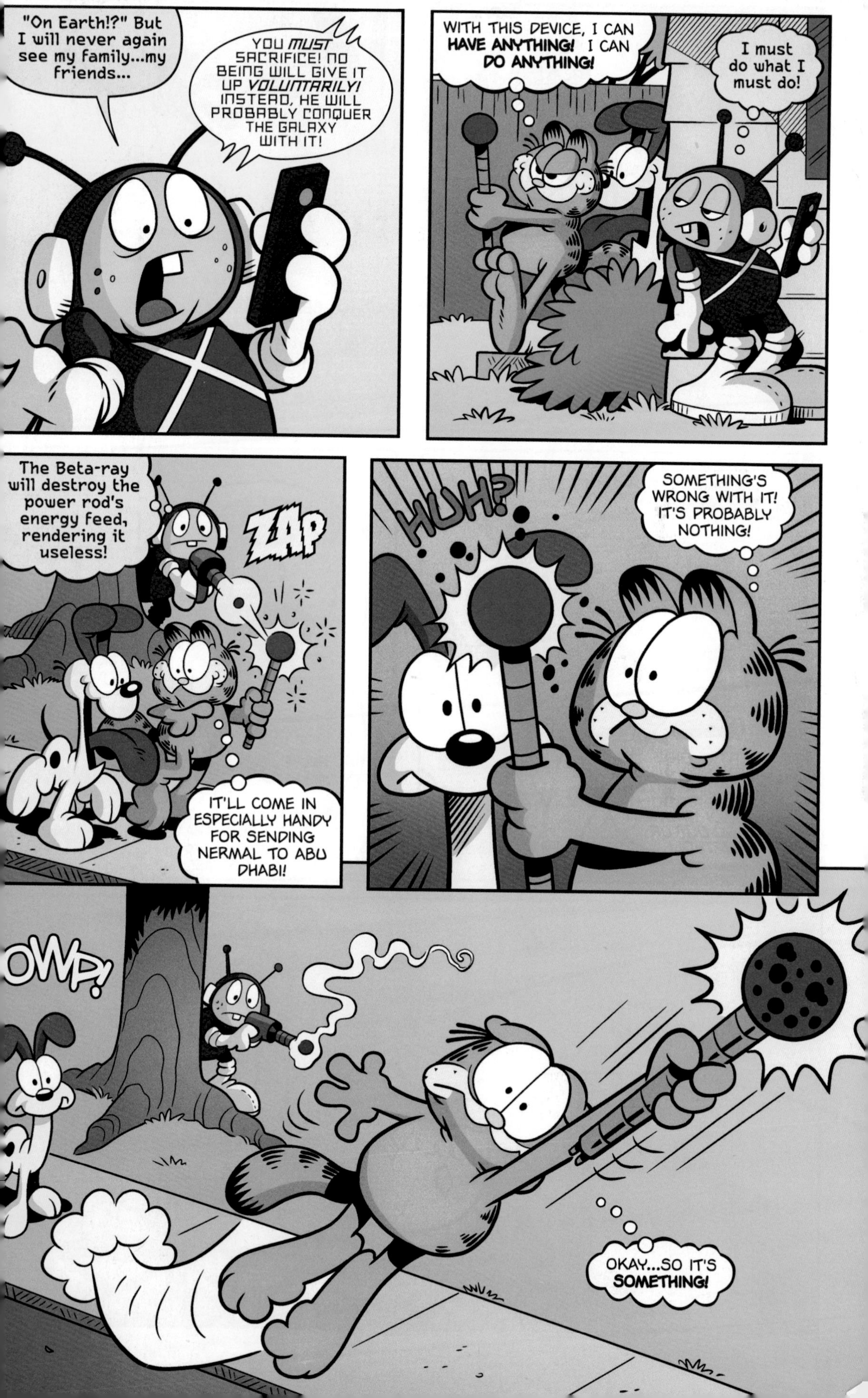
"On Earth!?" But I will never again see my family...my friends...
YOU MUST SACRIFICE! NO BEING WILL GIVE IT UP VOLUNTARILY! INSTEAD, HE WILL PROBABLY CONQUER THE GALAXY WITH IT!
WITH THIS DEVICE, I CAN HAVE ANYTHING! I CAN DO ANYTHING!
I must do what I must do!
The Beta-ray will destroy the power rod's energy feed, rendering it useless!
ZAP
IT'LL COME IN ESPECIALLY HANDY FOR SENDING NERMAL TO ABU DHABI!
HUH?
SOMETHING'S WRONG WITH IT! IT'S PROBABLY NOTHING!
OWP!
OKAY...SO IT'S SOMETHING!

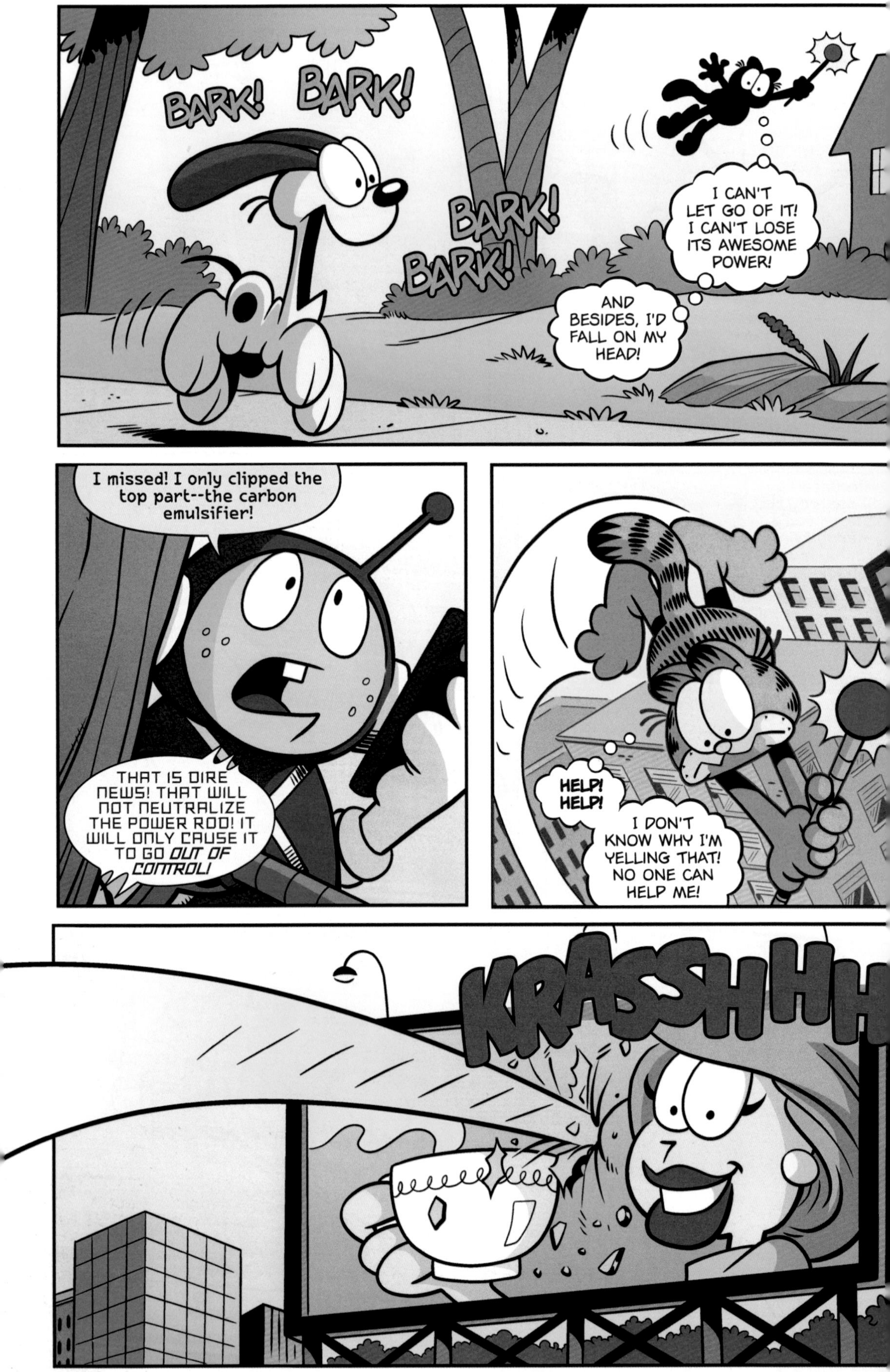
BARK! BARK!
BARK!
BARK!
I CAN'T LET GO OF IT! I CAN'T LOSE ITS AWESOME POWER!
AND BESIDES, I'D FALL ON MY HEAD!
I missed! I only clipped the top part--the carbon emulsifier!
THAT IS DIRE NEWS! THAT WILL NOT NEUTRALIZE THE POWER ROD! IT WILL ONLY CAUSE IT TO GO *OUT OF CONTROL!*
HELP! HELP!
I DON'T KNOW WHY I'M YELLING THAT! NO ONE CAN HELP ME!
KRASSHHH

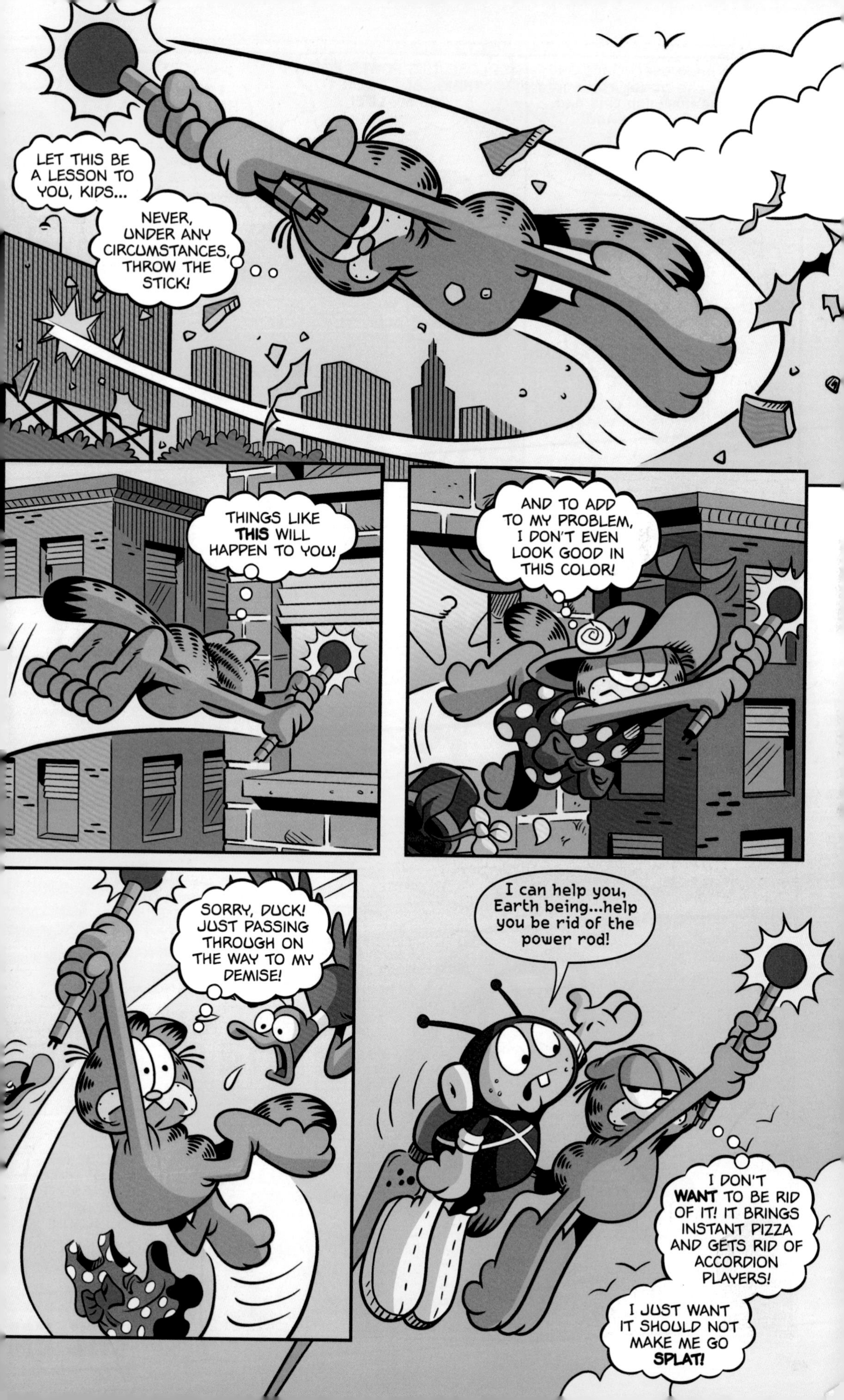
LET THIS BE A LESSON TO YOU, KIDS...
NEVER, UNDER ANY CIRCUMSTANCES, THROW THE STICK!
THINGS LIKE **THIS** WILL HAPPEN TO YOU!
AND TO ADD TO MY PROBLEM, I DON'T EVEN LOOK GOOD IN THIS COLOR!
SORRY, DUCK! JUST PASSING THROUGH ON THE WAY TO MY DEMISE!
I can help you, Earth being...help you be rid of the power rod!
I DON'T **WANT** TO BE RID OF IT! IT BRINGS INSTANT PIZZA AND GETS RID OF ACCORDION PLAYERS!
I JUST WANT IT SHOULD NOT MAKE ME GO **SPLAT!**

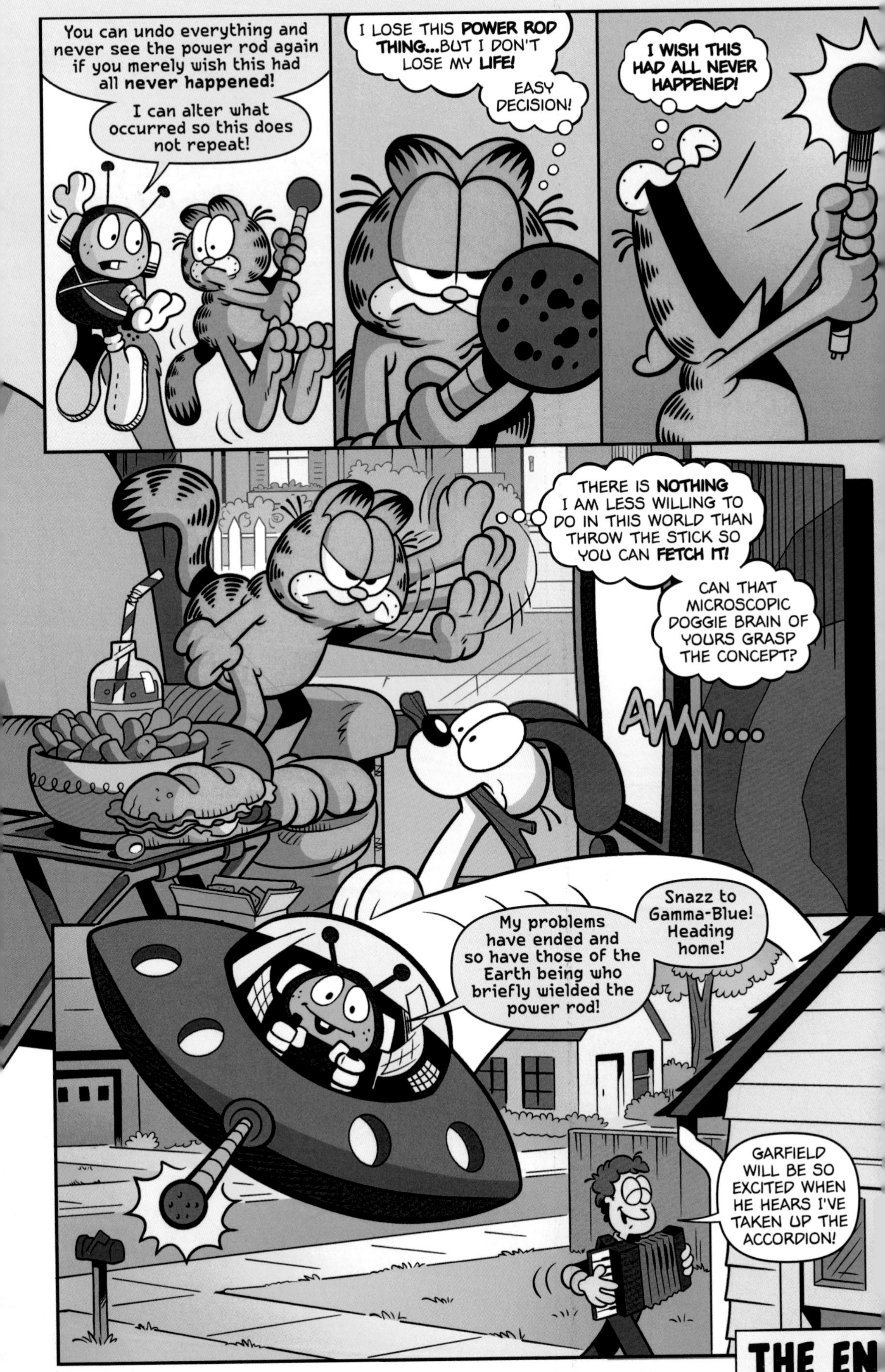
You can undo everything and never see the power rod again if you merely wish this had all **never happened!**
I can alter what occurred so this does not repeat!
I LOSE THIS **POWER ROD THING...**BUT I DON'T LOSE MY **LIFE!**
EASY DECISION!
I WISH THIS HAD ALL NEVER HAPPENED!
THERE IS **NOTHING** I AM LESS WILLING TO DO IN THIS WORLD THAN THROW THE STICK SO YOU CAN **FETCH IT!**
CAN THAT MICROSCOPIC DOGGIE BRAIN OF YOURS GRASP THE CONCEPT?
AWW...
My problems have ended and so have those of the Earth being who briefly wielded the power rod!
Snazz to Gamma-Blue! Heading home!
GARFIELD WILL BE SO EXCITED WHEN HE HEARS I'VE TAKEN UP THE ACCORDION!
THE EN

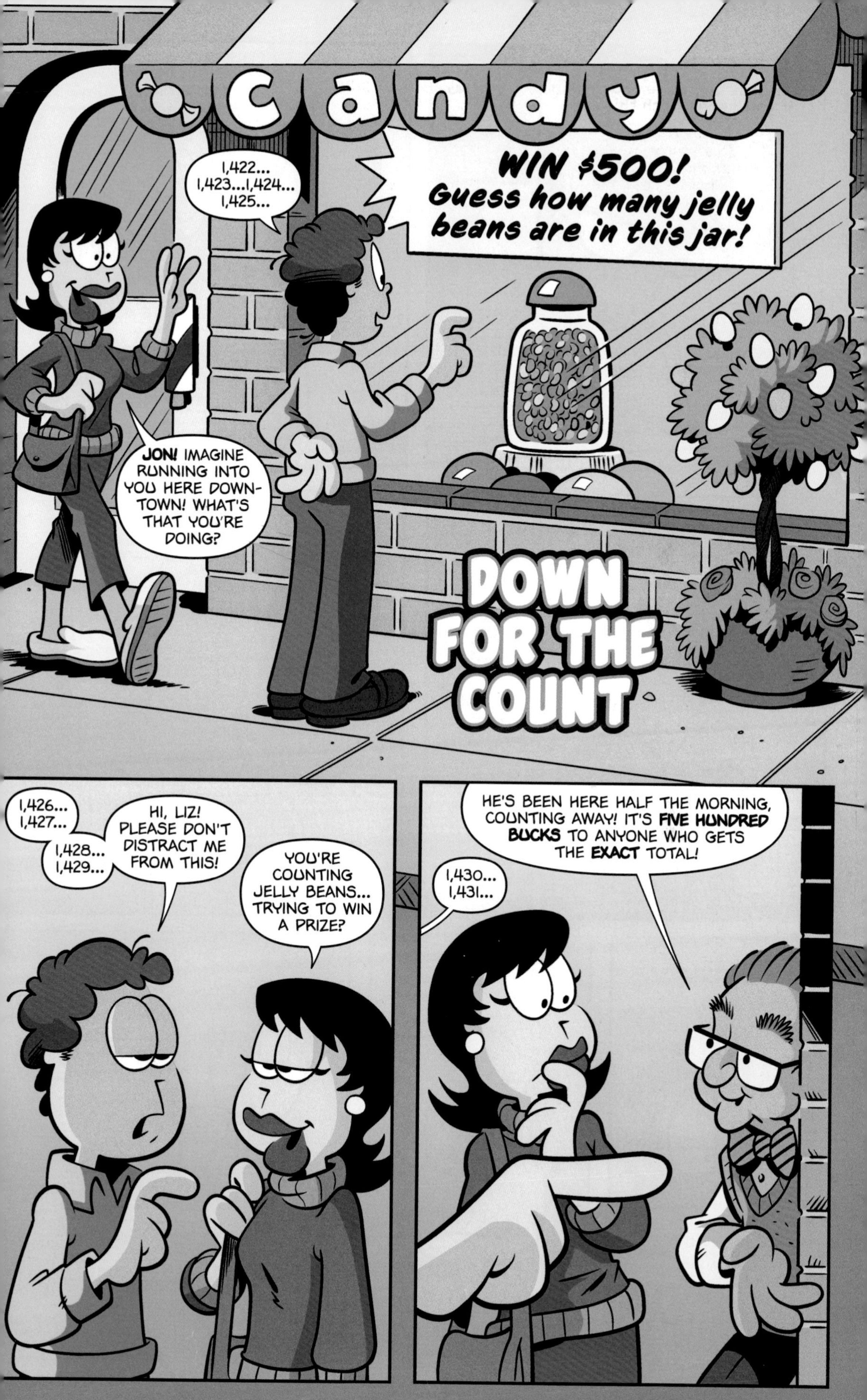
Candy
WIN $500! Guess how many jelly beans are in this jar!
1,422... 1,423...1,424... 1,425...
JON! IMAGINE RUNNING INTO YOU HERE DOWN-TOWN! WHAT'S THAT YOU'RE DOING?
DOWN FOR THE COUNT
1,426... 1,427...
1,428... 1,429...
HI, LIZ! PLEASE DON'T DISTRACT ME FROM THIS!
YOU'RE COUNTING JELLY BEANS... TRYING TO WIN A PRIZE?
HE'S BEEN HERE HALF THE MORNING, COUNTING AWAY! IT'S FIVE HUNDRED BUCKS TO ANYONE WHO GETS THE EXACT TOTAL!
1,430... 1,431...

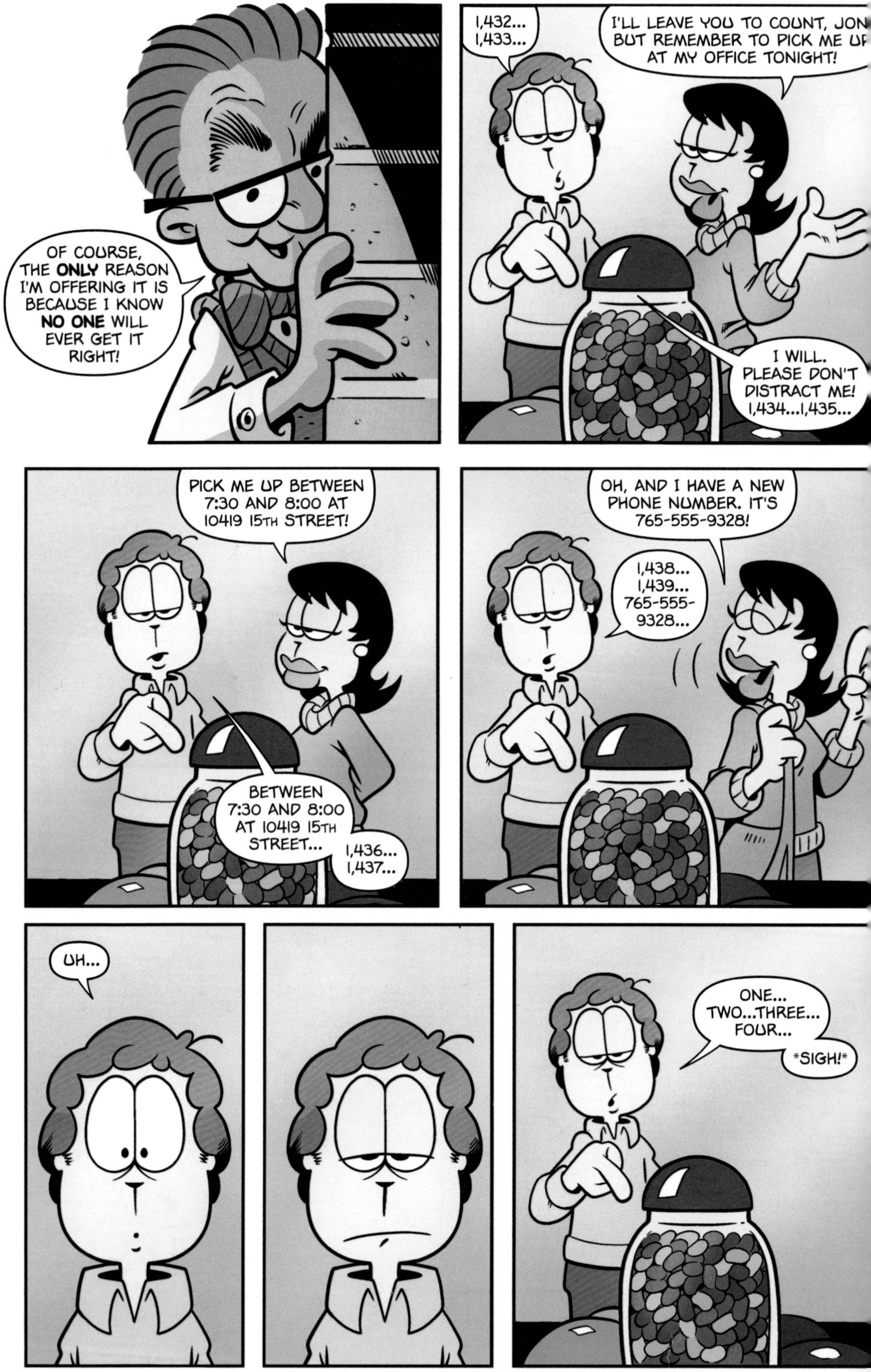
OF COURSE, THE **ONLY** REASON I'M OFFERING IT IS BECAUSE I KNOW **NO ONE** WILL EVER GET IT RIGHT!
1,432... 1,433...
I'LL LEAVE YOU TO COUNT, JON BUT REMEMBER TO PICK ME UP AT MY OFFICE TONIGHT!
I WILL. PLEASE DON'T DISTRACT ME! 1,434...1,435...
PICK ME UP BETWEEN 7:30 AND 8:00 AT 10419 15TH STREET!
BETWEEN 7:30 AND 8:00 AT 10419 15TH STREET...
1,436... 1,437...
OH, AND I HAVE A NEW PHONE NUMBER. IT'S 765-555-9328!
1,438... 1,439... 765-555-9328...
UH...
ONE... TWO...THREE... FOUR...
SIGH!

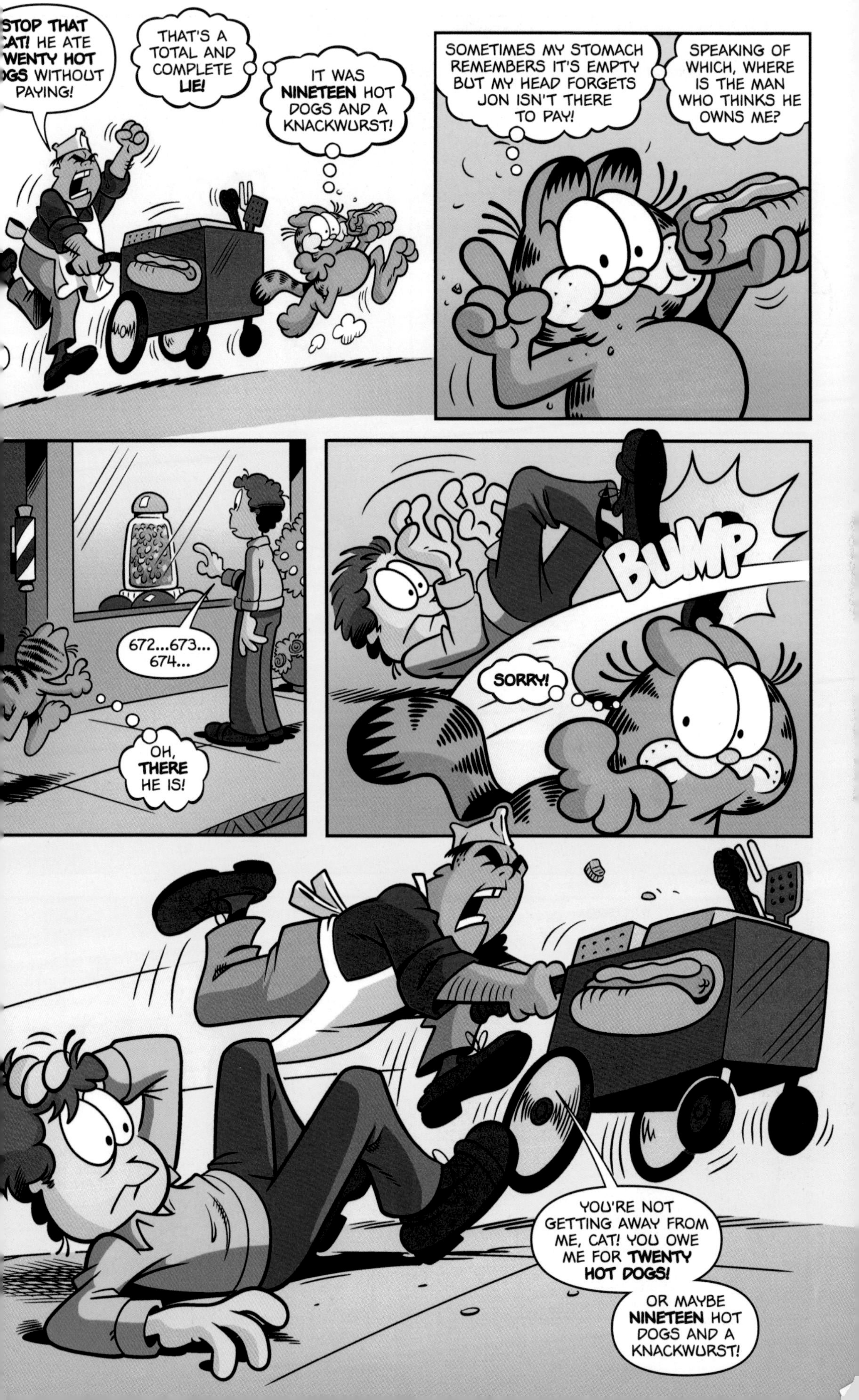

STOP THAT CAT! HE ATE TWENTY HOT DOGS WITHOUT PAYING!
THAT'S A TOTAL AND COMPLETE LIE!
IT WAS NINETEEN HOT DOGS AND A KNACKWURST!
SOMETIMES MY STOMACH REMEMBERS IT'S EMPTY BUT MY HEAD FORGETS JON ISN'T THERE TO PAY!
SPEAKING OF WHICH, WHERE IS THE MAN WHO THINKS HE OWNS ME?
672...673... 674...
OH, THERE HE IS!
BUMP
SORRY!
YOU'RE NOT GETTING AWAY FROM ME, CAT! YOU OWE ME FOR TWENTY HOT DOGS!
OR MAYBE NINETEEN HOT DOGS AND A KNACKWURST!

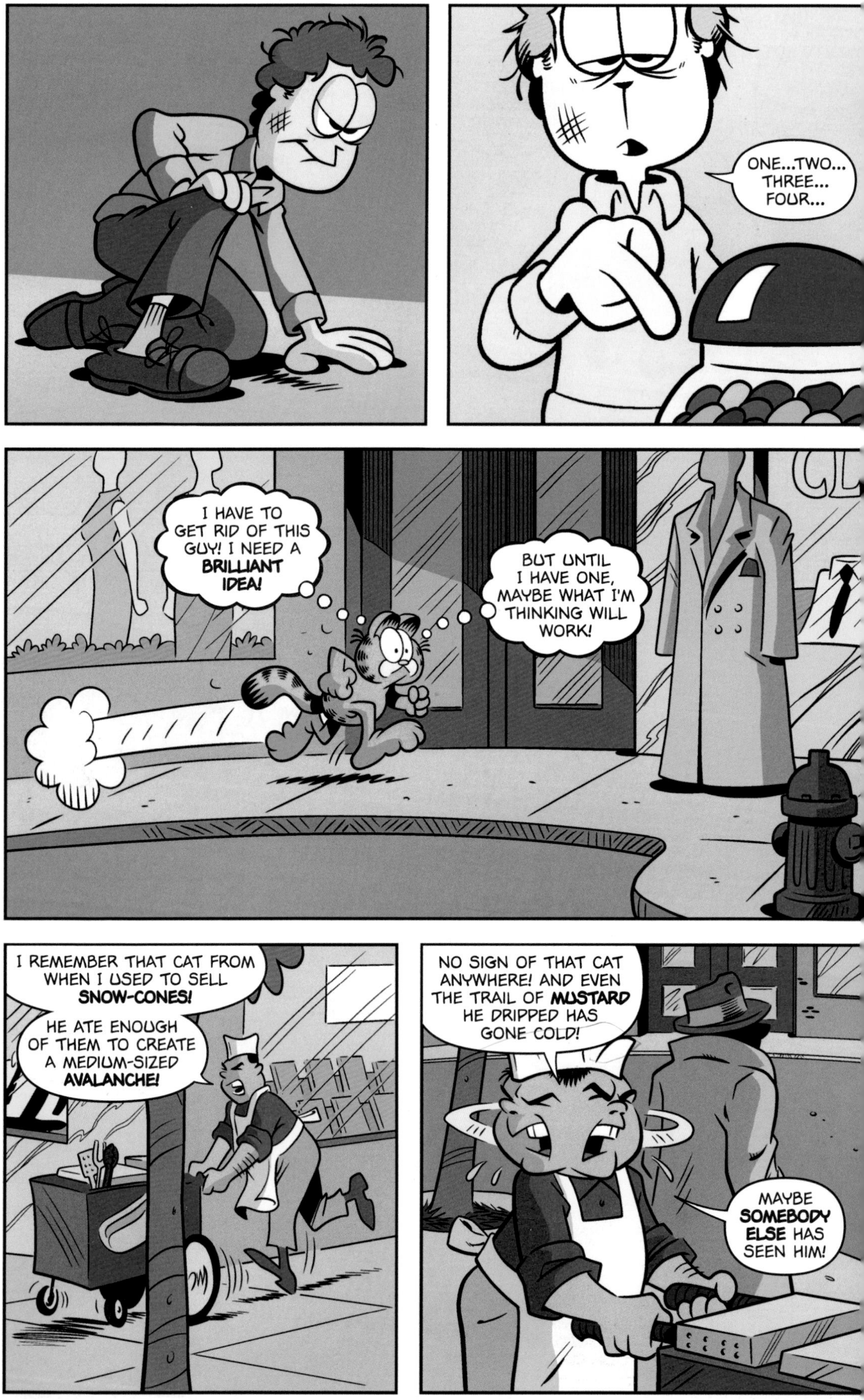
ONE...TWO... THREE... FOUR...
I HAVE TO GET RID OF THIS GUY! I NEED A **BRILLIANT IDEA!**
BUT UNTIL I HAVE ONE, MAYBE WHAT I'M THINKING WILL WORK!
I REMEMBER THAT CAT FROM WHEN I USED TO SELL **SNOW-CONES!**
HE ATE ENOUGH OF THEM TO CREATE A MEDIUM-SIZED **AVALANCHE!**
NO SIGN OF THAT CAT ANYWHERE! AND EVEN THE TRAIL OF **MUSTARD** HE DRIPPED HAS GONE COLD!
MAYBE **SOMEBODY ELSE** HAS SEEN HIM!

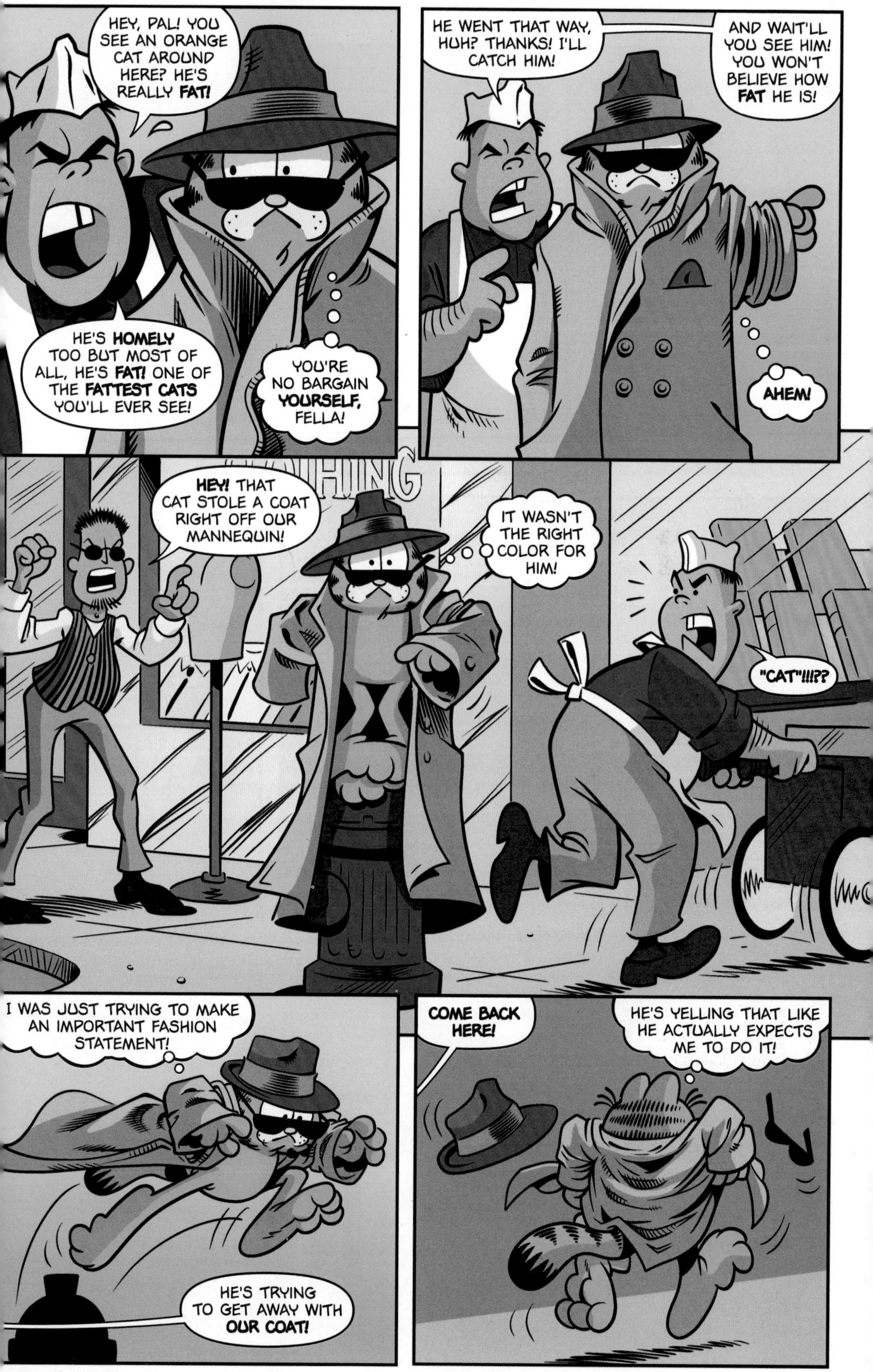
HEY, PAL! YOU SEE AN ORANGE CAT AROUND HERE? HE'S REALLY **FAT!**
HE'S **HOMELY** TOO BUT MOST OF ALL, HE'S **FAT!** ONE OF THE **FATTEST CATS** YOU'LL EVER SEE!
YOU'RE NO BARGAIN **YOURSELF,** FELLA!
HE WENT THAT WAY, HUH? THANKS! I'LL CATCH HIM!
AND WAIT'LL YOU SEE HIM! YOU WON'T BELIEVE HOW **FAT** HE IS!
AHEM!
HEY! THAT CAT STOLE A COAT RIGHT OFF OUR MANNEQUIN!
IT WASN'T THE RIGHT COLOR FOR HIM!
"CAT"!!!??
I WAS JUST TRYING TO MAKE AN IMPORTANT FASHION STATEMENT!
HE'S TRYING TO GET AWAY WITH **OUR COAT!**
COME BACK HERE!
HE'S YELLING THAT LIKE HE ACTUALLY EXPECTS ME TO DO IT!

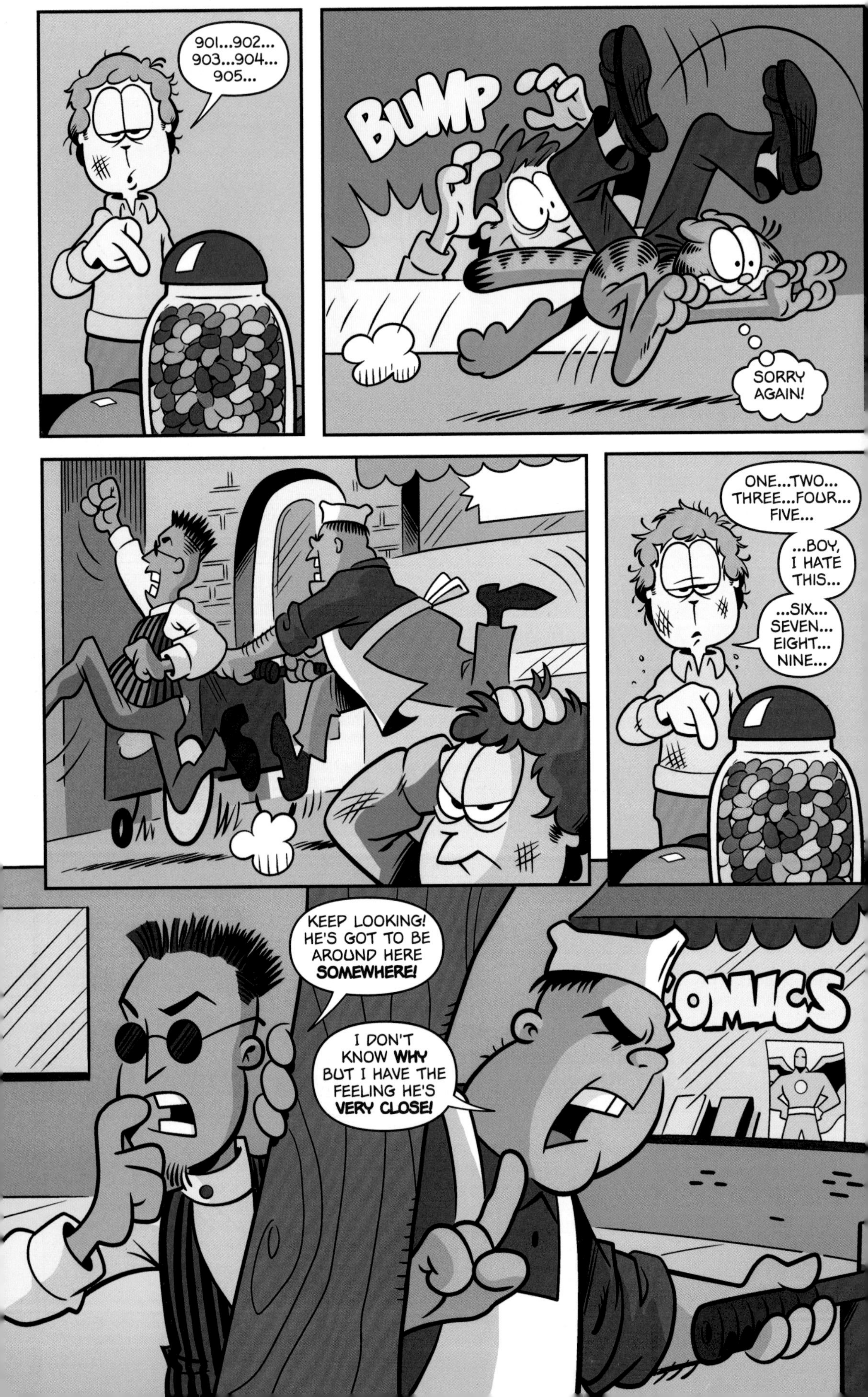
901...902...
903...904...
905...
BUMP
SORRY
AGAIN!
ONE...TWO...
THREE...FOUR...
FIVE...
...BOY,
I HATE
THIS...
...SIX...
SEVEN...
EIGHT...
NINE...
KEEP LOOKING!
HE'S GOT TO BE
AROUND HERE
SOMEWHERE!
OMICS
I DON'T
KNOW WHY
BUT I HAVE THE
FEELING HE'S
VERY CLOSE!

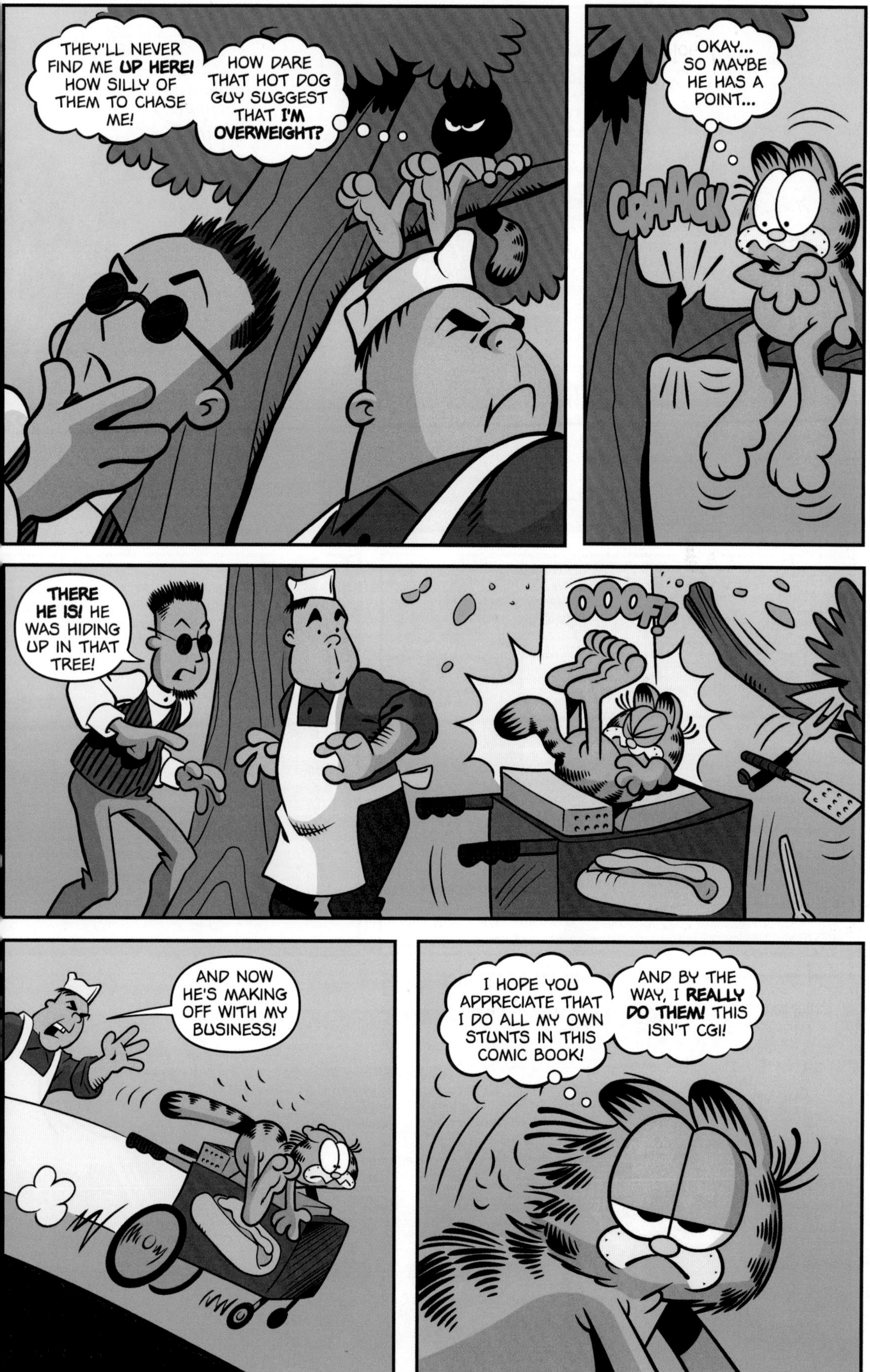
THEY'LL NEVER FIND ME UP HERE! HOW SILLY OF THEM TO CHASE ME!
HOW DARE THAT HOT DOG GUY SUGGEST THAT I'M OVERWEIGHT?
OKAY... SO MAYBE HE HAS A POINT...
CRAAACK
THERE HE IS! HE WAS HIDING UP IN THAT TREE!
OOOF!
AND NOW HE'S MAKING OFF WITH MY BUSINESS!
I HOPE YOU APPRECIATE THAT I DO ALL MY OWN STUNTS IN THIS COMIC BOOK!
AND BY THE WAY, I REALLY DO THEM! THIS ISN'T CGI!

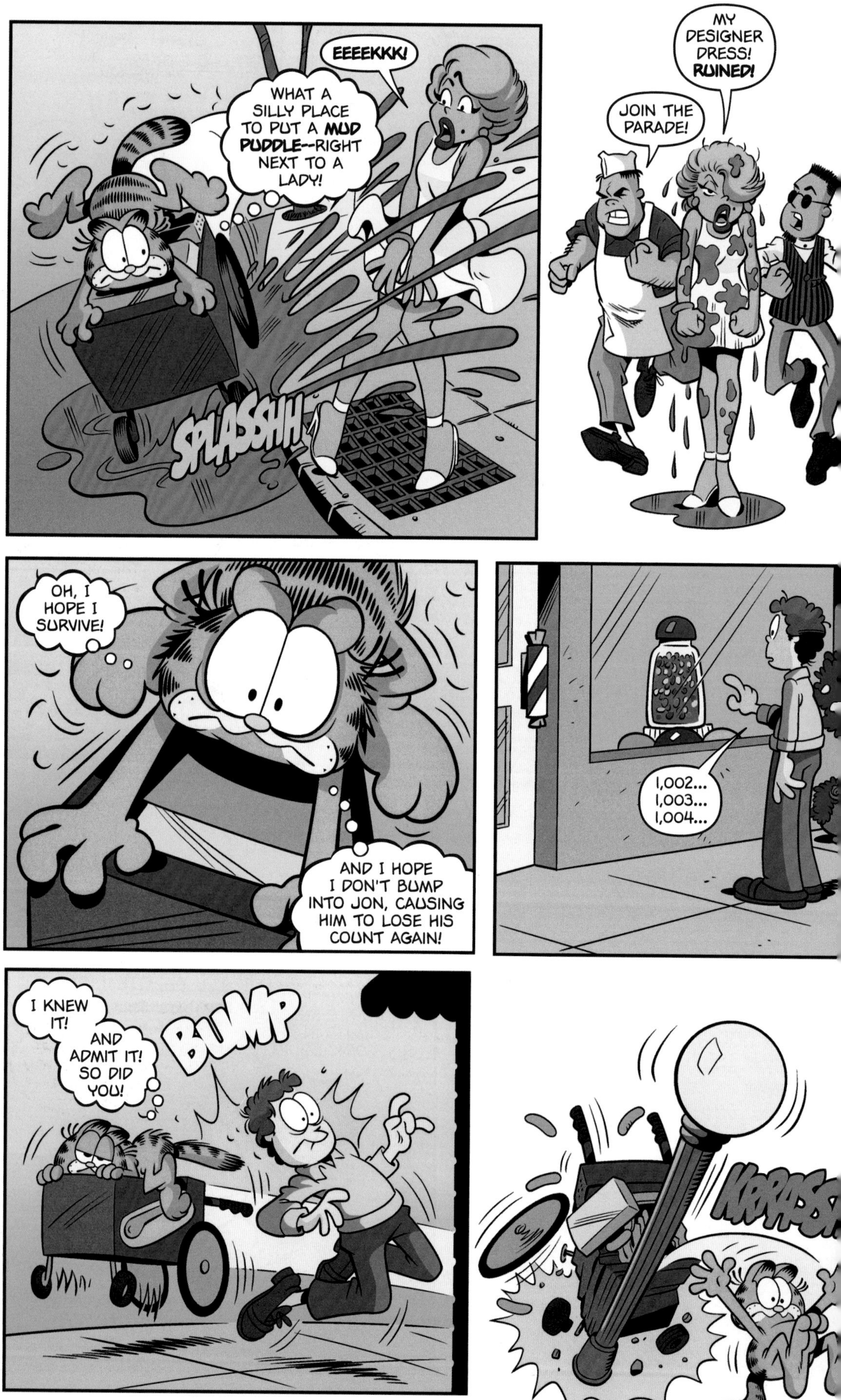
EEEEKKK!
WHAT A SILLY PLACE TO PUT A MUD PUDDLE--RIGHT NEXT TO A LADY!
SPLASSHH
JOIN THE PARADE!
MY DESIGNER DRESS! RUINED!
OH, I HOPE I SURVIVE!
AND I HOPE I DON'T BUMP INTO JON, CAUSING HIM TO LOSE HIS COUNT AGAIN!
1,002... 1,003... 1,004...
I KNEW IT!
AND ADMIT IT! SO DID YOU!
BUMP

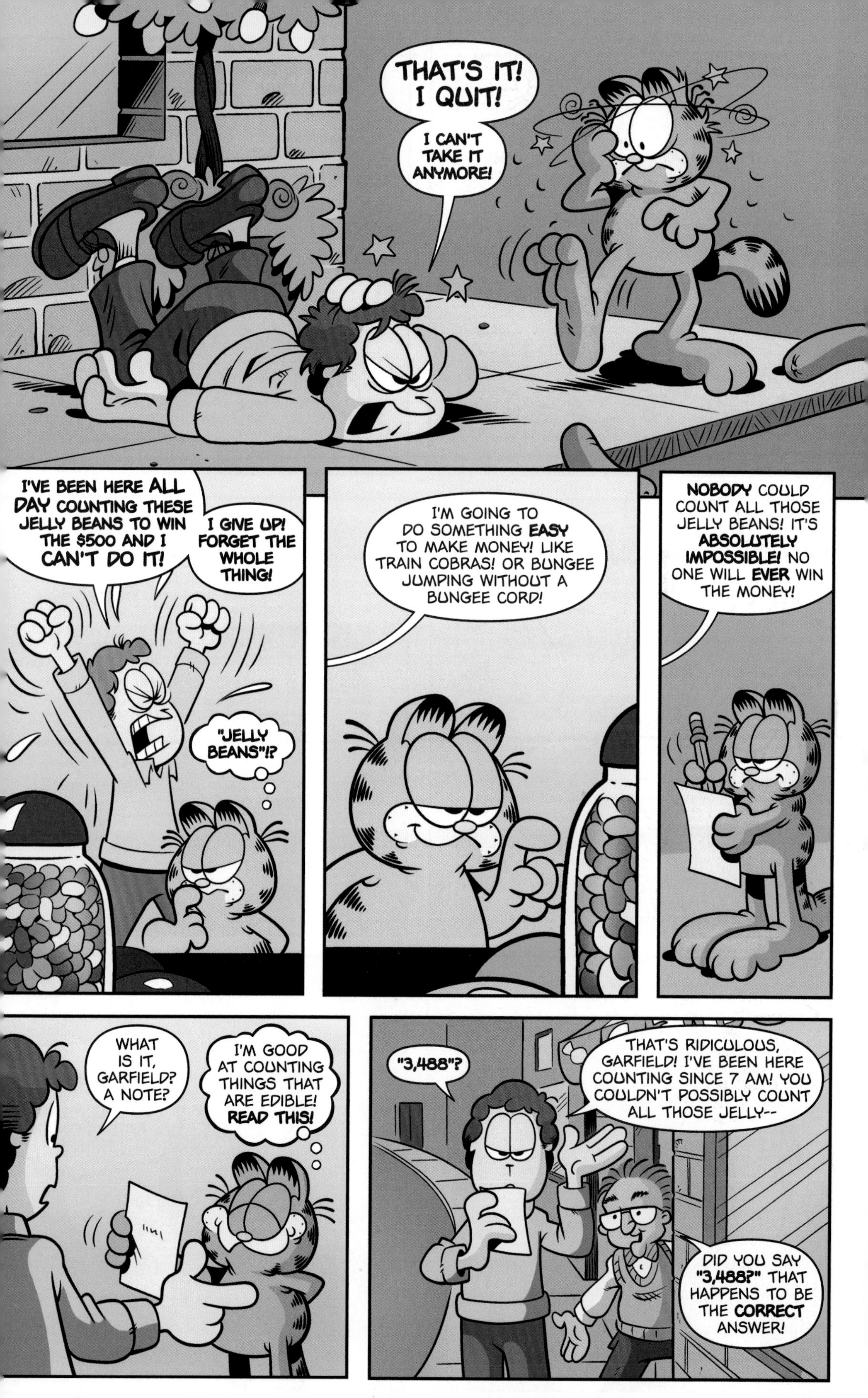
THAT'S IT! I QUIT!
I CAN'T TAKE IT ANYMORE!
I'VE BEEN HERE ALL DAY COUNTING THESE JELLY BEANS TO WIN THE $500 AND I CAN'T DO IT!
I GIVE UP! FORGET THE WHOLE THING!
"JELLY BEANS"!?
I'M GOING TO DO SOMETHING EASY TO MAKE MONEY! LIKE TRAIN COBRAS! OR BUNGEE JUMPING WITHOUT A BUNGEE CORD!
NOBODY COULD COUNT ALL THOSE JELLY BEANS! IT'S ABSOLUTELY IMPOSSIBLE! NO ONE WILL EVER WIN THE MONEY!
WHAT IS IT, GARFIELD? A NOTE?
I'M GOOD AT COUNTING THINGS THAT ARE EDIBLE! READ THIS!
"3,488"?
THAT'S RIDICULOUS, GARFIELD! I'VE BEEN HERE COUNTING SINCE 7 AM! YOU COULDN'T POSSIBLY COUNT ALL THOSE JELLY--
DID YOU SAY "3,488?" THAT HAPPENS TO BE THE CORRECT ANSWER!

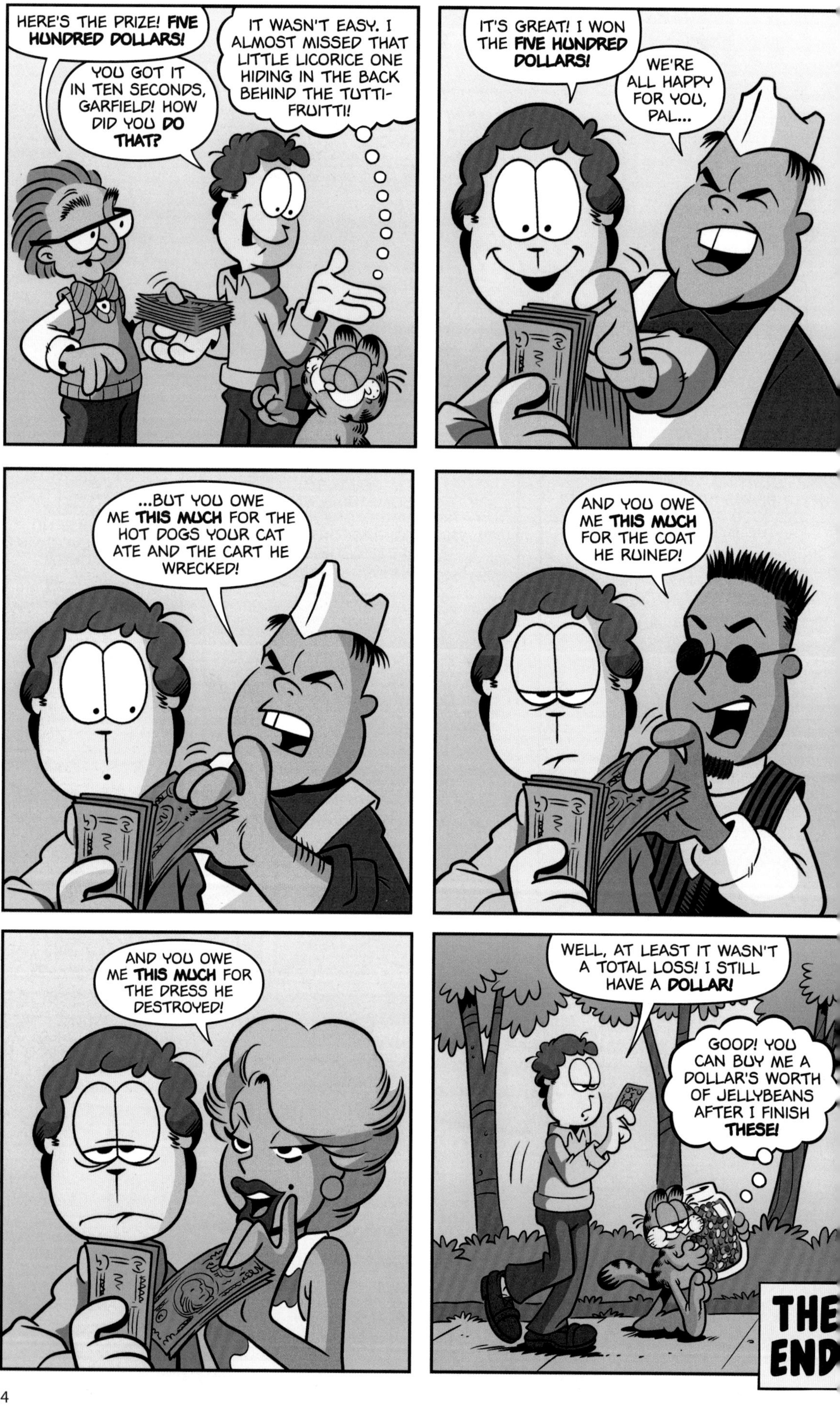
HERE'S THE PRIZE! **FIVE HUNDRED DOLLARS!**
YOU GOT IT IN TEN SECONDS, GARFIELD! HOW DID YOU **DO THAT?**
IT WASN'T EASY. I ALMOST MISSED THAT LITTLE LICORICE ONE HIDING IN THE BACK BEHIND THE TUTTI-FRUITTI!
IT'S GREAT! I WON THE **FIVE HUNDRED DOLLARS!**
WE'RE ALL HAPPY FOR YOU, PAL...
...BUT YOU OWE ME **THIS MUCH** FOR THE HOT DOGS YOUR CAT ATE AND THE CART HE WRECKED!
AND YOU OWE ME **THIS MUCH** FOR THE COAT HE RUINED!
AND YOU OWE ME **THIS MUCH** FOR THE DRESS HE DESTROYED!
WELL, AT LEAST IT WASN'T A TOTAL LOSS! I STILL HAVE A **DOLLAR!**
GOOD! YOU CAN BUY ME A DOLLAR'S WORTH OF JELLYBEANS AFTER I FINISH **THESE!**
THE END

CHAPTER THREE

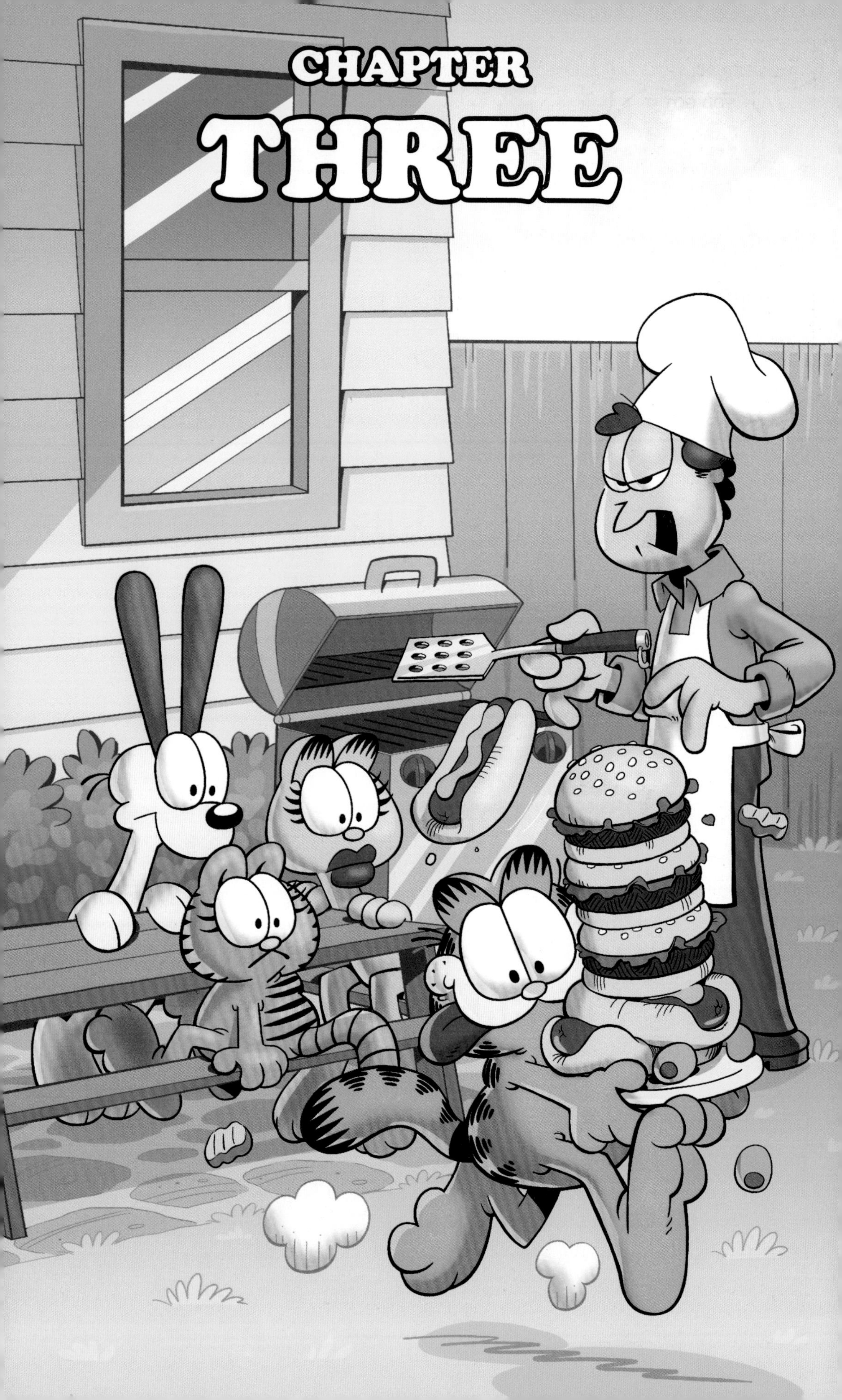

THE GREAT PIZZA NIGHTMARE
THE WONDERFUL WISHBONE

Written by
MARK EVANIER

Art by
GARY BARKER
AND DAN DAVIS

Colors by
LISA MOORE

Chapter Break Art by
GARY BARKER
WITH BRADEN LAMB

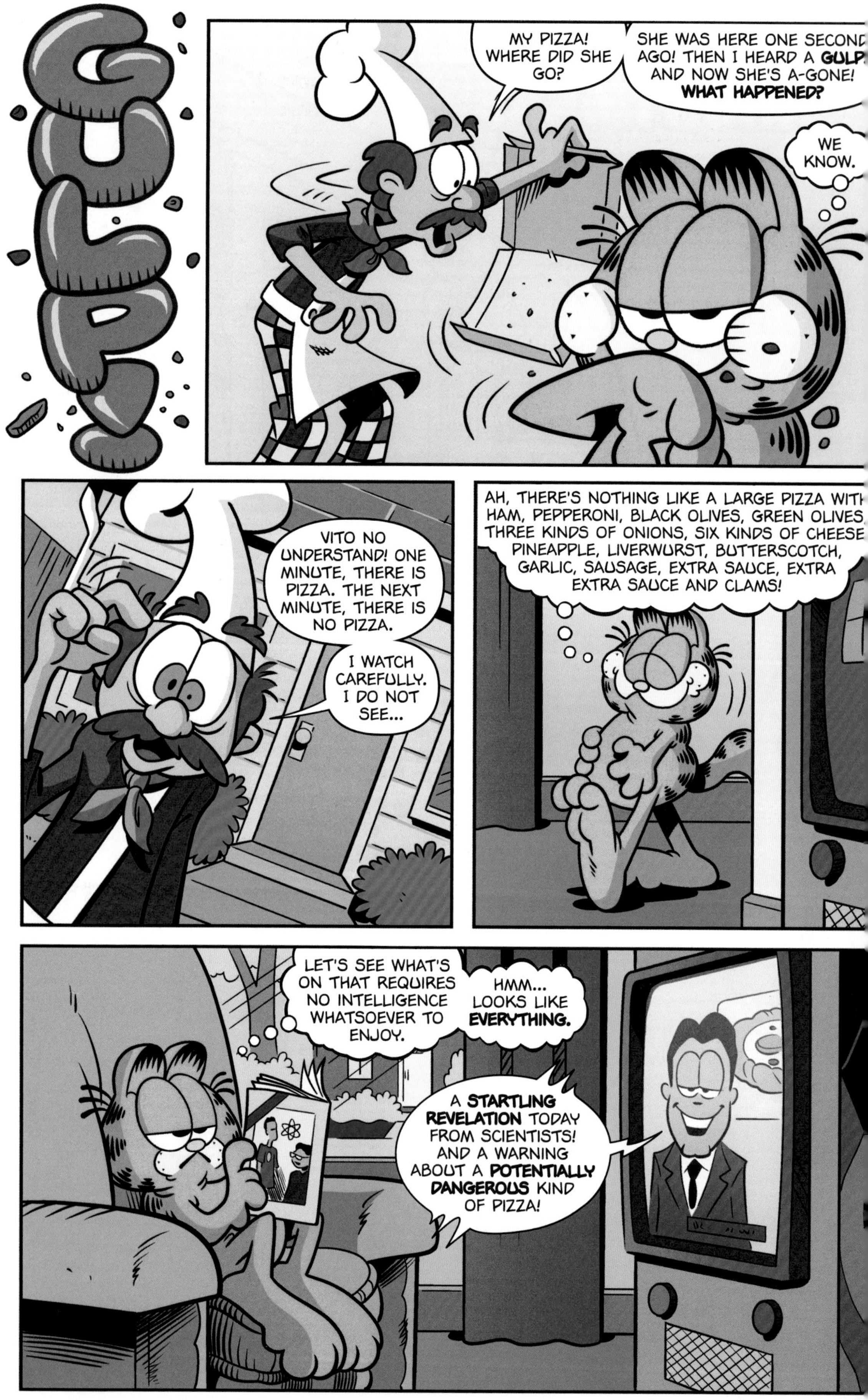

GULP
MY PIZZA! WHERE DID SHE GO?
SHE WAS HERE ONE SECOND AGO! THEN I HEARD A GULP, AND NOW SHE'S A-GONE! WHAT HAPPENED?
WE KNOW.
VITO NO UNDERSTAND! ONE MINUTE, THERE IS PIZZA. THE NEXT MINUTE, THERE IS NO PIZZA.
I WATCH CAREFULLY. I DO NOT SEE...
AH, THERE'S NOTHING LIKE A LARGE PIZZA WITH HAM, PEPPERONI, BLACK OLIVES, GREEN OLIVES, THREE KINDS OF ONIONS, SIX KINDS OF CHEESE, PINEAPPLE, LIVERWURST, BUTTERSCOTCH, GARLIC, SAUSAGE, EXTRA SAUCE, EXTRA EXTRA SAUCE AND CLAMS!
LET'S SEE WHAT'S ON THAT REQUIRES NO INTELLIGENCE WHATSOEVER TO ENJOY.
HMM... LOOKS LIKE EVERYTHING.
A STARTLING REVELATION TODAY FROM SCIENTISTS! AND A WARNING ABOUT A POTENTIALLY DANGEROUS KIND OF PIZZA!

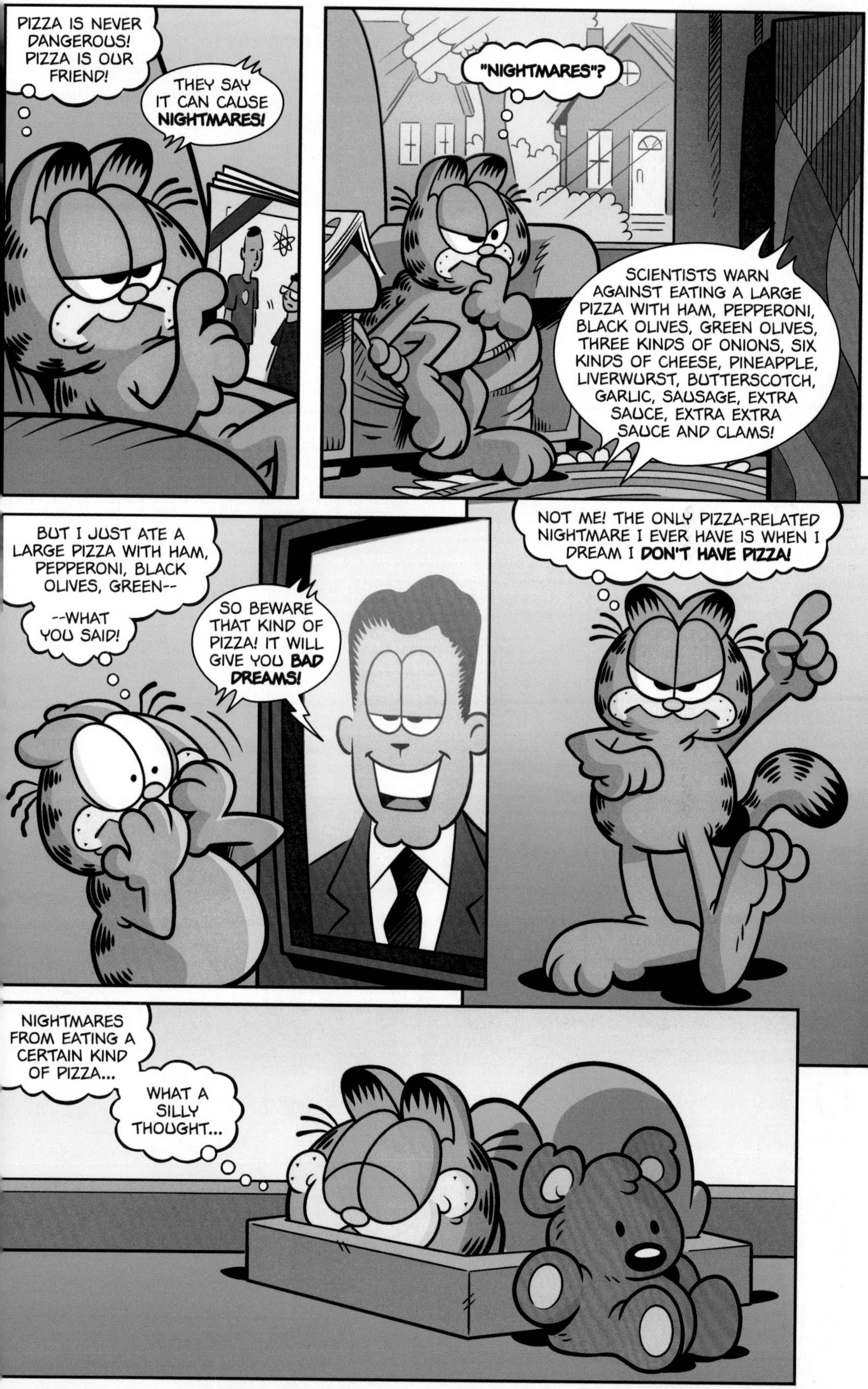

PIZZA IS NEVER DANGEROUS! PIZZA IS OUR FRIEND!
THEY SAY IT CAN CAUSE NIGHTMARES!
"NIGHTMARES"?
SCIENTISTS WARN AGAINST EATING A LARGE PIZZA WITH HAM, PEPPERONI, BLACK OLIVES, GREEN OLIVES, THREE KINDS OF ONIONS, SIX KINDS OF CHEESE, PINEAPPLE, LIVERWURST, BUTTERSCOTCH, GARLIC, SAUSAGE, EXTRA SAUCE, EXTRA EXTRA SAUCE AND CLAMS!
BUT I JUST ATE A LARGE PIZZA WITH HAM, PEPPERONI, BLACK OLIVES, GREEN--
--WHAT YOU SAID!
SO BEWARE THAT KIND OF PIZZA! IT WILL GIVE YOU BAD DREAMS!
NOT ME! THE ONLY PIZZA-RELATED NIGHTMARE I EVER HAVE IS WHEN I DREAM I DON'T HAVE PIZZA!
NIGHTMARES FROM EATING A CERTAIN KIND OF PIZZA...
WHAT A SILLY THOUGHT...

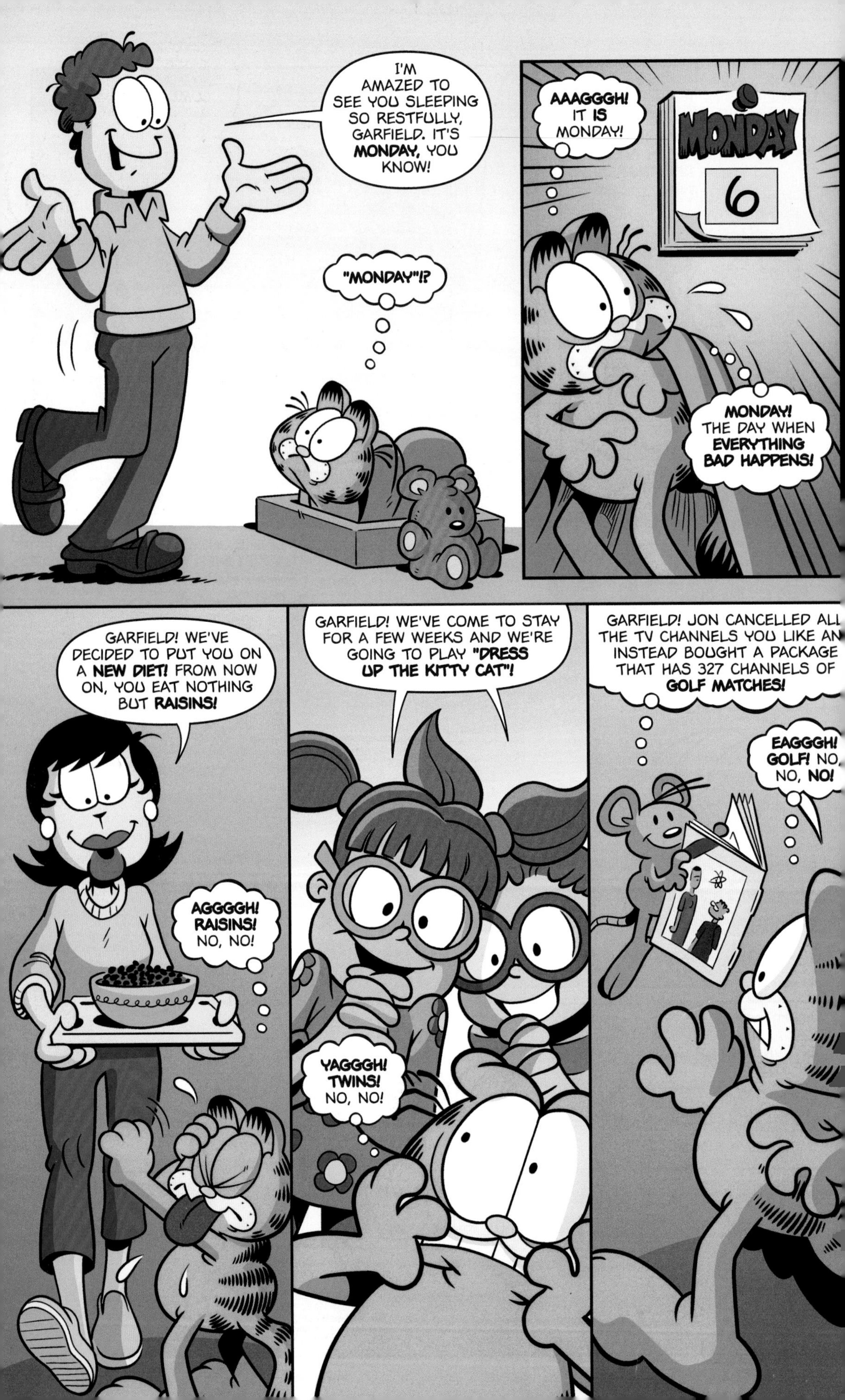
I'M AMAZED TO SEE YOU SLEEPING SO RESTFULLY, GARFIELD. IT'S **MONDAY,** YOU KNOW!
"MONDAY"!?
AAAGGGH! IT **IS** MONDAY!
MONDAY
6
MONDAY! THE DAY WHEN **EVERYTHING BAD HAPPENS!**
GARFIELD! WE'VE DECIDED TO PUT YOU ON A **NEW DIET!** FROM NOW ON, YOU EAT NOTHING BUT **RAISINS!**
AGGGGH! RAISINS! NO, NO!
GARFIELD! WE'VE COME TO STAY FOR A FEW WEEKS AND WE'RE GOING TO PLAY **"DRESS UP THE KITTY CAT"!**
YAGGGH! TWINS! NO, NO!
GARFIELD! JON CANCELLED ALL THE TV CHANNELS YOU LIKE AN INSTEAD BOUGHT A PACKAGE THAT HAS 327 CHANNELS OF **GOLF MATCHES!**
EAGGGH! GOLF! NO, NO, **NO!**

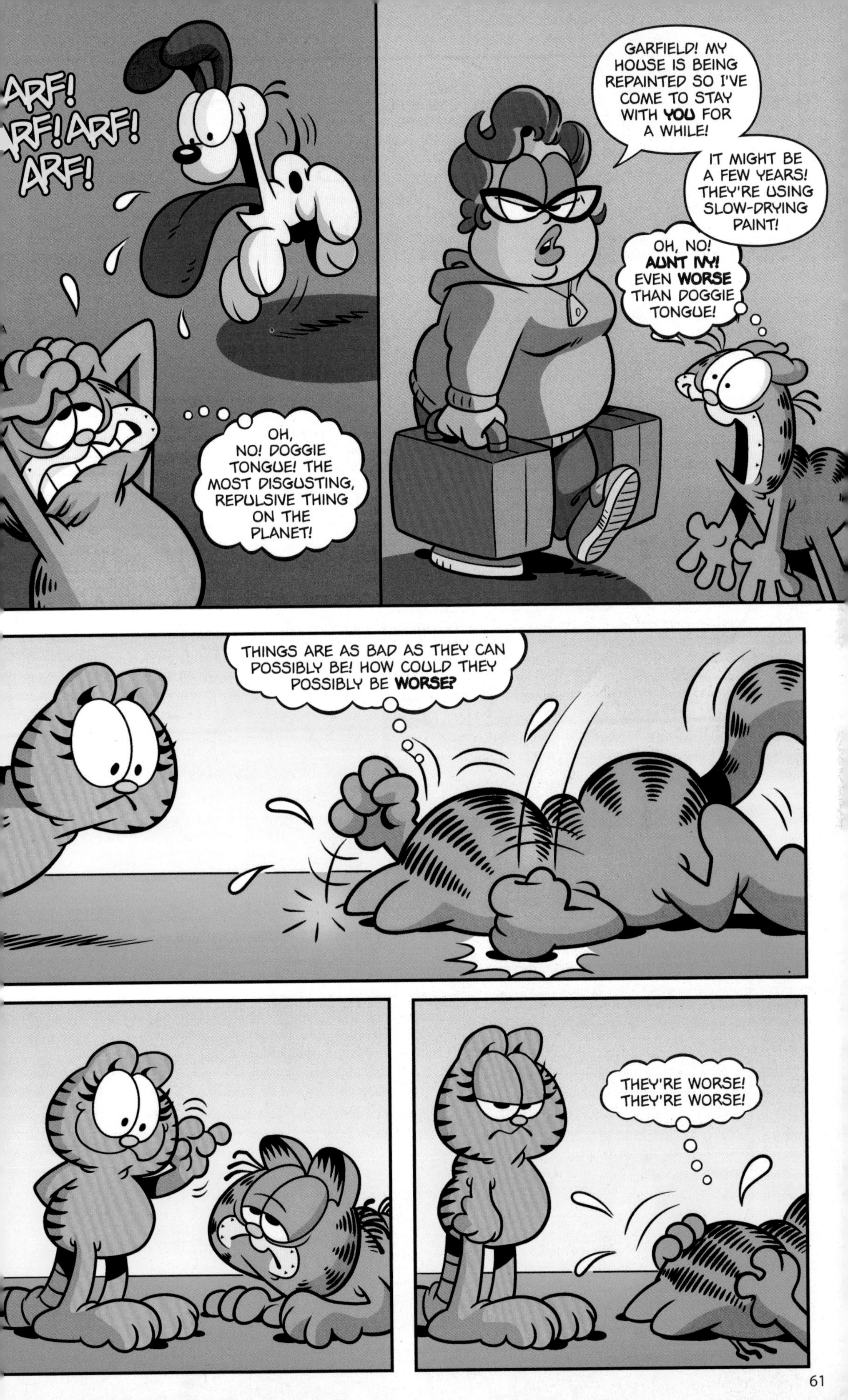
ARF! ARF! ARF! ARF!
OH, NO! DOGGIE TONGUE! THE MOST DISGUSTING, REPULSIVE THING ON THE PLANET!
GARFIELD! MY HOUSE IS BEING REPAINTED SO I'VE COME TO STAY WITH **YOU** FOR A WHILE!
IT MIGHT BE A FEW YEARS! THEY'RE USING SLOW-DRYING PAINT!
OH, NO! **AUNT IVY!** EVEN **WORSE** THAN DOGGIE TONGUE!
THINGS ARE AS BAD AS THEY CAN POSSIBLY BE! HOW COULD THEY POSSIBLY BE **WORSE?**
THEY'RE WORSE! THEY'RE WORSE!

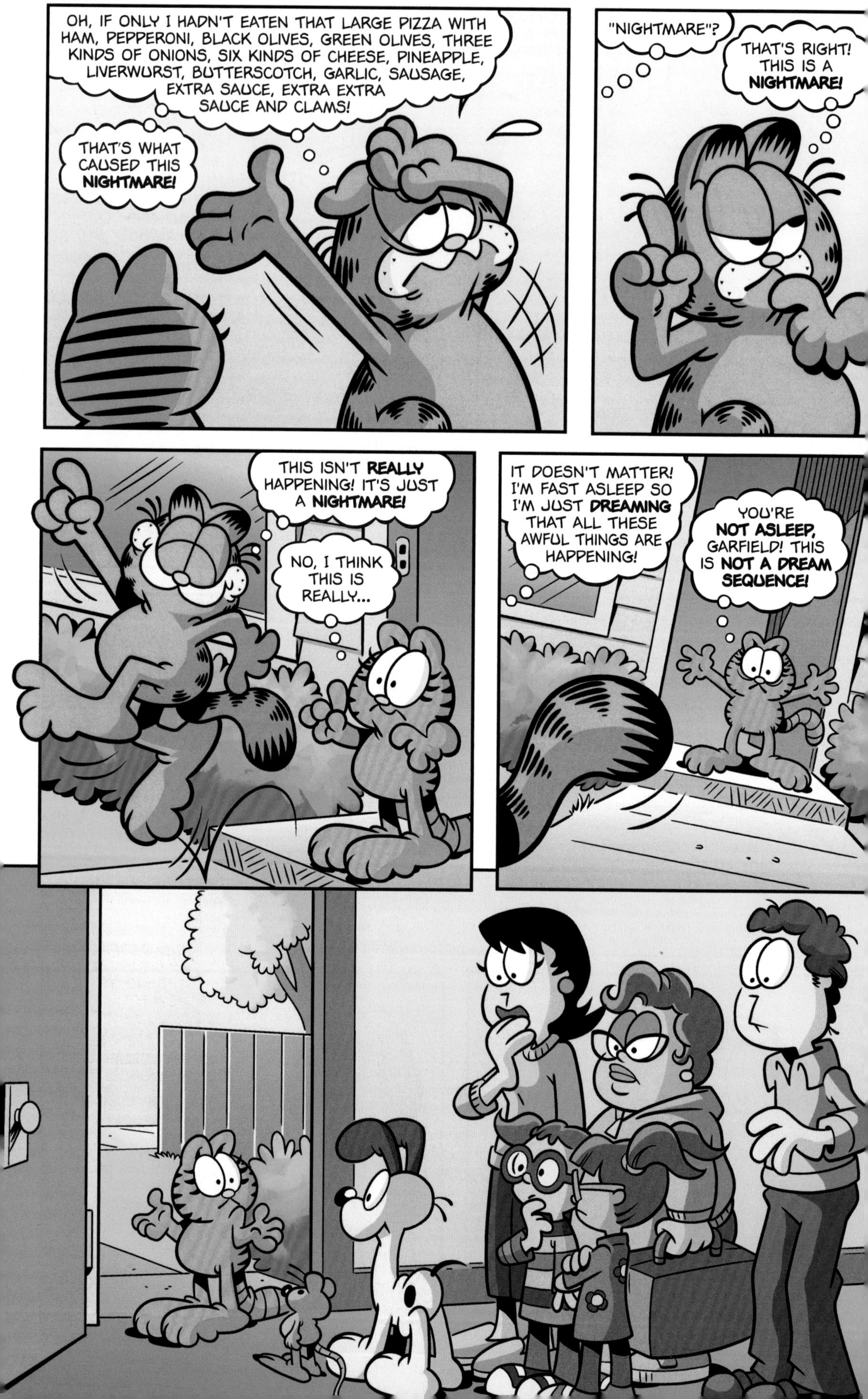

OH, IF ONLY I HADN'T EATEN THAT LARGE PIZZA WITH HAM, PEPPERONI, BLACK OLIVES, GREEN OLIVES, THREE KINDS OF ONIONS, SIX KINDS OF CHEESE, PINEAPPLE, LIVERWURST, BUTTERSCOTCH, GARLIC, SAUSAGE, EXTRA SAUCE, EXTRA EXTRA SAUCE AND CLAMS!
THAT'S WHAT CAUSED THIS **NIGHTMARE!**
"NIGHTMARE"?
THAT'S RIGHT! THIS IS A **NIGHTMARE!**
THIS ISN'T **REALLY** HAPPENING! IT'S JUST A **NIGHTMARE!**
NO, I THINK THIS IS REALLY...
IT DOESN'T MATTER! I'M FAST ASLEEP SO I'M JUST **DREAMING** THAT ALL THESE AWFUL THINGS ARE HAPPENING!
YOU'RE **NOT ASLEEP,** GARFIELD! THIS IS **NOT A DREAM SEQUENCE!**

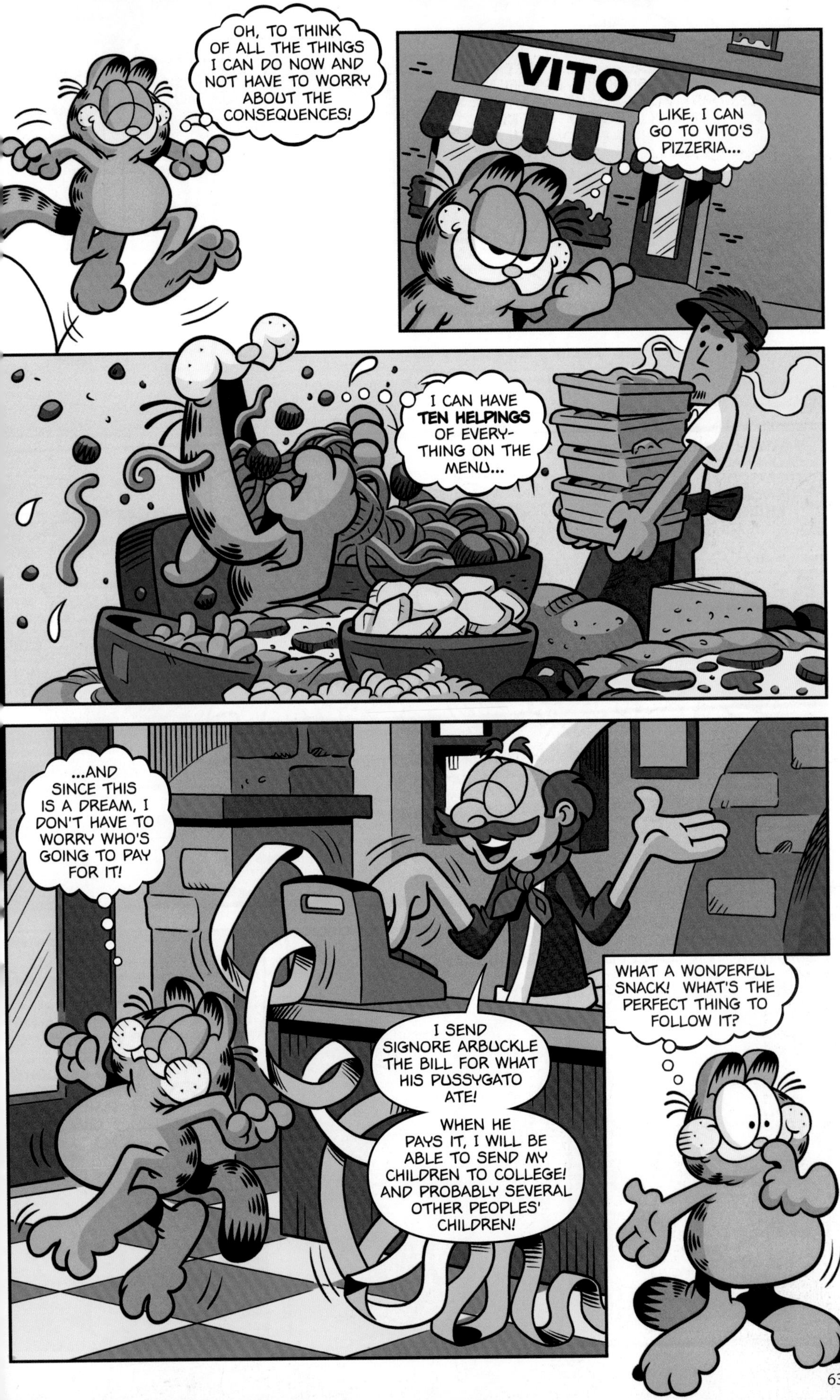
OH, TO THINK OF ALL THE THINGS I CAN DO NOW AND NOT HAVE TO WORRY ABOUT THE CONSEQUENCES!
VITO
LIKE, I CAN GO TO VITO'S PIZZERIA...
I CAN HAVE TEN HELPINGS OF EVERY-THING ON THE MENU...
...AND SINCE THIS IS A DREAM, I DON'T HAVE TO WORRY WHO'S GOING TO PAY FOR IT!
I SEND SIGNORE ARBUCKLE THE BILL FOR WHAT HIS PUSSYGATO ATE!
WHEN HE PAYS IT, I WILL BE ABLE TO SEND MY CHILDREN TO COLLEGE! AND PROBABLY SEVERAL OTHER PEOPLES' CHILDREN!
WHAT A WONDERFUL SNACK! WHAT'S THE PERFECT THING TO FOLLOW IT?

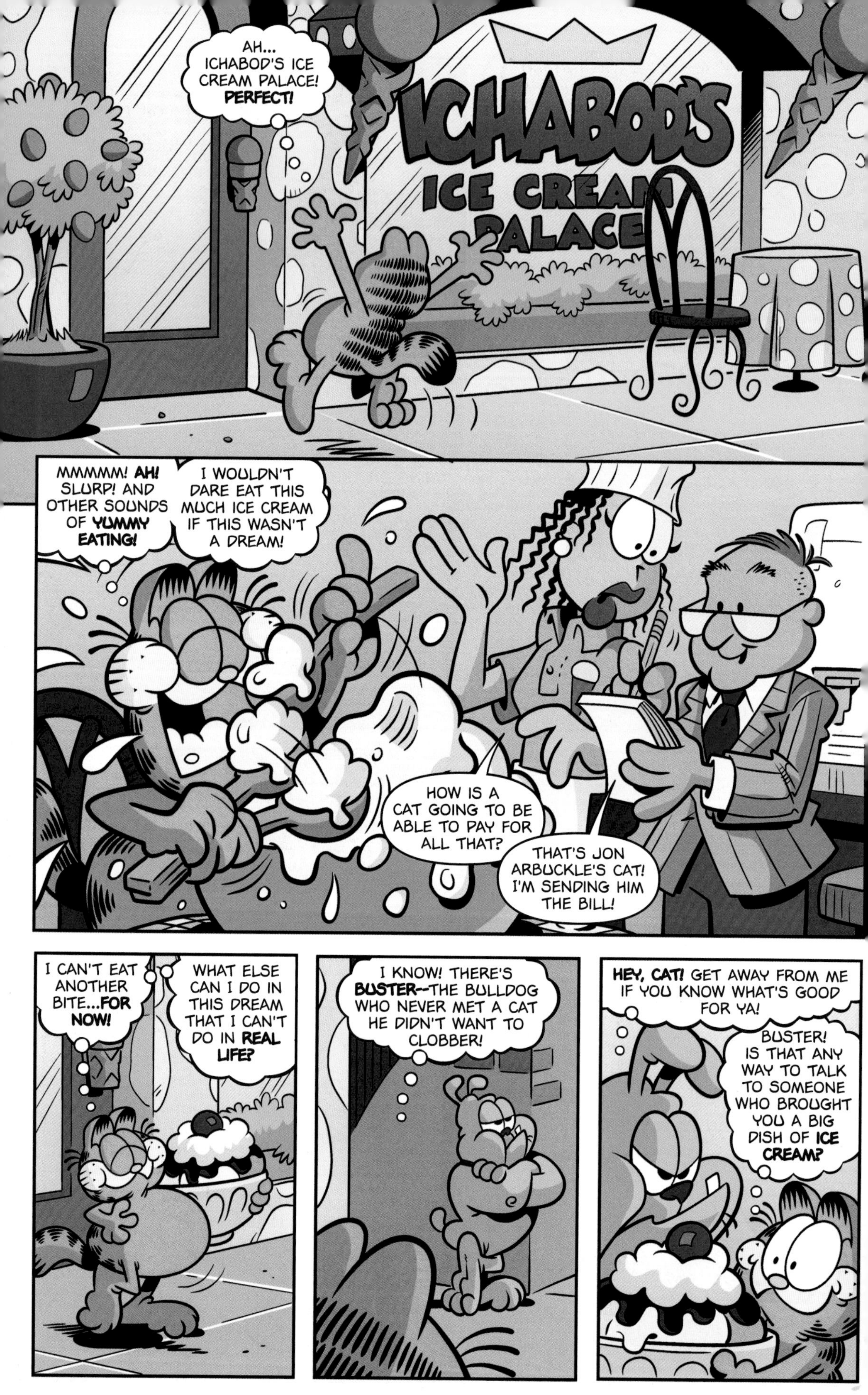

AH... ICHABOD'S ICE CREAM PALACE! **PERFECT!**
ICHABOD'S ICE CREAM PALACE
MMMMM! **AH!** SLURP! AND OTHER SOUNDS OF **YUMMY EATING!**
I WOULDN'T DARE EAT THIS MUCH ICE CREAM IF THIS WASN'T A DREAM!
HOW IS A CAT GOING TO BE ABLE TO PAY FOR ALL THAT?
THAT'S JON ARBUCKLE'S CAT! I'M SENDING HIM THE BILL!
I CAN'T EAT ANOTHER BITE...**FOR NOW!**
WHAT ELSE CAN I DO IN THIS DREAM THAT I CAN'T DO IN **REAL LIFE?**
I KNOW! THERE'S **BUSTER**--THE BULLDOG WHO NEVER MET A CAT HE DIDN'T WANT TO CLOBBER!
HEY, CAT! GET AWAY FROM ME IF YOU KNOW WHAT'S GOOD FOR YA!
BUSTER! IS THAT ANY WAY TO TALK TO SOMEONE WHO BROUGHT YOU A BIG DISH OF **ICE CREAM?**

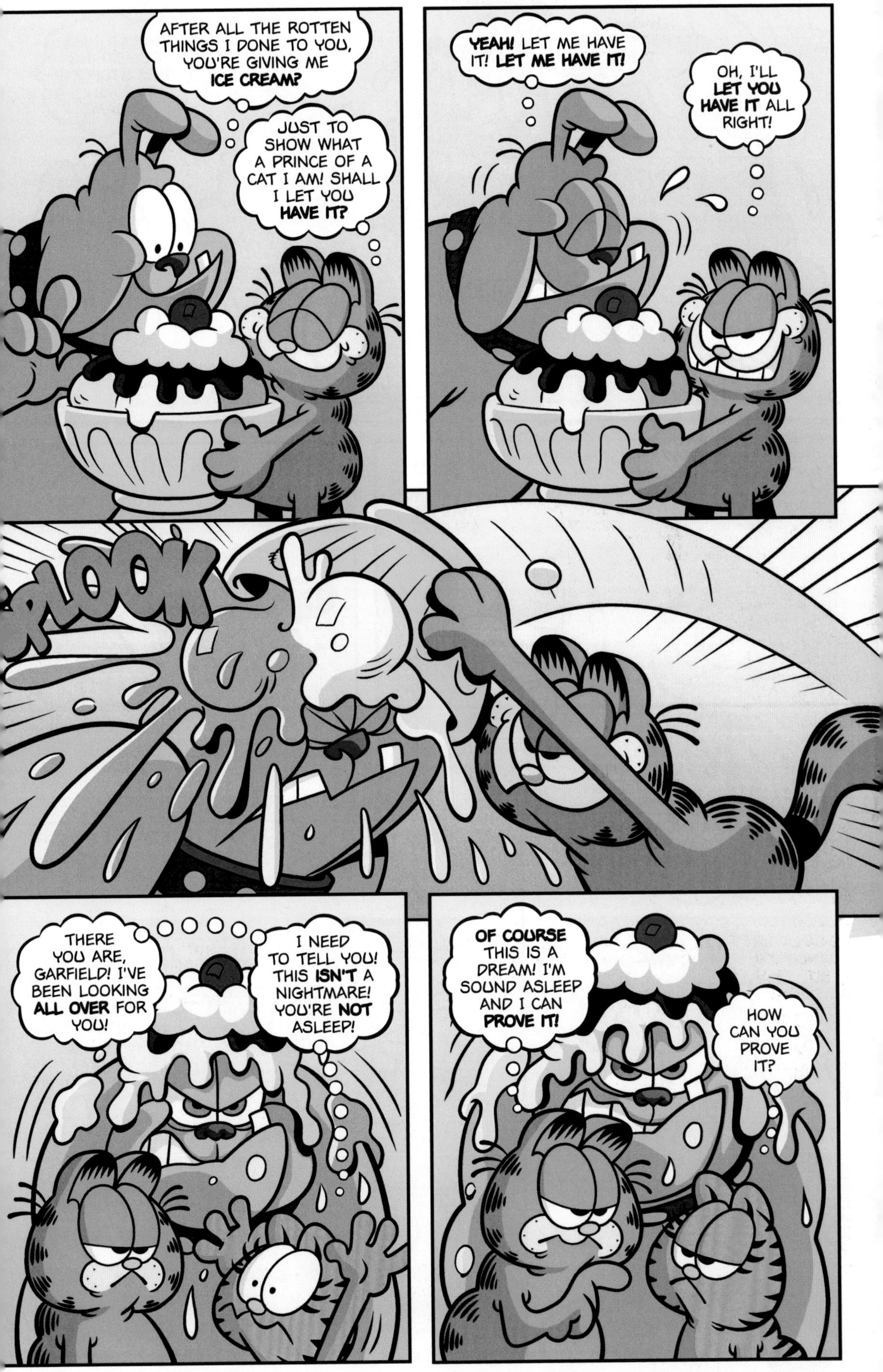

AFTER ALL THE ROTTEN THINGS I DONE TO YOU, YOU'RE GIVING ME **ICE CREAM?**
JUST TO SHOW WHAT A PRINCE OF A CAT I AM! SHALL I LET YOU **HAVE IT?**
YEAH! LET ME HAVE IT! **LET ME HAVE IT!**
OH, I'LL **LET YOU HAVE IT** ALL RIGHT!
PLOOK
THERE YOU ARE, GARFIELD! I'VE BEEN LOOKING **ALL OVER** FOR YOU!
I NEED TO TELL YOU! THIS **ISN'T** A NIGHTMARE! YOU'RE **NOT** ASLEEP!
OF COURSE THIS IS A DREAM! I'M SOUND ASLEEP AND I CAN **PROVE IT!**
HOW CAN YOU PROVE IT?

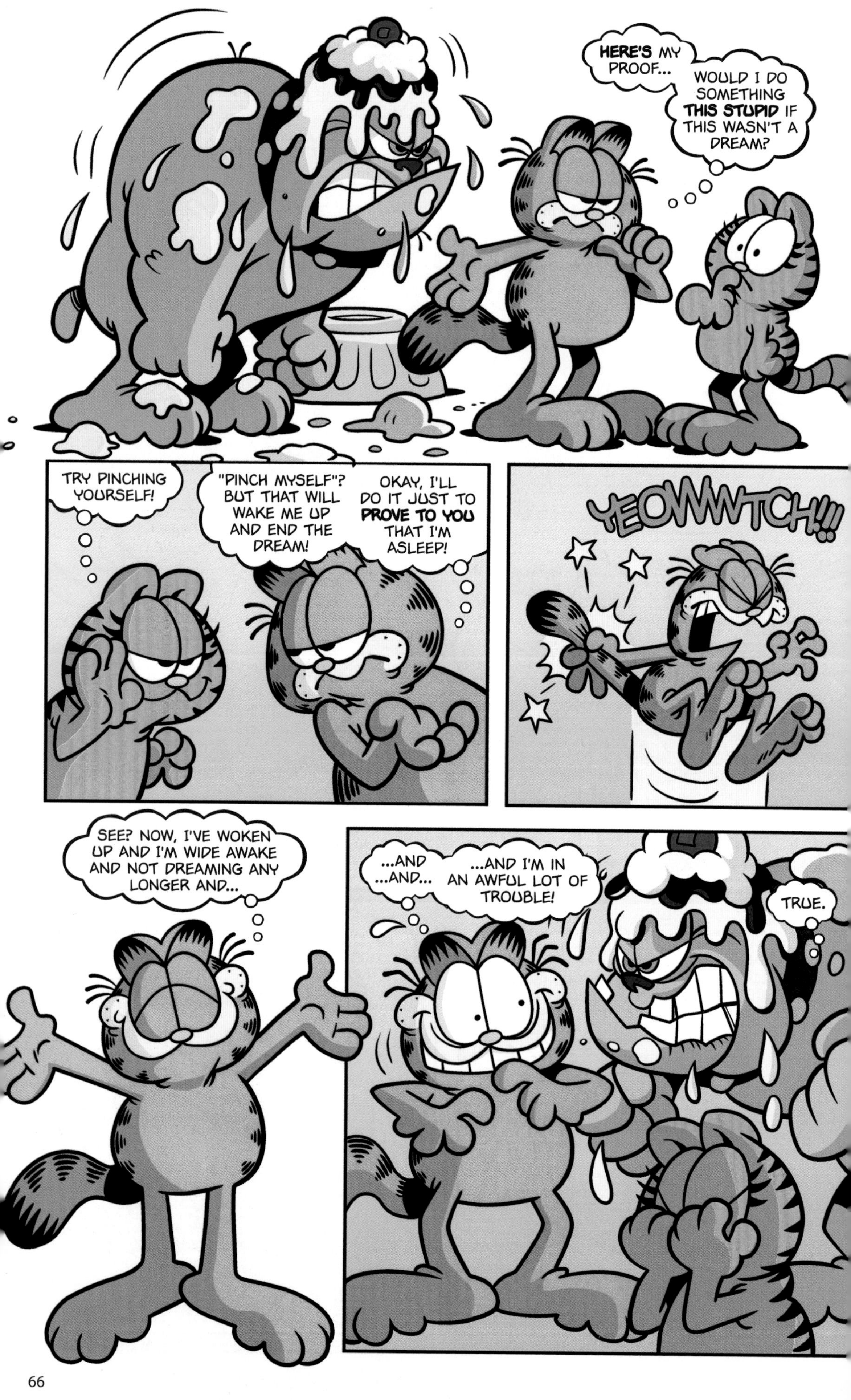

HERE'S MY PROOF...
WOULD I DO SOMETHING **THIS STUPID** IF THIS WASN'T A DREAM?
TRY PINCHING YOURSELF!
"PINCH MYSELF"? BUT THAT WILL WAKE ME UP AND END THE DREAM!
OKAY, I'LL DO IT JUST TO **PROVE TO YOU** THAT I'M ASLEEP!
YEOWWWTCH!!!
SEE? NOW, I'VE WOKEN UP AND I'M WIDE AWAKE AND NOT DREAMING ANY LONGER AND...
...AND ...AND...
...AND I'M IN AN AWFUL LOT OF TROUBLE!
TRUE.

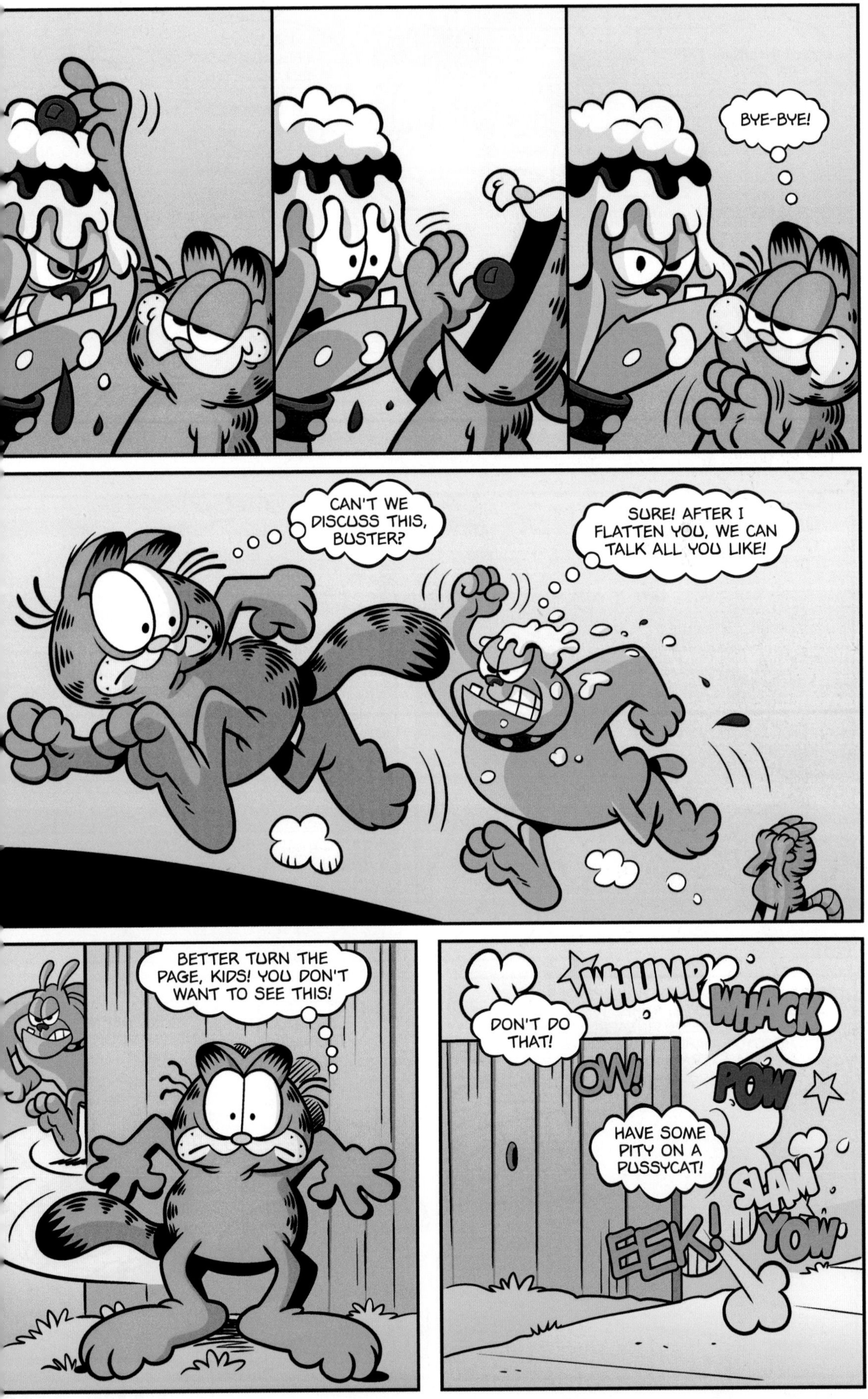
BYE-BYE!
CAN'T WE DISCUSS THIS, BUSTER?
SURE! AFTER I FLATTEN YOU, WE CAN TALK ALL YOU LIKE!
BETTER TURN THE PAGE, KIDS! YOU DON'T WANT TO SEE THIS!
WHUMP
WHACK
DON'T DO THAT!
OW!
POW
HAVE SOME PITY ON A PUSSYCAT!
SLAM
EEK!
YOW

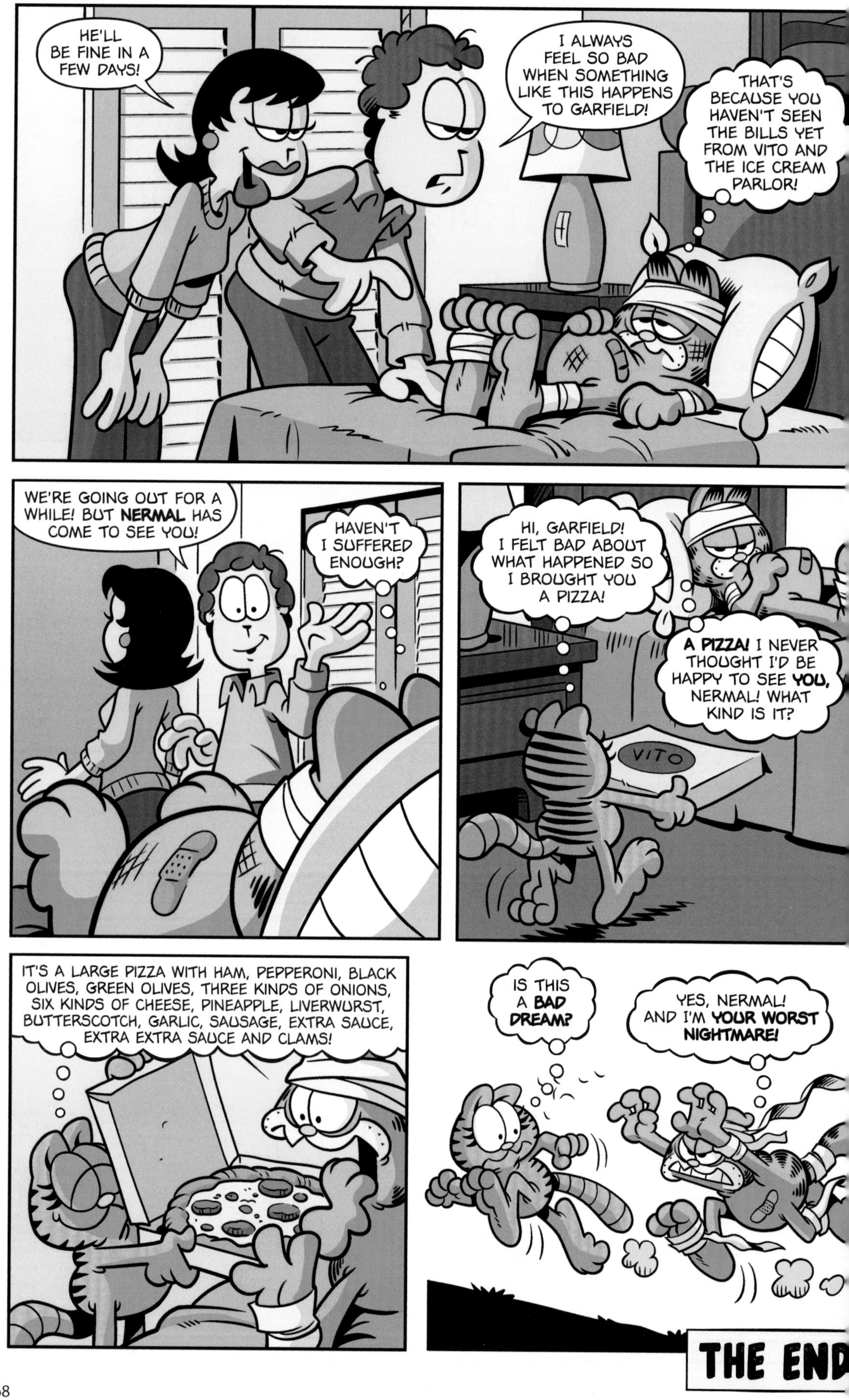

HE'LL BE FINE IN A FEW DAYS!
I ALWAYS FEEL SO BAD WHEN SOMETHING LIKE THIS HAPPENS TO GARFIELD!
THAT'S BECAUSE YOU HAVEN'T SEEN THE BILLS YET FROM VITO AND THE ICE CREAM PARLOR!
WE'RE GOING OUT FOR A WHILE! BUT **NERMAL** HAS COME TO SEE YOU!
HAVEN'T I SUFFERED ENOUGH?
HI, GARFIELD! I FELT BAD ABOUT WHAT HAPPENED SO I BROUGHT YOU A PIZZA!
VITO
A PIZZA! I NEVER THOUGHT I'D BE HAPPY TO SEE **YOU,** NERMAL! WHAT KIND IS IT?
IT'S A LARGE PIZZA WITH HAM, PEPPERONI, BLACK OLIVES, GREEN OLIVES, THREE KINDS OF ONIONS, SIX KINDS OF CHEESE, PINEAPPLE, LIVERWURST, BUTTERSCOTCH, GARLIC, SAUSAGE, EXTRA SAUCE, EXTRA EXTRA SAUCE AND CLAMS!
IS THIS A **BAD DREAM?**
YES, NERMAL! AND I'M **YOUR WORST NIGHTMARE!**
THE END

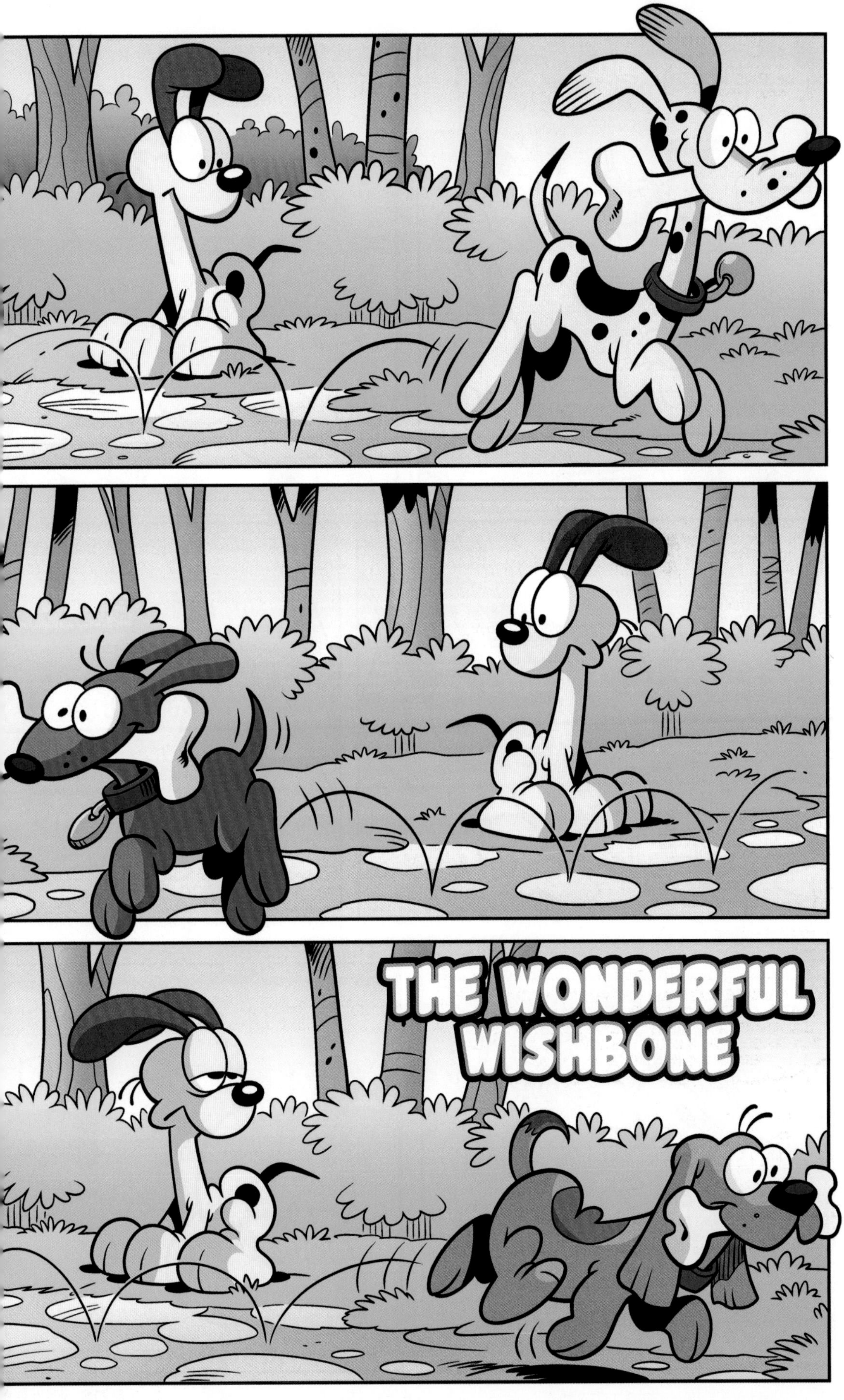
THE WONDERFUL WISHBONE

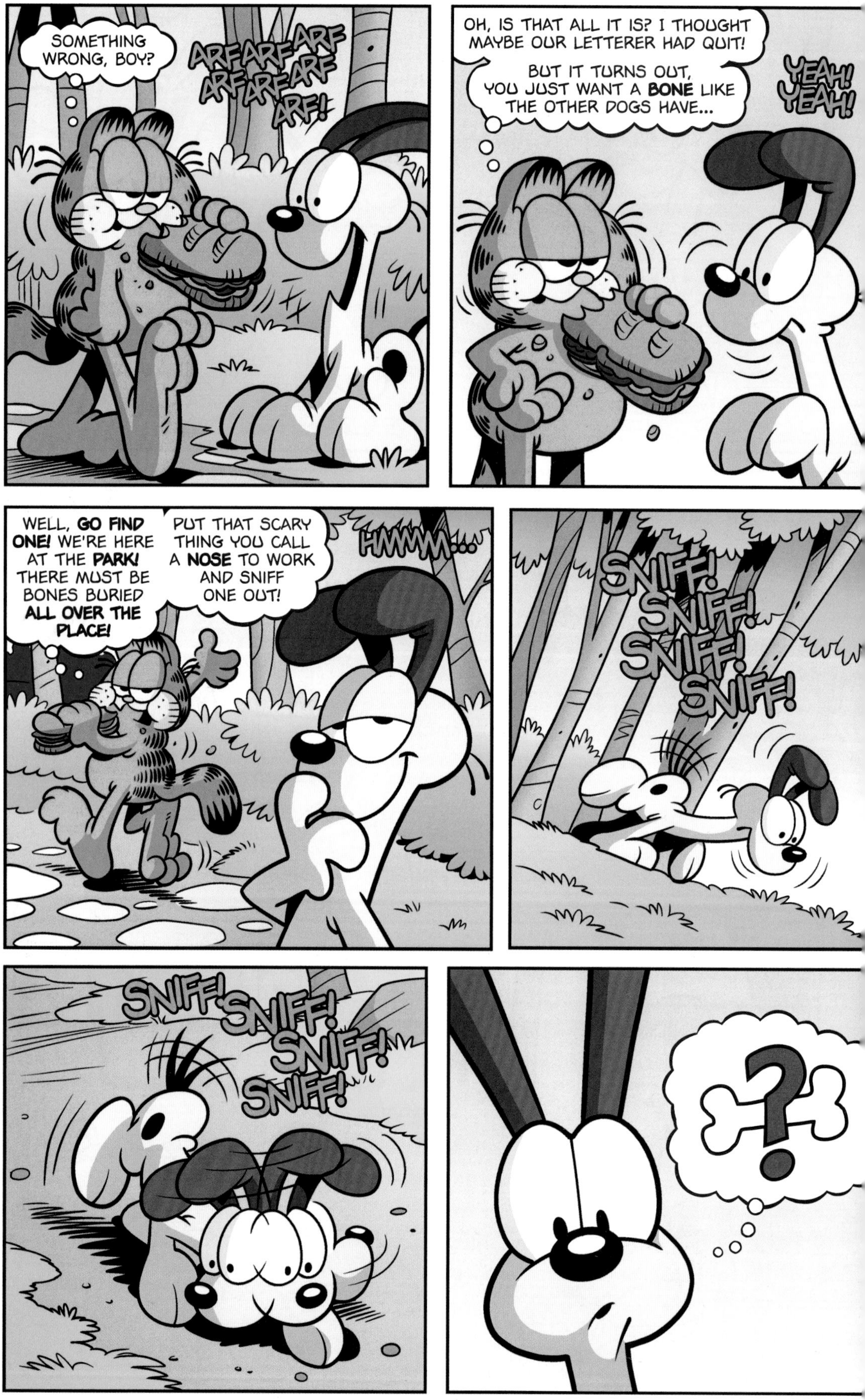
SOMETHING WRONG, BOY?
ARFARFARF ARFARFARF ARF!
OH, IS THAT ALL IT IS? I THOUGHT MAYBE OUR LETTERER HAD QUIT!
BUT IT TURNS OUT, YOU JUST WANT A **BONE** LIKE THE OTHER DOGS HAVE...
YEAH! YEAH!
WELL, **GO FIND ONE!** WE'RE HERE AT THE **PARK!** THERE MUST BE BONES BURIED **ALL OVER THE PLACE!**
PUT THAT SCARY THING YOU CALL A **NOSE** TO WORK AND SNIFF ONE OUT!
HMMM...
SNIFF! SNIFF! SNIFF! SNIFF!
SNIFF! SNIFF! SNIFF! SNIFF!
?

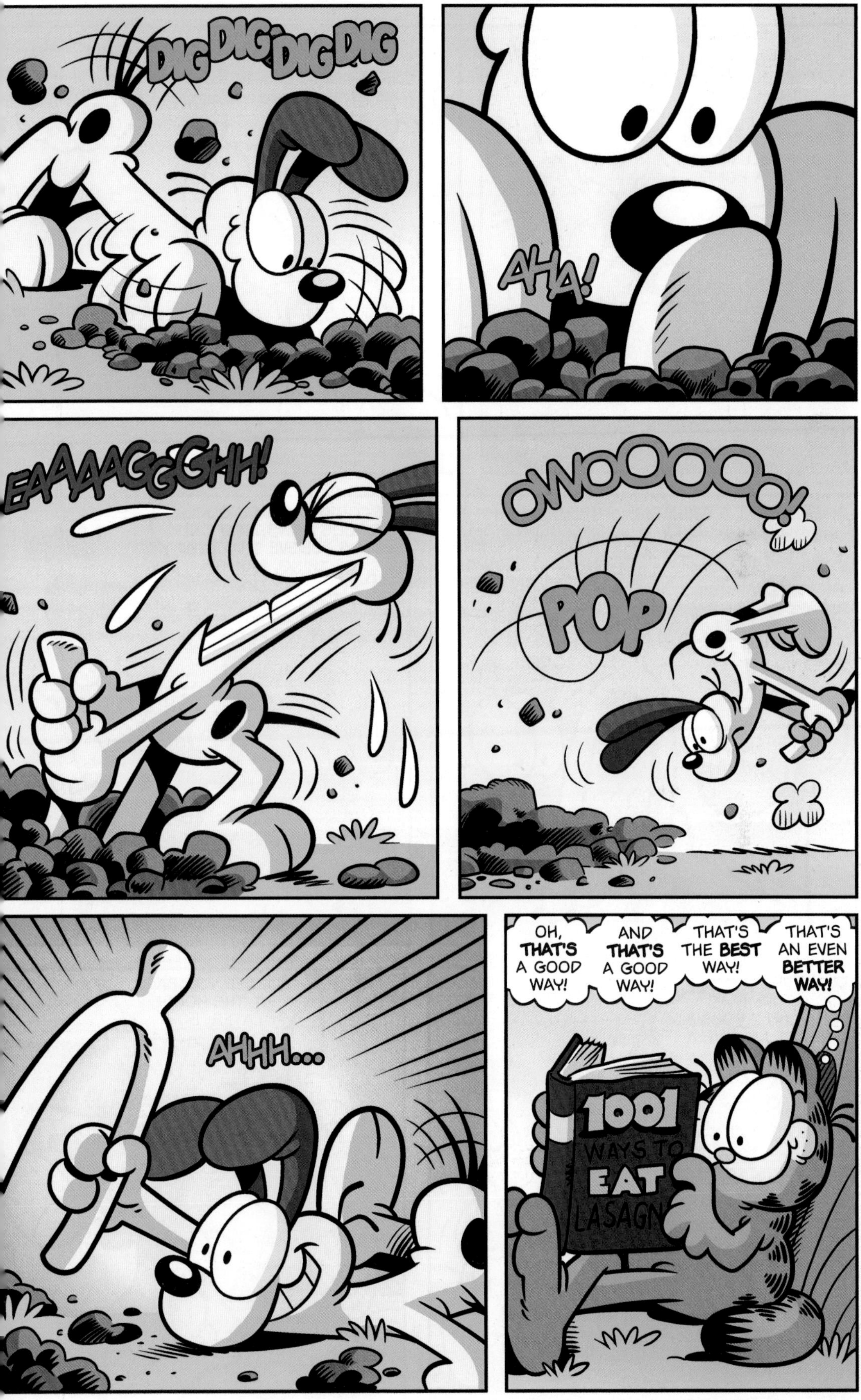
DIG DIG DIG DIG
AHA!
EAAAAGGGHH!
OWOOOOOO!
POP
AHHH...
OH, THAT'S A GOOD WAY!
AND THAT'S A GOOD WAY!
THAT'S THE BEST WAY!
THAT'S AN EVEN BETTER WAY!
1001 WAYS TO EAT LASAGN

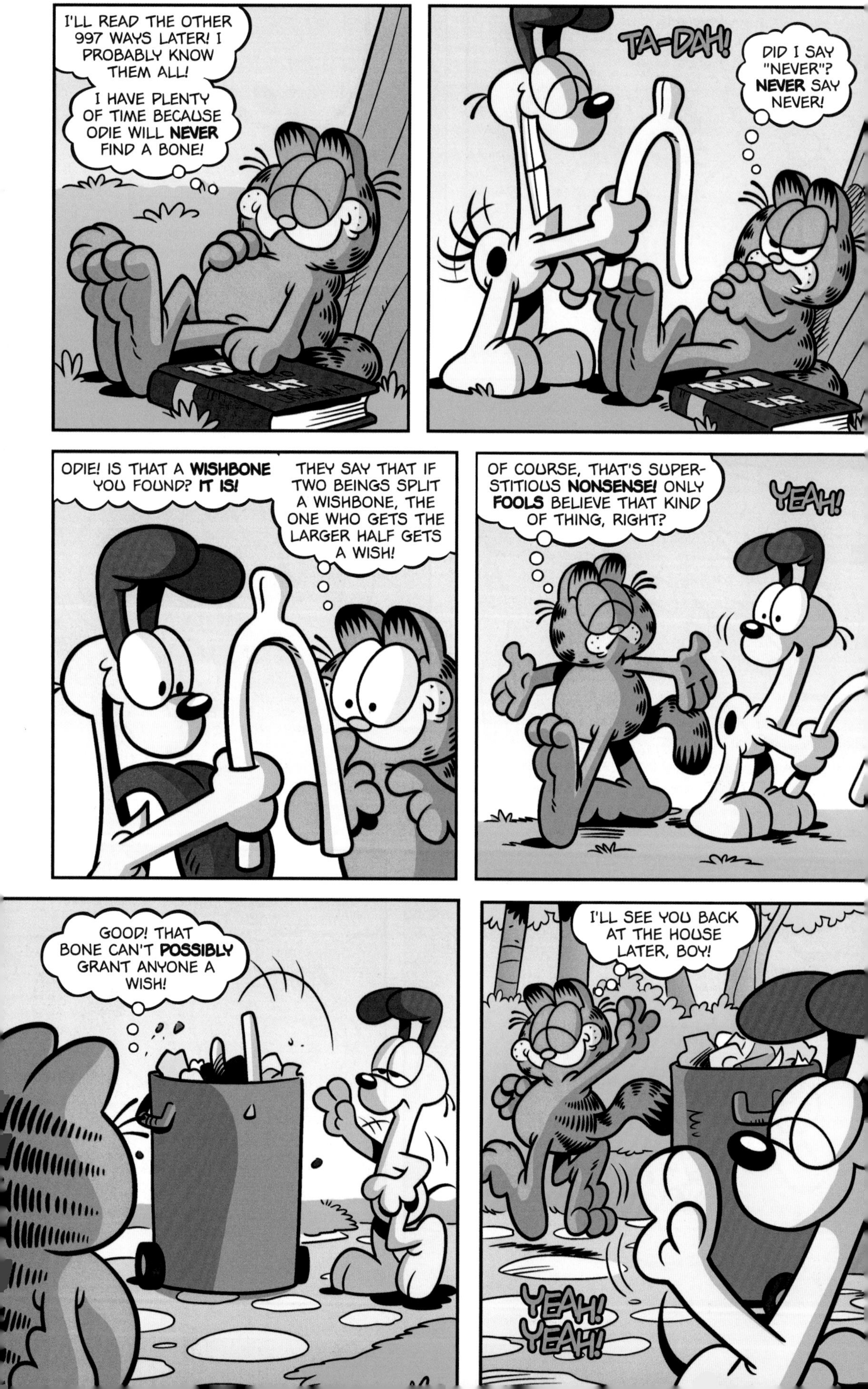
I'LL READ THE OTHER 997 WAYS LATER! I PROBABLY KNOW THEM ALL!
I HAVE PLENTY OF TIME BECAUSE ODIE WILL **NEVER** FIND A BONE!
TA-DAH!
DID I SAY "NEVER"? **NEVER** SAY NEVER!
ODIE! IS THAT A **WISHBONE** YOU FOUND? **IT IS!**
THEY SAY THAT IF TWO BEINGS SPLIT A WISHBONE, THE ONE WHO GETS THE LARGER HALF GETS A WISH!
OF COURSE, THAT'S SUPER-STITIOUS **NONSENSE!** ONLY **FOOLS** BELIEVE THAT KIND OF THING, RIGHT?
YEAH!
GOOD! THAT BONE CAN'T **POSSIBLY** GRANT ANYONE A WISH!
I'LL SEE YOU BACK AT THE HOUSE LATER, BOY!
YEAH! YEAH!

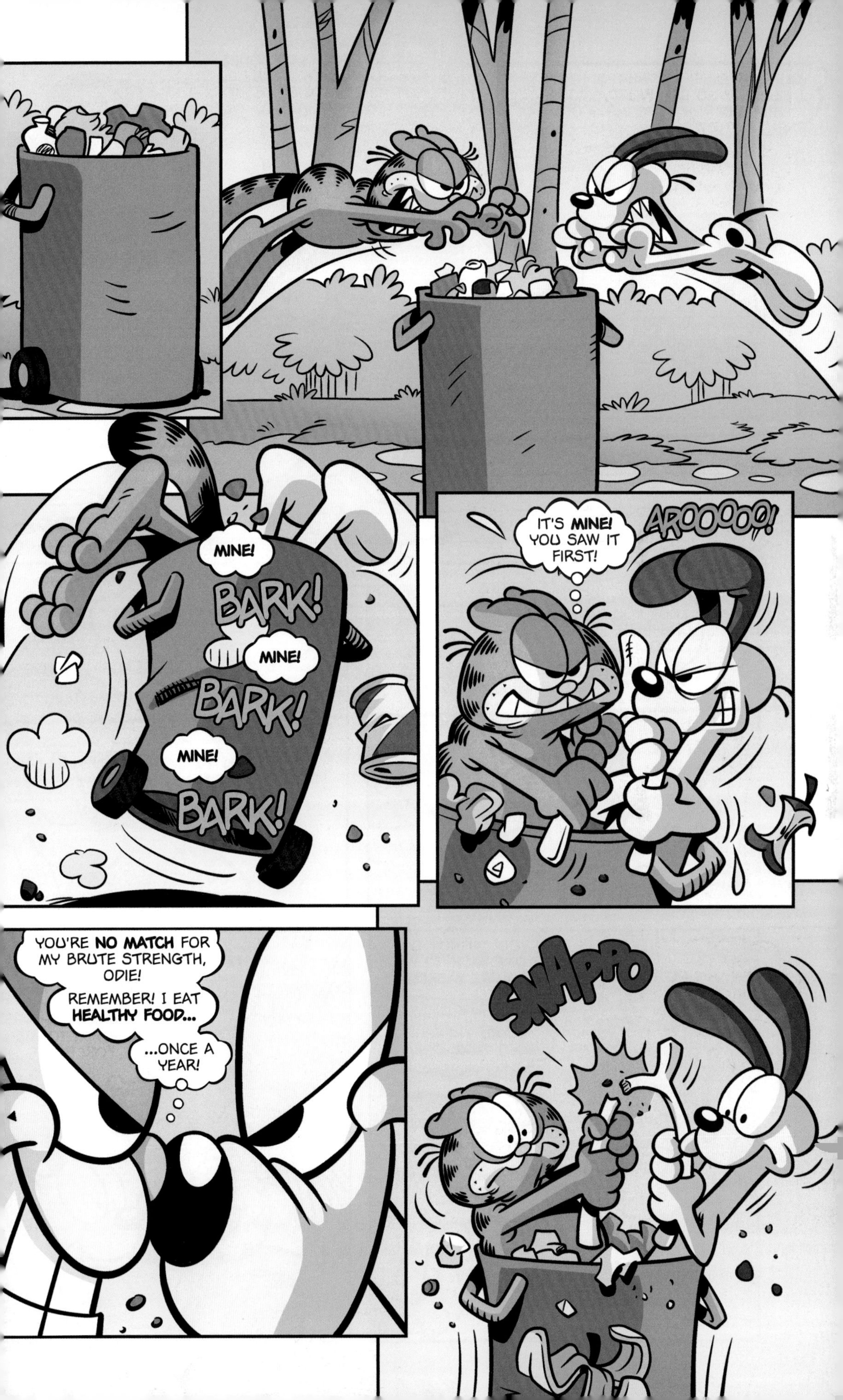

MINE!
BARK!
MINE!
BARK!
MINE!
BARK!
IT'S MINE! YOU SAW IT FIRST!
AROOOOOO!
YOU'RE NO MATCH FOR MY BRUTE STRENGTH, ODIE!
REMEMBER! I EAT HEALTHY FOOD...
...ONCE A YEAR!
SNAPPO

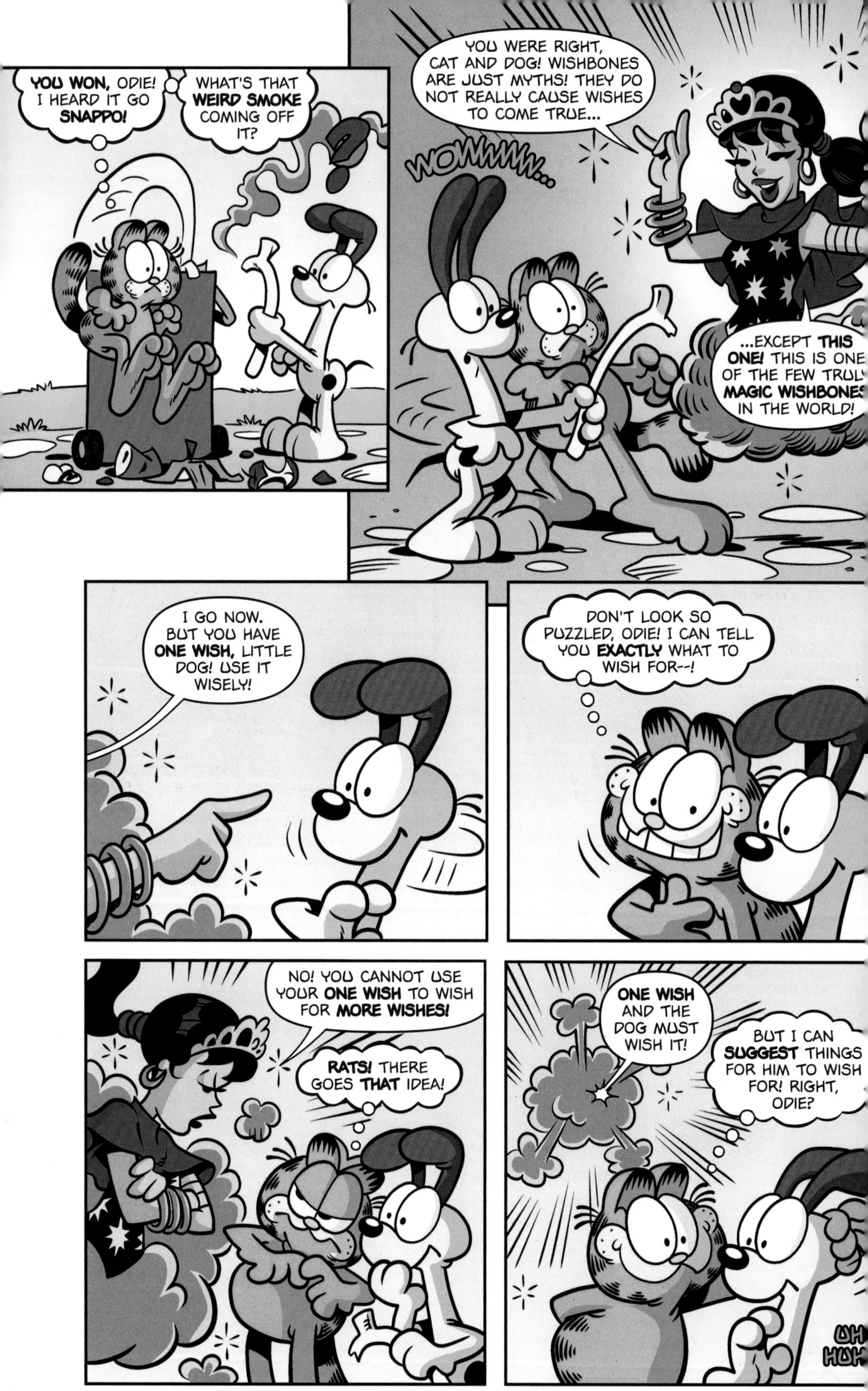

YOU WON, ODIE! I HEARD IT GO SNAPPO!
WHAT'S THAT WEIRD SMOKE COMING OFF IT?
YOU WERE RIGHT, CAT AND DOG! WISHBONES ARE JUST MYTHS! THEY DO NOT REALLY CAUSE WISHES TO COME TRUE...
WOWWWW...
...EXCEPT THIS ONE! THIS IS ONE OF THE FEW TRULY MAGIC WISHBONES IN THE WORLD!
I GO NOW. BUT YOU HAVE ONE WISH, LITTLE DOG! USE IT WISELY!
DON'T LOOK SO PUZZLED, ODIE! I CAN TELL YOU EXACTLY WHAT TO WISH FOR--!
NO! YOU CANNOT USE YOUR ONE WISH TO WISH FOR MORE WISHES!
RATS! THERE GOES THAT IDEA!
ONE WISH AND THE DOG MUST WISH IT!
BUT I CAN SUGGEST THINGS FOR HIM TO WISH FOR! RIGHT, ODIE?
UH HUH

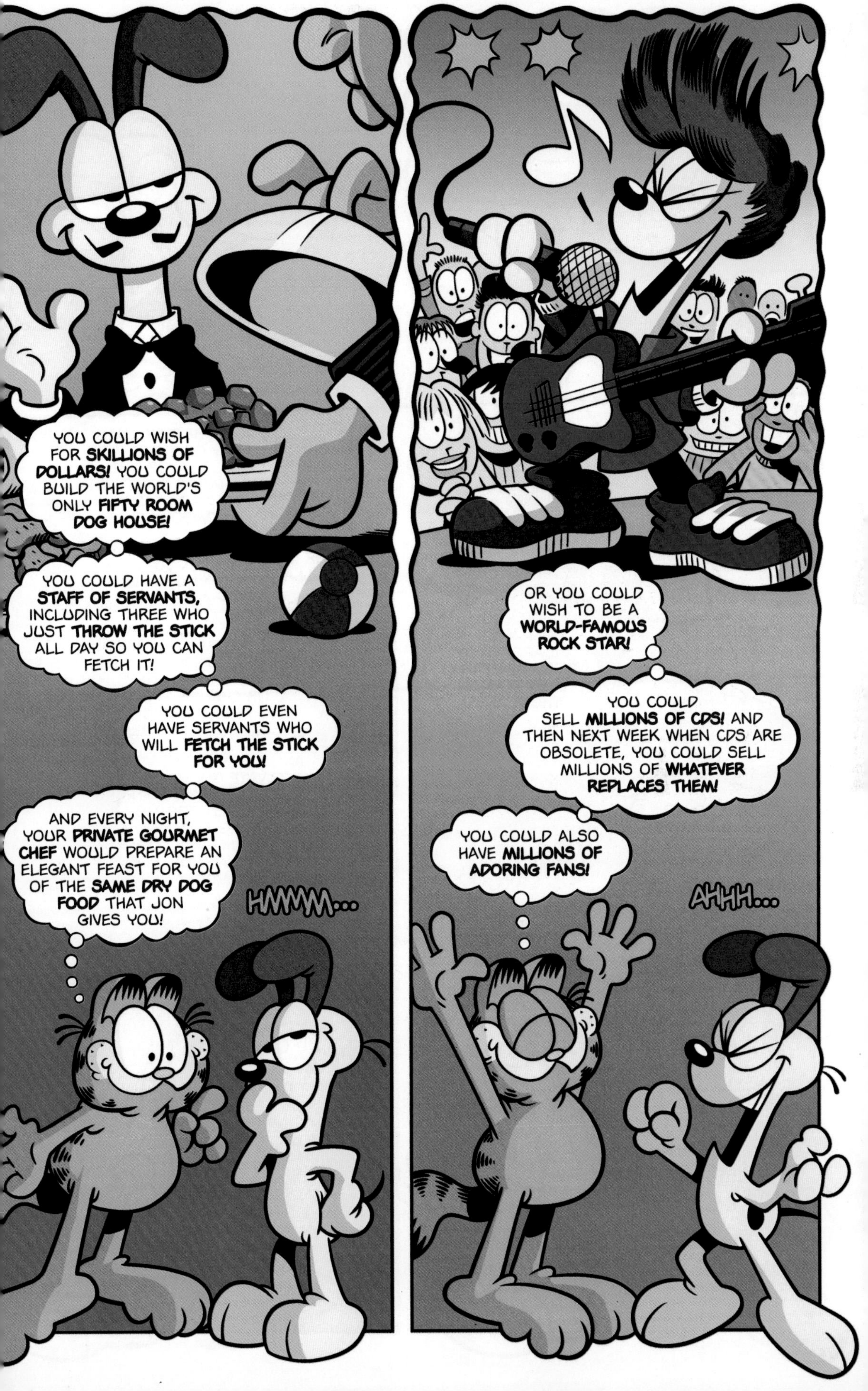

YOU COULD WISH FOR **SKILLIONS OF DOLLARS!** YOU COULD BUILD THE WORLD'S ONLY **FIFTY ROOM DOG HOUSE!**
YOU COULD HAVE A **STAFF OF SERVANTS,** INCLUDING THREE WHO JUST **THROW THE STICK** ALL DAY SO YOU CAN FETCH IT!
YOU COULD EVEN HAVE SERVANTS WHO WILL **FETCH THE STICK FOR YOU!**
AND EVERY NIGHT, YOUR **PRIVATE GOURMET CHEF** WOULD PREPARE AN ELEGANT FEAST FOR YOU OF THE **SAME DRY DOG FOOD** THAT JON GIVES YOU!
HMMM...
OR YOU COULD WISH TO BE A **WORLD-FAMOUS ROCK STAR!**
YOU COULD SELL **MILLIONS OF CDS!** AND THEN NEXT WEEK WHEN CDS ARE OBSOLETE, YOU COULD SELL MILLIONS OF **WHATEVER REPLACES THEM!**
YOU COULD ALSO HAVE **MILLIONS OF ADORING FANS!**
AHHH...

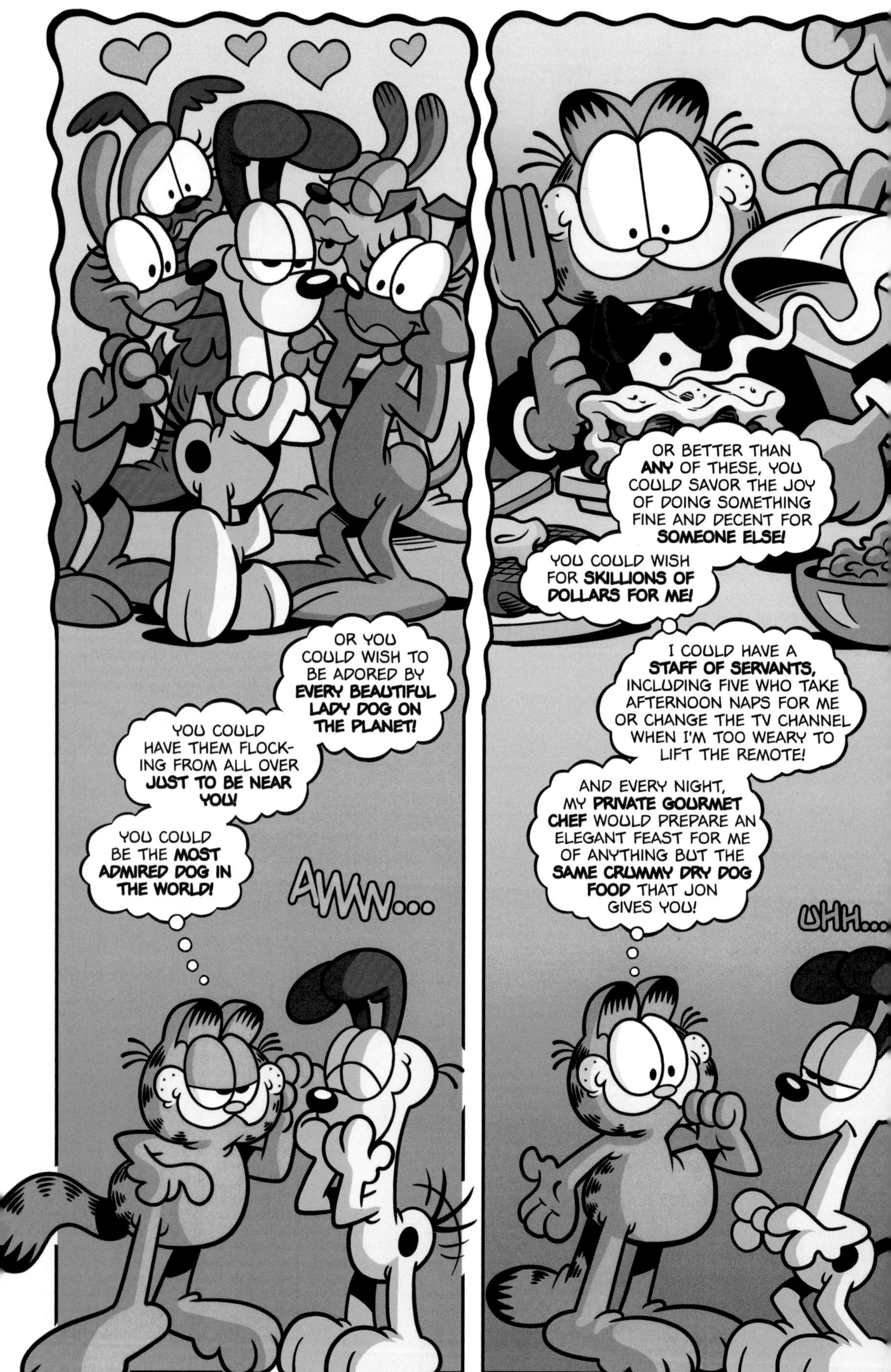

YOU COULD BE THE MOST ADMIRED DOG IN THE WORLD!
YOU COULD HAVE THEM FLOCKING FROM ALL OVER JUST TO BE NEAR YOU!
OR YOU COULD WISH TO BE ADORED BY EVERY BEAUTIFUL LADY DOG ON THE PLANET!
AWW...
YOU COULD WISH FOR SKILLIONS OF DOLLARS FOR ME!
I COULD HAVE A STAFF OF SERVANTS, INCLUDING FIVE WHO TAKE AFTERNOON NAPS FOR ME OR CHANGE THE TV CHANNEL WHEN I'M TOO WEARY TO LIFT THE REMOTE!
AND EVERY NIGHT, MY PRIVATE GOURMET CHEF WOULD PREPARE AN ELEGANT FEAST FOR ME OF ANYTHING BUT THE SAME CRUMMY DRY DOG FOOD THAT JON GIVES YOU!
OR BETTER THAN ANY OF THESE, YOU COULD SAVOR THE JOY OF DOING SOMETHING FINE AND DECENT FOR SOMEONE ELSE!
UHH...

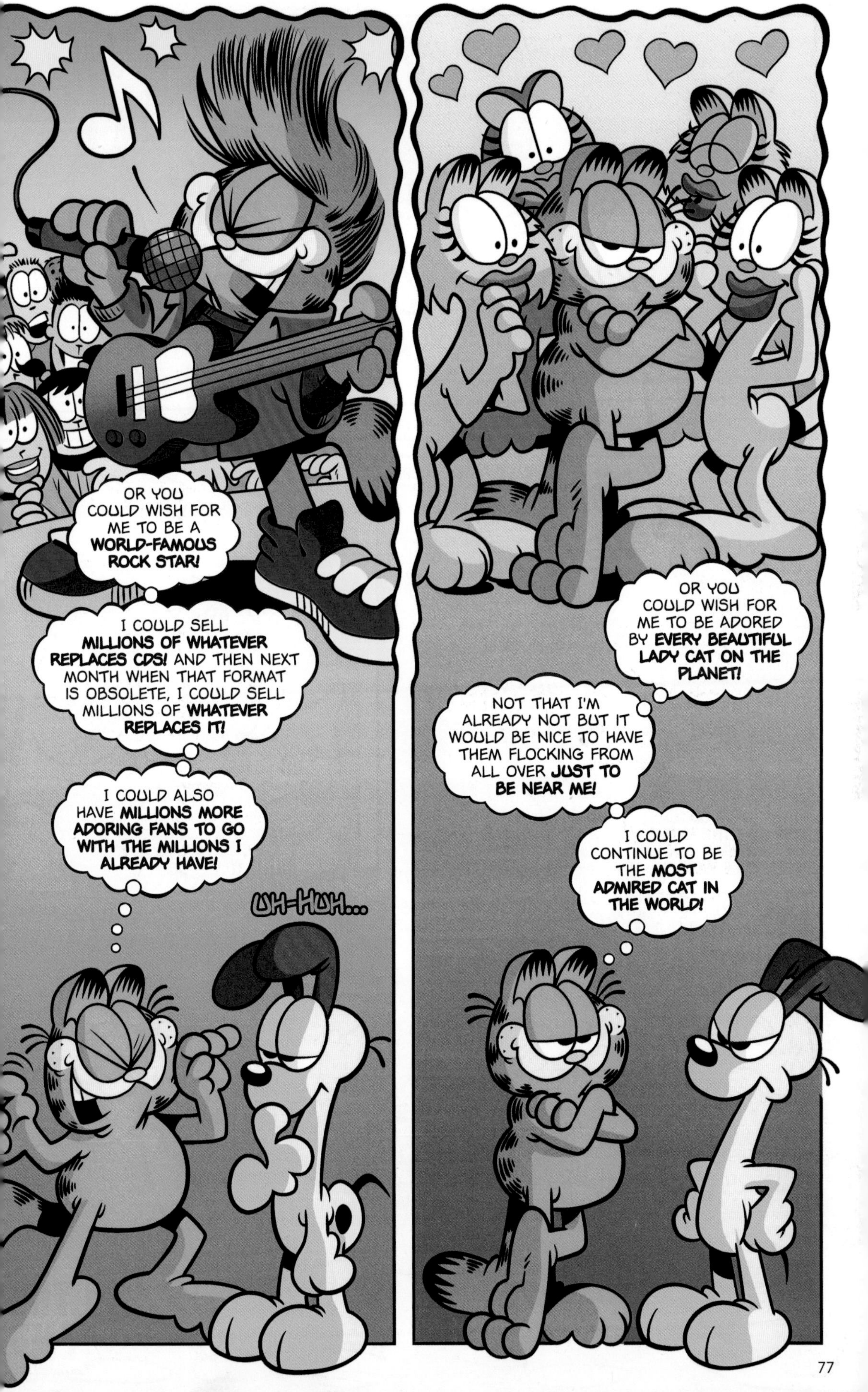

OR YOU COULD WISH FOR ME TO BE A WORLD-FAMOUS ROCK STAR!
I COULD SELL MILLIONS OF WHATEVER REPLACES CDS! AND THEN NEXT MONTH WHEN THAT FORMAT IS OBSOLETE, I COULD SELL MILLIONS OF WHATEVER REPLACES IT!
I COULD ALSO HAVE MILLIONS MORE ADORING FANS TO GO WITH THE MILLIONS I ALREADY HAVE!
UH-HUH...
OR YOU COULD WISH FOR ME TO BE ADORED BY EVERY BEAUTIFUL LADY CAT ON THE PLANET!
NOT THAT I'M ALREADY NOT BUT IT WOULD BE NICE TO HAVE THEM FLOCKING FROM ALL OVER JUST TO BE NEAR ME!
I COULD CONTINUE TO BE THE MOST ADMIRED CAT IN THE WORLD!

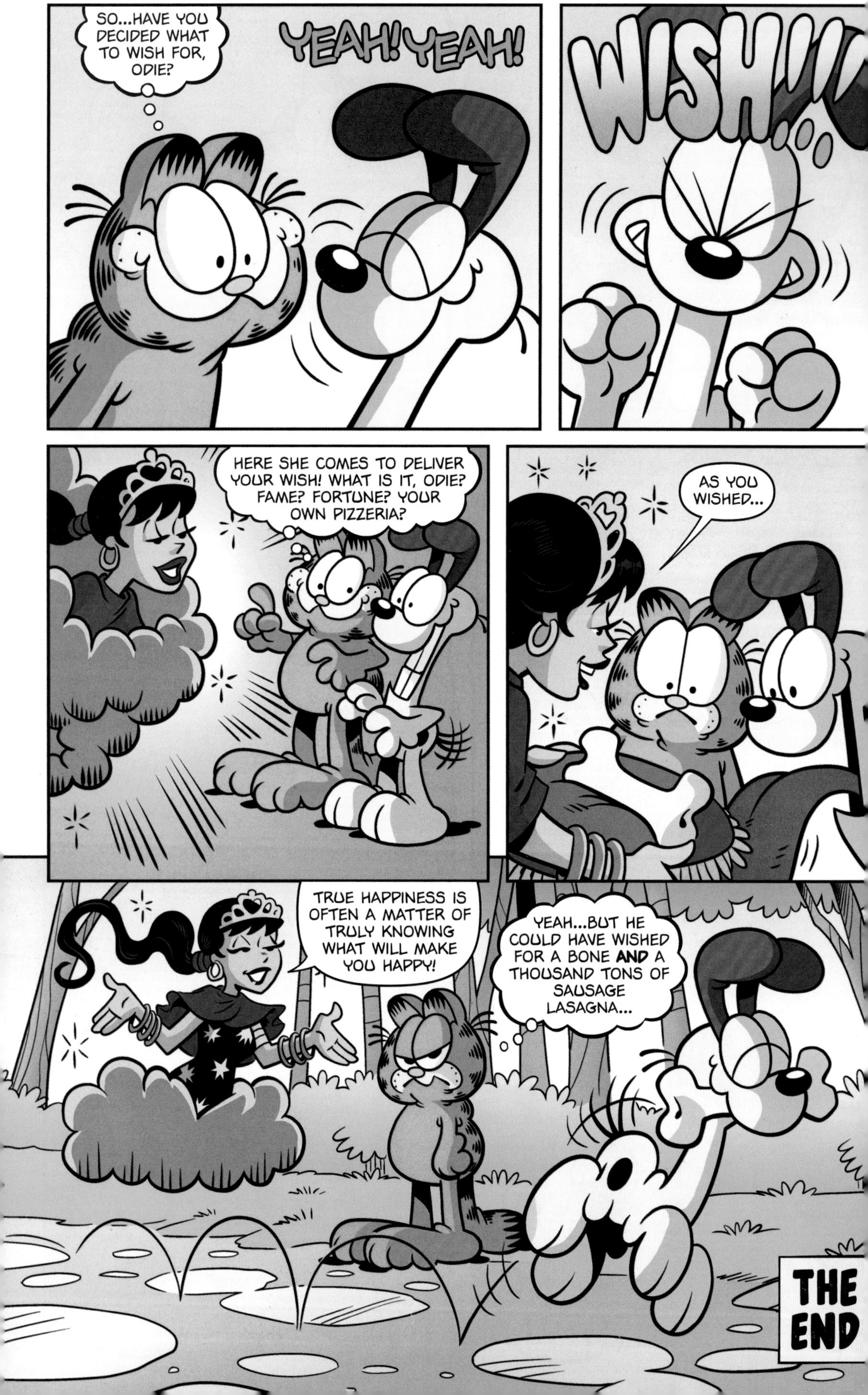

SO...HAVE YOU DECIDED WHAT TO WISH FOR, ODIE?
YEAH! YEAH!
WISH!!!
HERE SHE COMES TO DELIVER YOUR WISH! WHAT IS IT, ODIE? FAME? FORTUNE? YOUR OWN PIZZERIA?
AS YOU WISHED...
TRUE HAPPINESS IS OFTEN A MATTER OF TRULY KNOWING WHAT WILL MAKE YOU HAPPY!
YEAH...BUT HE COULD HAVE WISHED FOR A BONE AND A THOUSAND TONS OF SAUSAGE LASAGNA...
THE END

CHAPTER FOUR

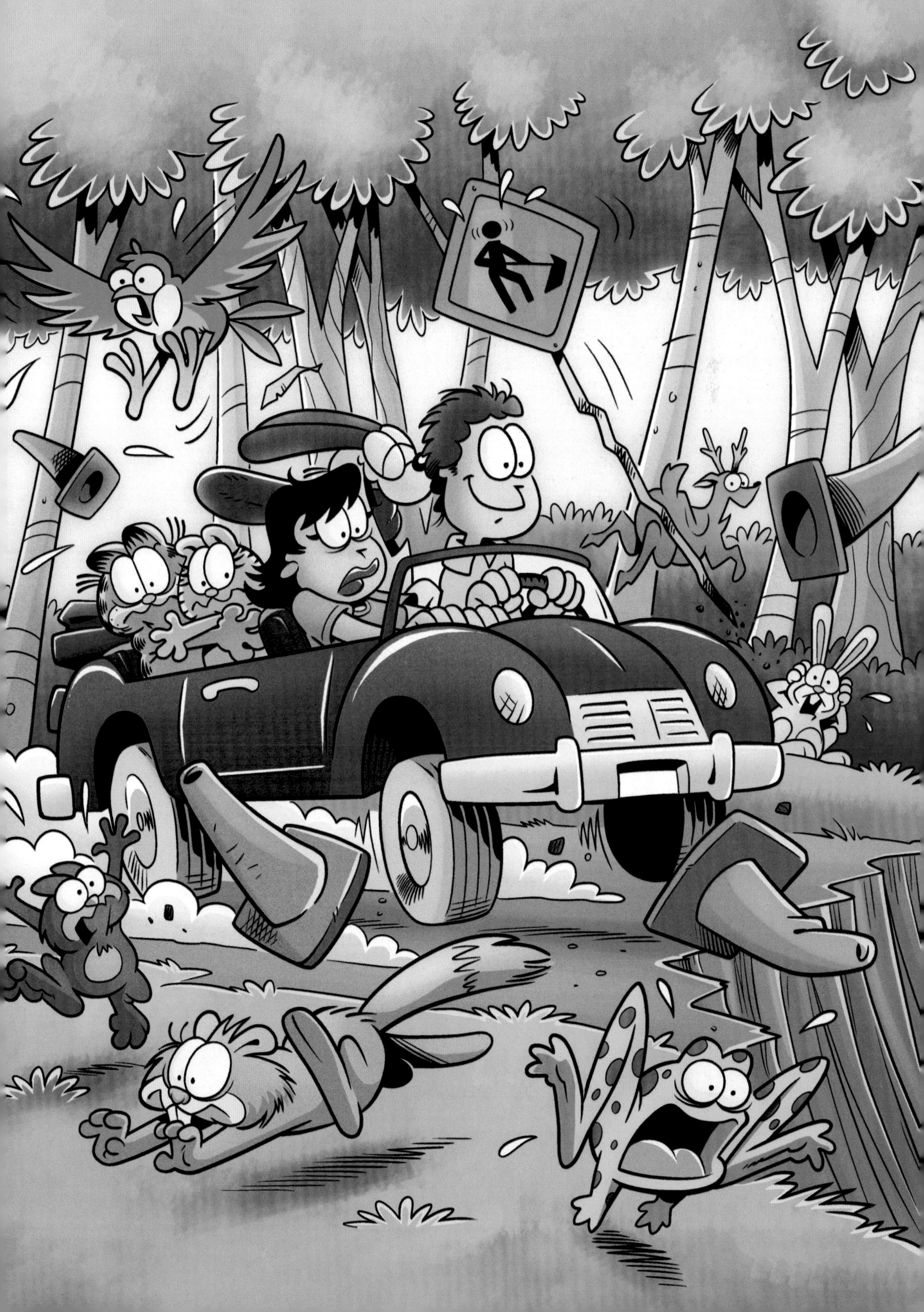

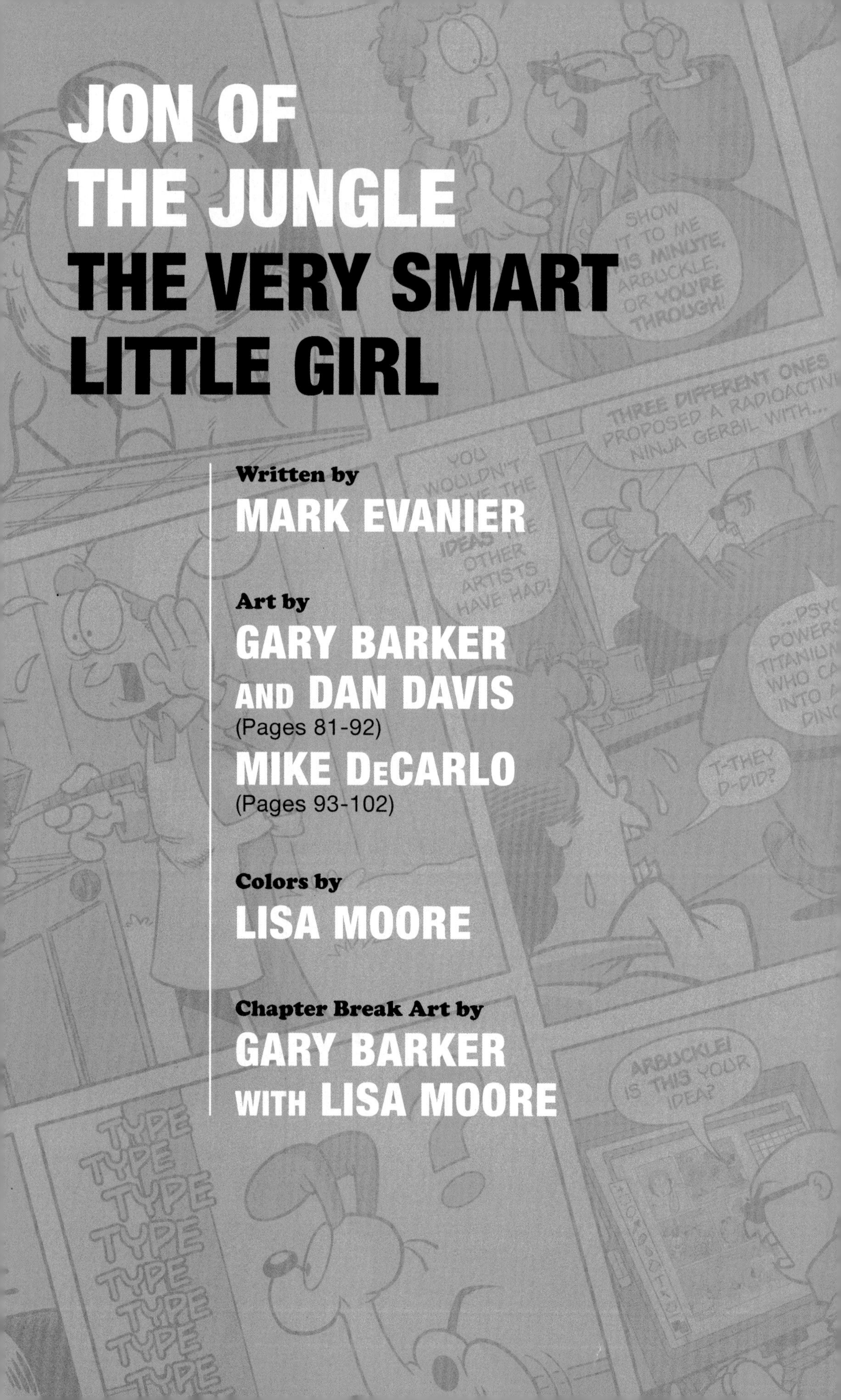
SHOW IT TO ME THIS MINUTE, ARBUCKLE, OR YOU'RE THROUGH!
T-THEY D-DID?
ARBUCKLE! IS THIS YOUR IDEA?

JON OF THE JUNGLE
THE VERY SMART LITTLE GIRL

Written by
MARK EVANIER

Art by
GARY BARKER AND DAN DAVIS
(Pages 81-92)
MIKE DeCARLO
(Pages 93-102)

Colors by
LISA MOORE

Chapter Break Art by
GARY BARKER WITH LISA MOORE

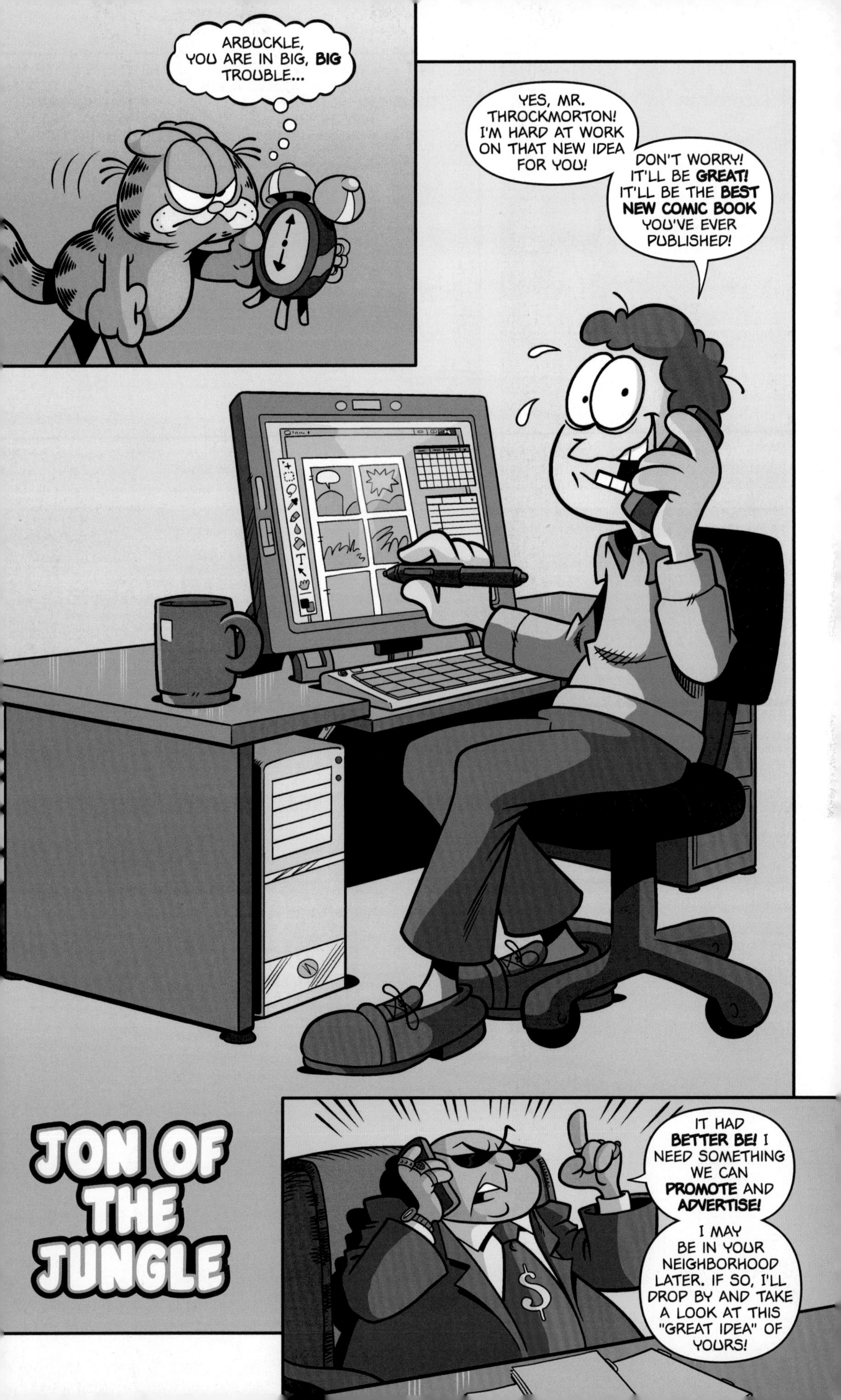
ARBUCKLE, YOU ARE IN BIG, BIG TROUBLE...
YES, MR. THROCKMORTON! I'M HARD AT WORK ON THAT NEW IDEA FOR YOU!
DON'T WORRY! IT'LL BE GREAT! IT'LL BE THE BEST NEW COMIC BOOK YOU'VE EVER PUBLISHED!
JON OF THE JUNGLE
IT HAD BETTER BE! I NEED SOMETHING WE CAN PROMOTE AND ADVERTISE!
I MAY BE IN YOUR NEIGHBORHOOD LATER. IF SO, I'LL DROP BY AND TAKE A LOOK AT THIS "GREAT IDEA" OF YOURS!

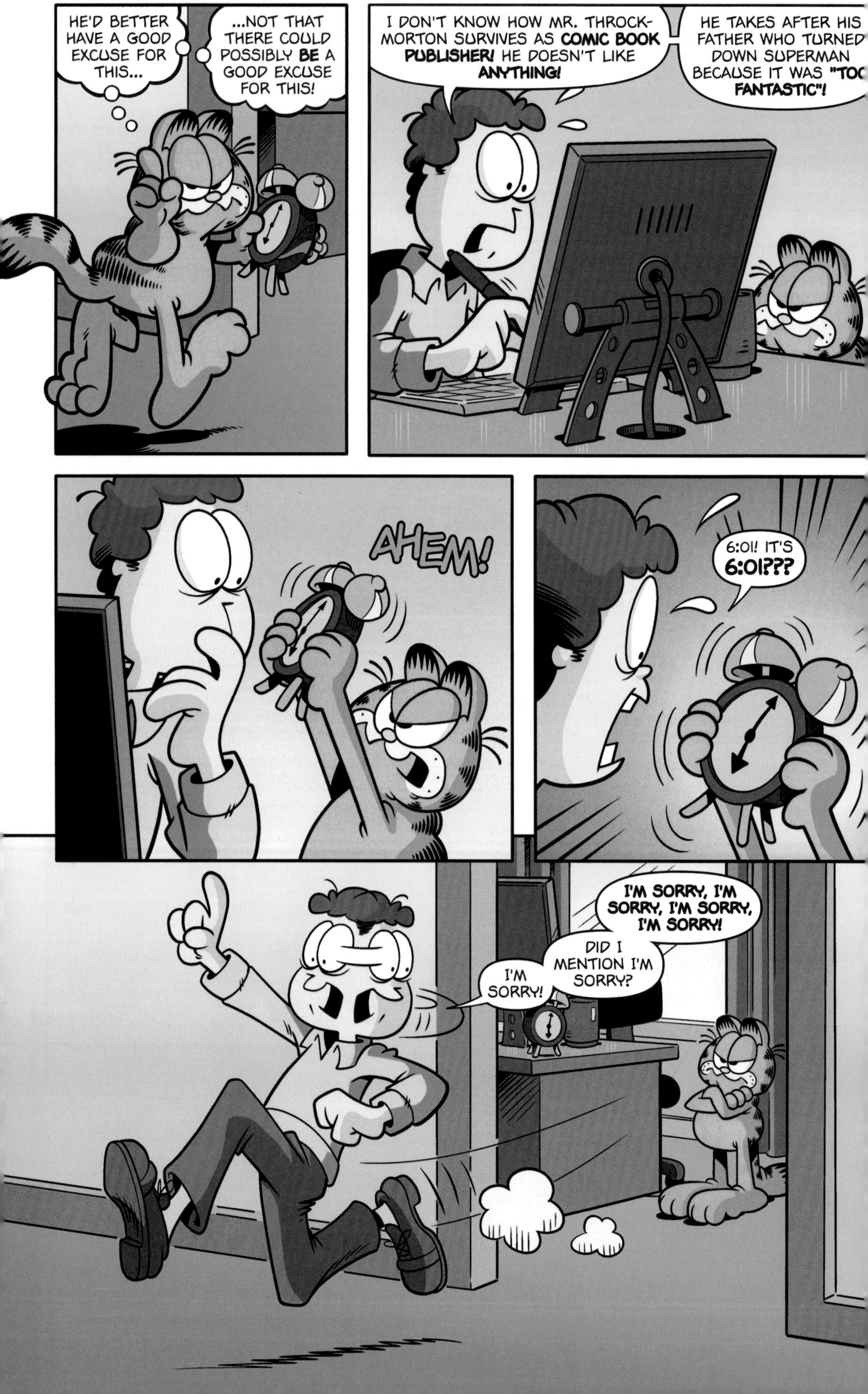

HE'D BETTER HAVE A GOOD EXCUSE FOR THIS...
...NOT THAT THERE COULD POSSIBLY BE A GOOD EXCUSE FOR THIS!
I DON'T KNOW HOW MR. THROCKMORTON SURVIVES AS COMIC BOOK PUBLISHER! HE DOESN'T LIKE ANYTHING!
HE TAKES AFTER HIS FATHER WHO TURNED DOWN SUPERMAN BECAUSE IT WAS "TOO FANTASTIC"!
AHEM!
6:01! IT'S 6:01???
I'M SORRY!
DID I MENTION I'M SORRY?
I'M SORRY, I'M SORRY, I'M SORRY, I'M SORRY!

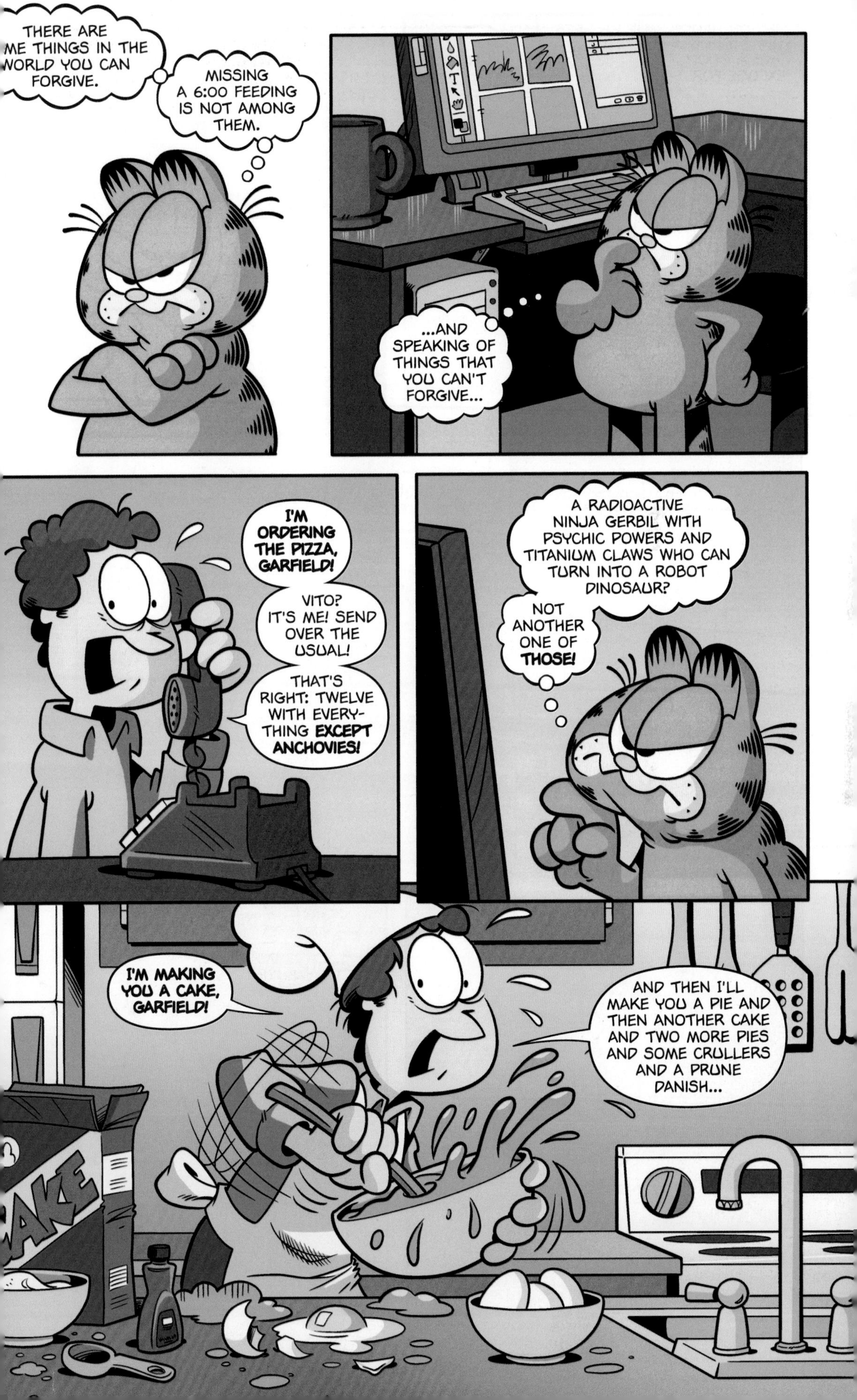
THERE ARE ME THINGS IN THE WORLD YOU CAN FORGIVE.
MISSING A 6:00 FEEDING IS NOT AMONG THEM.
...AND SPEAKING OF THINGS THAT YOU CAN'T FORGIVE...
I'M ORDERING THE PIZZA, GARFIELD!
VITO? IT'S ME! SEND OVER THE USUAL!
THAT'S RIGHT: TWELVE WITH EVERY-THING EXCEPT ANCHOVIES!
A RADIOACTIVE NINJA GERBIL WITH PSYCHIC POWERS AND TITANIUM CLAWS WHO CAN TURN INTO A ROBOT DINOSAUR?
NOT ANOTHER ONE OF THOSE!
I'M MAKING YOU A CAKE, GARFIELD!
AND THEN I'LL MAKE YOU A PIE AND THEN ANOTHER CAKE AND TWO MORE PIES AND SOME CRULLERS AND A PRUNE DANISH...
AKE

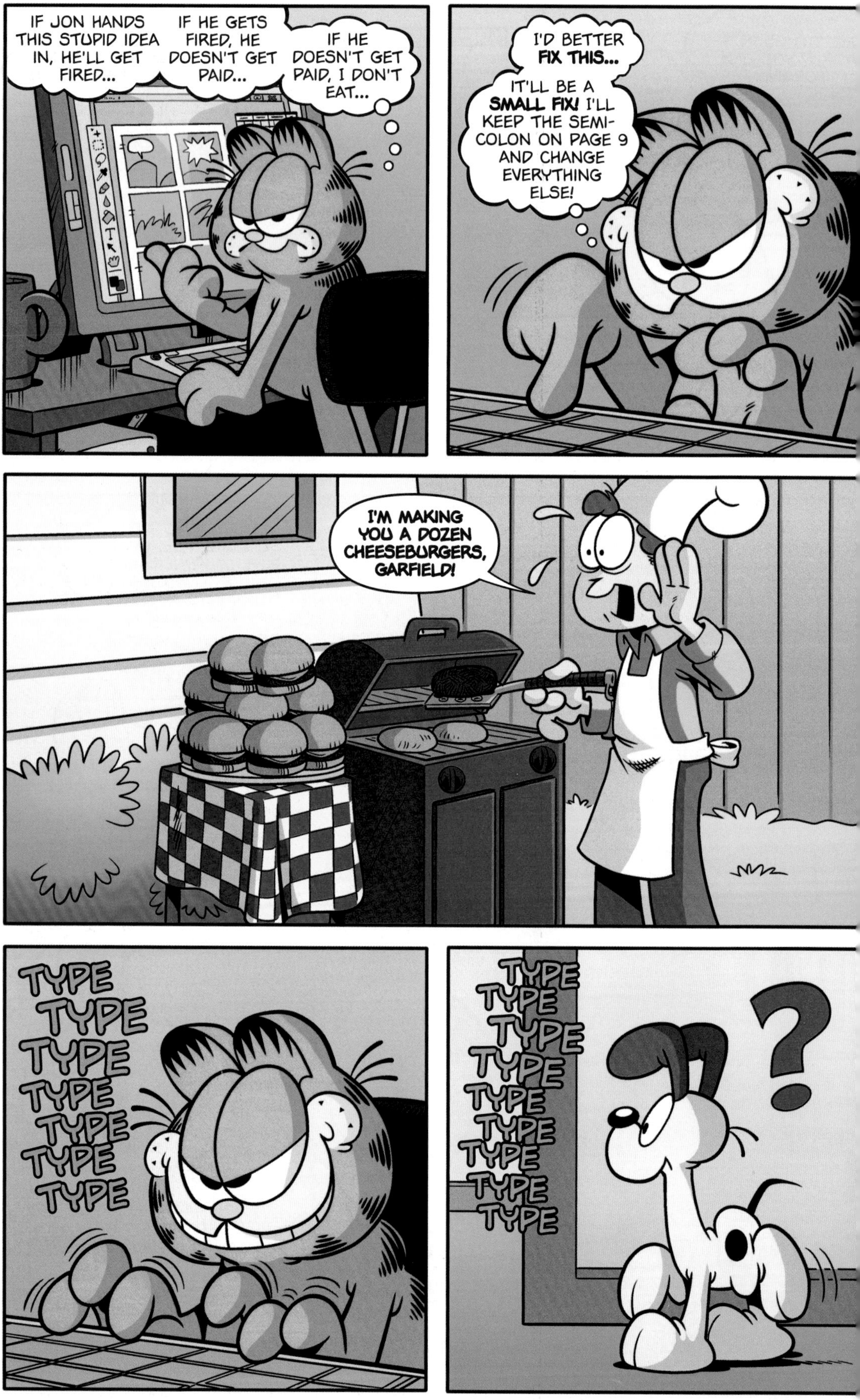
IF JON HANDS THIS STUPID IDEA IN, HE'LL GET FIRED...
IF HE GETS FIRED, HE DOESN'T GET PAID...
IF HE DOESN'T GET PAID, I DON'T EAT...
I'D BETTER **FIX THIS...**
IT'LL BE A **SMALL FIX!** I'LL KEEP THE SEMI-COLON ON PAGE 9 AND CHANGE EVERYTHING ELSE!
I'M MAKING YOU A DOZEN CHEESEBURGERS, GARFIELD!
TYPE TYPE TYPE TYPE TYPE TYPE TYPE
TYPE TYPE TYPE TYPE TYPE TYPE TYPE TYPE TYPE
?

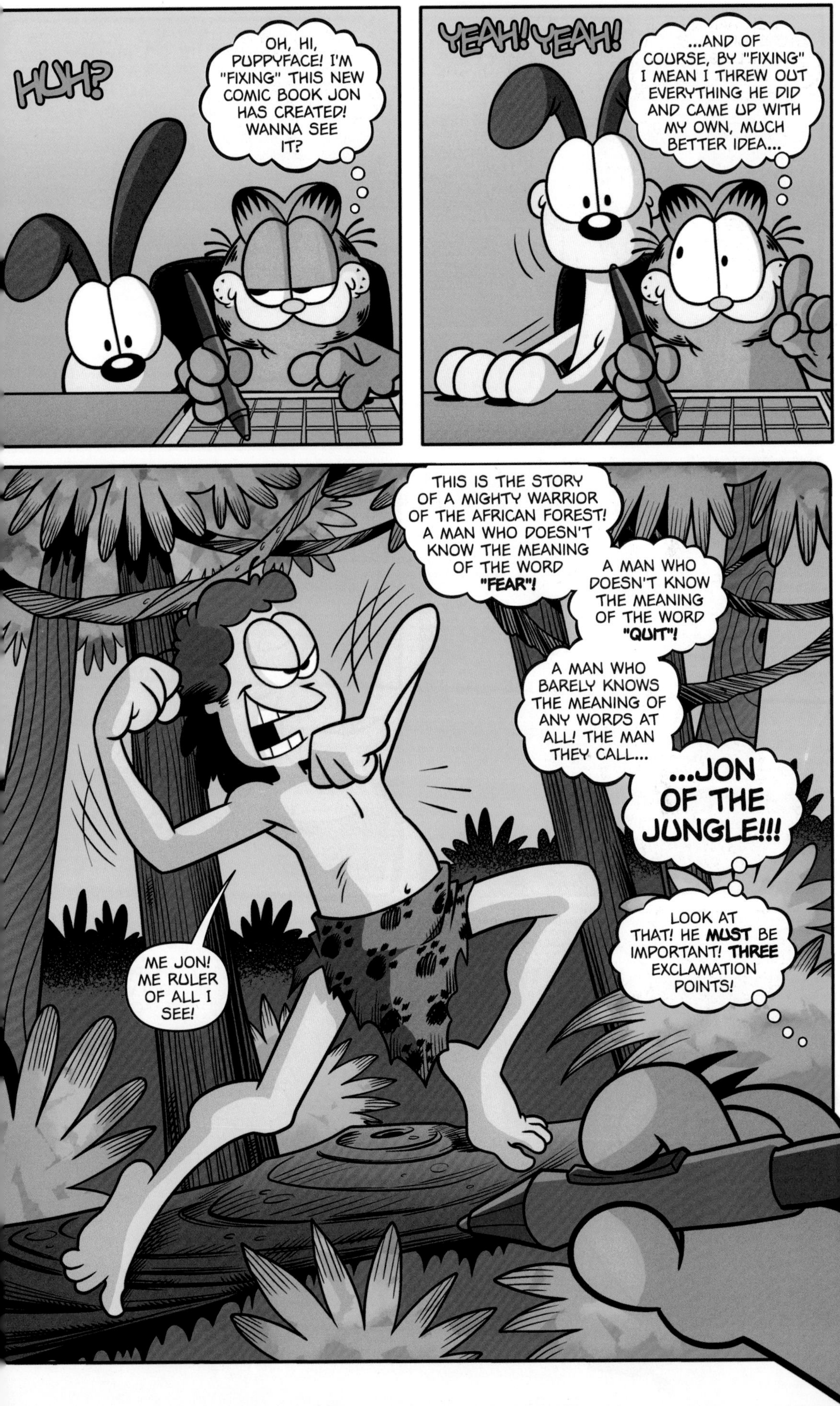
HUH?
OH, HI, PUPPYFACE! I'M "FIXING" THIS NEW COMIC BOOK JON HAS CREATED! WANNA SEE IT?
YEAH! YEAH!
...AND OF COURSE, BY "FIXING" I MEAN I THREW OUT EVERYTHING HE DID AND CAME UP WITH MY OWN, MUCH BETTER IDEA...
THIS IS THE STORY OF A MIGHTY WARRIOR OF THE AFRICAN FOREST! A MAN WHO DOESN'T KNOW THE MEANING OF THE WORD "FEAR"!
A MAN WHO DOESN'T KNOW THE MEANING OF THE WORD "QUIT"!
A MAN WHO BARELY KNOWS THE MEANING OF ANY WORDS AT ALL! THE MAN THEY CALL...
...JON OF THE JUNGLE!!!
ME JON! ME RULER OF ALL I SEE!
LOOK AT THAT! HE MUST BE IMPORTANT! THREE EXCLAMATION POINTS!

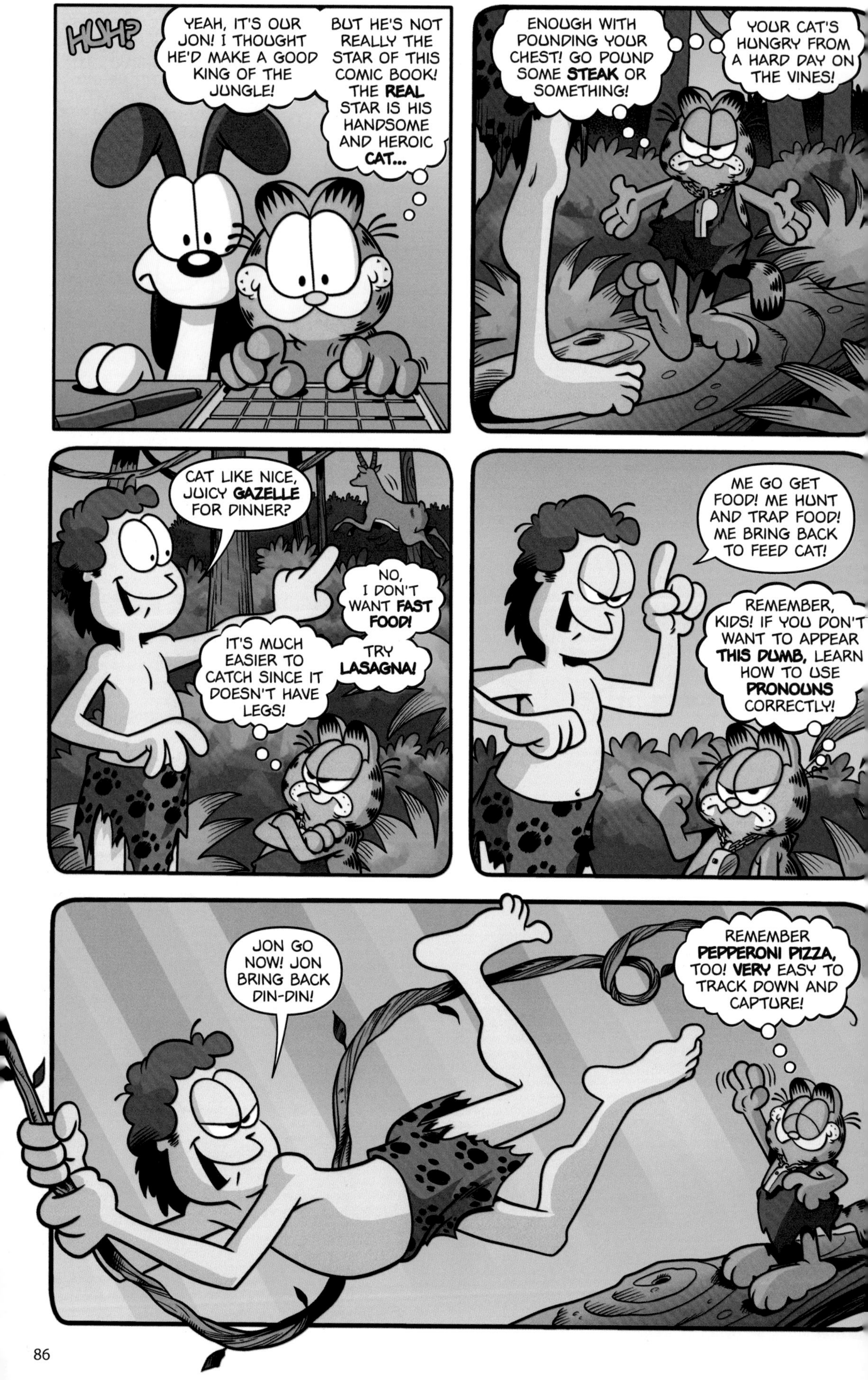
HUH?
YEAH, IT'S OUR JON! I THOUGHT HE'D MAKE A GOOD KING OF THE JUNGLE!
BUT HE'S NOT REALLY THE STAR OF THIS COMIC BOOK! THE REAL STAR IS HIS HANDSOME AND HEROIC CAT...
ENOUGH WITH POUNDING YOUR CHEST! GO POUND SOME STEAK OR SOMETHING!
YOUR CAT'S HUNGRY FROM A HARD DAY ON THE VINES!
CAT LIKE NICE, JUICY GAZELLE FOR DINNER?
NO, I DON'T WANT FAST FOOD!
IT'S MUCH EASIER TO CATCH SINCE IT DOESN'T HAVE LEGS!
TRY LASAGNA!
ME GO GET FOOD! ME HUNT AND TRAP FOOD! ME BRING BACK TO FEED CAT!
REMEMBER, KIDS! IF YOU DON'T WANT TO APPEAR THIS DUMB, LEARN HOW TO USE PRONOUNS CORRECTLY!
JON GO NOW! JON BRING BACK DIN-DIN!
REMEMBER PEPPERONI PIZZA, TOO! VERY EASY TO TRACK DOWN AND CAPTURE!

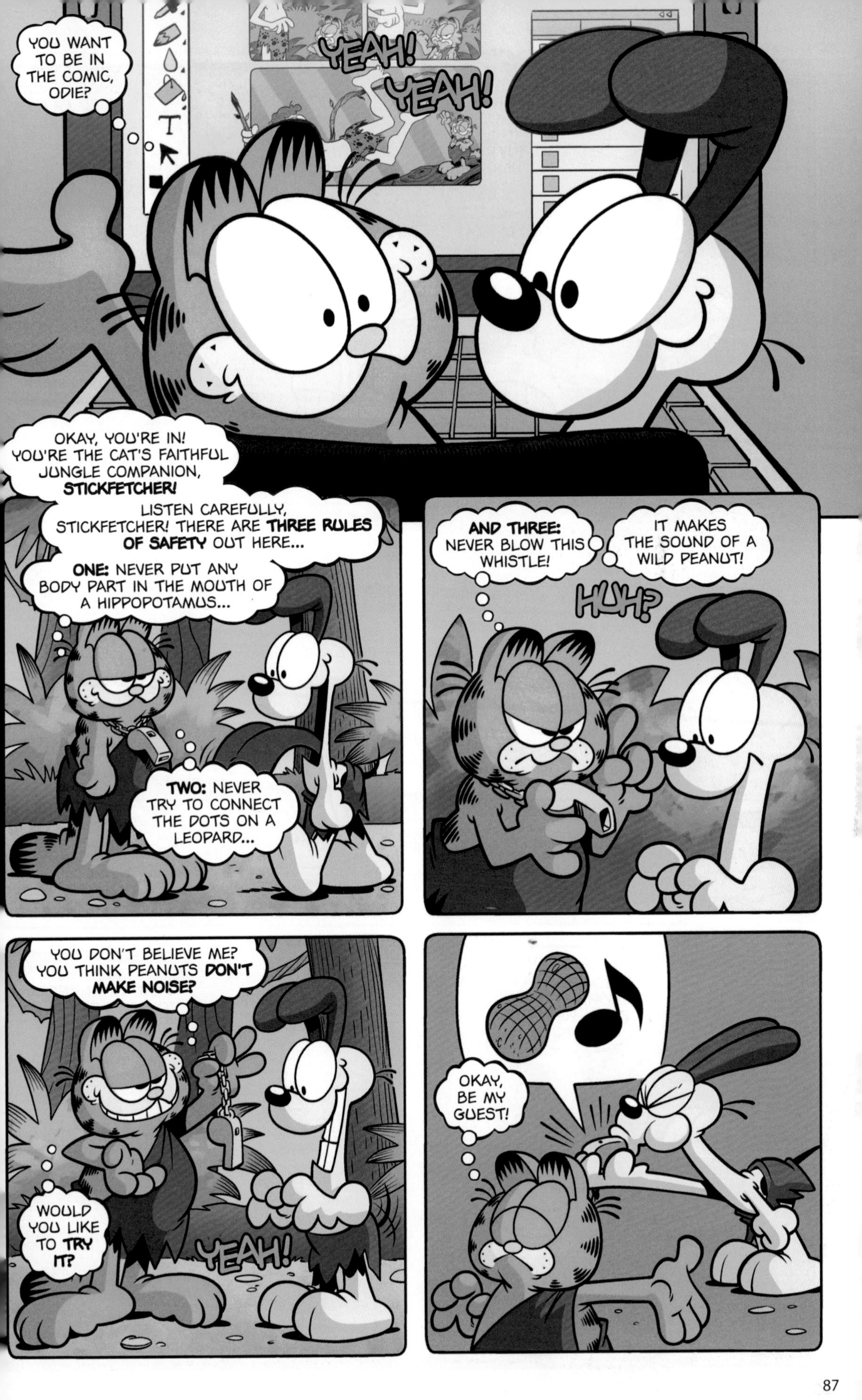

YOU WANT TO BE IN THE COMIC, ODIE?
YEAH! YEAH!
OKAY, YOU'RE IN! YOU'RE THE CAT'S FAITHFUL JUNGLE COMPANION, **STICKFETCHER!**
LISTEN CAREFULLY, STICKFETCHER! THERE ARE **THREE RULES OF SAFETY** OUT HERE...
ONE: NEVER PUT ANY BODY PART IN THE MOUTH OF A HIPPOPOTAMUS...
TWO: NEVER TRY TO CONNECT THE DOTS ON A LEOPARD...
AND THREE: NEVER BLOW THIS WHISTLE!
IT MAKES THE SOUND OF A WILD PEANUT!
HUH?
YOU DON'T BELIEVE ME? YOU THINK PEANUTS **DON'T MAKE NOISE?**
WOULD YOU LIKE TO **TRY IT?**
YEAH!
OKAY, BE MY GUEST!

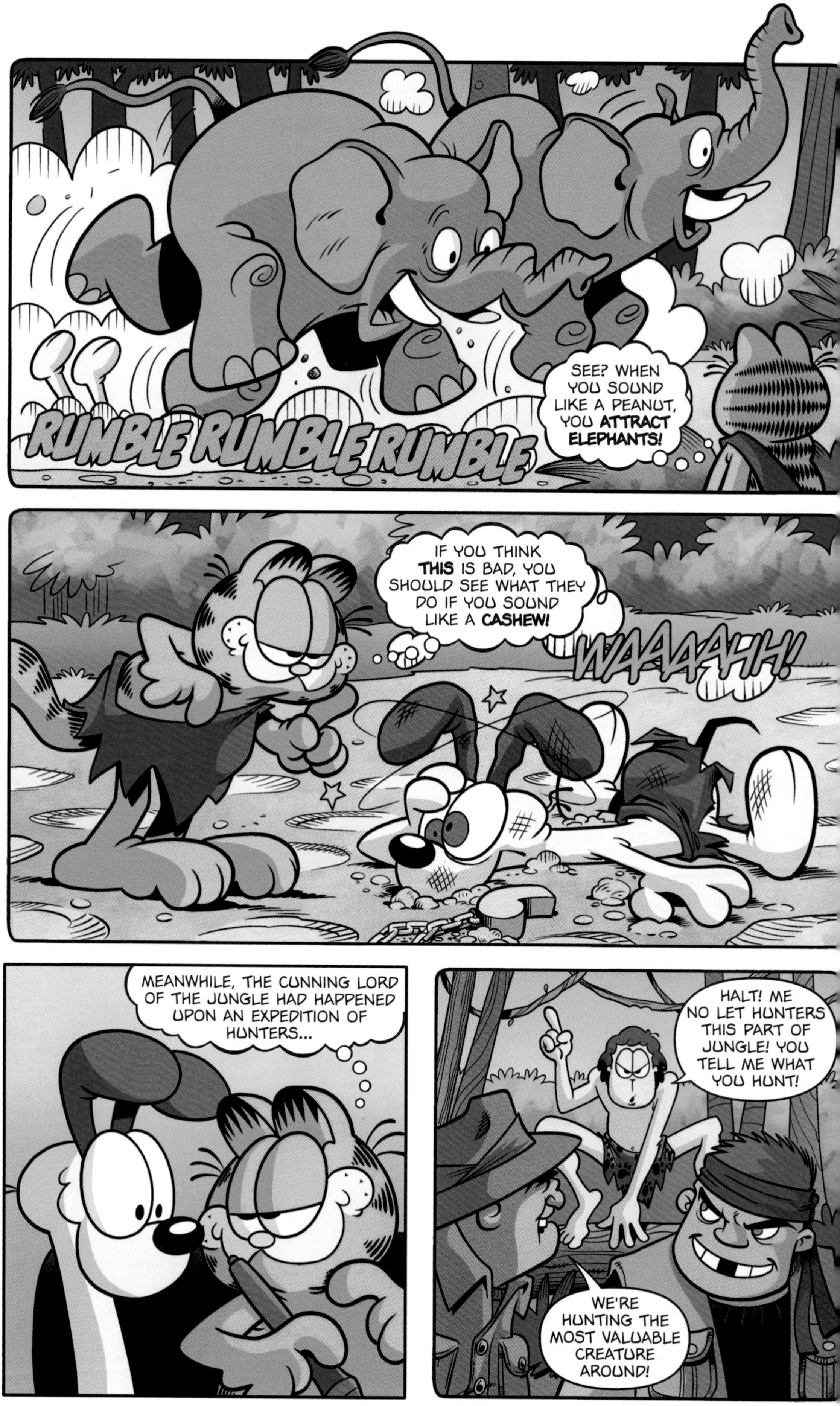
RUMBLE RUMBLE RUMBLE
SEE? WHEN YOU SOUND LIKE A PEANUT, YOU ATTRACT ELEPHANTS!
IF YOU THINK THIS IS BAD, YOU SHOULD SEE WHAT THEY DO IF YOU SOUND LIKE A CASHEW!
WAAAAHH!
MEANWHILE, THE CUNNING LORD OF THE JUNGLE HAD HAPPENED UPON AN EXPEDITION OF HUNTERS...
HALT! ME NO LET HUNTERS THIS PART OF JUNGLE! YOU TELL ME WHAT YOU HUNT!
WE'RE HUNTING THE MOST VALUABLE CREATURE AROUND!

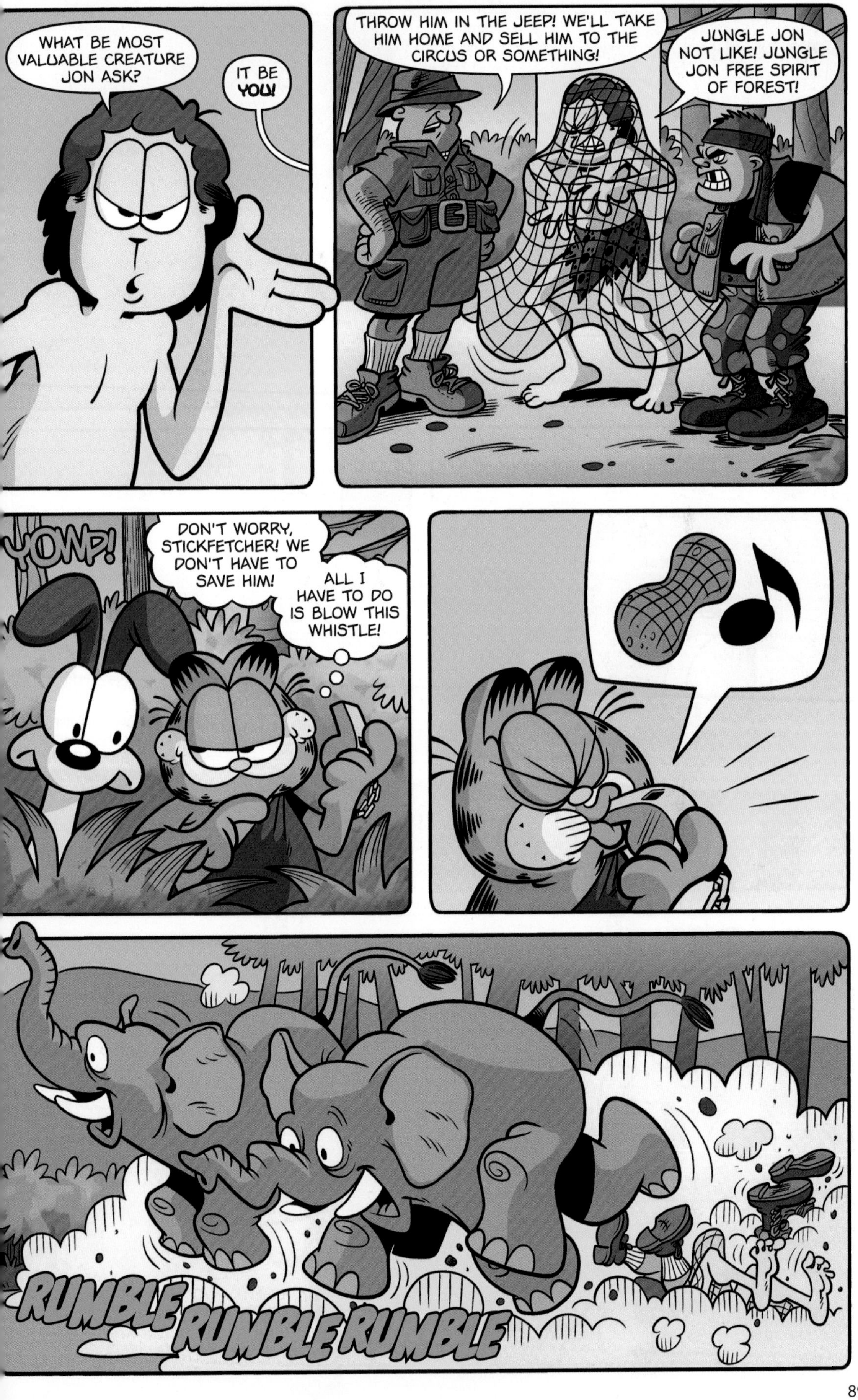
WHAT BE MOST VALUABLE CREATURE JON ASK?
IT BE YOU!
THROW HIM IN THE JEEP! WE'LL TAKE HIM HOME AND SELL HIM TO THE CIRCUS OR SOMETHING!
JUNGLE JON NOT LIKE! JUNGLE JON FREE SPIRIT OF FOREST!
YOWP!
DON'T WORRY, STICKFETCHER! WE DON'T HAVE TO SAVE HIM!
ALL I HAVE TO DO IS BLOW THIS WHISTLE!
RUMBLE RUMBLE RUMBLE

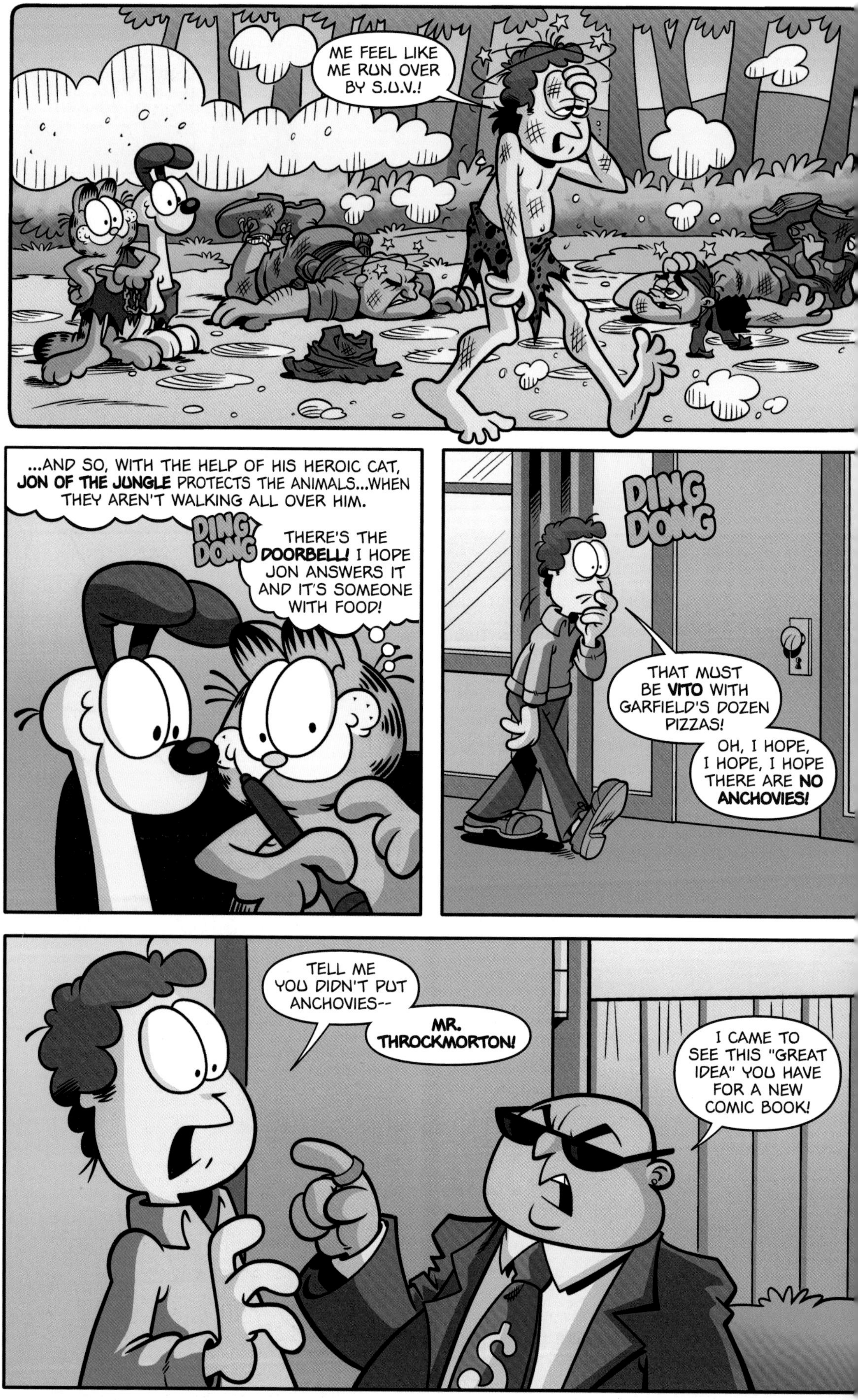
ME FEEL LIKE ME RUN OVER BY S.U.V.!
...AND SO, WITH THE HELP OF HIS HEROIC CAT, JON OF THE JUNGLE PROTECTS THE ANIMALS...WHEN THEY AREN'T WALKING ALL OVER HIM.
DING DONG
THERE'S THE DOORBELL! I HOPE JON ANSWERS IT AND IT'S SOMEONE WITH FOOD!
DING DONG
THAT MUST BE VITO WITH GARFIELD'S DOZEN PIZZAS!
OH, I HOPE, I HOPE, I HOPE THERE ARE NO ANCHOVIES!
TELL ME YOU DIDN'T PUT ANCHOVIES--
MR. THROCKMORTON!
I CAME TO SEE THIS "GREAT IDEA" YOU HAVE FOR A NEW COMIC BOOK!

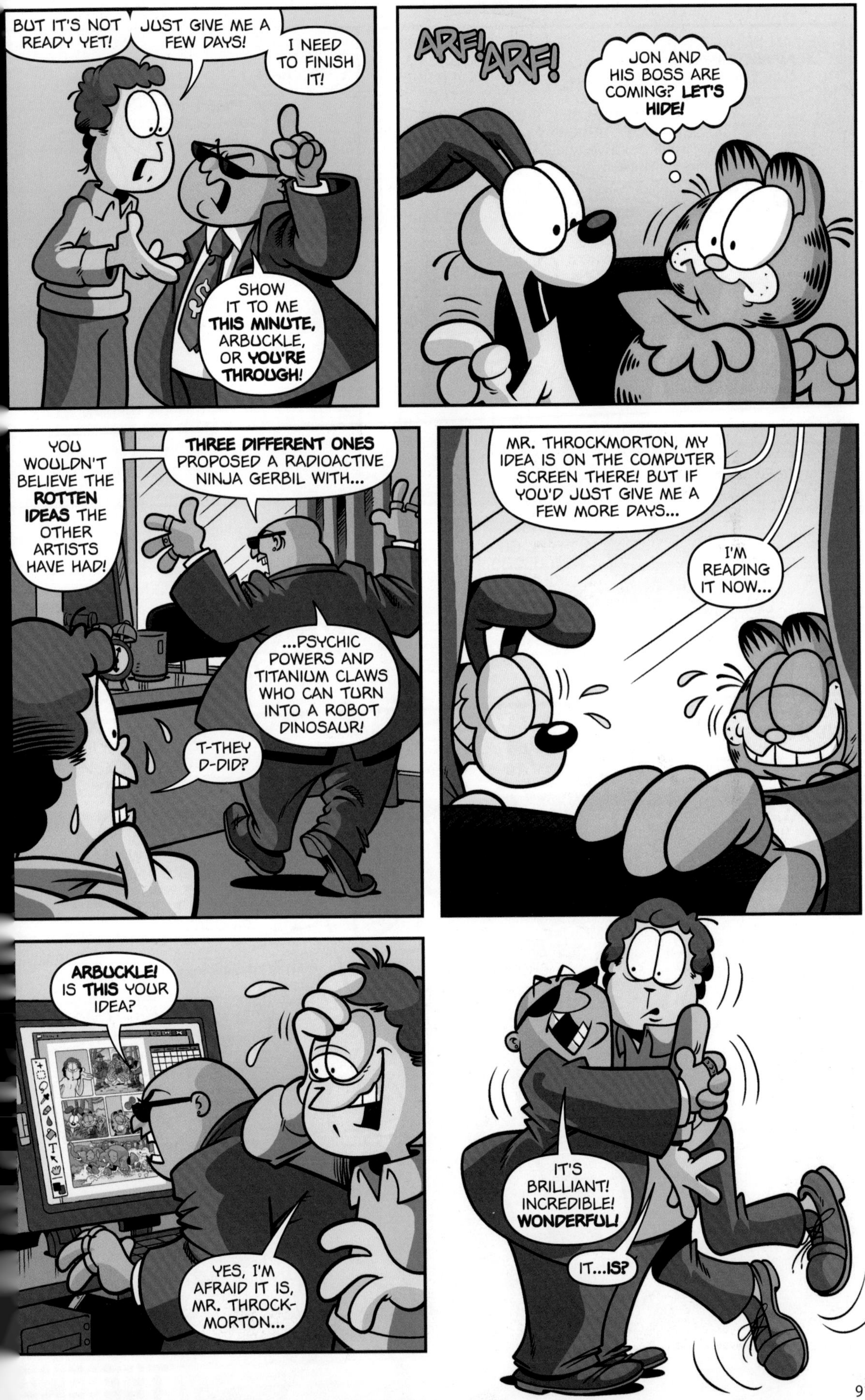
BUT IT'S NOT READY YET!
JUST GIVE ME A FEW DAYS!
I NEED TO FINISH IT!
SHOW IT TO ME THIS MINUTE, ARBUCKLE, OR YOU'RE THROUGH!
ARF! ARF!
JON AND HIS BOSS ARE COMING? LET'S HIDE!
YOU WOULDN'T BELIEVE THE ROTTEN IDEAS THE OTHER ARTISTS HAVE HAD!
THREE DIFFERENT ONES PROPOSED A RADIOACTIVE NINJA GERBIL WITH...
...PSYCHIC POWERS AND TITANIUM CLAWS WHO CAN TURN INTO A ROBOT DINOSAUR!
T-THEY D-DID?
MR. THROCKMORTON, MY IDEA IS ON THE COMPUTER SCREEN THERE! BUT IF YOU'D JUST GIVE ME A FEW MORE DAYS...
I'M READING IT NOW...
ARBUCKLE! IS THIS YOUR IDEA?
YES, I'M AFRAID IT IS, MR. THROCK-MORTON...
IT'S BRILLIANT! INCREDIBLE! WONDERFUL!
IT...IS?

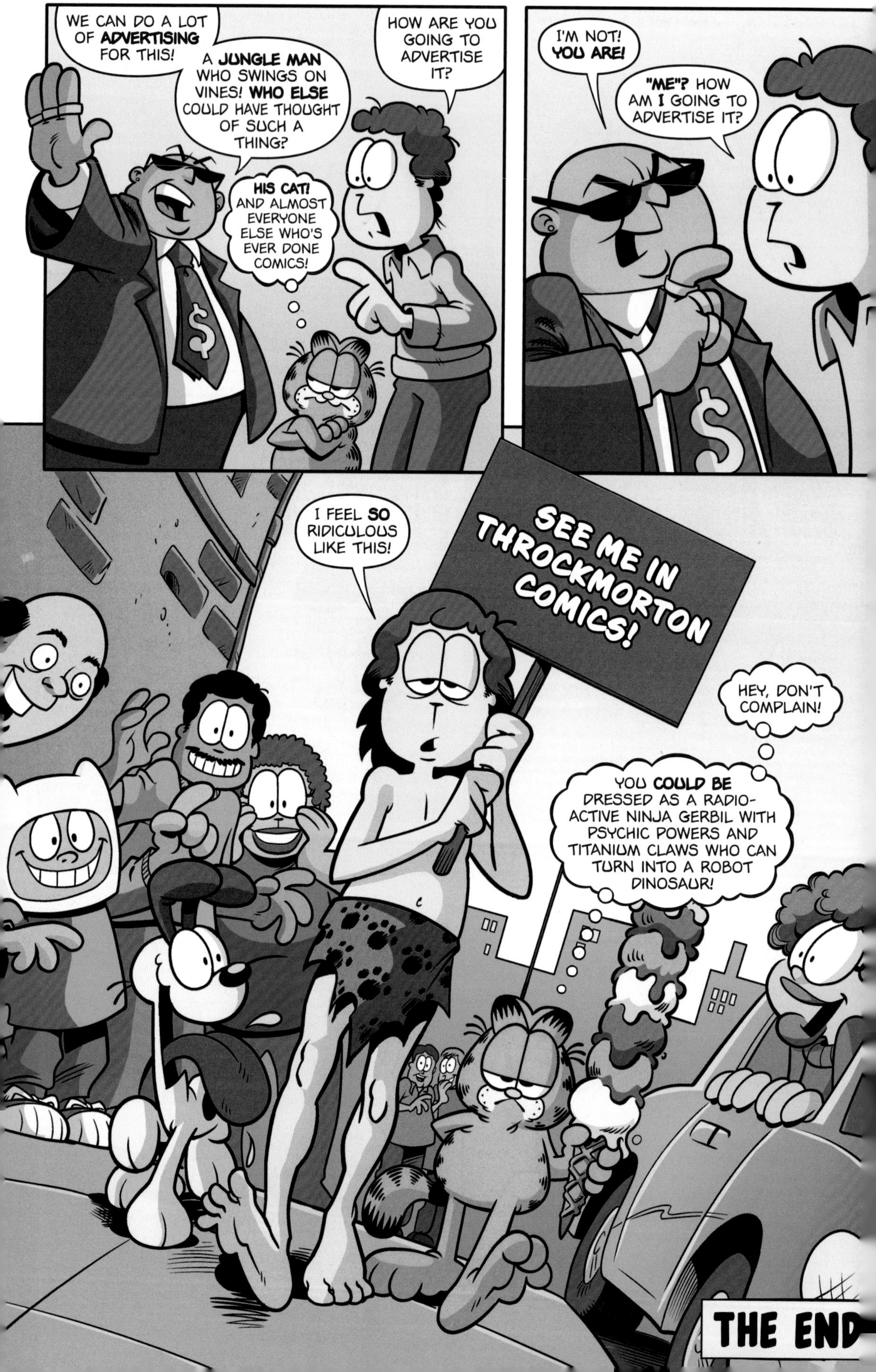
WE CAN DO A LOT OF **ADVERTISING** FOR THIS!
A **JUNGLE MAN** WHO SWINGS ON VINES! **WHO ELSE** COULD HAVE THOUGHT OF SUCH A THING?
HOW ARE YOU GOING TO ADVERTISE IT?
HIS CAT! AND ALMOST EVERYONE ELSE WHO'S EVER DONE COMICS!
I'M NOT! **YOU ARE!**
"ME"? HOW AM **I** GOING TO ADVERTISE IT?
I FEEL **SO** RIDICULOUS LIKE THIS!
SEE ME IN THROCKMORTON COMICS!
HEY, DON'T COMPLAIN!
YOU **COULD BE** DRESSED AS A RADIO-ACTIVE NINJA GERBIL WITH PSYCHIC POWERS AND TITANIUM CLAWS WHO CAN TURN INTO A ROBOT DINOSAUR!
THE END

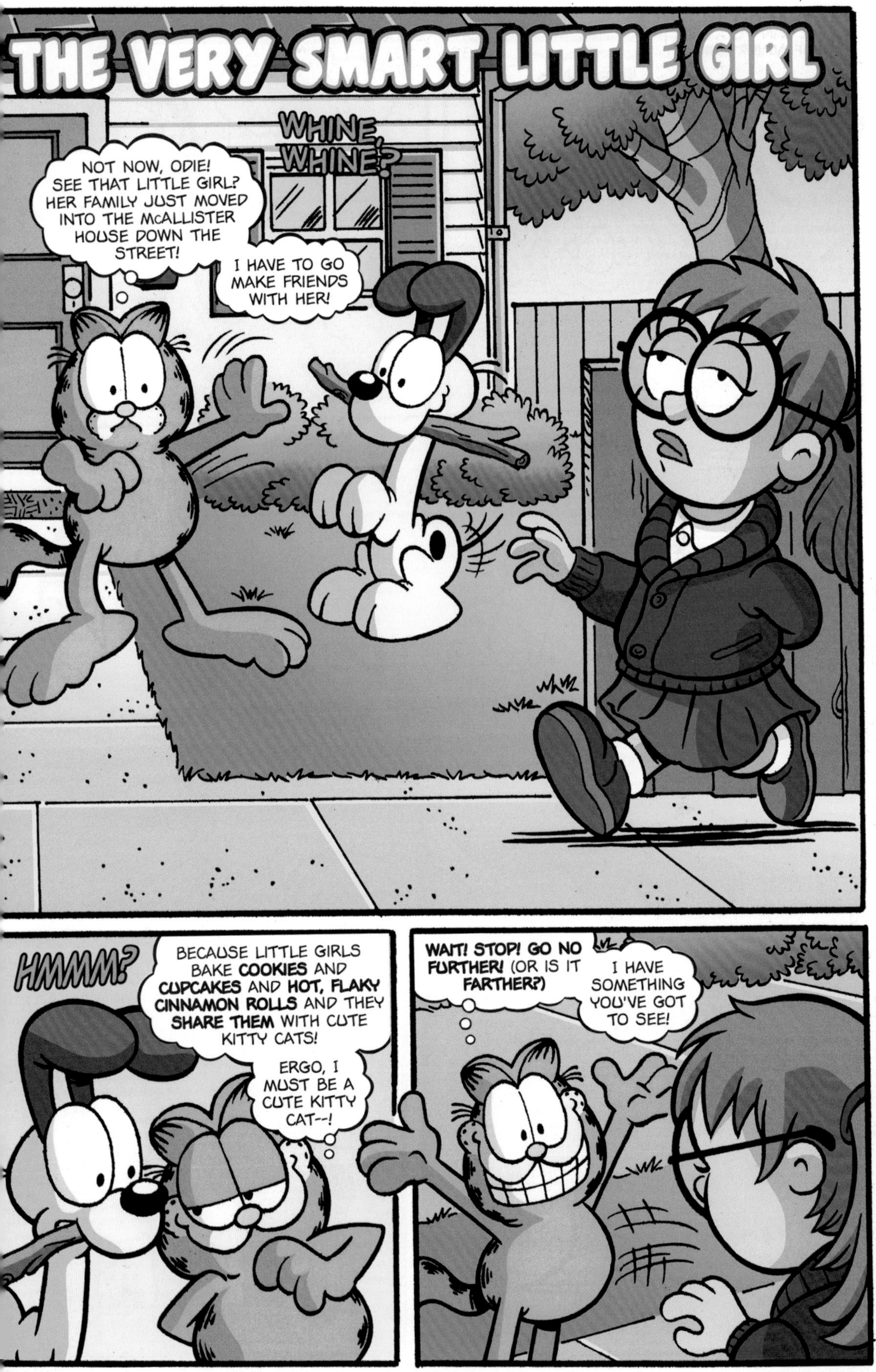
THE VERY SMART LITTLE GIRL
WHINE, WHINE?
NOT NOW, ODIE! SEE THAT LITTLE GIRL? HER FAMILY JUST MOVED INTO THE McALLISTER HOUSE DOWN THE STREET!
I HAVE TO GO MAKE FRIENDS WITH HER!
HMMM?
BECAUSE LITTLE GIRLS BAKE COOKIES AND CUPCAKES AND HOT, FLAKY CINNAMON ROLLS AND THEY SHARE THEM WITH CUTE KITTY CATS!
ERGO, I MUST BE A CUTE KITTY CAT--!
WAIT! STOP! GO NO FURTHER! (OR IS IT FARTHER?)
I HAVE SOMETHING YOU'VE GOT TO SEE!

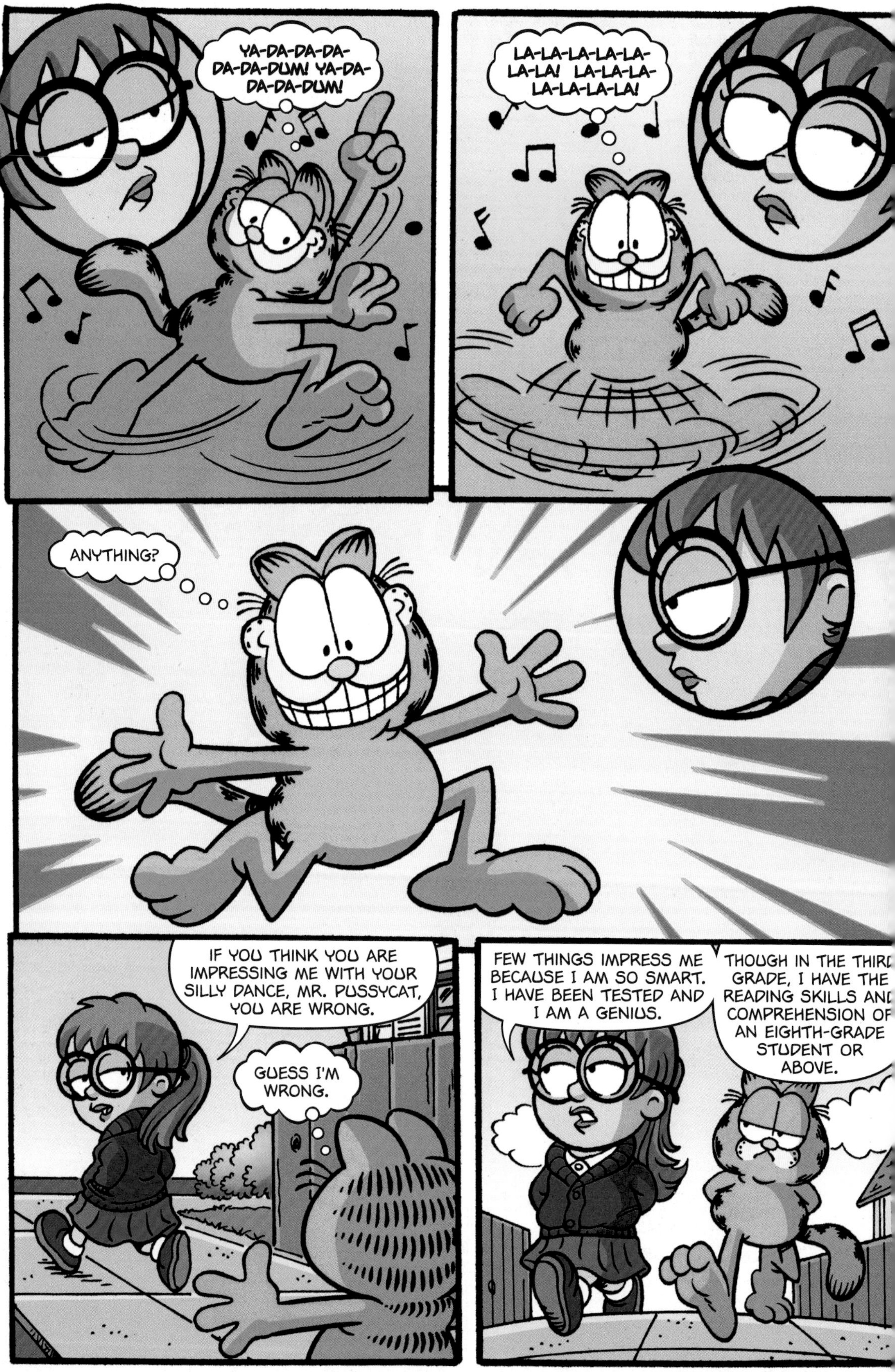
YA-DA-DA-DA-DA-DA-DUM! YA-DA-DA-DA-DUM!
LA-LA-LA-LA-LA-LA-LA! LA-LA-LA-LA-LA-LA-LA!
ANYTHING?
IF YOU THINK YOU ARE IMPRESSING ME WITH YOUR SILLY DANCE, MR. PUSSYCAT, YOU ARE WRONG.
GUESS I'M WRONG.
FEW THINGS IMPRESS ME BECAUSE I AM SO SMART. I HAVE BEEN TESTED AND I AM A GENIUS.
THOUGH IN THE THIRD GRADE, I HAVE THE READING SKILLS AND COMPREHENSION OF AN EIGHTH-GRADE STUDENT OR ABOVE.

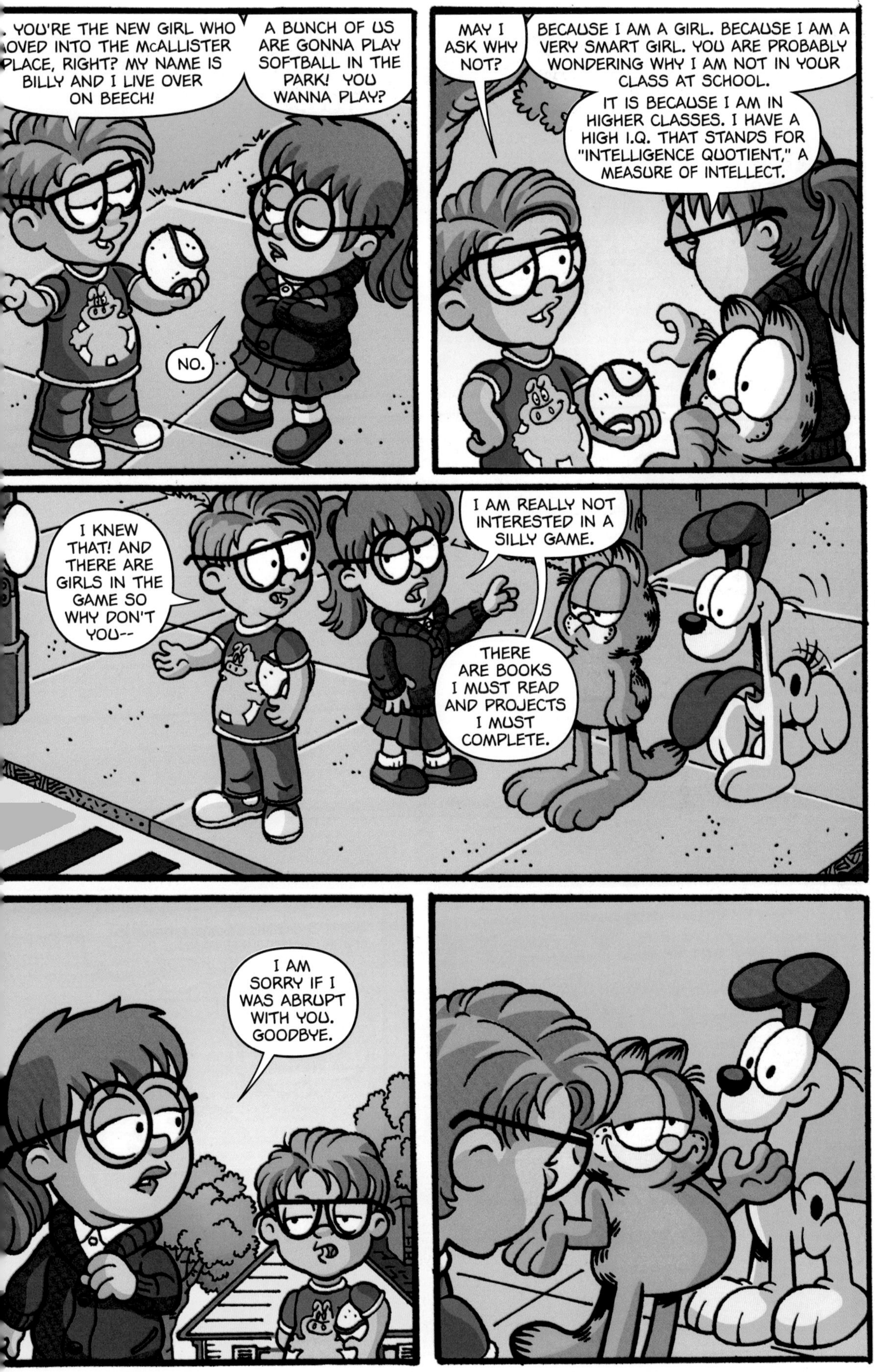

. YOU'RE THE NEW GIRL WHO
OVED INTO THE McALLISTER
PLACE, RIGHT? MY NAME IS
BILLY AND I LIVE OVER
ON BEECH!
A BUNCH OF US ARE GONNA PLAY SOFTBALL IN THE PARK! YOU WANNA PLAY?
NO.
MAY I ASK WHY NOT?
BECAUSE I AM A GIRL. BECAUSE I AM A VERY SMART GIRL. YOU ARE PROBABLY WONDERING WHY I AM NOT IN YOUR CLASS AT SCHOOL.
IT IS BECAUSE I AM IN HIGHER CLASSES. I HAVE A HIGH I.Q. THAT STANDS FOR "INTELLIGENCE QUOTIENT," A MEASURE OF INTELLECT.
I KNEW THAT! AND THERE ARE GIRLS IN THE GAME SO WHY DON'T YOU--
I AM REALLY NOT INTERESTED IN A SILLY GAME.
THERE ARE BOOKS I MUST READ AND PROJECTS I MUST COMPLETE.
I AM SORRY IF I WAS ABRUPT WITH YOU. GOODBYE.

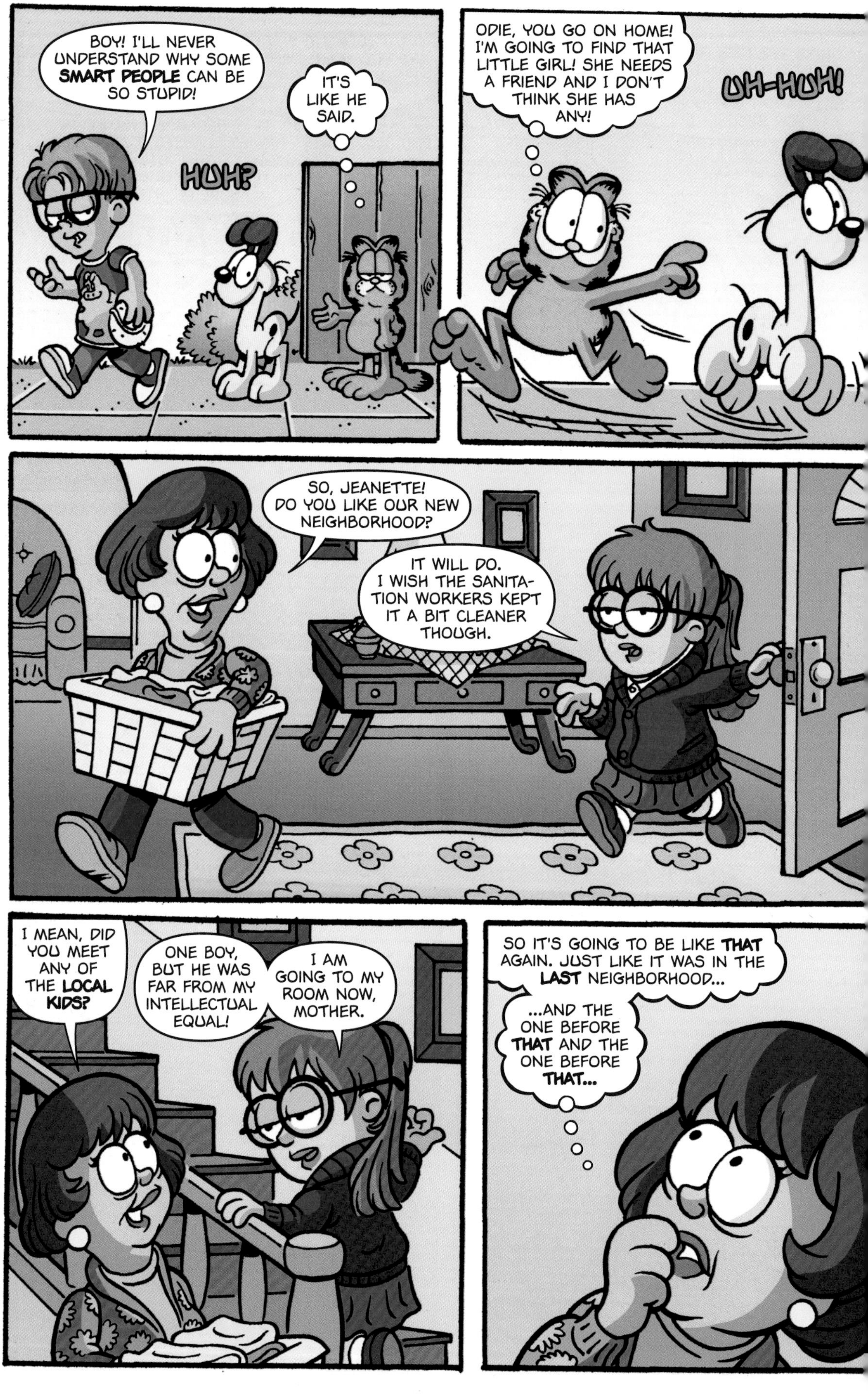
BOY! I'LL NEVER UNDERSTAND WHY SOME **SMART PEOPLE** CAN BE SO STUPID!
HUH?
IT'S LIKE HE SAID.
ODIE, YOU GO ON HOME! I'M GOING TO FIND THAT LITTLE GIRL! SHE NEEDS A FRIEND AND I DON'T THINK SHE HAS ANY!
UH-HUH!
SO, JEANETTE! DO YOU LIKE OUR NEW NEIGHBORHOOD?
IT WILL DO. I WISH THE SANITATION WORKERS KEPT IT A BIT CLEANER THOUGH.
I MEAN, DID YOU MEET ANY OF THE **LOCAL KIDS?**
ONE BOY, BUT HE WAS FAR FROM MY INTELLECTUAL EQUAL!
I AM GOING TO MY ROOM NOW, MOTHER.
SO IT'S GOING TO BE LIKE **THAT** AGAIN. JUST LIKE IT WAS IN THE **LAST** NEIGHBORHOOD...
...AND THE ONE BEFORE **THAT** AND THE ONE BEFORE **THAT...**

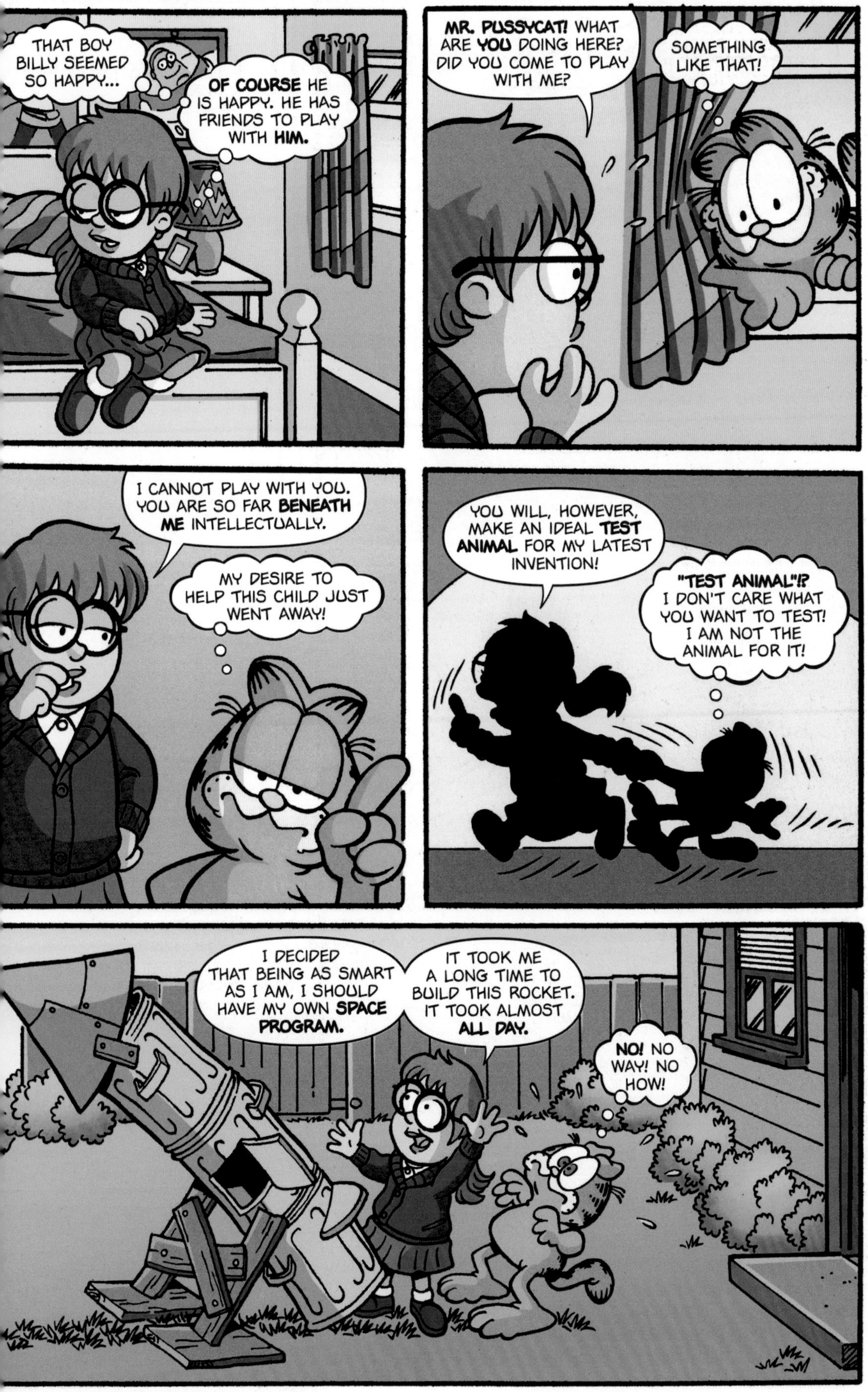

THAT BOY BILLY SEEMED SO HAPPY...
OF COURSE HE IS HAPPY. HE HAS FRIENDS TO PLAY WITH HIM.
MR. PUSSYCAT! WHAT ARE YOU DOING HERE? DID YOU COME TO PLAY WITH ME?
SOMETHING LIKE THAT!
I CANNOT PLAY WITH YOU. YOU ARE SO FAR BENEATH ME INTELLECTUALLY.
MY DESIRE TO HELP THIS CHILD JUST WENT AWAY!
YOU WILL, HOWEVER, MAKE AN IDEAL TEST ANIMAL FOR MY LATEST INVENTION!
"TEST ANIMAL"!? I DON'T CARE WHAT YOU WANT TO TEST! I AM NOT THE ANIMAL FOR IT!
I DECIDED THAT BEING AS SMART AS I AM, I SHOULD HAVE MY OWN SPACE PROGRAM.
IT TOOK ME A LONG TIME TO BUILD THIS ROCKET. IT TOOK ALMOST ALL DAY.
NO! NO WAY! NO HOW!

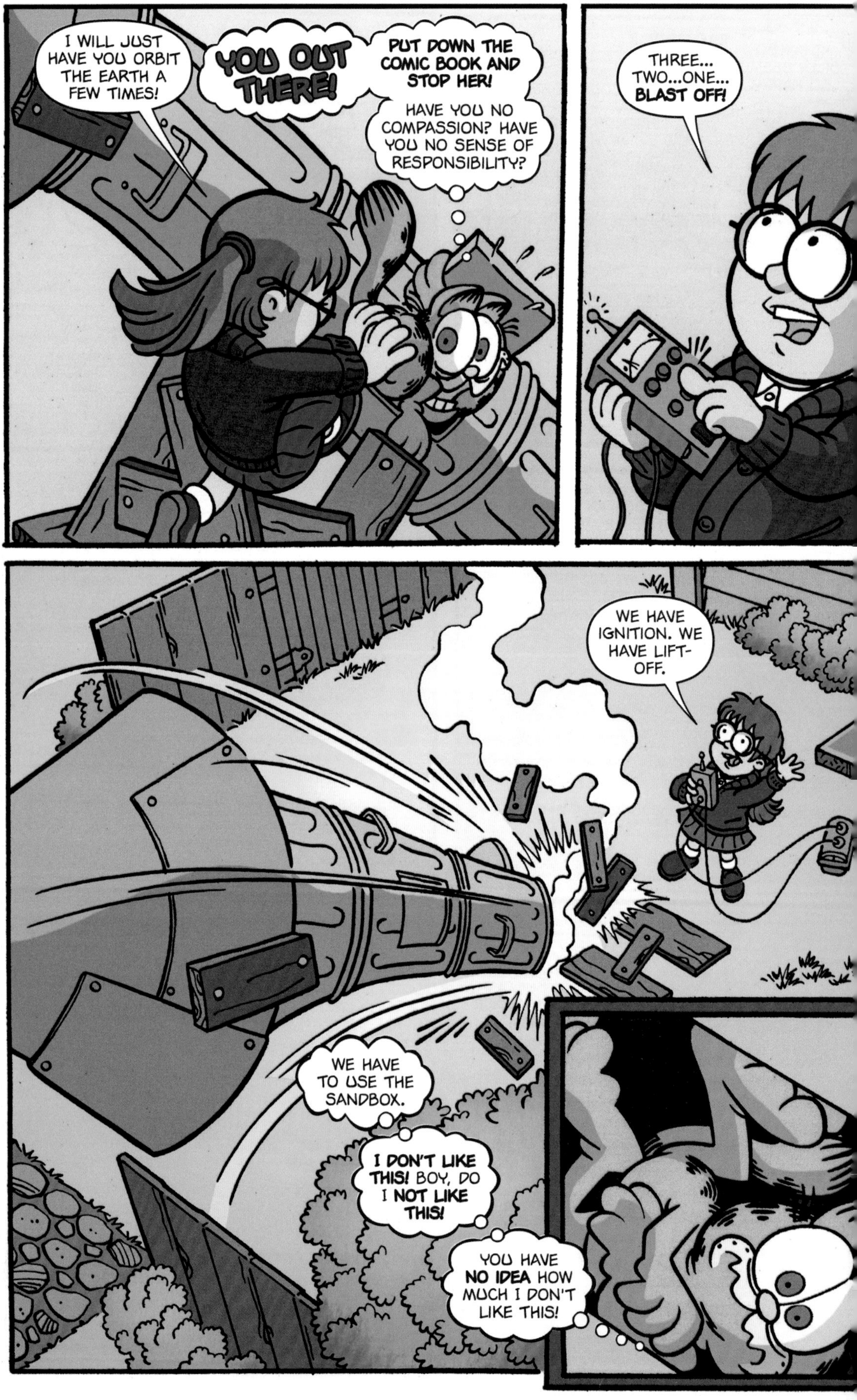
I WILL JUST HAVE YOU ORBIT THE EARTH A FEW TIMES!
YOU OUT THERE!
PUT DOWN THE COMIC BOOK AND STOP HER!
HAVE YOU NO COMPASSION? HAVE YOU NO SENSE OF RESPONSIBILITY?
THREE... TWO...ONE... BLAST OFF!
WE HAVE IGNITION. WE HAVE LIFT-OFF.
WE HAVE TO USE THE SANDBOX.
I DON'T LIKE THIS! BOY, DO I NOT LIKE THIS!
YOU HAVE NO IDEA HOW MUCH I DON'T LIKE THIS!

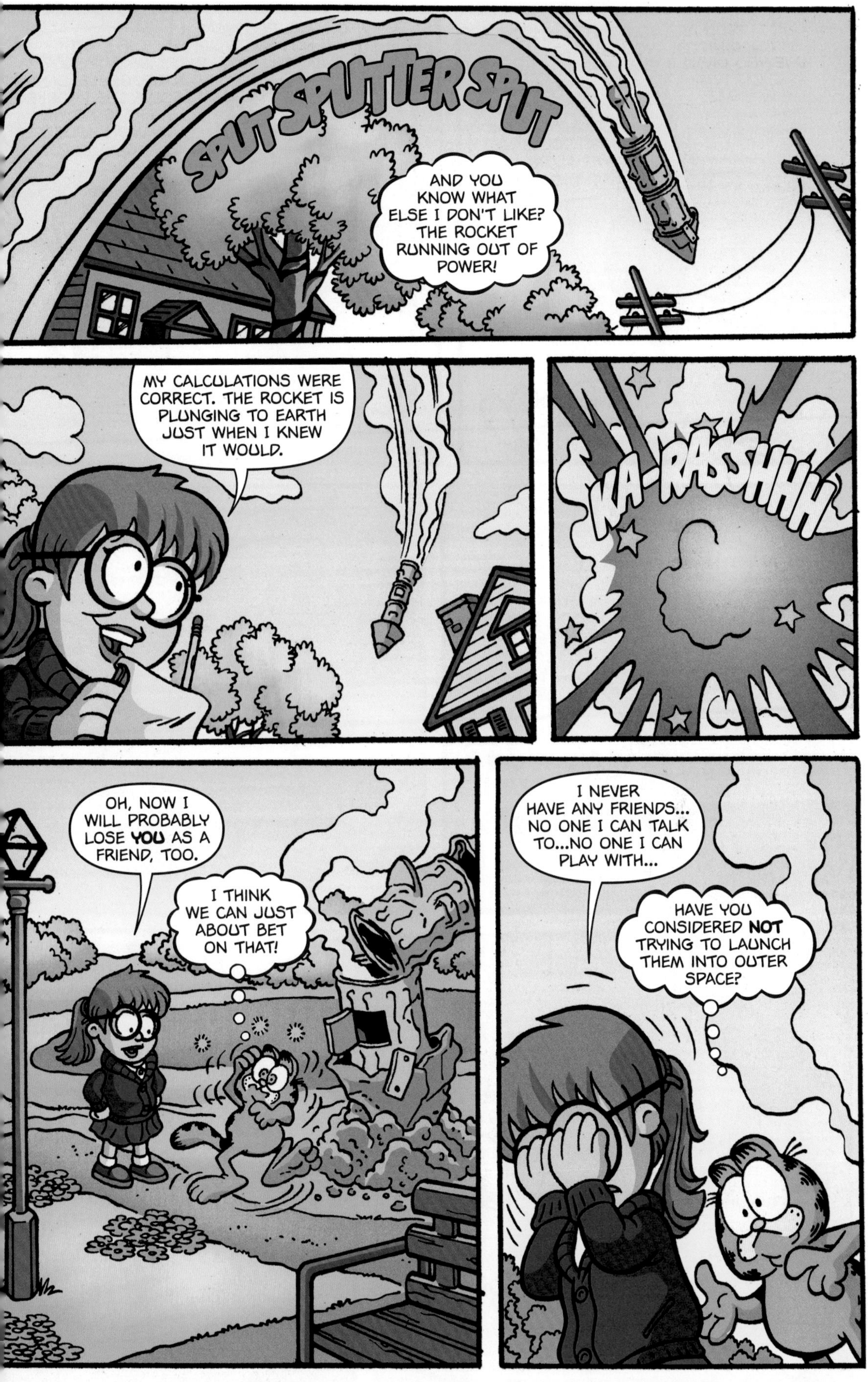
SPUT SPUTTER SPUT
AND YOU KNOW WHAT ELSE I DON'T LIKE? THE ROCKET RUNNING OUT OF POWER!
MY CALCULATIONS WERE CORRECT. THE ROCKET IS PLUNGING TO EARTH JUST WHEN I KNEW IT WOULD.
KA-RASSHHH
OH, NOW I WILL PROBABLY LOSE **YOU** AS A FRIEND, TOO.
I THINK WE CAN JUST ABOUT BET ON THAT!
I NEVER HAVE ANY FRIENDS... NO ONE I CAN TALK TO...NO ONE I CAN PLAY WITH...
HAVE YOU CONSIDERED **NOT** TRYING TO LAUNCH THEM INTO OUTER SPACE?

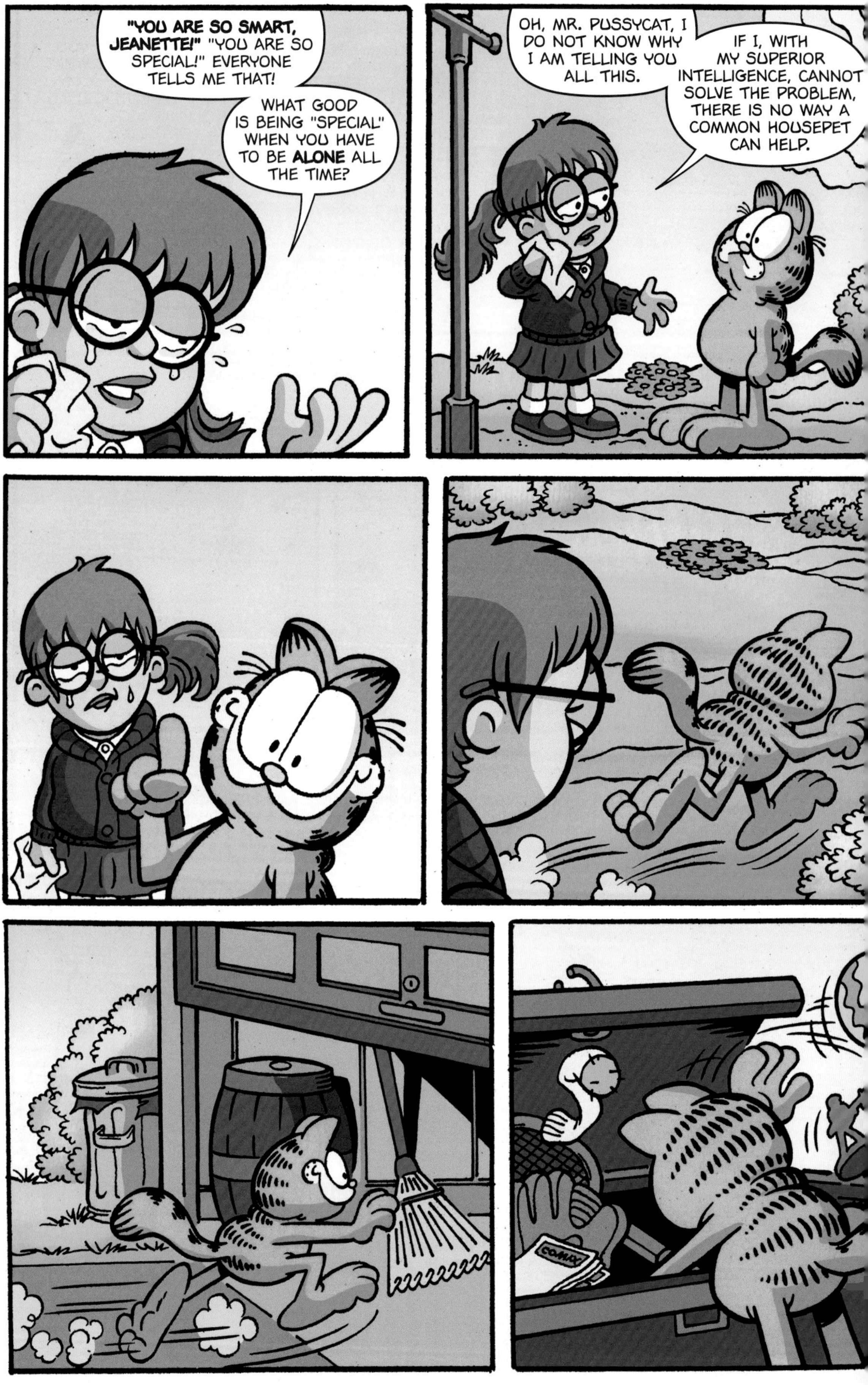
"YOU ARE SO SMART, JEANETTE!" "YOU ARE SO SPECIAL!" EVERYONE TELLS ME THAT!
WHAT GOOD IS BEING "SPECIAL" WHEN YOU HAVE TO BE ALONE ALL THE TIME?
OH, MR. PUSSYCAT, I DO NOT KNOW WHY I AM TELLING YOU ALL THIS.
IF I, WITH MY SUPERIOR INTELLIGENCE, CANNOT SOLVE THE PROBLEM, THERE IS NO WAY A COMMON HOUSEPET CAN HELP.
COMIX

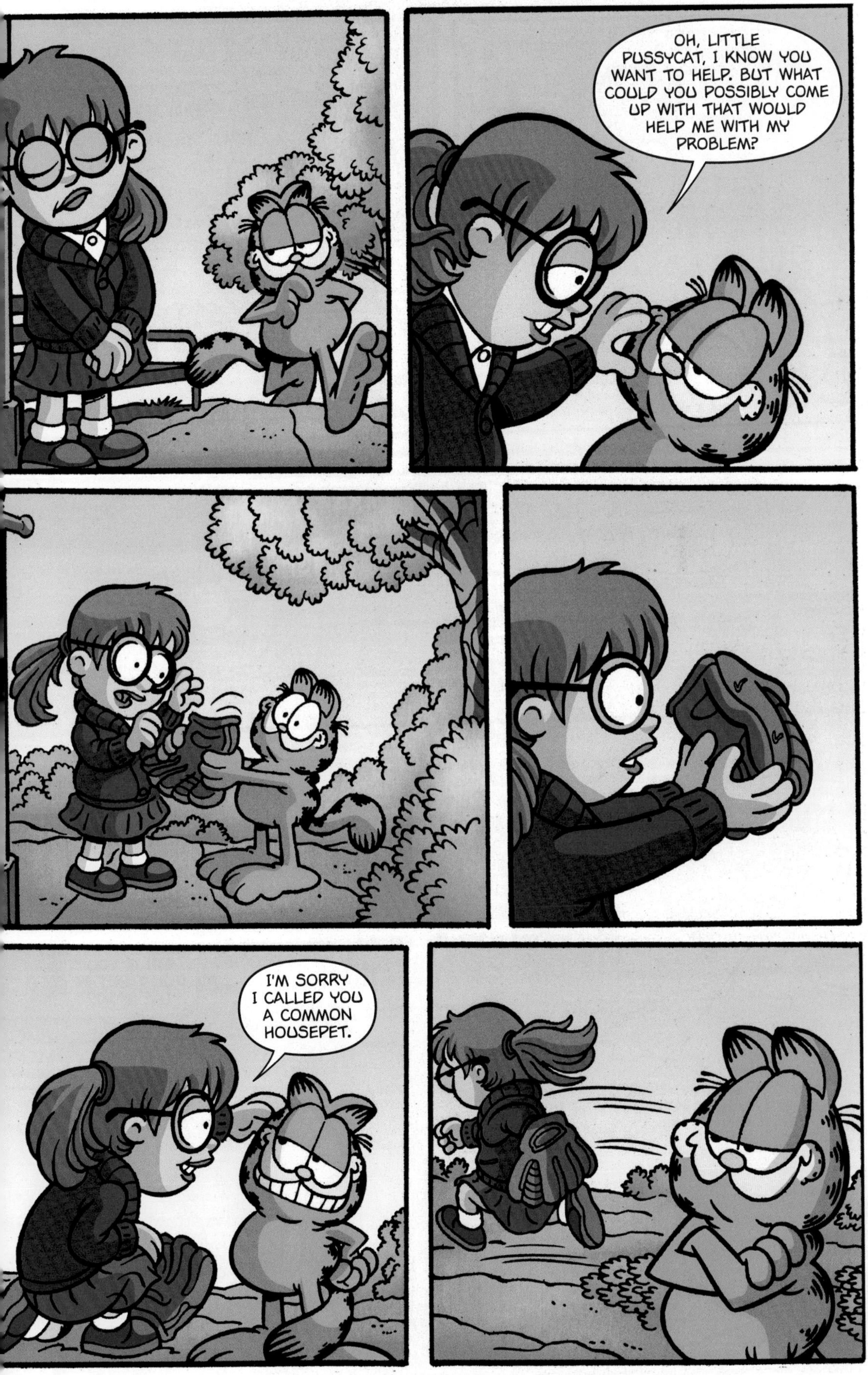

OH, LITTLE PUSSYCAT, I KNOW YOU WANT TO HELP. BUT WHAT COULD YOU POSSIBLY COME UP WITH THAT WOULD HELP ME WITH MY PROBLEM?
I'M SORRY I CALLED YOU A COMMON HOUSEPET.

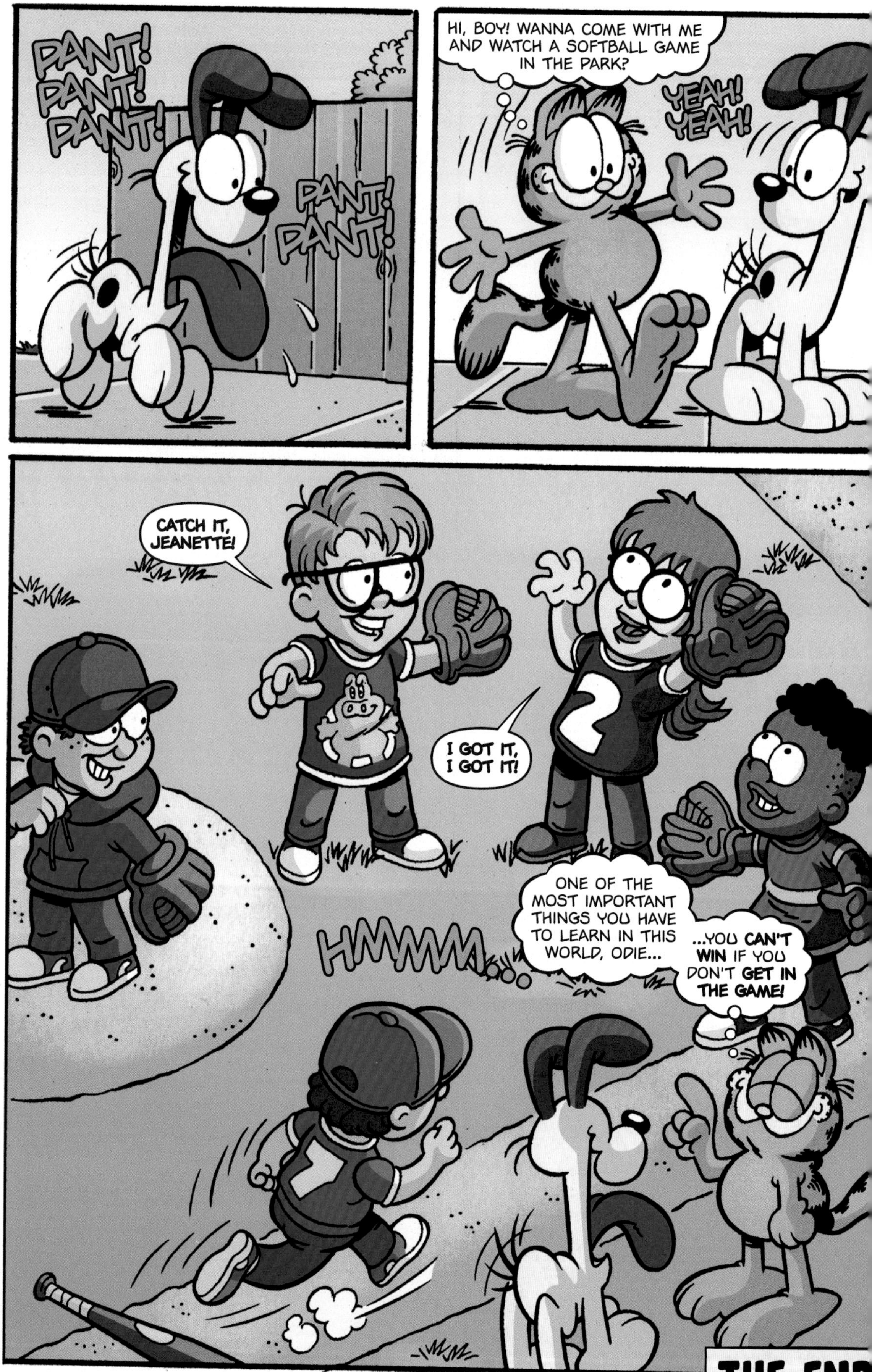
PANT! PANT! PANT!
PANT! PANT!
HI, BOY! WANNA COME WITH ME AND WATCH A SOFTBALL GAME IN THE PARK?
YEAH! YEAH!
CATCH IT, JEANETTE!
I GOT IT, I GOT IT!
HMMM...
ONE OF THE MOST IMPORTANT THINGS YOU HAVE TO LEARN IN THIS WORLD, ODIE...
...YOU CAN'T WIN IF YOU DON'T GET IN THE GAME!
THE END

CHAPTER FIVE

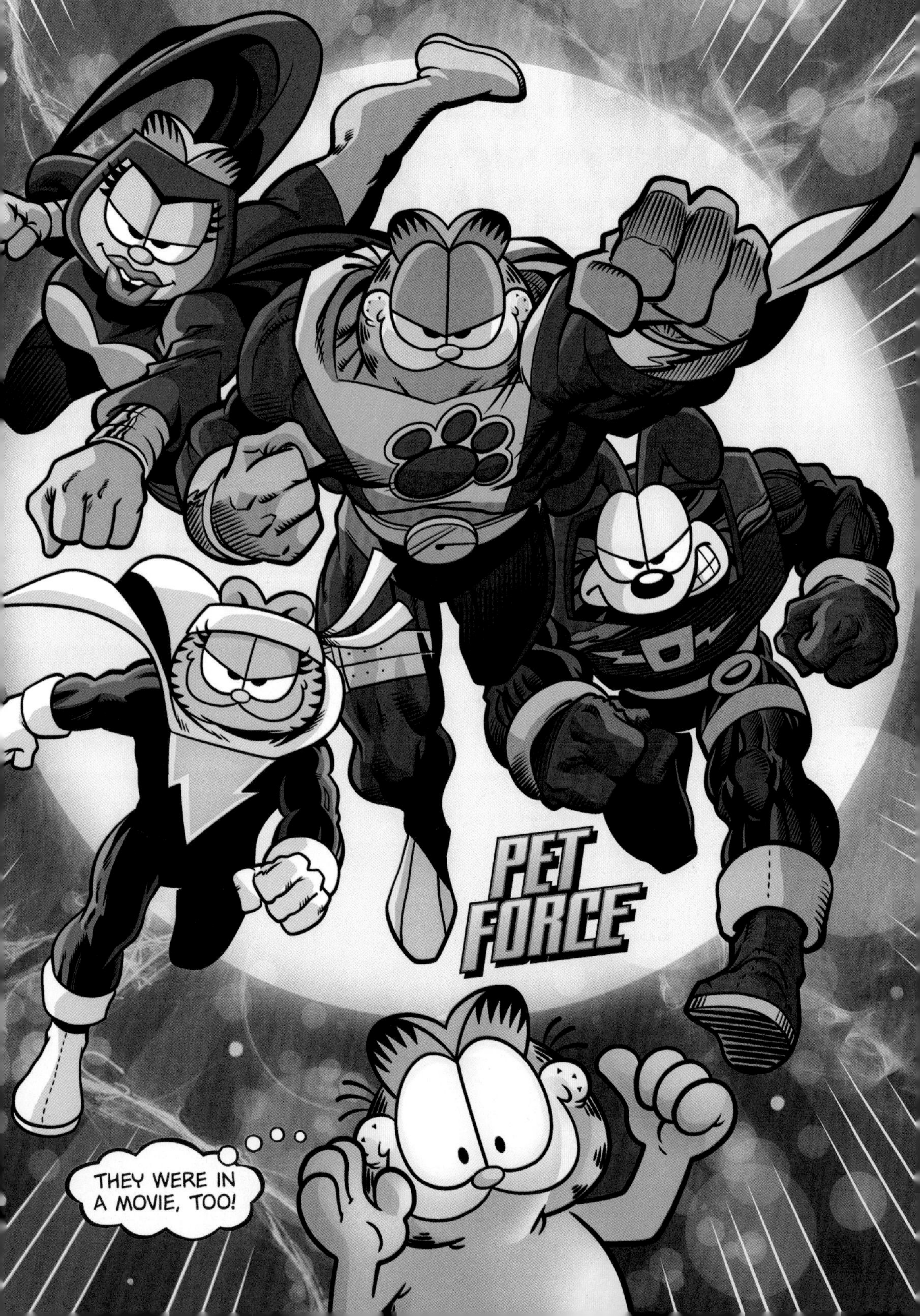
PET FORCE
THEY WERE IN A MOVIE, TOO!

THE MOUSE WHO WANTED TO BE A CAT
THE MOUSE WHO WANTED TO BE A DOG
PET FORCE: THE CREATURE STALKS!

Written by
MARK EVANIER

Art by
MIKE DeCARLO
(Pages 105-116)
GARY BARKER
AND DAN DAVIS
(Pages 117-126)

Colors by
LISA MOORE

Chapter Break Art by
GARY BARKER
AND DAN DAVIS
WITH LISA MOORE

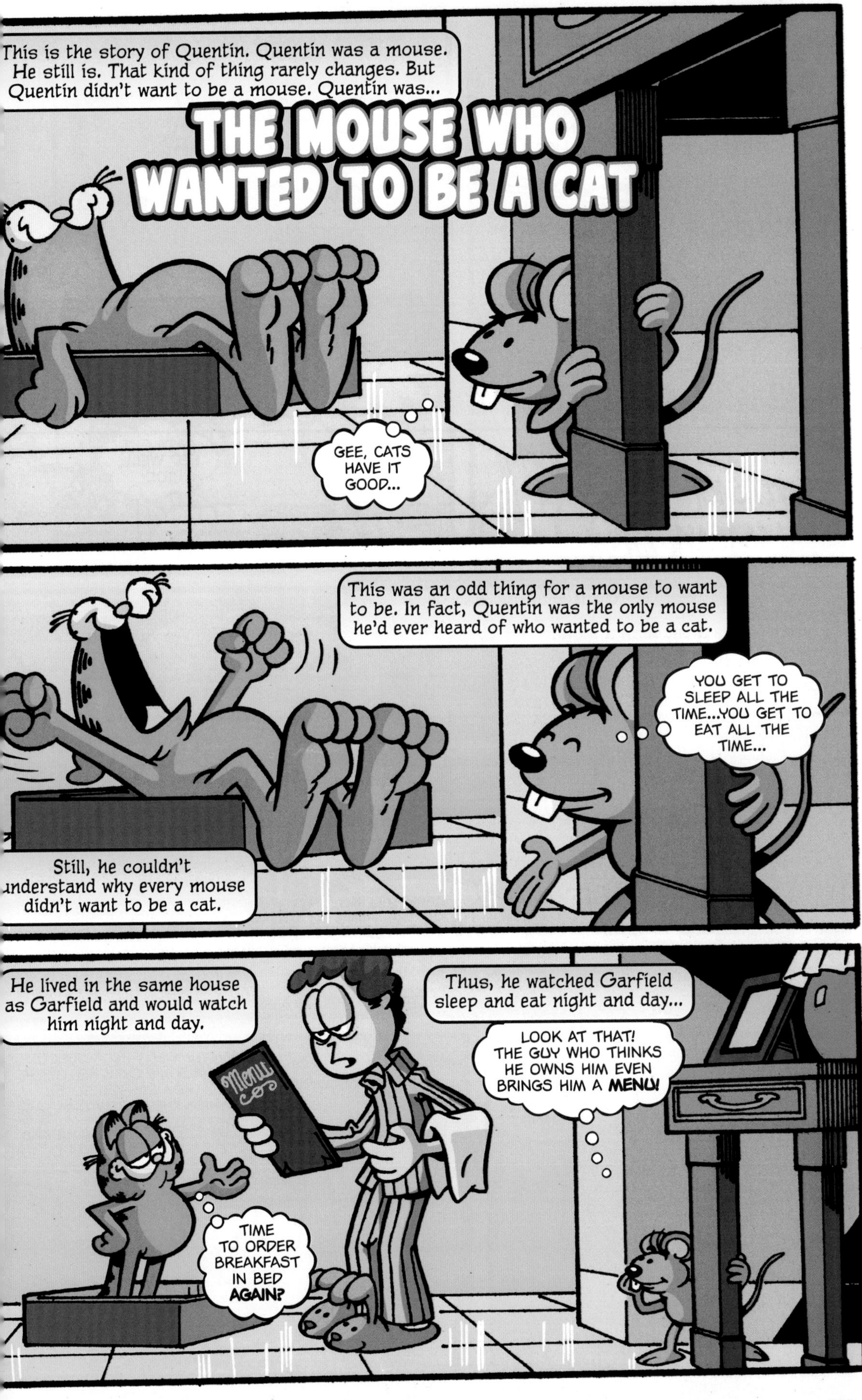

This is the story of Quentin. Quentin was a mouse. He still is. That kind of thing rarely changes. But Quentin didn't want to be a mouse. Quentin was...
THE MOUSE WHO WANTED TO BE A CAT
GEE, CATS HAVE IT GOOD...
This was an odd thing for a mouse to want to be. In fact, Quentin was the only mouse he'd ever heard of who wanted to be a cat.
YOU GET TO SLEEP ALL THE TIME...YOU GET TO EAT ALL THE TIME...
Still, he couldn't understand why every mouse didn't want to be a cat.
He lived in the same house as Garfield and would watch him night and day.
Thus, he watched Garfield sleep and eat night and day...
LOOK AT THAT! THE GUY WHO THINKS HE OWNS HIM EVEN BRINGS HIM A MENU!
Menu
TIME TO ORDER BREAKFAST IN BED AGAIN?

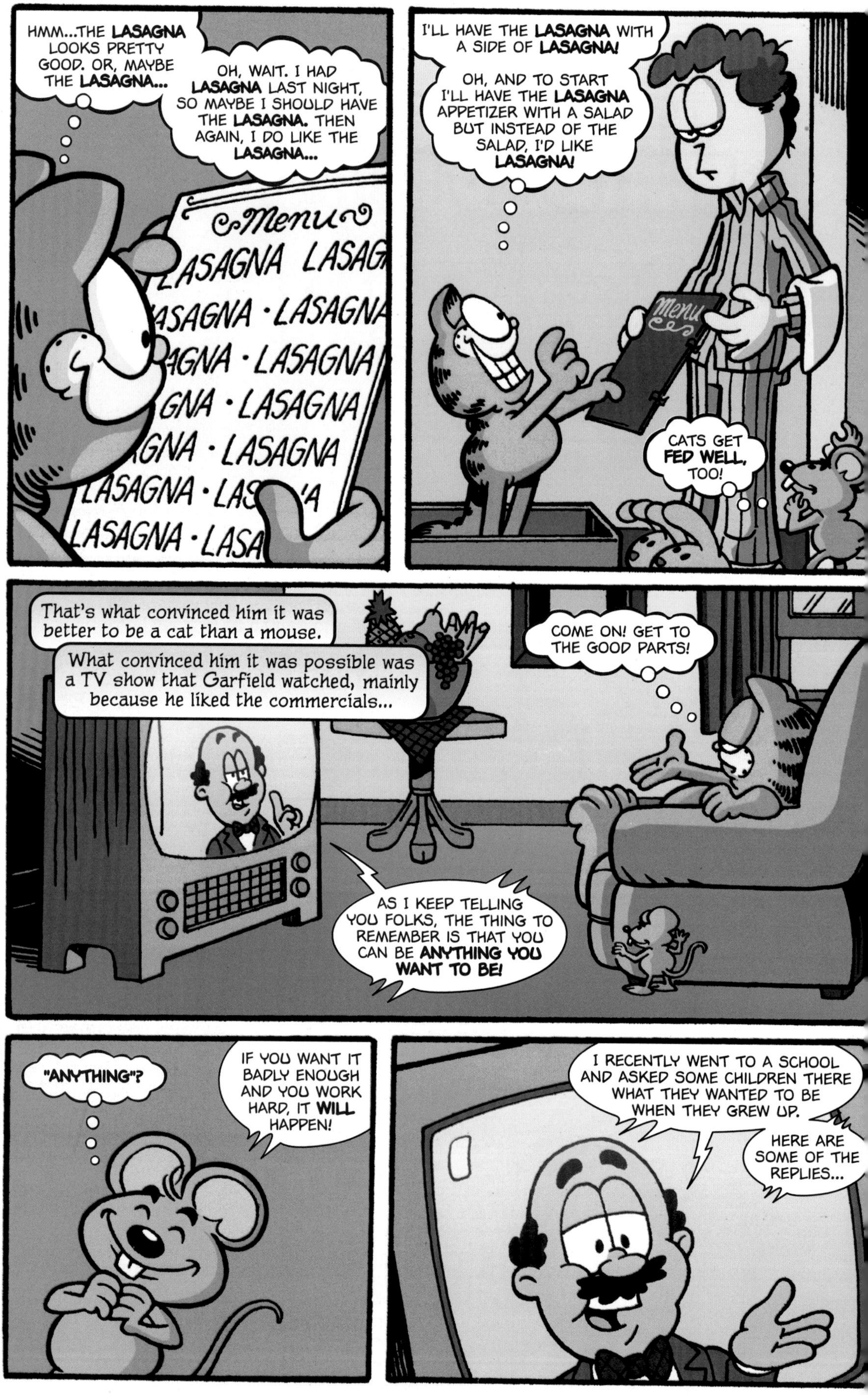
HMM...THE LASAGNA LOOKS PRETTY GOOD. OR, MAYBE THE LASAGNA...
OH, WAIT. I HAD LASAGNA LAST NIGHT, SO MAYBE I SHOULD HAVE THE LASAGNA. THEN AGAIN, I DO LIKE THE LASAGNA...
Menu
LASAGNA LASAG
ASAGNA · LASAGNA
AGNA · LASAGNA
GNA · LASAGNA
GNA · LASAGNA
LASAGNA · LAS A
LASAGNA · LASA
I'LL HAVE THE LASAGNA WITH A SIDE OF LASAGNA!
OH, AND TO START I'LL HAVE THE LASAGNA APPETIZER WITH A SALAD BUT INSTEAD OF THE SALAD, I'D LIKE LASAGNA!
Menu
CATS GET FED WELL, TOO!
That's what convinced him it was better to be a cat than a mouse.
What convinced him it was possible was a TV show that Garfield watched, mainly because he liked the commercials...
COME ON! GET TO THE GOOD PARTS!
AS I KEEP TELLING YOU FOLKS, THE THING TO REMEMBER IS THAT YOU CAN BE ANYTHING YOU WANT TO BE!
"ANYTHING"?
IF YOU WANT IT BADLY ENOUGH AND YOU WORK HARD, IT WILL HAPPEN!
I RECENTLY WENT TO A SCHOOL AND ASKED SOME CHILDREN THERE WHAT THEY WANTED TO BE WHEN THEY GREW UP.
HERE ARE SOME OF THE REPLIES...

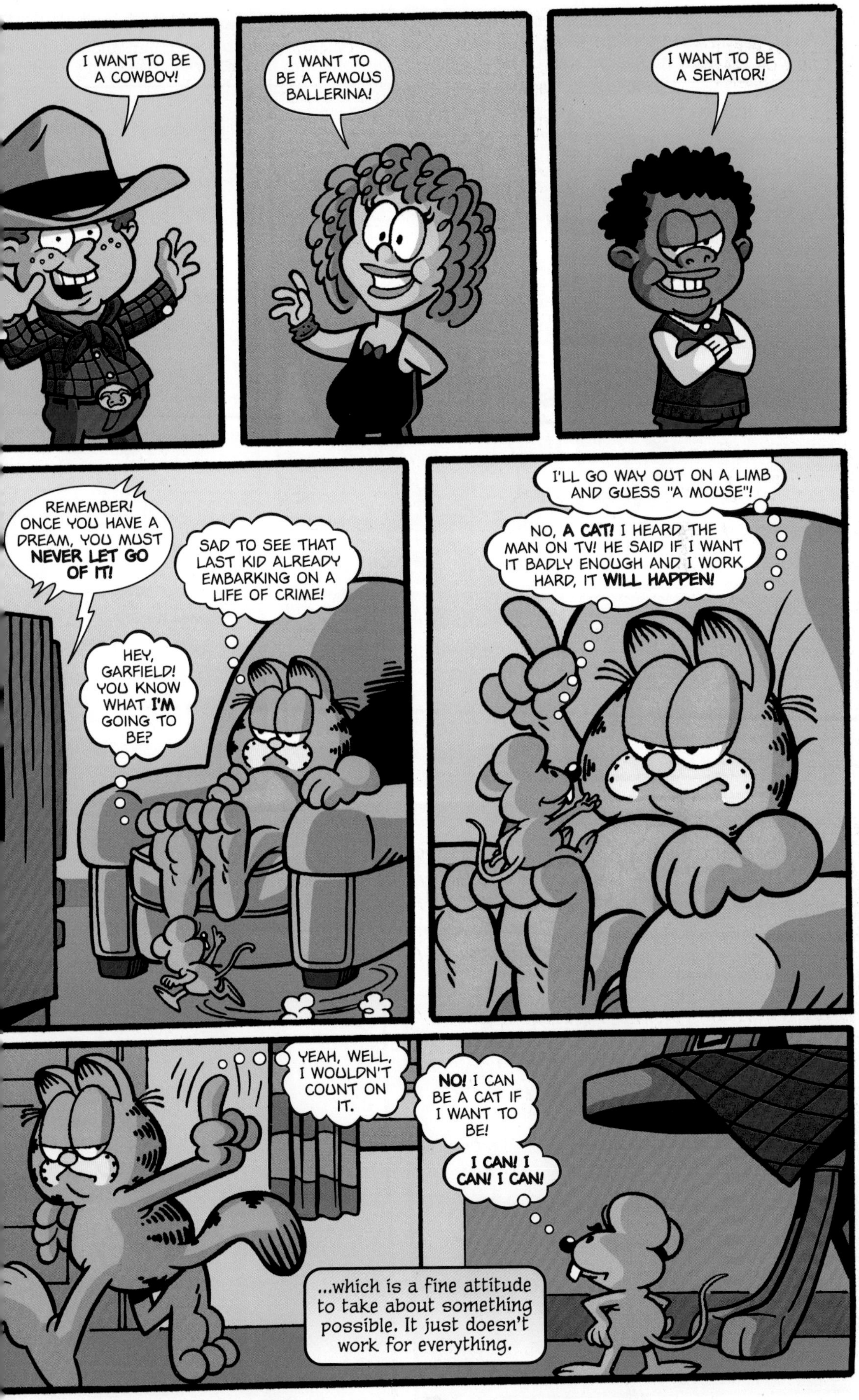
I WANT TO BE A COWBOY!
I WANT TO BE A FAMOUS BALLERINA!
I WANT TO BE A SENATOR!
REMEMBER! ONCE YOU HAVE A DREAM, YOU MUST NEVER LET GO OF IT!
SAD TO SEE THAT LAST KID ALREADY EMBARKING ON A LIFE OF CRIME!
HEY, GARFIELD! YOU KNOW WHAT I'M GOING TO BE?
I'LL GO WAY OUT ON A LIMB AND GUESS "A MOUSE"!
NO, A CAT! I HEARD THE MAN ON TV! HE SAID IF I WANT IT BADLY ENOUGH AND I WORK HARD, IT WILL HAPPEN!
YEAH, WELL, I WOULDN'T COUNT ON IT.
NO! I CAN BE A CAT IF I WANT TO BE!
I CAN! I CAN! I CAN!
...which is a fine attitude to take about something possible. It just doesn't work for everything.

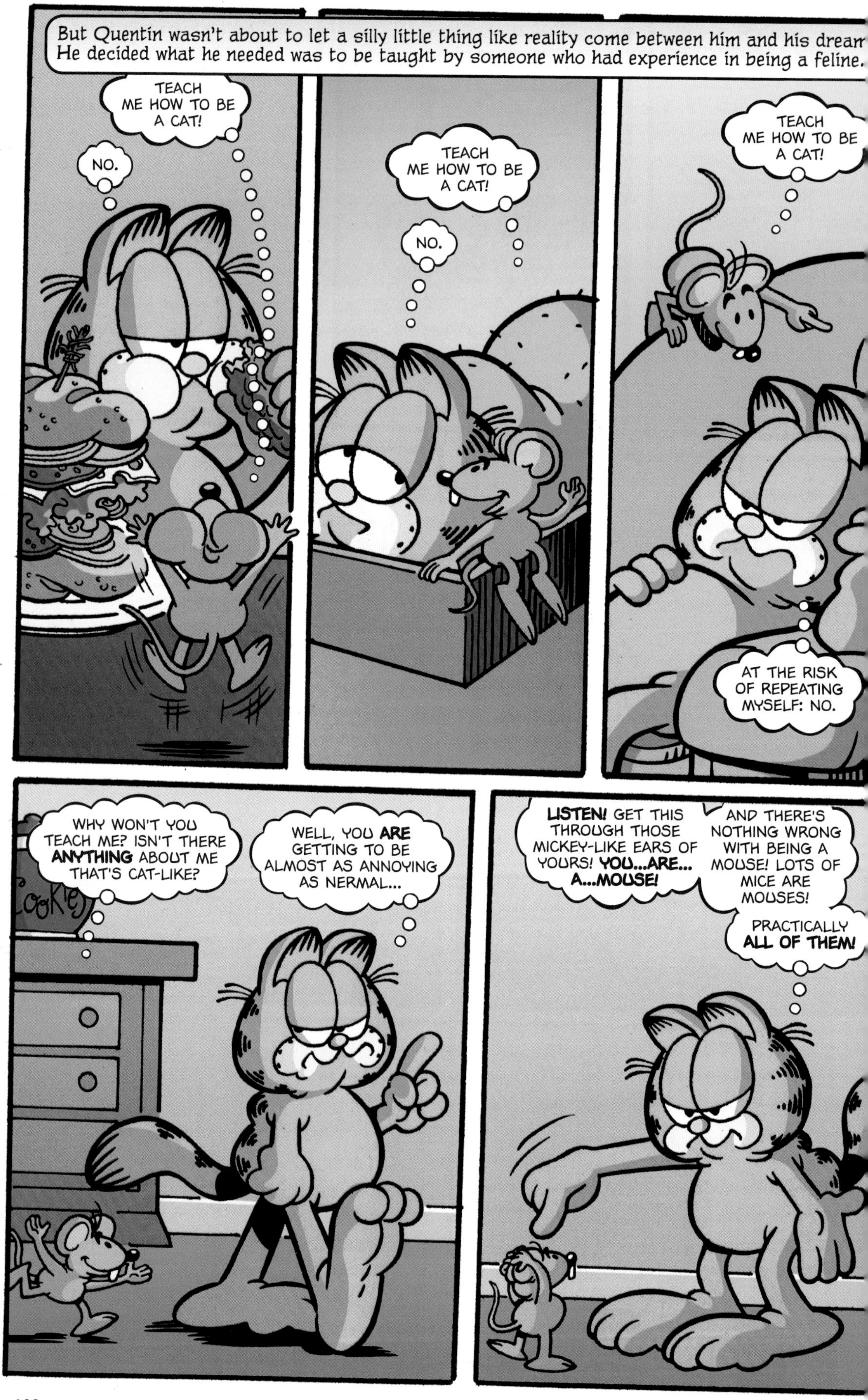

But Quentin wasn't about to let a silly little thing like reality come between him and his drean
He decided what he needed was to be taught by someone who had experience in being a feline.
TEACH ME HOW TO BE A CAT!
NO.
TEACH ME HOW TO BE A CAT!
NO.
TEACH ME HOW TO BE A CAT!
AT THE RISK OF REPEATING MYSELF: NO.
WHY WON'T YOU TEACH ME? ISN'T THERE **ANYTHING** ABOUT ME THAT'S CAT-LIKE?
WELL, YOU **ARE** GETTING TO BE ALMOST AS ANNOYING AS NERMAL...
LISTEN! GET THIS THROUGH THOSE MICKEY-LIKE EARS OF YOURS! **YOU...ARE... A...MOUSE!**
AND THERE'S NOTHING WRONG WITH BEING A MOUSE! LOTS OF MICE ARE MOUSES!
PRACTICALLY **ALL OF THEM!**

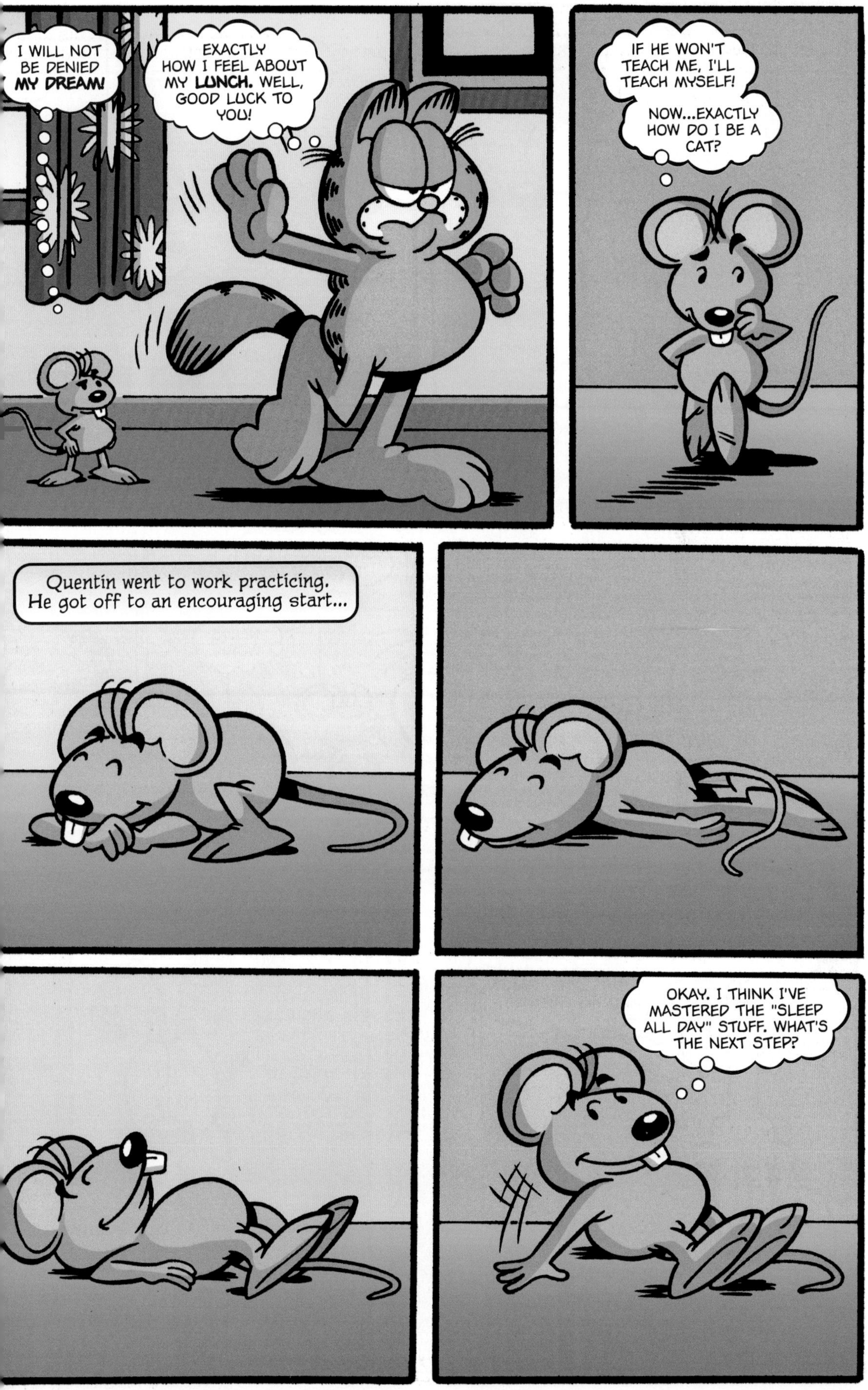
I WILL NOT BE DENIED **MY DREAM!**
EXACTLY HOW I FEEL ABOUT MY **LUNCH.** WELL, GOOD LUCK TO YOU!
IF HE WON'T TEACH ME, I'LL TEACH MYSELF!
NOW...EXACTLY HOW DO I BE A CAT?
Quentin went to work practicing. He got off to an encouraging start...
OKAY. I THINK I'VE MASTERED THE "SLEEP ALL DAY" STUFF. WHAT'S THE NEXT STEP?

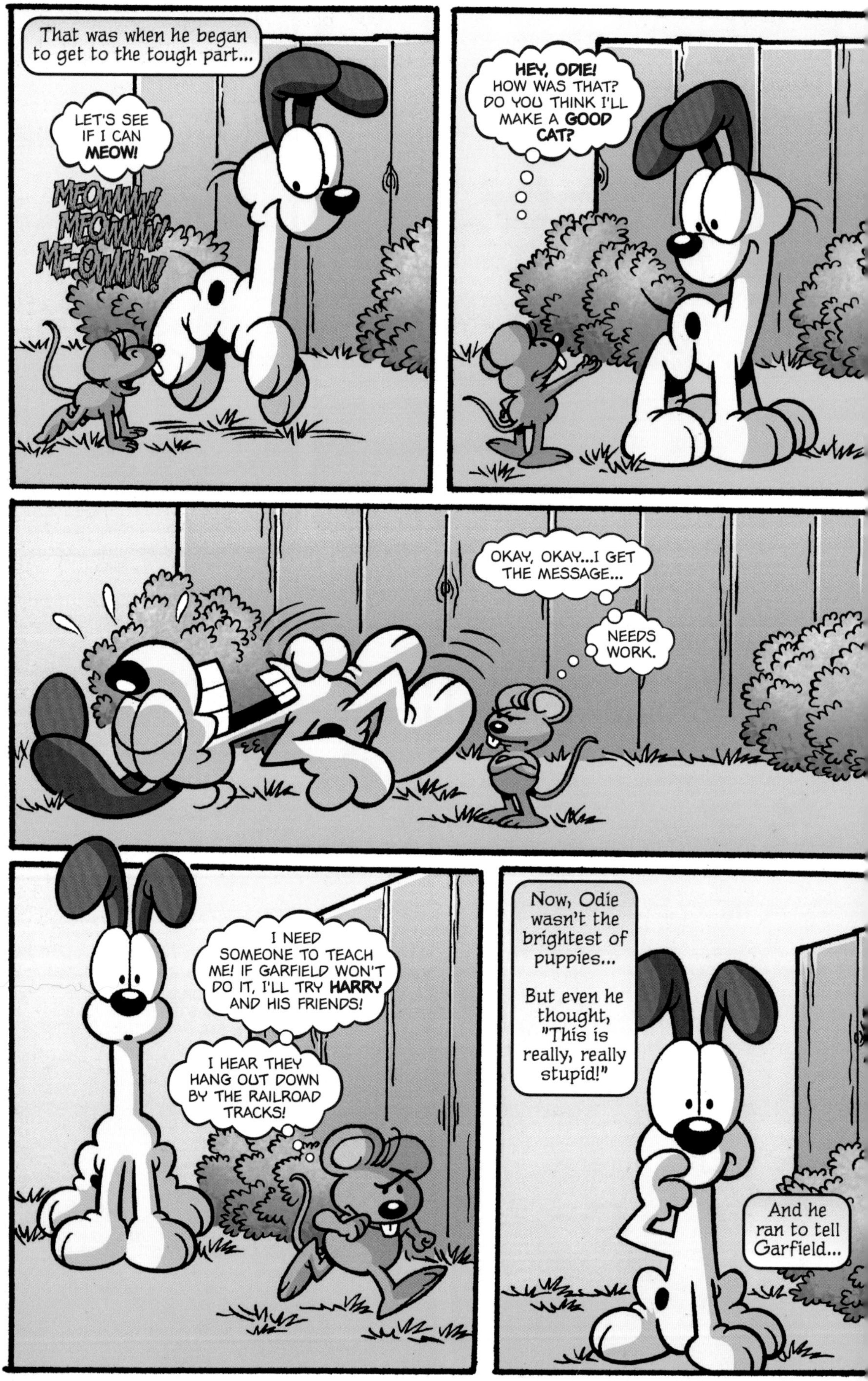
That was when he began to get to the tough part...
LET'S SEE IF I CAN MEOW!
MEOWWW! MEOWWW! ME-OWWW!
HEY, ODIE! HOW WAS THAT? DO YOU THINK I'LL MAKE A GOOD CAT?
OKAY, OKAY...I GET THE MESSAGE...
NEEDS WORK.
I NEED SOMEONE TO TEACH ME! IF GARFIELD WON'T DO IT, I'LL TRY HARRY AND HIS FRIENDS!
I HEAR THEY HANG OUT DOWN BY THE RAILROAD TRACKS!
Now, Odie wasn't the brightest of puppies...
But even he thought, "This is really, really stupid!"
And he ran to tell Garfield...

...who agreed:

THAT IS REALLY, REALLY STUPID!

QUENTIN'S NOT GOING TO GET HIS DREAM OF **BECOMING** A CAT...

...BUT HE MIGHT WIND UP **INSIDE ONE!**

YOWP!

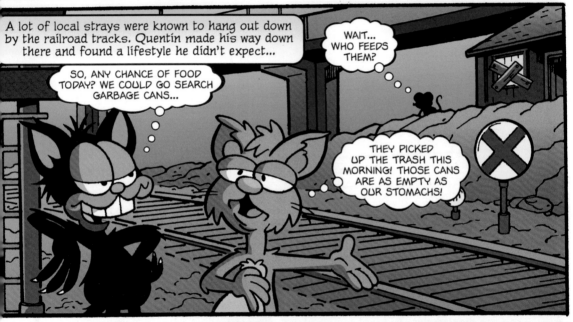

A lot of local strays were known to hang out down by the railroad tracks. Quentin made his way down there and found a lifestyle he didn't expect...

SO, ANY CHANCE OF FOOD TODAY? WE COULD GO SEARCH GARBAGE CANS...

WAIT... WHO FEEDS THEM?

THEY PICKED UP THE TRASH THIS MORNING! THOSE CANS ARE AS EMPTY AS OUR STOMACHS!

I THOUGHT PEOPLE FED CATS...LIKE THAT JON GUY DOES...

THEY FEED THEM AND PET THEM AND PAMPER THEM AND BUY THEM LITTLE TOYS AND LET THEM WATCH CABLE TV...

MAYBE BEING A MOUSE ISN'T SO BAD...

But as too often happens in life, just when he was about to do something smart...

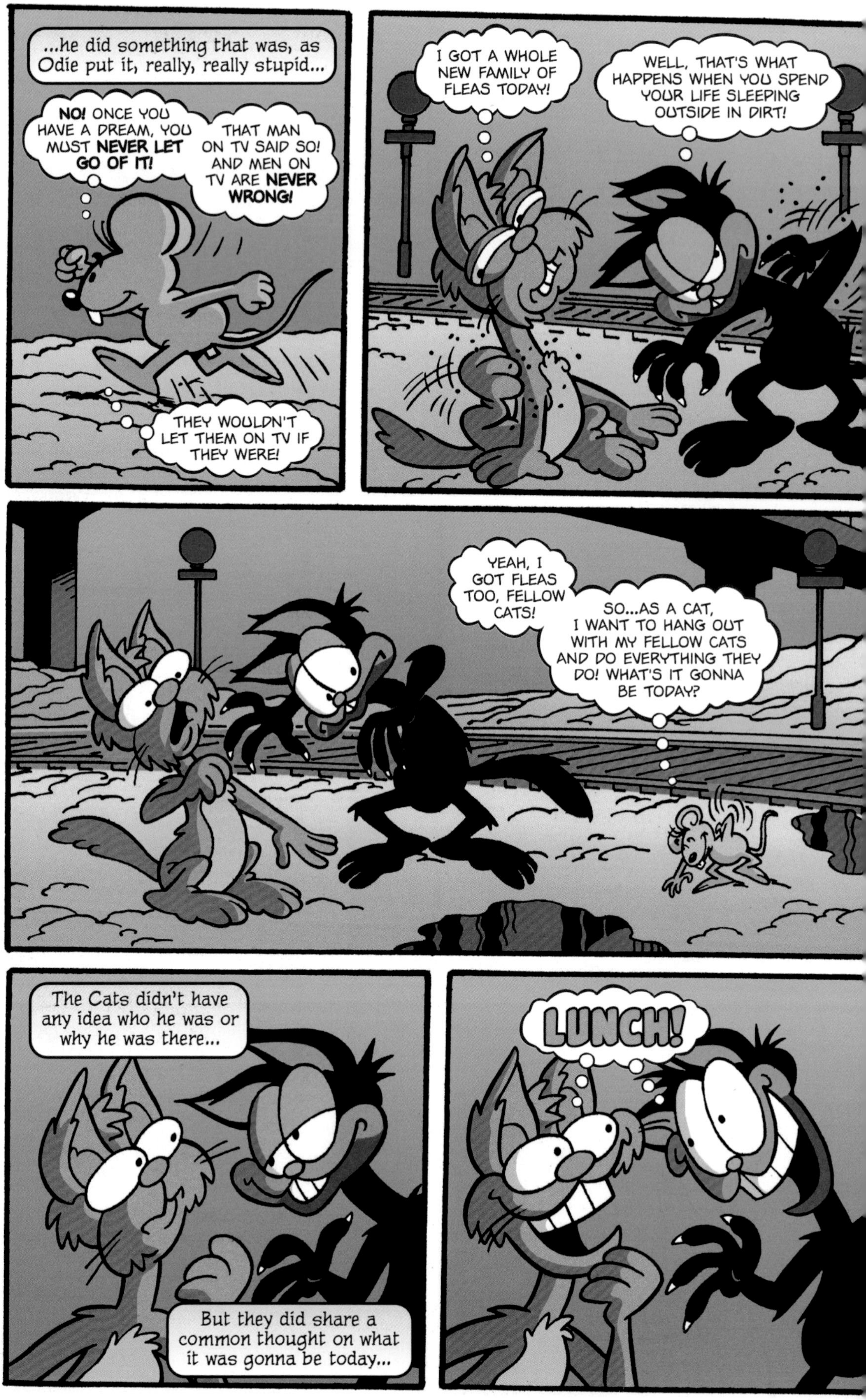

...he did something that was, as Odie put it, really, really stupid...
NO! ONCE YOU HAVE A DREAM, YOU MUST NEVER LET GO OF IT!
THAT MAN ON TV SAID SO! AND MEN ON TV ARE NEVER WRONG!
THEY WOULDN'T LET THEM ON TV IF THEY WERE!
I GOT A WHOLE NEW FAMILY OF FLEAS TODAY!
WELL, THAT'S WHAT HAPPENS WHEN YOU SPEND YOUR LIFE SLEEPING OUTSIDE IN DIRT!
YEAH, I GOT FLEAS TOO, FELLOW CATS!
SO...AS A CAT, I WANT TO HANG OUT WITH MY FELLOW CATS AND DO EVERYTHING THEY DO! WHAT'S IT GONNA BE TODAY?
The Cats didn't have any idea who he was or why he was there...
But they did share a common thought on what it was gonna be today...
LUNCH!

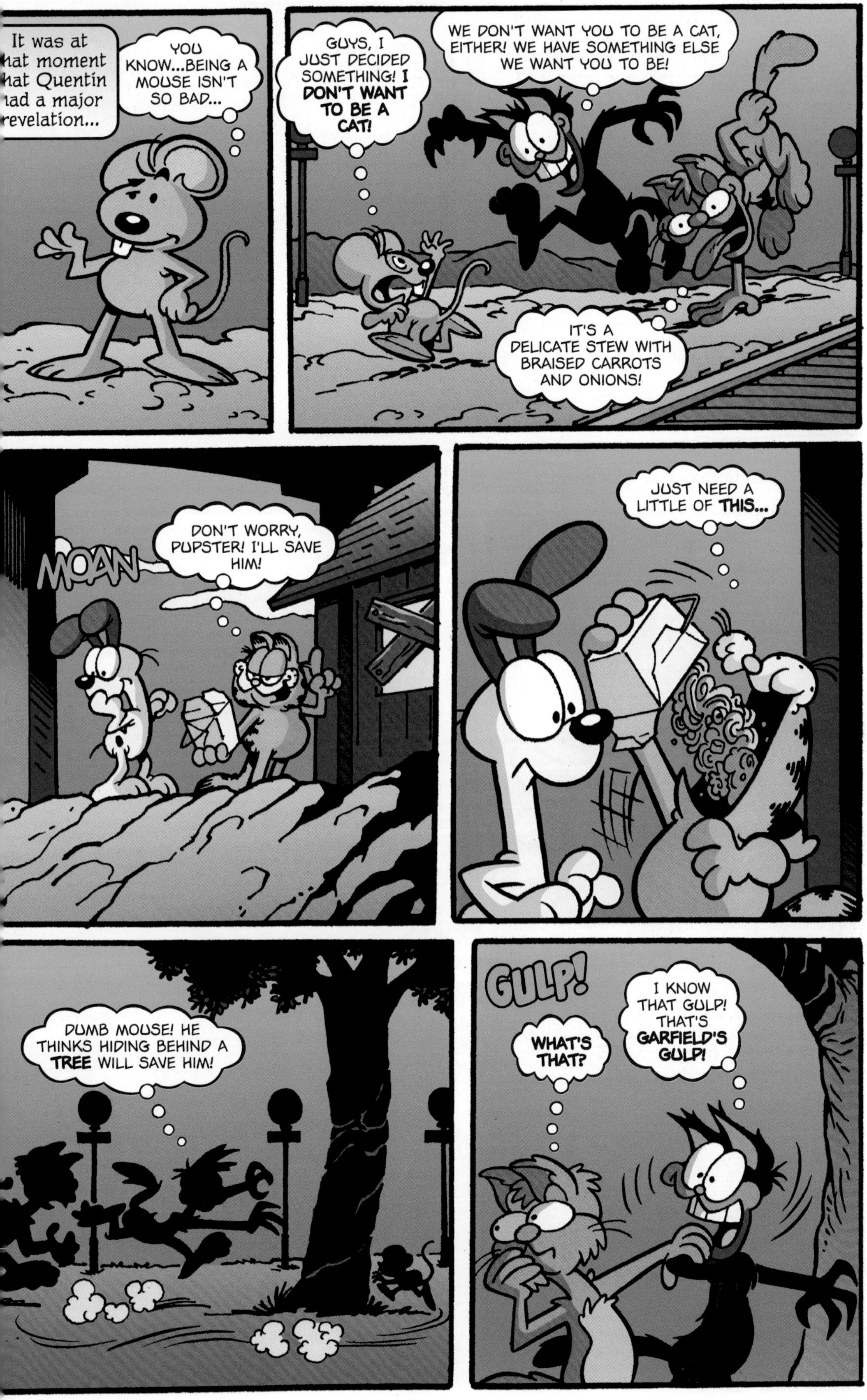
It was at that moment that Quentin had a major revelation...
YOU KNOW...BEING A MOUSE ISN'T SO BAD...
GUYS, I JUST DECIDED SOMETHING! I DON'T WANT TO BE A CAT!
WE DON'T WANT YOU TO BE A CAT, EITHER! WE HAVE SOMETHING ELSE WE WANT YOU TO BE!
IT'S A DELICATE STEW WITH BRAISED CARROTS AND ONIONS!
MOAN
DON'T WORRY, PUPSTER! I'LL SAVE HIM!
JUST NEED A LITTLE OF THIS...
DUMB MOUSE! HE THINKS HIDING BEHIND A TREE WILL SAVE HIM!
GULP!
WHAT'S THAT?
I KNOW THAT GULP! THAT'S GARFIELD'S GULP!

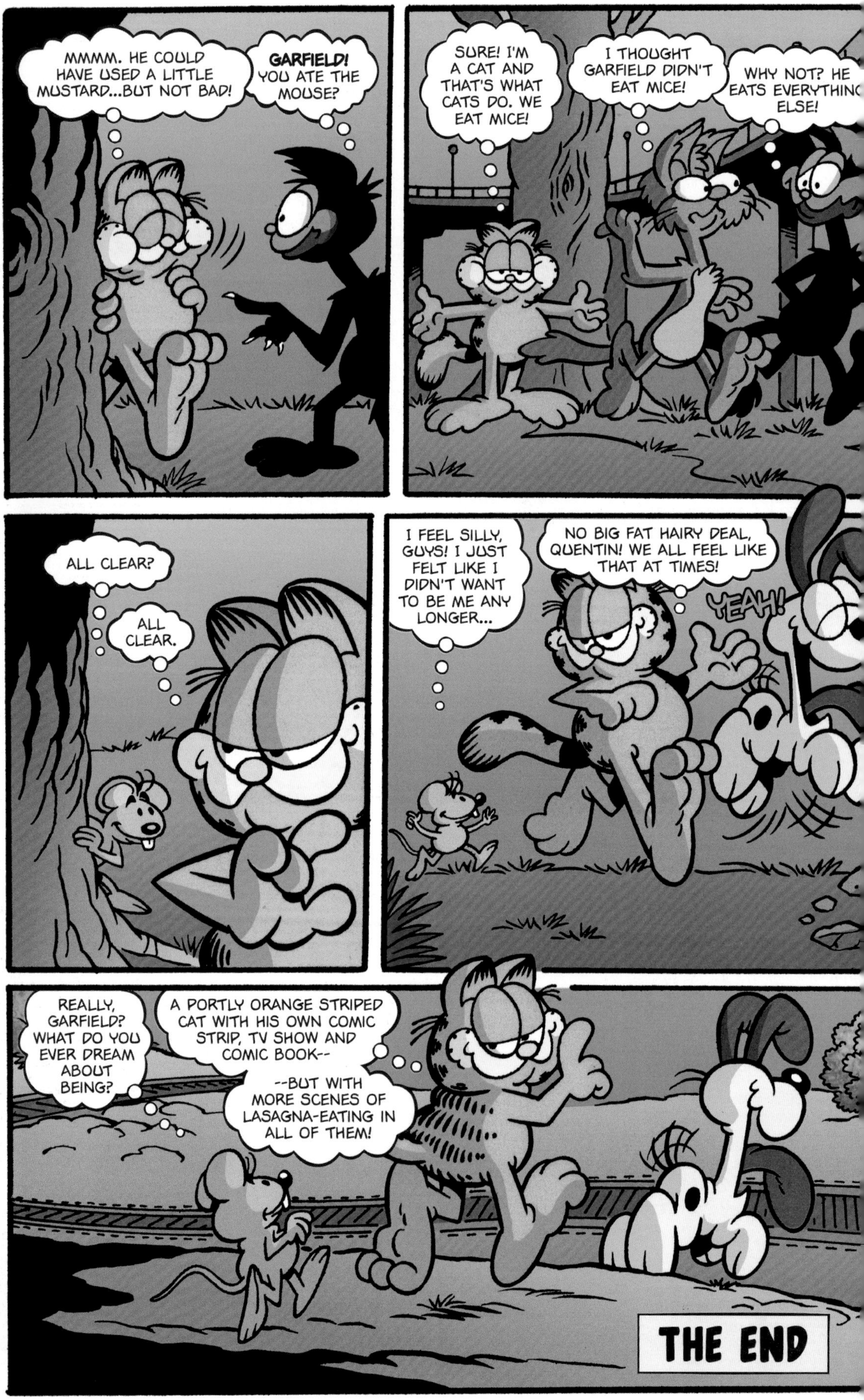

MMMM. HE COULD HAVE USED A LITTLE MUSTARD...BUT NOT BAD!
GARFIELD! YOU ATE THE MOUSE?
SURE! I'M A CAT AND THAT'S WHAT CATS DO. WE EAT MICE!
I THOUGHT GARFIELD DIDN'T EAT MICE!
ALL CLEAR?
ALL CLEAR.
I FEEL SILLY, GUYS! I JUST FELT LIKE I DIDN'T WANT TO BE ME ANY LONGER...
NO BIG FAT HAIRY DEAL, QUENTIN! WE ALL FEEL LIKE THAT AT TIMES!
YEAH!
REALLY, GARFIELD? WHAT DO YOU EVER DREAM ABOUT BEING?
A PORTLY ORANGE STRIPED CAT WITH HIS OWN COMIC STRIP, TV SHOW AND COMIC BOOK--
--BUT WITH MORE SCENES OF LASAGNA-EATING IN ALL OF THEM!
THE END

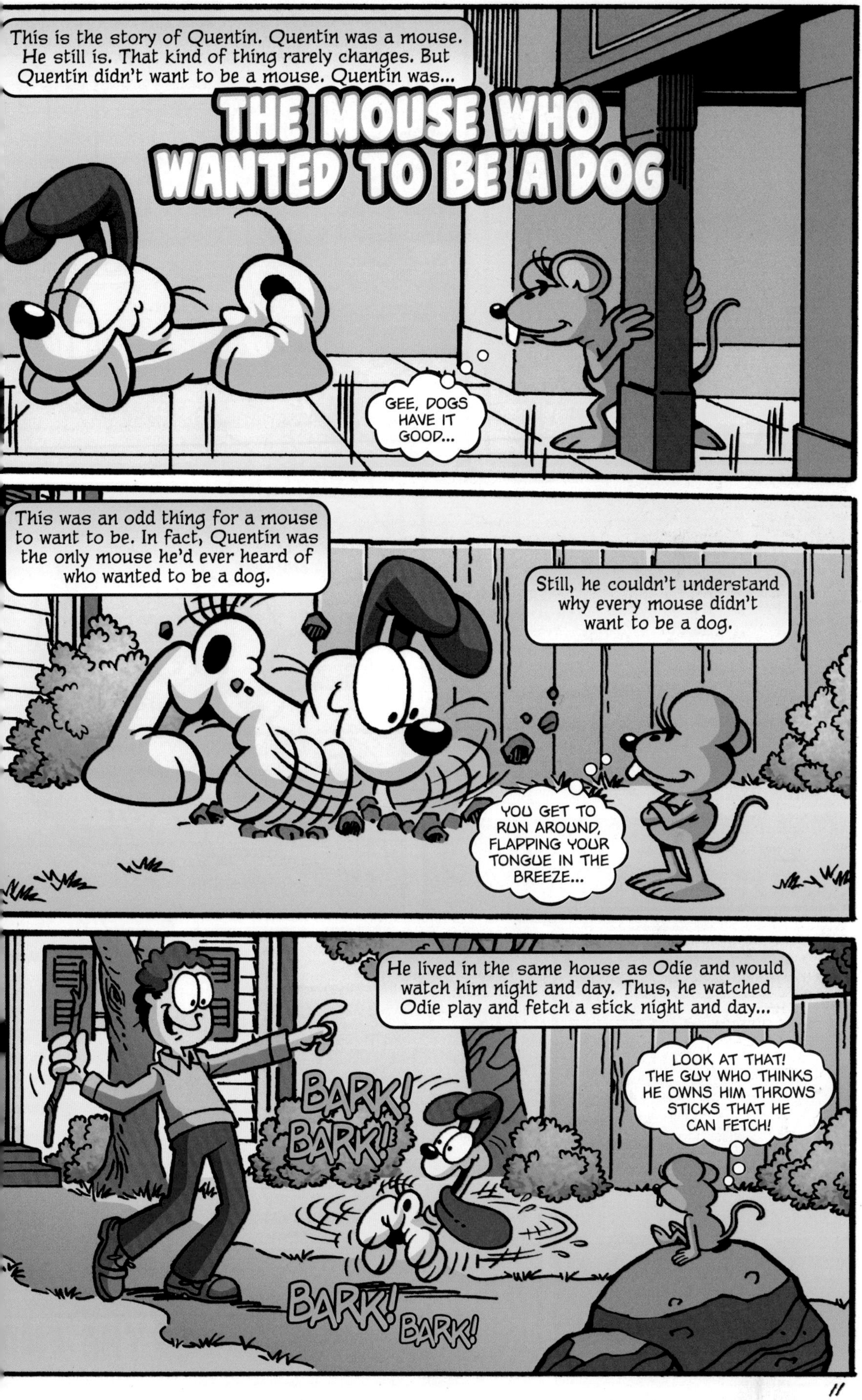

This is the story of Quentin. Quentin was a mouse. He still is. That kind of thing rarely changes. But Quentin didn't want to be a mouse. Quentin was...
THE MOUSE WHO WANTED TO BE A DOG
GEE, DOGS HAVE IT GOOD...
This was an odd thing for a mouse to want to be. In fact, Quentin was the only mouse he'd ever heard of who wanted to be a dog.
Still, he couldn't understand why every mouse didn't want to be a dog.
YOU GET TO RUN AROUND, FLAPPING YOUR TONGUE IN THE BREEZE...
He lived in the same house as Odie and would watch him night and day. Thus, he watched Odie play and fetch a stick night and day...
LOOK AT THAT! THE GUY WHO THINKS HE OWNS HIM THROWS STICKS THAT HE CAN FETCH!
BARK! BARK!!
BARK! BARK!

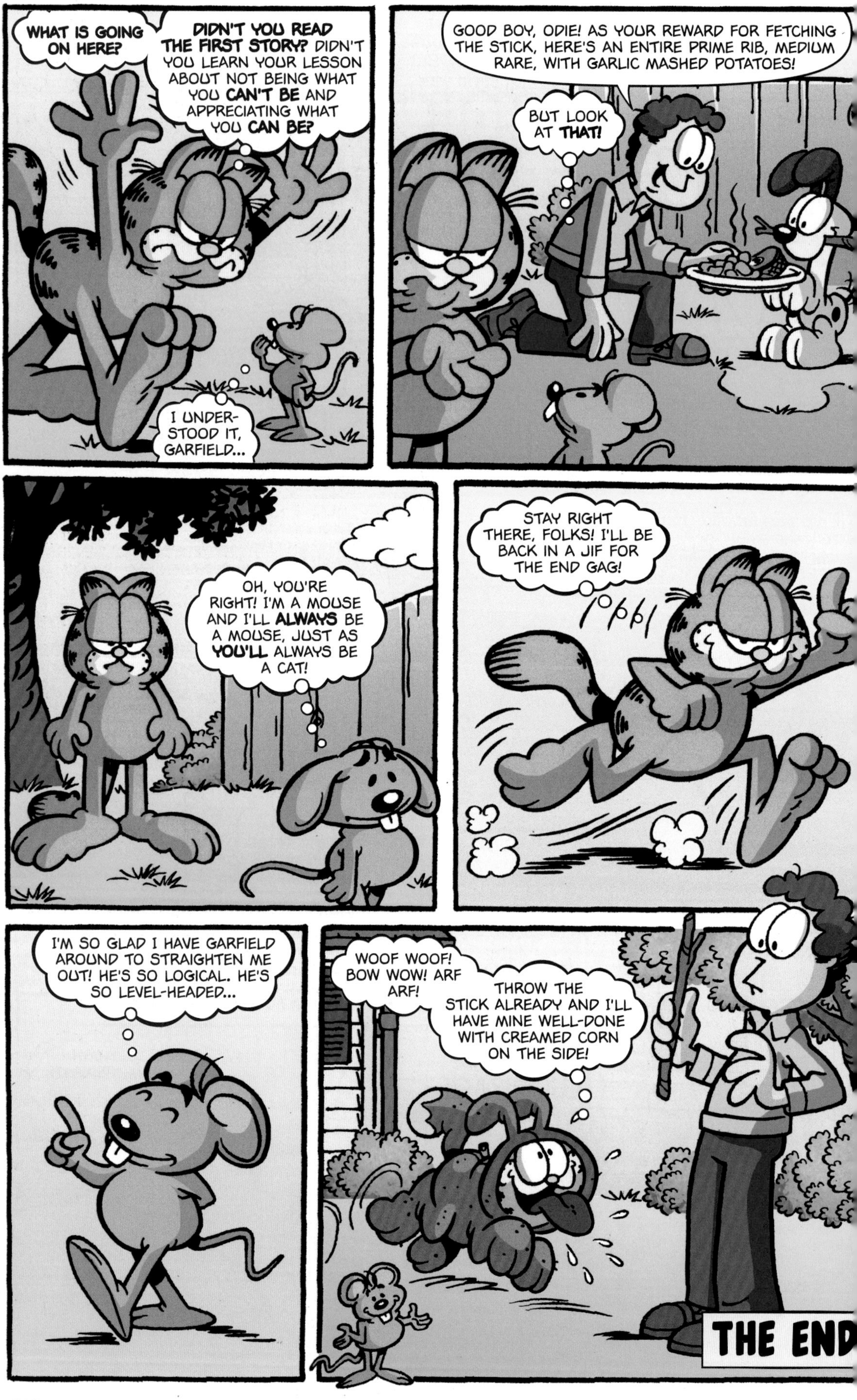
WHAT IS GOING ON HERE?
DIDN'T YOU READ THE FIRST STORY? DIDN'T YOU LEARN YOUR LESSON ABOUT NOT BEING WHAT YOU CAN'T BE AND APPRECIATING WHAT YOU CAN BE?
I UNDER-STOOD IT, GARFIELD...
GOOD BOY, ODIE! AS YOUR REWARD FOR FETCHING THE STICK, HERE'S AN ENTIRE PRIME RIB, MEDIUM RARE, WITH GARLIC MASHED POTATOES!
BUT LOOK AT THAT!
OH, YOU'RE RIGHT! I'M A MOUSE AND I'LL ALWAYS BE A MOUSE, JUST AS YOU'LL ALWAYS BE A CAT!
STAY RIGHT THERE, FOLKS! I'LL BE BACK IN A JIF FOR THE END GAG!
I'M SO GLAD I HAVE GARFIELD AROUND TO STRAIGHTEN ME OUT! HE'S SO LOGICAL. HE'S SO LEVEL-HEADED...
WOOF WOOF! BOW WOW! ARF ARF!
THROW THE STICK ALREADY AND I'LL HAVE MINE WELL-DONE WITH CREAMED CORN ON THE SIDE!
THE END

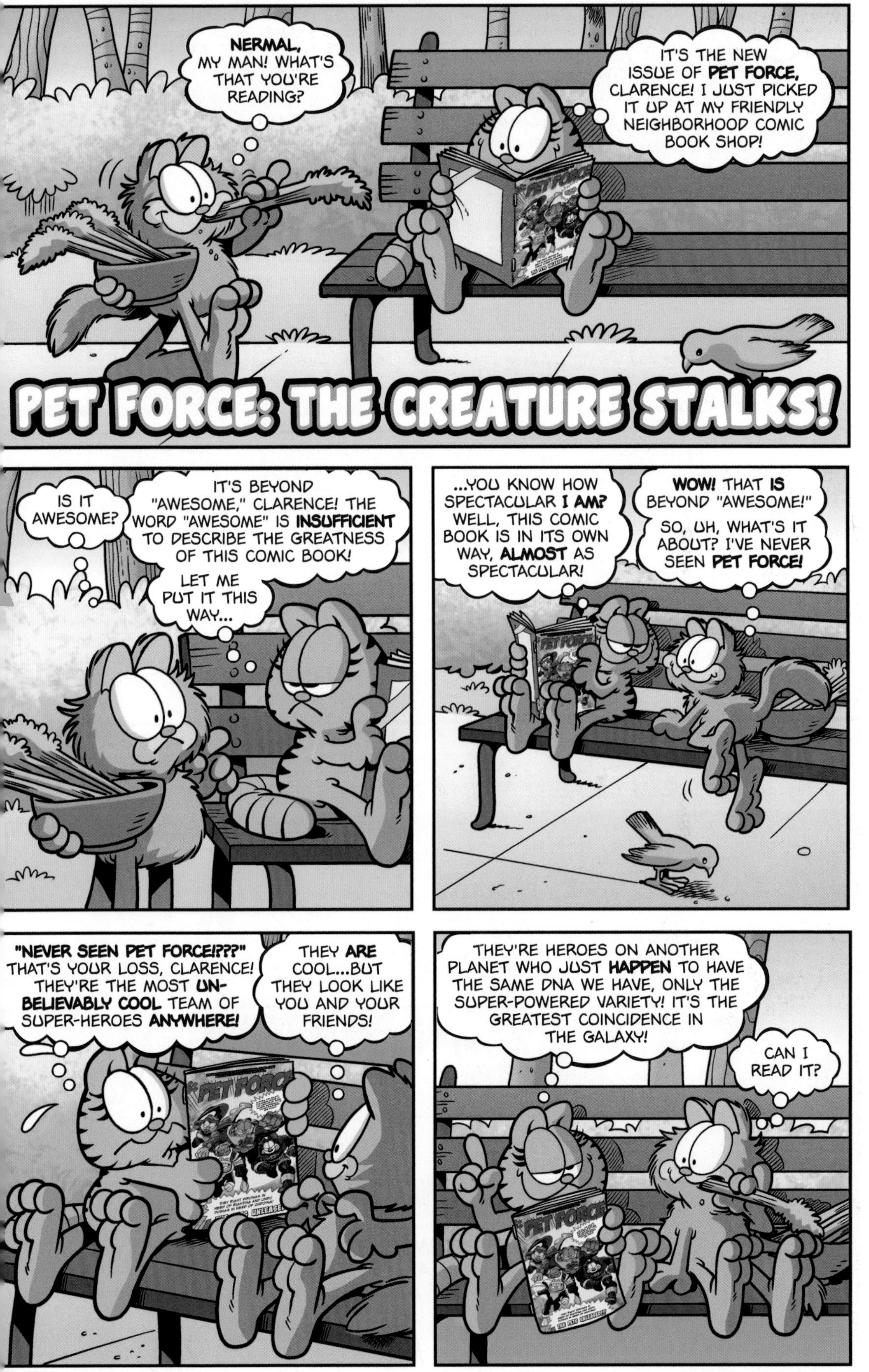
NERMAL, MY MAN! WHAT'S THAT YOU'RE READING?
IT'S THE NEW ISSUE OF PET FORCE, CLARENCE! I JUST PICKED IT UP AT MY FRIENDLY NEIGHBORHOOD COMIC BOOK SHOP!
PET FORCE: THE CREATURE STALKS!
IS IT AWESOME?
IT'S BEYOND "AWESOME," CLARENCE! THE WORD "AWESOME" IS INSUFFICIENT TO DESCRIBE THE GREATNESS OF THIS COMIC BOOK!
LET ME PUT IT THIS WAY...
...YOU KNOW HOW SPECTACULAR I AM? WELL, THIS COMIC BOOK IS IN ITS OWN WAY, ALMOST AS SPECTACULAR!
WOW! THAT IS BEYOND "AWESOME!"
SO, UH, WHAT'S IT ABOUT? I'VE NEVER SEEN PET FORCE!
"NEVER SEEN PET FORCE!???" THAT'S YOUR LOSS, CLARENCE! THEY'RE THE MOST UN-BELIEVABLY COOL TEAM OF SUPER-HEROES ANYWHERE!
THEY ARE COOL...BUT THEY LOOK LIKE YOU AND YOUR FRIENDS!
THEY'RE HEROES ON ANOTHER PLANET WHO JUST HAPPEN TO HAVE THE SAME DNA WE HAVE, ONLY THE SUPER-POWERED VARIETY! IT'S THE GREATEST COINCIDENCE IN THE GALAXY!
CAN I READ IT?

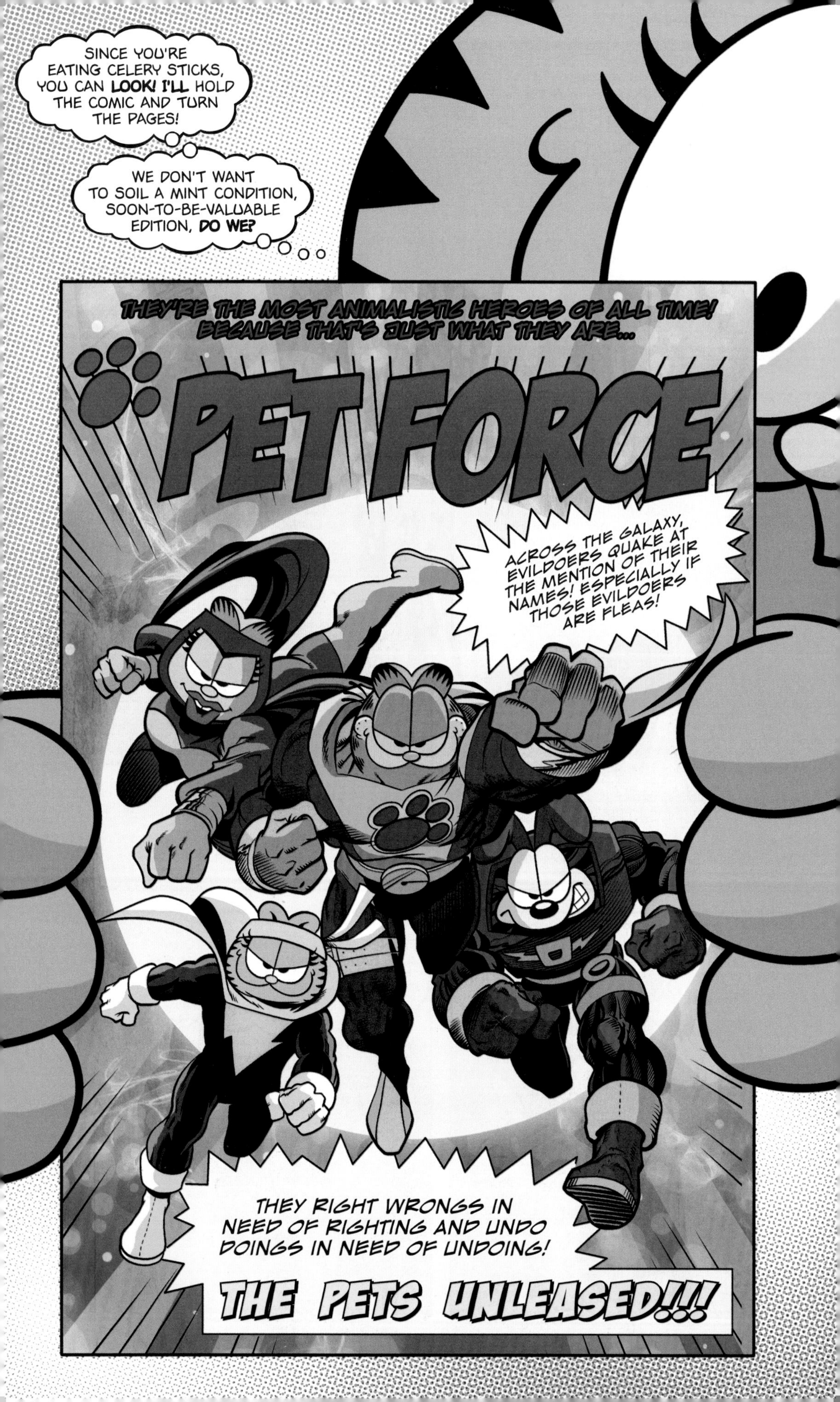

SINCE YOU'RE EATING CELERY STICKS, YOU CAN LOOK! I'LL HOLD THE COMIC AND TURN THE PAGES!
WE DON'T WANT TO SOIL A MINT CONDITION, SOON-TO-BE-VALUABLE EDITION, DO WE?
THEY'RE THE MOST ANIMALISTIC HEROES OF ALL TIME! BECAUSE THAT'S JUST WHAT THEY ARE...
PET FORCE
ACROSS THE GALAXY, EVILDOERS QUAKE AT THE MENTION OF THEIR NAMES! ESPECIALLY IF THOSE EVILDOERS ARE FLEAS!
THEY RIGHT WRONGS IN NEED OF RIGHTING AND UNDO DOINGS IN NEED OF UNDOING!
THE PETS UNLEASED!!!

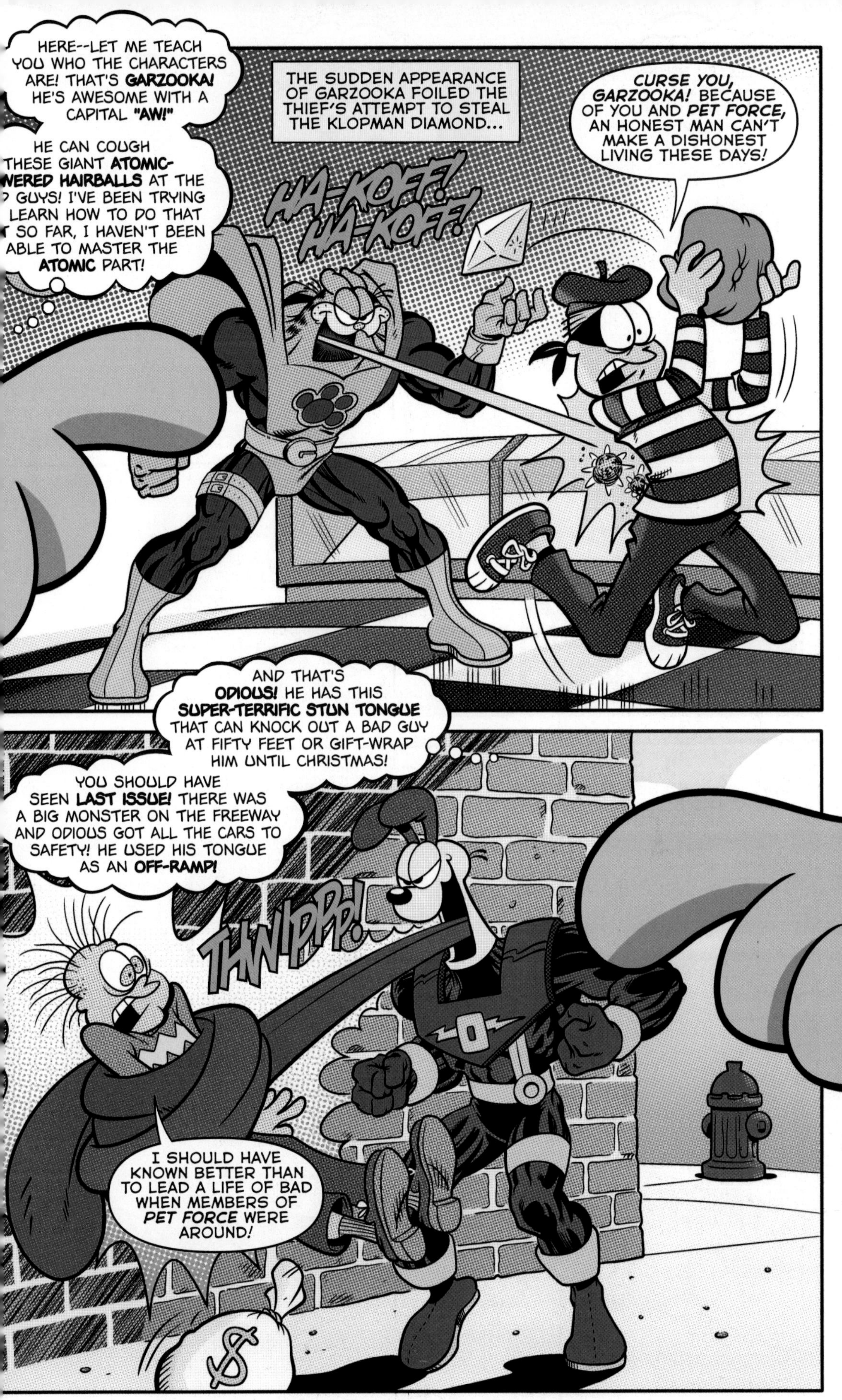

HERE--LET ME TEACH YOU WHO THE CHARACTERS ARE! THAT'S GARZOOKA! HE'S AWESOME WITH A CAPITAL "AW!"
HE CAN COUGH THESE GIANT ATOMIC-WERED HAIRBALLS AT THE GUYS! I'VE BEEN TRYING LEARN HOW TO DO THAT SO FAR, I HAVEN'T BEEN ABLE TO MASTER THE ATOMIC PART!
THE SUDDEN APPEARANCE OF GARZOOKA FOILED THE THIEF'S ATTEMPT TO STEAL THE KLOPMAN DIAMOND...
CURSE YOU, GARZOOKA! BECAUSE OF YOU AND PET FORCE, AN HONEST MAN CAN'T MAKE A DISHONEST LIVING THESE DAYS!
HA-KOFF! HA-KOFF!
AND THAT'S ODIOUS! HE HAS THIS SUPER-TERRIFIC STUN TONGUE THAT CAN KNOCK OUT A BAD GUY AT FIFTY FEET OR GIFT-WRAP HIM UNTIL CHRISTMAS!
YOU SHOULD HAVE SEEN LAST ISSUE! THERE WAS A BIG MONSTER ON THE FREEWAY AND ODIOUS GOT ALL THE CARS TO SAFETY! HE USED HIS TONGUE AS AN OFF-RAMP!
THWIPPP!
I SHOULD HAVE KNOWN BETTER THAN TO LEAD A LIFE OF BAD WHEN MEMBERS OF PET FORCE WERE AROUND!

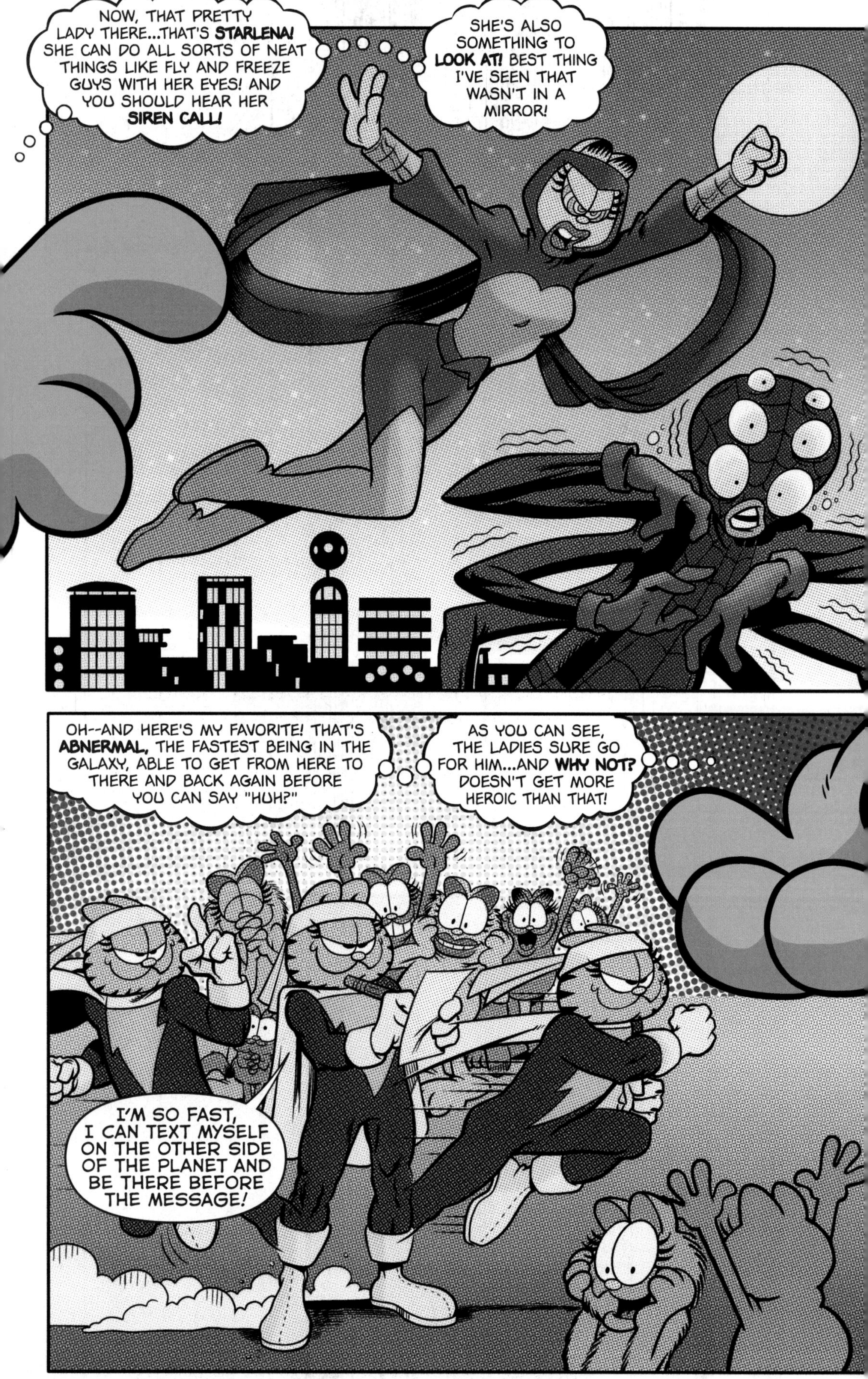
NOW, THAT PRETTY LADY THERE...THAT'S STARLENA! SHE CAN DO ALL SORTS OF NEAT THINGS LIKE FLY AND FREEZE GUYS WITH HER EYES! AND YOU SHOULD HEAR HER SIREN CALL!
SHE'S ALSO SOMETHING TO LOOK AT! BEST THING I'VE SEEN THAT WASN'T IN A MIRROR!
OH--AND HERE'S MY FAVORITE! THAT'S ABNERMAL, THE FASTEST BEING IN THE GALAXY, ABLE TO GET FROM HERE TO THERE AND BACK AGAIN BEFORE YOU CAN SAY "HUH?"
AS YOU CAN SEE, THE LADIES SURE GO FOR HIM...AND WHY NOT? DOESN'T GET MORE HEROIC THAN THAT!
I'M SO FAST, I CAN TEXT MYSELF ON THE OTHER SIDE OF THE PLANET AND BE THERE BEFORE THE MESSAGE!

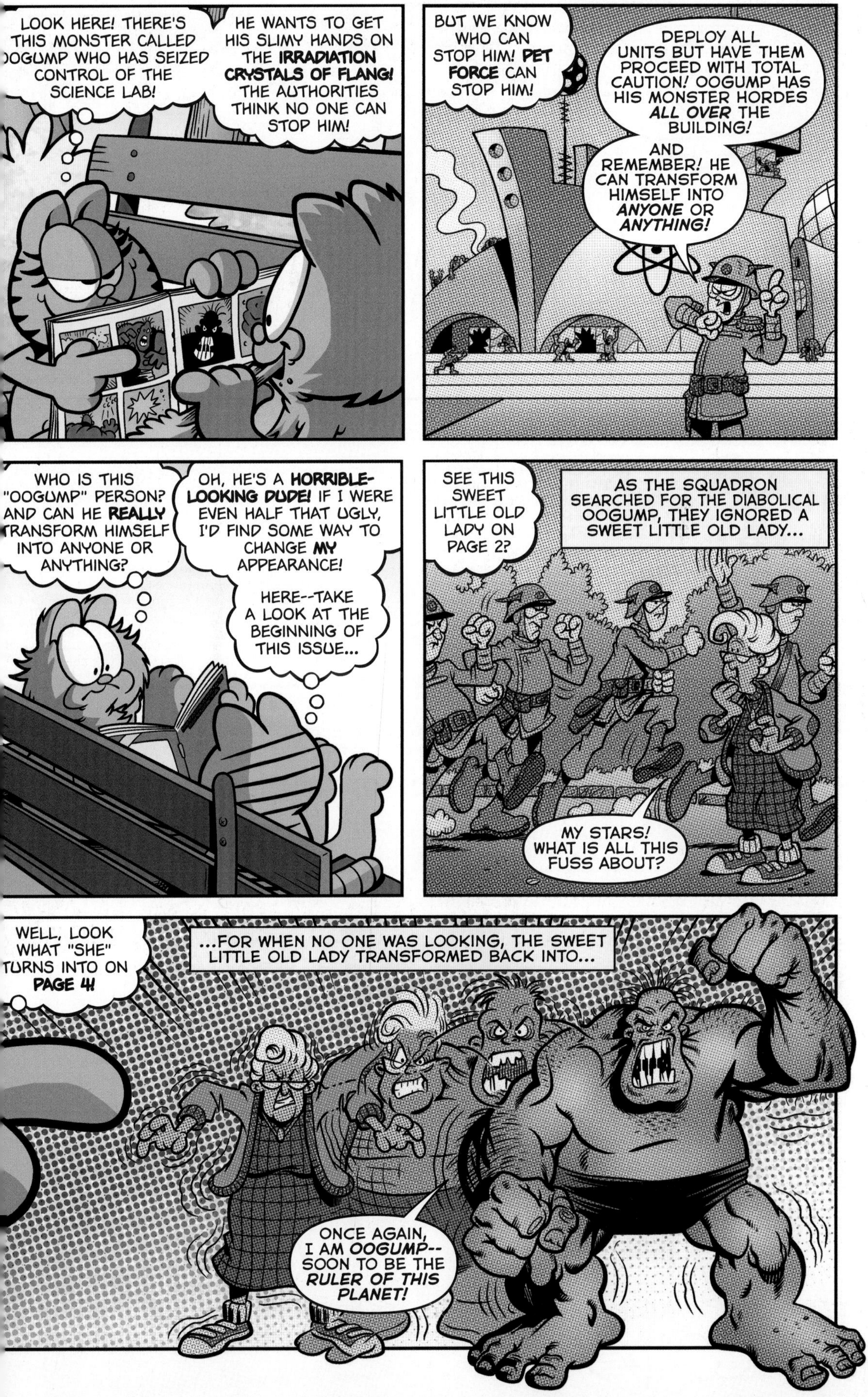
LOOK HERE! THERE'S THIS MONSTER CALLED OOGUMP WHO HAS SEIZED CONTROL OF THE SCIENCE LAB!
HE WANTS TO GET HIS SLIMY HANDS ON THE IRRADIATION CRYSTALS OF FLANG! THE AUTHORITIES THINK NO ONE CAN STOP HIM!
BUT WE KNOW WHO CAN STOP HIM! PET FORCE CAN STOP HIM!
DEPLOY ALL UNITS BUT HAVE THEM PROCEED WITH TOTAL CAUTION! OOGUMP HAS HIS MONSTER HORDES ALL OVER THE BUILDING!
AND REMEMBER! HE CAN TRANSFORM HIMSELF INTO ANYONE OR ANYTHING!
WHO IS THIS "OOGUMP" PERSON? AND CAN HE REALLY TRANSFORM HIMSELF INTO ANYONE OR ANYTHING?
OH, HE'S A HORRIBLE-LOOKING DUDE! IF I WERE EVEN HALF THAT UGLY, I'D FIND SOME WAY TO CHANGE MY APPEARANCE!
HERE--TAKE A LOOK AT THE BEGINNING OF THIS ISSUE...
SEE THIS SWEET LITTLE OLD LADY ON PAGE 2?
AS THE SQUADRON SEARCHED FOR THE DIABOLICAL OOGUMP, THEY IGNORED A SWEET LITTLE OLD LADY...
MY STARS! WHAT IS ALL THIS FUSS ABOUT?
WELL, LOOK WHAT "SHE" TURNS INTO ON PAGE 4!
...FOR WHEN NO ONE WAS LOOKING, THE SWEET LITTLE OLD LADY TRANSFORMED BACK INTO...
ONCE AGAIN, I AM OOGUMP-- SOON TO BE THE RULER OF THIS PLANET!

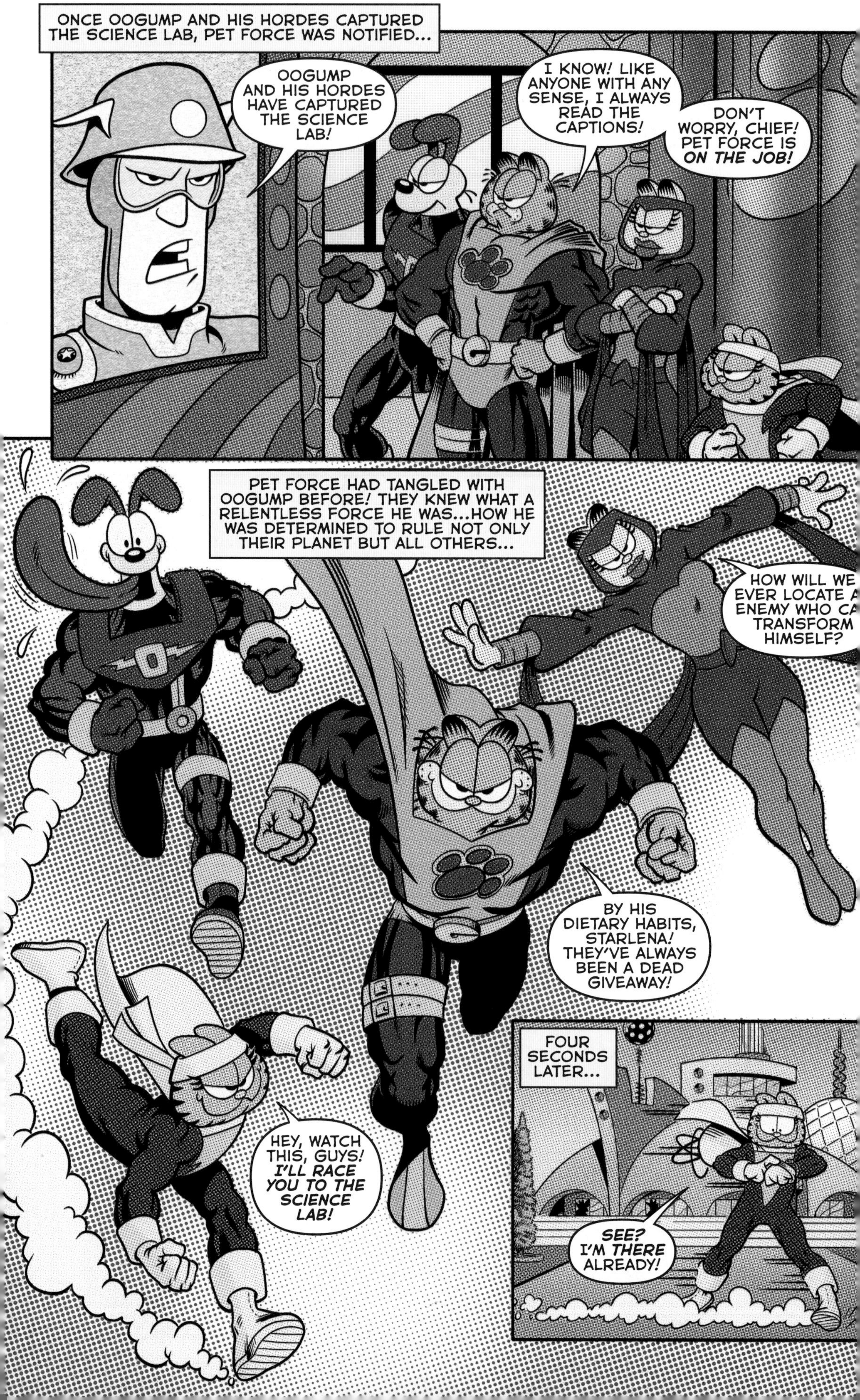
ONCE OOGUMP AND HIS HORDES CAPTURED THE SCIENCE LAB, PET FORCE WAS NOTIFIED...
OOGUMP AND HIS HORDES HAVE CAPTURED THE SCIENCE LAB!
I KNOW! LIKE ANYONE WITH ANY SENSE, I ALWAYS READ THE CAPTIONS!
DON'T WORRY, CHIEF! PET FORCE IS ON THE JOB!
PET FORCE HAD TANGLED WITH OOGUMP BEFORE! THEY KNEW WHAT A RELENTLESS FORCE HE WAS...HOW HE WAS DETERMINED TO RULE NOT ONLY THEIR PLANET BUT ALL OTHERS...
HOW WILL WE EVER LOCATE A ENEMY WHO CA TRANSFORM HIMSELF?
BY HIS DIETARY HABITS, STARLENA! THEY'VE ALWAYS BEEN A DEAD GIVEAWAY!
HEY, WATCH THIS, GUYS! I'LL RACE YOU TO THE SCIENCE LAB!
FOUR SECONDS LATER...
SEE? I'M THERE ALREADY!

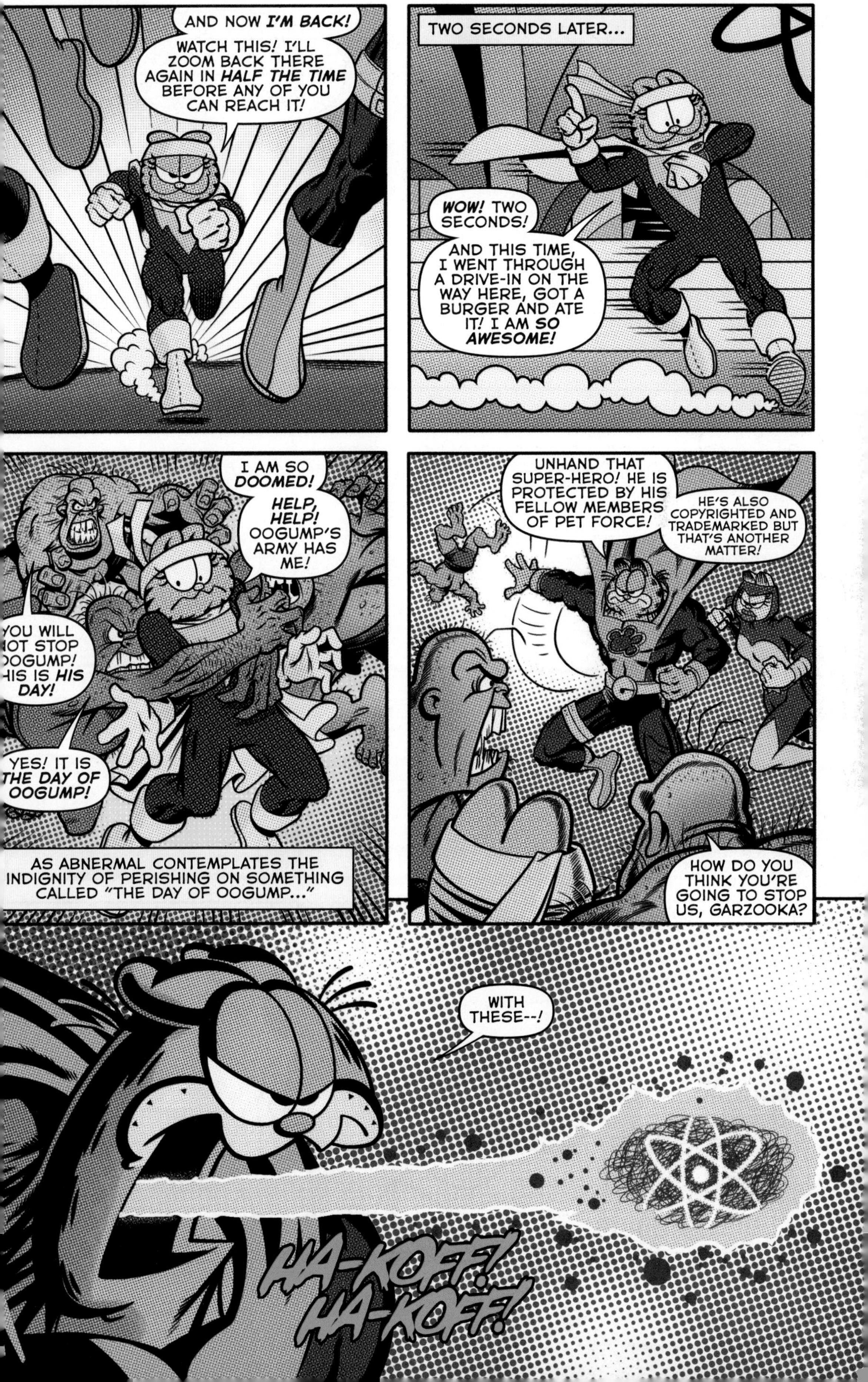
AND NOW I'M BACK!
WATCH THIS! I'LL ZOOM BACK THERE AGAIN IN HALF THE TIME BEFORE ANY OF YOU CAN REACH IT!
TWO SECONDS LATER...
WOW! TWO SECONDS!
AND THIS TIME, I WENT THROUGH A DRIVE-IN ON THE WAY HERE, GOT A BURGER AND ATE IT! I AM SO AWESOME!
I AM SO DOOMED!
HELP, HELP! OOGUMP'S ARMY HAS ME!
YOU WILL NOT STOP OOGUMP! THIS IS HIS DAY!
YES! IT IS THE DAY OF OOGUMP!
AS ABNERMAL CONTEMPLATES THE INDIGNITY OF PERISHING ON SOMETHING CALLED "THE DAY OF OOGUMP..."
UNHAND THAT SUPER-HERO! HE IS PROTECTED BY HIS FELLOW MEMBERS OF PET FORCE!
HE'S ALSO COPYRIGHTED AND TRADEMARKED BUT THAT'S ANOTHER MATTER!
HOW DO YOU THINK YOU'RE GOING TO STOP US, GARZOOKA?
WITH THESE--!
HA-KOFF! HA-KOFF!

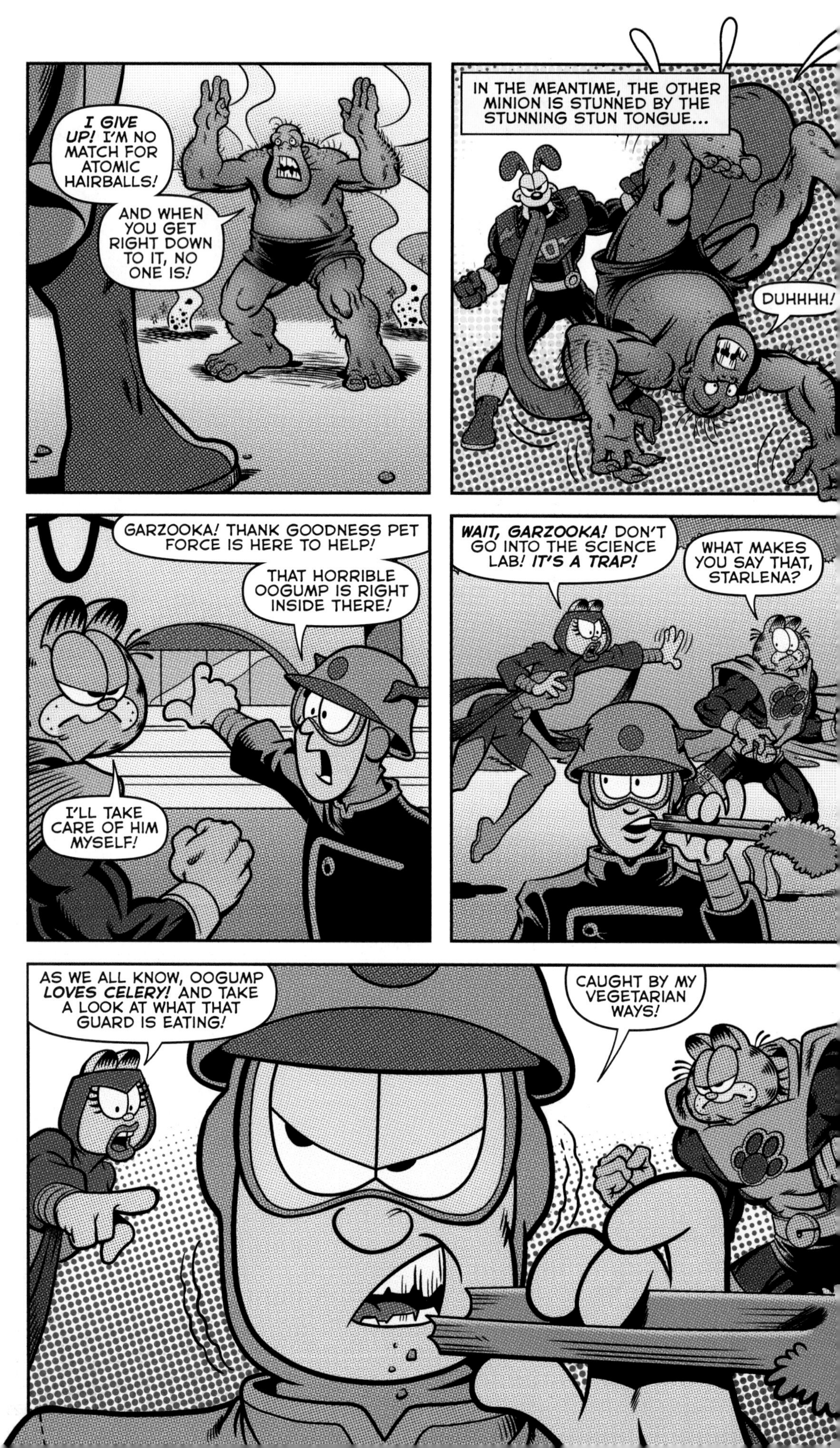
I GIVE UP! I'M NO MATCH FOR ATOMIC HAIRBALLS!
AND WHEN YOU GET RIGHT DOWN TO IT, NO ONE IS!
IN THE MEANTIME, THE OTHER MINION IS STUNNED BY THE STUNNING STUN TONGUE...
DUHHHH!
GARZOOKA! THANK GOODNESS PET FORCE IS HERE TO HELP!
THAT HORRIBLE OOGUMP IS RIGHT INSIDE THERE!
I'LL TAKE CARE OF HIM MYSELF!
WAIT, GARZOOKA! DON'T GO INTO THE SCIENCE LAB! IT'S A TRAP!
WHAT MAKES YOU SAY THAT, STARLENA?
AS WE ALL KNOW, OOGUMP LOVES CELERY! AND TAKE A LOOK AT WHAT THAT GUARD IS EATING!
CAUGHT BY MY VEGETARIAN WAYS!

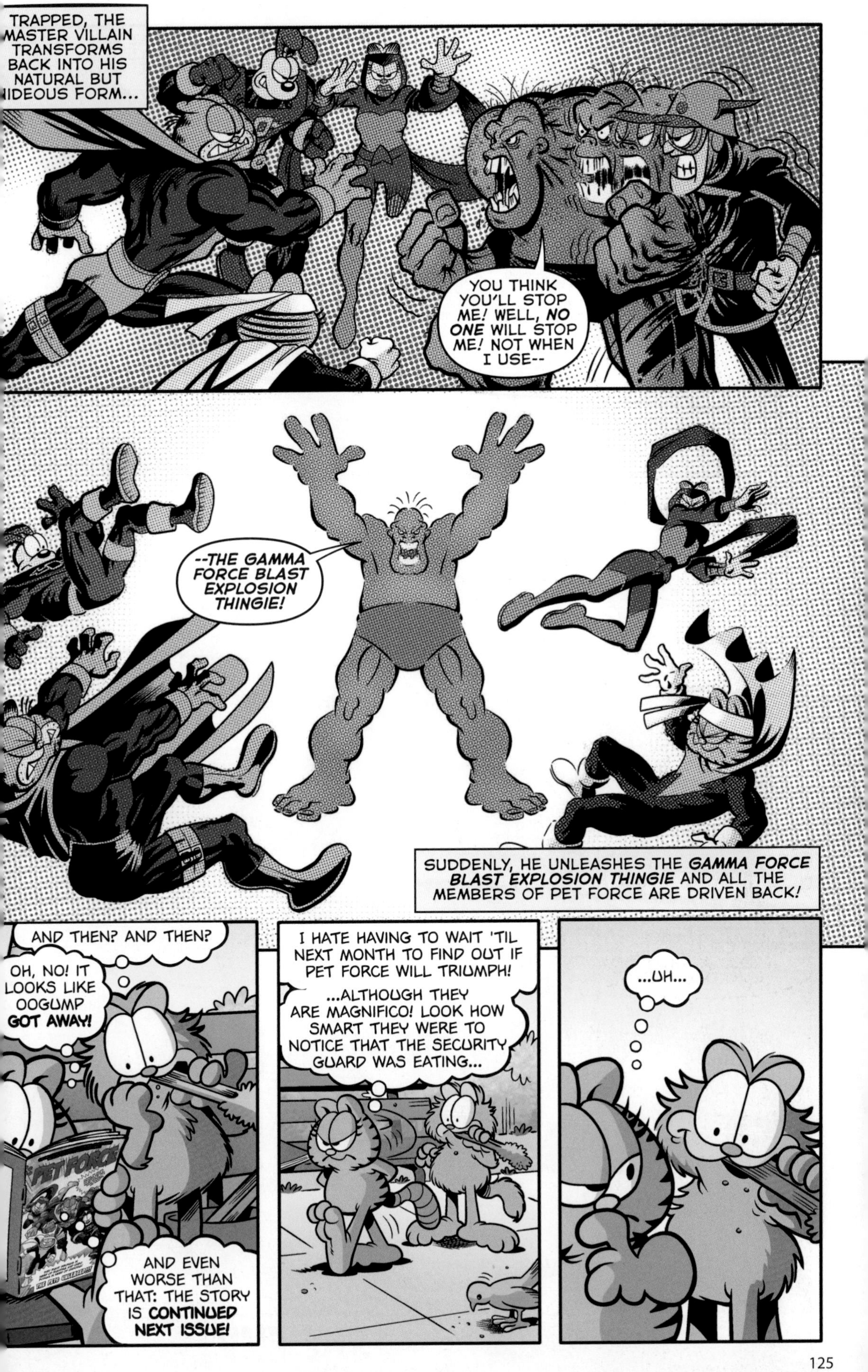

TRAPPED, THE MASTER VILLAIN TRANSFORMS BACK INTO HIS NATURAL BUT HIDEOUS FORM...
YOU THINK YOU'LL STOP ME! WELL, NO ONE WILL STOP ME! NOT WHEN I USE--
--THE GAMMA FORCE BLAST EXPLOSION THINGIE!
SUDDENLY, HE UNLEASHES THE GAMMA FORCE BLAST EXPLOSION THINGIE AND ALL THE MEMBERS OF PET FORCE ARE DRIVEN BACK!
AND THEN? AND THEN?
OH, NO! IT LOOKS LIKE OOGUMP GOT AWAY!
AND EVEN WORSE THAN THAT: THE STORY IS CONTINUED NEXT ISSUE!
I HATE HAVING TO WAIT 'TIL NEXT MONTH TO FIND OUT IF PET FORCE WILL TRIUMPH!
...ALTHOUGH THEY ARE MAGNIFICO! LOOK HOW SMART THEY WERE TO NOTICE THAT THE SECURITY GUARD WAS EATING...
...UH...

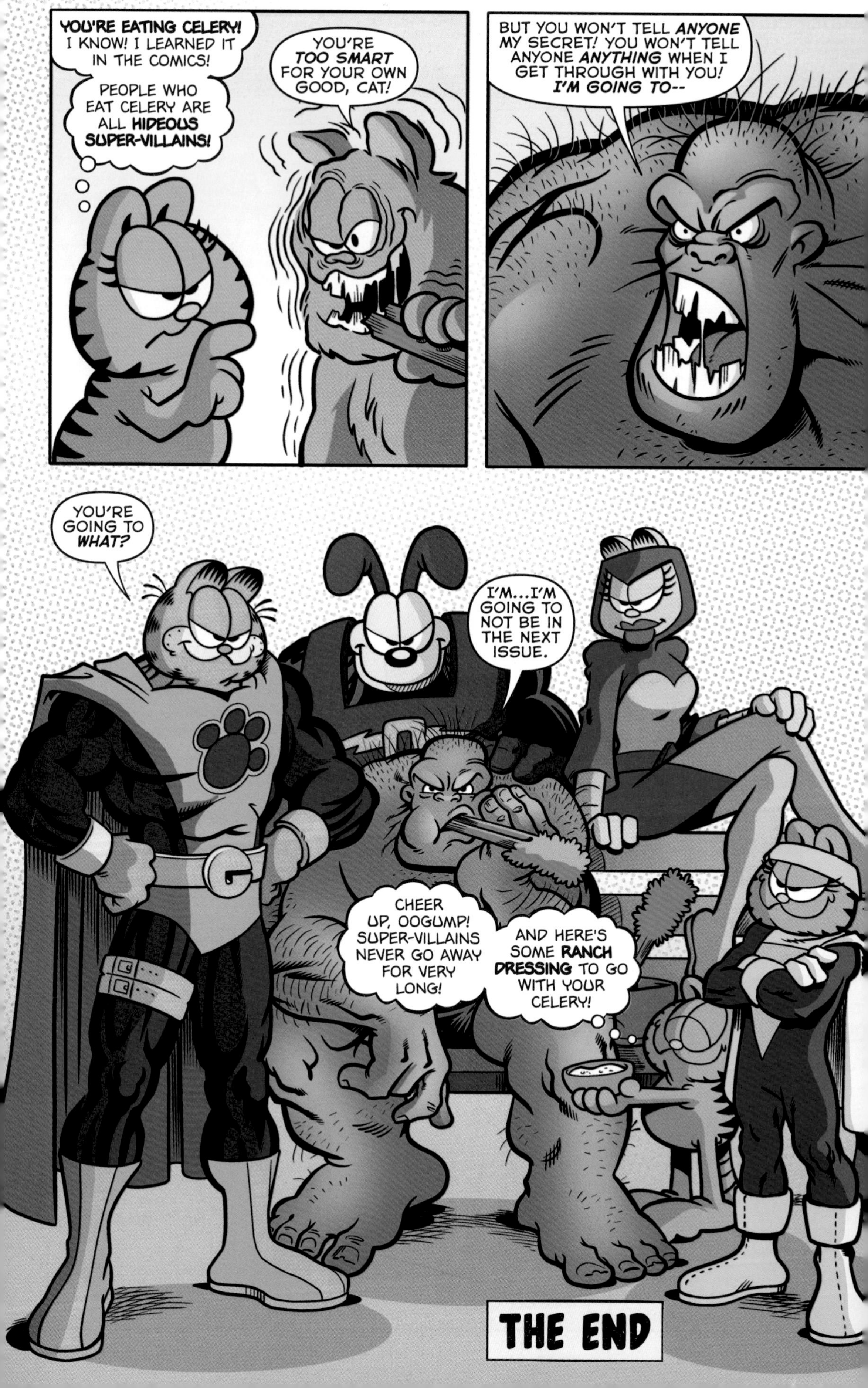

YOU'RE EATING CELERY! I KNOW! I LEARNED IT IN THE COMICS!
PEOPLE WHO EAT CELERY ARE ALL HIDEOUS SUPER-VILLAINS!
YOU'RE TOO SMART FOR YOUR OWN GOOD, CAT!
BUT YOU WON'T TELL ANYONE MY SECRET! YOU WON'T TELL ANYONE ANYTHING WHEN I GET THROUGH WITH YOU! I'M GOING TO--
YOU'RE GOING TO WHAT?
I'M...I'M GOING TO NOT BE IN THE NEXT ISSUE.
CHEER UP, OOGUMP! SUPER-VILLAINS NEVER GO AWAY FOR VERY LONG!
AND HERE'S SOME RANCH DRESSING TO GO WITH YOUR CELERY!
THE END

CHAPTER SIX

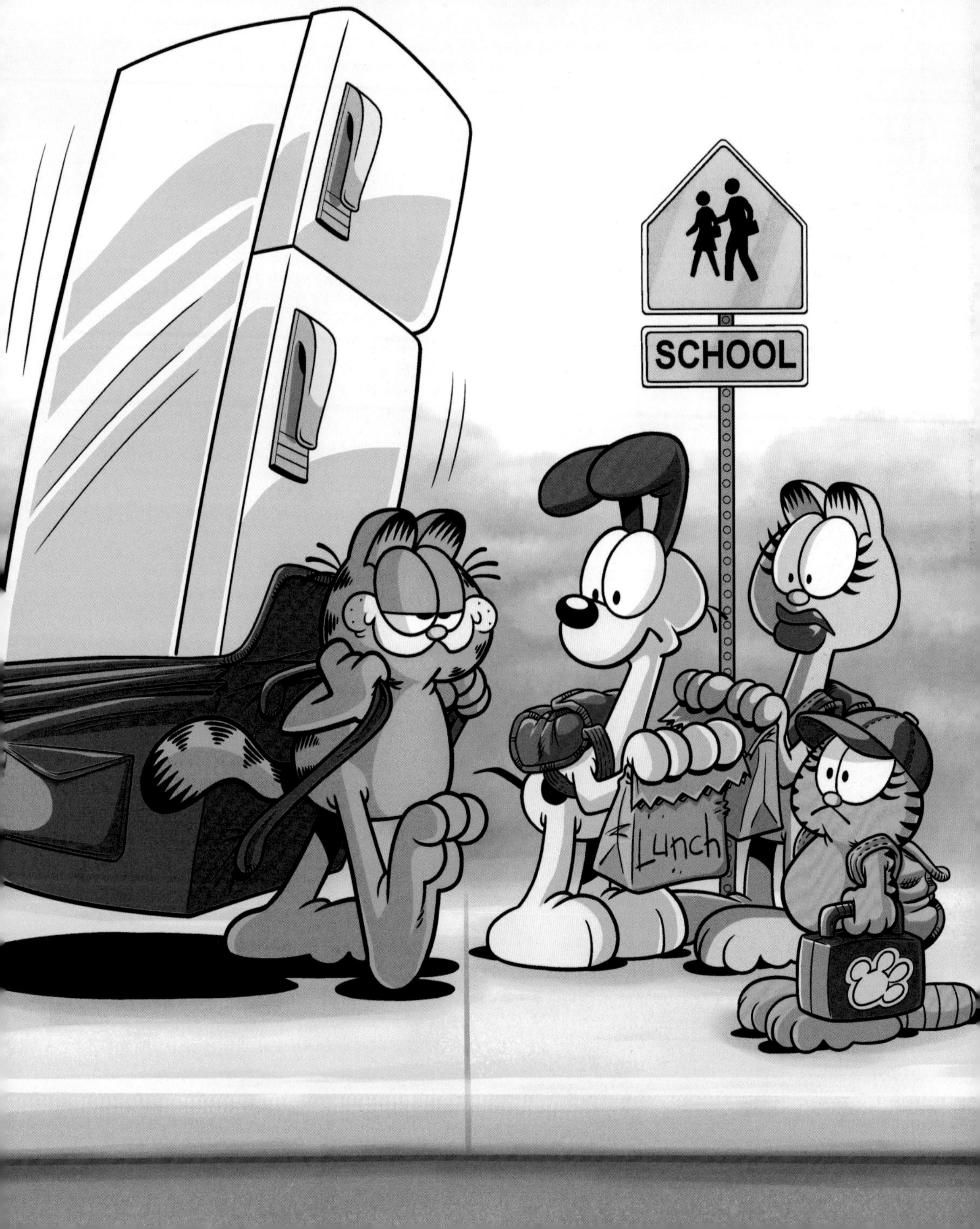

SCHOOL
Lunch

THE PHARAOH'S PET
TRICK OR TREATMENT!

Written by
MARK EVANIER

Art by
MIKE DeCARLO
(Pages 129-140)
GARY BARKER
AND DAN DAVIS
(Pages 141-150)

Colors by
LISA MOORE

Chapter Break Art by
GARY BARKER
AND DAN DAVIS
WITH LISA MOORE

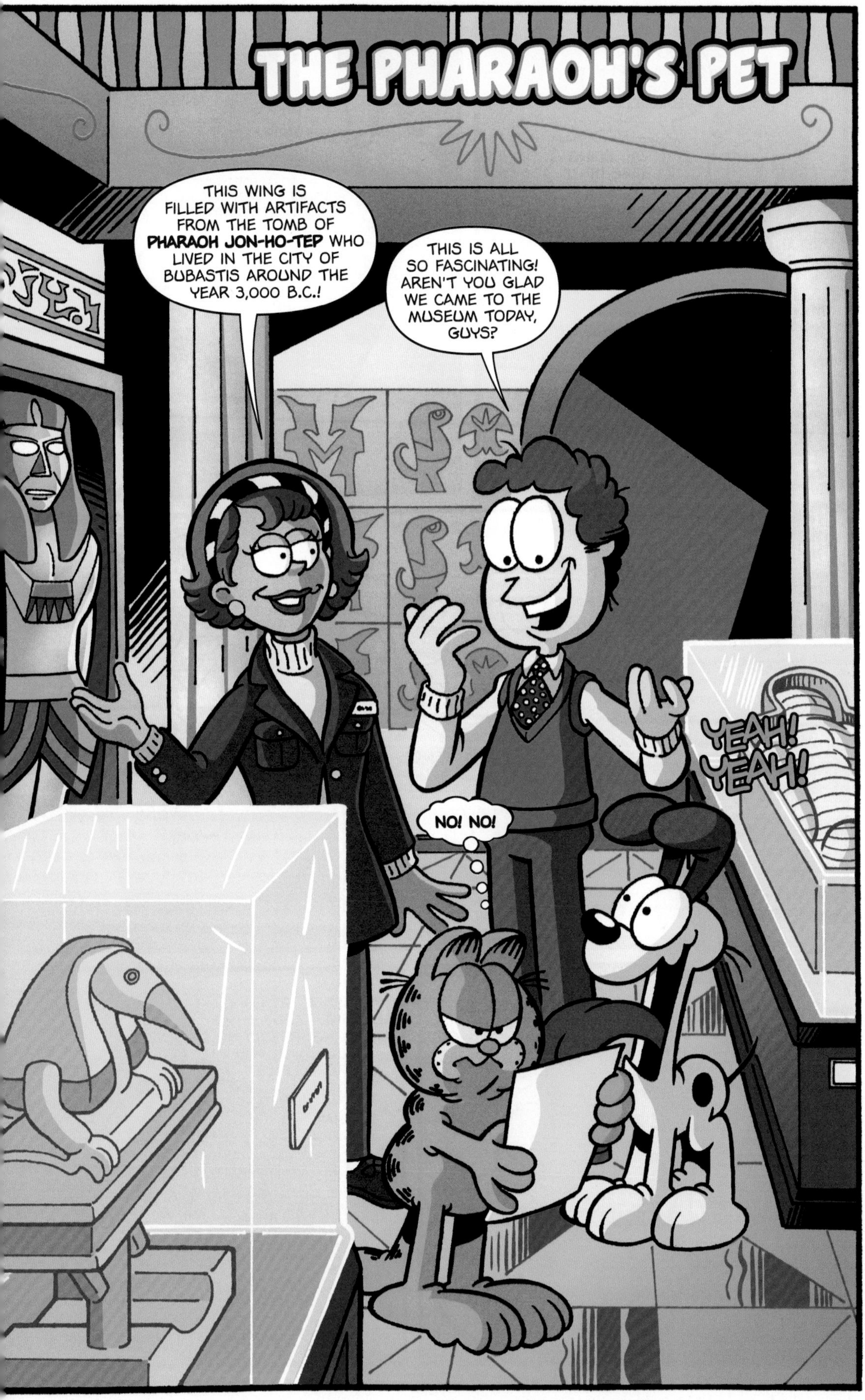
THE PHARAOH'S PET
THIS WING IS FILLED WITH ARTIFACTS FROM THE TOMB OF **PHARAOH JON-HO-TEP** WHO LIVED IN THE CITY OF BUBASTIS AROUND THE YEAR 3,000 B.C.!
THIS IS ALL SO FASCINATING! AREN'T YOU GLAD WE CAME TO THE MUSEUM TODAY, GUYS?
NO! NO!
YEAH! YEAH!

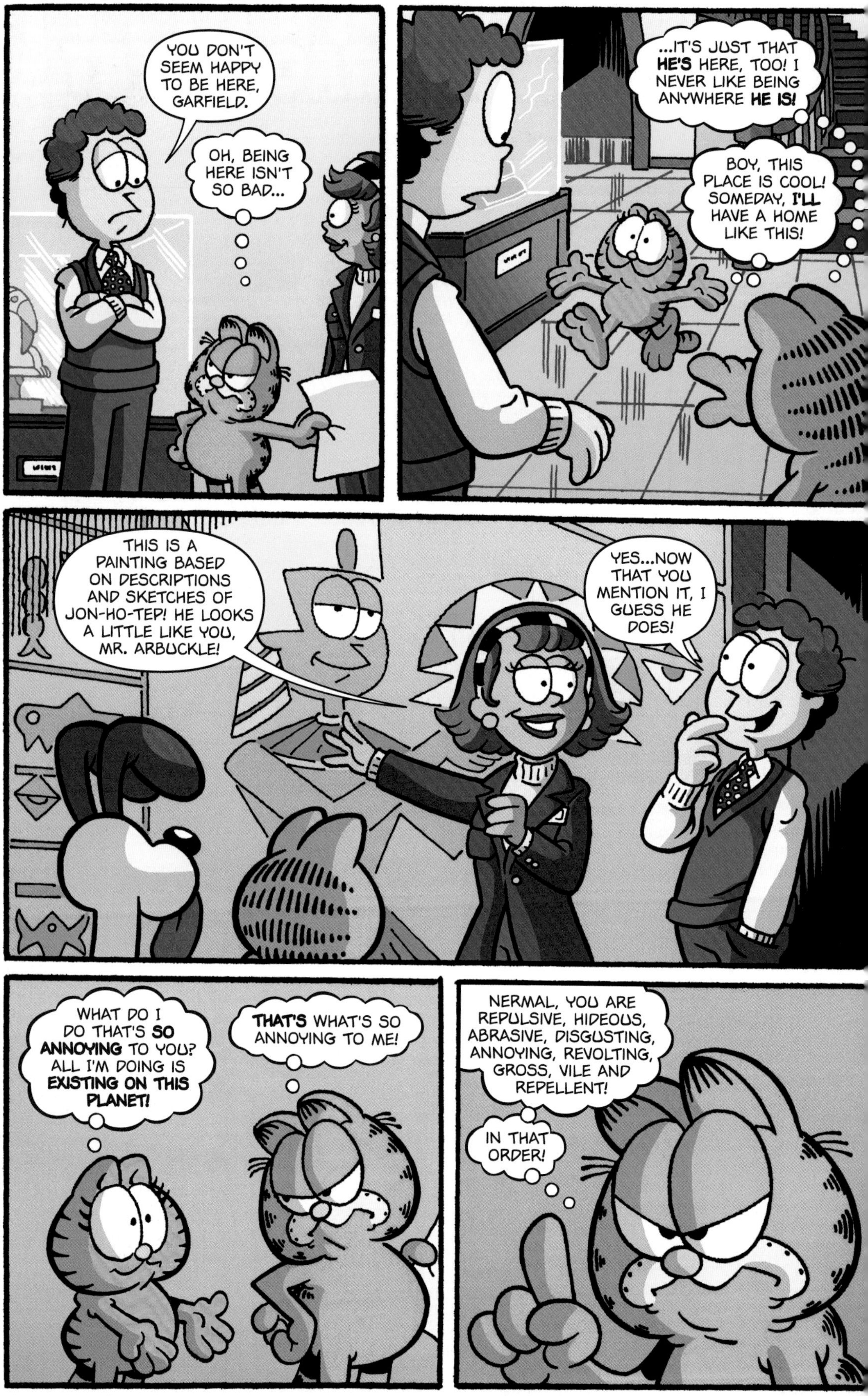
YOU DON'T SEEM HAPPY TO BE HERE, GARFIELD.
OH, BEING HERE ISN'T SO BAD...
...IT'S JUST THAT HE'S HERE, TOO! I NEVER LIKE BEING ANYWHERE HE IS!
BOY, THIS PLACE IS COOL! SOMEDAY, I'LL HAVE A HOME LIKE THIS!
THIS IS A PAINTING BASED ON DESCRIPTIONS AND SKETCHES OF JON-HO-TEP! HE LOOKS A LITTLE LIKE YOU, MR. ARBUCKLE!
YES...NOW THAT YOU MENTION IT, I GUESS HE DOES!
WHAT DO I DO THAT'S SO ANNOYING TO YOU? ALL I'M DOING IS EXISTING ON THIS PLANET!
THAT'S WHAT'S SO ANNOYING TO ME!
NERMAL, YOU ARE REPULSIVE, HIDEOUS, ABRASIVE, DISGUSTING, ANNOYING, REVOLTING, GROSS, VILE AND REPELLENT!
IN THAT ORDER!

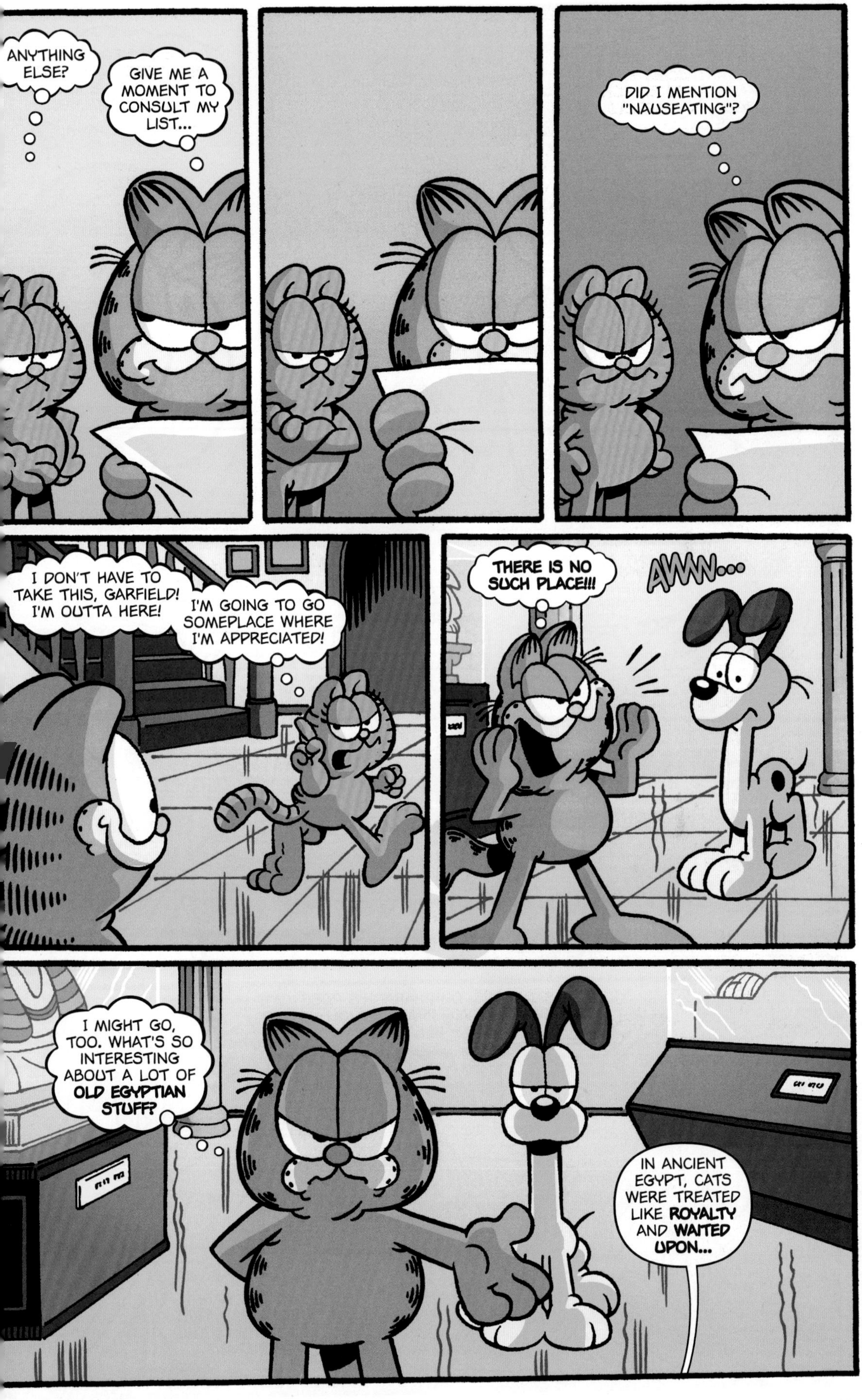

ANYTHING ELSE?
GIVE ME A MOMENT TO CONSULT MY LIST...
DID I MENTION "NAUSEATING"?
I DON'T HAVE TO TAKE THIS, GARFIELD! I'M OUTTA HERE!
I'M GOING TO GO SOMEPLACE WHERE I'M APPRECIATED!
THERE IS NO SUCH PLACE!!!
AWWW...
I MIGHT GO, TOO. WHAT'S SO INTERESTING ABOUT A LOT OF OLD EGYPTIAN STUFF?
IN ANCIENT EGYPT, CATS WERE TREATED LIKE ROYALTY AND WAITED UPON...

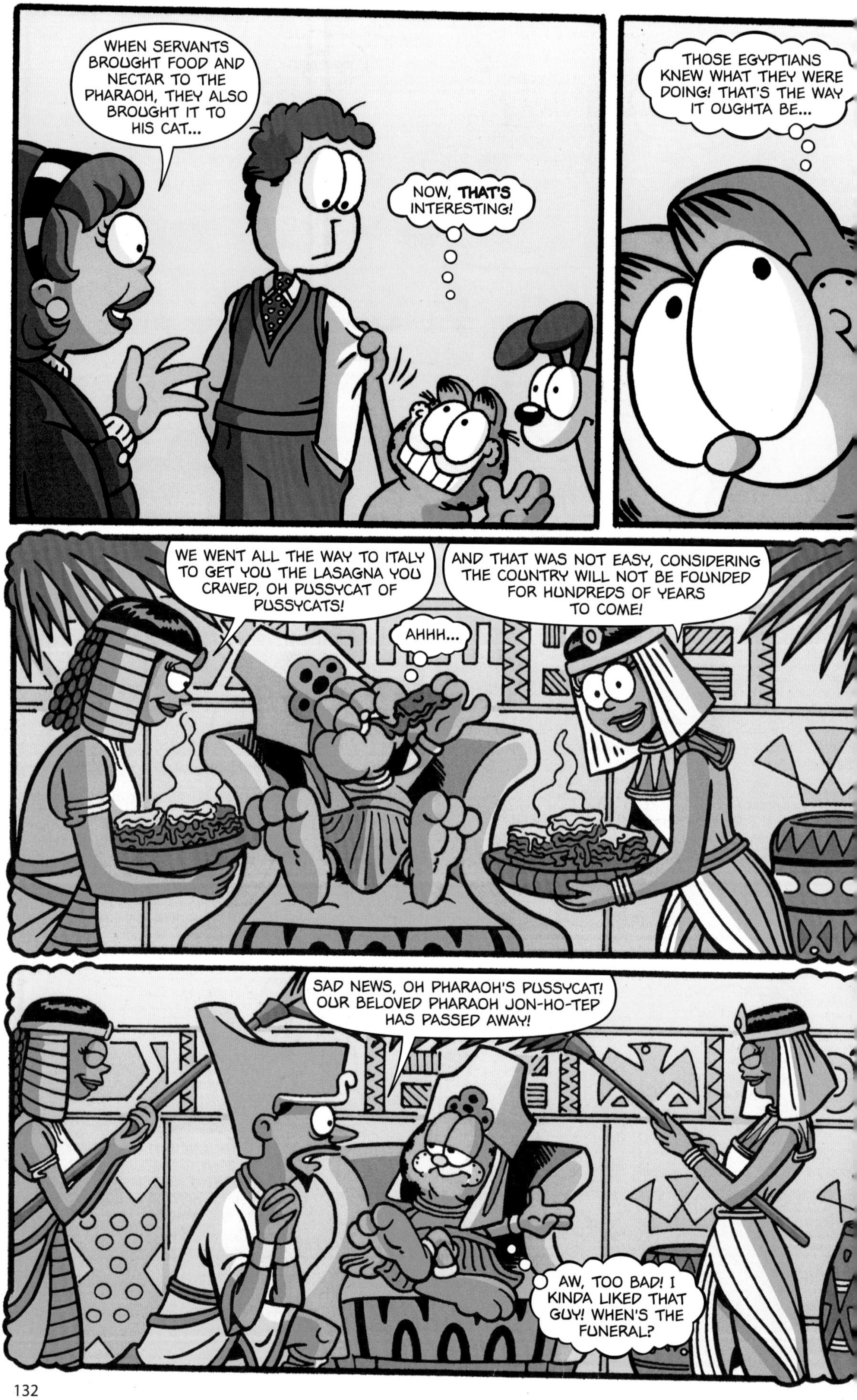

WHEN SERVANTS BROUGHT FOOD AND NECTAR TO THE PHARAOH, THEY ALSO BROUGHT IT TO HIS CAT...
NOW, **THAT'S** INTERESTING!
THOSE EGYPTIANS KNEW WHAT THEY WERE DOING! THAT'S THE WAY IT OUGHTA BE...
WE WENT ALL THE WAY TO ITALY TO GET YOU THE LASAGNA YOU CRAVED, OH PUSSYCAT OF PUSSYCATS!
AHHH...
AND THAT WAS NOT EASY, CONSIDERING THE COUNTRY WILL NOT BE FOUNDED FOR HUNDREDS OF YEARS TO COME!
SAD NEWS, OH PHARAOH'S PUSSYCAT! OUR BELOVED PHARAOH JON-HO-TEP HAS PASSED AWAY!
AW, TOO BAD! I KINDA LIKED THAT GUY! WHEN'S THE FUNERAL?

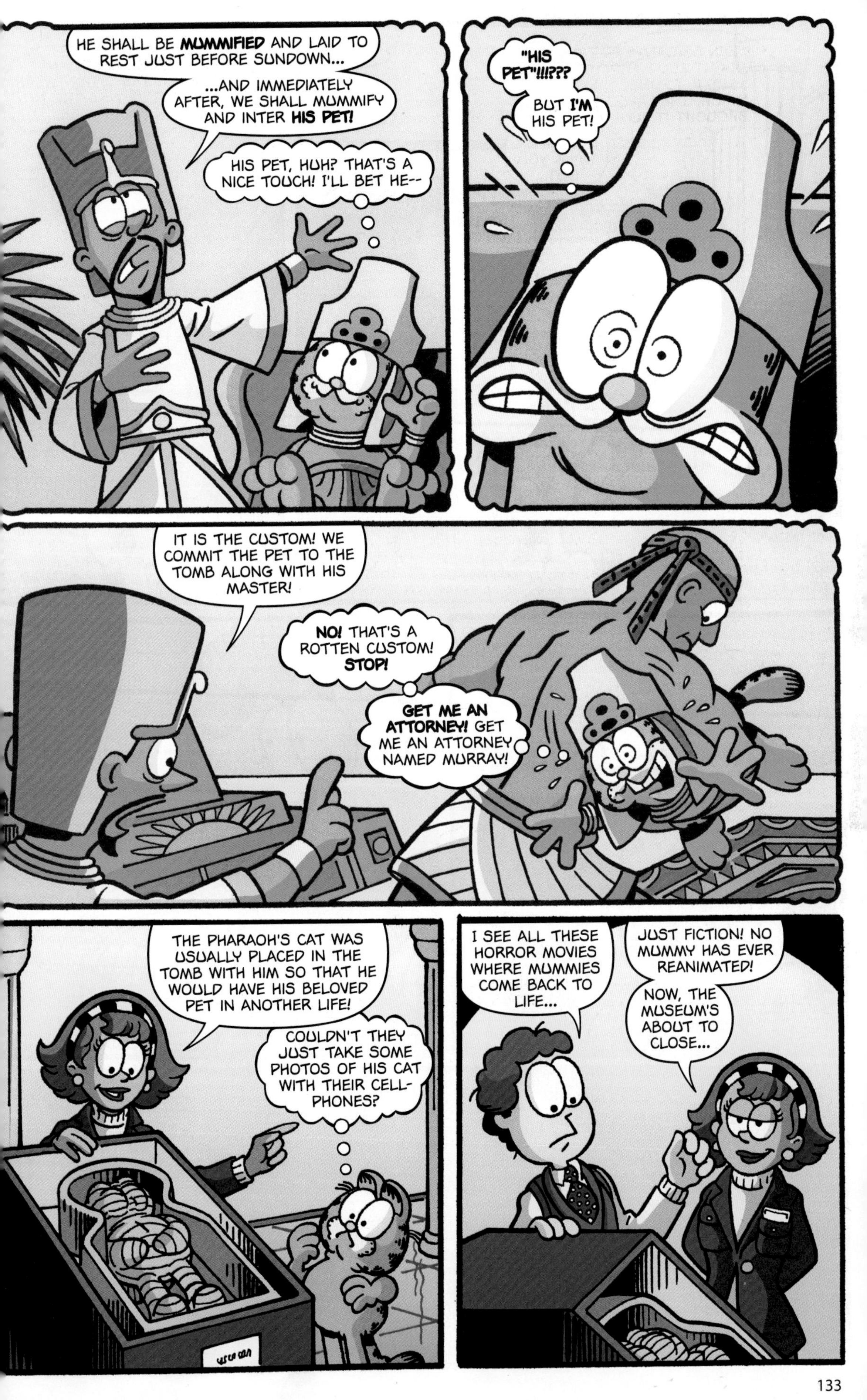
HE SHALL BE MUMMIFIED AND LAID TO REST JUST BEFORE SUNDOWN...
...AND IMMEDIATELY AFTER, WE SHALL MUMMIFY AND INTER HIS PET!
HIS PET, HUH? THAT'S A NICE TOUCH! I'LL BET HE--
"HIS PET"!!!???
BUT I'M HIS PET!
IT IS THE CUSTOM! WE COMMIT THE PET TO THE TOMB ALONG WITH HIS MASTER!
NO! THAT'S A ROTTEN CUSTOM! STOP!
GET ME AN ATTORNEY! GET ME AN ATTORNEY NAMED MURRAY!
THE PHARAOH'S CAT WAS USUALLY PLACED IN THE TOMB WITH HIM SO THAT HE WOULD HAVE HIS BELOVED PET IN ANOTHER LIFE!
COULDN'T THEY JUST TAKE SOME PHOTOS OF HIS CAT WITH THEIR CELL-PHONES?
I SEE ALL THESE HORROR MOVIES WHERE MUMMIES COME BACK TO LIFE...
JUST FICTION! NO MUMMY HAS EVER REANIMATED!
NOW, THE MUSEUM'S ABOUT TO CLOSE...

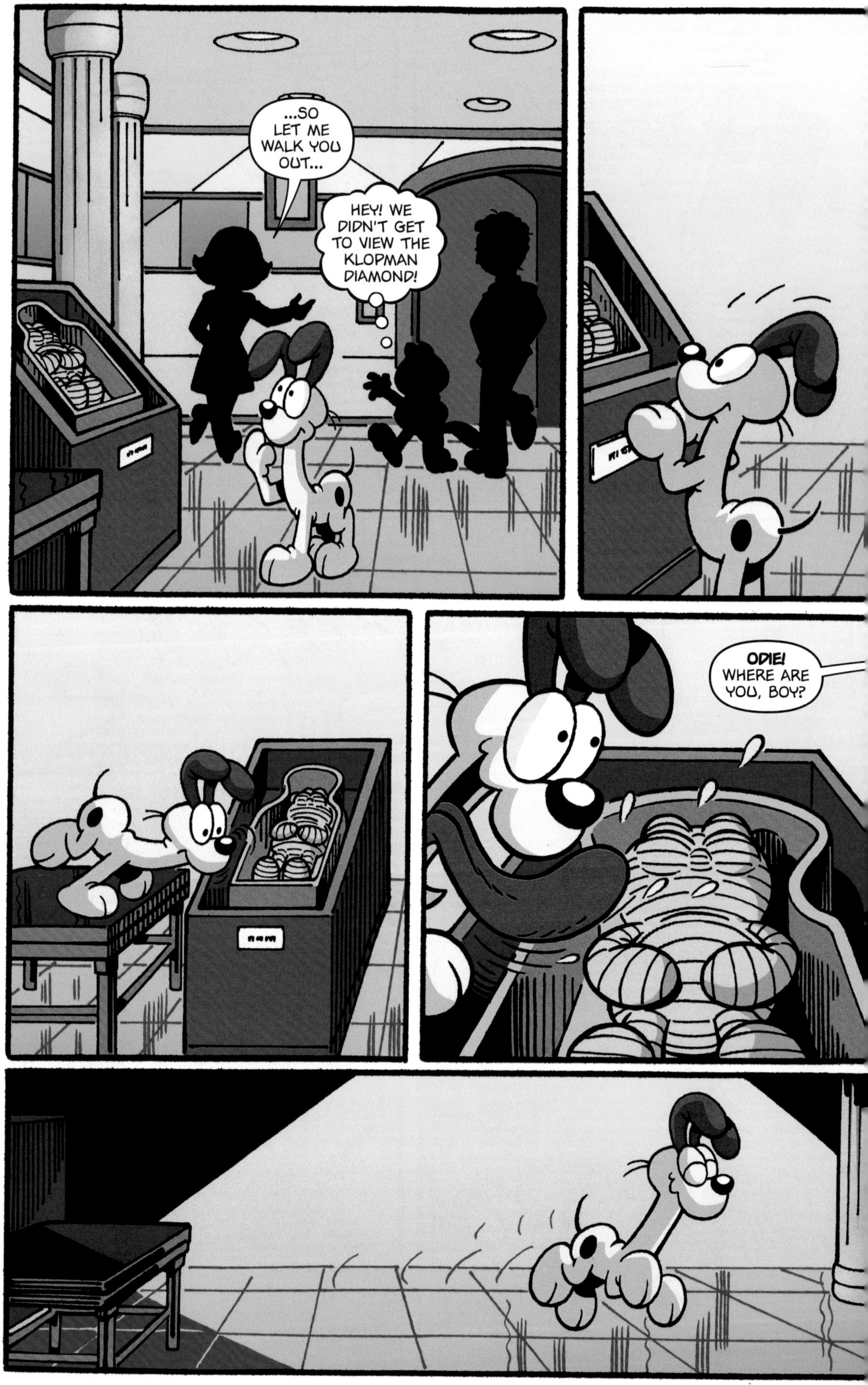
...SO LET ME WALK YOU OUT...
HEY! WE DIDN'T GET TO VIEW THE KLOPMAN DIAMOND!
ODIE! WHERE ARE YOU, BOY?

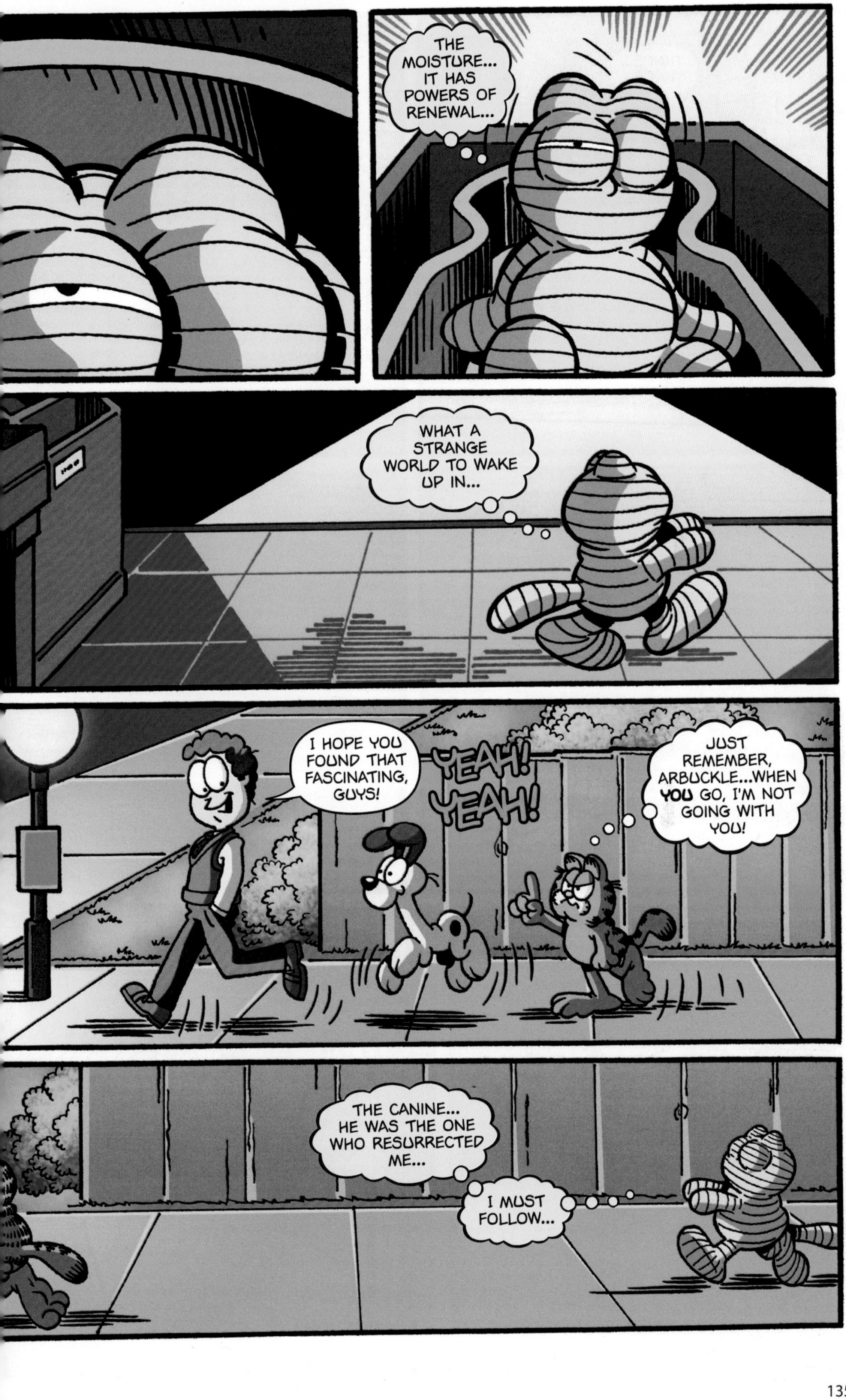

THE MOISTURE... IT HAS POWERS OF RENEWAL...
WHAT A STRANGE WORLD TO WAKE UP IN...
I HOPE YOU FOUND THAT FASCINATING, GUYS!
YEAH! YEAH!
JUST REMEMBER, ARBUCKLE...WHEN YOU GO, I'M NOT GOING WITH YOU!
THE CANINE... HE WAS THE ONE WHO RESURRECTED ME...
I MUST FOLLOW...

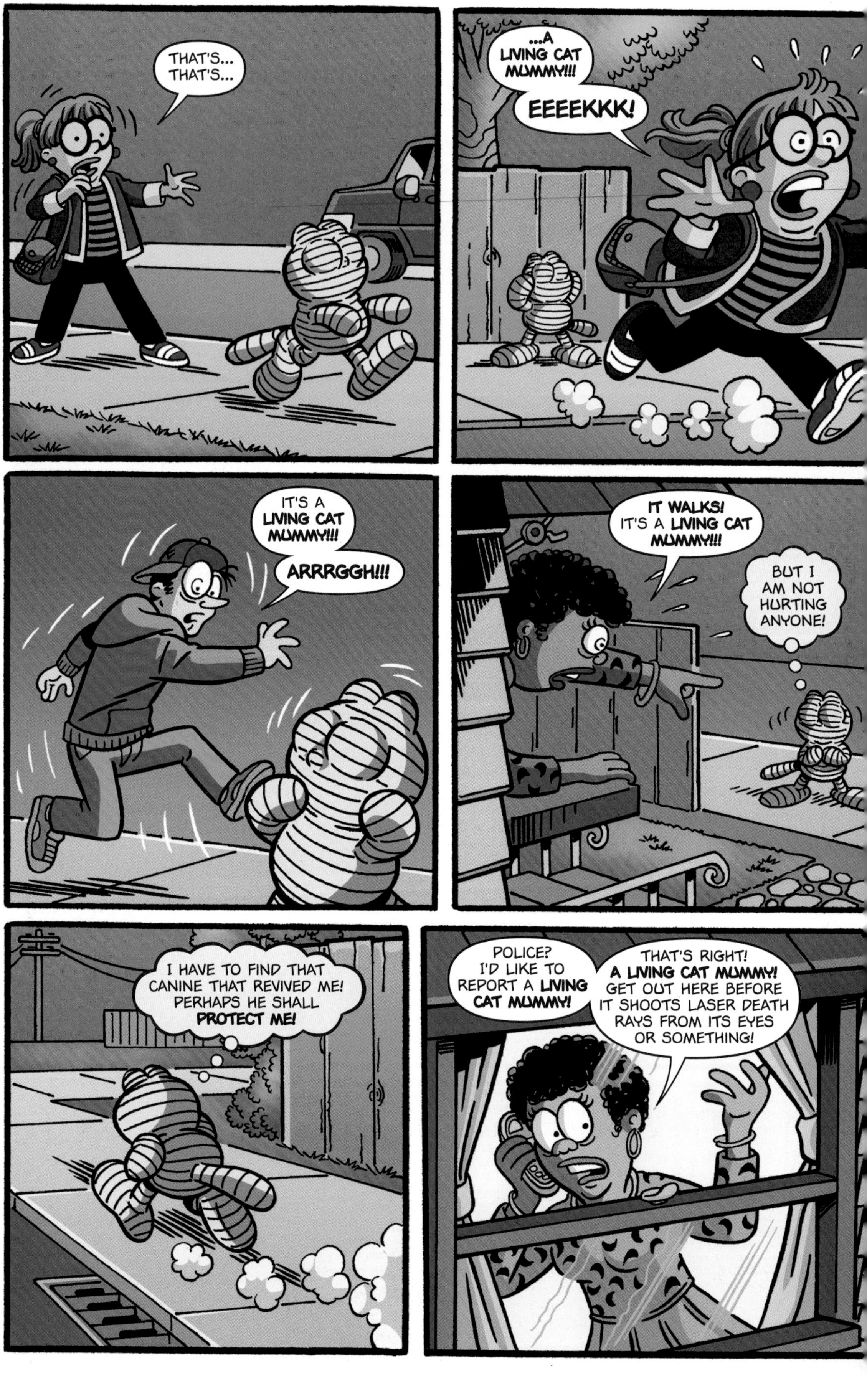

THAT'S... THAT'S...
...A LIVING CAT MUMMY!!!
EEEEKKK!
IT'S A LIVING CAT MUMMY!!!
ARRRGGH!!!
IT WALKS! IT'S A LIVING CAT MUMMY!!!
BUT I AM NOT HURTING ANYONE!
I HAVE TO FIND THAT CANINE THAT REVIVED ME! PERHAPS HE SHALL PROTECT ME!
POLICE? I'D LIKE TO REPORT A LIVING CAT MUMMY!
THAT'S RIGHT! A LIVING CAT MUMMY! GET OUT HERE BEFORE IT SHOOTS LASER DEATH RAYS FROM ITS EYES OR SOMETHING!

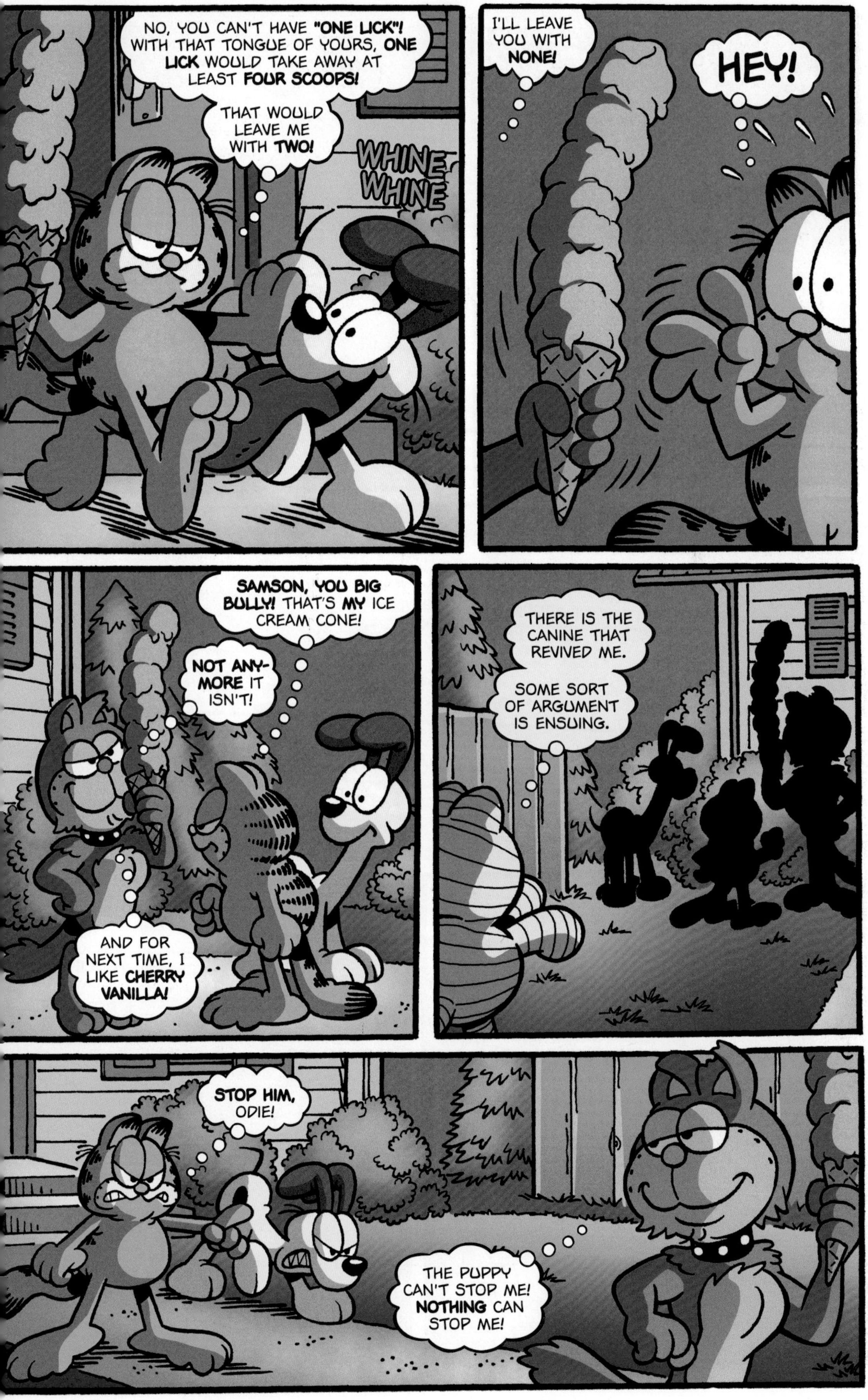
NO, YOU CAN'T HAVE "ONE LICK"! WITH THAT TONGUE OF YOURS, ONE LICK WOULD TAKE AWAY AT LEAST FOUR SCOOPS!
THAT WOULD LEAVE ME WITH TWO!
WHINE WHINE
I'LL LEAVE YOU WITH NONE!
HEY!
SAMSON, YOU BIG BULLY! THAT'S MY ICE CREAM CONE!
NOT ANYMORE IT ISN'T!
AND FOR NEXT TIME, I LIKE CHERRY VANILLA!
THERE IS THE CANINE THAT REVIVED ME.
SOME SORT OF ARGUMENT IS ENSUING.
STOP HIM, ODIE!
THE PUPPY CAN'T STOP ME! NOTHING CAN STOP ME!

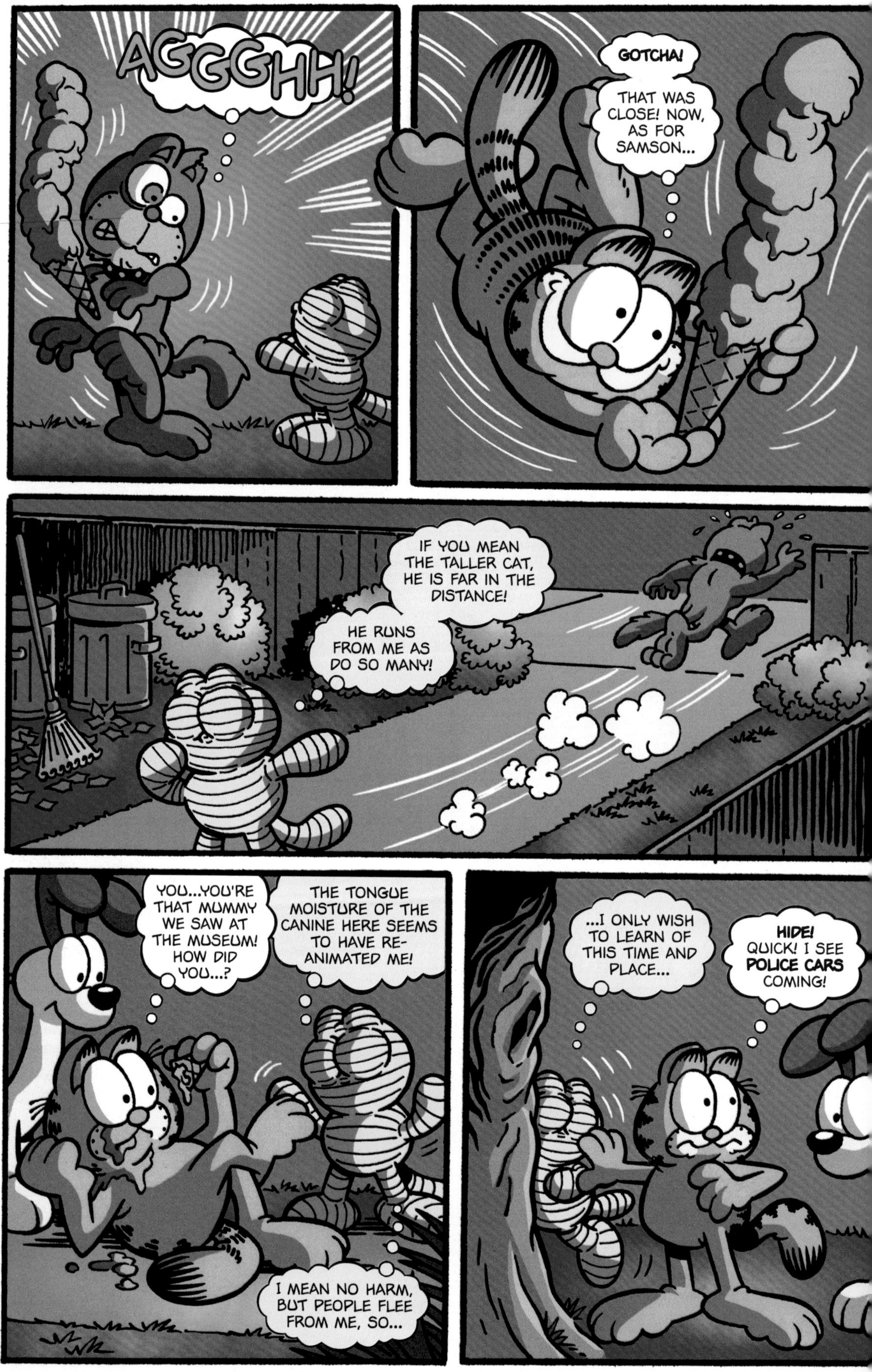
AGGGHH!
GOTCHA!
THAT WAS CLOSE! NOW, AS FOR SAMSON...
IF YOU MEAN THE TALLER CAT, HE IS FAR IN THE DISTANCE!
HE RUNS FROM ME AS DO SO MANY!
YOU...YOU'RE THAT MUMMY WE SAW AT THE MUSEUM! HOW DID YOU...?
THE TONGUE MOISTURE OF THE CANINE HERE SEEMS TO HAVE RE-ANIMATED ME!
I MEAN NO HARM, BUT PEOPLE FLEE FROM ME, SO...
...I ONLY WISH TO LEARN OF THIS TIME AND PLACE...
HIDE! QUICK! I SEE POLICE CARS COMING!

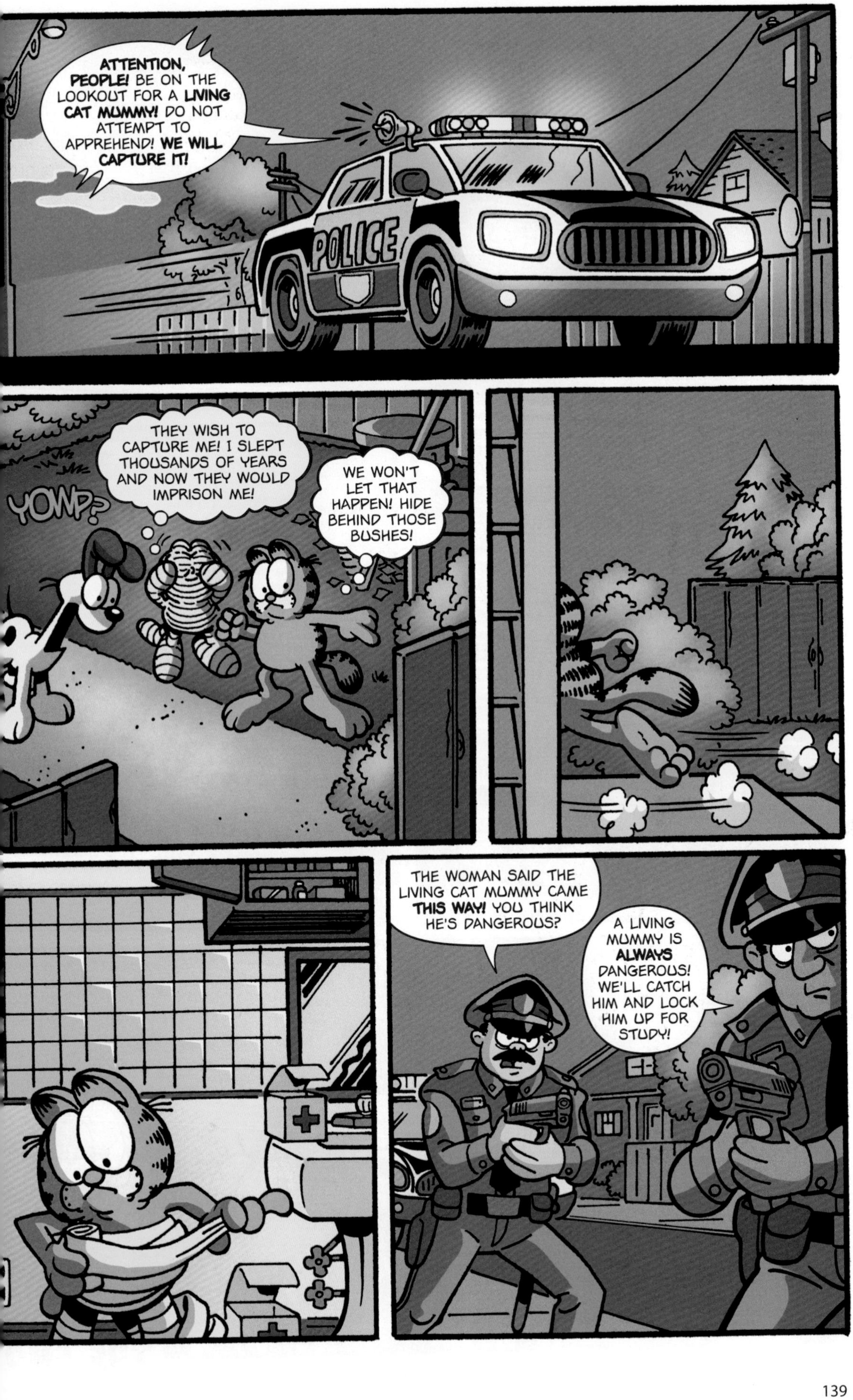

ATTENTION, PEOPLE! BE ON THE LOOKOUT FOR A LIVING CAT MUMMY! DO NOT ATTEMPT TO APPREHEND! WE WILL CAPTURE IT!
POLICE
THEY WISH TO CAPTURE ME! I SLEPT THOUSANDS OF YEARS AND NOW THEY WOULD IMPRISON ME!
YOWP?
WE WON'T LET THAT HAPPEN! HIDE BEHIND THOSE BUSHES!
THE WOMAN SAID THE LIVING CAT MUMMY CAME THIS WAY! YOU THINK HE'S DANGEROUS?
A LIVING MUMMY IS ALWAYS DANGEROUS! WE'LL CATCH HIM AND LOCK HIM UP FOR STUDY!

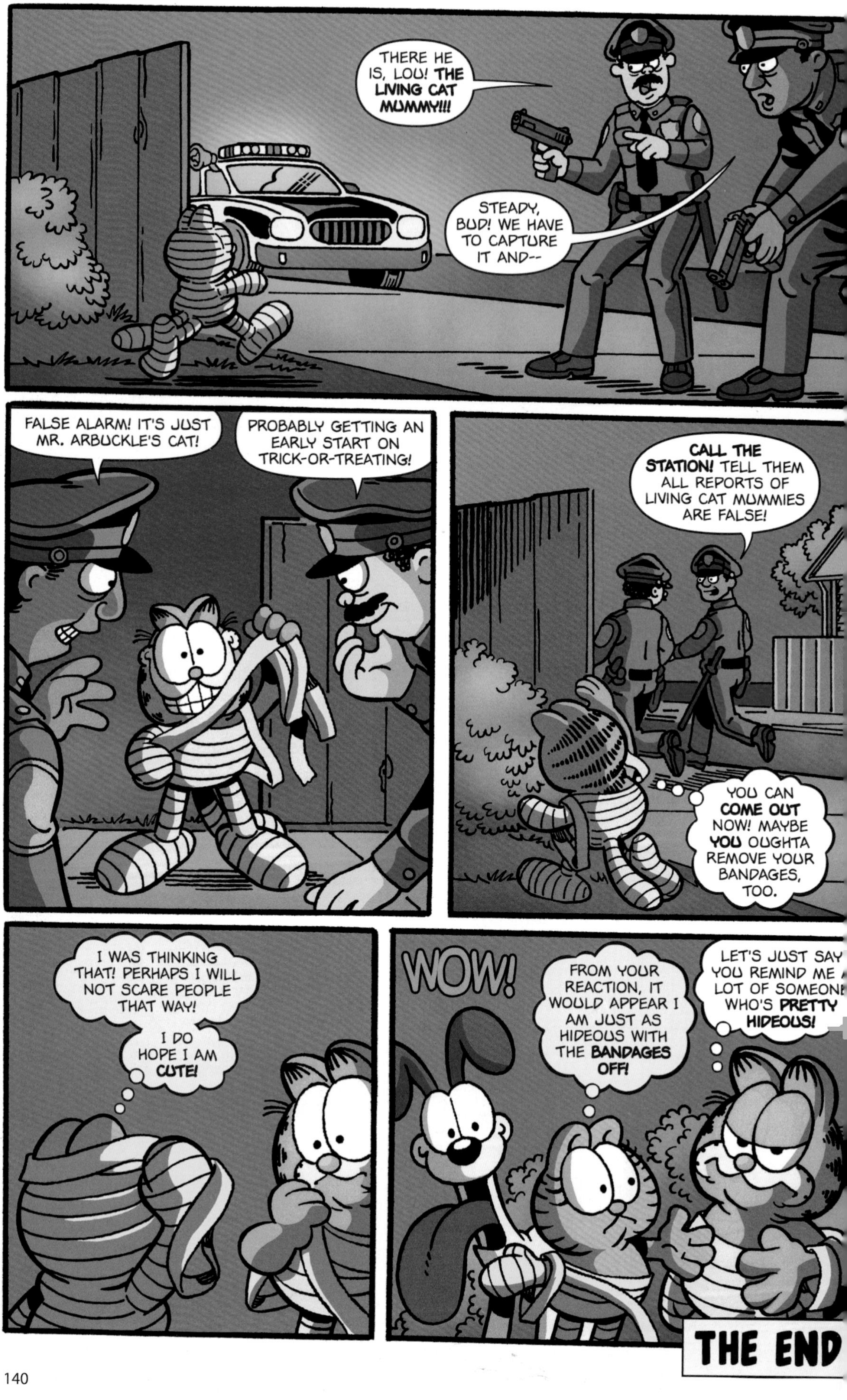
THERE HE IS, LOU! THE LIVING CAT MUMMY!!!
STEADY, BUD! WE HAVE TO CAPTURE IT AND--
FALSE ALARM! IT'S JUST MR. ARBUCKLE'S CAT!
PROBABLY GETTING AN EARLY START ON TRICK-OR-TREATING!
CALL THE STATION! TELL THEM ALL REPORTS OF LIVING CAT MUMMIES ARE FALSE!
YOU CAN COME OUT NOW! MAYBE YOU OUGHTA REMOVE YOUR BANDAGES, TOO.
I WAS THINKING THAT! PERHAPS I WILL NOT SCARE PEOPLE THAT WAY!
I DO HOPE I AM CUTE!
WOW!
FROM YOUR REACTION, IT WOULD APPEAR I AM JUST AS HIDEOUS WITH THE BANDAGES OFF!
LET'S JUST SAY YOU REMIND ME A LOT OF SOMEONE WHO'S PRETTY HIDEOUS!
THE END

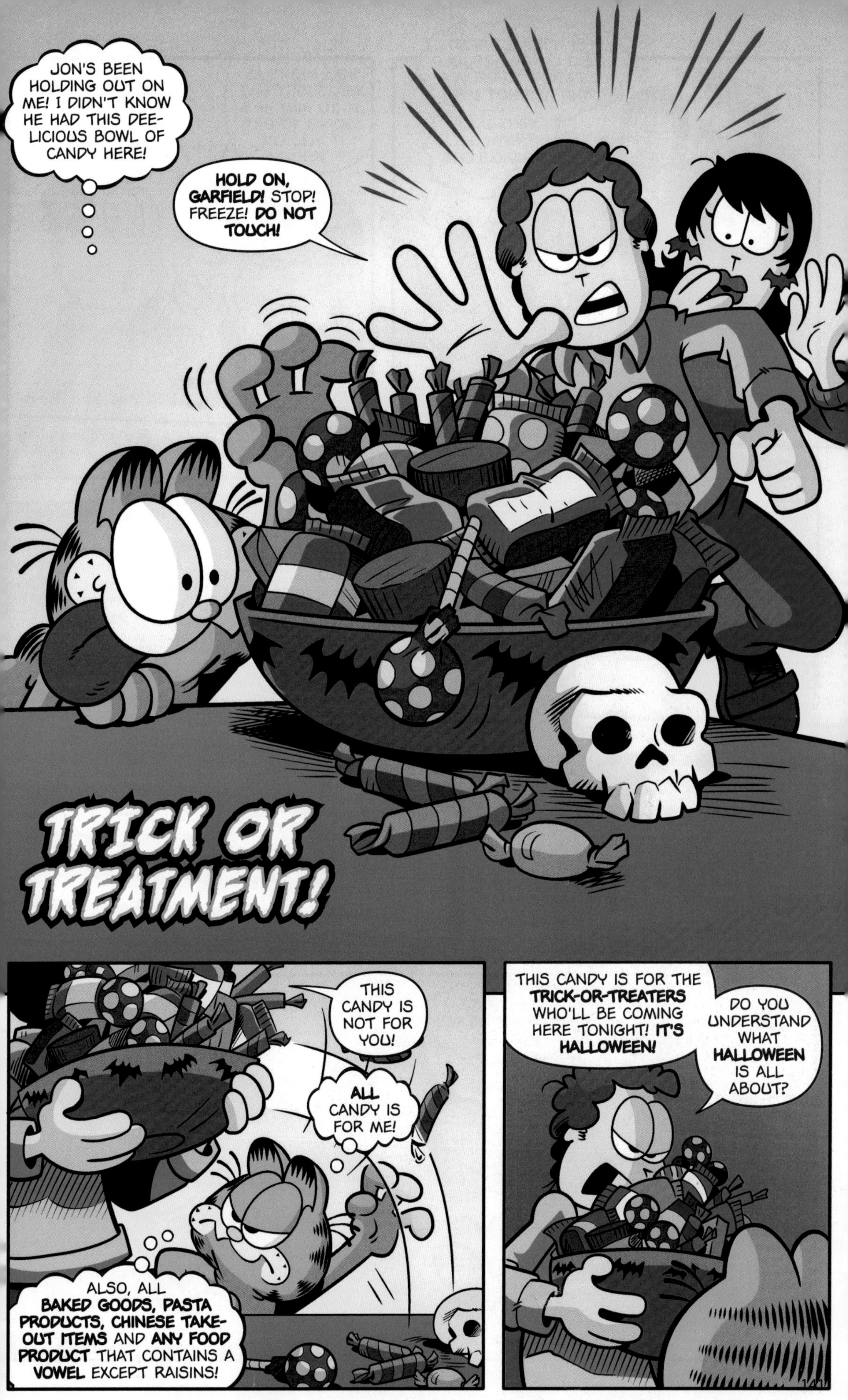

JON'S BEEN HOLDING OUT ON ME! I DIDN'T KNOW HE HAD THIS DEE-LICIOUS BOWL OF CANDY HERE!
HOLD ON, GARFIELD! STOP! FREEZE! DO NOT TOUCH!
TRICK OR TREATMENT!
THIS CANDY IS NOT FOR YOU!
ALL CANDY IS FOR ME!
ALSO, ALL BAKED GOODS, PASTA PRODUCTS, CHINESE TAKE-OUT ITEMS AND ANY FOOD PRODUCT THAT CONTAINS A VOWEL EXCEPT RAISINS!
THIS CANDY IS FOR THE TRICK-OR-TREATERS WHO'LL BE COMING HERE TONIGHT! IT'S HALLOWEEN!
DO YOU UNDERSTAND WHAT HALLOWEEN IS ALL ABOUT?

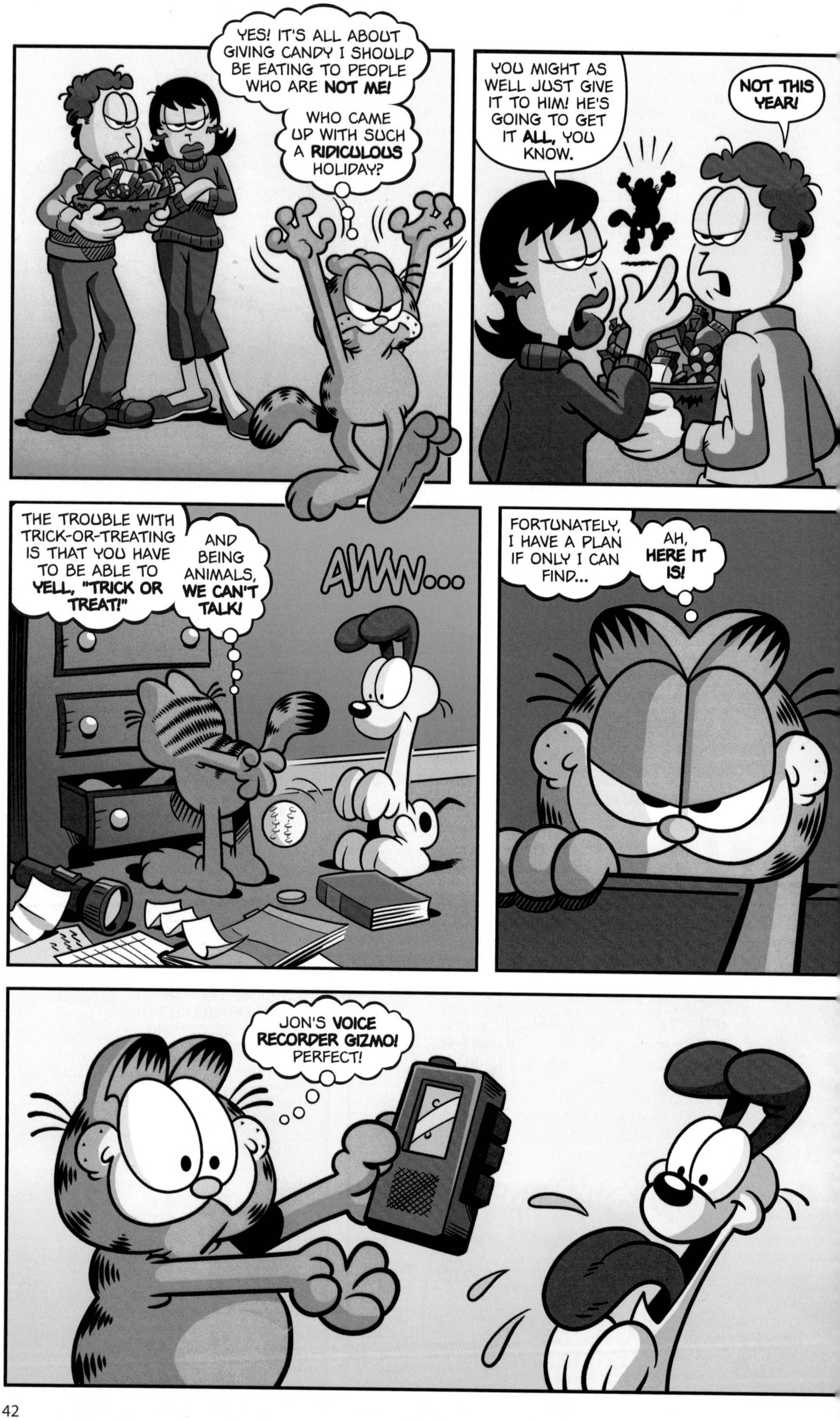

YES! IT'S ALL ABOUT GIVING CANDY I SHOULD BE EATING TO PEOPLE WHO ARE **NOT ME!**
WHO CAME UP WITH SUCH A **RIDICULOUS** HOLIDAY?
YOU MIGHT AS WELL JUST GIVE IT TO HIM! HE'S GOING TO GET IT **ALL**, YOU KNOW.
NOT THIS YEAR!
THE TROUBLE WITH TRICK-OR-TREATING IS THAT YOU HAVE TO BE ABLE TO **YELL, "TRICK OR TREAT!"**
AND BEING ANIMALS, **WE CAN'T TALK!**
AWW...
FORTUNATELY, I HAVE A PLAN IF ONLY I CAN FIND...
AH, **HERE IT IS!**
JON'S **VOICE RECORDER GIZMO!** PERFECT!

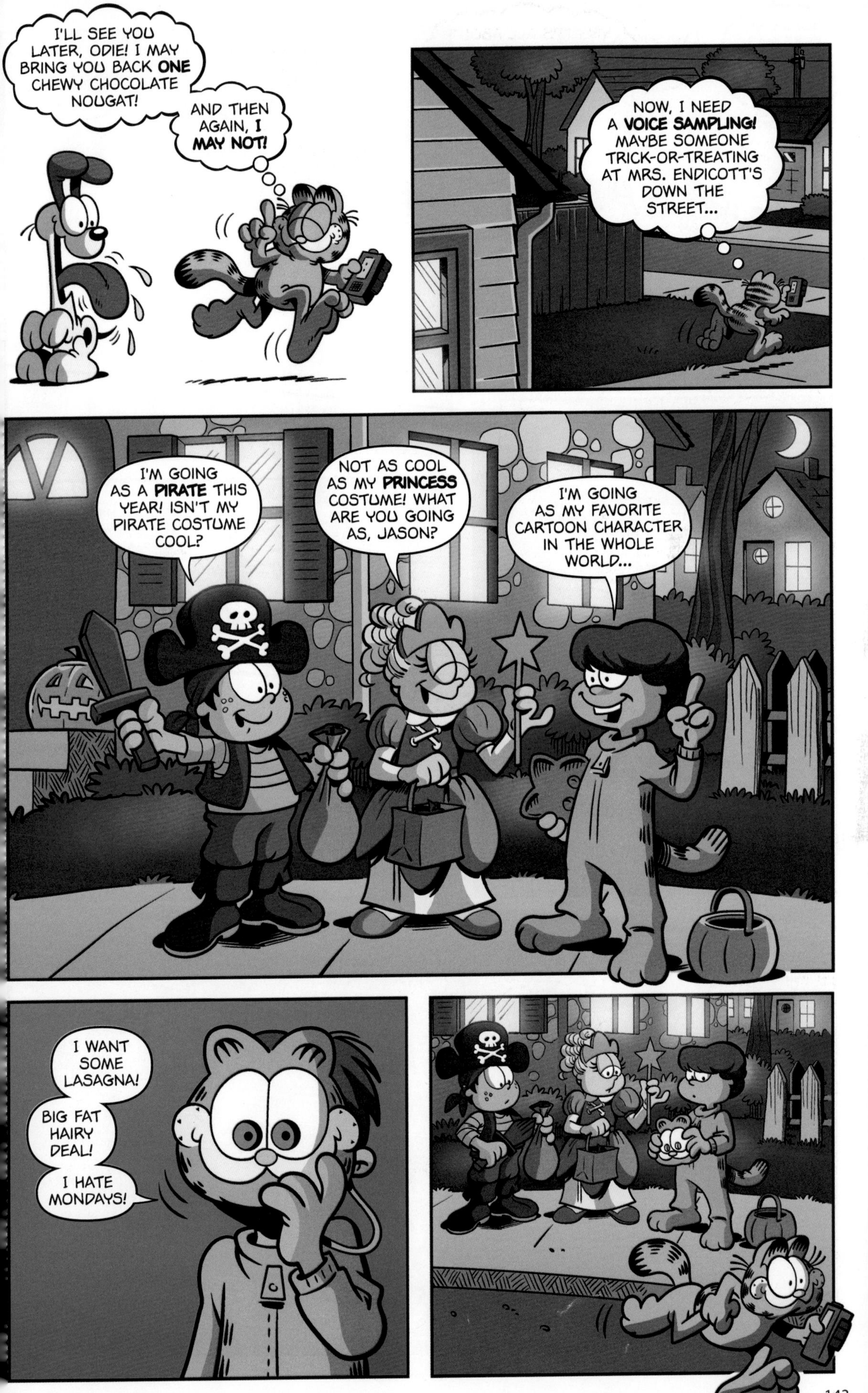

I'LL SEE YOU LATER, ODIE! I MAY BRING YOU BACK ONE CHEWY CHOCOLATE NOUGAT!
AND THEN AGAIN, I MAY NOT!
NOW, I NEED A VOICE SAMPLING! MAYBE SOMEONE TRICK-OR-TREATING AT MRS. ENDICOTT'S DOWN THE STREET...
I'M GOING AS A PIRATE THIS YEAR! ISN'T MY PIRATE COSTUME COOL?
NOT AS COOL AS MY PRINCESS COSTUME! WHAT ARE YOU GOING AS, JASON?
I'M GOING AS MY FAVORITE CARTOON CHARACTER IN THE WHOLE WORLD...
I WANT SOME LASAGNA!
BIG FAT HAIRY DEAL!
I HATE MONDAYS!

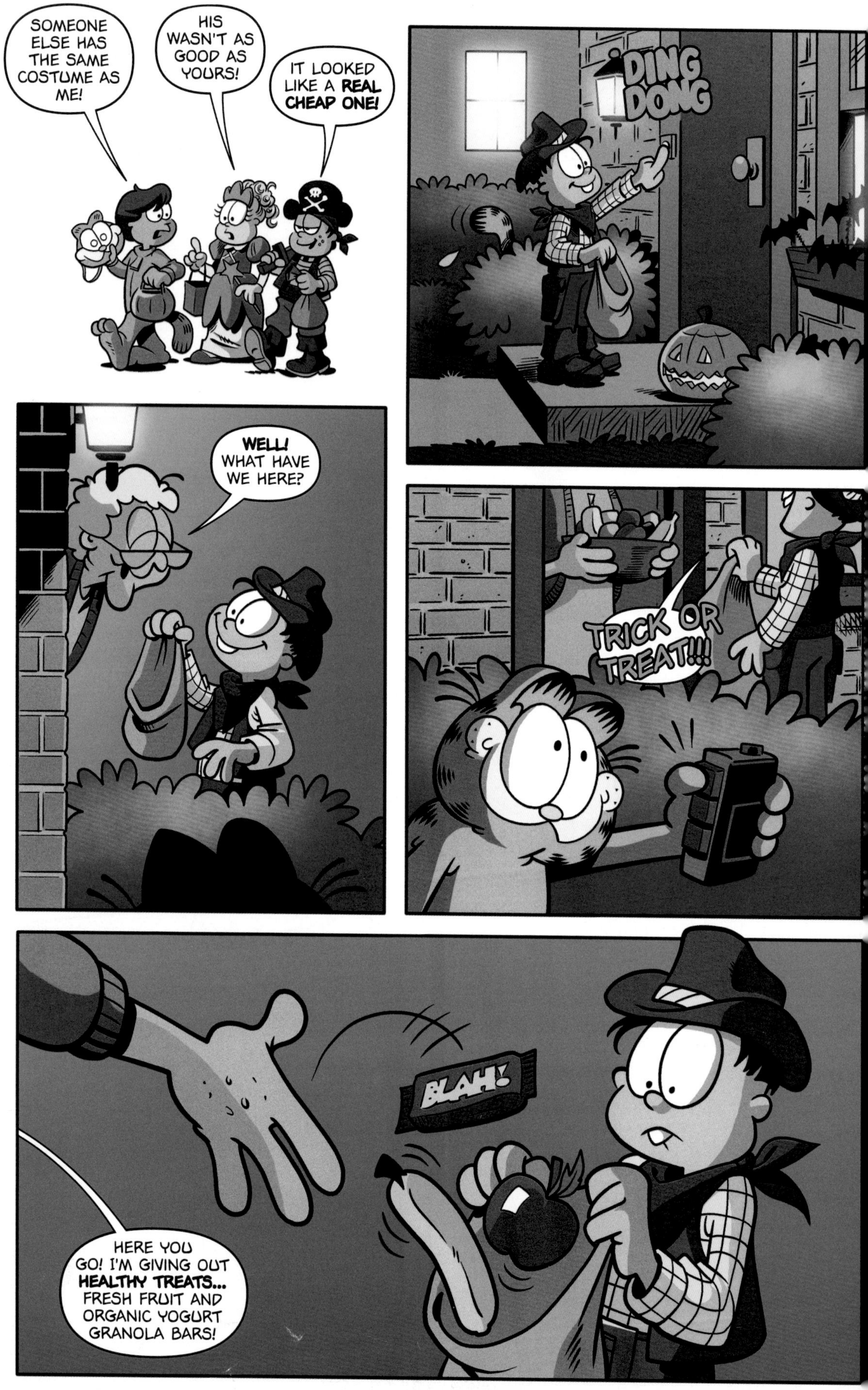
SOMEONE ELSE HAS THE SAME COSTUME AS ME!
HIS WASN'T AS GOOD AS YOURS!
IT LOOKED LIKE A **REAL CHEAP ONE!**
DING DONG
WELL! WHAT HAVE WE HERE?
TRICK OR TREAT!!!
BLAH!
HERE YOU GO! I'M GIVING OUT **HEALTHY TREATS...** FRESH FRUIT AND ORGANIC YOGURT GRANOLA BARS!

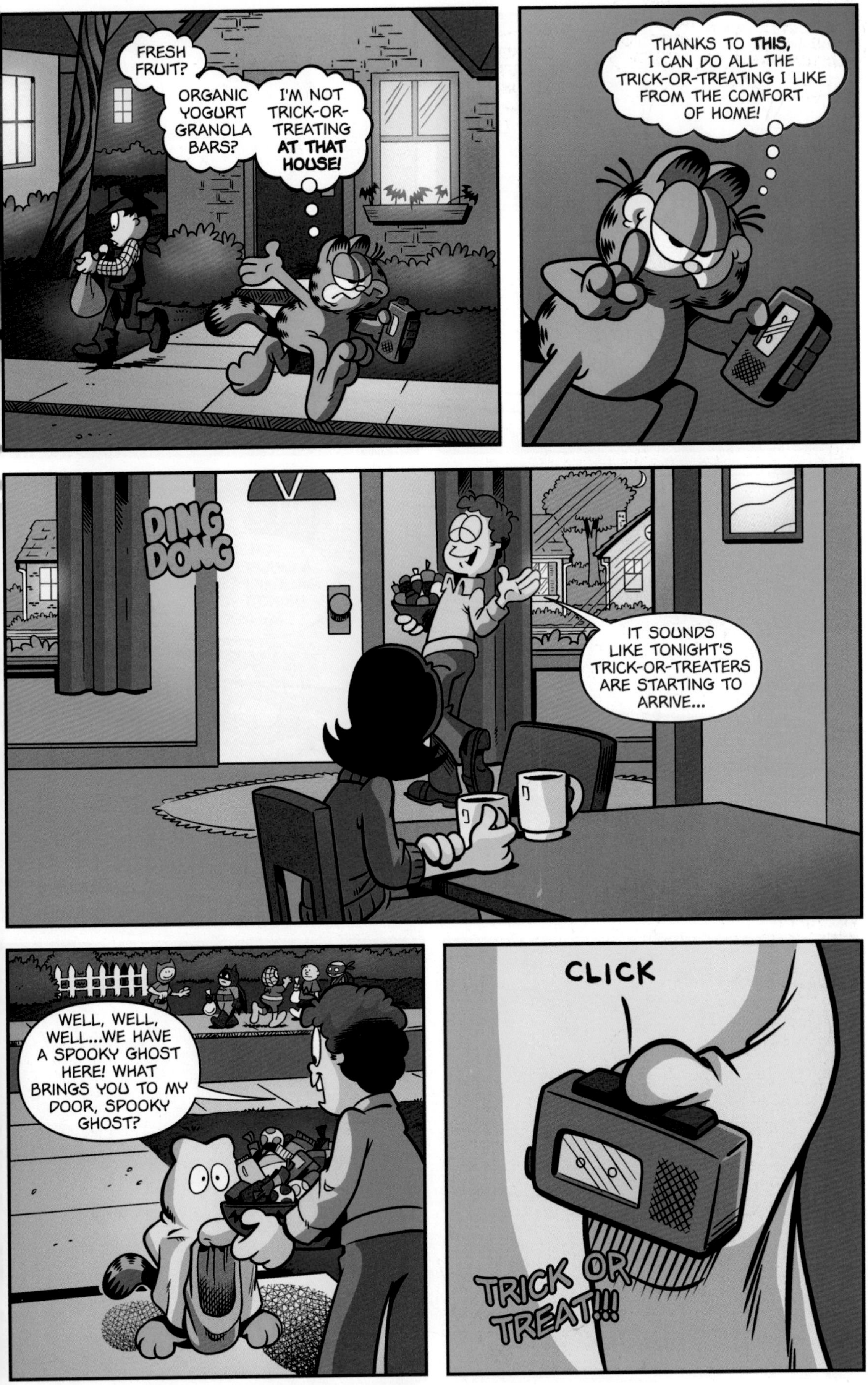
FRESH FRUIT?
ORGANIC YOGURT GRANOLA BARS?
I'M NOT TRICK-OR-TREATING AT THAT HOUSE!
THANKS TO THIS, I CAN DO ALL THE TRICK-OR-TREATING I LIKE FROM THE COMFORT OF HOME!
DING DONG
IT SOUNDS LIKE TONIGHT'S TRICK-OR-TREATERS ARE STARTING TO ARRIVE...
WELL, WELL, WELL...WE HAVE A SPOOKY GHOST HERE! WHAT BRINGS YOU TO MY DOOR, SPOOKY GHOST?
CLICK
TRICK OR TREAT!!!

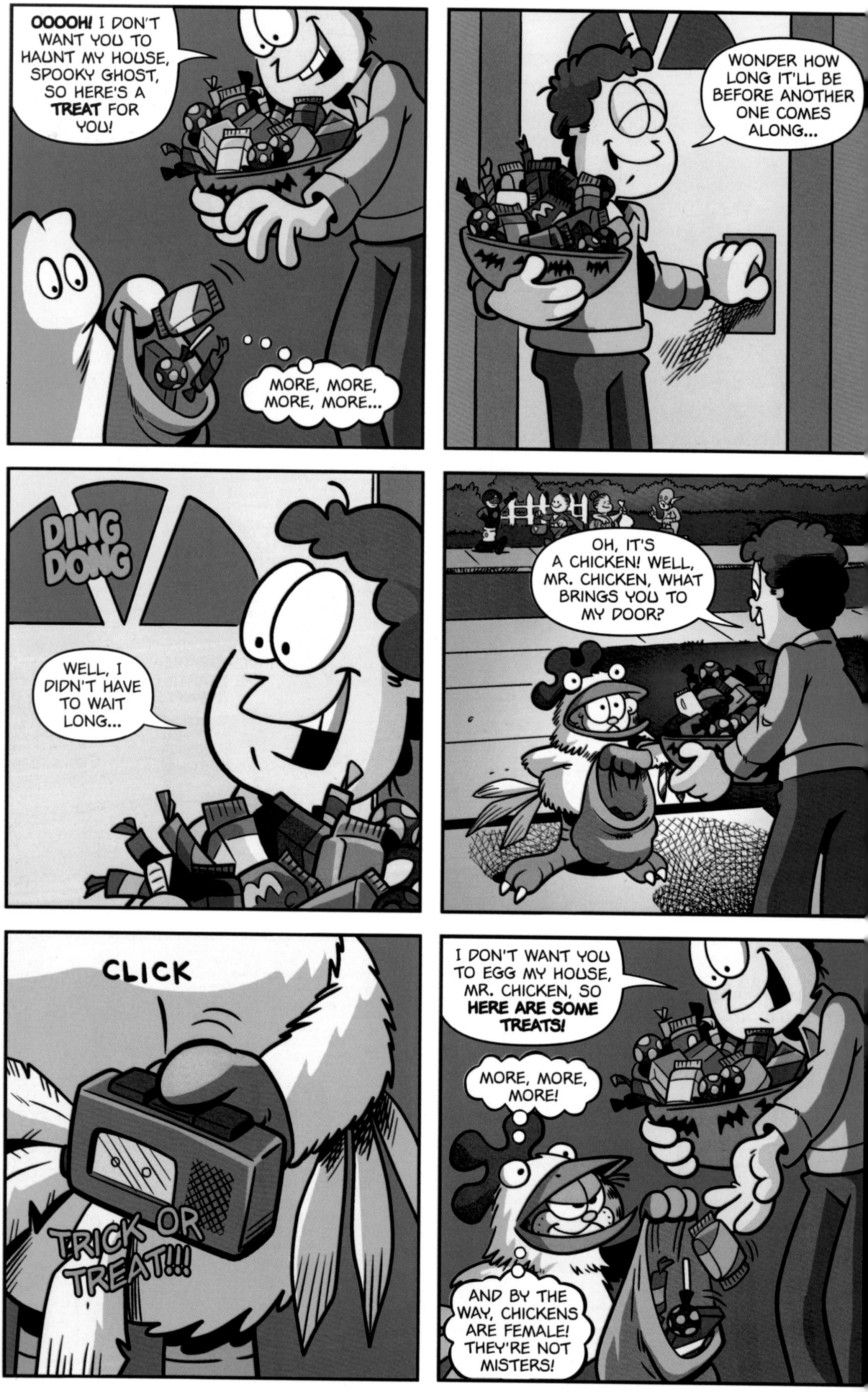
OOOOH! I DON'T WANT YOU TO HAUNT MY HOUSE, SPOOKY GHOST, SO HERE'S A TREAT FOR YOU!
MORE, MORE, MORE, MORE...
WONDER HOW LONG IT'LL BE BEFORE ANOTHER ONE COMES ALONG...
DING DONG
WELL, I DIDN'T HAVE TO WAIT LONG...
OH, IT'S A CHICKEN! WELL, MR. CHICKEN, WHAT BRINGS YOU TO MY DOOR?
CLICK
TRICK OR TREAT!!!
I DON'T WANT YOU TO EGG MY HOUSE, MR. CHICKEN, SO HERE ARE SOME TREATS!
MORE, MORE, MORE!
AND BY THE WAY, CHICKENS ARE FEMALE! THEY'RE NOT MISTERS!

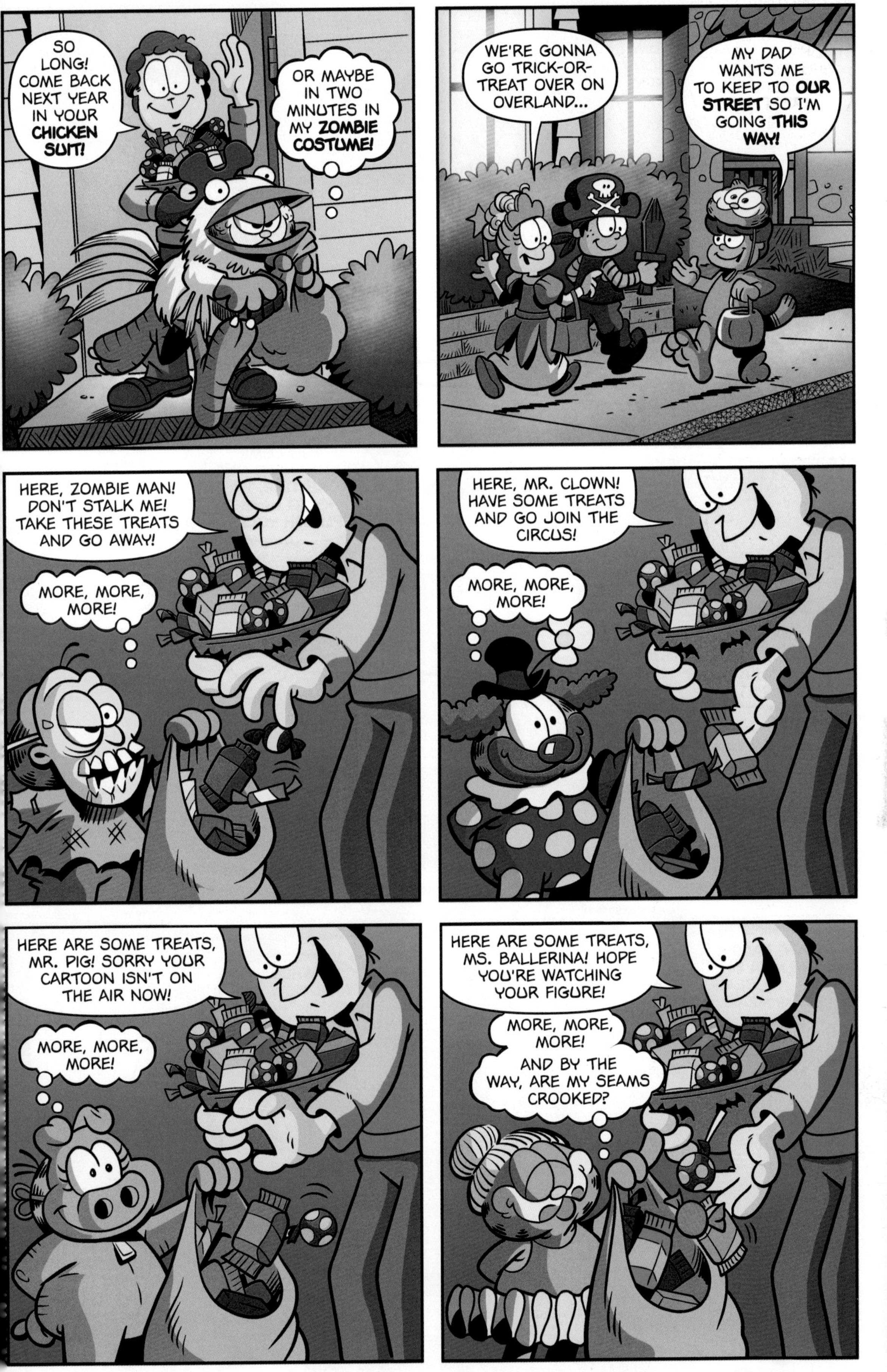
SO LONG! COME BACK NEXT YEAR IN YOUR CHICKEN SUIT!
OR MAYBE IN TWO MINUTES IN MY ZOMBIE COSTUME!
WE'RE GONNA GO TRICK-OR-TREAT OVER ON OVERLAND...
MY DAD WANTS ME TO KEEP TO OUR STREET SO I'M GOING THIS WAY!
HERE, ZOMBIE MAN! DON'T STALK ME! TAKE THESE TREATS AND GO AWAY!
MORE, MORE, MORE!
HERE, MR. CLOWN! HAVE SOME TREATS AND GO JOIN THE CIRCUS!
MORE, MORE, MORE!
HERE ARE SOME TREATS, MR. PIG! SORRY YOUR CARTOON ISN'T ON THE AIR NOW!
MORE, MORE, MORE!
HERE ARE SOME TREATS, MS. BALLERINA! HOPE YOU'RE WATCHING YOUR FIGURE!
MORE, MORE, MORE!
AND BY THE WAY, ARE MY SEAMS CROOKED?

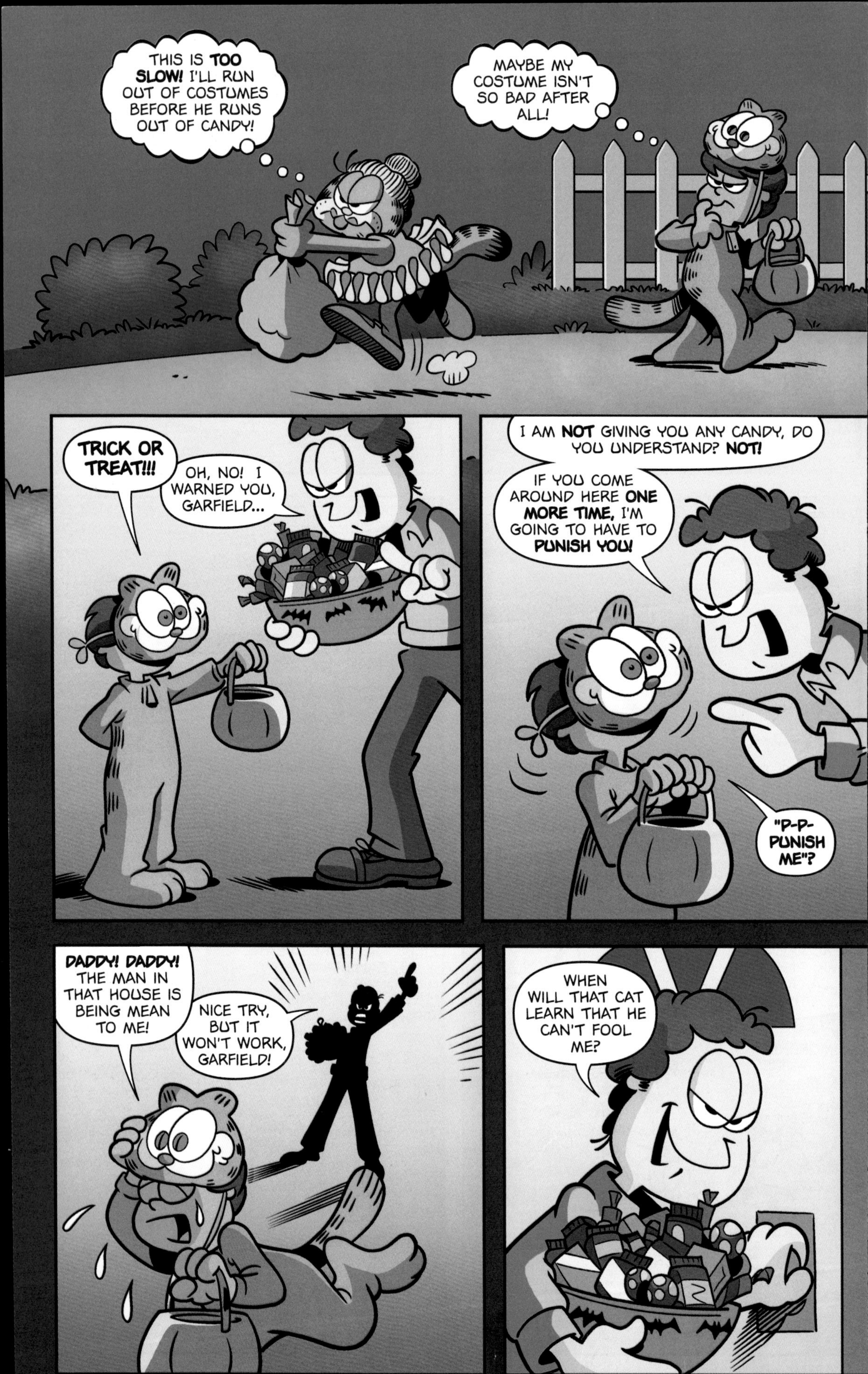
THIS IS TOO SLOW! I'LL RUN OUT OF COSTUMES BEFORE HE RUNS OUT OF CANDY!
MAYBE MY COSTUME ISN'T SO BAD AFTER ALL!
TRICK OR TREAT!!!
OH, NO! I WARNED YOU, GARFIELD...
I AM NOT GIVING YOU ANY CANDY, DO YOU UNDERSTAND? NOT!
IF YOU COME AROUND HERE ONE MORE TIME, I'M GOING TO HAVE TO PUNISH YOU!
"P-P-PUNISH ME"?
DADDY! DADDY! THE MAN IN THAT HOUSE IS BEING MEAN TO ME!
NICE TRY, BUT IT WON'T WORK, GARFIELD!
WHEN WILL THAT CAT LEARN THAT HE CAN'T FOOL ME?

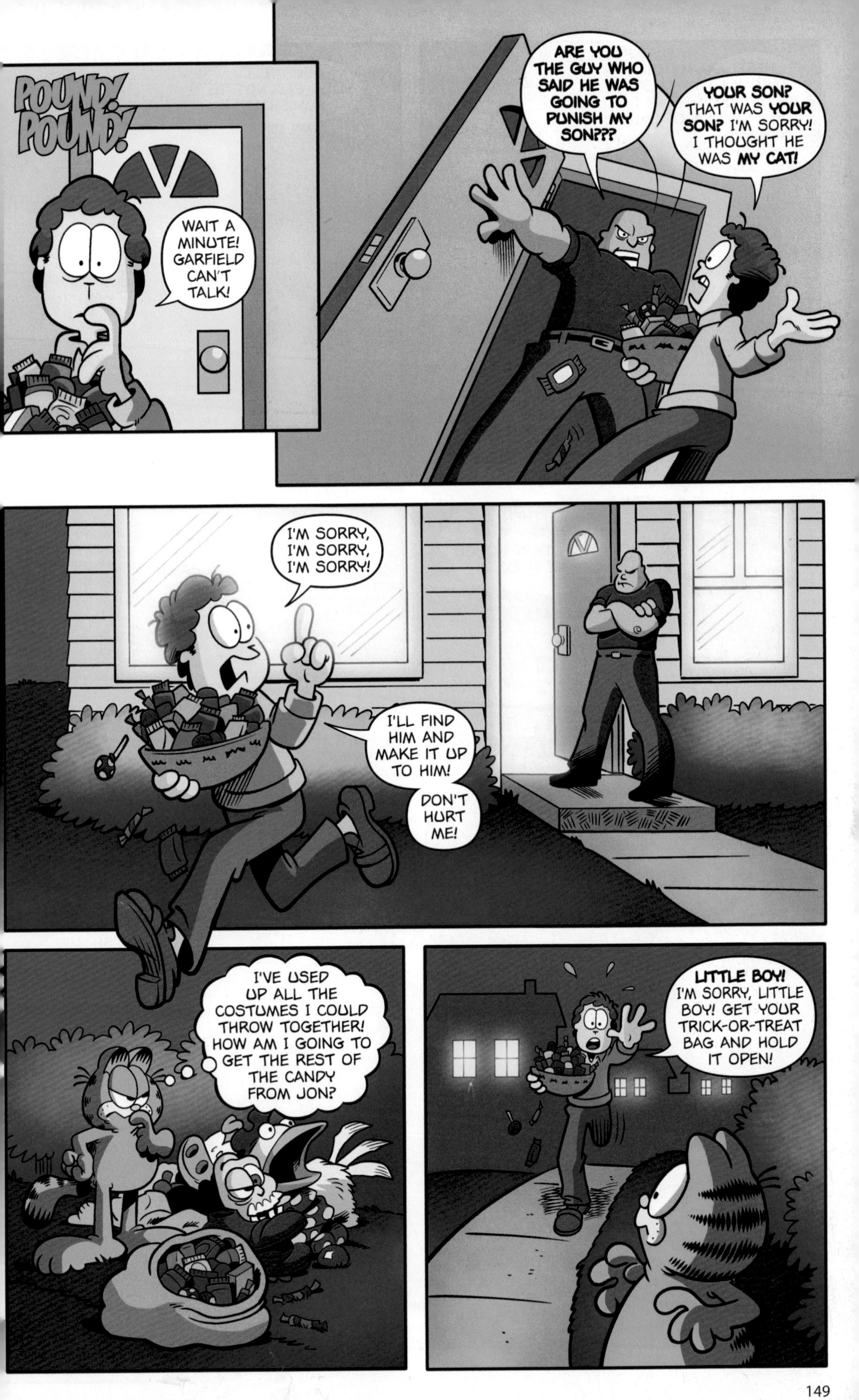
POUND! POUND!
WAIT A MINUTE! GARFIELD CAN'T TALK!
ARE YOU THE GUY WHO SAID HE WAS GOING TO PUNISH MY SON???
YOUR SON? THAT WAS YOUR SON? I'M SORRY! I THOUGHT HE WAS MY CAT!
I'M SORRY, I'M SORRY, I'M SORRY!
I'LL FIND HIM AND MAKE IT UP TO HIM!
DON'T HURT ME!
I'VE USED UP ALL THE COSTUMES I COULD THROW TOGETHER! HOW AM I GOING TO GET THE REST OF THE CANDY FROM JON?
LITTLE BOY! I'M SORRY, LITTLE BOY! GET YOUR TRICK-OR-TREAT BAG AND HOLD IT OPEN!

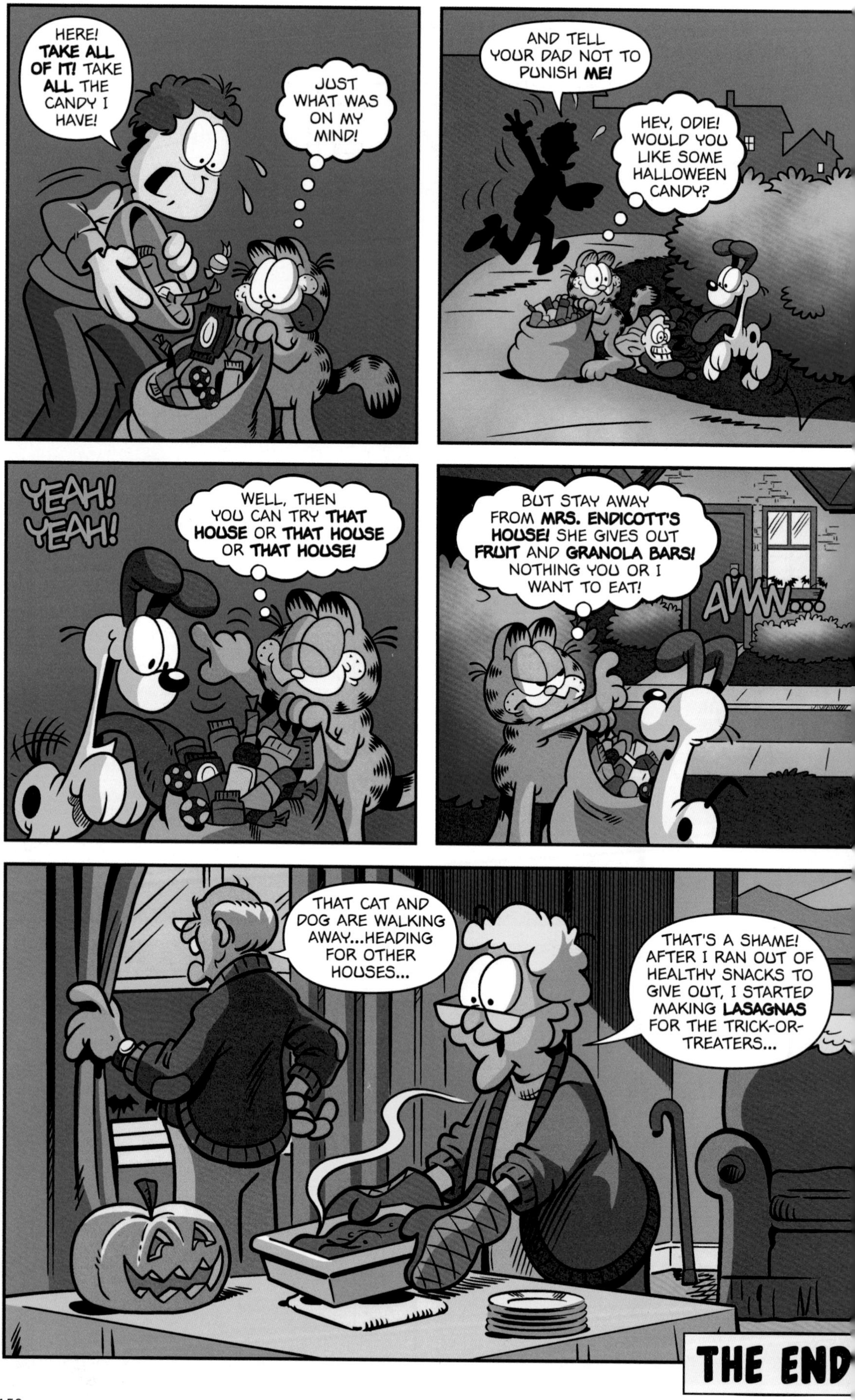

HERE! TAKE ALL OF IT! TAKE ALL THE CANDY I HAVE!
JUST WHAT WAS ON MY MIND!
AND TELL YOUR DAD NOT TO PUNISH ME!
HEY, ODIE! WOULD YOU LIKE SOME HALLOWEEN CANDY?
YEAH! YEAH!
WELL, THEN YOU CAN TRY THAT HOUSE OR THAT HOUSE OR THAT HOUSE!
BUT STAY AWAY FROM MRS. ENDICOTT'S HOUSE! SHE GIVES OUT FRUIT AND GRANOLA BARS! NOTHING YOU OR I WANT TO EAT!
AWW
THAT CAT AND DOG ARE WALKING AWAY...HEADING FOR OTHER HOUSES...
THAT'S A SHAME! AFTER I RAN OUT OF HEALTHY SNACKS TO GIVE OUT, I STARTED MAKING LASAGNAS FOR THE TRICK-OR-TREATERS...
THE END

CHAPTER SEVEN

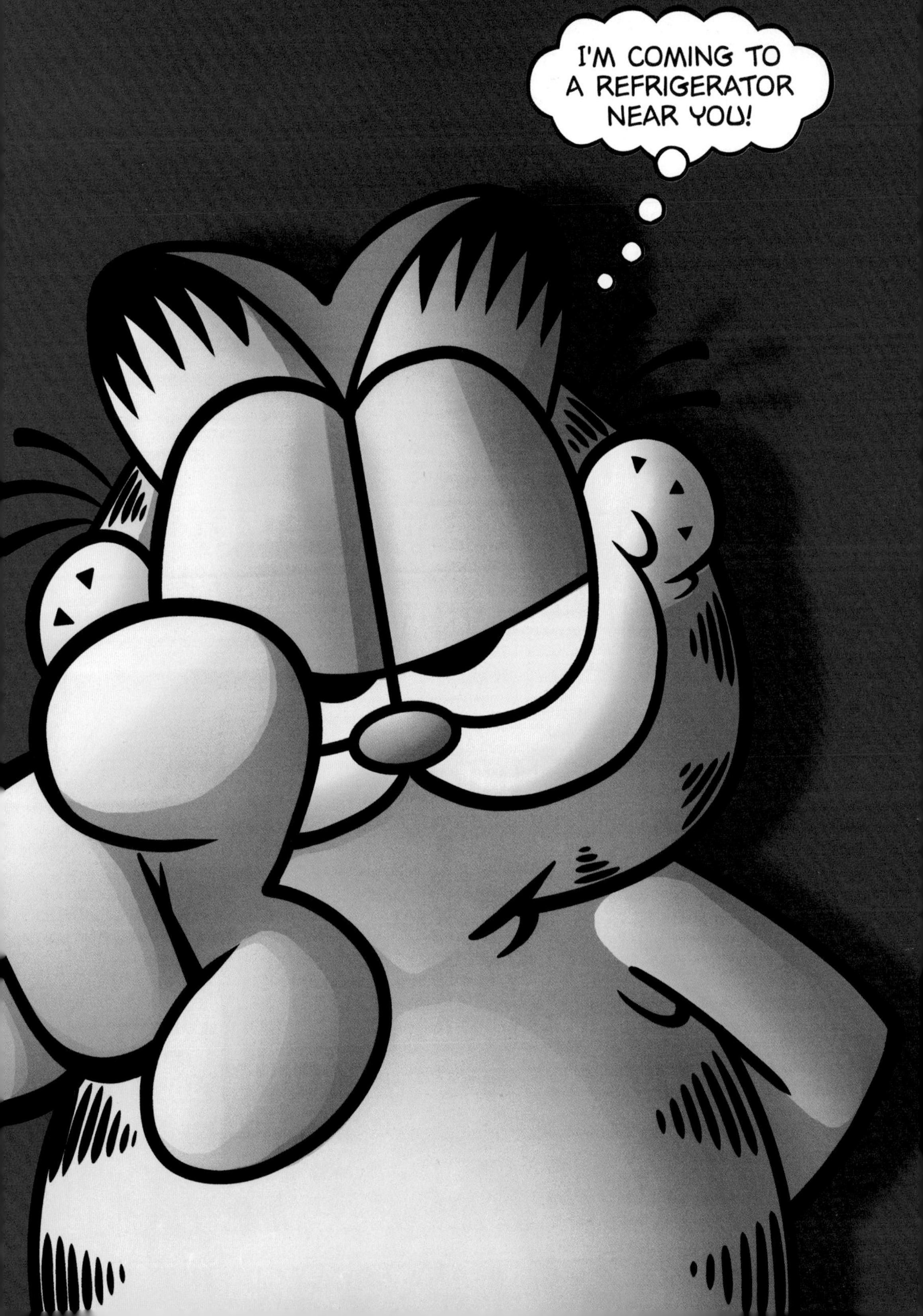
I'M COMING TO A REFRIGERATOR NEAR YOU!

THE CAT WITH NO NAME
THANKSGIVING DAZE

Written by
MARK EVANIER

Art by
ANDY HIRSCH
AND DAN DAVIS
WITH MARK
AND STEPHANIE HEIKE
(Pages 153-164)
MIKE DeCARLO
(Pages 165-174)

Colors by
LISA MOORE

Chapter Break Art by
GARY BARKER
AND DAN DAVIS
WITH LISA MOORE

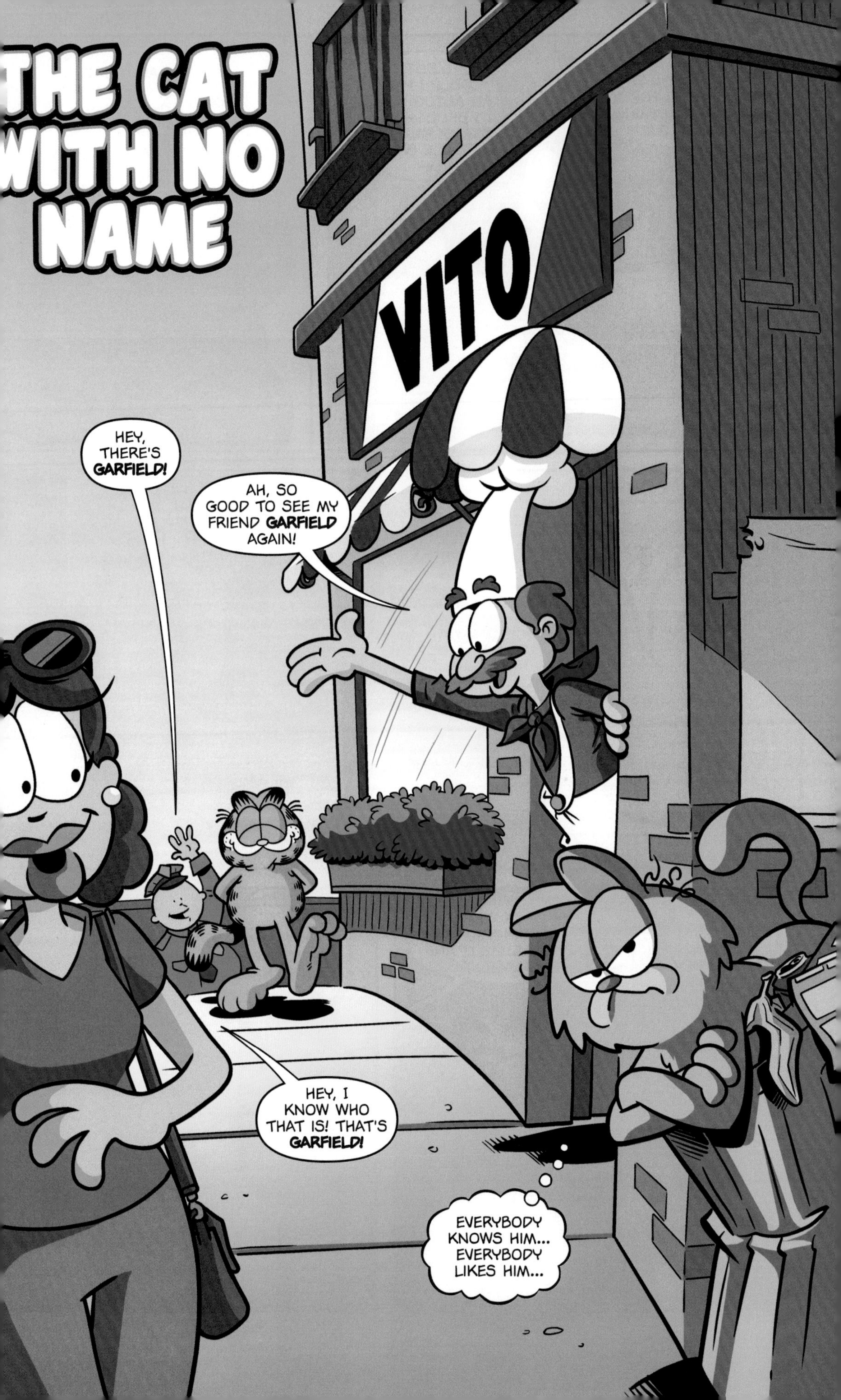

THE CAT WITH NO NAME
VITO
HEY, THERE'S GARFIELD!
AH, SO GOOD TO SEE MY FRIEND GARFIELD AGAIN!
HEY, I KNOW WHO THAT IS! THAT'S GARFIELD!
EVERYBODY KNOWS HIM... EVERYBODY LIKES HIM...

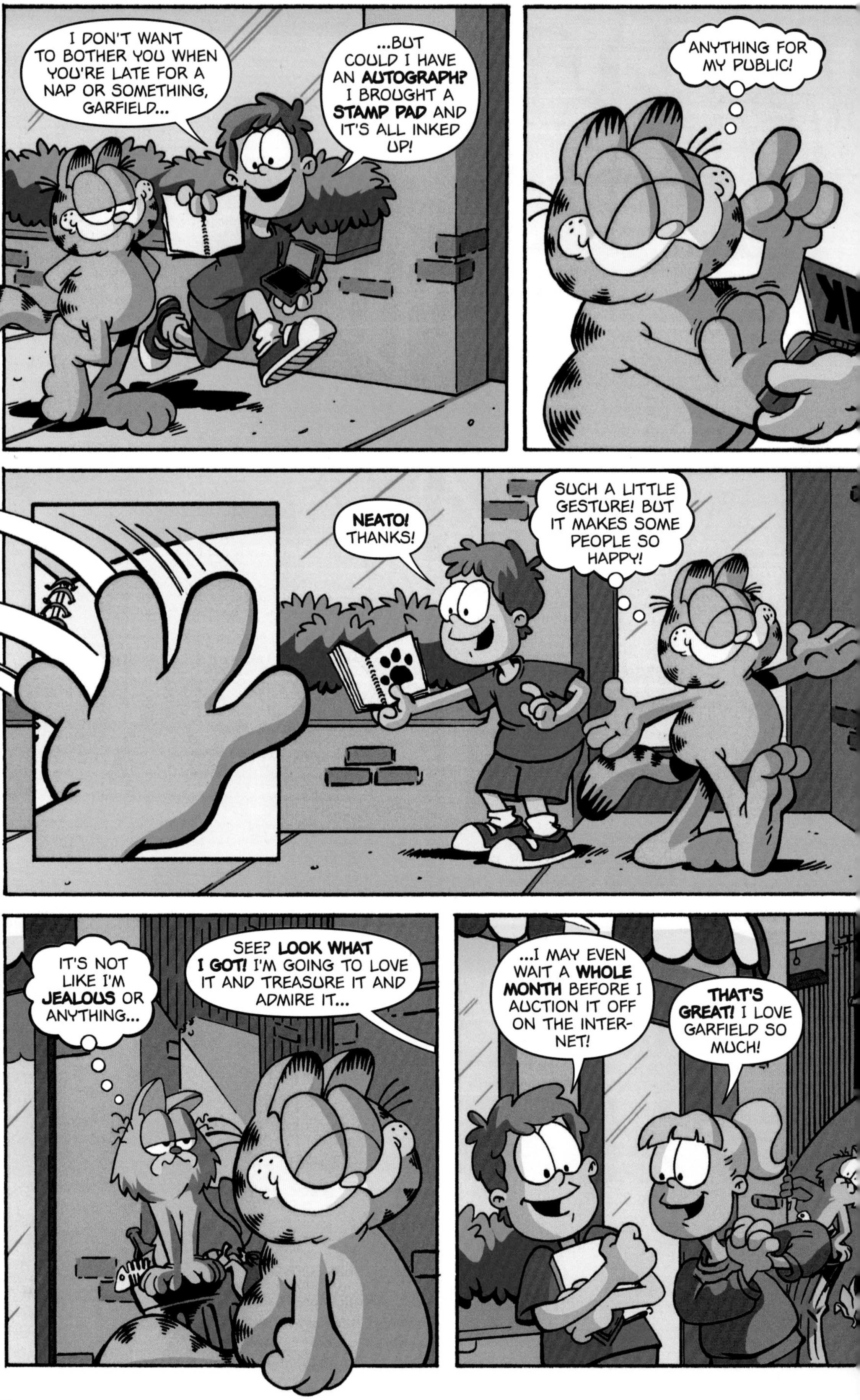
I DON'T WANT TO BOTHER YOU WHEN YOU'RE LATE FOR A NAP OR SOMETHING, GARFIELD...
...BUT COULD I HAVE AN **AUTOGRAPH?** I BROUGHT A **STAMP PAD** AND IT'S ALL INKED UP!
ANYTHING FOR MY PUBLIC!
NEATO! THANKS!
SUCH A LITTLE GESTURE! BUT IT MAKES SOME PEOPLE SO HAPPY!
IT'S NOT LIKE I'M **JEALOUS** OR ANYTHING...
SEE? **LOOK WHAT I GOT!** I'M GOING TO LOVE IT AND TREASURE IT AND ADMIRE IT...
...I MAY EVEN WAIT A **WHOLE MONTH** BEFORE I AUCTION IT OFF ON THE INTER-NET!
THAT'S GREAT! I LOVE GARFIELD SO MUCH!

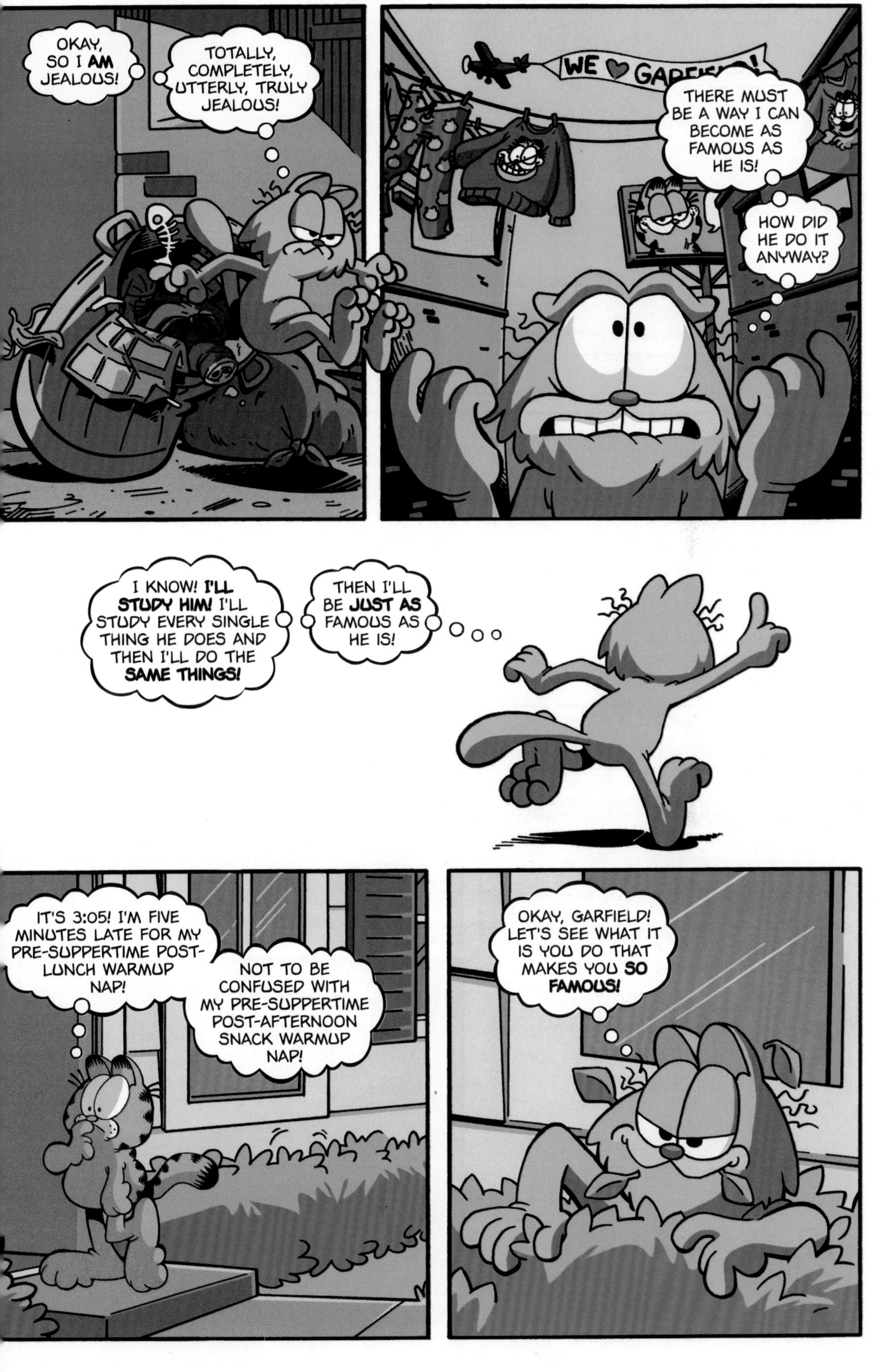
OKAY, SO I **AM** JEALOUS!
TOTALLY, COMPLETELY, UTTERLY, TRULY JEALOUS!
WE ♥ GARFIELD!
THERE MUST BE A WAY I CAN BECOME AS FAMOUS AS HE IS!
HOW DID HE DO IT ANYWAY?
I KNOW! **I'LL STUDY HIM!** I'LL STUDY EVERY SINGLE THING HE DOES AND THEN I'LL DO THE **SAME THINGS!**
THEN I'LL BE **JUST AS** FAMOUS AS HE IS!
IT'S 3:05! I'M FIVE MINUTES LATE FOR MY PRE-SUPPERTIME POST-LUNCH WARMUP NAP!
NOT TO BE CONFUSED WITH MY PRE-SUPPERTIME POST-AFTERNOON SNACK WARMUP NAP!
OKAY, GARFIELD! LET'S SEE WHAT IT IS YOU DO THAT MAKES YOU **SO FAMOUS!**

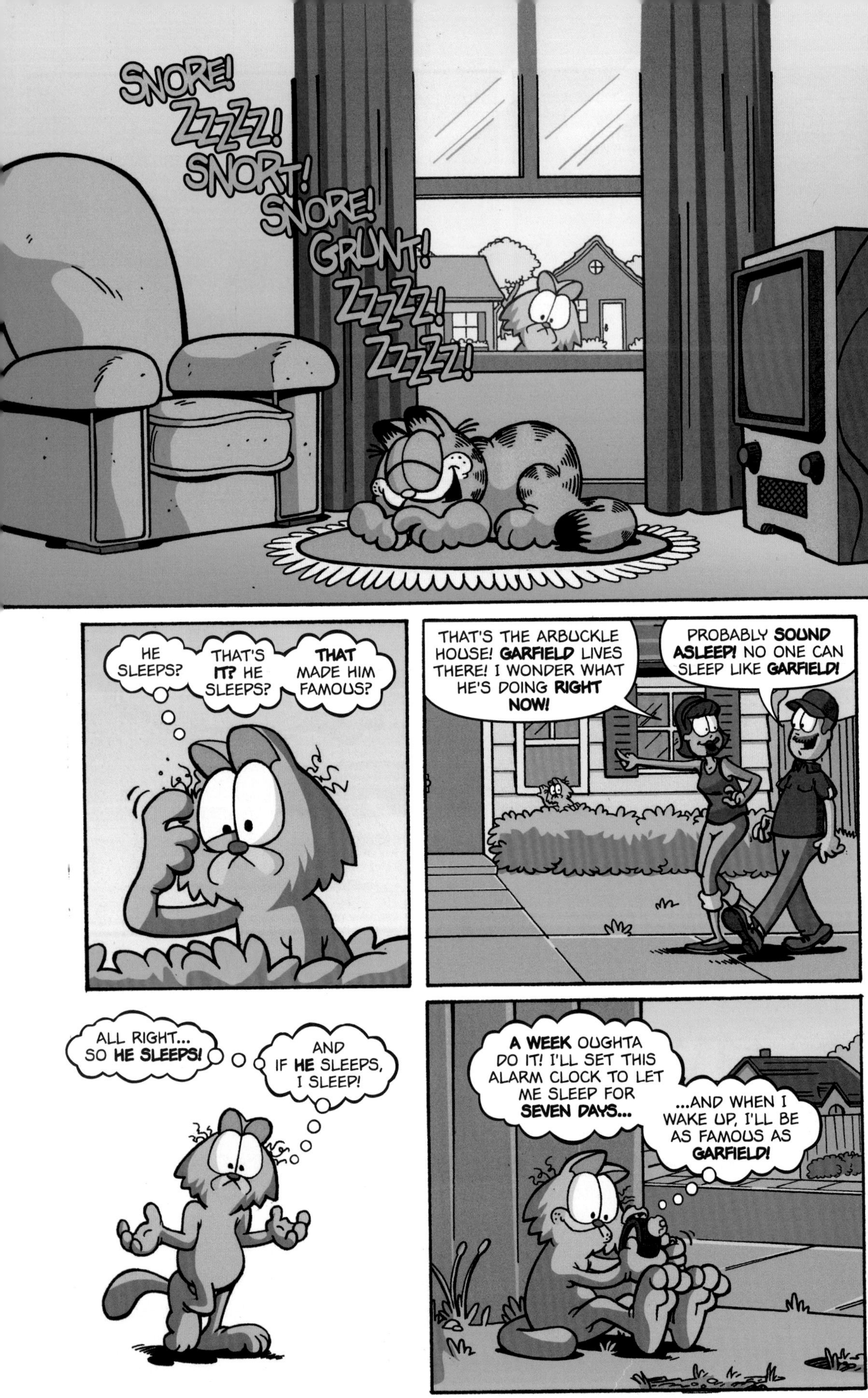
SNORE!
ZZZZZ!
SNORT!
SNORE!
GRUNT!
ZZZZZ!
ZZZZZ!
HE SLEEPS?
THAT'S IT? HE SLEEPS?
THAT MADE HIM FAMOUS?
THAT'S THE ARBUCKLE HOUSE! GARFIELD LIVES THERE! I WONDER WHAT HE'S DOING RIGHT NOW!
PROBABLY SOUND ASLEEP! NO ONE CAN SLEEP LIKE GARFIELD!
ALL RIGHT... SO HE SLEEPS!
AND IF HE SLEEPS, I SLEEP!
A WEEK OUGHTA DO IT! I'LL SET THIS ALARM CLOCK TO LET ME SLEEP FOR SEVEN DAYS...
...AND WHEN I WAKE UP, I'LL BE AS FAMOUS AS GARFIELD!

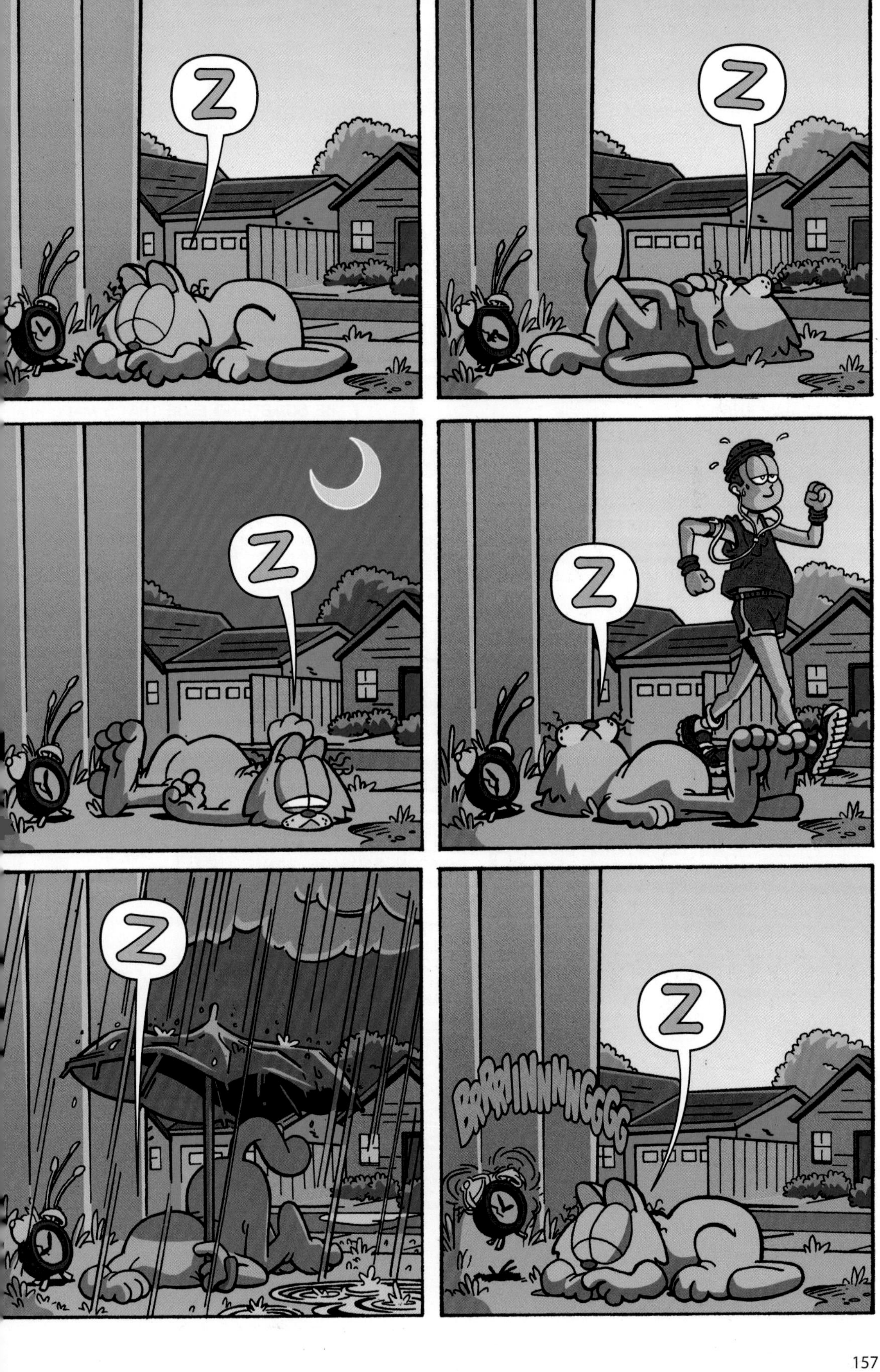
Z
Z
Z
Z
Z
BRRRINNNNGGGG
Z

AHHHH....
YAWWWWNN!

TIME TO GET UP AND SEE HOW FAMOUS I AM!

DO YOU KNOW THAT CAT?

NO BUT HE'S ALWAYS SLEEPING IN THAT EMPTY LOT! HE'LL NEVER AMOUNT TO **ANYTHING!**

YOU KNOW WHO **REALLY** KNOWS HOW TO SLEEP? **GARFIELD!**

OH, HE'S **FAMOUS** FOR HIS SLEEPING!

GRRRRR.

ALL RIGHT! THERE MUST BE **SOMETHING ELSE** THAT'S MADE HIM FAMOUS! **NO ONE** COULD GET FAMOUS JUST BY **SLEEPING!**

MAYBE RIP VAN WINKLE, BUT THAT'S ABOUT IT!

I MADE FIFTY PANCAKES, SIXTY WAFFLES, THREE DOZEN EGGS, BACON, SAUSAGE, HAM, POTATOES, PASTRY AND MORE PASTRY!

IS THERE **ANYTHING ELSE** YOU'D LIKE WITH YOUR **BREAKFAST?**

YES! LUNCH!!!

EAT! CHEW SLURP YUM! GUL GNA BUR

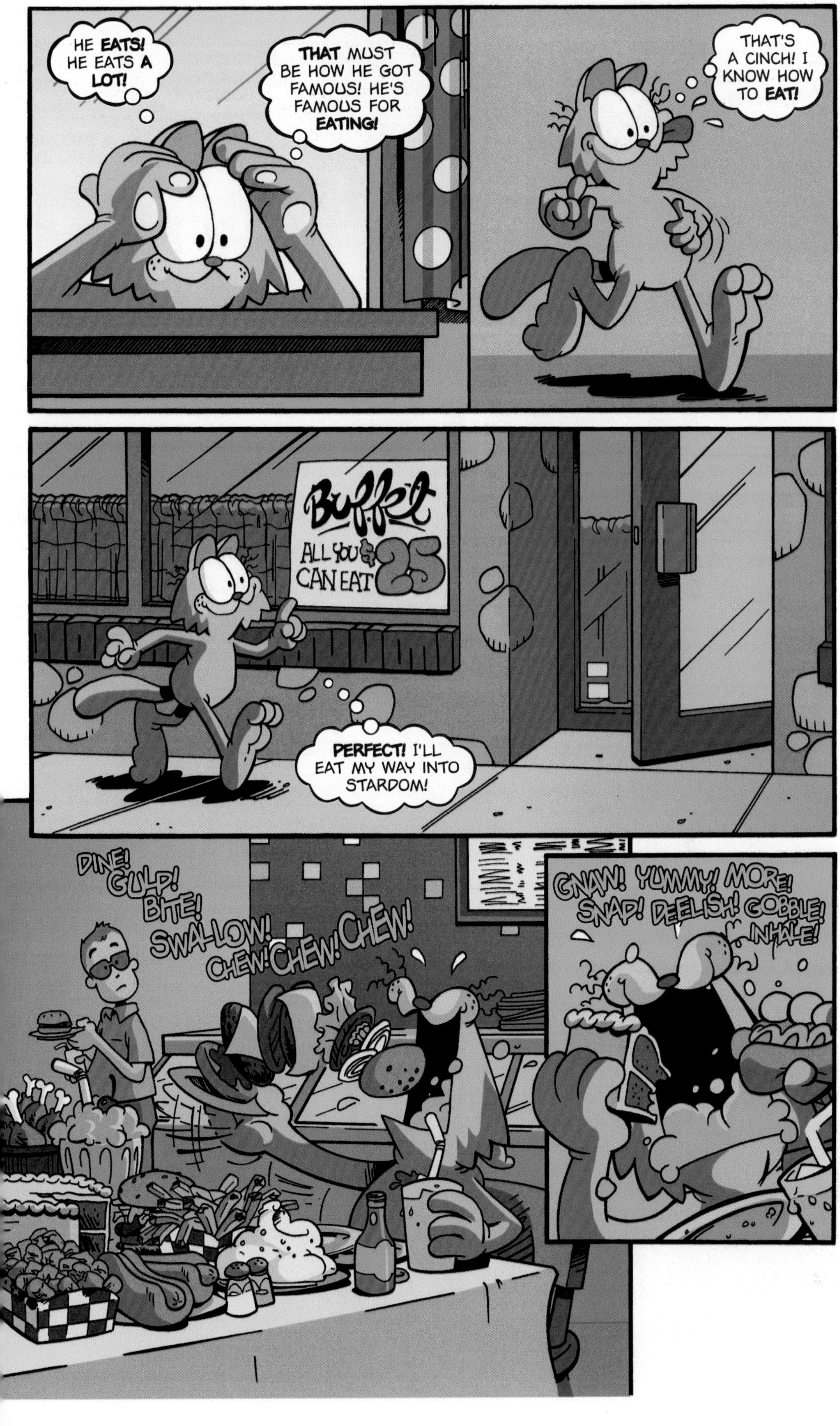
HE EATS! HE EATS A LOT!
THAT MUST BE HOW HE GOT FAMOUS! HE'S FAMOUS FOR EATING!
THAT'S A CINCH! I KNOW HOW TO EAT!
Buffet
ALL YOU CAN EAT 25
PERFECT! I'LL EAT MY WAY INTO STARDOM!
DINE! GULP! BITE! SWALLOW! CHEW! CHEW! CHEW!
GNAW! YUMMY! MORE! SNAP! DEELISH! GOBBLE! INHALE!

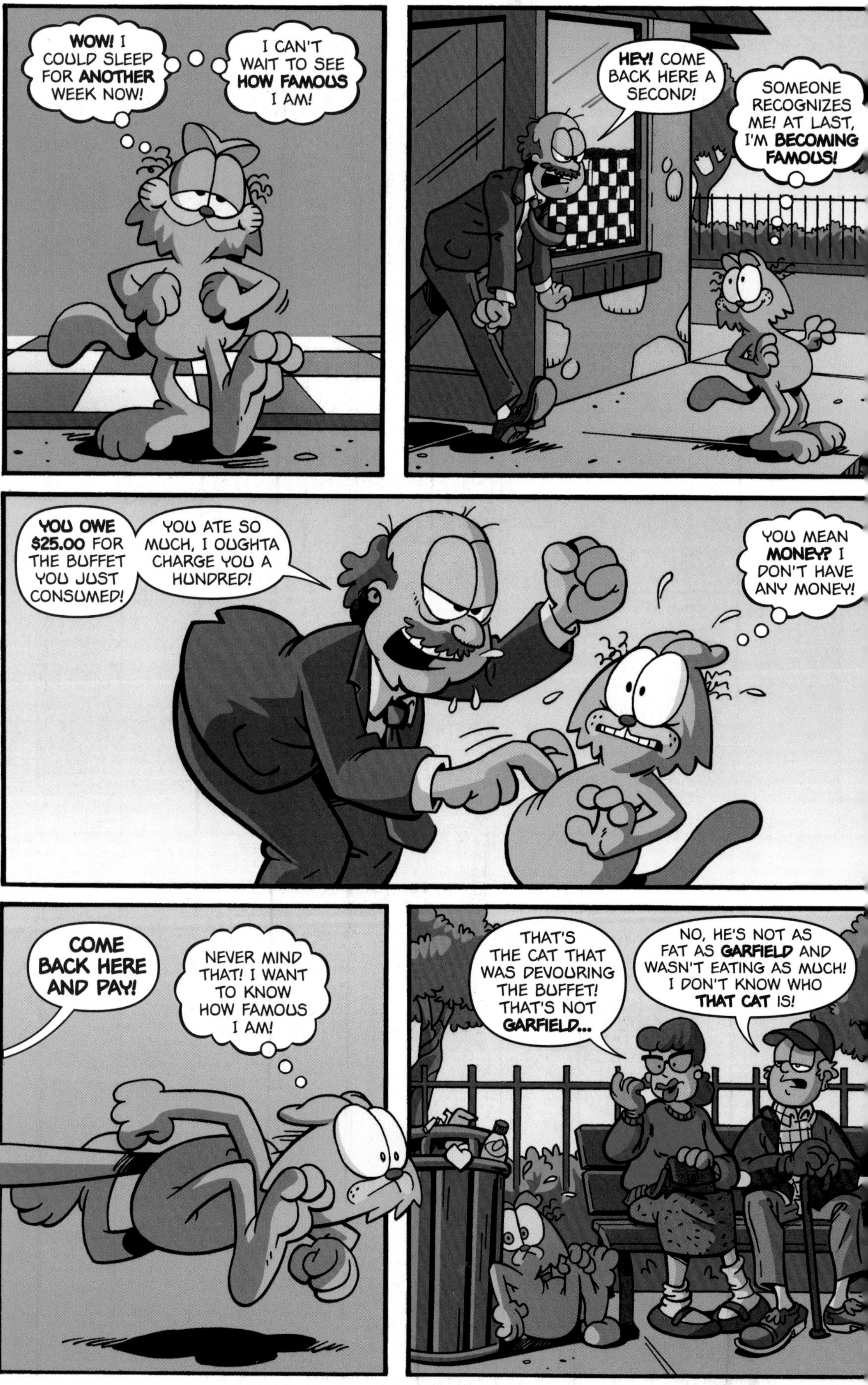
WOW! I COULD SLEEP FOR ANOTHER WEEK NOW!
I CAN'T WAIT TO SEE HOW FAMOUS I AM!
HEY! COME BACK HERE A SECOND!
SOMEONE RECOGNIZES ME! AT LAST, I'M BECOMING FAMOUS!
YOU OWE $25.00 FOR THE BUFFET YOU JUST CONSUMED!
YOU ATE SO MUCH, I OUGHTA CHARGE YOU A HUNDRED!
YOU MEAN MONEY? I DON'T HAVE ANY MONEY!
COME BACK HERE AND PAY!
NEVER MIND THAT! I WANT TO KNOW HOW FAMOUS I AM!
THAT'S THE CAT THAT WAS DEVOURING THE BUFFET! THAT'S NOT GARFIELD...
NO, HE'S NOT AS FAT AS GARFIELD AND WASN'T EATING AS MUCH! I DON'T KNOW WHO THAT CAT IS!

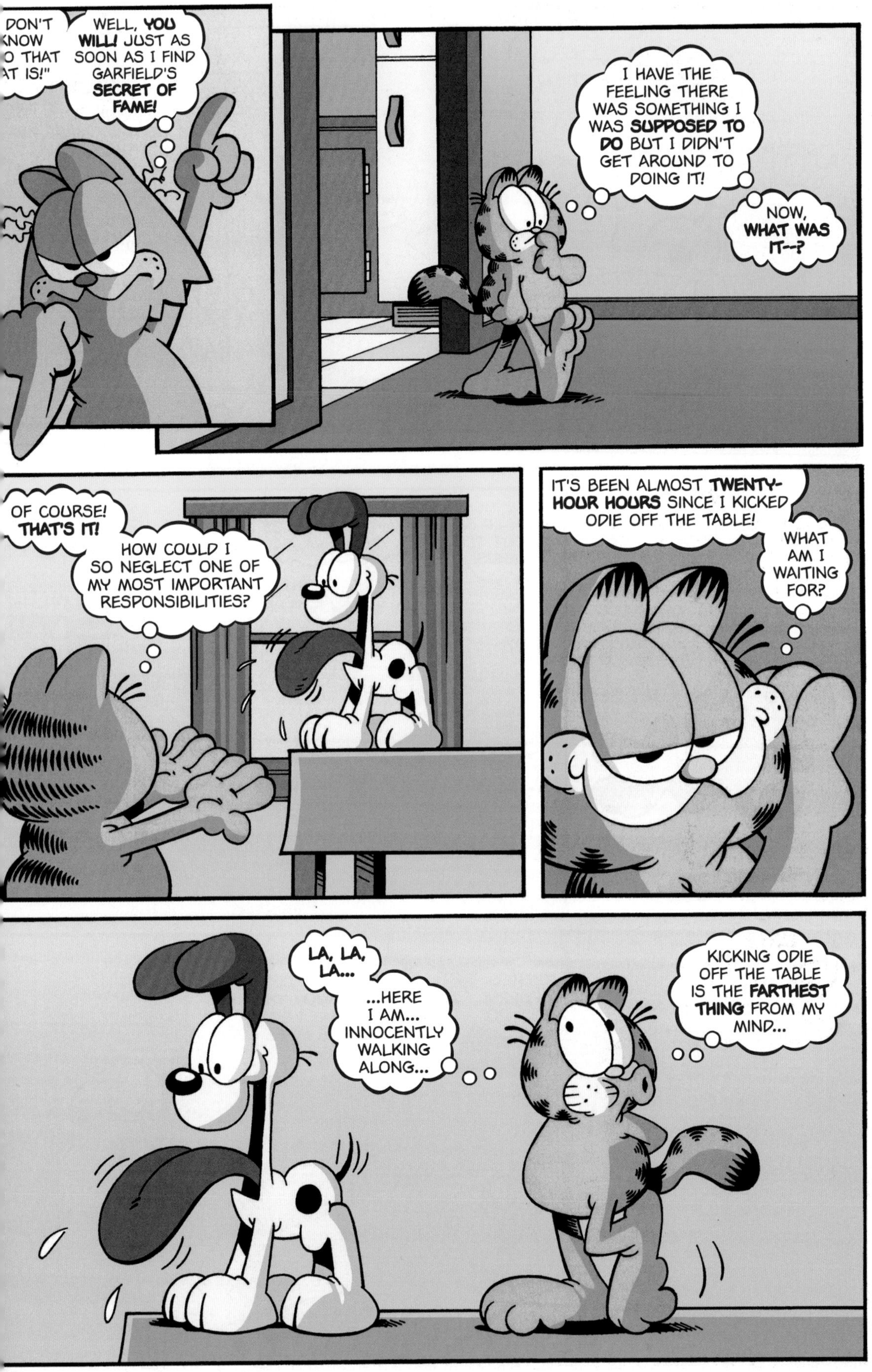
DON'T KNOW O THAT AT IS!"
WELL, **YOU WILL!** JUST AS SOON AS I FIND GARFIELD'S **SECRET OF FAME!**
I HAVE THE FEELING THERE WAS SOMETHING I WAS **SUPPOSED TO DO** BUT I DIDN'T GET AROUND TO DOING IT!
NOW, **WHAT WAS IT--?**
OF COURSE! **THAT'S IT!**
HOW COULD I SO NEGLECT ONE OF MY MOST IMPORTANT RESPONSIBILITIES?
IT'S BEEN ALMOST **TWENTY-HOUR HOURS** SINCE I KICKED ODIE OFF THE TABLE!
WHAT AM I WAITING FOR?
LA, LA, LA...
...HERE I AM... INNOCENTLY WALKING ALONG...
KICKING ODIE OFF THE TABLE IS THE **FARTHEST THING** FROM MY MIND...

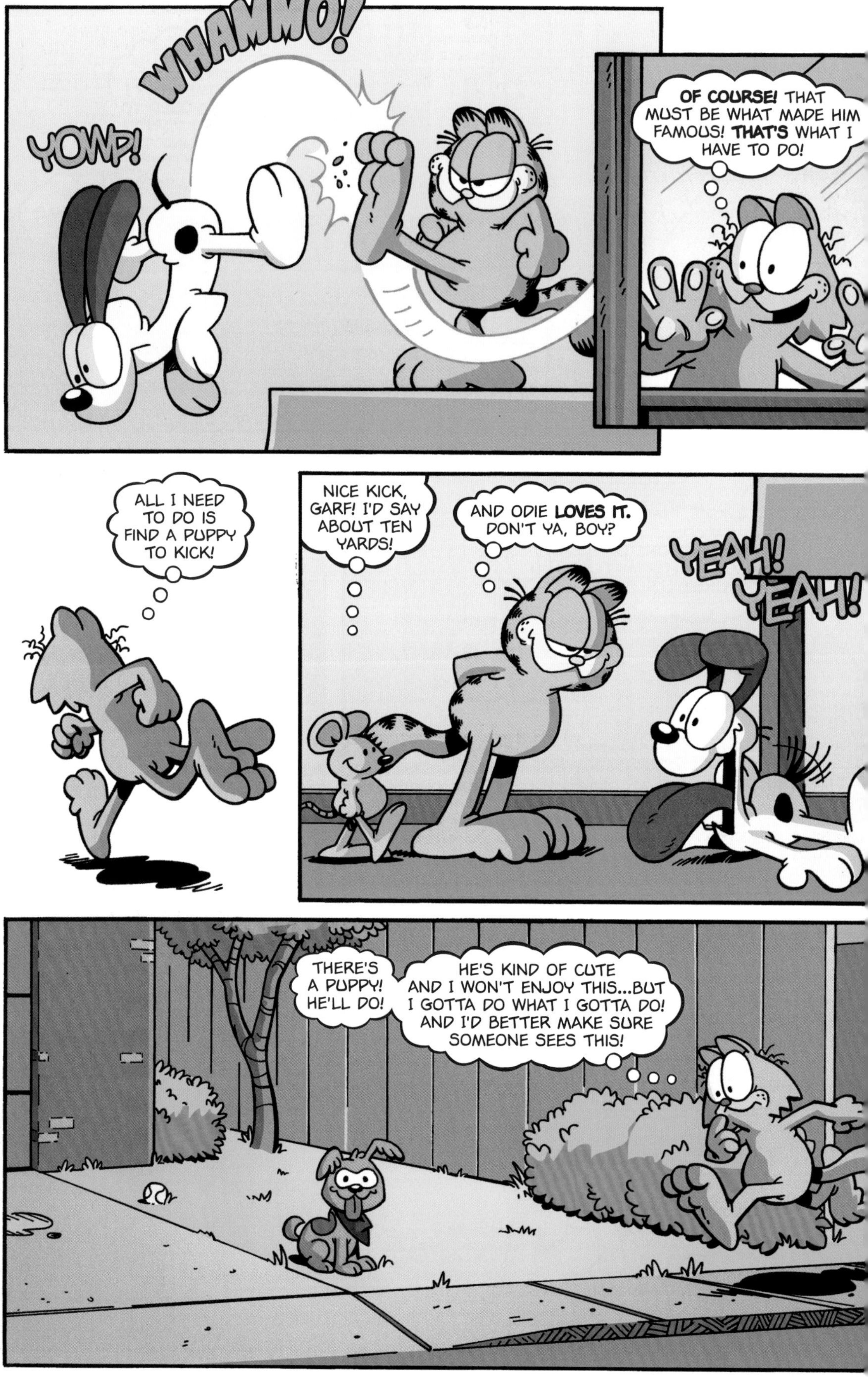
WHAMMO!
YOWP!
OF COURSE! THAT MUST BE WHAT MADE HIM FAMOUS! THAT'S WHAT I HAVE TO DO!
ALL I NEED TO DO IS FIND A PUPPY TO KICK!
NICE KICK, GARF! I'D SAY ABOUT TEN YARDS!
AND ODIE LOVES IT. DON'T YA, BOY?
YEAH! YEAH!
THERE'S A PUPPY! HE'LL DO!
HE'S KIND OF CUTE AND I WON'T ENJOY THIS...BUT I GOTTA DO WHAT I GOTTA DO! AND I'D BETTER MAKE SURE SOMEONE SEES THIS!

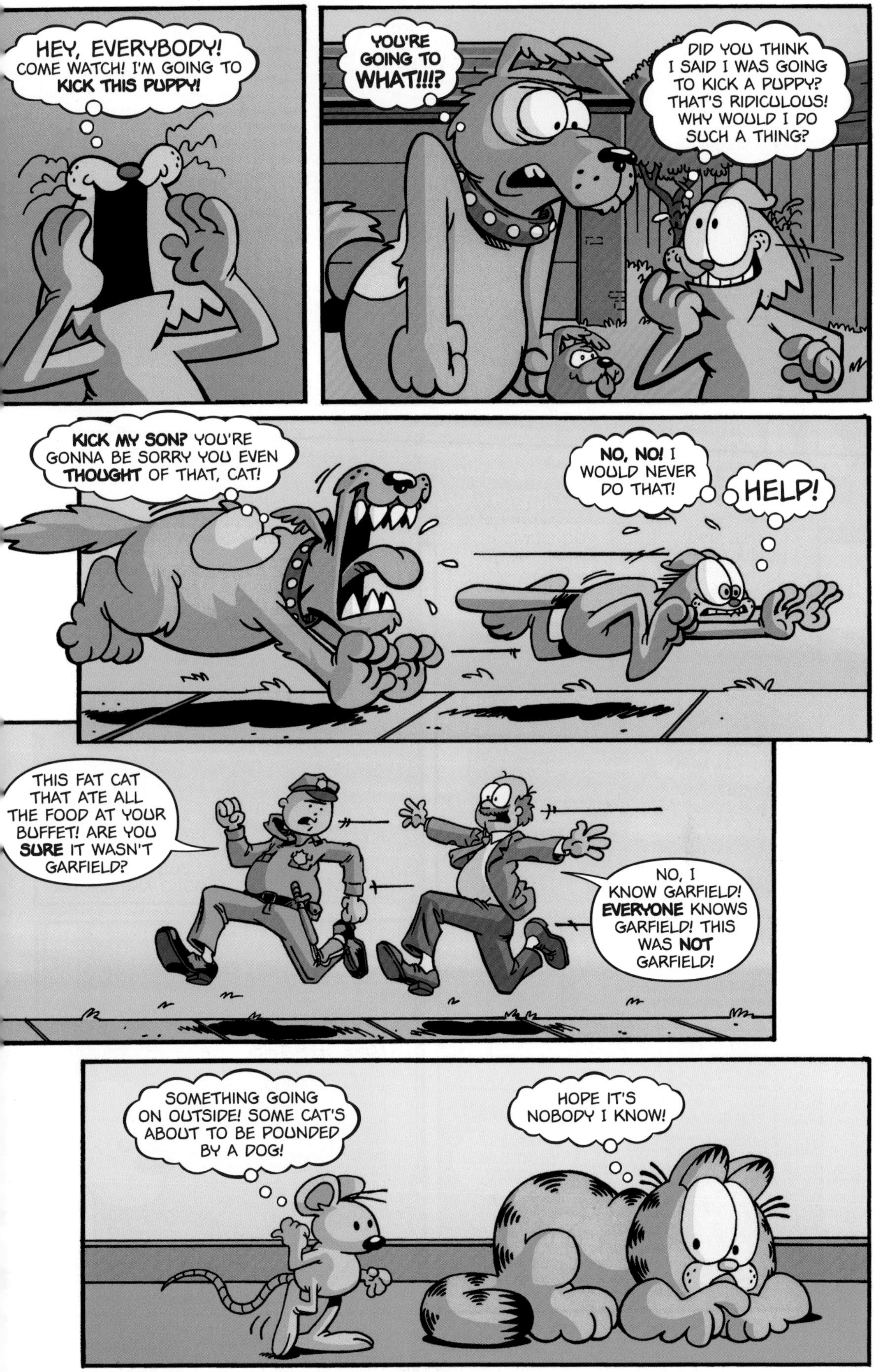
HEY, EVERYBODY! COME WATCH! I'M GOING TO KICK THIS PUPPY!
YOU'RE GOING TO WHAT!!!?
DID YOU THINK I SAID I WAS GOING TO KICK A PUPPY? THAT'S RIDICULOUS! WHY WOULD I DO SUCH A THING?
KICK MY SON? YOU'RE GONNA BE SORRY YOU EVEN THOUGHT OF THAT, CAT!
NO, NO! I WOULD NEVER DO THAT!
HELP!
THIS FAT CAT THAT ATE ALL THE FOOD AT YOUR BUFFET! ARE YOU SURE IT WASN'T GARFIELD?
NO, I KNOW GARFIELD! EVERYONE KNOWS GARFIELD! THIS WAS NOT GARFIELD!
SOMETHING GOING ON OUTSIDE! SOME CAT'S ABOUT TO BE POUNDED BY A DOG!
HOPE IT'S NOBODY I KNOW!

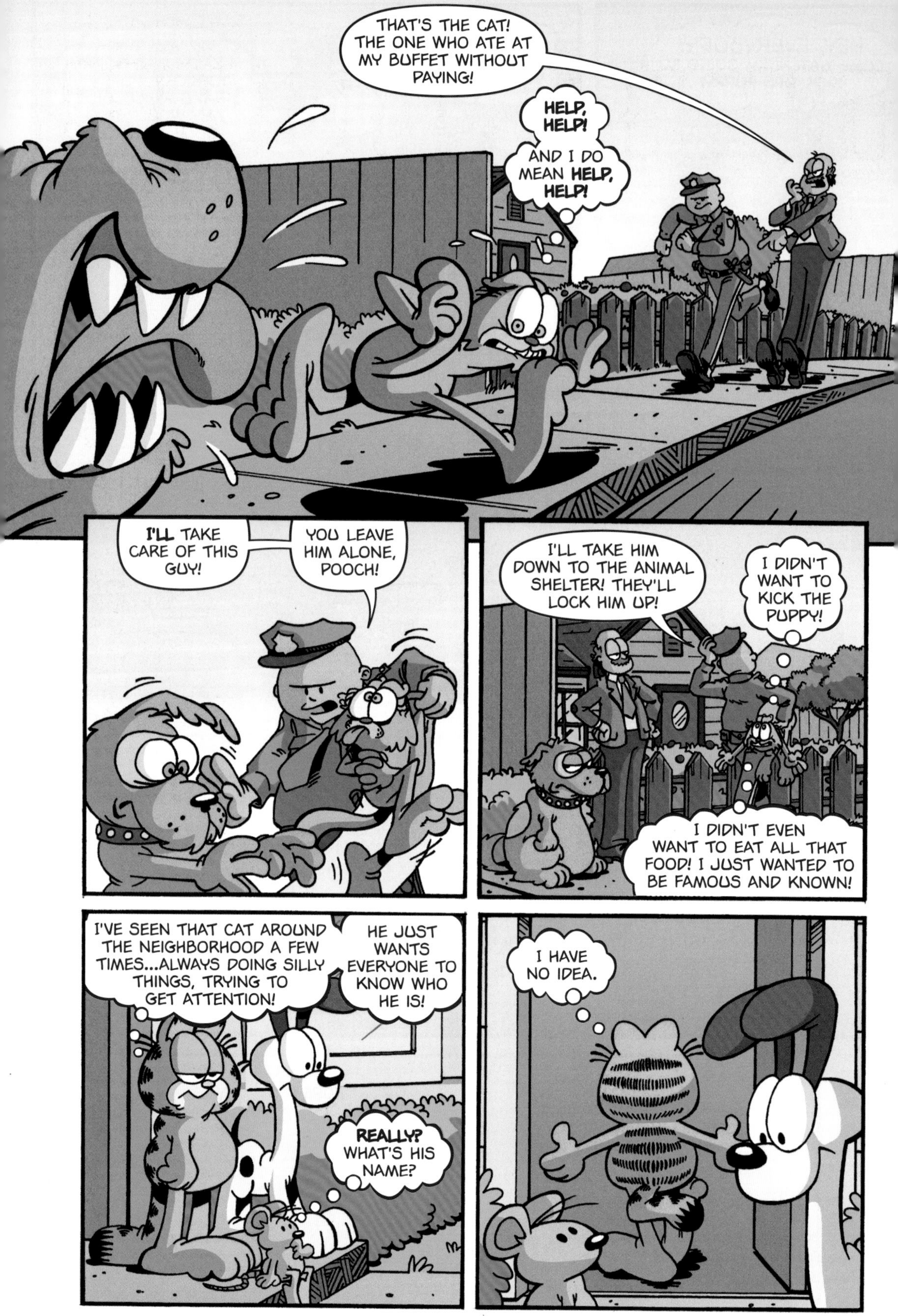
THAT'S THE CAT! THE ONE WHO ATE AT MY BUFFET WITHOUT PAYING!
HELP, HELP!
AND I DO MEAN HELP, HELP!
I'LL TAKE CARE OF THIS GUY!
YOU LEAVE HIM ALONE, POOCH!
I'LL TAKE HIM DOWN TO THE ANIMAL SHELTER! THEY'LL LOCK HIM UP!
I DIDN'T WANT TO KICK THE PUPPY!
I DIDN'T EVEN WANT TO EAT ALL THAT FOOD! I JUST WANTED TO BE FAMOUS AND KNOWN!
I'VE SEEN THAT CAT AROUND THE NEIGHBORHOOD A FEW TIMES...ALWAYS DOING SILLY THINGS, TRYING TO GET ATTENTION!
HE JUST WANTS EVERYONE TO KNOW WHO HE IS!
REALLY? WHAT'S HIS NAME?
I HAVE NO IDEA.

THE END

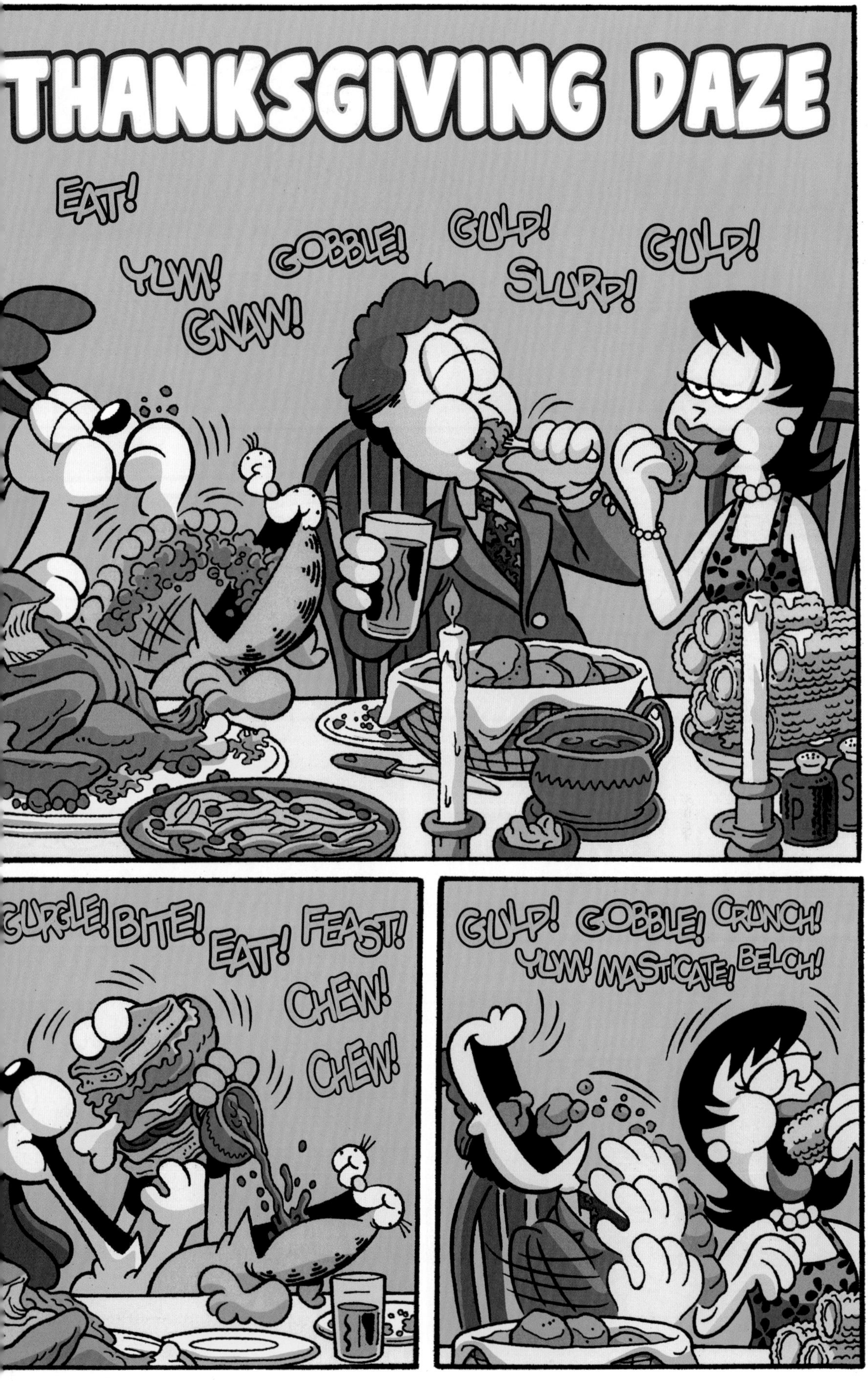
THANKSGIVING DAZE
EAT!
YUM!
GNAW!
GOBBLE!
GULP!
SLURP!
GULP!
GURGLE! BITE!
EAT! FEAST!
CHEW!
CHEW!
GULP! GOBBLE! CRUNCH!
YUM! MASTICATE! BELCH!

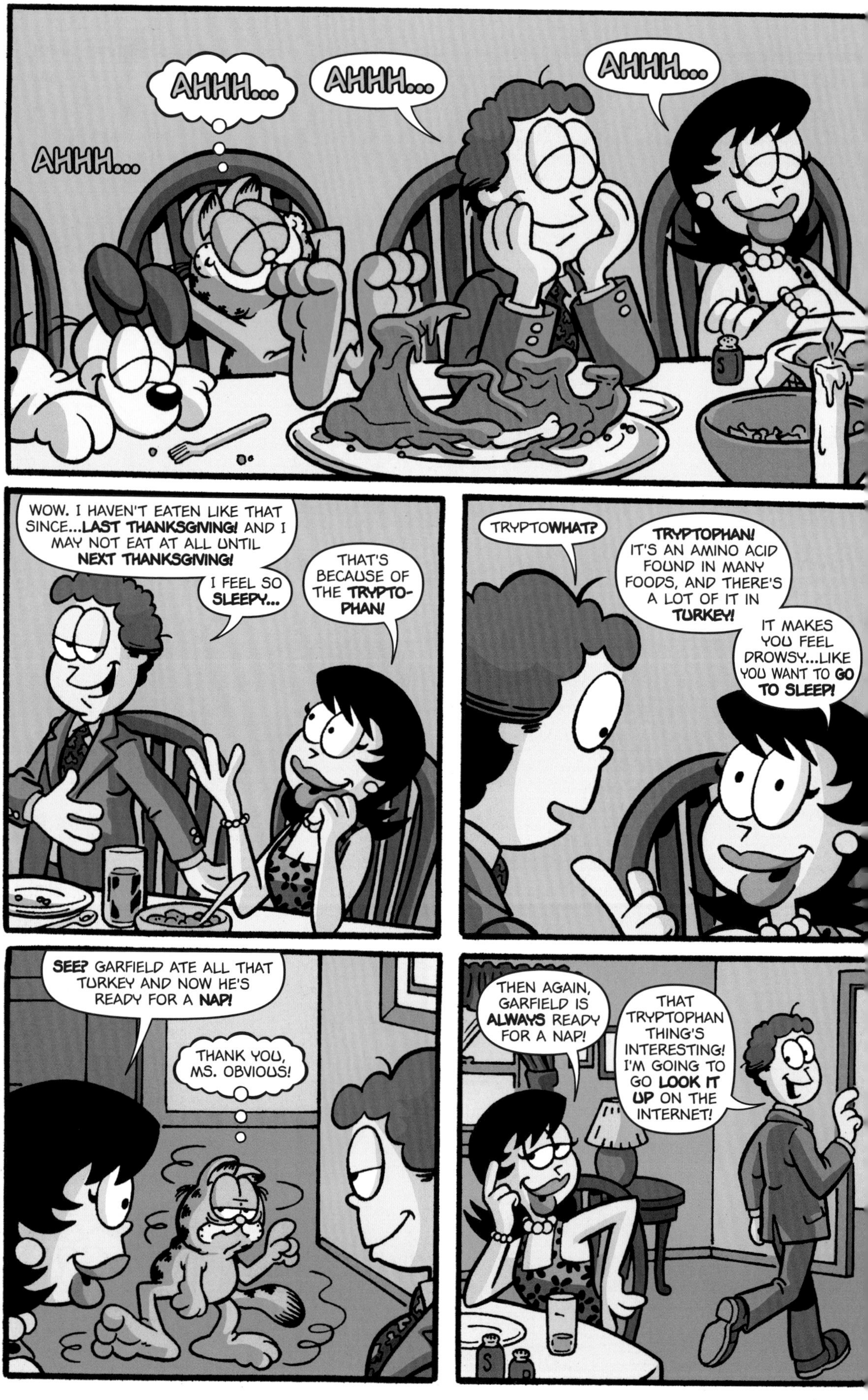
AHHH...
AHHH...
AHHH...
AHHH...
WOW. I HAVEN'T EATEN LIKE THAT SINCE...LAST THANKSGIVING! AND I MAY NOT EAT AT ALL UNTIL NEXT THANKSGIVING!
I FEEL SO SLEEPY...
THAT'S BECAUSE OF THE TRYPTO-PHAN!
TRYPTOWHAT?
TRYPTOPHAN! IT'S AN AMINO ACID FOUND IN MANY FOODS, AND THERE'S A LOT OF IT IN TURKEY!
IT MAKES YOU FEEL DROWSY...LIKE YOU WANT TO GO TO SLEEP!
SEE? GARFIELD ATE ALL THAT TURKEY AND NOW HE'S READY FOR A NAP!
THANK YOU, MS. OBVIOUS!
THEN AGAIN, GARFIELD IS ALWAYS READY FOR A NAP!
THAT TRYPTOPHAN THING'S INTERESTING! I'M GOING TO GO LOOK IT UP ON THE INTERNET!

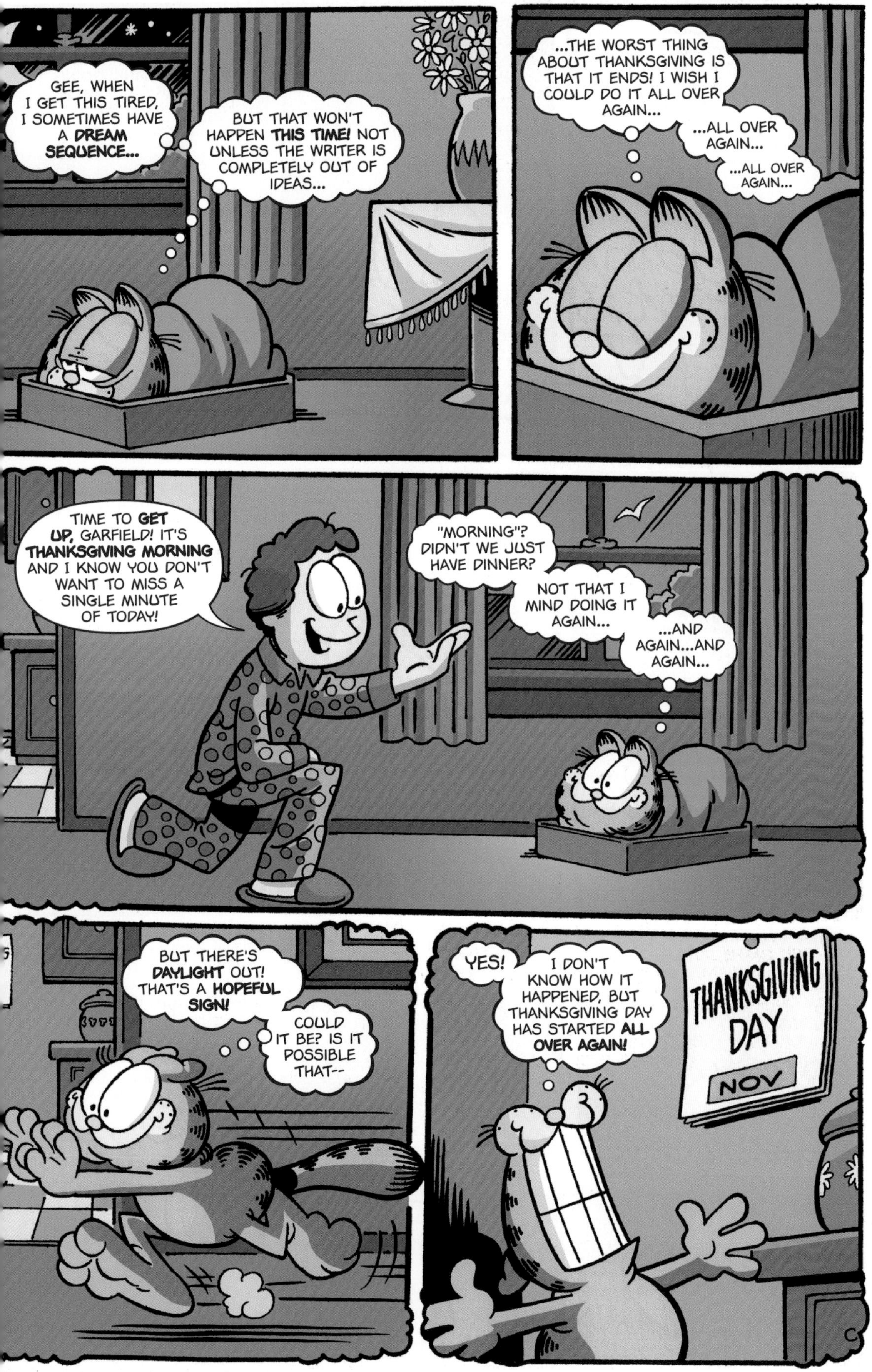

GEE, WHEN I GET THIS TIRED, I SOMETIMES HAVE A **DREAM SEQUENCE...**
BUT THAT WON'T HAPPEN **THIS TIME!** NOT UNLESS THE WRITER IS COMPLETELY OUT OF IDEAS...
...THE WORST THING ABOUT THANKSGIVING IS THAT IT ENDS! I WISH I COULD DO IT ALL OVER AGAIN...
...ALL OVER AGAIN...
...ALL OVER AGAIN...
TIME TO **GET UP,** GARFIELD! IT'S **THANKSGIVING MORNING** AND I KNOW YOU DON'T WANT TO MISS A SINGLE MINUTE OF TODAY!
"MORNING"? DIDN'T WE JUST HAVE DINNER?
NOT THAT I MIND DOING IT AGAIN...
...AND AGAIN...AND AGAIN...
BUT THERE'S **DAYLIGHT** OUT! THAT'S A **HOPEFUL SIGN!**
COULD IT BE? IS IT POSSIBLE THAT--
YES!
I DON'T KNOW HOW IT HAPPENED, BUT THANKSGIVING DAY HAS STARTED **ALL OVER AGAIN!**
THANKSGIVING DAY
NOV

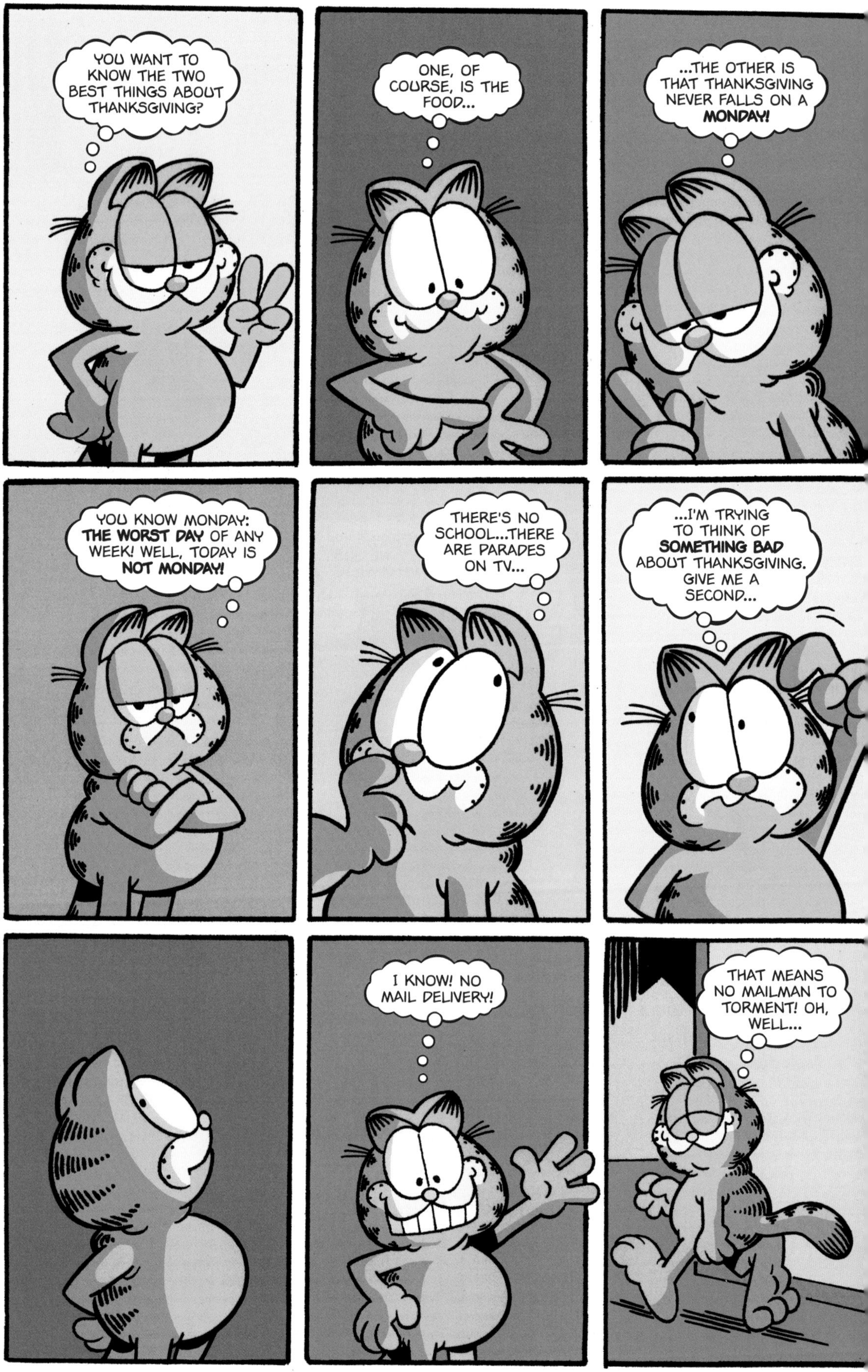
YOU WANT TO KNOW THE TWO BEST THINGS ABOUT THANKSGIVING?
ONE, OF COURSE, IS THE FOOD...
...THE OTHER IS THAT THANKSGIVING NEVER FALLS ON A **MONDAY!**
YOU KNOW MONDAY: **THE WORST DAY** OF ANY WEEK! WELL, TODAY IS **NOT MONDAY!**
THERE'S NO SCHOOL...THERE ARE PARADES ON TV...
...I'M TRYING TO THINK OF **SOMETHING BAD** ABOUT THANKSGIVING. GIVE ME A SECOND...
I KNOW! NO MAIL DELIVERY!
THAT MEANS NO MAILMAN TO TORMENT! OH, WELL...

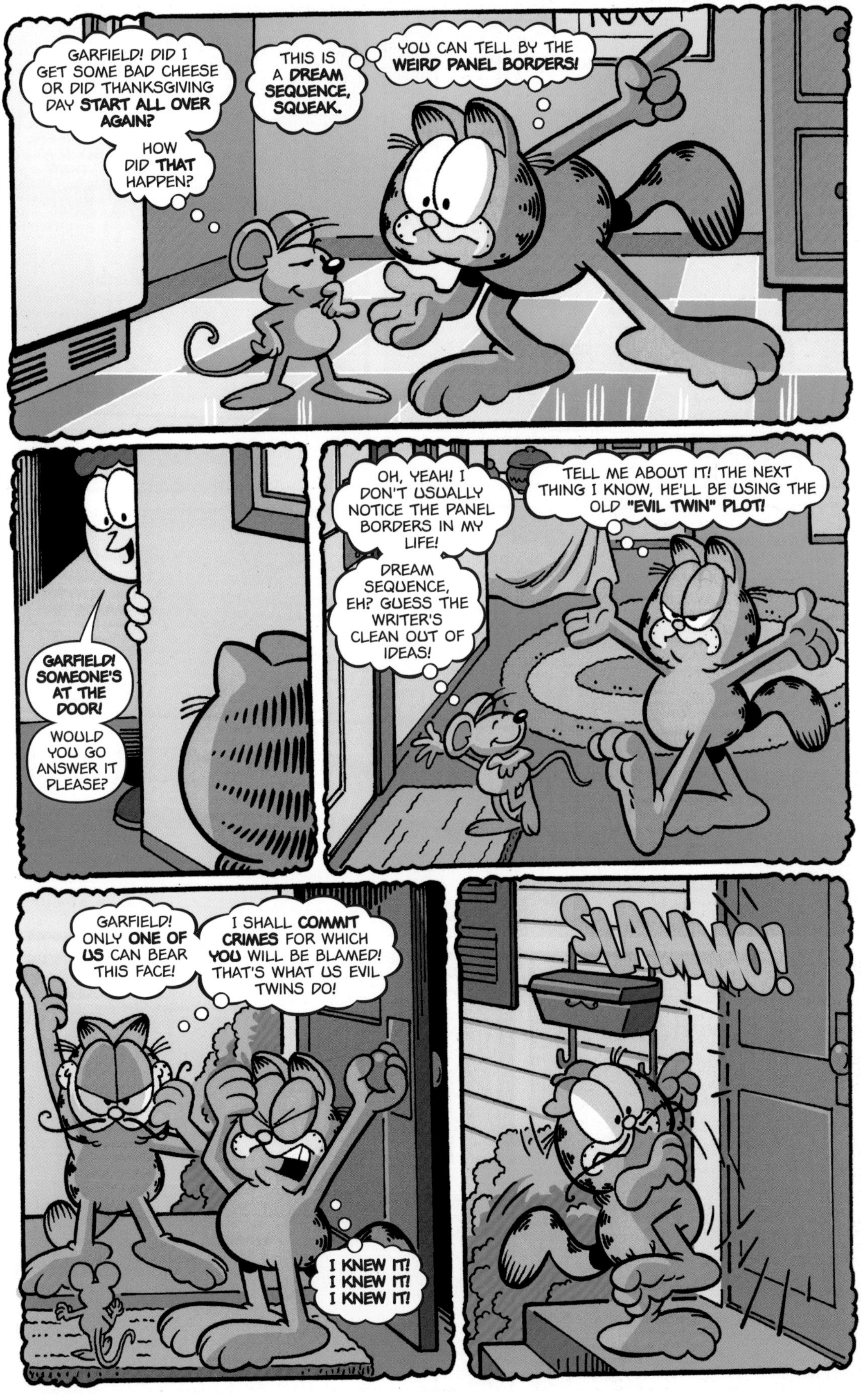

GARFIELD! DID I GET SOME BAD CHEESE OR DID THANKSGIVING DAY **START ALL OVER AGAIN?**
HOW DID **THAT** HAPPEN?
THIS IS A **DREAM SEQUENCE, SQUEAK.**
YOU CAN TELL BY THE **WEIRD PANEL BORDERS!**
GARFIELD! SOMEONE'S AT THE DOOR!
WOULD YOU GO ANSWER IT PLEASE?
OH, YEAH! I DON'T USUALLY NOTICE THE PANEL BORDERS IN MY LIFE!
DREAM SEQUENCE, EH? GUESS THE WRITER'S CLEAN OUT OF IDEAS!
TELL ME ABOUT IT! THE NEXT THING I KNOW, HE'LL BE USING THE OLD **"EVIL TWIN" PLOT!**
GARFIELD! ONLY **ONE OF US** CAN BEAR THIS FACE!
I SHALL **COMMIT CRIMES** FOR WHICH **YOU** WILL BE BLAMED! THAT'S WHAT US EVIL TWINS DO!
I KNEW IT! I KNEW IT! I KNEW IT!
SLAMMO!

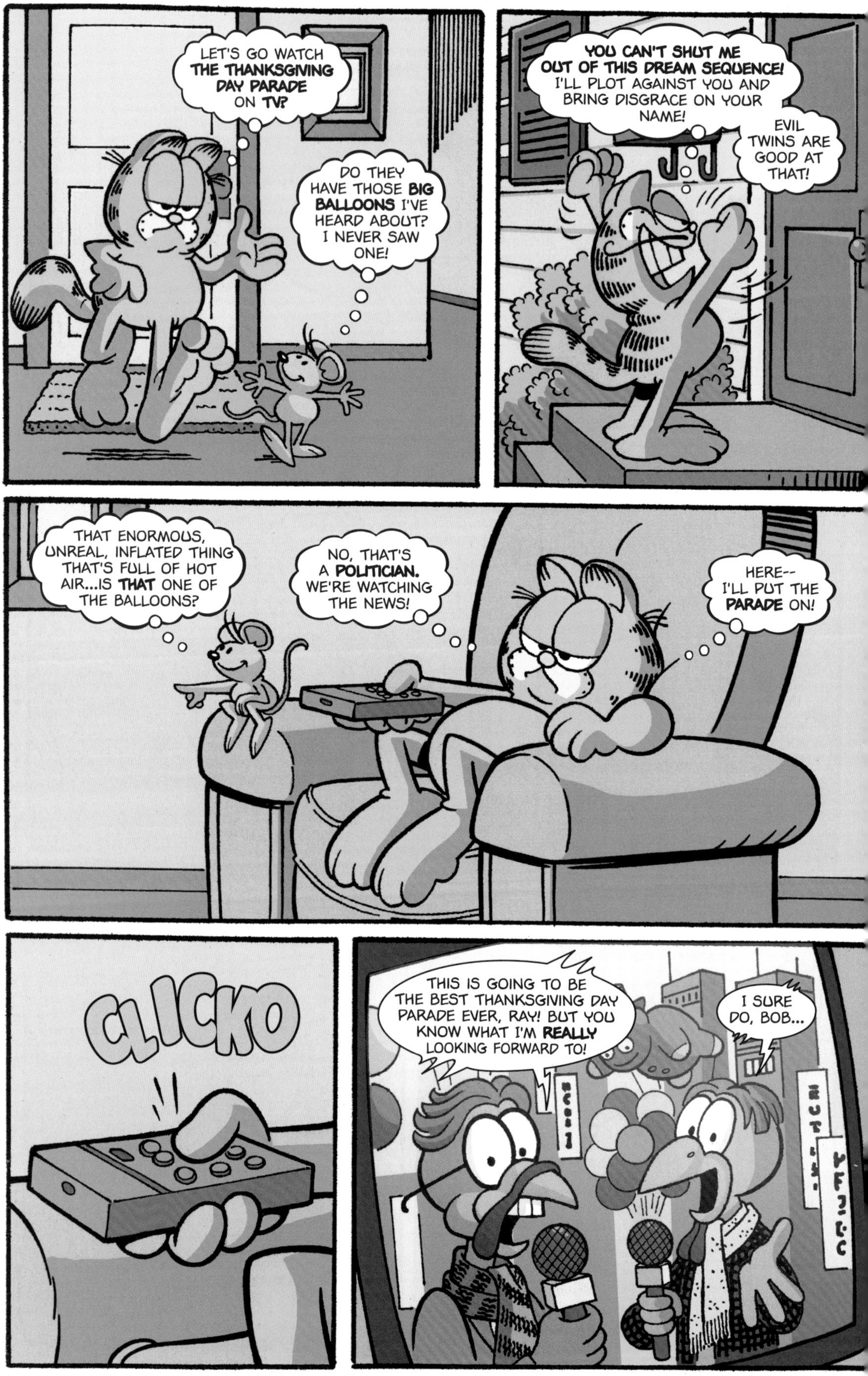

LET'S GO WATCH **THE THANKSGIVING DAY PARADE** ON **TV?**
DO THEY HAVE THOSE **BIG BALLOONS** I'VE HEARD ABOUT? I NEVER SAW ONE!
YOU CAN'T SHUT ME OUT OF THIS DREAM SEQUENCE! I'LL PLOT AGAINST YOU AND BRING DISGRACE ON YOUR NAME!
EVIL TWINS ARE GOOD AT THAT!
THAT ENORMOUS, UNREAL, INFLATED THING THAT'S FULL OF HOT AIR...IS **THAT** ONE OF THE BALLOONS?
NO, THAT'S A **POLITICIAN.** WE'RE WATCHING THE NEWS!
HERE-- I'LL PUT THE **PARADE** ON!
CLICKO
THIS IS GOING TO BE THE BEST THANKSGIVING DAY PARADE EVER, RAY! BUT YOU KNOW WHAT I'M **REALLY** LOOKING FORWARD TO!
I SURE DO, BOB...

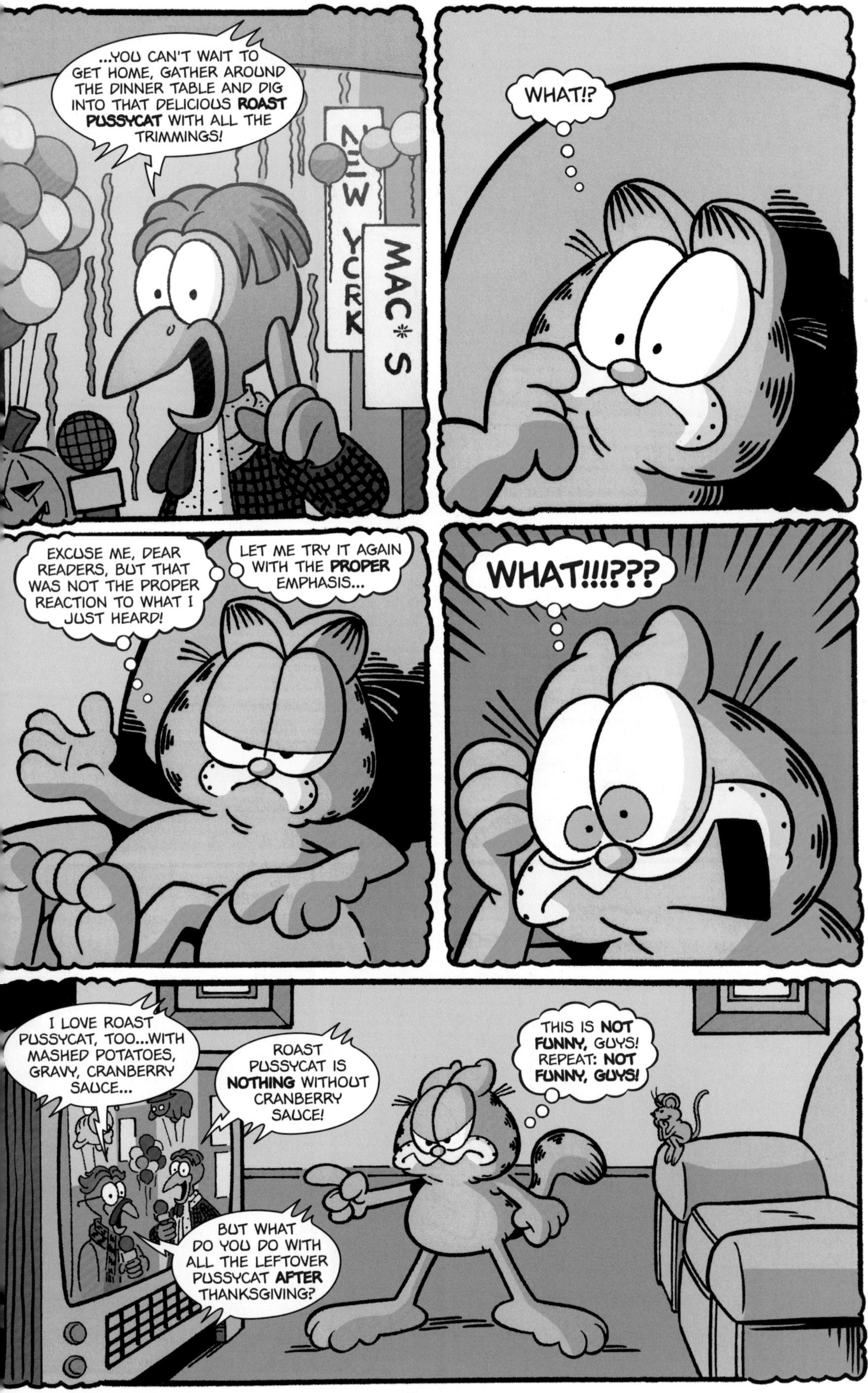
...YOU CAN'T WAIT TO GET HOME, GATHER AROUND THE DINNER TABLE AND DIG INTO THAT DELICIOUS **ROAST PUSSYCAT** WITH ALL THE TRIMMINGS!
NEW YORK
MAC*S
WHAT!?
EXCUSE ME, DEAR READERS, BUT THAT WAS NOT THE PROPER REACTION TO WHAT I JUST HEARD!
LET ME TRY IT AGAIN WITH THE **PROPER** EMPHASIS...
WHAT!!!???
I LOVE ROAST PUSSYCAT, TOO...WITH MASHED POTATOES, GRAVY, CRANBERRY SAUCE...
ROAST PUSSYCAT IS **NOTHING** WITHOUT CRANBERRY SAUCE!
BUT WHAT DO YOU DO WITH ALL THE LEFTOVER PUSSYCAT **AFTER** THANKSGIVING?
THIS IS **NOT FUNNY**, GUYS! REPEAT: **NOT FUNNY, GUYS!**

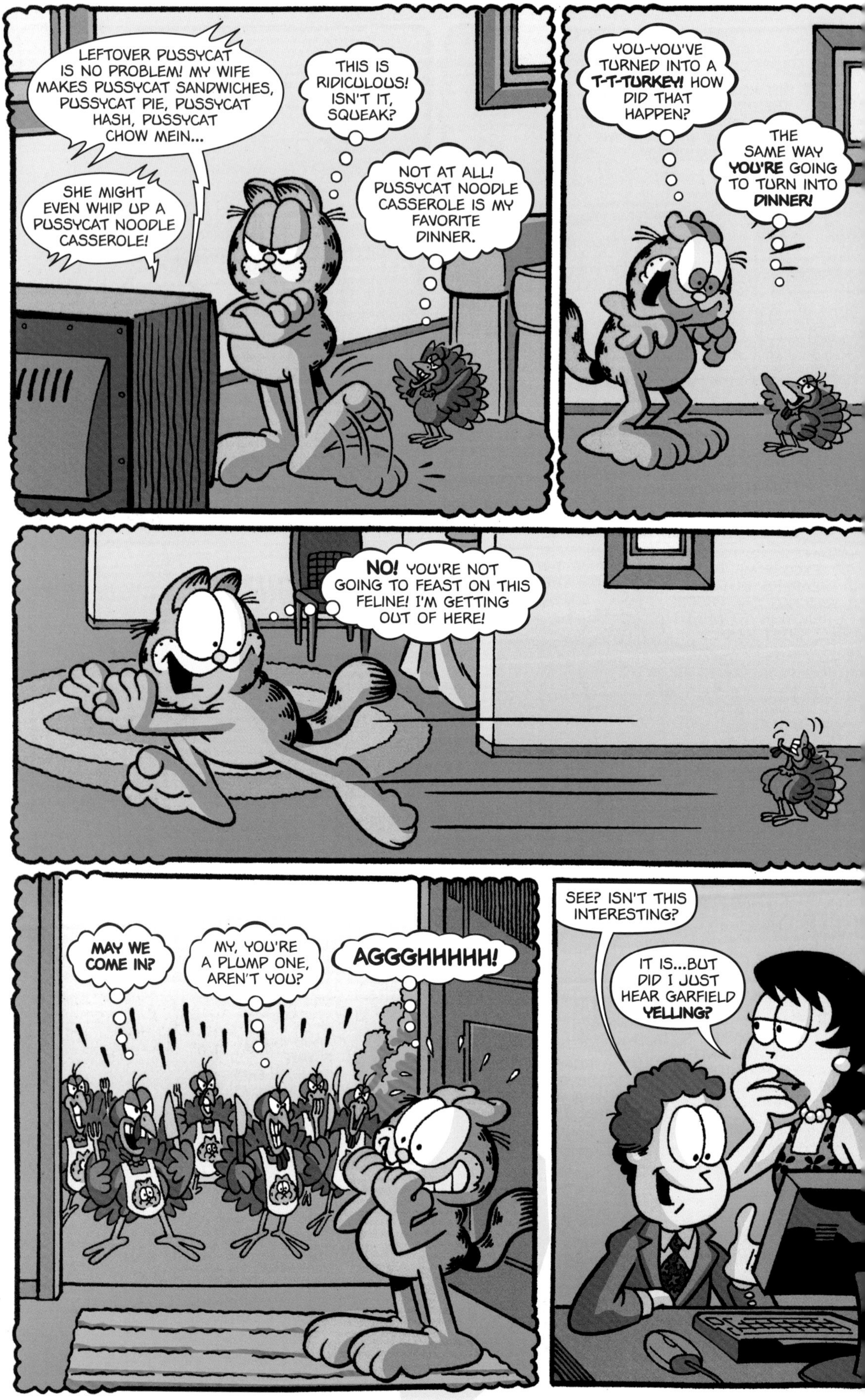

LEFTOVER PUSSYCAT IS NO PROBLEM! MY WIFE MAKES PUSSYCAT SANDWICHES, PUSSYCAT PIE, PUSSYCAT HASH, PUSSYCAT CHOW MEIN...
SHE MIGHT EVEN WHIP UP A PUSSYCAT NOODLE CASSEROLE!
THIS IS RIDICULOUS! ISN'T IT, SQUEAK?
NOT AT ALL! PUSSYCAT NOODLE CASSEROLE IS MY FAVORITE DINNER.
YOU-YOU'VE TURNED INTO A T-T-TURKEY! HOW DID THAT HAPPEN?
THE SAME WAY YOU'RE GOING TO TURN INTO DINNER!
NO! YOU'RE NOT GOING TO FEAST ON THIS FELINE! I'M GETTING OUT OF HERE!
MAY WE COME IN?
MY, YOU'RE A PLUMP ONE, AREN'T YOU?
AGGGHHHHH!
SEE? ISN'T THIS INTERESTING?
IT IS...BUT DID I JUST HEAR GARFIELD YELLING?

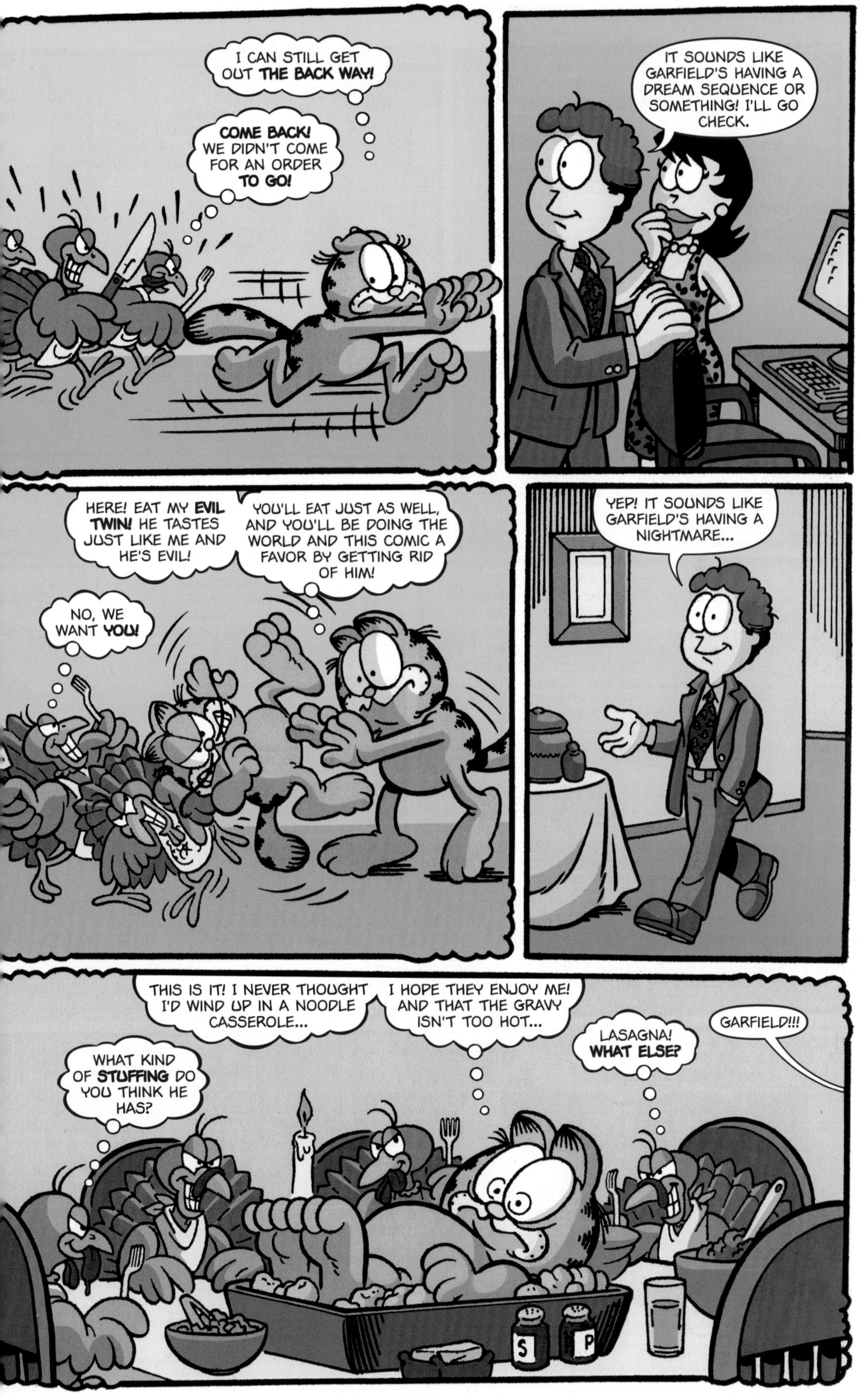
I CAN STILL GET OUT **THE BACK WAY!**
COME BACK! WE DIDN'T COME FOR AN ORDER **TO GO!**
IT SOUNDS LIKE GARFIELD'S HAVING A DREAM SEQUENCE OR SOMETHING! I'LL GO CHECK.
HERE! EAT MY **EVIL TWIN!** HE TASTES JUST LIKE ME AND HE'S EVIL!
YOU'LL EAT JUST AS WELL, AND YOU'LL BE DOING THE WORLD AND THIS COMIC A FAVOR BY GETTING RID OF HIM!
NO, WE WANT **YOU!**
YEP! IT SOUNDS LIKE GARFIELD'S HAVING A NIGHTMARE...
WHAT KIND OF **STUFFING** DO YOU THINK HE HAS?
THIS IS IT! I NEVER THOUGHT I'D WIND UP IN A NOODLE CASSEROLE...
I HOPE THEY ENJOY ME! AND THAT THE GRAVY ISN'T TOO HOT...
LASAGNA! **WHAT ELSE?**
GARFIELD!!!
S
P

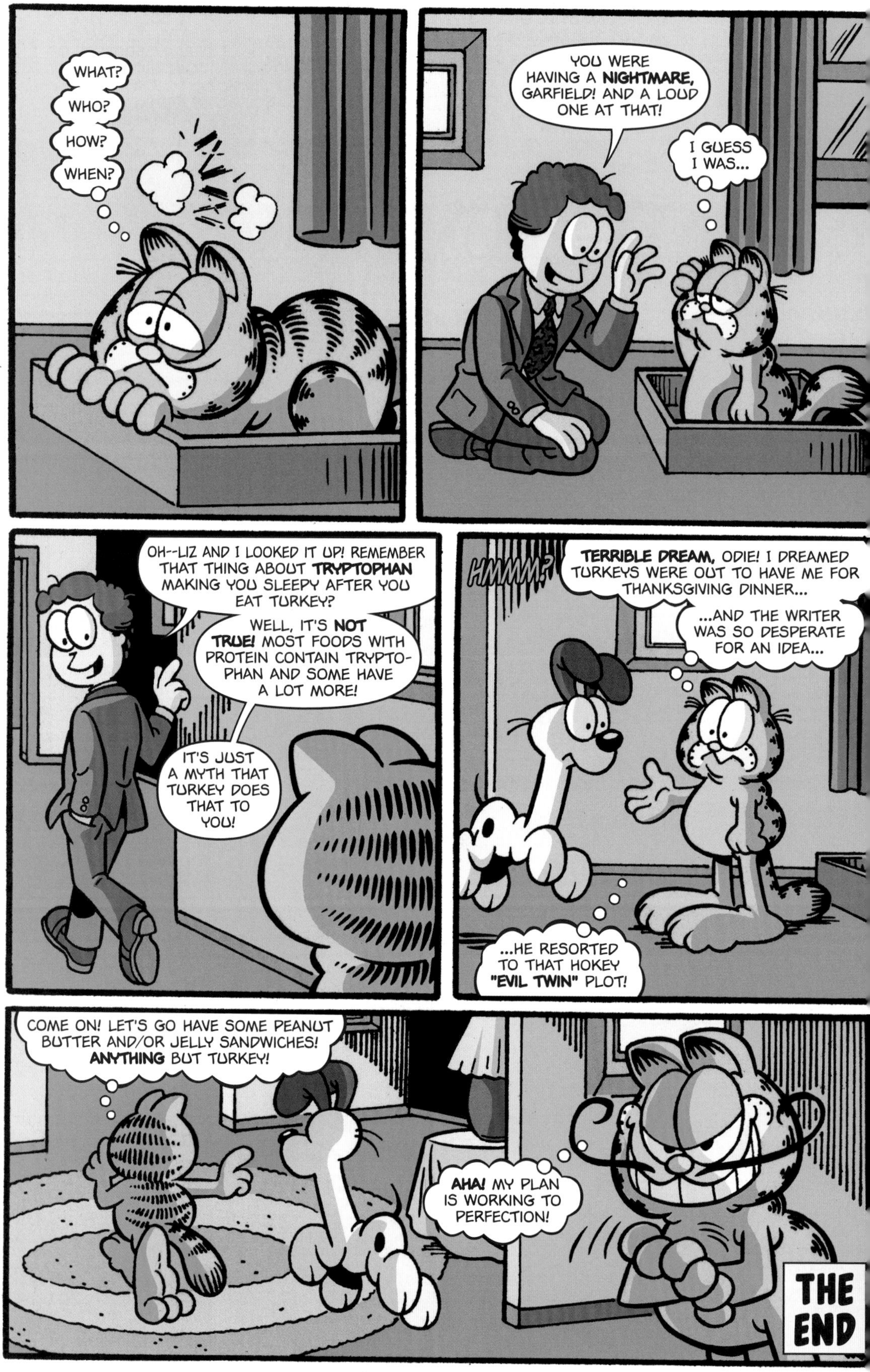

WHAT?
WHO?
HOW?
WHEN?
YOU WERE HAVING A NIGHTMARE, GARFIELD! AND A LOUD ONE AT THAT!
I GUESS I WAS...
OH--LIZ AND I LOOKED IT UP! REMEMBER THAT THING ABOUT TRYPTOPHAN MAKING YOU SLEEPY AFTER YOU EAT TURKEY?
WELL, IT'S NOT TRUE! MOST FOODS WITH PROTEIN CONTAIN TRYPTO-PHAN AND SOME HAVE A LOT MORE!
IT'S JUST A MYTH THAT TURKEY DOES THAT TO YOU!
HMMM?
TERRIBLE DREAM, ODIE! I DREAMED TURKEYS WERE OUT TO HAVE ME FOR THANKSGIVING DINNER...
...AND THE WRITER WAS SO DESPERATE FOR AN IDEA...
...HE RESORTED TO THAT HOKEY "EVIL TWIN" PLOT!
COME ON! LET'S GO HAVE SOME PEANUT BUTTER AND/OR JELLY SANDWICHES! ANYTHING BUT TURKEY!
AHA! MY PLAN IS WORKING TO PERFECTION!
THE END

CHAPTER EIGHT

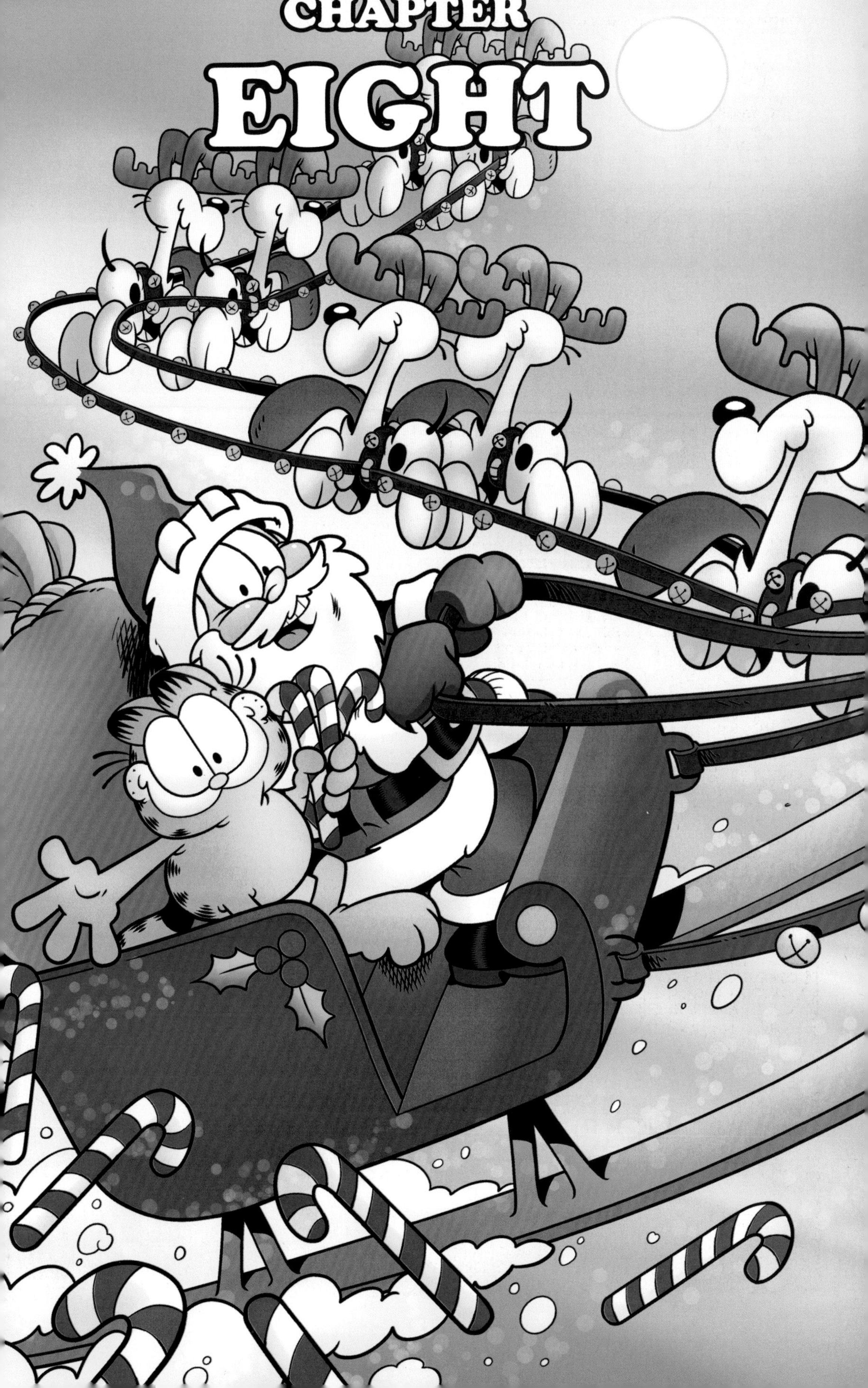

THE NEVER-ENDING TALE OF SANTA MOUSE
SNOW PROBLEM

Written by
MARK EVANIER
(Pages 177-188)
SCOTT NICKEL
(Pages 189-198)

Art by
ANDY HIRSCH
WITH MARK
AND STEPHANIE HEIKE
(Pages 177-188)
MIKE DeCARLO
(Pages 189-198)

Colors by
LISA MOORE

Chapter Break Art by
GARY BARKER
AND DAN DAVIS
WITH LISA MOORE

The Never-Ending Tale of Santa Mouse

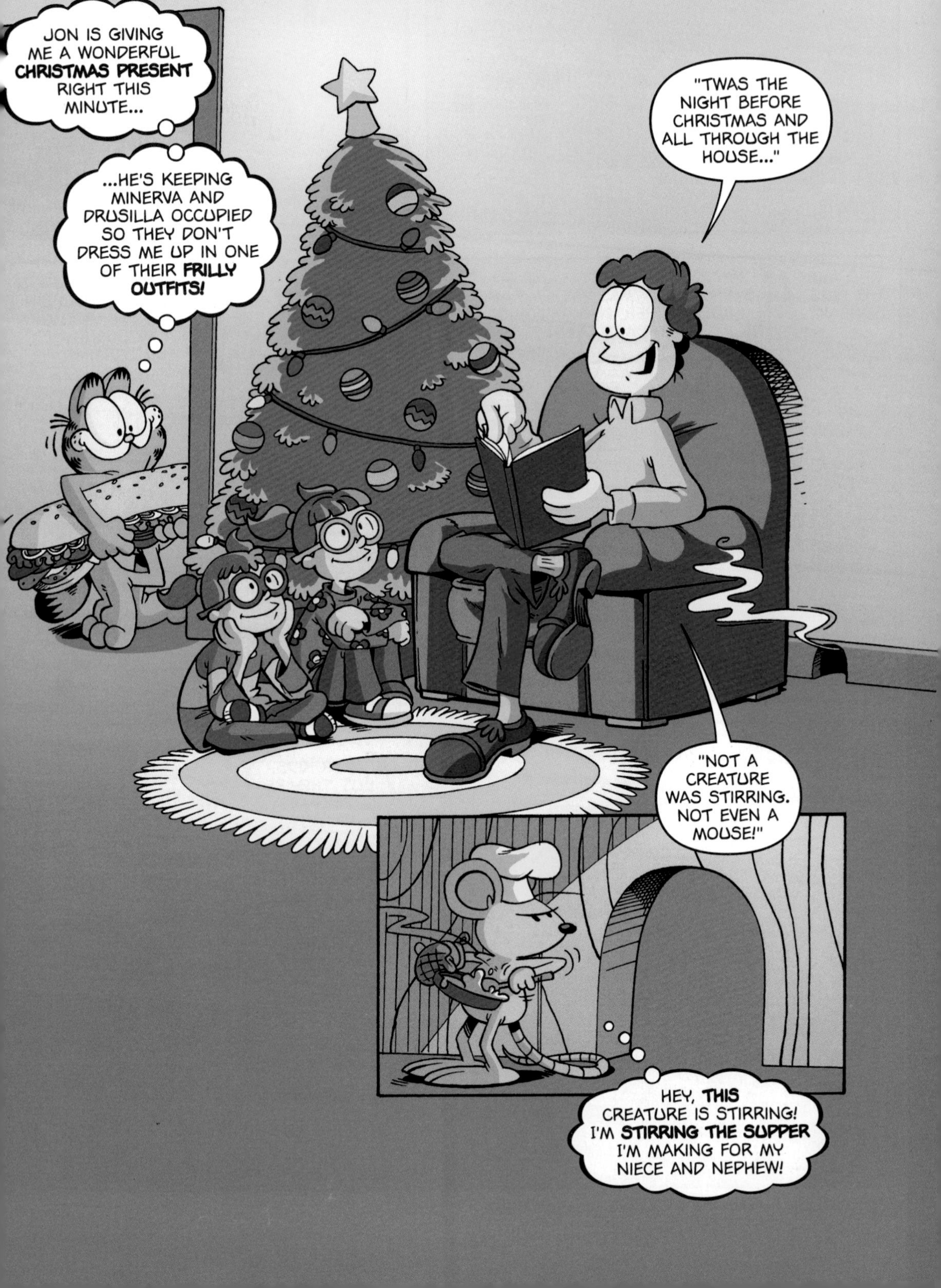

JON IS GIVING ME A WONDERFUL CHRISTMAS PRESENT RIGHT THIS MINUTE...
...HE'S KEEPING MINERVA AND DRUSILLA OCCUPIED SO THEY DON'T DRESS ME UP IN ONE OF THEIR FRILLY OUTFITS!
"TWAS THE NIGHT BEFORE CHRISTMAS AND ALL THROUGH THE HOUSE..."
"NOT A CREATURE WAS STIRRING. NOT EVEN A MOUSE!"
HEY, THIS CREATURE IS STIRRING! I'M STIRRING THE SUPPER I'M MAKING FOR MY NIECE AND NEPHEW!

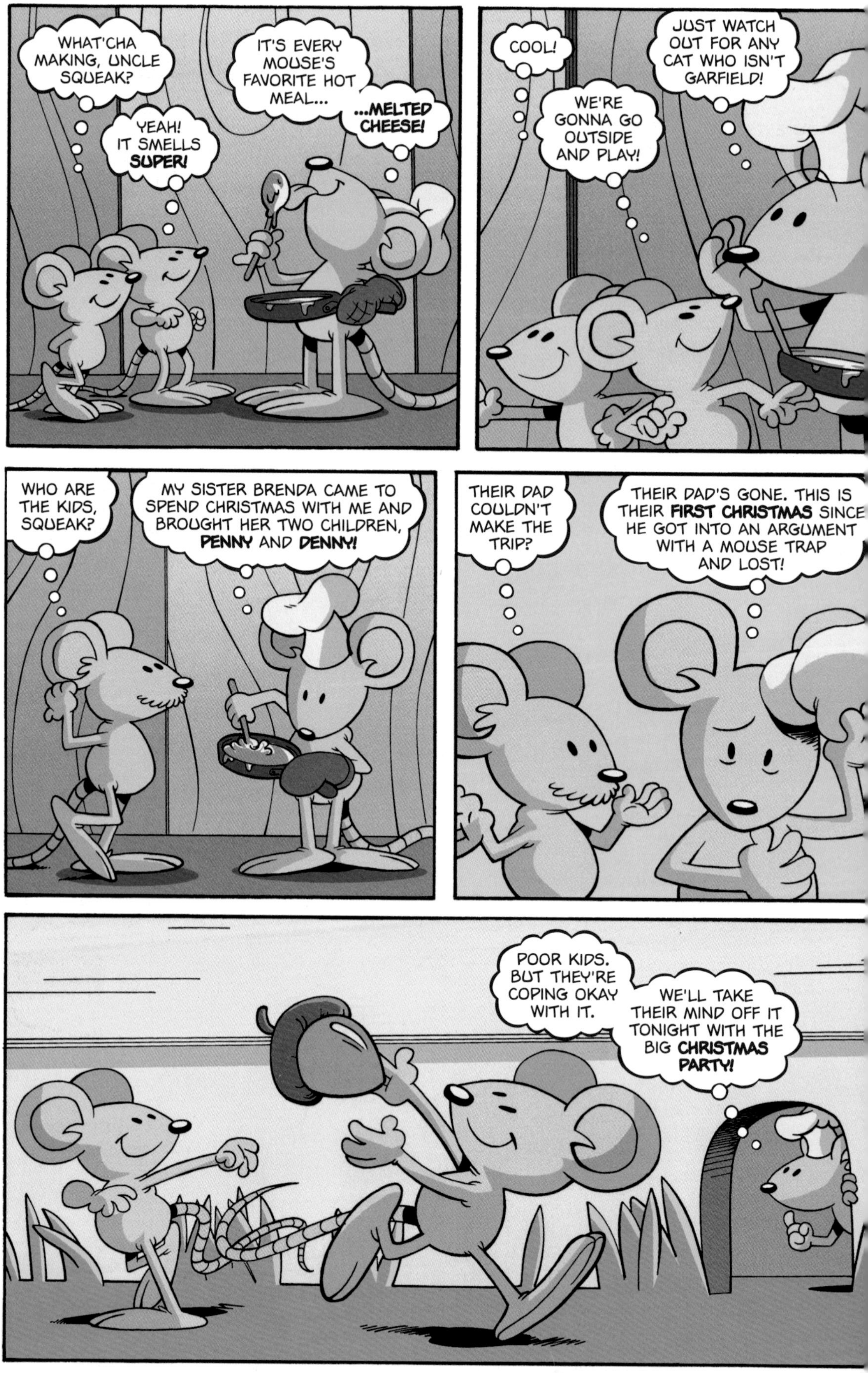
WHAT'CHA MAKING, UNCLE SQUEAK?
YEAH! IT SMELLS SUPER!
IT'S EVERY MOUSE'S FAVORITE HOT MEAL...
...MELTED CHEESE!
COOL!
WE'RE GONNA GO OUTSIDE AND PLAY!
JUST WATCH OUT FOR ANY CAT WHO ISN'T GARFIELD!
WHO ARE THE KIDS, SQUEAK?
MY SISTER BRENDA CAME TO SPEND CHRISTMAS WITH ME AND BROUGHT HER TWO CHILDREN, PENNY AND DENNY!
THEIR DAD COULDN'T MAKE THE TRIP?
THEIR DAD'S GONE. THIS IS THEIR FIRST CHRISTMAS SINCE HE GOT INTO AN ARGUMENT WITH A MOUSE TRAP AND LOST!
POOR KIDS. BUT THEY'RE COPING OKAY WITH IT.
WE'LL TAKE THEIR MIND OFF IT TONIGHT WITH THE BIG CHRISTMAS PARTY!

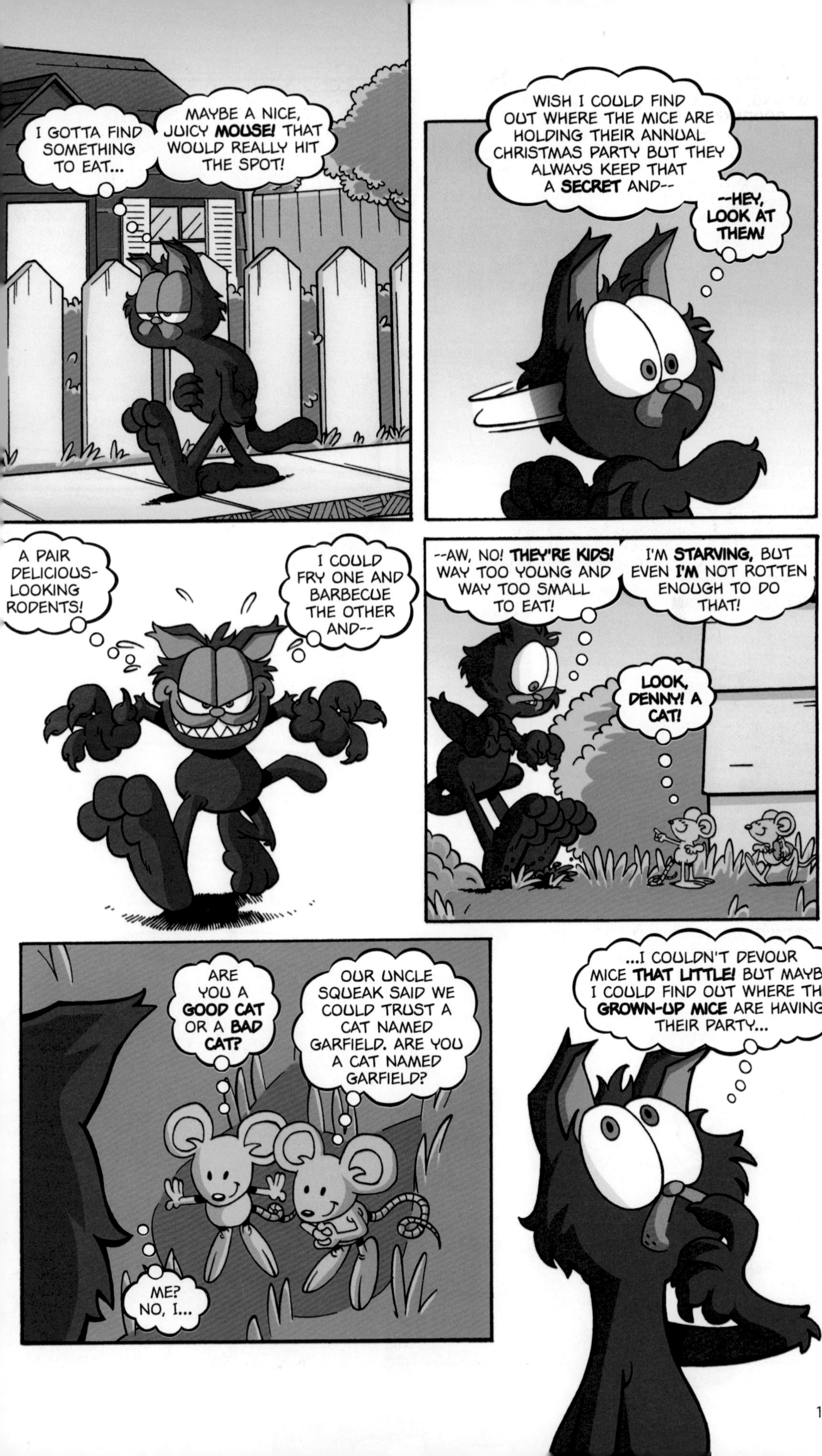
I GOTTA FIND SOMETHING TO EAT...
MAYBE A NICE, JUICY **MOUSE!** THAT WOULD REALLY HIT THE SPOT!
WISH I COULD FIND OUT WHERE THE MICE ARE HOLDING THEIR ANNUAL CHRISTMAS PARTY BUT THEY ALWAYS KEEP THAT A **SECRET** AND--
--HEY, LOOK AT THEM!
A PAIR DELICIOUS-LOOKING RODENTS!
I COULD FRY ONE AND BARBECUE THE OTHER AND--
--AW, NO! **THEY'RE KIDS!** WAY TOO YOUNG AND WAY TOO SMALL TO EAT!
I'M **STARVING,** BUT EVEN **I'M** NOT ROTTEN ENOUGH TO DO THAT!
LOOK, DENNY! A CAT!
ARE YOU A **GOOD CAT** OR A **BAD CAT?**
OUR UNCLE SQUEAK SAID WE COULD TRUST A CAT NAMED GARFIELD. ARE YOU A CAT NAMED GARFIELD?
ME? NO, I...
...I COULDN'T DEVOUR MICE **THAT LITTLE!** BUT MAYBE I COULD FIND OUT WHERE THE **GROWN-UP MICE** ARE HAVING THEIR PARTY...

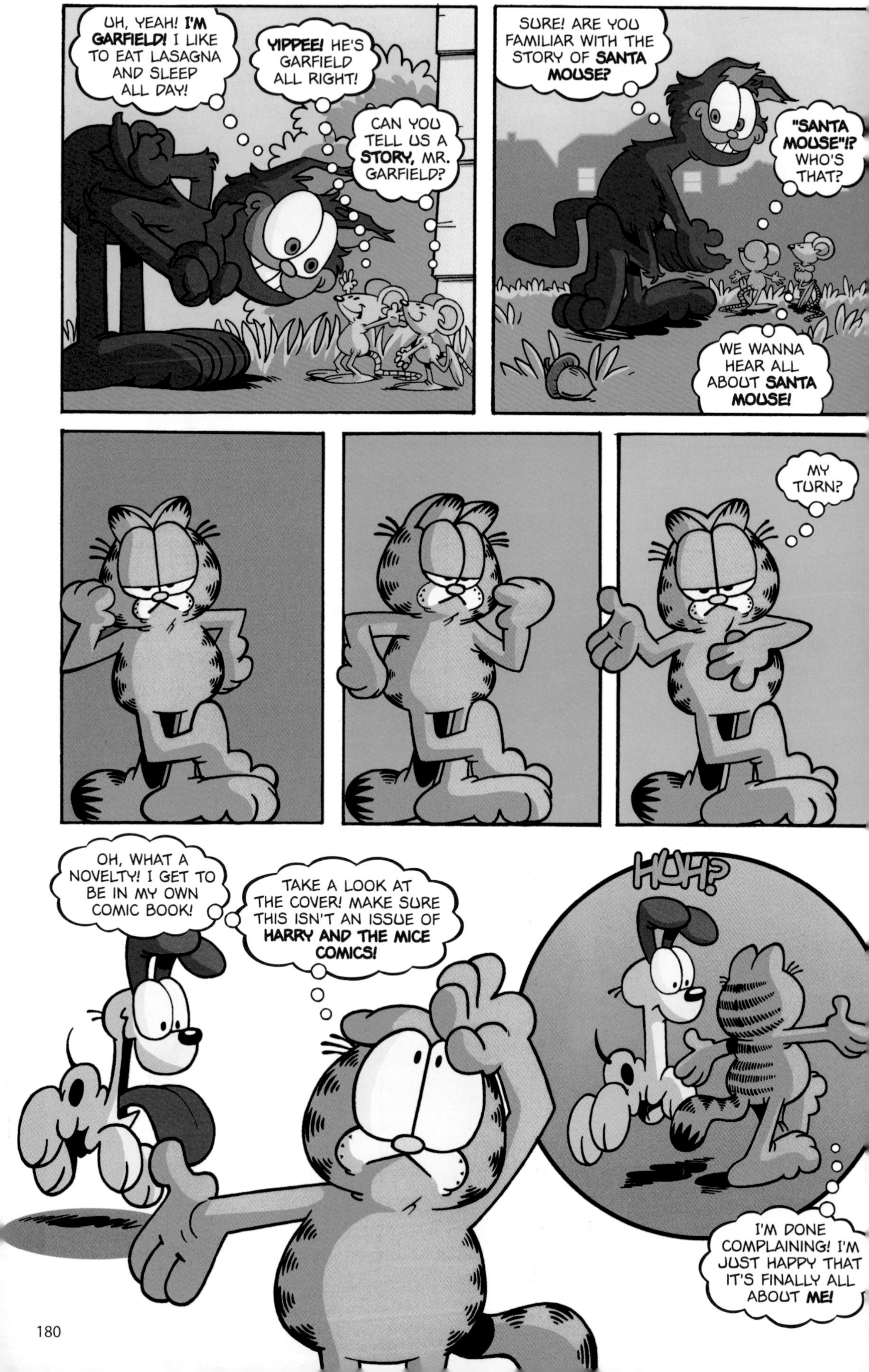

UH, YEAH! I'M GARFIELD! I LIKE TO EAT LASAGNA AND SLEEP ALL DAY!
YIPPEE! HE'S GARFIELD ALL RIGHT!
CAN YOU TELL US A STORY, MR. GARFIELD?
SURE! ARE YOU FAMILIAR WITH THE STORY OF SANTA MOUSE?
"SANTA MOUSE"!? WHO'S THAT?
WE WANNA HEAR ALL ABOUT SANTA MOUSE!
MY TURN?
OH, WHAT A NOVELTY! I GET TO BE IN MY OWN COMIC BOOK!
TAKE A LOOK AT THE COVER! MAKE SURE THIS ISN'T AN ISSUE OF HARRY AND THE MICE COMICS!
HUH?
I'M DONE COMPLAINING! I'M JUST HAPPY THAT IT'S FINALLY ALL ABOUT ME!

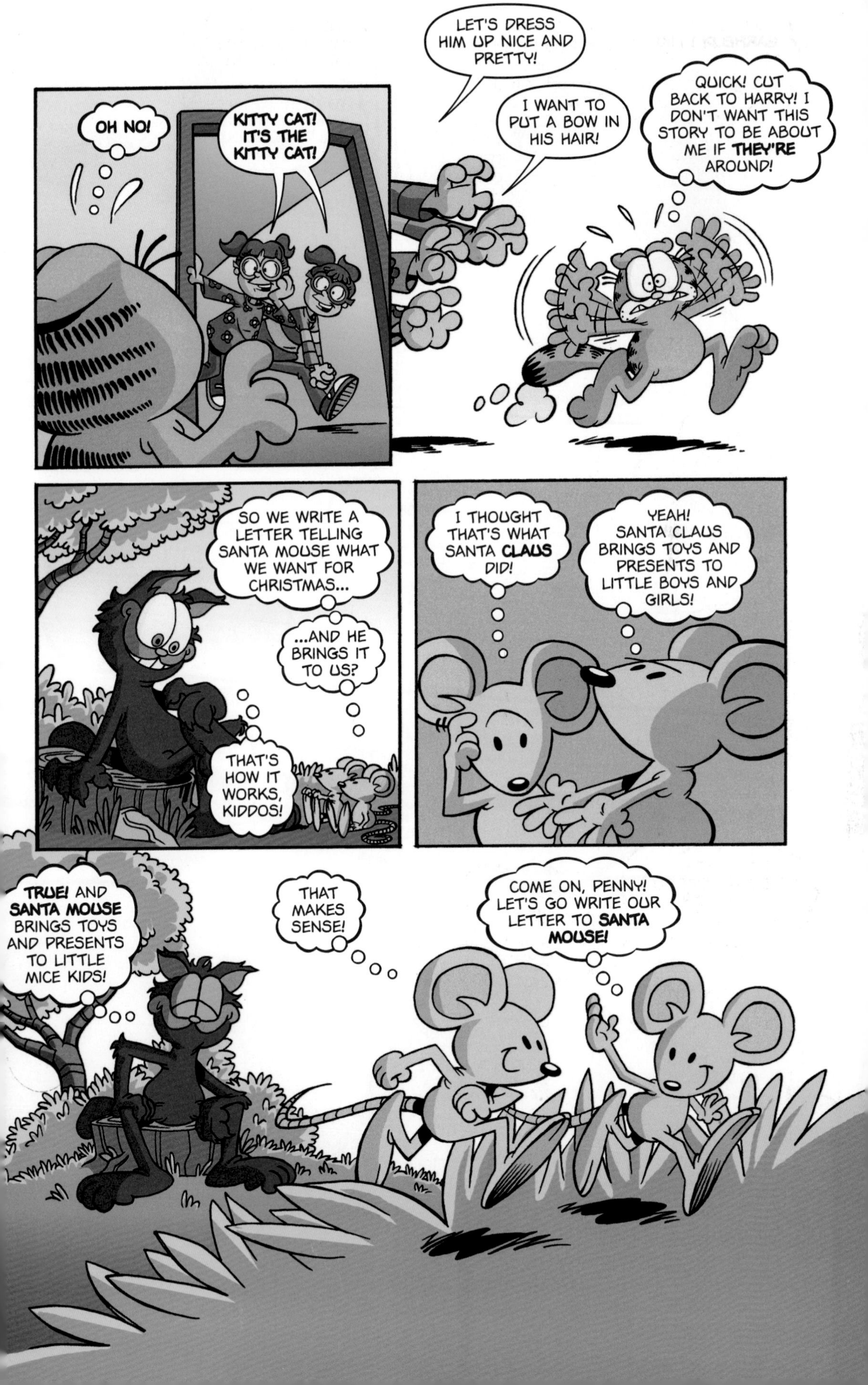
OH NO!
KITTY CAT! IT'S THE KITTY CAT!
LET'S DRESS HIM UP NICE AND PRETTY!
I WANT TO PUT A BOW IN HIS HAIR!
QUICK! CUT BACK TO HARRY! I DON'T WANT THIS STORY TO BE ABOUT ME IF **THEY'RE** AROUND!
SO WE WRITE A LETTER TELLING SANTA MOUSE WHAT WE WANT FOR CHRISTMAS...
...AND HE BRINGS IT TO US?
THAT'S HOW IT WORKS, KIDDOS!
I THOUGHT THAT'S WHAT SANTA **CLAUS** DID!
YEAH! SANTA CLAUS BRINGS TOYS AND PRESENTS TO LITTLE BOYS AND GIRLS!
TRUE! AND **SANTA MOUSE** BRINGS TOYS AND PRESENTS TO LITTLE MICE KIDS!
THAT MAKES SENSE!
COME ON, PENNY! LET'S GO WRITE OUR LETTER TO **SANTA MOUSE!**

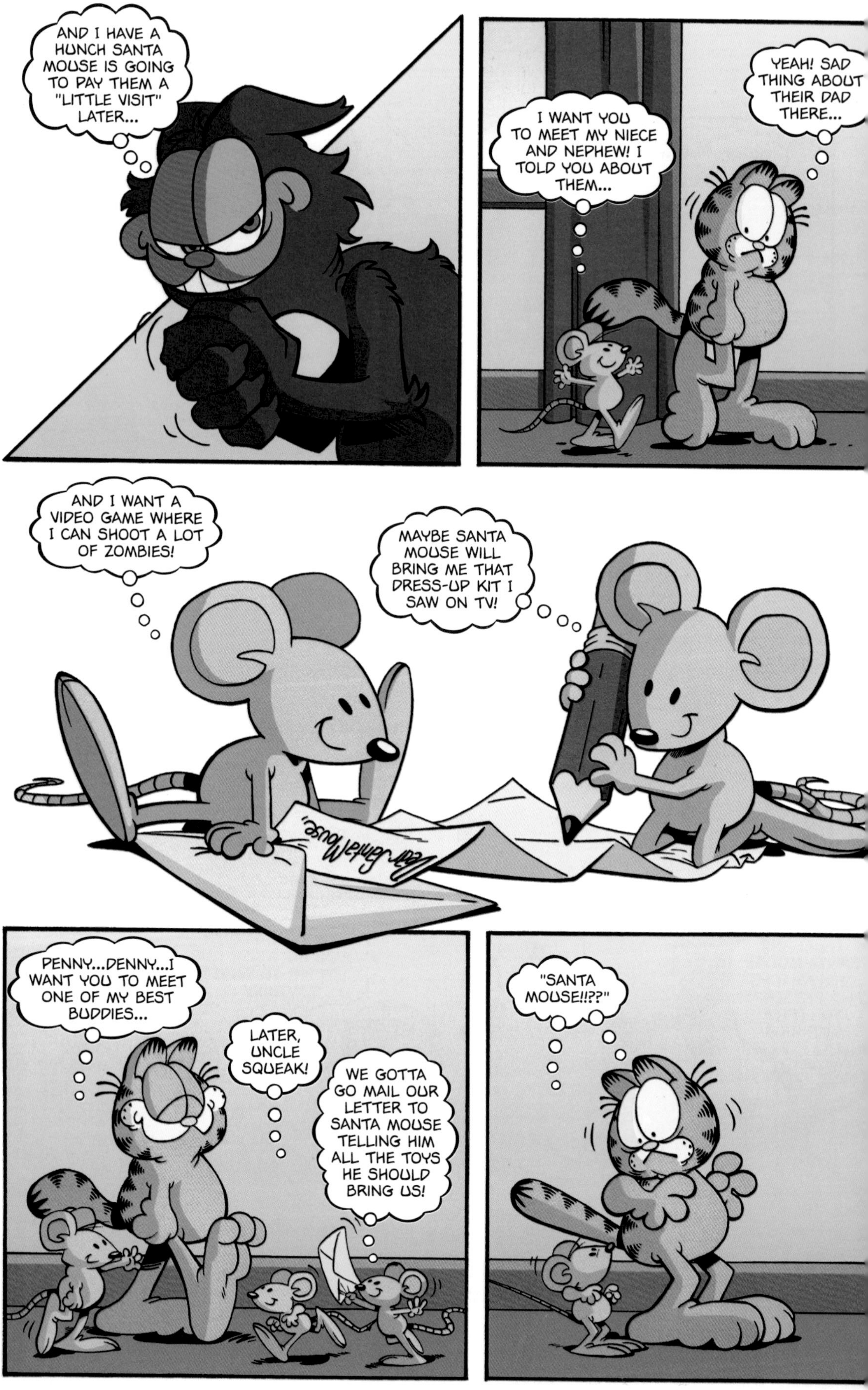
AND I HAVE A HUNCH SANTA MOUSE IS GOING TO PAY THEM A "LITTLE VISIT" LATER...
I WANT YOU TO MEET MY NIECE AND NEPHEW! I TOLD YOU ABOUT THEM...
YEAH! SAD THING ABOUT THEIR DAD THERE...
AND I WANT A VIDEO GAME WHERE I CAN SHOOT A LOT OF ZOMBIES!
MAYBE SANTA MOUSE WILL BRING ME THAT DRESS-UP KIT I SAW ON TV!
Dear Santa Mouse,
PENNY...DENNY...I WANT YOU TO MEET ONE OF MY BEST BUDDIES...
LATER, UNCLE SQUEAK!
WE GOTTA GO MAIL OUR LETTER TO SANTA MOUSE TELLING HIM ALL THE TOYS HE SHOULD BRING US!
"SANTA MOUSE!!??"

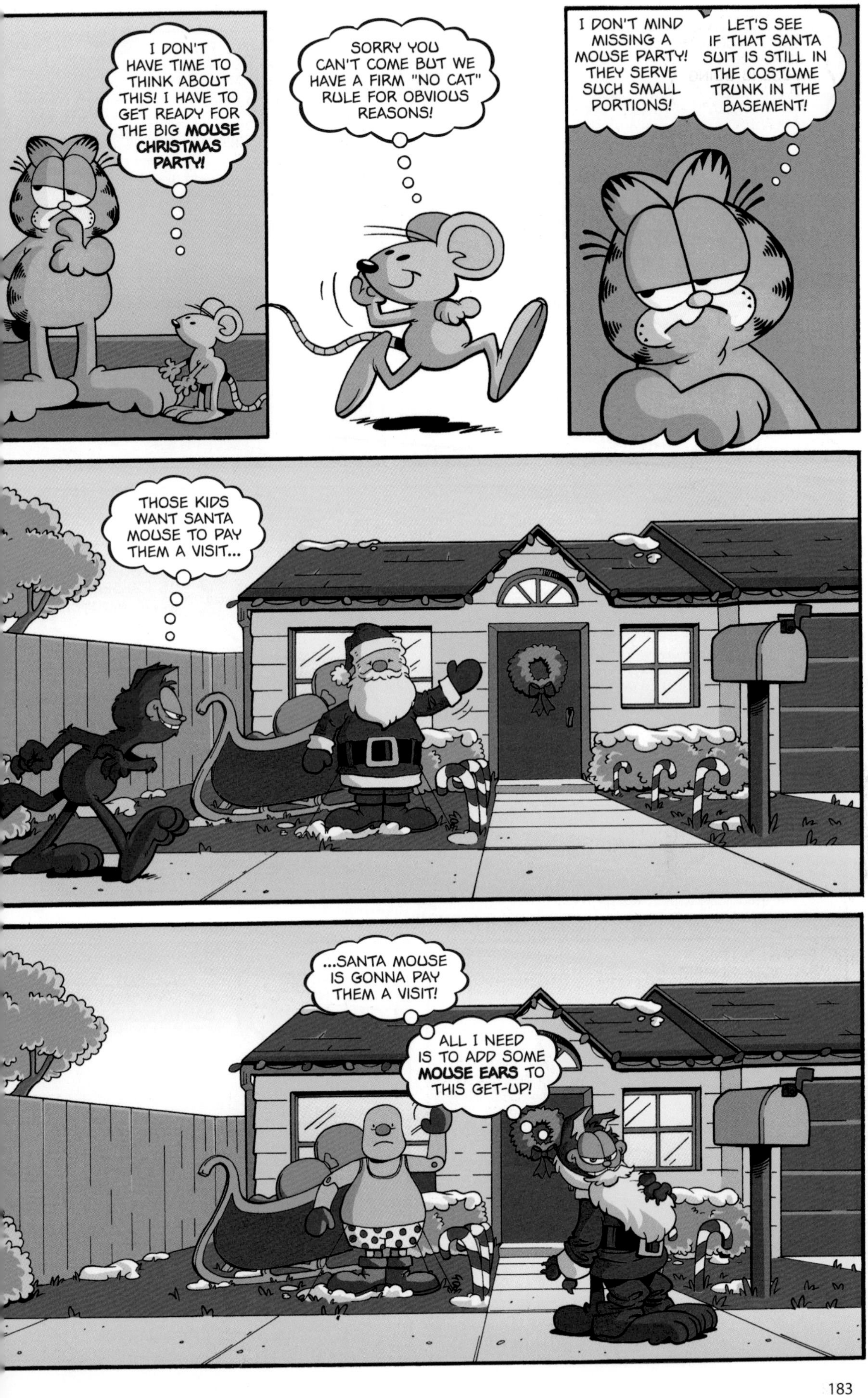
I DON'T HAVE TIME TO THINK ABOUT THIS! I HAVE TO GET READY FOR THE BIG **MOUSE CHRISTMAS PARTY!**
SORRY YOU CAN'T COME BUT WE HAVE A FIRM "NO CAT" RULE FOR OBVIOUS REASONS!
I DON'T MIND MISSING A MOUSE PARTY! THEY SERVE SUCH SMALL PORTIONS!
LET'S SEE IF THAT SANTA SUIT IS STILL IN THE COSTUME TRUNK IN THE BASEMENT!
THOSE KIDS WANT SANTA MOUSE TO PAY THEM A VISIT...
...SANTA MOUSE IS GONNA PAY THEM A VISIT!
ALL I NEED IS TO ADD SOME **MOUSE EARS** TO THIS GET-UP!

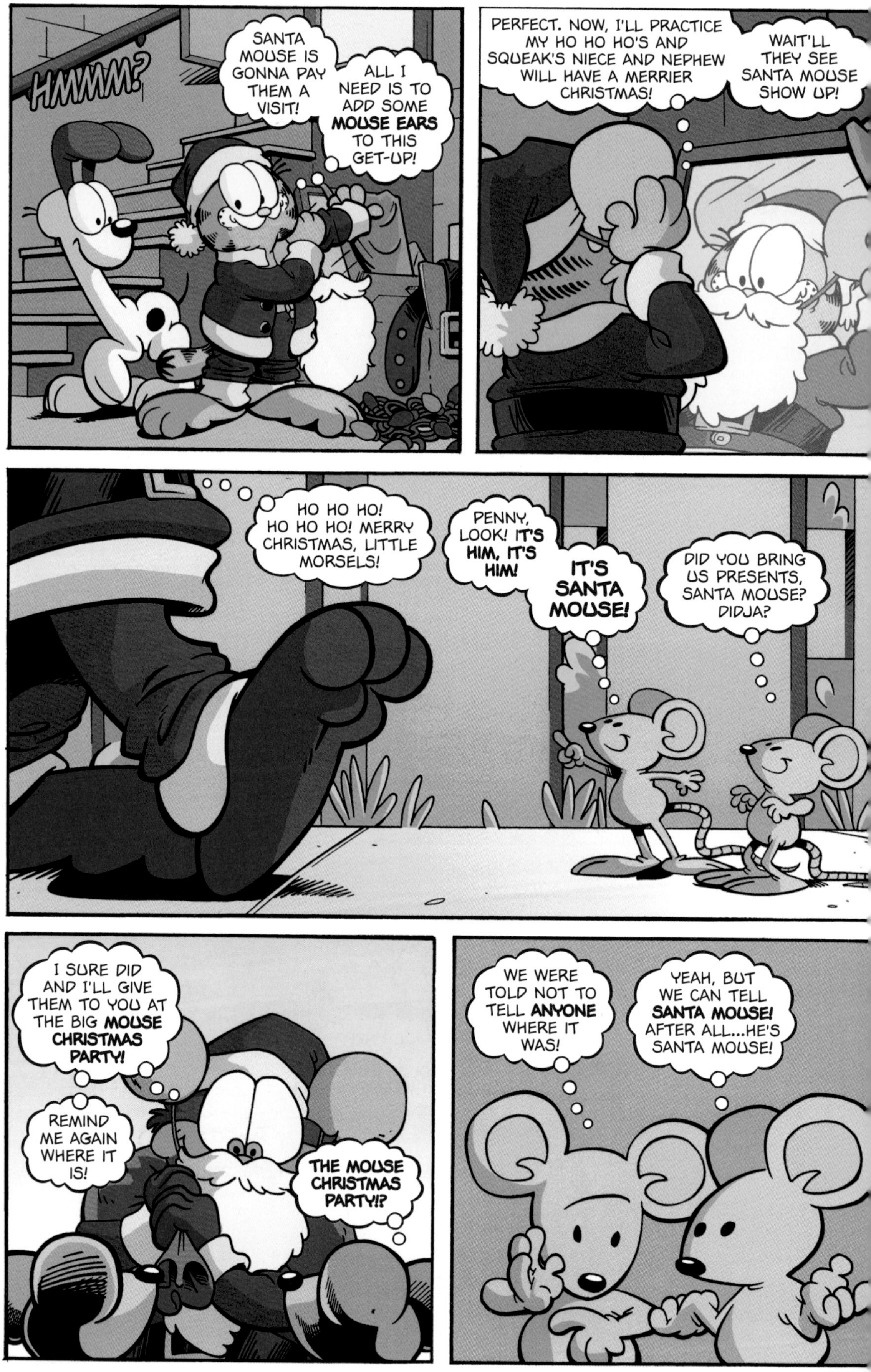
HMMM?
SANTA MOUSE IS GONNA PAY THEM A VISIT!
ALL I NEED IS TO ADD SOME **MOUSE EARS** TO THIS GET-UP!
PERFECT. NOW, I'LL PRACTICE MY HO HO HO'S AND SQUEAK'S NIECE AND NEPHEW WILL HAVE A MERRIER CHRISTMAS!
WAIT'LL THEY SEE SANTA MOUSE SHOW UP!
HO HO HO! HO HO HO! MERRY CHRISTMAS, LITTLE MORSELS!
PENNY, LOOK! **IT'S HIM, IT'S HIM!**
IT'S SANTA MOUSE!
DID YOU BRING US PRESENTS, SANTA MOUSE? DIDJA?
I SURE DID AND I'LL GIVE THEM TO YOU AT THE BIG **MOUSE CHRISTMAS PARTY!**
REMIND ME AGAIN WHERE IT IS!
THE MOUSE CHRISTMAS PARTY!?
WE WERE TOLD NOT TO TELL **ANYONE** WHERE IT WAS!
YEAH, BUT WE CAN TELL **SANTA MOUSE!** AFTER ALL...HE'S SANTA MOUSE!

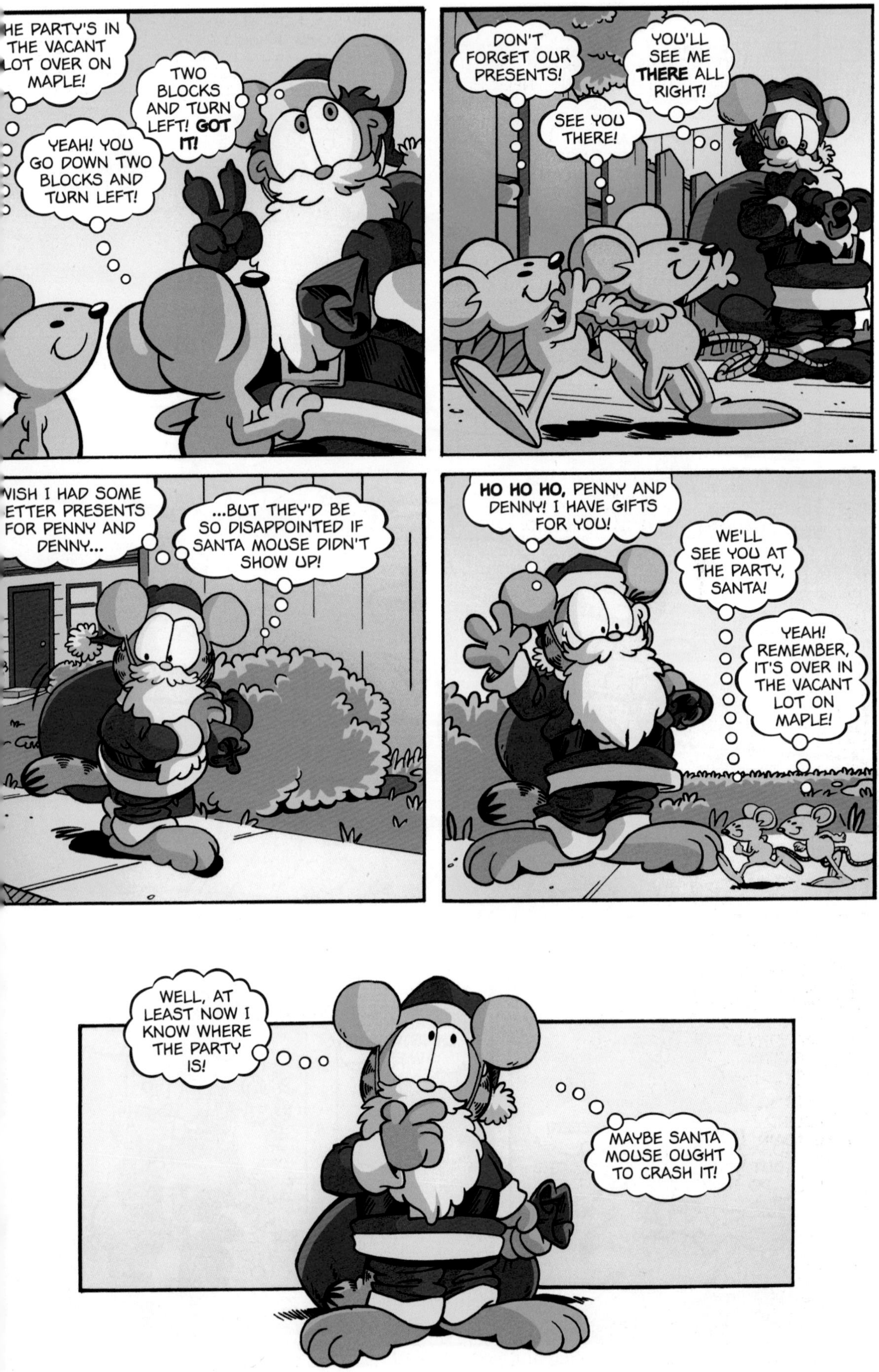
HE PARTY'S IN THE VACANT LOT OVER ON MAPLE!
TWO BLOCKS AND TURN LEFT! GOT IT!
YEAH! YOU GO DOWN TWO BLOCKS AND TURN LEFT!
DON'T FORGET OUR PRESENTS!
YOU'LL SEE ME THERE ALL RIGHT!
SEE YOU THERE!
VISH I HAD SOME ETTER PRESENTS FOR PENNY AND DENNY...
...BUT THEY'D BE SO DISAPPOINTED IF SANTA MOUSE DIDN'T SHOW UP!
HO HO HO, PENNY AND DENNY! I HAVE GIFTS FOR YOU!
WE'LL SEE YOU AT THE PARTY, SANTA!
YEAH! REMEMBER, IT'S OVER IN THE VACANT LOT ON MAPLE!
WELL, AT LEAST NOW I KNOW WHERE THE PARTY IS!
MAYBE SANTA MOUSE OUGHT TO CRASH IT!

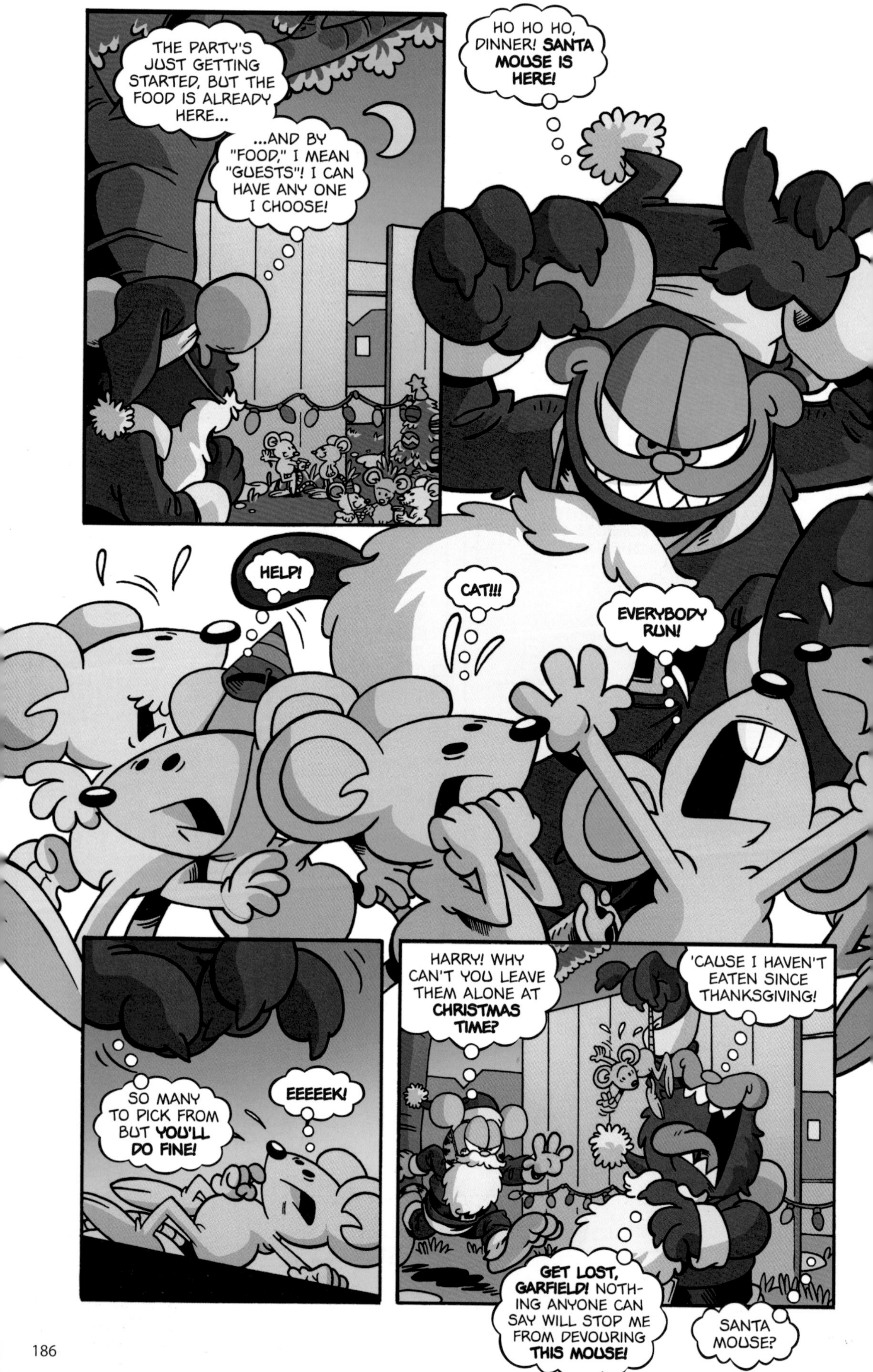

THE PARTY'S JUST GETTING STARTED, BUT THE FOOD IS ALREADY HERE...
...AND BY "FOOD," I MEAN "GUESTS"! I CAN HAVE ANY ONE I CHOOSE!
HO HO HO, DINNER! SANTA MOUSE IS HERE!
HELP!
CAT!!!
EVERYBODY RUN!
SO MANY TO PICK FROM BUT YOU'LL DO FINE!
EEEEEK!
HARRY! WHY CAN'T YOU LEAVE THEM ALONE AT CHRISTMAS TIME?
'CAUSE I HAVEN'T EATEN SINCE THANKSGIVING!
GET LOST, GARFIELD! NOTHING ANYONE CAN SAY WILL STOP ME FROM DEVOURING THIS MOUSE!
SANTA MOUSE?

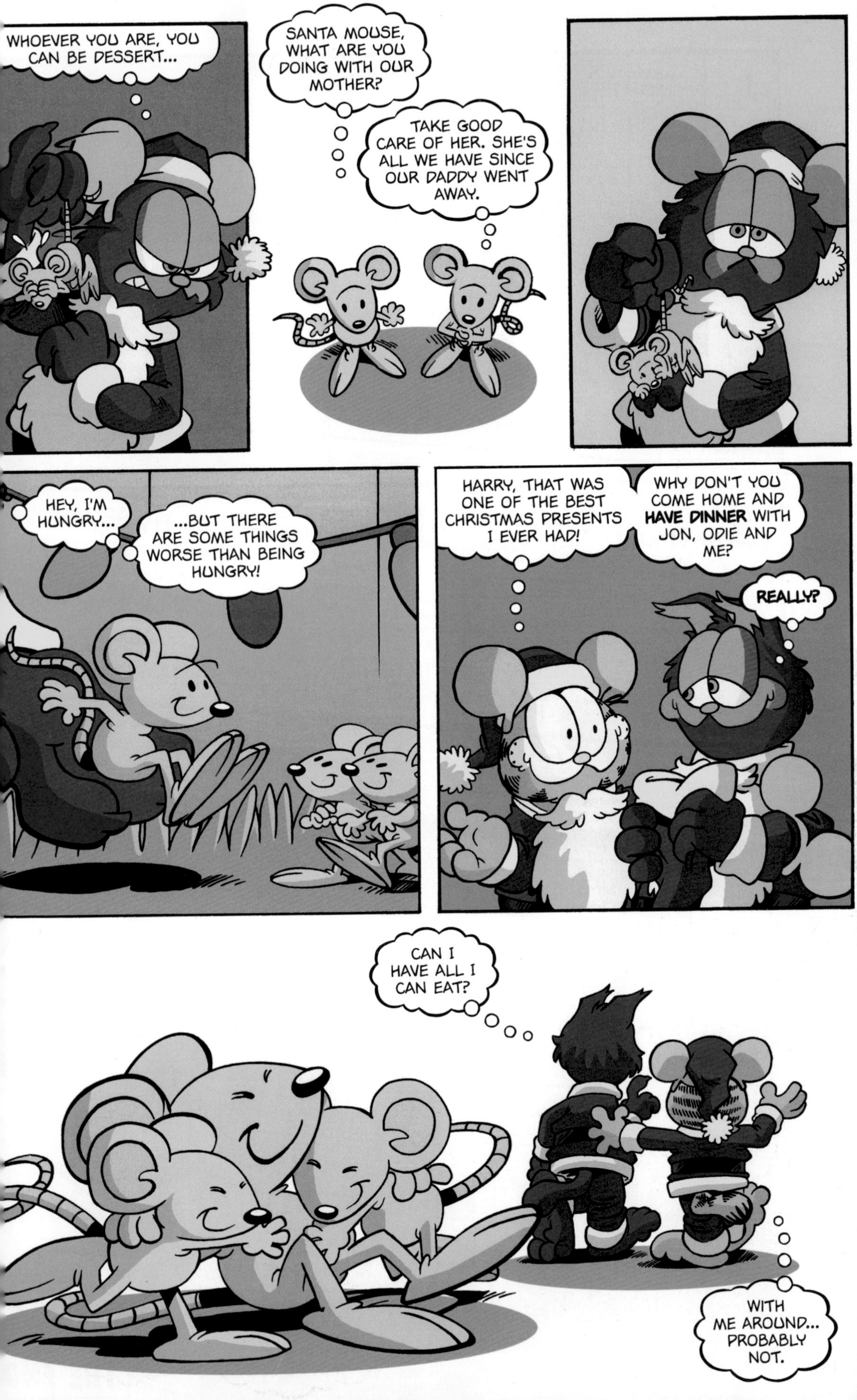
WHOEVER YOU ARE, YOU CAN BE DESSERT...
SANTA MOUSE, WHAT ARE YOU DOING WITH OUR MOTHER?
TAKE GOOD CARE OF HER. SHE'S ALL WE HAVE SINCE OUR DADDY WENT AWAY.
HEY, I'M HUNGRY...
...BUT THERE ARE SOME THINGS WORSE THAN BEING HUNGRY!
HARRY, THAT WAS ONE OF THE BEST CHRISTMAS PRESENTS I EVER HAD!
WHY DON'T YOU COME HOME AND **HAVE DINNER** WITH JON, ODIE AND ME?
REALLY?
CAN I HAVE ALL I CAN EAT?
WITH ME AROUND... PROBABLY NOT.

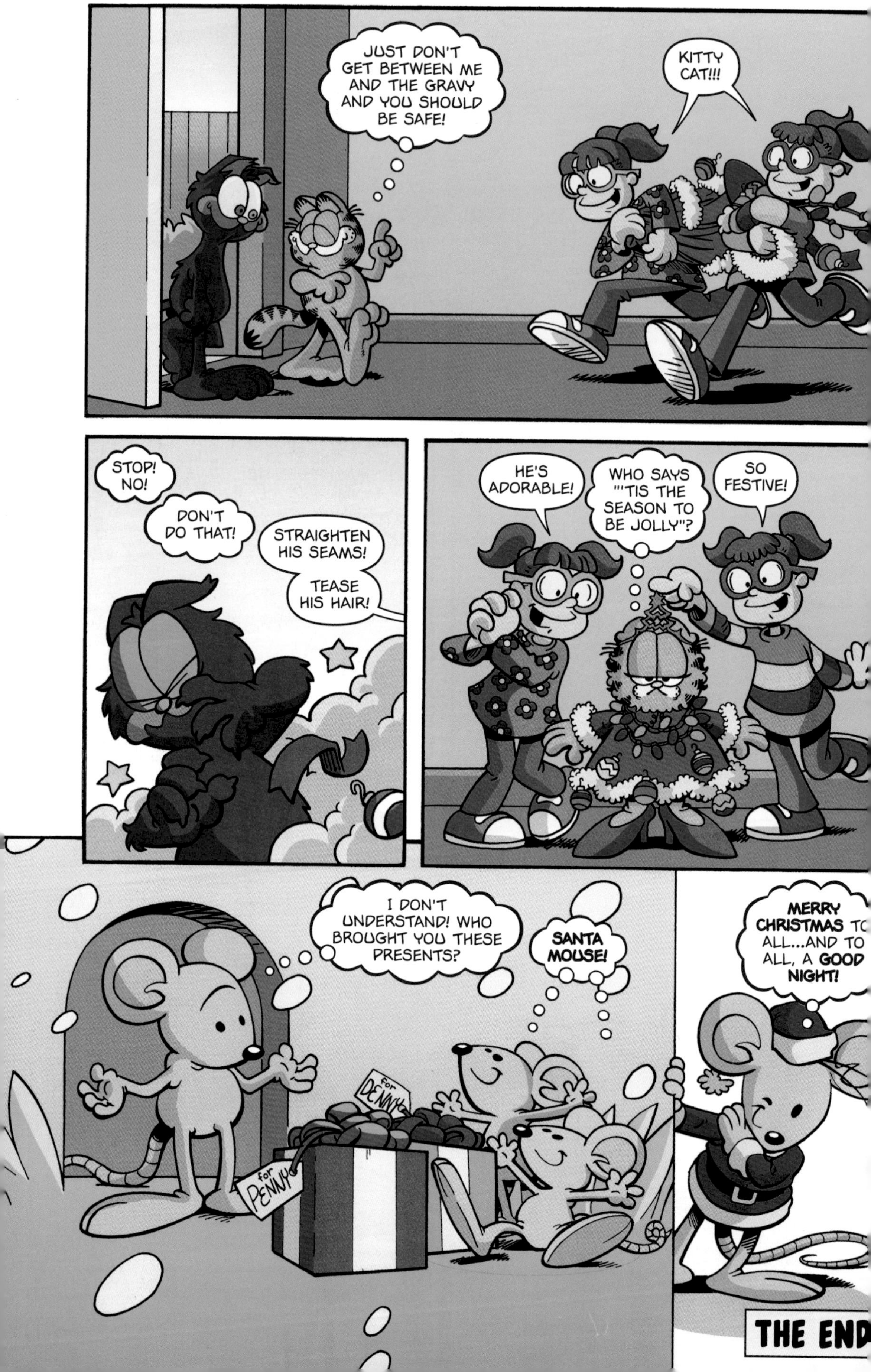
JUST DON'T GET BETWEEN ME AND THE GRAVY AND YOU SHOULD BE SAFE!
KITTY CAT!!!
STOP! NO!
DON'T DO THAT!
STRAIGHTEN HIS SEAMS!
TEASE HIS HAIR!
HE'S ADORABLE!
WHO SAYS "'TIS THE SEASON TO BE JOLLY"?
SO FESTIVE!
I DON'T UNDERSTAND! WHO BROUGHT YOU THESE PRESENTS?
SANTA MOUSE!
for DENNY
for PENNY
MERRY CHRISTMAS TO ALL...AND TO ALL, A GOOD NIGHT!
THE END

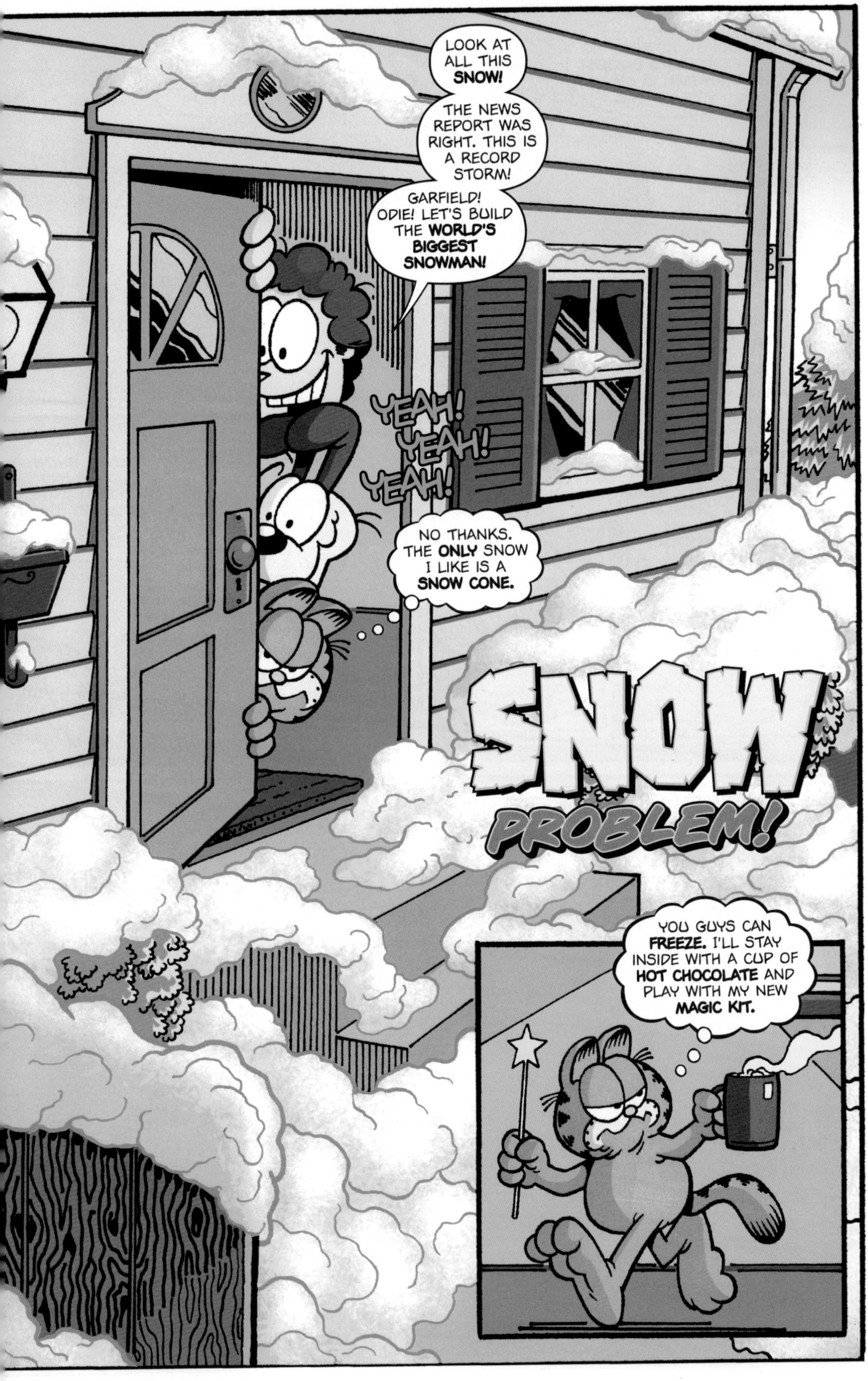
LOOK AT ALL THIS SNOW!
THE NEWS REPORT WAS RIGHT. THIS IS A RECORD STORM!
GARFIELD! ODIE! LET'S BUILD THE WORLD'S BIGGEST SNOWMAN!
YEAH! YEAH! YEAH!
NO THANKS. THE ONLY SNOW I LIKE IS A SNOW CONE.
SNOW PROBLEM!
YOU GUYS CAN FREEZE. I'LL STAY INSIDE WITH A CUP OF HOT CHOCOLATE AND PLAY WITH MY NEW MAGIC KIT.

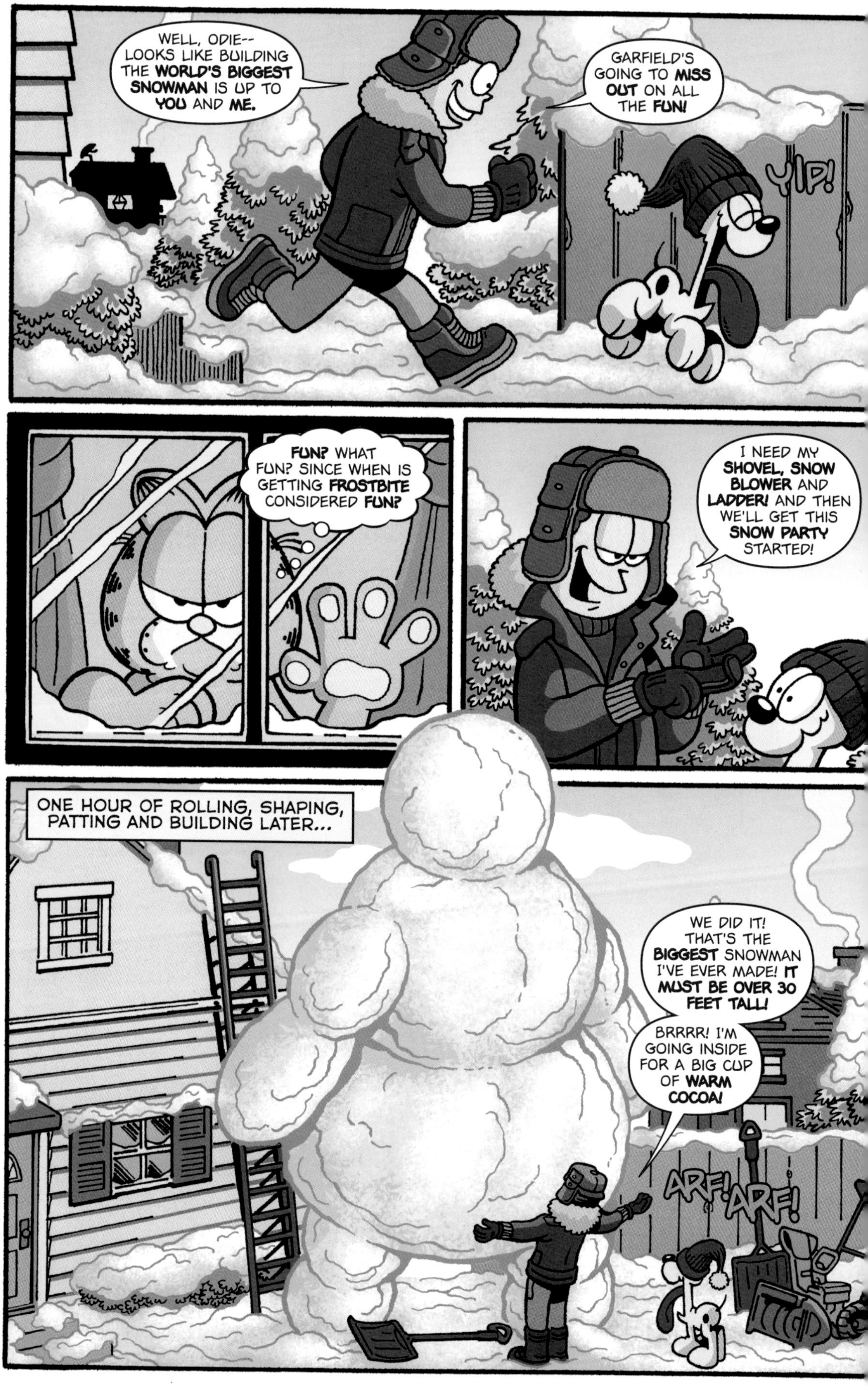
WELL, ODIE-- LOOKS LIKE BUILDING THE WORLD'S BIGGEST SNOWMAN IS UP TO YOU AND ME.
GARFIELD'S GOING TO MISS OUT ON ALL THE FUN!
YIP!
FUN? WHAT FUN? SINCE WHEN IS GETTING FROSTBITE CONSIDERED FUN?
I NEED MY SHOVEL, SNOW BLOWER AND LADDER! AND THEN WE'LL GET THIS SNOW PARTY STARTED!
ONE HOUR OF ROLLING, SHAPING, PATTING AND BUILDING LATER...
WE DID IT! THAT'S THE BIGGEST SNOWMAN I'VE EVER MADE! IT MUST BE OVER 30 FEET TALL!
BRRRR! I'M GOING INSIDE FOR A BIG CUP OF WARM COCOA!
ARF! ARF!

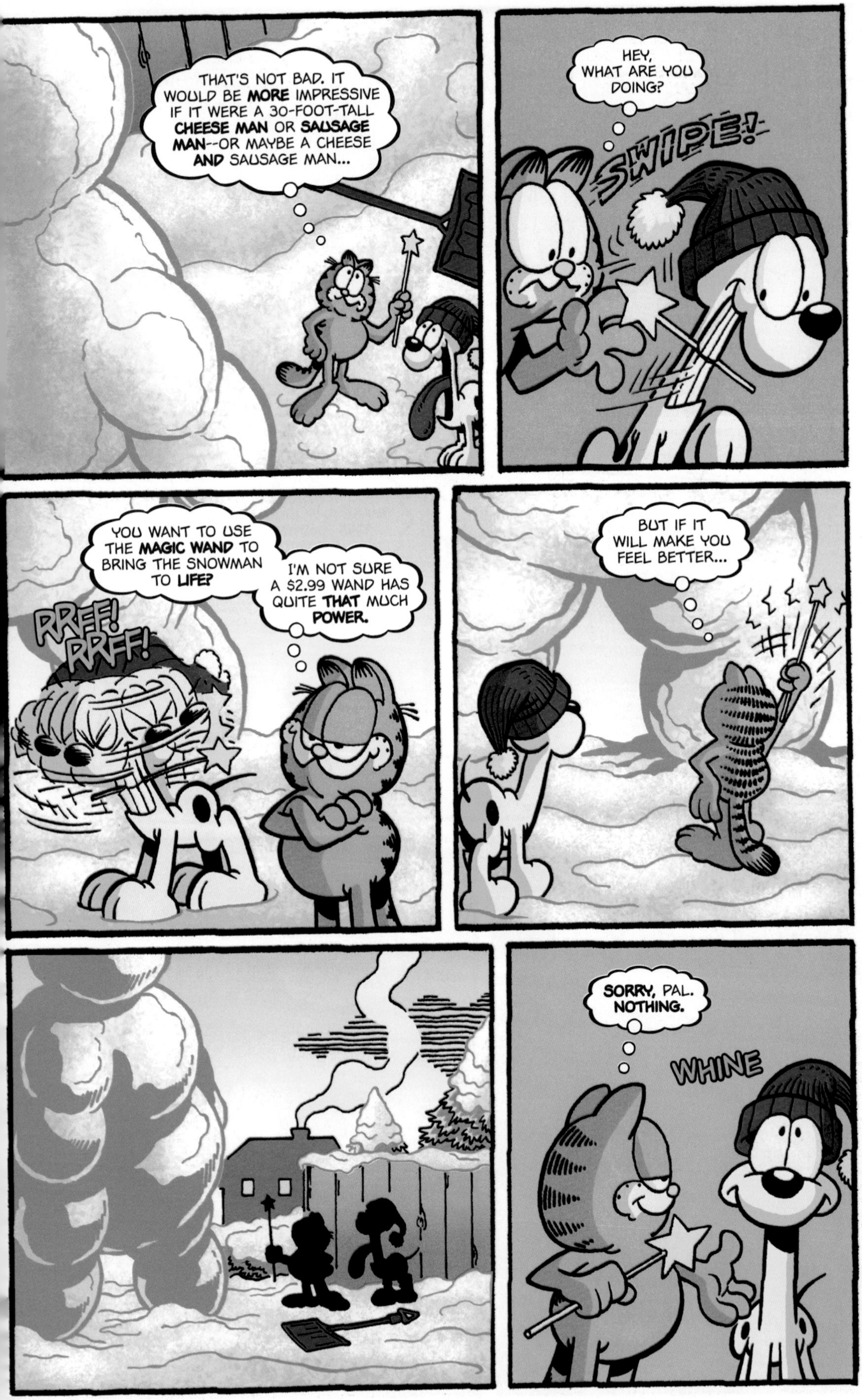
THAT'S NOT BAD. IT WOULD BE MORE IMPRESSIVE IF IT WERE A 30-FOOT-TALL CHEESE MAN OR SAUSAGE MAN--OR MAYBE A CHEESE AND SAUSAGE MAN...
HEY, WHAT ARE YOU DOING?
SWIPE!
YOU WANT TO USE THE MAGIC WAND TO BRING THE SNOWMAN TO LIFE?
I'M NOT SURE A $2.99 WAND HAS QUITE THAT MUCH POWER.
RRFF! RRFF!
BUT IF IT WILL MAKE YOU FEEL BETTER...
SORRY, PAL. NOTHING.
WHINE

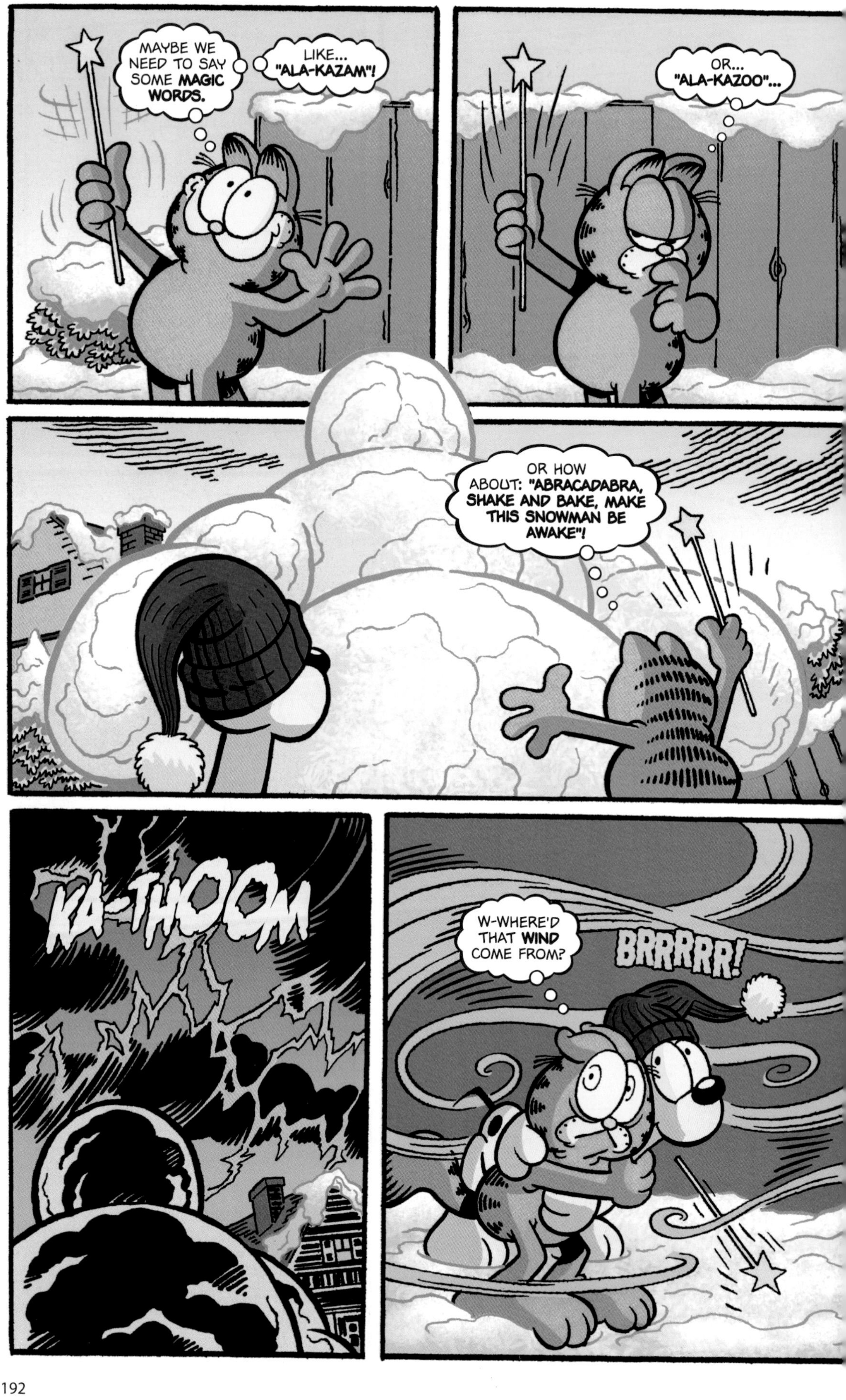
MAYBE WE NEED TO SAY SOME MAGIC WORDS.
LIKE... "ALA-KAZAM"!
OR... "ALA-KAZOO"...
OR HOW ABOUT: "ABRACADABRA, SHAKE AND BAKE, MAKE THIS SNOWMAN BE AWAKE"!
KA-THOOM
W-WHERE'D THAT WIND COME FROM?
BRRRRR!

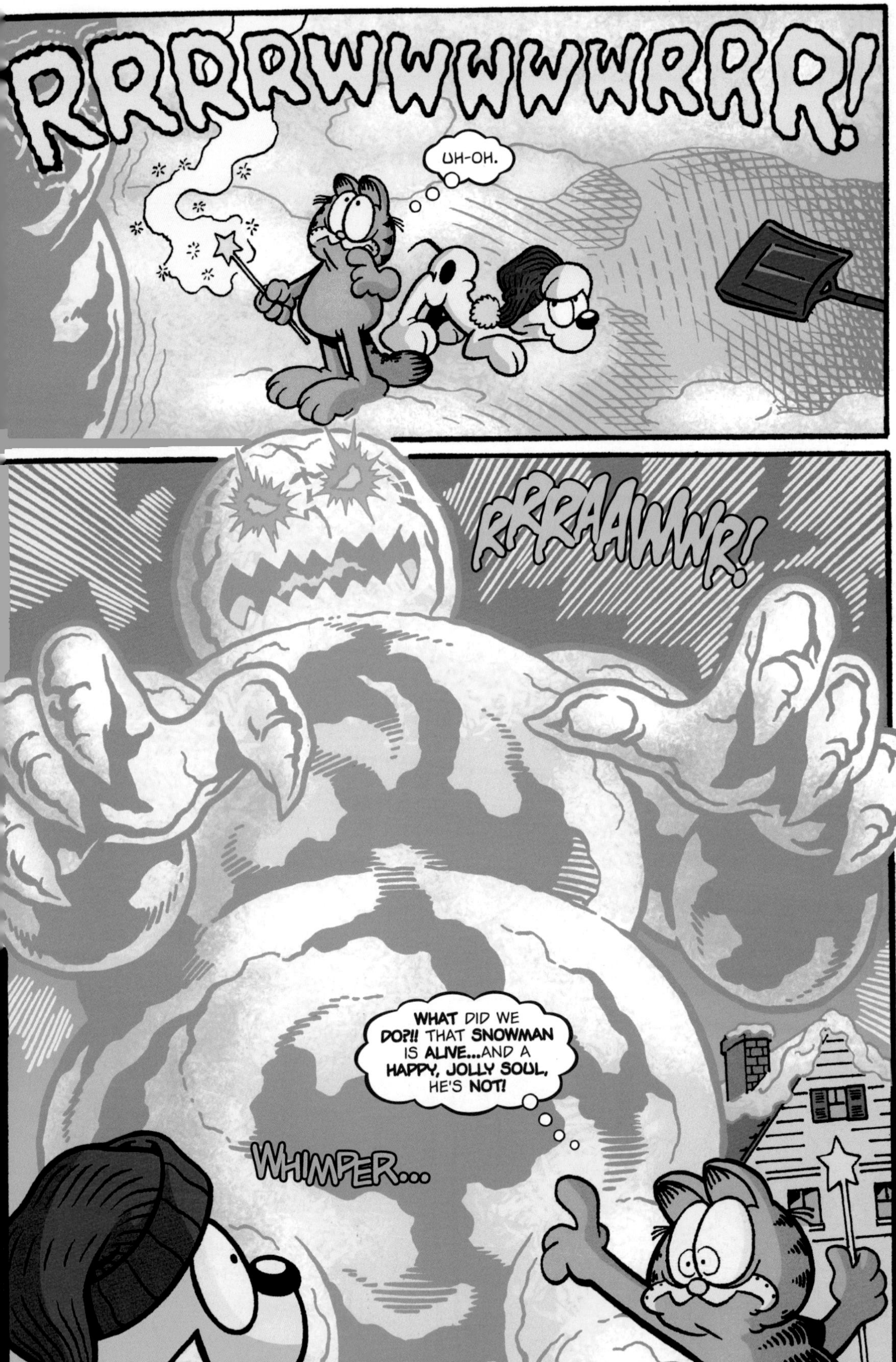
RRRRWWWWWRRR!
UH-OH.
RRRAAWWR!
WHAT DID WE DO?!! THAT SNOWMAN IS ALIVE...AND A HAPPY, JOLLY SOUL, HE'S NOT!
WHIMPER...

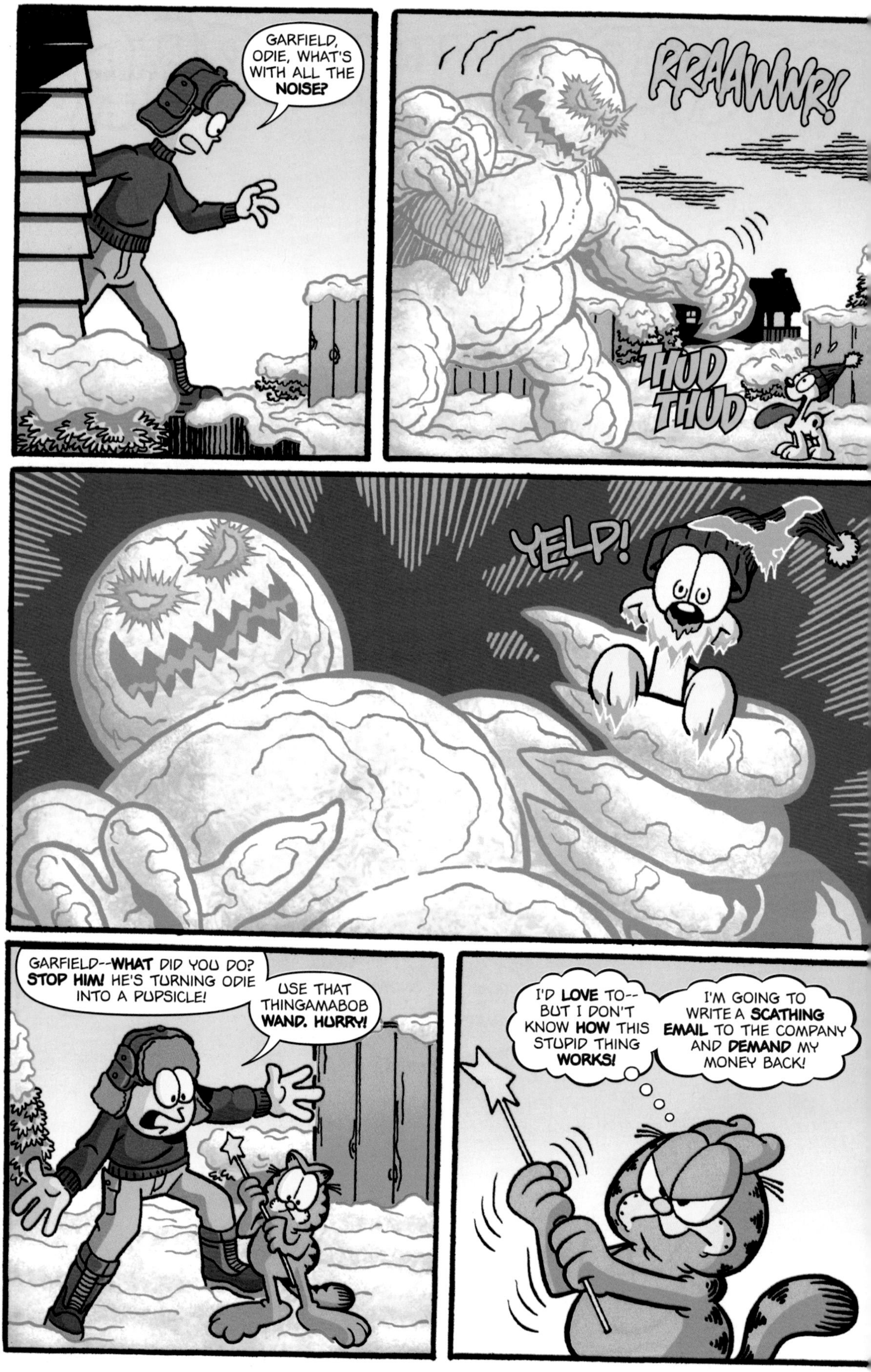
GARFIELD, ODIE, WHAT'S WITH ALL THE **NOISE?**
RRAAWWR!
THUD THUD
YELP!
GARFIELD--**WHAT** DID YOU DO? **STOP HIM!** HE'S TURNING ODIE INTO A PUPSICLE!
USE THAT THINGAMABOB **WAND. HURRY!**
I'D **LOVE** TO-- BUT I DON'T KNOW **HOW** THIS STUPID THING **WORKS!**
I'M GOING TO WRITE A **SCATHING EMAIL** TO THE COMPANY AND **DEMAND** MY MONEY BACK!

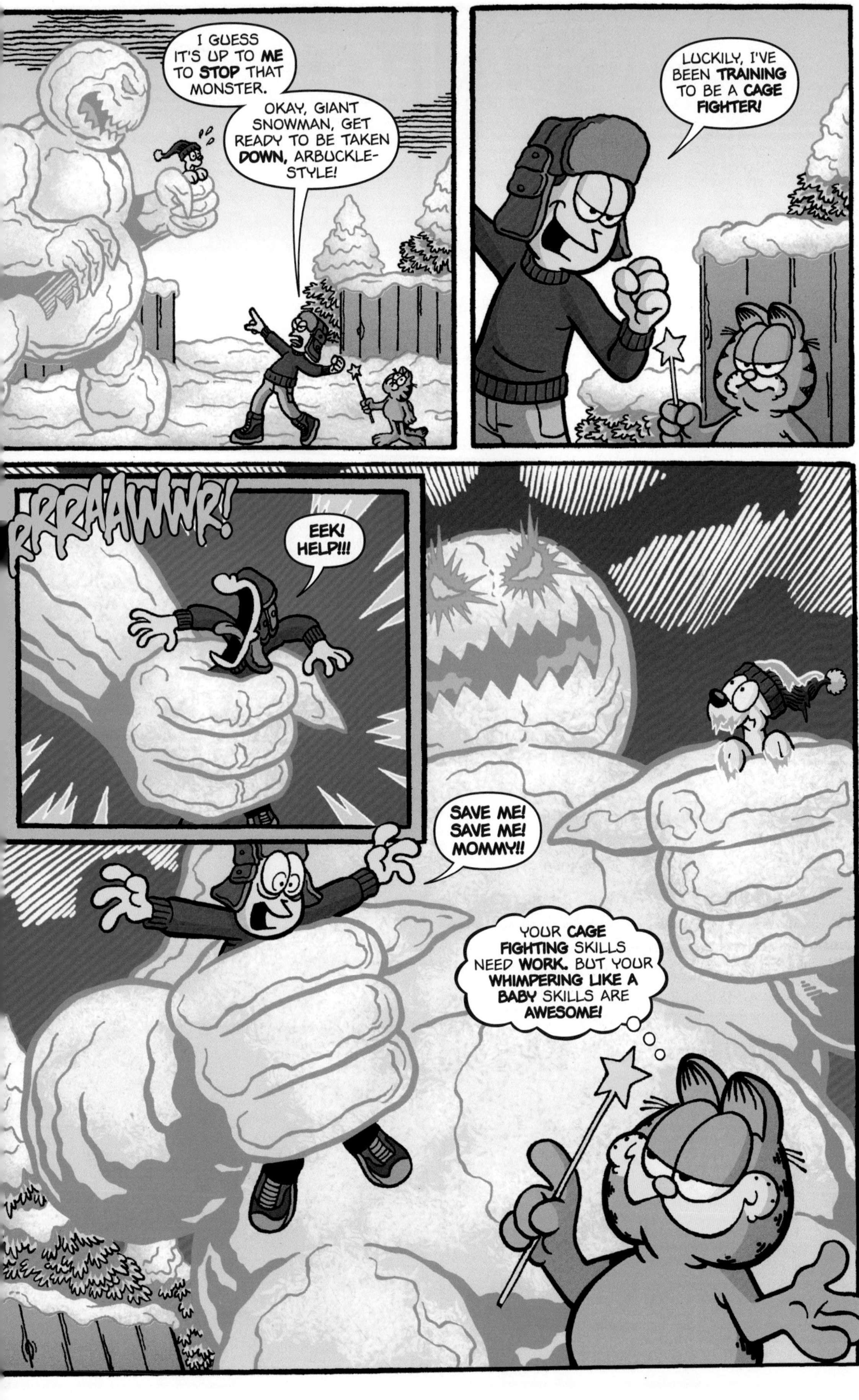

I GUESS IT'S UP TO ME TO STOP THAT MONSTER.
OKAY, GIANT SNOWMAN, GET READY TO BE TAKEN DOWN, ARBUCKLE-STYLE!
LUCKILY, I'VE BEEN TRAINING TO BE A CAGE FIGHTER!
RRRAAWWR!
EEK! HELP!!!
SAVE ME! SAVE ME! MOMMY!!
YOUR CAGE FIGHTING SKILLS NEED WORK. BUT YOUR WHIMPERING LIKE A BABY SKILLS ARE AWESOME!

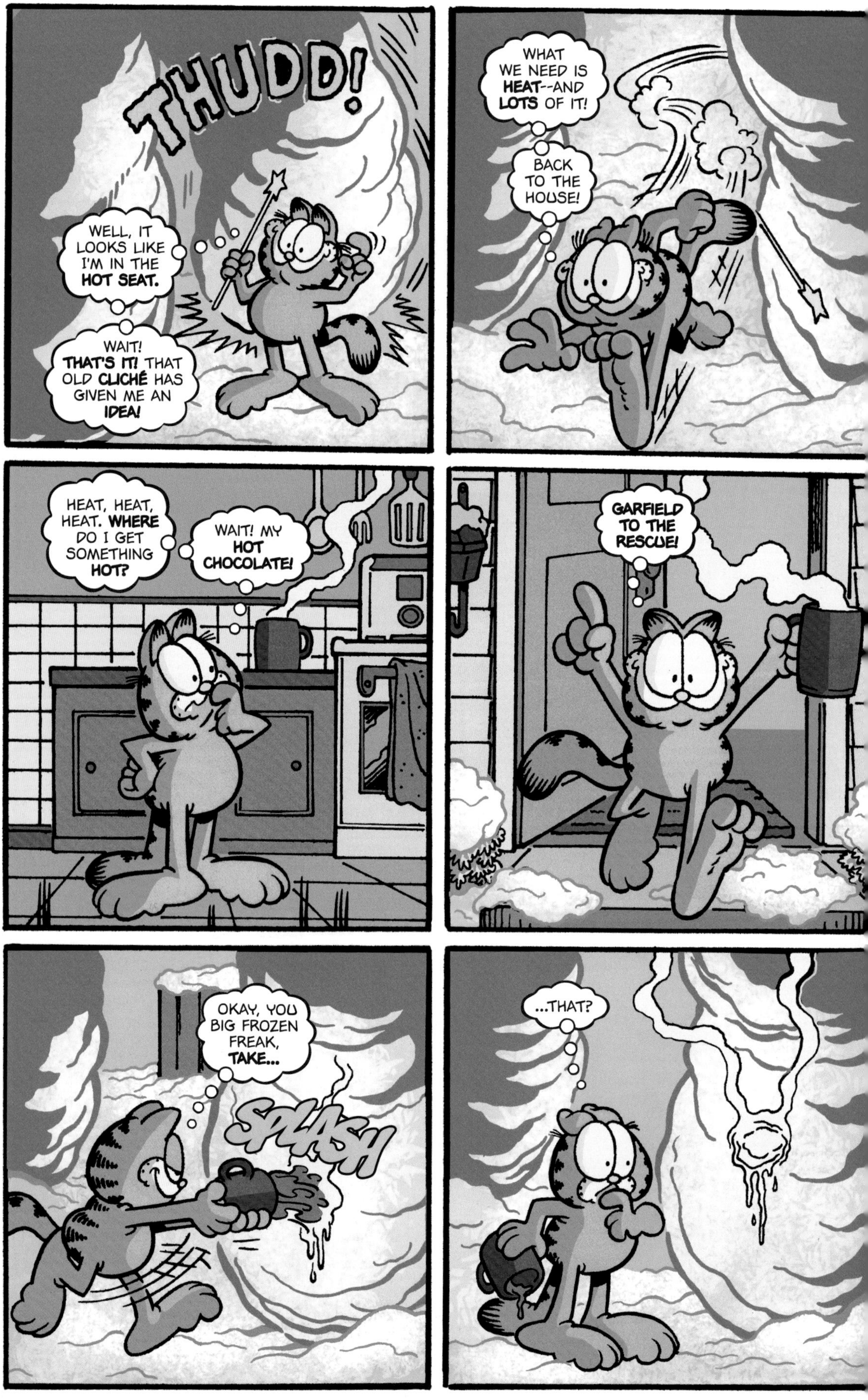
THUDD!
WELL, IT LOOKS LIKE I'M IN THE **HOT SEAT.**
WAIT! **THAT'S IT!** THAT OLD **CLICHÉ** HAS GIVEN ME AN **IDEA!**
WHAT WE NEED IS **HEAT**--AND **LOTS** OF IT!
BACK TO THE HOUSE!
HEAT, HEAT, HEAT. **WHERE** DO I GET SOMETHING **HOT?**
WAIT! MY **HOT CHOCOLATE!**
GARFIELD TO THE RESCUE!
OKAY, YOU BIG FROZEN FREAK, **TAKE...**
SPLASH
...THAT?

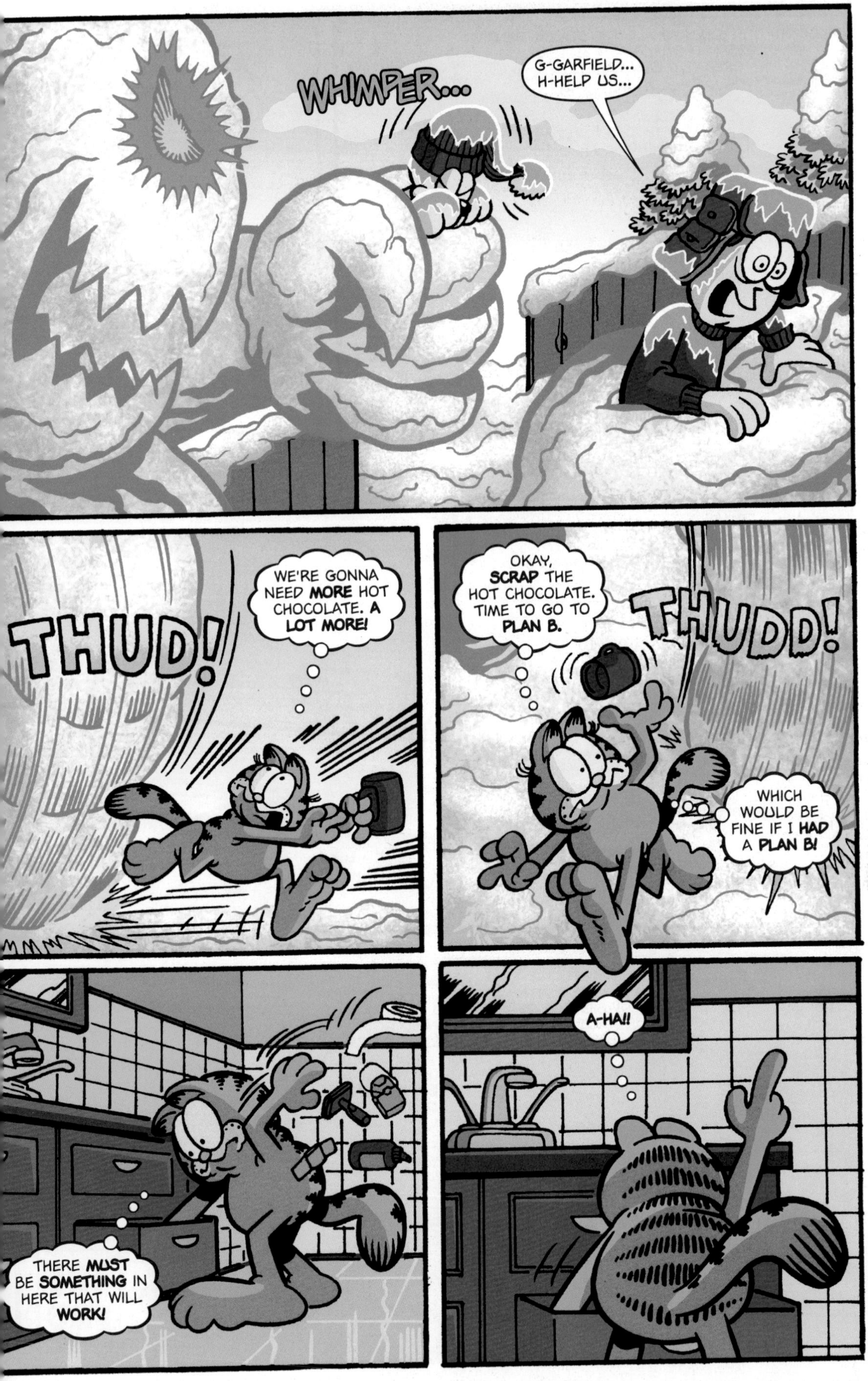
WHIMPER...
G-GARFIELD...
H-HELP US...
THUD!
WE'RE GONNA NEED MORE HOT CHOCOLATE. A LOT MORE!
OKAY, SCRAP THE HOT CHOCOLATE. TIME TO GO TO PLAN B.
THUDD!
WHICH WOULD BE FINE IF I HAD A PLAN B!
THERE MUST BE SOMETHING IN HERE THAT WILL WORK!
A-HA!!

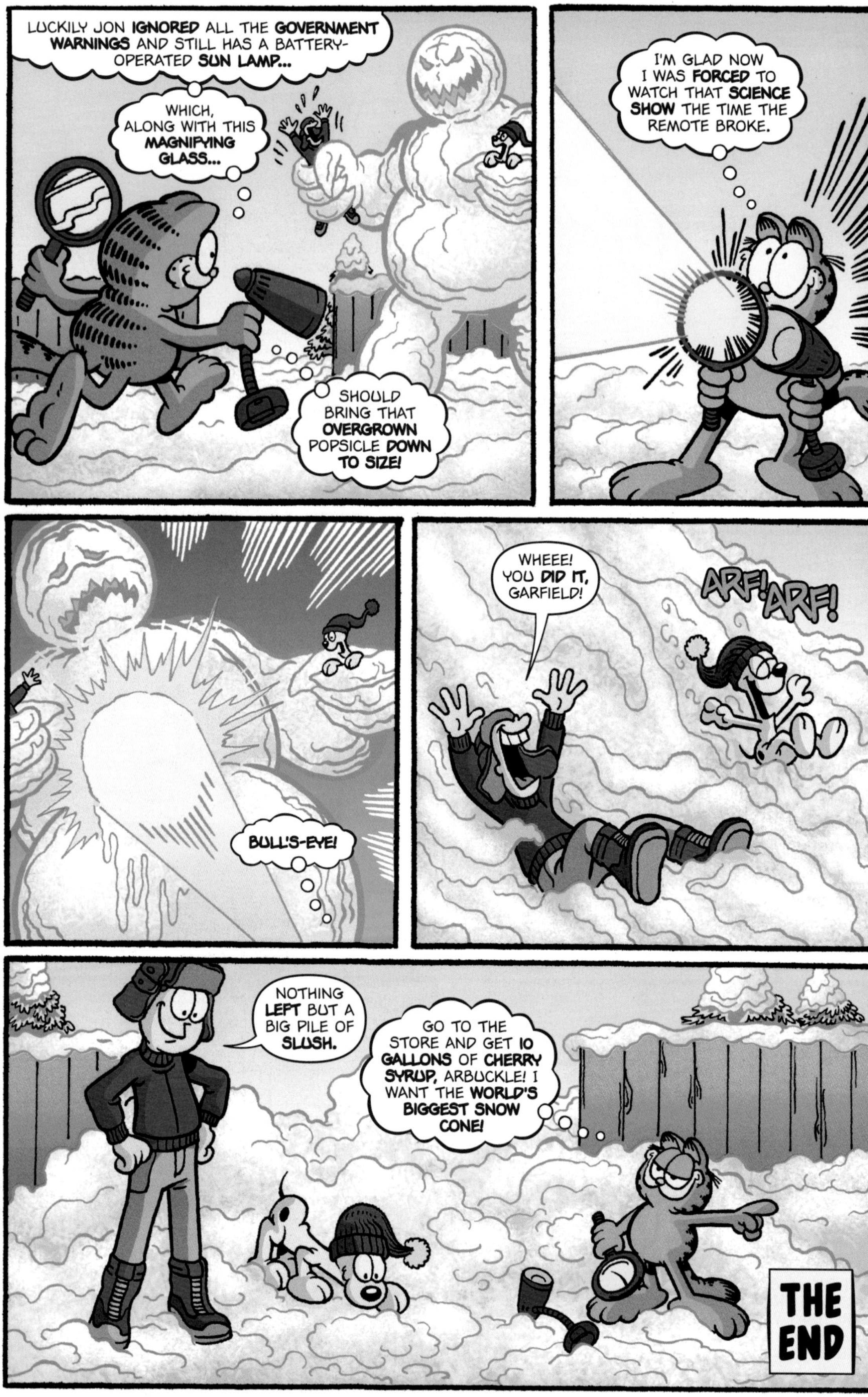
LUCKILY JON IGNORED ALL THE GOVERNMENT WARNINGS AND STILL HAS A BATTERY-OPERATED SUN LAMP...
WHICH, ALONG WITH THIS MAGNIFYING GLASS...
SHOULD BRING THAT OVERGROWN POPSICLE DOWN TO SIZE!
I'M GLAD NOW I WAS FORCED TO WATCH THAT SCIENCE SHOW THE TIME THE REMOTE BROKE.
BULL'S-EYE!
WHEEE! YOU DID IT, GARFIELD!
ARF! ARF!
NOTHING LEFT BUT A BIG PILE OF SLUSH.
GO TO THE STORE AND GET 10 GALLONS OF CHERRY SYRUP, ARBUCKLE! I WANT THE WORLD'S BIGGEST SNOW CONE!
THE END

COVER GALLERY

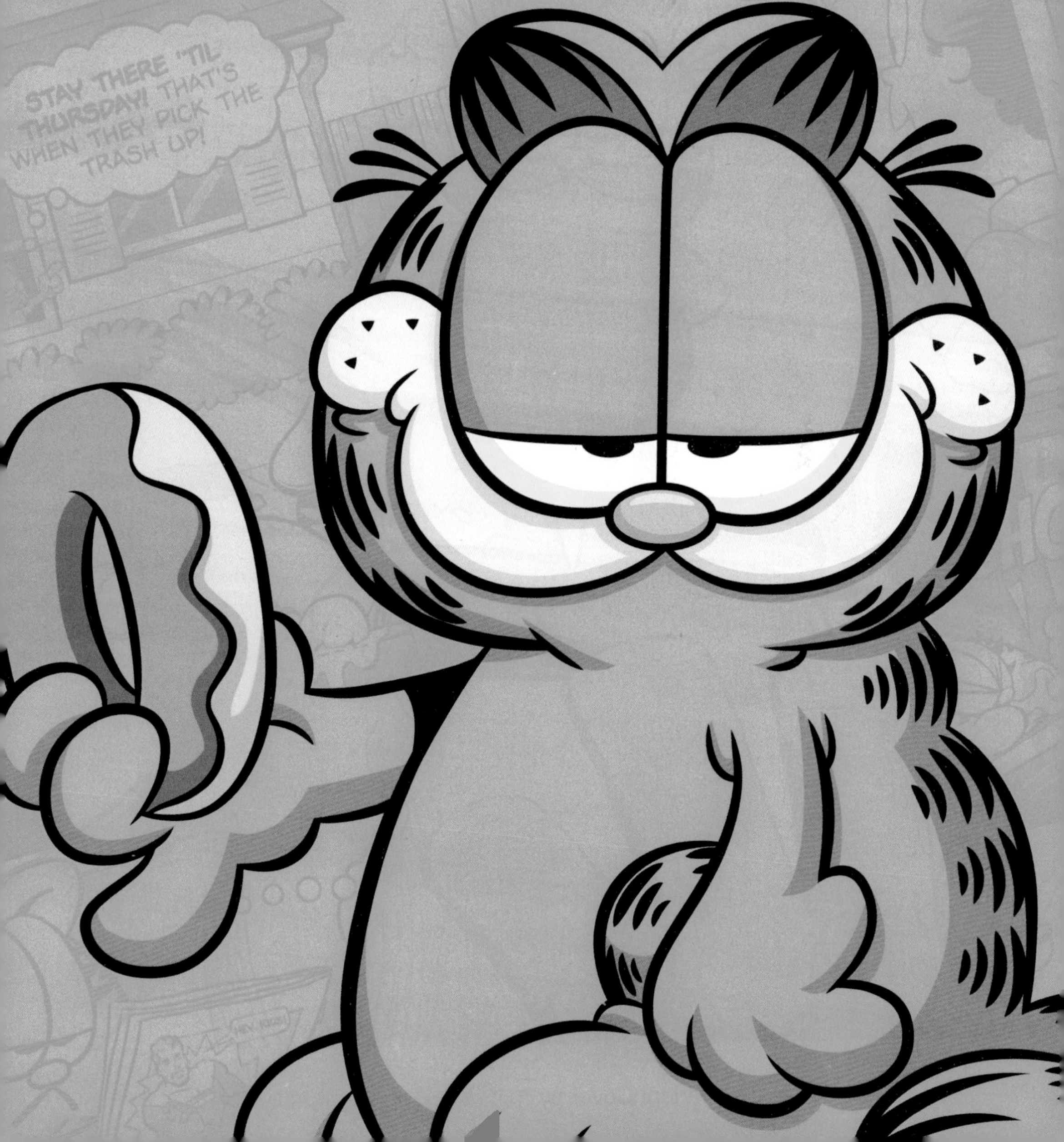
STAY THERE 'TIL THURSDAY! THAT'S WHEN THEY PICK THE TRASH UP!

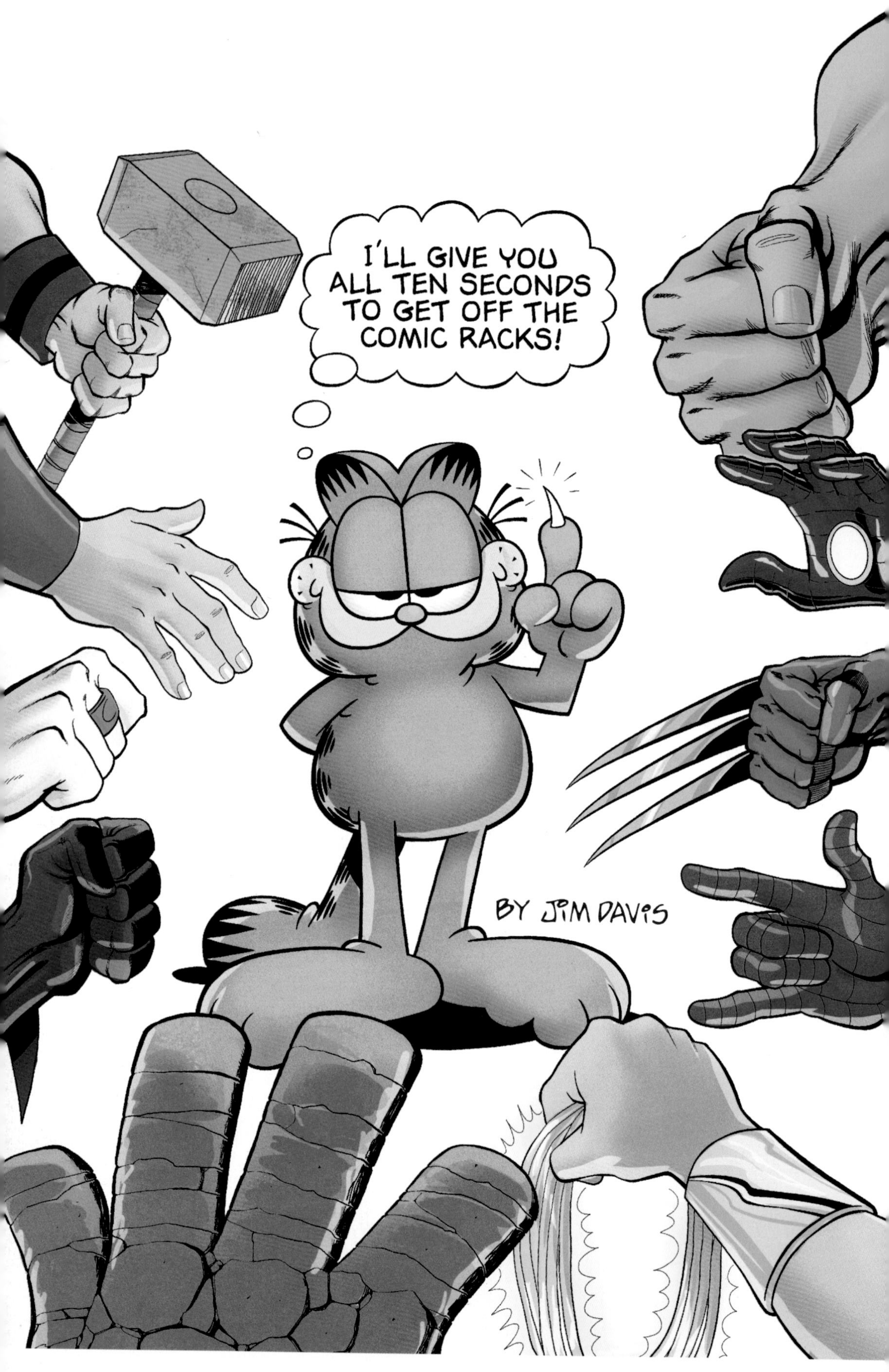
I'LL GIVE YOU ALL TEN SECONDS TO GET OFF THE COMIC RACKS!
BY JIM DAVIS

Garfield #1 Variant Cover by **GARY BARKER** with **BRADEN LAMB**

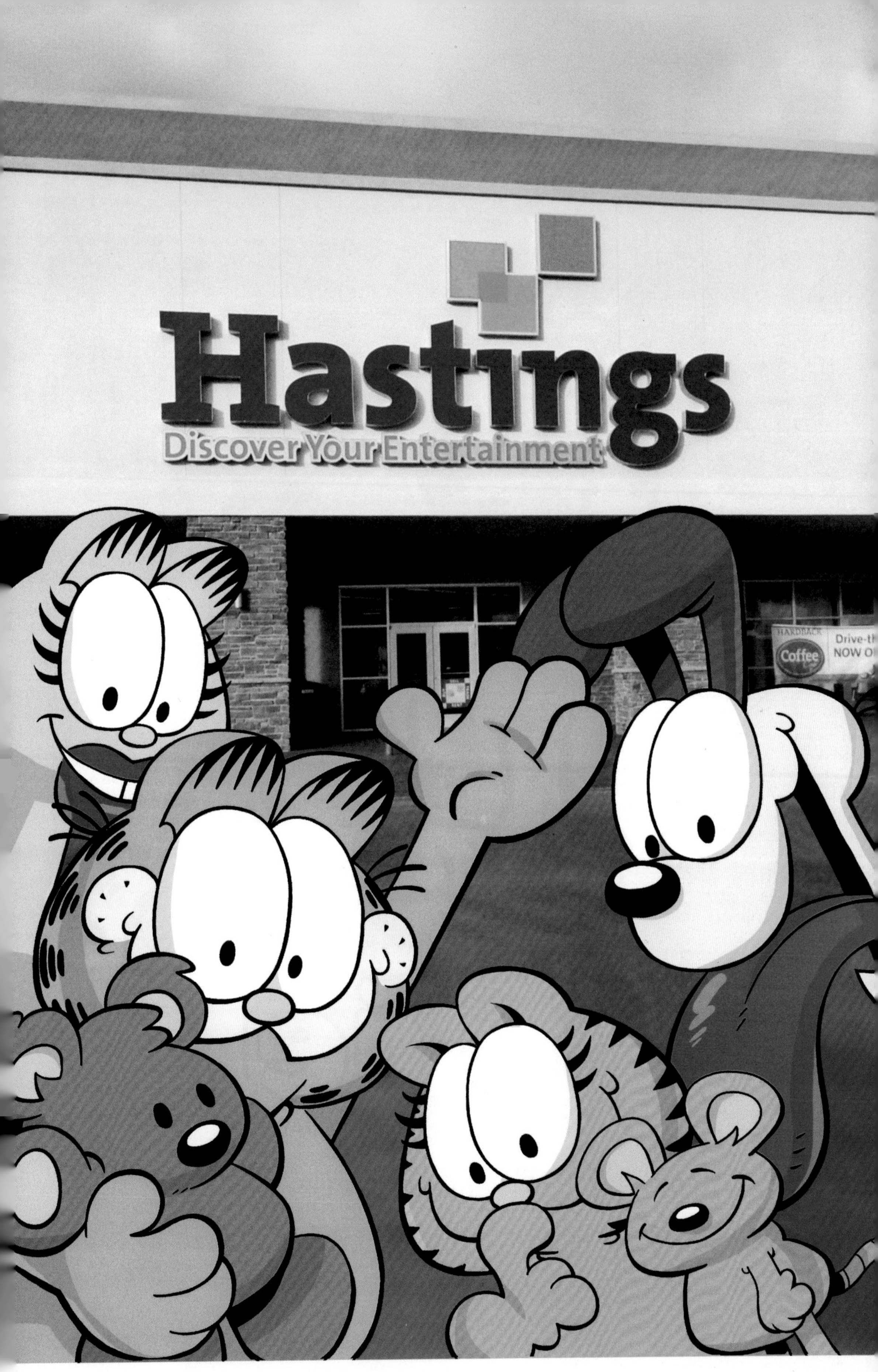
Hastings
Discover Your Entertainment
HARDBACK
Coffee

Garfield #1 Hastings Exclusive Variant Cover by **GARY BARKER**

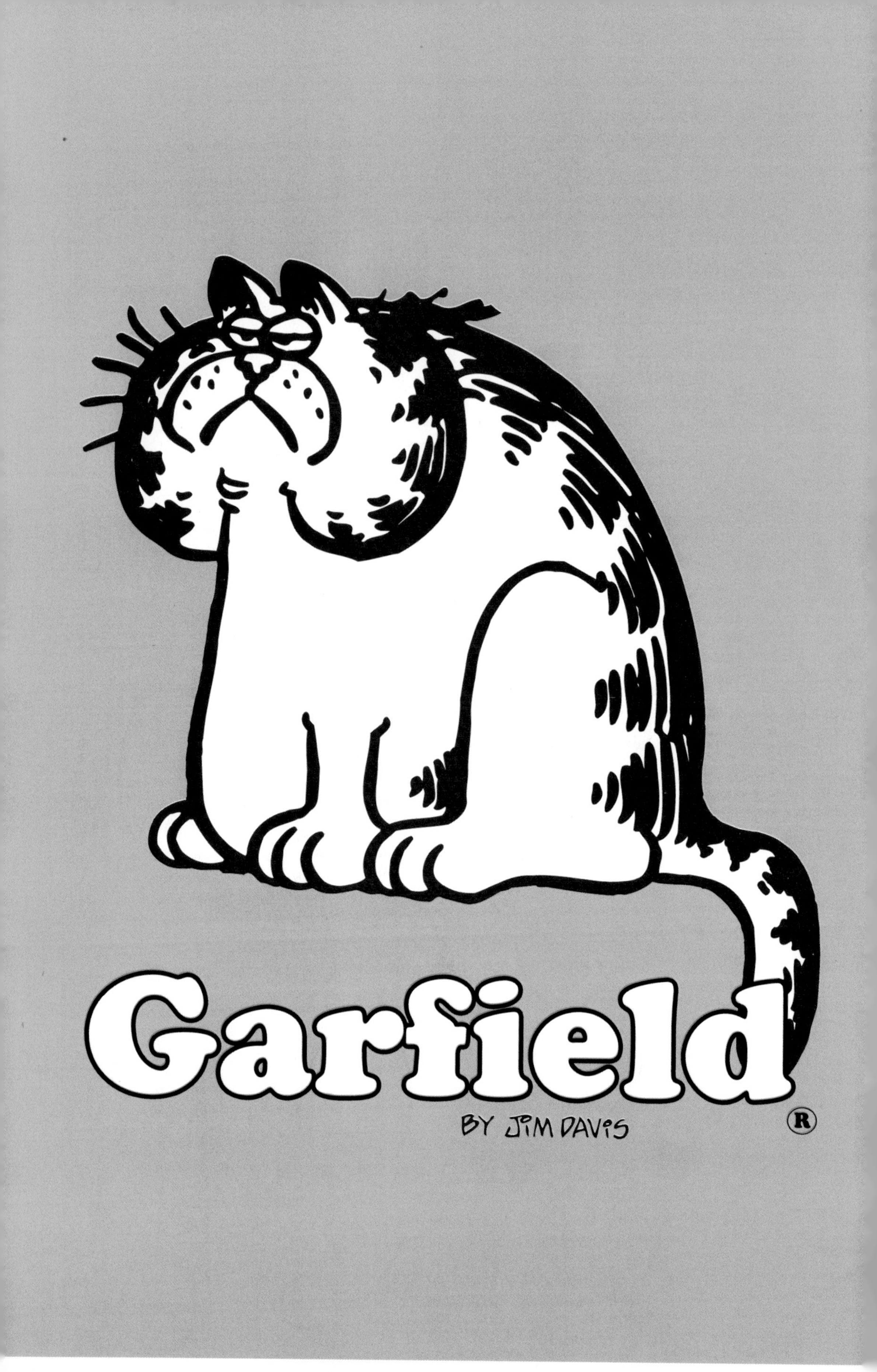
Garfield
BY JIM DAVIS
®

Garfield #1 Variant Cover by **JIM DAVIS**

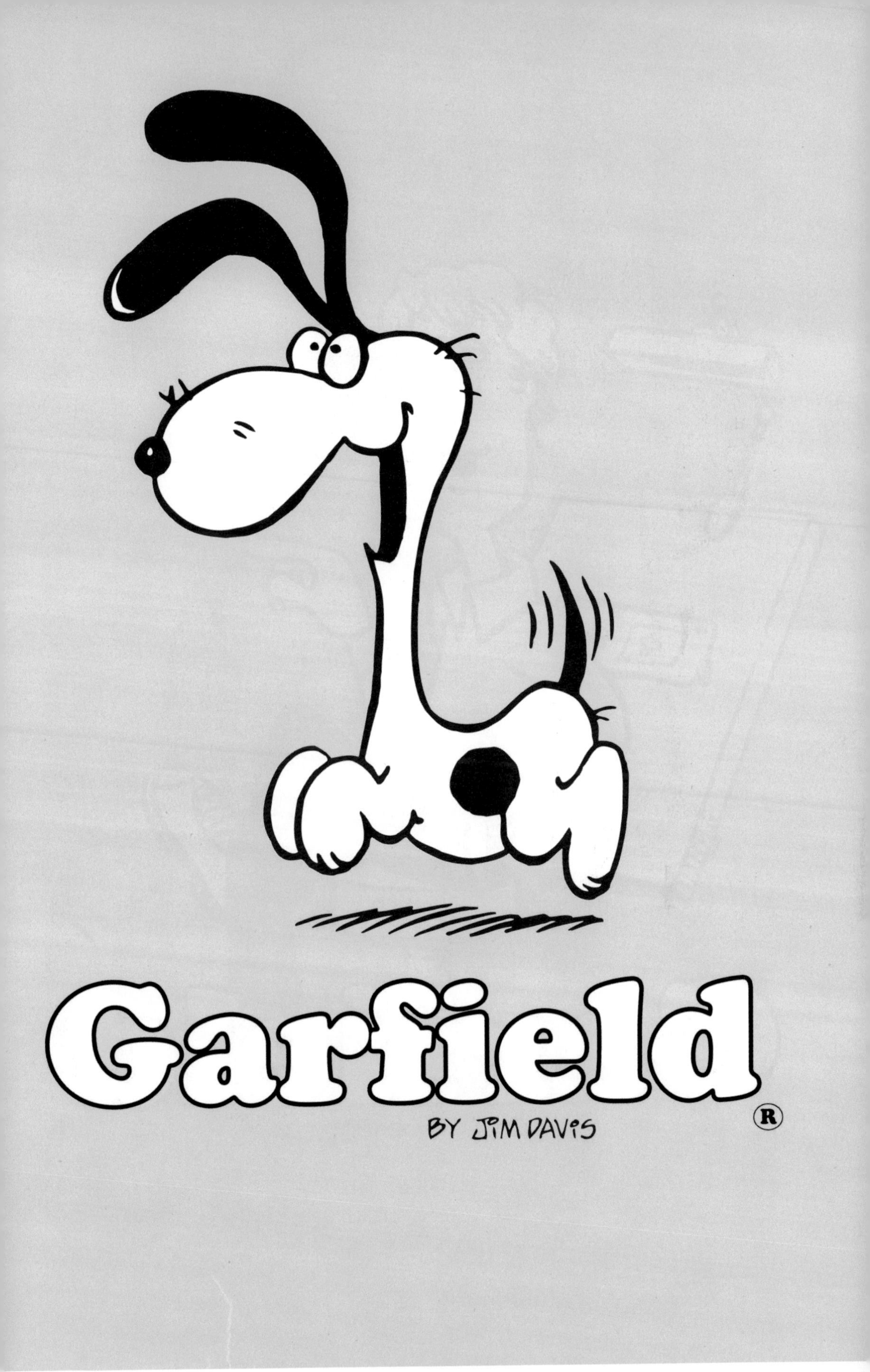
Garfield
BY JIM DAVIS

Garfield #2 Variant Cover by **JIM DAVIS**

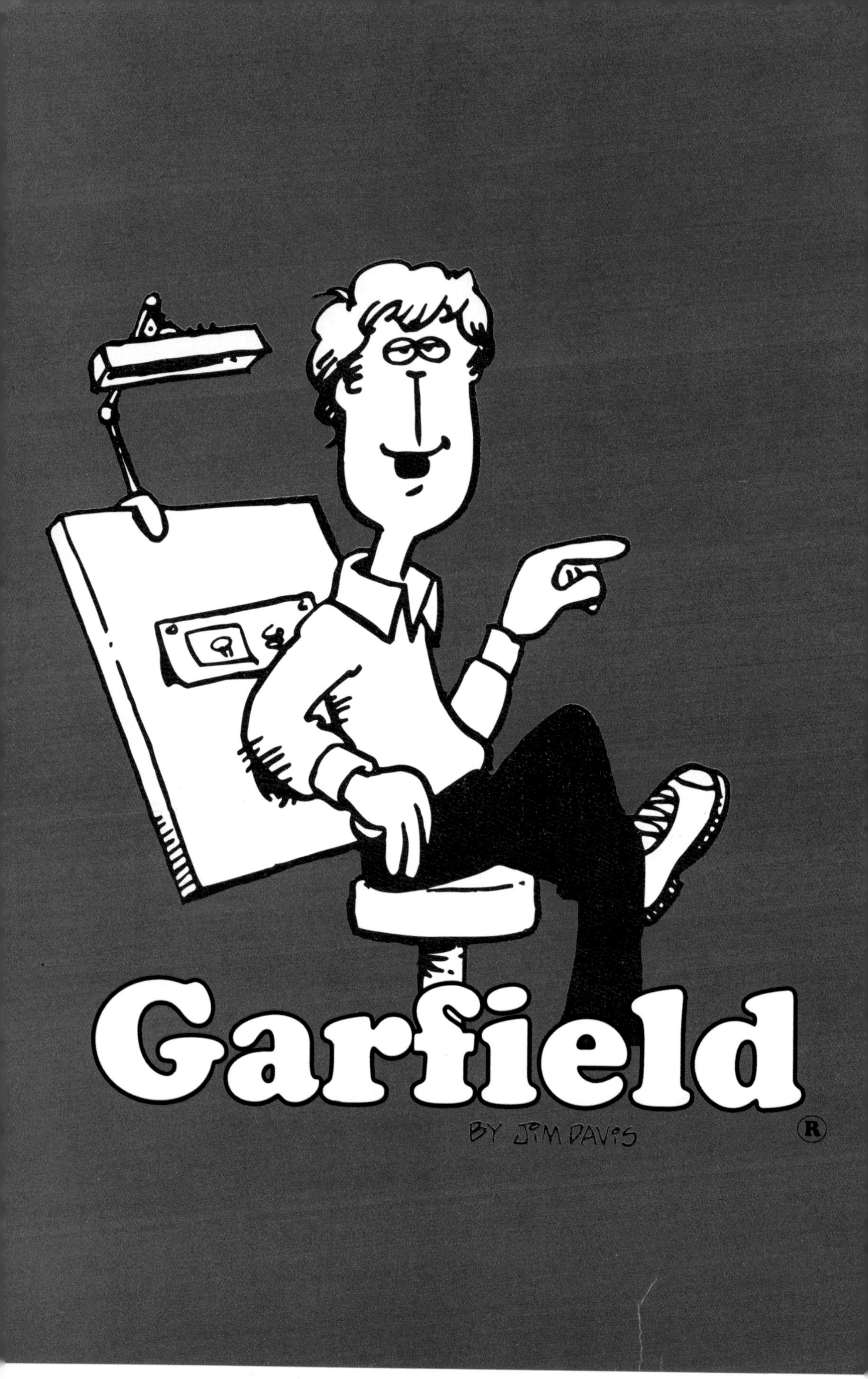
Garfield
BY JIM DAVIS

Garfield #3 Variant Cover by **JIM DAVIS**

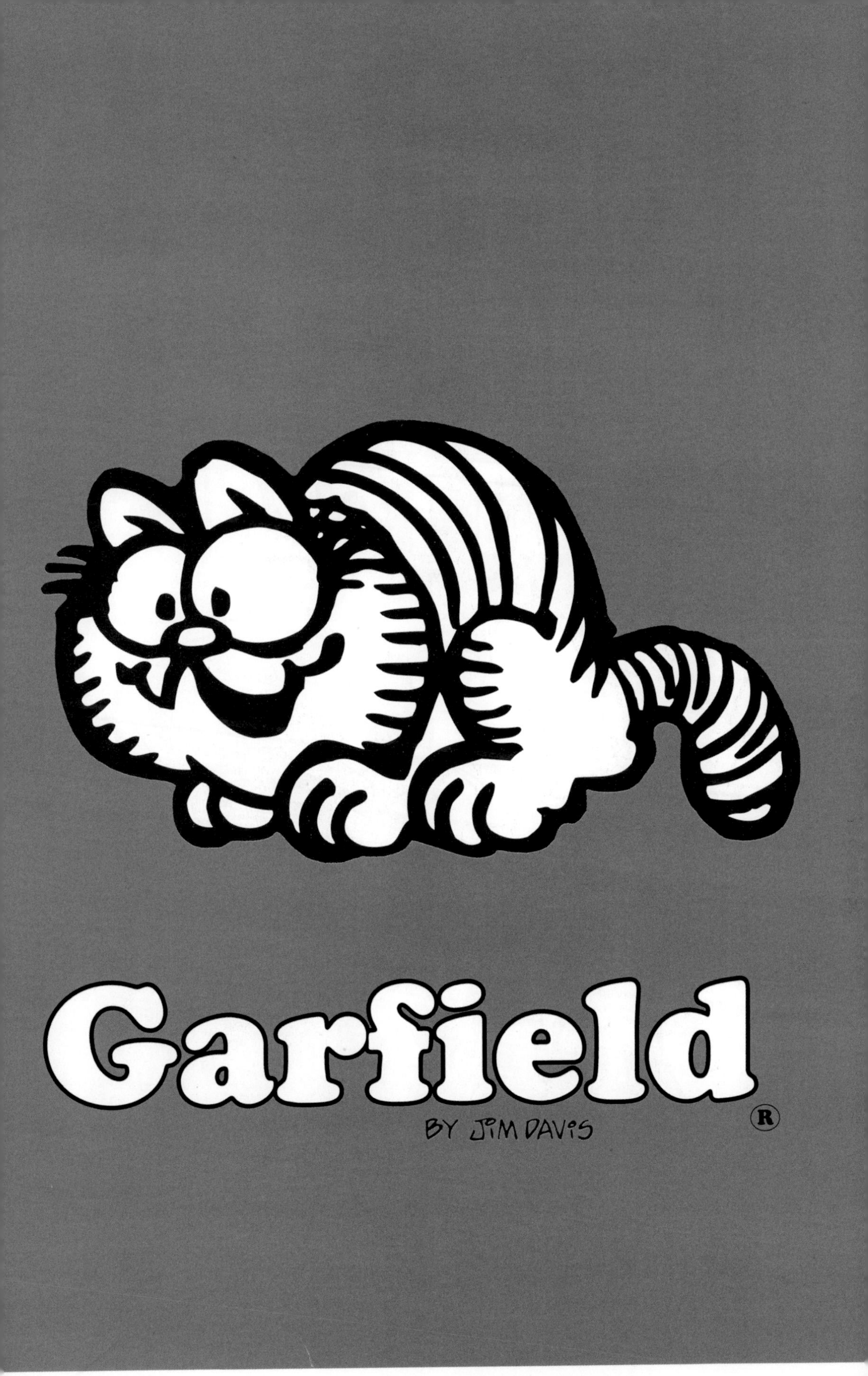
Garfield
BY JIM DAVIS
®

Garfield #4 Variant Cover by **JIM DAVIS**

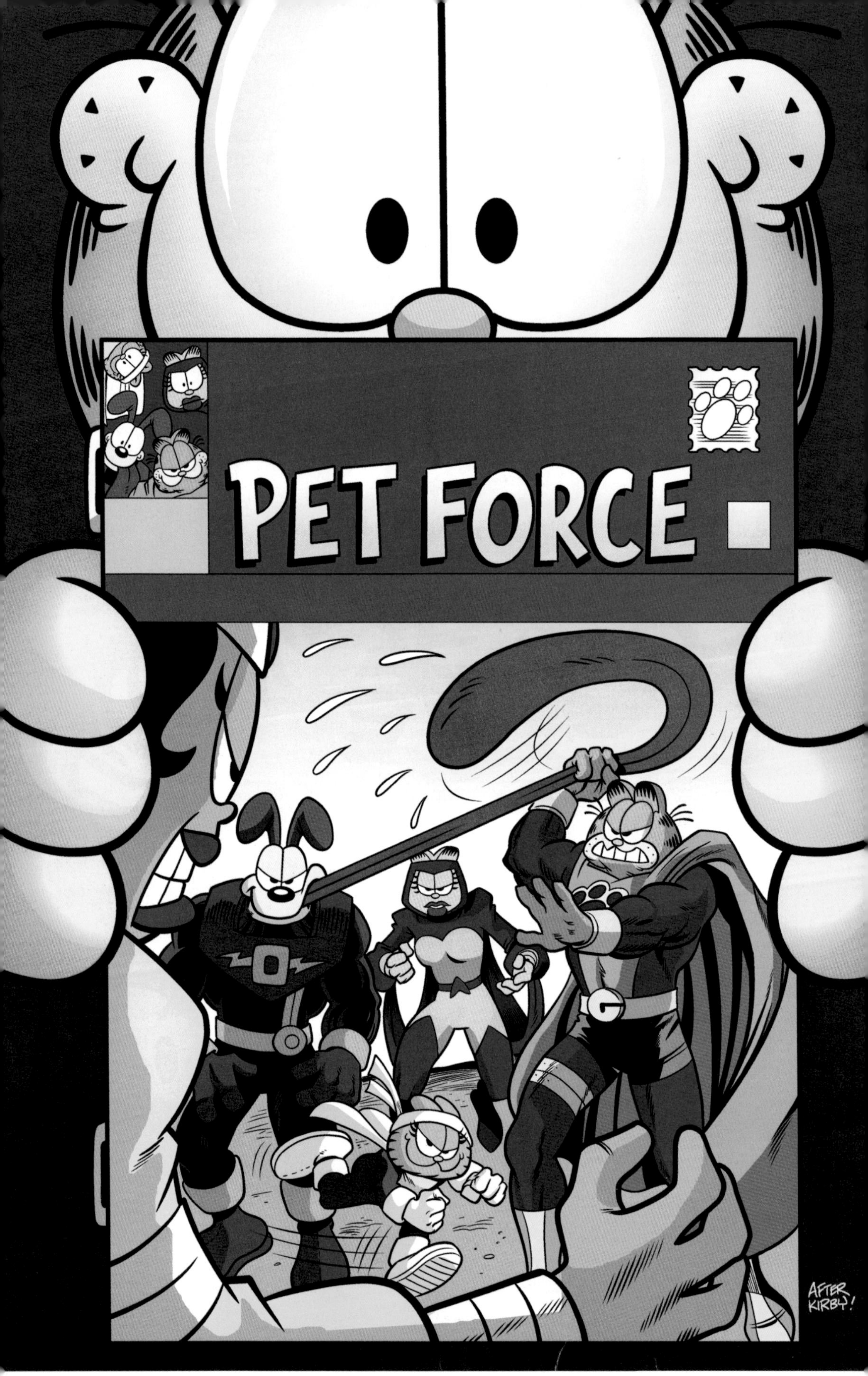
PET FORCE
AFTER KIRBY!

Garfield #5 Variant Cover by **GARY BARKER** and **DAN DAVIS** with **LISA MOORE**

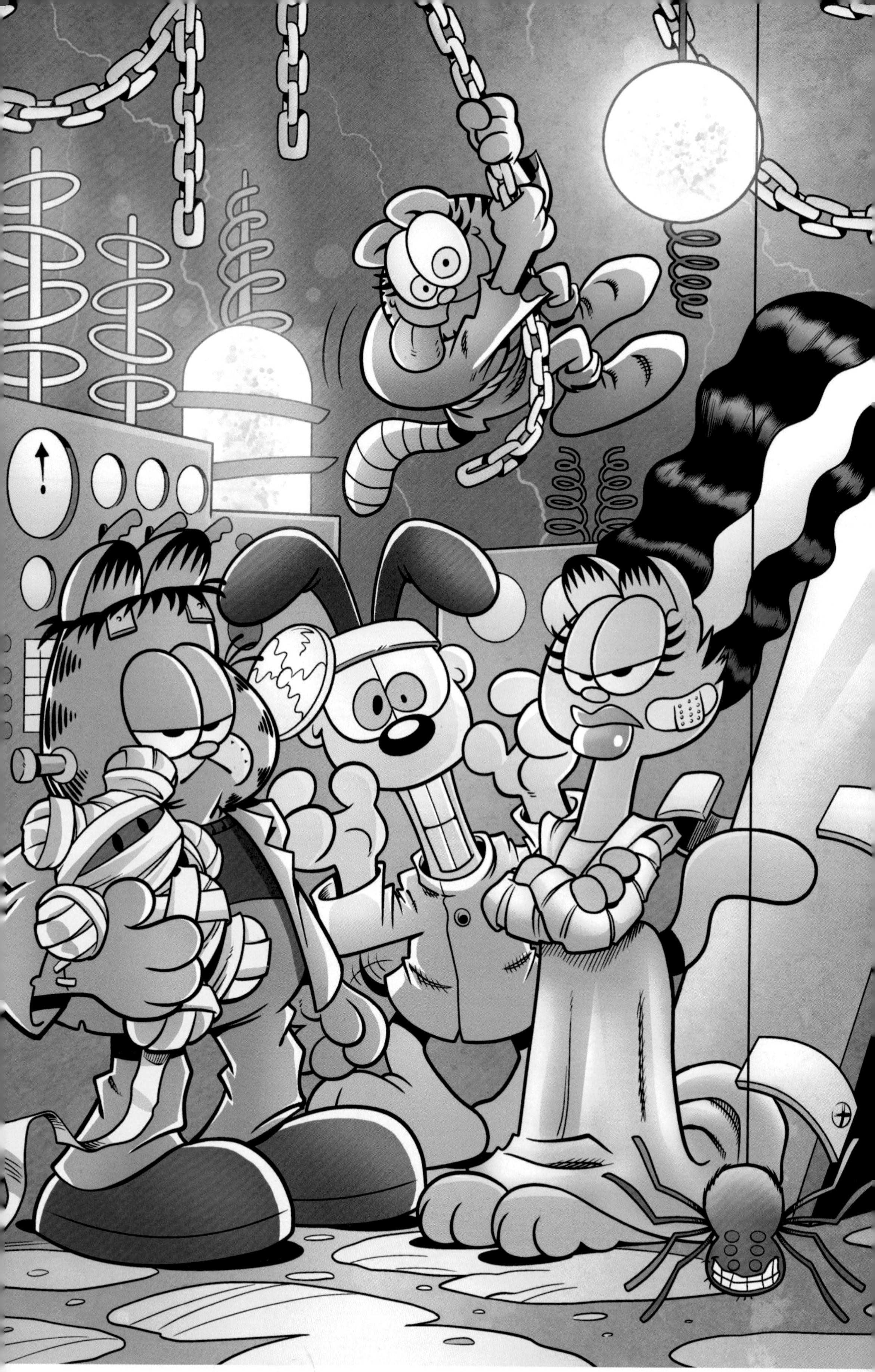

Garfield #6 Variant Cover by **GARY BARKER** and **DAN DAVIS** with **LISA MOORE**

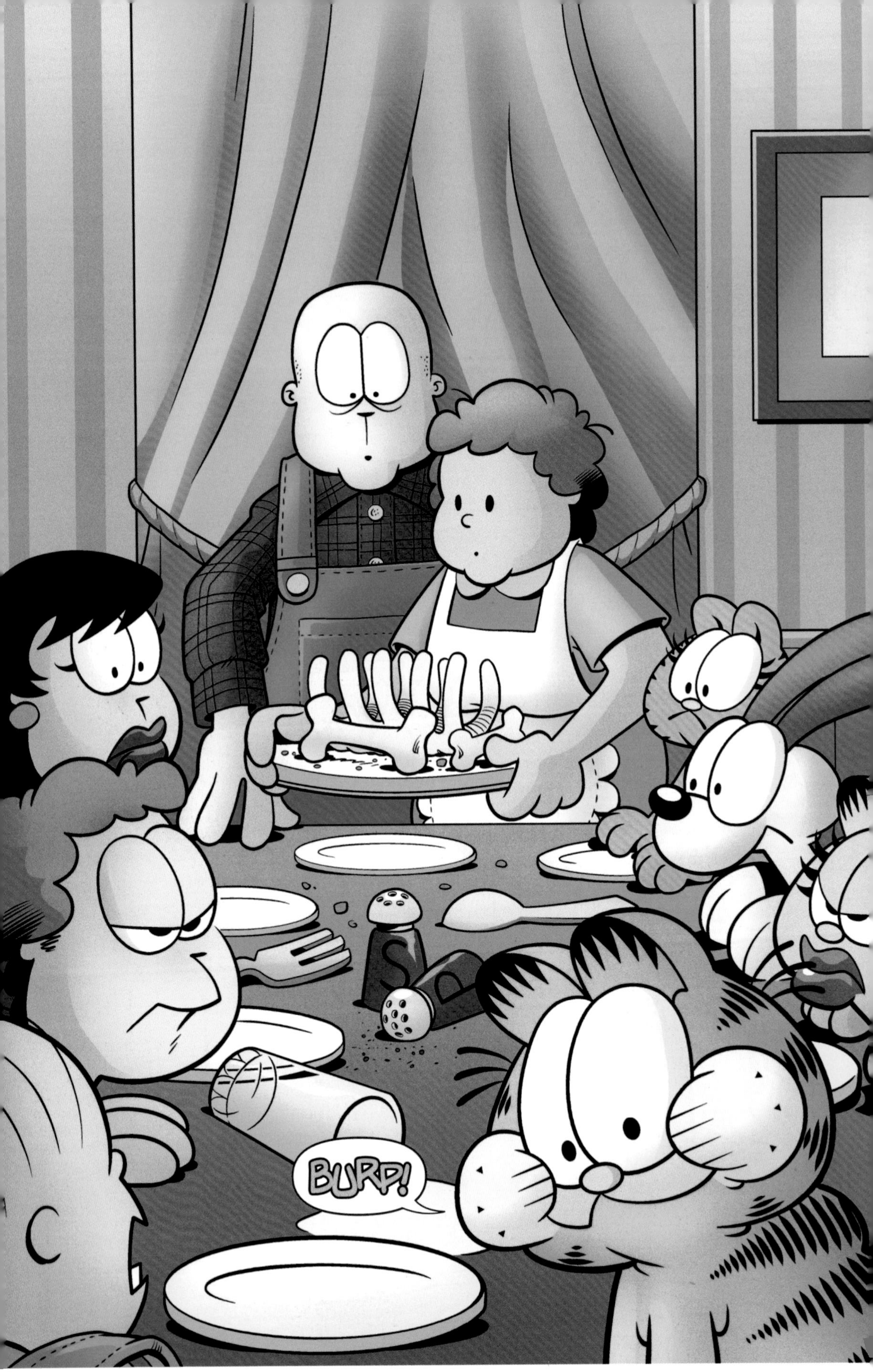
BURP!

Garfield #7 Variant Cover by **GARY BARKER** and **DAN DAVIS** with **LISA MOORE**

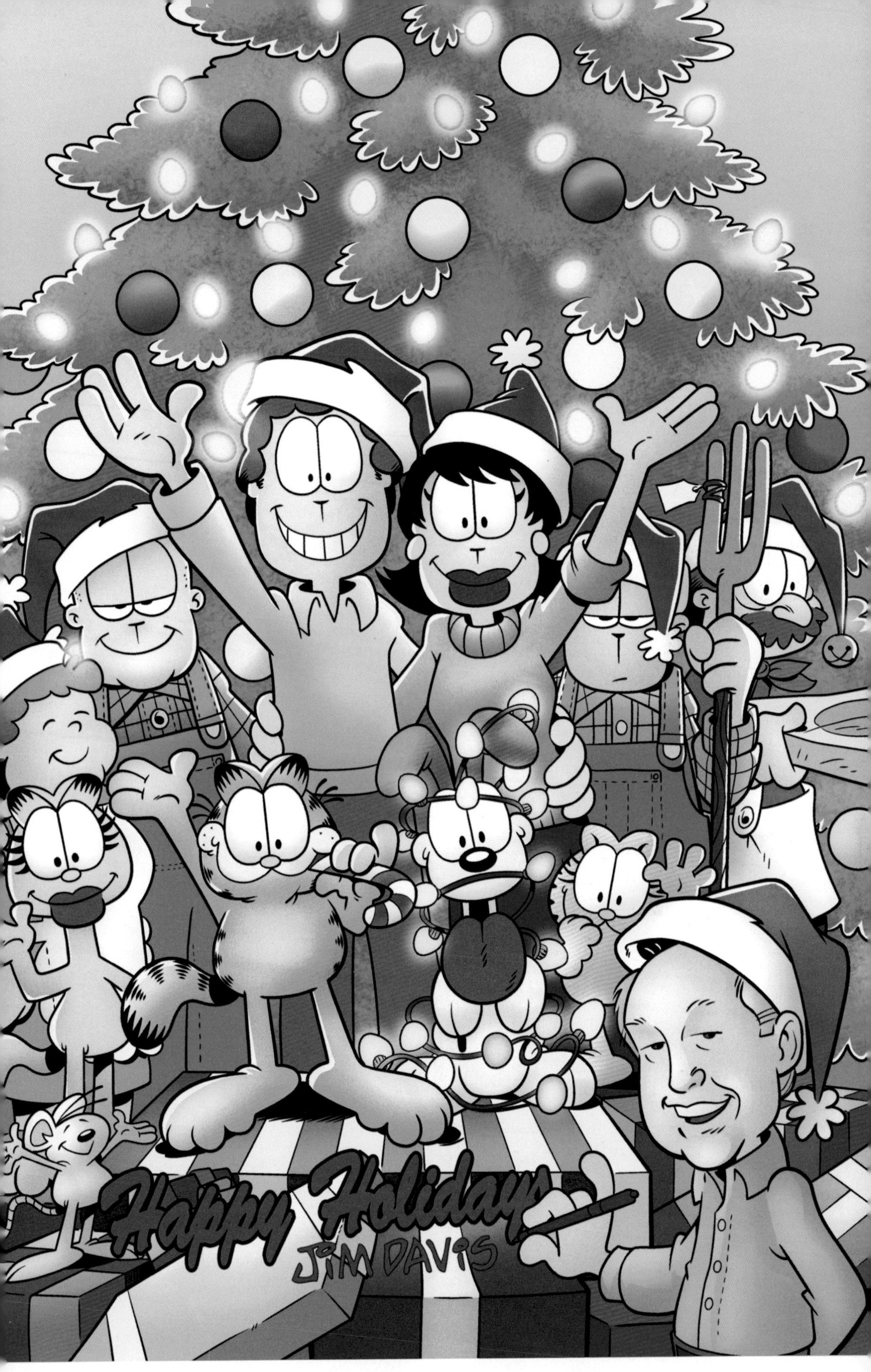
Happy Holidays
JIM DAVIS

Garfield #8 Variant Cover by **GARY BARKER** and **DAN DAVIS** with **LISA MOORE**

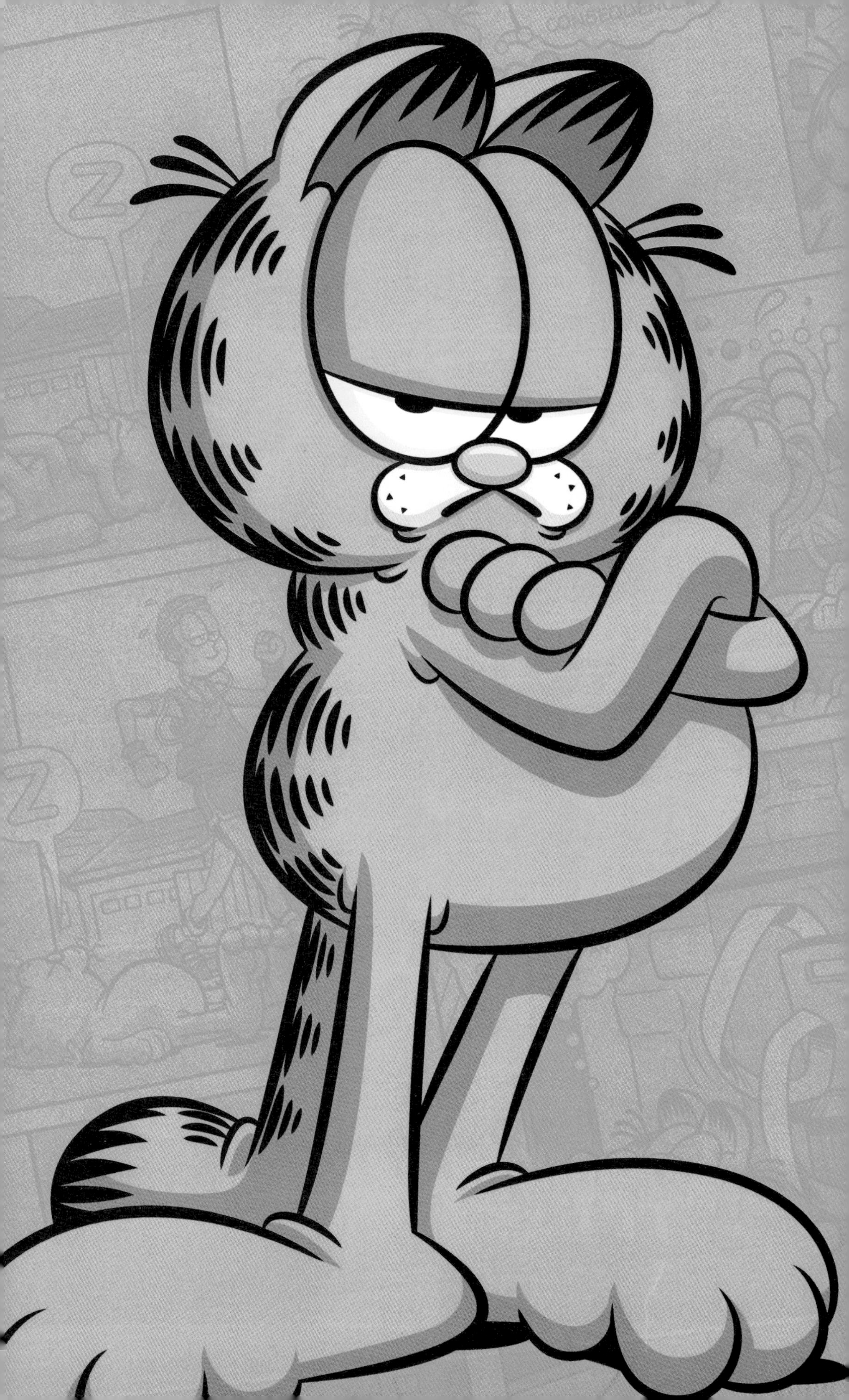

HI, THERE... I'M JON ARBUCKLE. I'M A CARTOONIST, AND THIS IS MY CAT, GARFIELD.
JIM DAVIS 6-19
HI, THERE. I'M GARFIELD. I'M A CAT, AND THIS IS MY CARTOONIST, JON.
OUR ONLY THOUGHT IS TO ENTERTAIN YOU.
FEED ME.

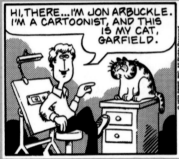

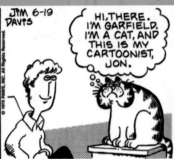

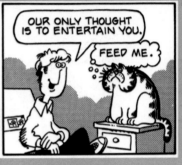

Garfield & Jon
First appearance
June 19, 1978

IS THAT ALL YOU HAVE, THE ONE SUITCASE?
NOT EXACTLY
HERE BOY!
OH, LAWSEY, LAWSEY, LAWSEY.
8-8
JIM DAVIS

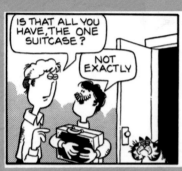

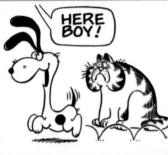

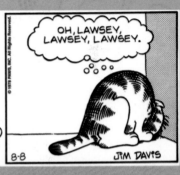

Odie
First appearance
August 8, 1978

GUESS WHAT, GARFIELD? WHILE MOM AND DAD'RE ON A WEEK'S VACATION, WE'RE GOING TO BABY-SIT FOR THEIR KITTEN
9-3
MEET NERMAL
WAKE ME IN A WEEK
© 1979 PAWS, INC. All Rights Reserved.
JIM DAVIS

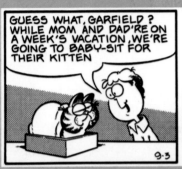

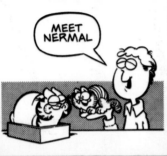

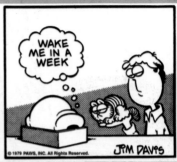

Nermal
First appearance
September 3, 1979

45TH GARFIELD

IT'S A CAT'S LIFE

PASTE

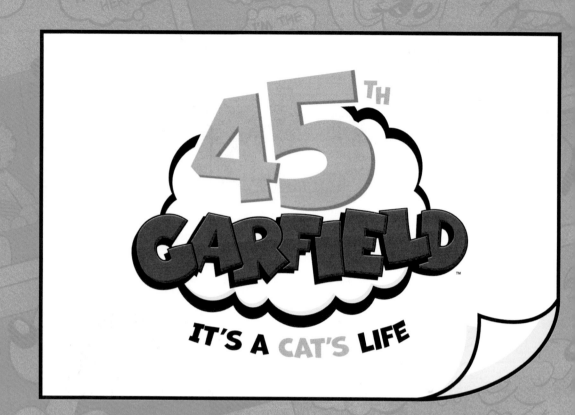

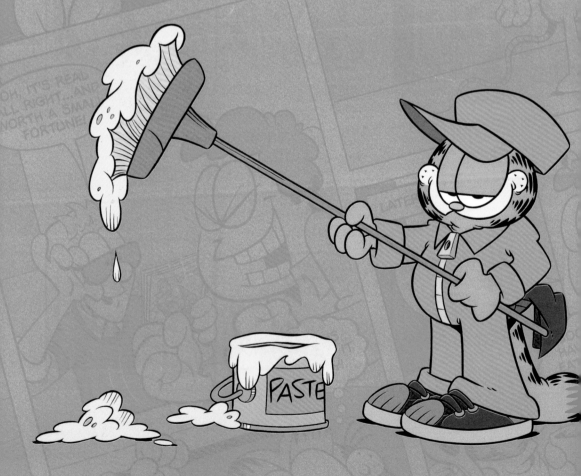

1978

1980

1994

1998

2007

2010

2017

2023

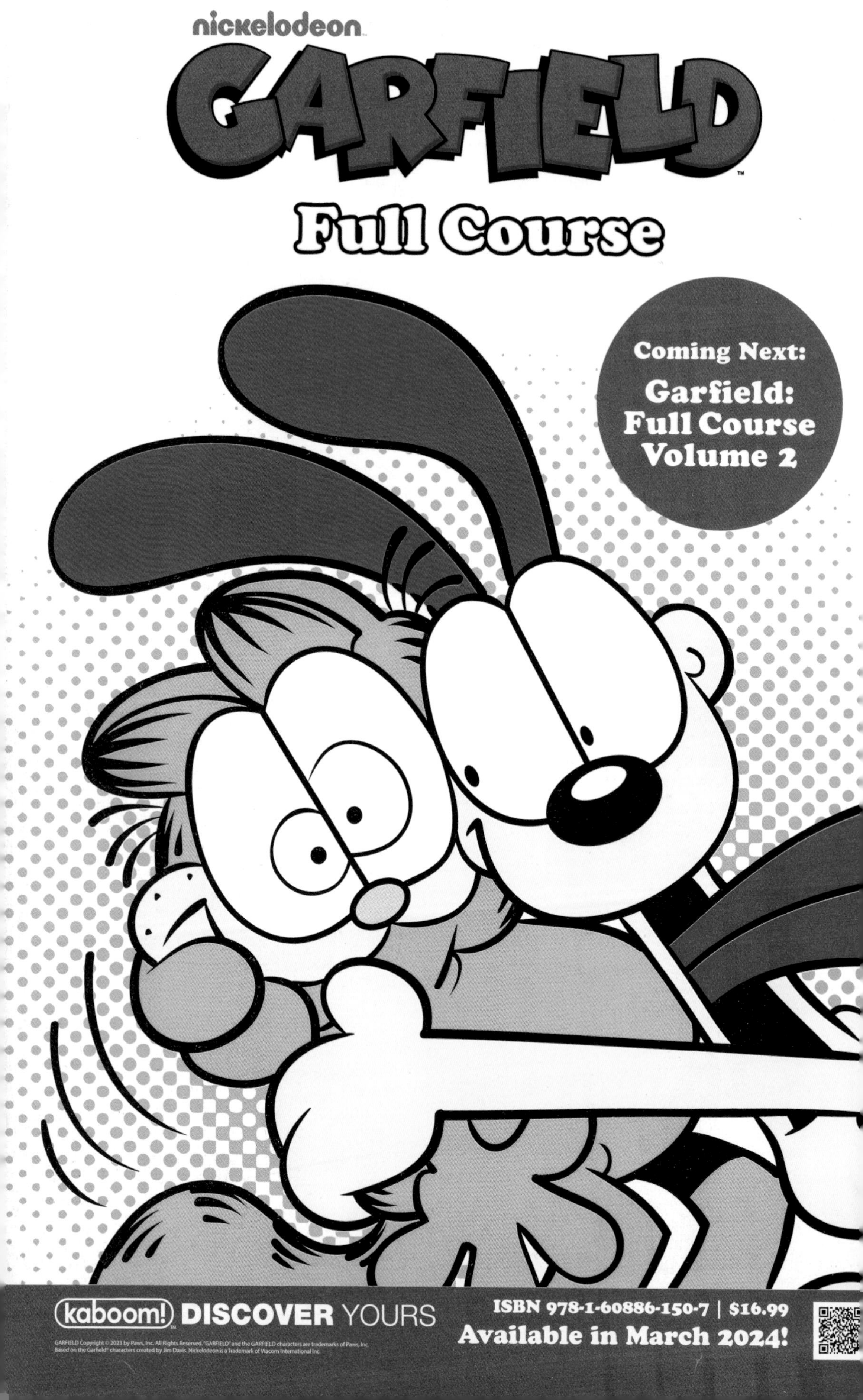

nickelodeon
GARFIELD
Full Course
Coming Next:
Garfield: Full Course Volume 2
kaboom! DISCOVER YOURS
ISBN 978-1-60886-150-7 | $16.99
Available in March 2024!
GARFIELD Copyright © 2023 by Paws, Inc. All Rights Reserved. "GARFIELD" and the GARFIELD characters are trademarks of Paws, Inc. Based on the Garfield® characters created by Jim Davis. Nickelodeon is a Trademark of Viacom International Inc.

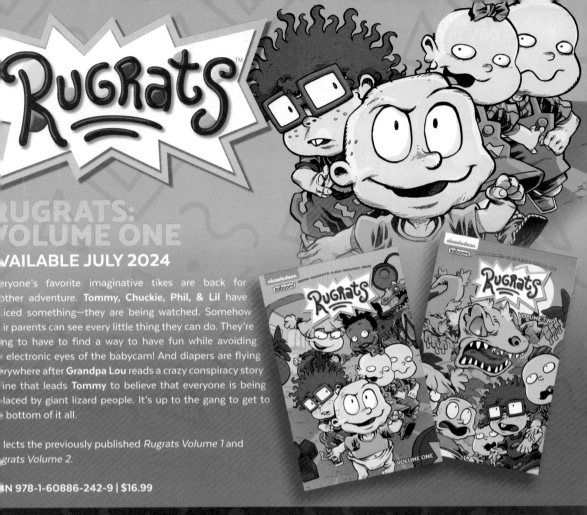

RUGRATS: VOLUME ONE

VAILABLE JULY 2024

eryone's favorite imaginative tikes are back for other adventure. **Tommy, Chuckie, Phil, & Lil** have iced something—they are being watched. Somehow ir parents can see every little thing they can do. They're ng to have to find a way to have fun while avoiding electronic eyes of the babycam! And diapers are flying rywhere after **Grandpa Lou** reads a crazy conspiracy story ine that leads **Tommy** to believe that everyone is being laced by giant lizard people. It's up to the gang to get to bottom of it all.

llects the previously published *Rugrats Volume 1* and *grats Volume 2.*

3N 978-1-60886-242-9 | $16.99

nickelodeon
kaboom!
Rugrats
VOLUME ONE
Rugrats
VOLUME TWO

RUGRATS: VOLUME TWO

VAILABLE DECEMBER 2024

llects *Rugrats The Last Token* Graphic Novel, *Rugrats C is for Chanukah,* d *Rugrats R is for Reptar.*

Rugrats
THE LAST TOKEN
nickelodeon
kaboom!
#1
Rugrats
C IS FOR CHANUKAH
nickelodeon
kaboom!
#1
Rugrats
R IS FOR REPTAR

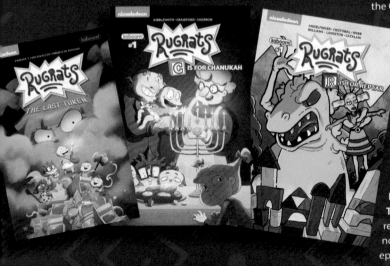

It's a Rugrats family vacation to the mountains, complete with **Grandpa Lou** and **Boris** arguing over which holiday is better–Chanukah or Christmas. **Boris** is determined to win and starts giving **Tommy** and the babies a history lesson on the Golem which sets imaginations ablaze. **Tommy, Chuckie, Phil & Lil** now feel that they have to save Chanukah from the Golem before it can steal the holiday away for good! Back at the Pickles house, babies and adults come together to share their favorite **Reptar** stories when the power goes out! **Stu and Drew** take the babies to the local arcade for a relaxing day of pizza and games. But the arcade's token stock goes down to one and a frenzy breaks loose upon the arcade floor. When **Tommy** gets his hands on the only remaining token left in the building, the noble fellowship of babies take on an epic quest to save the day.